The Piano Teacher

by

David F Pennant

Silver Lining Books
Woking

The Piano Teacher

Published by Silver Lining Books
30 Oriental Road
Woking
Surrey
GU22 7AW

ISBN 0-9550053-0-2

Water Aid receives a contribution for every copy sold.

By the same author
The Priorities of Jesus, which tells the story of his fifteen year
search for the aim of the church.

www.silverliningbooks.co.uk

Part The First

A Bomb in the Piano Stool

Why on earth, Bruce Winter asked himself, was he still travelling by train, in this day and age? Then he spotted the unintended pun and smiled. On earth indeed!

The truth was, he felt lonely. All these other people rushing to work looked so full of purpose and ready for the day. It must be nice to feel fulfilled. He was almost unnoticeable in this crowd, he thought to himself, trundling along in a stopping service, sitting by the window. These slam door trains ought to have been phased out years ago! But still, they served his purpose, and not just his; the carriage was surprisingly full. Perhaps the small sum the government paid you to travel did attract a few people. At all events, the 0745 stopping train to London would go on running for several years yet.

He was one among many, he reflected. As to his age, he was neither old nor young. Anyway, what did age matter? Nobody would look twice at him, he reckoned, jammed in next door to a complete stranger, clutching his improving literature, despite his jet black hair, of which he was secretly rather proud. They might have wondered at somebody taking the trouble to bring a book to read on a journey which lasted just six minutes, but most people were not observant enough to notice that he got in and out at consecutive stations. They were too busy looking out of the windows.

They had good reason. It was extraordinary seeing the teenagers swooping about like swallows in the sky. It did look such fun! But even more remarkable, to Bruce, was the speed with which it had all come about. Who could have foretold that the two discoveries would come out of the blue, and so close to each other, that would make the move into the skies possible?

Infinite energy! Well, virtually infinite. Nobody had even dreamt that such a thing was possible. It was ridiculous, really. His granddad had told him so often that the world's reserves of fossil

3

fuels would run out some day, and that they should be carefully preserved, that it had become a deep-rooted part of his thinking. That was the real reason why he did not run a car. People thought that it was because his piano teacher's income would not allow it, but really, it was out of concern for the environment. "Preserve some of the world's precious resources for your grandchildren!" He could just hear his granddad saying it. Not that he was ever likely to have any grandchildren, but that was another matter, and it was best not to go down that path so early in the day.

Now there was no reason to worry about the oil and coal reserves. Fossil fuels not just by name, but by nature too.

Then the discovery of anti-gravity! And by the same people who had cracked the energy business. That seemed to suggest that the two were linked in some way. Anyway, you had to hand it to those boys. Although the energy breakthrough was out in the open, they had managed to keep their anti-gravity invention secret even to the stage of marketing the flying suits. It really did not seem possible to believe that nobody could discover how they worked. All over the world, the finest brains were taking the suits apart as best they could, and coming up with... nothing! It was not just intriguing; it was the ultimate mystery of all time, Bruce reckoned. You would have thought that somebody somewhere would have been able to work out how it was done.

You also had to admire their marketing. The earliest suits had been clumsy affairs, but the newest ones did not just have automatic temperature control, keeping you warm in Winter and cool in Summer, but they could also be tailored to you for a perfect fit. How wise they were to keep the price down to a level where the teenagers could afford them. That was always going to have been the mass market. Although there was a lot of jealousy about against Skywear (what a good name), it was limited to those scientists and engineers who wished they could have been the ones to scoop the prize. The young people had nothing but praise for Skywear, which must be just what they wanted.

Funny how he had assumed the inventors were men. Perhaps they were women? Whoever it was, they certainly understood how to make the girls look shapely. Take that one for instance, doing loop the loops near the carriage window. He supposed the young people liked to come down low, in order to be seen. Why, wasn't that Araminta? Yes, it was! Impulsively, he waved, then immediately regretted it. Oh dear, she had seen him, and waved back vigorously. Then she shot off skywards to join a group of friends. They made off into the middle distance.

That was a foolish thing to do. He looked around inside the carriage, to see if anyone else had noticed the interchange between them. A young woman sitting diagonally opposite him caught his eye, and smiled. She had seen. He smiled back. He had noticed her before. She had a book like him; that was curious.

It was time to get out. He was always worried that he would get carried away in his thoughts and miss the station. It had not happened yet, but there was always a first time. Daydreaming was deeply embedded in his nature; he had developed sufficient self-knowledge to have grasped that! He must try and stay focussed enough each day to get off the train.

It was an eight minute walk to the school. Down the few steps from the station entrance, across the forecourt, and into the little alley. So far, the occasional cyclists coming the other way had always slowed down, but Bruce was anticipating a collision one day, so he marched quickly along peering ahead, ready to fall backwards into the hedge if required. Today there was no incident, and he was able to step through the gap in the wire netting behind the bike shed and make his way to the music block. Somewhat unofficial, maybe, but it did save going all round by the gate, and Bruce preferred to slip in unobserved.

Step confidently into the old building, pass through two fire doors, unlock the little practice room, and put his bag on top of the piano. Open the window to its fullest extent, this being the beginning of May. This was only two inches, as there was some sort of catch on it, for security purposes. There must be a way of overriding that, Bruce reckoned, but he had never found it. No matter. For one thing, he did not want the caretaker shouting at him if he left the window wide open by mistake. Better to be safe than sorry.

He always felt secure when he was in the little practice room. Apart from the occasional quick visit from Jane, the Head of Music, or Sue, the second in the department, no other adult troubled him in there. It was just a matter of giving the pupils their lessons, and then locking up and leaving for the station again. It was a good arrangement.

0803. Seven minutes to practise, before Simon would arrive at 0810, since it was Thursday. Then Araminta at 0840, then those two scamps Beccy and Simna who learned together at 0910, when first lesson was beginning, and then three more individual pupils afterwards. The older pupils had their lesson before the school day started. The arrangement worked well; the building was quiet, and they did not have to miss class time.

Simon was punctual. He had been learning for eight months. He had made a good start. His note reading was poor, like most of them, but he was able to grasp the music quickly, and make it his own. He showed real promise.

Then it was time for Araminta. He always looked forward to her lesson; he had managed to work out why. It was because she talked to him. The hardest pupils were the ones who did not say a word from start to finish; he found having to make all the running in the lesson a strain. However, he was getting better at it; he did not find silent pupils so threatening as he had at first. Everything becomes easier with practice, he thought.

"Good morning, Mr. Winter, and how are you today?"

Araminta had burst in. Whatever you do, make a good entry; he had learned about that in drama lessons at school. She was bright and cheerful, as usual. Her high cheek bones tended to make her stand out from the crowd.

"Good morning, Araminta. I'm fine thanks. How are things with you?"

"Couldn't be better, thanks," she chirped, as she settled onto the piano stool. "I saw you in the train."

He had wondered how long it would take for that topic to come up.

"You have got your sky-diving down to a fine art. Isn't it rather dangerous coming so low?"

"Not at all, Mr. Winter." He liked the way she used his name. "There are safety devices built into the suit. You couldn't crash if you wanted to. The sensors slow you down before you hit anything. That's also true for power cables; the suit detects the presence of the magnetic field, and prevents you from flying into them. It's disconcerting at first, but you soon get used to the suit overriding your intentions. In fact, it can be rather fun. You should try it."

That too had been inevitable. "An old fogy like me?"

"Nonsense. It only takes a few hours to master the basics, and after a week or two, you'll be getting along fine. Think of it as the aerial equivalent of snowboarding."

Bruce grimaced. He had tried skiing in the Alps on several holidays for young people; that had been bad enough. His knees had got so tired! He needed to stop every few hundred yards to cope with the ache, and there was a limit to how long you could pretend to be admiring the view. He had never ventured on to snowboarding. It looked very difficult. After a few years he had stopped going. For one thing, everyone said that if you went with Snowbiz three times, you were guaranteed to end up with a life partner; if not, you got your money back. The guarantee had failed in his case.

"I think I will stay on *terra firma*," he said, hearing how feeble that sounded as he spoke the words. "But if I change my mind, I will come to you for advice. Now, what are you going to play me today?"

Araminta got out her book of Grade Seven pieces. She played well, he had to acknowledge. With her gifts and talents and bright personality, she would soon be making some young man very happy. They worked at some points of technique until the bell went.

The two twelve year olds Simna and Beccy were such a challenge, because they chattered so much! They were already in full flow as they stormed the door – that was how their entry felt to

Bruce. Part of him was pleased, because it meant that they felt at home and comfortable in the lesson. They threw down their bags and settled happily on their stools. They had a keyboard each, one on each side of him.

Every time Beccy came for a lesson, Bruce found himself thinking of the same verse from the Song of Solomon; 'I am dark but lovely, daughters of Jerusalem.' This was rather nonsensical, because Simna, being coffee coloured, was actually the darker of the two, but in her case it was her natural colour. In Beccy's case, it was caused either by exotic holidays, or by a sun tan machine. If it was the latter, he hoped she had taken good advice regarding health. Same with the former, come to think of it. Simna seemed to have been born with a permanent impish grin. He was glad he was not a classroom teacher, as he would need to get cross from time to time, and it would have been impossible with Simna, he felt.

It was such hard work keeping them focussed on playing! One week, their concentration had been so poor that they had only worked through four bars of music, and even those were not thoroughly grasped. However, they both had some talent, and they did practise, unlike some of his other pupils, so he did not feel uncomfortable with their progress. Also, they did not hold the record; with one of his adult pupils at home, the whole half hour had been spent on one bar of music! Still, it was the hardest bar in the book, as Bruce had pointed out. Also it was good to remember the story about Sir Edward Elgar, the composer. On one occasion, friends were staying with the Elgars, and after breakfast, the rest of the family took them out on a long walk, leaving Sir Edward in peace to compose. When they returned four hours later, Sir Edward had composed... just one bar! If it was in common time, with four beats to the bar, then the average rate of progress for that composition was one beat per hour. Mind you, Bruce reflected, I bet it was a good bar. There was nothing shoddy about Elgar's music.

His morning's lessons were soon over; six today, which meant that, allowing for the fifteen minute break at 1010, he was leaving the building at 1127. It was touch and go whether he would catch the 1133 home, but it was often late, so he might manage it if he strode along briskly.

He climbed the steps to the platform, and glanced at the monitor. What nonsense was this – thirteen minutes late? How ridiculous. He hated waiting for trains. He settled on an uncomfortable bench. There were no young people flying; they were all in class. It was a shame that people of his age had not gone in for it. The few sky-cars were high enough not to intrude. Indeed, they could hardly be seen from the ground. They were still very expensive at present, but they would become cheaper, leading to clogged skies; hence the government payout for travelling on public transport. Sometimes governments took wise decisions! Bruce settled down to wait.

```
1. From: Mission 12
To: Undisclosed recipients
Sent:
```

We're on our way! This is the first chance I have had of sending news. The launch went flawlessly, as far as I could tell. Big Nimp seems pretty happy about it, I reckon. Oh, I'd better explain. When we were young, my sister could not pronounce the word computer properly; she called our desktop PC the nimputer. The name stuck, and it soon got shortened to nimp.

Big Nimp is the onboard machine. Its size and skills are breathtaking. Take the display, for example. The solid grey steel wall, eight metres high by twelve metres wide, converts to a huge screen in an instant. It must be made of something other than steel, really. The amount of information Big Nimp can throw up at once is too much for me. It gives me vertigo!

little nimp lives in my pocket. I'll tell you about him later. I don't really need him, to be truthful, as Big Nimp could do everything with no trouble, but I like little nimp. He's my friend.

He gives me a feeling of security. That's why I keep him in lower case.

You will want to know about the spaceship. Well, she's big. She tapers to a point at the front, which is what you would expect, so that if we were to hit anything, there is a chance that it might glance off us. However, at the speed we will be going, the slightest bump, even with something microscopic, would be enough to blow us to smithereens. It's scary, really. I just hope the route planners were up to the job. It's all very well saying that their instruments are state of the art, and that with radio telescopes dotted round the solar system, the resolution is unbelievable, but it only takes one small slip and we are done for. I prefer not to think about it, but you might like to, which is why I have put it in the first email to get it out of the way.

The engines are amazing. There is no sound at all, not even a hum, and no vibrations either. We are not going very fast yet, but with the constant acceleration, our speed will build over the coming months. We speed up by one gee by day, and two at night; gee means the force of gravity in case anyone still does not know that. At two gees, your body weight doubles. Of course, day and night mean nothing on board, but they have programmed everything to a twenty-four hour clock for my benefit! It was one of the conditions I made when I accepted the job. It preserves my body clock, and my sanity. I actually find I sleep better under two gees at night. When it gets to ten p.m., a claxon sounds and a loud voice says, "It's time to clean your teeth and get into bed. Two gee acceleration in fifteen minutes." At least, that's what I've got it set on at present. I'll probably change it in a few days. Big Nimp is quite happy for me to mess around with the settings as long as I don't want

to do anything that will upset the mission. Then at 0615, we go back to one gee. The deceleration wakes me up, and I leap out of bed. I've always been an early riser - can't bear slacking in bed.
All for now. Be in touch again soon!
Bruce

PS. Big Nimp corrects any spelling mistakes I make and adds the date and time before sending.

Ah, here was the train. It had long since ceased to be interesting trying to work out where they had got to from the viewpoint of the train window. He knew the area too well. Still, the journey was quickly over, and as his house was only a short walk from the station, he was soon advancing up the little path, putting his key in the lock and letting himself in. Close the door firmly! He had never had an intruder, but you could not be too careful.

He called it his house, but it was only rented. It was a three bedroom bungalow belonging to Marjorie, a retired academic, who lived in the four bedroom house next door. The bungalow had been built for Marjorie's elderly mother. When the mother had died, Marjorie decided to let it. The rent would add to her pension.

Both houses were detached and swathed in Virginia creeper; they were set back five yards from the road, and they shared the large garden. This suited Bruce, as he could play his piano as loud as he wanted without disturbing anybody. "Love your neighbour, even if he plays the trombone," ran the Jewish proverb; this was all very well, but Bruce did not want to run the risk of irritating anybody. They might get cross with him.

Bruce only needed the one bedroom, with a spare one in case anyone came to stay. However, the third one was so full of Marjorie's things, that it was more of a junk room than anything else. Since the sitting room shelves were full to overflowing, she had started piling up books on the floor in the third bedroom as well. There were also boxes and boxes of cuttings from the Look-Book in there, as the weekly Lookout Literary Digest was affectionately known, going back a long way. Even though she had been retired for years, she kept herself up to date in her subject. She was a remarkable lady in many ways.

1158 was a bit late for mid-morning coffee. He had made one later than that on occasion, but today he decided to be virtuous, and wait until after lunch for his next Caffeine. There was an occasional pupil due at 1230, Sandra, a retired lady who kept on saying she was no good but was actually doing quite well. "Learning the piano is like climbing a mountain," he would tell her. "If you keep on putting one foot in front of the other, and don't give up, then you should get to a good height one day." Nobody ever gets to the top, he reflected. Even the greatest pianists are still learning.

Then there would be a break until 3.45, when the after school pupils would start arriving, keeping him occupied until 7.30. Then after a hasty tea, there was another adult due at 8.10.

He had taken a pupil at 8.50 before now, but really, it was a mistake; he was in danger of falling asleep during the lesson. What he liked to do was to read for an hour after the final pupil had left, before tuning in to the BBC news on the TV at 10 p.m. Sometimes he would watch the whole bulletin, but often, the headlines were enough to convince him that nothing of interest was happening, and he would switch off again and turn in for the night.

It was wonderful how many pupils he had, Bruce reflected. He could not understand why he was so popular. Some weeks he gave over forty lessons! Still, the thing to do was to enjoy his success. He did; it was a pleasure to see his pupils gradually improve.

There had been a pleasing development for him earlier in the year. The new shopping centre in the town comprised a large glass dome, four stories tall, in an oblong shape, with shops on each side of it. At the bottom, there were tables and chairs, and various food outlets. Bruce had suggested to the centre manager that a grand piano playing background music down there would improve the ambience, and to his delight, the idea had been taken up. They had kindly booked him, among others, to play once a month on a Friday, from midday until 4 p.m.

It was a real challenge. Bruce aimed to play a wide range of music, from the classics through to pop, with the main emphasis on

12

films and shows. He hoped that everybody would recognise at least one tune while they were shopping or drinking their hot chocolate. He was never satisfied with how he played – that went with the role of being a musician, he had decided – but he had received enough positive feedback to feel that he was doing alright. The only negative comment from someone seated at a table, passed on by one of the waiters, was that he played too loud. Although this hurt at the time, it was helpful feedback. He had been trying to fill the whole space with his music. He realised that this was not appropriate; it was better to play in an intimate manner, so that people who overheard, as it were, had the choice to listen, or to ignore it. So now he played at drawing room volume, and it felt better, and less pushy.

The only disappointment was that he had scattered his business cards around on the little ledges between the food tables, not too ostentatiously, but enough, in the hopes that people might pick them up, leading to more invitations to play. However, as far as he could make out, not a single one had been taken in the five sessions so far. Oh well. Never mind. The important thing was to do a good job. Something might come of it one day.

1202. He made himself do some chores. It was no good leaving the washing up indefinitely. Letters should be dealt with as they arrive; that was his attitude. No bills outstanding; that was good. Just sweep up that bit of dust there; mustn't allow the place to look untidy. Keep standards up!

```
2. From: Mission 12
To: Undisclosed recipients
Sent:
```

```
There is something I don't understand about the
ship. The floor area is large, about the size of
a football pitch, split into various rooms, some
big, some small. Everywhere is carpeted in a
light brown colour; it looks pretty long-wearing,
which seems a bit daft as I am the only person
who will ever walk on it. The overall floor shape
```

is rather like a large fat pear, with the pointed
bit aimed forward. Here's the bit I can't get.
The acceleration force is down through my feet to
the floor, but we are rushing forward to one
side, as it were. I would have expected to be
standing on a side wall, if you see what I mean.
How on earth do they do that? I just can't
imagine how the apparent direction of gravity can
be changed through ninety degrees. It makes no
sense. But then, I never was much good at
science, so why should I be able to understand
it? However, the arrangement certainly makes it
more comfortable for me, and saves a lot of
running up and down stairs. I think it was very
thoughtful of them.
    Bruce

Friday did have a different feel to the other working days, he
thought, as he boarded the train next morning. Ah, the diagonal girl
was there again. It is a good thing people can't read your thoughts,
he reflected; diagonal girl was not much of a compliment. It
sounded like something out of a painting by Picasso. He was
intrigued to know what book she was reading. The secret was to
observe without being seen.

What was it… Proust! Now this was something. A nice-looking
girl reading Proust, before eight in the morning!

It took him several minutes to work up the courage to say
something. He wanted to formulate the words just right. Now he
was ready. He leaned across.

"Excuse me, but I am impressed to see you reading Proust on
the train. Did you know that another Frenchman, Jean Jacques
Rameau, said that it does not matter what you teach as long as it is
difficult?" It sounded rather academic and know-all when he put it
into words.

She smiled back. Lovely brown hair.

"Actually, it was Rousseau who said that. Rameau was a French
composer. But you were close – you got the right nationality."

Bruce could have kicked himself. He had meant to say Rousseau. How could he be so stupid? He was always hopeless when talking to girls. What would she think of him now? Oh well, never mind. He had put his foot in it yet again. Thank goodness it was time to get out.

"Oh yes. Stupid of me. Sorry. Bye."

"Bye."

He saw her settling into her book as the train pulled out of the station. Instead of impressing her with his knowledge, he had made himself look stupid. And classical music was his own subject too, which made it worse! He felt all hot and bothered as he made his way to the school. He was such a nit-wit!

The lessons were uneventful, except that one of his less talented pupils named Michael told him the following Friday but one was an Inset Day, only he called it an Insect Day. "Do you mean you will be playing me the Beatles, or Adam and the Ants?" Bruce asked. It was good to keep the lessons on a cheerful footing, and humour was a help, he had found.

"No, it's a day off from school."

"Oh yes, in-service training for the staff, I believe. Thank you for letting me know, Michael."

The music staff were not good at warning him about changes to the timetable. Once before on an Inset Day, he had turned up as usual, been disappointed that the first pupil had not arrived, and then finally tumbled to the truth at about 0850 when not only had the second pupil not come, but there were none of the usual shouting hordes in the corridor either. It was a good thing that he had learned to make use of every spare moment. The forty-seven minutes of scales and arpeggios must have done him some good, even if he could not actually feel the benefit. Also, it was no use allowing a setback like that to make him feel unimportant; his significance did not rest on how other people perceived him. All the same, it would have been nice to have been told. This time, now he knew about the Inset Day, he could plan ahead, and make use of the day off.

"So I will see you next Friday as usual, but not the one after," Bruce said as Michael was leaving. Good to be crystal clear.

3. From: Mission 12
To: Undisclosed recipients
Sent:

Silly me! Take no notice of my last email. We are not rushing forwards at all; we are speeding upwards. At least, I think that must be it. There are no windows, so you can't see which way we are going by looking out. Come to think of it, even if you could look out, the stars are so far away, you could stare for ages and not see any difference in their layout. As I say, the engines are silent, and we are not going through atmosphere like an aeroplane, so there is no sense of direction. The only changes in momentum are when we speed up to two gees or down to one gee, as I told you before. Sorry if I repeat things. I'm not very clever about that.

Anyway, if I am right that we are going upwards, it means that the ship is far larger than I thought. I never had a proper view of it when I was taken on board. My level is just one segment of it, like a flat in an apartment block. There is no lift up or down, but I don't mind; there's plenty of room for me here. I have space to walk and take exercise to keep fit.

I said there are no windows, but there is the observation chamber, for looking at the stars. At one side of the ship there is a short flight of stairs upwards into a small lobby or vestibule, and then you step into the special chair and strap yourself in. It's fully adjustable, not only in its backrest and headrest, but in width as well. It's important to be snugly fitted, as it were, because when you press the little button, you are rolled forward through the ship's outside wall and into the glass bubble and locked onto the rotating wheel. The wheel does a full circle every thirty-five minutes. The speed of rotation varies a little - it's slower when you are the right way up, and faster when you are head down. I did not like being upside down to begin with - I never liked rides at fairgrounds when I was a teenager, but I'm getting used to it. Still, it's worth it for the view. There is no atmosphere, as I said, and no light pollution, and so you can see ever so many stars. I think there may be a magnifying effect built into the glass as well, making everything look larger. Every part of the view is amazing, but the centre of the galaxy is best. I think that gazing at the Milky Way is the best experience I have ever had in my life. The only sad thing is that there is nobody to share it with.

When you've had enough, you press the other button and get taken back in again. I like it.

Bruce

Saturday morning was busy; it was a popular time with pupils. He always felt drained by Saturday lunchtime. However, once the last pupil had left, and he had eaten some bread and cheese (plenty of pickle), the weekend gave space for reading. He made a coffee, went through to his armchair, and reached for a favourite book. Yes, Profiles of the Future had some wonderful quotes in the opening chapters, which demonstrated how difficult it was to foretell the future. Take this one for example, by a famous American astronomer named Simon Newcomb, on the notion of building an aeroplane.

'The demonstration that no possible combination of known substances, known forms of machinery and known forms of force, can be united in a practical machine by which man shall fly long distances through the air, seems to the writer as complete as it is possible for the demonstration of any physical fact to be.' What fun it was to read that!

Nobody could have foreseen the arrival of virtually unlimited energy, it seemed to Bruce. And yet, it was here. It had burst on the world a mere eight months earlier. The ramifications were going to be immense. A major concern, it seemed to Bruce, was that with oil losing much of its importance, the inevitable shift in power between the Middle East and the rest of the world could turn out to be very tricky. Doubtless the politicians were all scratching their heads at what was likely to come.

A question of more immediate concern to him, arising from the anti-gravity discovery, was how the new transport was going to be managed. As sky vehicles began to multiply, what safety arrangements would be needed?

Bruce enjoyed thinking about new technology, and the flying cars gave him plenty of scope for thought. How were the skies to be managed in order to avoid collisions between vehicles? Something along the lines of the current air traffic control, no doubt. However, ground cars at street level had always travelled much closer to each other than aeroplanes. As the prices of the new vehicles fell, and the skies became increasingly crowded, there would be mounting pressure for each sky-car to use minimal airspace. Maybe the day would come when manual flying would have to be prohibited, at least in the busiest areas, and they would all need to become computer controlled. You would enter your destination, and then the sky-car would fly itself, using satellites for navigation, and radar for sensing other vehicles and obstructions. It seemed to Bruce that the scope for regulations was endless. The new transport was a civil servant's dream come true; a guarantee of a job for life.

Maybe the anti-gravity drive would even allow homes to float in the air. If so, there was no obvious reason why one should not live above the sea, in a house gripped in position against the elements by invisible moorings, as it were. Bruce dismissed the thought; speculating along those lines was for another day. There was more to consider regarding the sky-car.

Danger to pedestrians from ground cars had always been an issue, but society was willing to tolerate the few thousand road deaths that they caused each year. In addition, although it was possible to fill a van with explosives and explode it as a bomb, the problem was limited in scope, and not impossible to contain. In contrast, sky-cars posed a new threat. Could the makers guarantee that a sky-car's anti-gravity drive would never break down, allowing it to plummet down like a missile, accidentally or on purpose? He was sure that there had not been an incident of this kind before now, as if there had been, it would have been widely reported. A falling car could cause an immense problem. So too could something dropped from a sky-car. Supposing a baby fell out? It would not just die itself; if it hit somebody, coming from a sufficient height, it might kill them too. Even worse was the idea of a deliberate attack from the air. These sky-cars differed from helicopter gun ships only by not carrying weapons. It was only a matter of time before the criminals started arming them.

Bruce wondered whether the sensing technology, which prevented the flying suits from hitting objects or from crash landing, might be adaptable. What about a shield around the sky-car, which not only prevented collisions with other objects, but which also stopped anything from being dropped, thrown, or maybe even fired out? Bruce smiled as he found himself imagining a sky-car surrounded by an invisible circular force field, at the bottom of which lay a baby's rattle and pet toys, thrust out of the windows by a disgruntled infant, only to float along in mid air just underneath the sky-car. Perhaps each vehicle could be fitted with a vacuuming system, so that the long-suffering mum could reach down a length of hose and suck the discarded item back up again. Such a feature might even prove to be a selling point. Never lose anything ever again. What fun!

Also, what about privacy laws? He did not want nosey youngsters hovering over his garden when he was sitting out in it. Would we all have cameras pointing skywards above our properties in a few years' time, to discourage snoopers?

There was plenty to occupy the mind, and not just his. Still, the benefits for mankind clearly outweighed any teething problems over the new technology. Bruce could hardly begin to imagine what changes to society would emerge. One thing was certain; the world would never look the same again. All those films and TV programmes made before the advent of sky-diving and -driving would soon begin to look very antiquated.

Another facet of the new discoveries, which excited Bruce, was that getting into orbit must have suddenly become ridiculously cheap. The implications for space exploration and travel were immense. The sky was no longer the limit...

```
4. From: Mission 12
To: Undisclosed recipients
Sent:
```

When I said that about there being nobody else to share the experience with, at the end of my last email, I don't want you to misunderstand me. I was chosen because I was able to be on my own and not mind. Yes, in order to apply, you had to be resourceful and reliable and dedicated, but the main thing was to be self-sufficient. Out of the twelve hundred candidates, I came out on top in that one. I'll tell you why it was later in the trip.

I want to explain about the trip odometer, at least, that's what I call it. Big Nimp can output information in various displays in different rooms. Although the big one is brilliant for films and TV, for travel information I prefer what I call the diddy screen, one metre by one metre. It is in a small side room where I make tea sometimes. Of course, Big Nimp does the catering, and all I need to say is "Tea for one, please" and he obliges, but I like making my own tea, actually. I don't think he's grasped about warming the pot. The ship's designers were quite happy about my request for a little gyp room. That means a place with a sink with hot and cold taps, and an electric kettle and a small fridge, if you don't know.

What I like to do is to brew up, and then settle back and watch the numbers going round on the odometer. Big Nimp likes to show our distance travelled in Astronomical Units. I'd better explain that. One Astronomical Unit is the distance between the sun and the earth, about ninety million miles. Oh dear, I should not have mentioned the earth, you'll have to excuse me…

Saturday afternoon was not a good time to go to the supermarket, as everyone else in the world seemed to want to go then as well. It was all so slow. Not that he needed to buy much; he had found that it was best to take a basket rather than a trolley, and then he could go to the special checkout for baskets. The man on that till was one of the more efficient ones, and as Bruce paid in cash, it made the queuing bearably short. No, the problem in the supermarket was not one of getting out with the supplies. It was seeing all the other people buying for their families that upset him.

It had been even harder before than it was now. A year or two back, he would sometimes feel low for the rest of the day after a visit to the supermarket. It was the young mums pushing infants in trolleys that affected him most. Some man or other had managed to scoop them up. What had they got that he hadn't? It was a constant challenge to him that he had not found a girl to share his life with. Added to that was the feeling that time was passing. He had tried to convince himself that there were still single girls around at his age, but it was not easy.

It was not just a matter of finding love. Bruce believed he would be a good family man. Time and again, he would see the mums trying to control the older children, telling them "No!" and "I've told you before!" and the like. He was sure he could do better as a parent; he had taken note of the other kind of mum who carried on a continuous conversation with their toddler. "Yes we need Marmalade; which pot do you think Daddy would like?" or, "Can you lift me down two tins of Sweetcorn?" or "Which cereal would you like this week?" That would be his model, as a dad. He would spend time with his children, and talk to them, not brush them off,

21

as he had seen other men do. They did not know what they were doing, he thought. How could they take such treasures for granted?

He had definitely made progress with his feelings. Although passing close to the young women still hurt, he was getting used to it. It was a dull ache rather than a stabbing pain. He felt it was something he had to put up with, rather like having the toothache. No point in complaining all the time.

A visit to the market for some summer fruit, and then he could walk home. It was not far. Sometimes he would bump into an acquaintance while he was out in the shops, but not often. Apart from Bill, whom he would see next day, he did not have any real friends.

That was one of the reasons he went to church on Sunday mornings. It was a good place to meet people. He had always believed in God; that was no problem, but church puzzled him. The Sunday meetings were all very well, but where was their practical love and concern for the beaten-up person in the gutter? That side of things seemed to be left to him to do on his own, if he wanted, during the week. But he felt so helpless! He hated passing the ones that sat on a blanket at the side of the pavement as you approached the shops. These people were in obvious need; but what could he do, acting as one individual? It needed group action. But the group was too busy singing to have any time for the hopeless and homeless; at least, that was how he saw it; but he did not like to say anything, because it sounded critical, and anyway, he knew nothing, so he kept quiet about it. The thing to do, he felt, was to put up with the worship and the teaching on Sunday mornings in order to enjoy meeting the people afterwards over coffee.

This week, he could not concentrate on the singing for thinking about the ones on the blankets. He hated giving money to them; he felt he was being robbed, and it would go on alcohol, or cigarettes, probably. Still, what they did with their money was their affair, not his. He also hated walking past without giving anything. Jesus had said, 'Give to him who asks,' and he was worried about ignoring that. It was better to give than not, he had decided.

When he got his coffee, he made his way over to Bill. They had met at church, and got on well together. They were a similar age. Bill had sandy coloured hair, and an honest, somewhat serious face. He held down an office job which bored him, and which bored Bruce even more. By mutual agreement, they never talked about Bill's work.

Bill was having trouble with his Swedish girlfriend Gnilla yet again. She was somewhat petite, and tended to get hurt rather easily, Bruce thought. Gnilla worked in a florist's shop; she was very gifted in making bouquets. She was not a believer, and did not come to church. It was most depressing hearing of their troubles. Bruce listened carefully, and then for the hundredth time, said that he really had not got any suggestions. He was not a good person to ask.

Bill and he had committed themselves to learning New Testament Greek a while back, so as to be able to read the Bible in the original language. Bill had only lasted about a month before giving up, but Bruce had kept at it, encouraged by the classics teacher at the school, whom he had met one morning break over a coffee. Greek had proved easier than he had expected. Indeed, after a while, he had gone on to Old Testament Hebrew as well. He had enjoyed the challenge.

Bruce knew several young people who had gone off to Bible College over the years. One of the things which puzzled him was why they were so reluctant to try the Greek and Hebrew. They almost boasted of their inability with languages. Strange, really, and rather worrying, he thought.

After exchanging news, Bill and he agreed to go to a film together on Tuesday evening. That would be nice: something to look forward to.

```
5. From: Mission 12
To: Undisclosed recipients
Sent:
```

```
Sorry to have broken off. I hoped I would not
mind leaving the earth for ever, but the truth
is, I am homesick. I used to attempt to silence
```

my feelings by pretending they were not there, but it never worked properly, and now I'm trying a different tack. I just speak them out. I am homesick, I am homesick, I am homesick! I don't know if it is any more successful than trying to silence them. I think it is reasonable to be upset about leaving so much behind. I know I can see whatever I want on the screen; every TV programme and film ever made is in the memory banks somewhere, but it's not the same. I hope you understand.

I should add that I don't always make the tea myself; I let Big Nimp do it sometimes. I don't want him to feel left out.

Anyway, the trip odometer. There are all sorts of ways Big Nimp can show the information, but the one I like best is Miles Travelled So Far. The number of noughts at the left hand end is depressing, but the thing to do is to look at the right hand numbers. The units column is turning over so fast that it is a complete blur. I have tried to resolve it by concentrating on it and then closing my eye, and seeing if I can discern a number. I can't! In fact, I can't do it for the tens column either. That's a blur too. The hundreds column turns over slowly enough for me to be able to count along with it, but only just. I have to count as fast as I can. I reckon we are doing about six hundred miles a second by now. To get the idea, try saying the numbers over so that you get to six after one second. Like this :- 01234567890123456789012345678901234567890123456789. I use little nimp as a watch to calculate our speed in miles per hour. Yes I know Big Nimp could flash the speed up on the screen if I asked him, but it's more fun to work it out. Also, it's good to keep using my brain to help prevent getting Alzheimer's. I read about that once in a magazine.

I remember my granddad once telling me that the Voyager probe was doing about fifty miles a second when it got to Neptune. That was back in the late 1980s. It seemed very impressive then. It's nothing now.

I want to tell you about my granddad, but not yet.

But here is something interesting. Imagine driving at fifty miles an hour along a country road in your car. Approaching Neptune, Voyager was doing the distance that you would drive in an hour in just one second. Now imagine a much faster ship doing in one second the distance that Voyager travelled in an hour. Do you get it? Well, guess what; that is the speed of light! So you could say that in one sense, Voyager was doing half the speed of light, but if you did, it would be very misleading. Not a good idea.

I'm looking forward to one day next week. At about half past ten in the morning, we will have done a tenth of a light year. I've got it all planned. The big screen will have nothing on it except Light Years Travelled, in huge white letters on a black ground, and at the moment it turns over from 0.0 to 0.1, I will salute and then dance a jig. I haven't decided the music yet, but maybe the jig from Holst's St. Paul's Suite for Strings would be good, I don't know. I'll let you know later.

Holst wrote the music for a girls' school. St. Paul's School in London, in fact. He was director of music there. But you probably knew that before.

The young people must have been good violinists in those days!

Bruce

It was soon Thursday again. However, this week, the train journey was not routine. Soon after they left the station, the passengers began pointing out of the windows, up into the sky, and commenting to each other. Bruce looked up to see what the fuss was about, and was horrified.

A group of young people were flying in formation, about three hundred yards away. They had arranged themselves into capital letters. Two of them twisted double, were holding onto a third, who was straight out, forming a tolerable B. Next came an R, again formed from three more of them. After this was a W, made up by four more youngsters. The final one was the least convincing letter, which was hardly surprising. How could any two people form a convincing S shape when lying on the ground, let alone when flying along in the sky?

The whole set were coming closer. Bruce had no doubt it was done for his benefit, and sure enough, as they swooped down low over the train, he could see Araminta forming the upright of the B, waving at him cheerfully. He hoped nobody on the train would connect the young people with him. He glanced nervously at the diagonal girl, but she was engrossed in her Sartre, surprisingly, despite the volume of comments in the carriage. He reckoned she would have finished it by next day; she had only started it on Monday. She was a quick reader. The Proust had only taken her five days.

Why BRWS, he asked himself. Was it just a young person's idea of a trendy spelling of his name? Or did they know that in ancient Hebrew, W and a long O were the same letter? Probably the former. He did not think anybody at the school knew of his interest in Hebrew.

When Araminta came in to her lesson, she made no reference to the fly-past.

"Mr. Winter, I want to learn *Liebestraum*, by Liszt."

"Araminta, it's a great piece, but I think at your stage of development, it's out of the question." He had the feeling from her tone that this was a wind-up. "It's very difficult, way beyond me; I have never even tried it. Can I recommend something simpler?"

"What does *Liebestraum* mean, Mr. Winter?"

Now he was sure it was a wind-up, but a good-humoured one, not hostile or unkind.

"It means Dream of Love, Araminta. Now, I think this piece is more realistic," he said, reaching for a book of Easy Classics. "*La Donna E Mobile*, from Verdi's opera Rigoletto. It's a famous tune; the Count sings it in the second half." He played it through. "The Oom-Cha-Cha bass will do your left hand good."

"And what does the title of this one mean?"

"It means Woman is Fickle, Araminta." Two could play at that game.

She took the piece gracefully. "I will learn it, if I can do the Moonlight Sonata next."

This was realistic. "Well, the trouble is, there is no such piece." An opportunity to have a little fun.

"What do you mean, Mr. Winter; of course there is. It's ever so famous."

"Ah, but Beethoven himself would not have known what you were talking about." He reached for his copy. "It was only given the name Moonlight Sonata after his death, by someone who said it reminded him of the reflections of the moonlight on the ripples of Lake Lucerne. Beethoven just called it a *Sonata Quasi una Fantasia*, a Sonata like a Fantasia. Stand up a moment."

Araminta stood up to one side while Bruce sat on the stool. He turned to the last movement and let rip. He could manage the first few bars at the very fast speed required, which would be enough.

"Oh dear," said Araminta, "I think there is some mistake. I thought the Moonlight Sonata was a quiet, slow piece, not this loud rushing waterfall stuff."

"Oh, I see; you must mean the first movement," said Bruce, as if totally surprised. He turned back to the opening movement, and played the familiar theme. The young people never knew that there was more than one movement to a Sonata, and this was as good a way of pointing it out as he could think of.

"That's better."

Now for the punch line.

"You see at the top that it says Dedicated to Countess Julie somebody?"

"Yes."

"She was one of Beethoven's piano pupils. He hoped to marry her. He wrote her the first movement, and she was thrilled with it. Everything looked very promising. Then he added the second movement here." Bruce turned the pages to the *Allegretto*. "That was a bit harder, but never mind. She might manage to play it. Then he added the last movement. It is so tricky! *Presto Agitato* means very fast and agitated. Anyway, she couldn't take it; the piece was far too difficult, so she stormed off back to Italy in disgust, and that was the end of that relationship."

"Oh dear!" The young people always loved this story.

"Now Araminta, you won't let me down, will you? You will promise to work hard until you can play all three movements, won't you?"

Araminta knew she was cornered, but she also knew that he would not have made the suggestion unless he thought she could do it, and that was a compliment, so she felt pleased too. It was nice to have a challenge.

"Okay, Mr. Winter. You're on. All three movements."

Bruce thought that conversation might have eliminated any further fly-pasts for his benefit, but he was wrong. The following week, Thursday morning's journey was even worse. Twelve sky-divers had formed the word BROOS, this time, goodness knows how. He could not help admiring them, and feeling a little pleased. Even the diagonal girl was looking out this time, and he knew that she had grasped that it was him they were signalling to. Never mind.

Although the first O was convincing – two very athletic sixteen year olds with arched backs - the second O was not as good as the other letters. The two acrobats were much too close at the top. Then Bruce realised it was because the young people, a boy and girl, were kissing in mid flight. He suddenly felt incensed. I bet that is aimed at me, he thought. Has she grasped that I am so lonely?

It was at that moment that he suddenly knew what he was going to do on the Inset Day next morning, when he would not have to travel in to the school. Rather than staying at home, he was going to board the train as usual, and then he would show them.

6. From: Mission 12
To: Undisclosed recipients
Sent:

Big Nimp is very impressive. That's not meant to be a rhyme by the way. He's learned to understand my speech so well that I don't need to type these emails any more. I only need to speak them out. It saves a lot of work at the keyboard.

I've also found that he responds to any name. I discovered it when I said "Make us a pot of tea, Benito," and he didn't bat an eyelid. (Figuratively speaking). In fact, I asked him if he would like a cup, and he said yes. So now I make enough for two. Then when I've finished mine, I pour his cup down Grim Reaper's throat.

Oh dear, I haven't told you about Grim Reaper yet. Sorry.

Its real name is The Reprocessor or the The Reprogrammer or something like that. I can't actually remember. I think it is really what makes the mission feasible. Put simply, Grim Reaper can make anything out of anything. You put in waste and rubbish at one end, and whatever Big Nimp wants it to make comes out at the other. I can't begin to tell you how it is done. I think of it as magic. When I say waste and rubbish, I mean everything. I have followed the plumbing - the drains all go into it. The fresh water comes from it. I prefer not to think about that too much, but you have to agree it is amazing. I have never had the slightest complaint about any food or drink since I have been on board.

There are two ways in to Grim Reaper; the throat, as I call it, is for slops and liquids. I like to do the washing up myself rather than leave it to Big Nimp; it seems more homely, somehow. Mind you, it is not much more than the odd cup and saucer. Also, although I could let

29

the dirty water go down the plug-hole, from where it would end up in Grim Reaper as I said before, I prefer to wash up in a washing-up bowl so as to save the water, and then I carry it through to the throat, being careful not to slop any out on the way. I don't want to stain the carpet! If I pour the dirty water down quickly enough, there is a satisfying gurgle from somewhere deep down inside. I enjoy hearing it. It sounds a little like the satisfied belch my granddad sometimes did at the end of a good meal.

Come to think of it, the top of the throat looks rather like a gurgle jug shaped like a fish with an open mouth, which my granddad had. He said he had inherited it from one of the aunts.

Talking of Granddad and mechanical noises, I remember once going with him into the bank to draw money out from the bank machine. He pointed out to me that at a certain stage of the transaction, when he had keyed in the amount and pressed enter, the machine would make a little noise, "Urr - Urr;" he said it was just like the call of the Corncrake, a bird he remembered from his youth. Farm machinery had killed them all off on the mainland now, he explained, which is why you don't hear them any more. I did not like to correct him, but personally I thought the noise was more like the call of a Woodcock. Does a Corncrake repeat its note, anyway?

The other way into Grim Reaper is impressive. It looks like a solid metal wall until you get close to it, but as you do, it divides into a pair of doors which open inwards automatically, about the width of the French windows in Granddad's old home, but only half the height. The doors are at floor level, so you don't have to lift heavy items. When you have pushed whatever it is inside, the doors swing shut again, and become a solid wall; you cannot see any seam at all. Most fascinating. I call this entrance the mouth.

If you think about it, they could not afford to jettison anything from the ship, as it would become space debris, and could prove disastrous for a later mission. It's bad enough to have space debris in orbit around planets, where the speeds are small, but to have it floating around in deep space is an awful thought. As it is, everything gets reused.

Grim Reaper can also make things from scratch. There must be a lot of sand or something down below that can be used to fuel it. Fancy making a grand piano out of sand. I know it could do it, because Big Nimp once offered to make me one, but I said no. I don't want to play any music at present; I can't explain why.

Things that you order - well, Big Nimp actually places the order - come out of a hole and slide down some rollers. I have had rather fun with the rollers. I ordered a hand bell, and two metres of a thin metal strip, about an inch wide. When they came, I bent the metal round and round on itself until it was looped in several tight circles. When I released it, the circles expanded, like a large spring. I bolted one end onto Grim Reaper himself, and hung the hand bell on the other end so that it was suspended just above the rollers. Now, when anything comes down the rollers, there is a cheerful "Ding-a-ling ling!" which goes on for up to a minute, until the bell finally stops dancing about.

Big Nimp cannot understand it at all. He regards the bell as hopelessly antiquated. He keeps offering to sound a note for me himself when items come through. I decline. What he does not know is that I have very few memories of my home when I was still with my parents, but I do remember that the front door had a bell pull by it, which activated a suspended bell like the one

31

I have described. Is it so wrong of me to want to have one here? I had a wretched childhood, but there are a few happy memories. I thought I might recreate some of the things here and now that I remember. I feel safe doing it, as there is nobody here to tell me off.

Really, Grim Reaper is not unlike one of those machines they have at airports for X-raying the hand luggage, but it is much larger. From mouth to rollers is about twenty five metres, although it is hard to be sure, because the various small rooms you have to go through to get from the mouth to the rollers make it a long route on foot. It is a little confusing. You could say it was shaped like an enormous steam locomotive from the 1950s, especially as, although it reaches right up to the ceiling for most of its length, in two places it only rises three metres from the floor. The fact that its top is rounded at these points does make it look like a steam train's boiler. A bit like Gordon, really.

Back to its name; Grim Reaper. You've probably guessed why I call it that. I know that I am not going to live long enough to see this trip through, and when my time comes to go, I will be pushed in through the double doors. It is not a nice thought, but you have to face up to these things. At least I have the consolation of feeling that I am a link in a chain, and that my body will be of value to science when I am gone. In the meantime, the thing to do is to be faithful in fulfilling my part in the mission.

There is a happier side to it, of course. All I need to do is to say, "Sausage, Egg and Chips on a Postman Pat plate in bone china, please," and it comes in a few minutes. I still have not finished the first bottle of ketchup. I could have a new one each time, but that is wasteful; instead I keep the bottle in the fridge for next time. I hate waste. I also save the plates; I

have a nice collection, which is gradually
growing. I have explained to Big Nimp to do a
different design of plate each time.

Ah well. Happy days.

Come to think of it, what is going to do the
pushing when my time comes to go, I wonder?

Bruce

There was no need to feel nervous, Bruce told himself, as he
stood on the platform next morning. Would the train never arrive? It
was strange how often it had to be a few minutes late. He hated
wasting time, even though part of him appreciated that running the
trains was a complex business, and we all often make mistakes.
Perhaps he could afford to be a little more generous towards the
staff, who were doubtless trying their best.

Ah, here it was at last. Bruce found his usual seat. The diagonal
girl was there. He tried to settle into his book. What was this? She
was nudging his leg with her foot. "It's your station," she was
urging. "Time to get out."

"Thank you," he smiled, "but I'm going further today." He
could see she was puzzled. Oh dear, he had not foreseen this aspect
of things. He began to feel even more uncomfortable than before, if
possible. How far would she be travelling, he wondered?

As the train slowed for the next station, she stood up, ready to
get out. This was it, he realised. Why was his heart beating so
loudly? Was everybody in the carriage aware of the thumping
sound, he wondered?

He followed her onto the platform and made sure he kept close
to her in the small crowd as they walked out of the exit. They were
soon in a street lined with shops that he did not know. He had never
alighted here before. He strode quickly to catch up with her.
"Excuse me," he said, clearing his throat to try and dislodge the frog
that had taken up residence there. She stopped and looked at him.
"Look, I don't know how else to do this, but I could not bear to say
anything in front of the people in the carriage. What I was
wondering was, could I take you out for a meal some time?" Bruce
gave her no time to reply. "Think it over; here's my card. I would

be very pleased if you felt able to say yes. Thanks. Bye!" and with that, he turned on his heels and made his way back into the station.

The girl actually laughed out loud, but was careful that he should not hear it. Men! Really! All the same, he was rather sweet. And it was nice to be invited out.

Bruce made a point of not looking back to see where she was going. She needed to have space! The ball was now in her court. She would get in touch, he was sure of it. All the same, he felt hot all over as he sat on the platform waiting for a train home. No doubt, he could have handled it better, but at least he had managed to say something.

Had he allowed himself to watch where she went, he would have seen her walk thirty yards along the street, and then go into the second shop on the left. He would have realised from the posters outside that it was a newsagent. However, he would not have seen her buying a picture postcard and a stamp, and then writing a few words on it, before making her way out of the back of the shop onto a service road. There she paused for a moment to tear something in half from corner to corner – it might have been the postcard, it was hard to tell from a distance – before dropping the two halves into a convenient waste-bin. Then she set off along the service road walking away from the station until she came to a parked car. She got into the passenger seat, and the car moved off.

When the man from the council came to empty the waste-bin forty minutes later, it might have appeared odd to any passers-by that he should look inside the black bin liner before he gathered it up. But then on the other hand, it might have seemed the natural thing to do. Maybe the man had found valuables in waste-bins before now. Perhaps his philosophy of life was that you never know what lies round the next corner. There seemed nothing of importance in this bin, so he thrust the liner into the cart with the others before moving on.

```
7. From: Mission 12
   To: Undisclosed recipients
   Sent:
```

I am lonely! That is the bottom line. I tried
to get Big Nimp to make a virtual dog, to keep me
company, by holographic projection. The trouble
was that he had never seen a dog. I made an
interesting discovery about this. Even though
there are hours of video inside him about dogs,
and all the books you could dream of about them
as well, he cannot interpret them. To him, all
the information is just a string of digits.

I had to describe the animal. I did my best,
but when he had finished, the result was nothing
at all like a dog. This was my fault, not Big
Nimp's; my description was not clear enough. I
told the creature to sit, and it did so the first
time, which was ludicrous; I suppose Big Nimp
cannot understand about stubbornness. Then when I
tried to stroke what he had made, my hand passed
through the projection. It was quite useless,
really.

Then I had another idea. I feigned death, to
see what would happen. We used to play Dead Lions
when we were little. You lie on the floor without
moving or breathing, until the mother of the
child whose party it is declares the winner. I
used to be very good at it.

Anyway, I had not lost my touch. I lay as still
as I could for several minutes, and then quickly
opened my eyes and looked about me. I was just in
time to see two little robots, about eighteen
inches high, scuttling off out of the door. I ran
after them, but they had disappeared, into the
solid wall, it seemed to me. I tried coaxing them
out by saying "Kutchy Koo", but it was no use.
They did not reappear. I reckon their job is to
push bulky waste items into Grim Reaper's mouth.
I wonder why the furniture does not suffer that
fate. Strange.

That phrase Kutchy Koo was on a TV programme I
once saw. I've never forgotten it.

Bruce

35

Bruce had not expected her to get in touch on the Friday. She was probably at work. Anyway, she would need time to think it over. The only thing to do was to wait. Patience was not his strong point!

In the afternoon, one of his lessons was interrupted by the doorbell. That's funny, Bruce thought; I'm not expecting anybody now. It turned out to be a firm of builders offering to coat the house with a new high tech coating at a ridiculously cheap rate due to some special offer. Bruce had a stock response to such people.

"I'm sorry; it's not my house. It belongs to the lady that lives there," he pointed next door, "so ask her. Thank you."

By Saturday lunchtime, he was beginning to feel uncomfortable. The phone had not rung. Not that he could have taken a phone call that morning, as he had piano lessons all through. He never answered the phone when giving a lesson; people had to leave a message.

It was turning out to be the hottest day of the summer so far. After weighing it up over lunch, he decided he would go for a swim in the afternoon anyway, in the open air pool. The pool would be dreadfully crowded. He would also have to be careful where he looked. However, there was one of those narrow twisting rivers with a gentle current. He would be able to lie on his back there, quietly floating round and round the circuit, staring up at the sky. That should be alright. He liked lying on his back in a swimming pool, because then the water did not go up his nostrils. It was strange, because when he was a boy, he had happily swum under water. Nowadays he could not abide the water up his nose. This meant that when he was swimming on his front, breast stroke was Okay, but certainly not crawl.

As a boy, he had loved swimming pools. He used to go with a bunch of his school friends. Their main activity was splashing each other. The others just thrashed the water generally. Bruce had discovered that if he held his fingers close together, leaving no gaps, and moved his hand vigorously forwards over the surface of the pool, a powerful jet of water would shoot forwards. With practice, he had become very accurate with this. What he liked to do was to pause a moment or two in the middle of a fight, and wait until a friend of his opened his mouth to say something, and then strike. He could fill an open mouth with deadly accuracy anywhere up to fifteen feet away. The friend would collapse spluttering. It was hardly surprising that Bruce was undisputed king of the water when it came to splashing.

However, once they had got a bit older, and interest in girls had begun to kick in, it all went wrong. You could not splash girls; they did not like it. His group of friends had broken up, and nowadays, Bruce never really knew what to do in a swimming pool. There were the keen types who swam up and down endlessly, for the sake of fitness and health. He was not one of those; he never had to think about diet or anything of that kind. He stayed permanently slim. Diving had never appealed to him. So on the whole, he just floated and enjoyed getting cool. It was a bit dull really, but he could not think of anything better to do.

He gathered up his swimming things, locked the front door, and made his way to the pool. It was conveniently close to where he lived. There was a large crowd, but never mind that. After changing, he put his clothes in the locker, and put the elastic key band round his arm. Going through the cold shower was normally awful, but today it was lovely because of the heat. Oh dear, here were all the girls – he was out of the men only area now. Try to ignore them and their chattery laughter. Part of him was pleased that they were obviously enjoying themselves. He felt a stab of loneliness. Perhaps Bill would have joined him. He had not thought to ring.

At least the gentle river was fairly empty. Yes, this was fine; it had been a good idea to come here. The white fluffy clouds above were beautiful. Bruce found himself imagining them as castles and hillsides, delightful places to explore and roam.

"Hello Sir!"

"Hello Sir!"

He came to with a jerk. It was the two scamps. Acknowledge the daughters of Jerusalem.

"Hello Beccy, Hello Simna. What on earth are you doing here?" Take the offensive.

"Having a swim, sir. But what are you doing here?"

Why shouldn't he be allowed to swim too he wondered. Did they need to sound quite so surprised?

"Oh, just having a general wallow. I expect you know the song?"

Naturally, they did not.

"'Mud, mud," he sang, not too loudly, "glorious mud! Nothing quite like it for cooling the blood. So follow me follow, down to the hollow, and there let us wallow in glor...- i - ous mud!' Sadly, there isn't a mud-bath closer than Africa, so I have to put up with this water instead, which is a bitter disappointment, but I am bearing it bravely."

The girls loved that. He needed to keep the initiative.

"You know, you swim like a crocodile, Beccy."

"Like a crocodile?"

"Crocodiles have scales that are very important to them, and as a pianist, so do you."

"Very funny," said Simna. "And what do I swim like?"

"You swim like the big fish in the book of Jonah, because you are having a whale of a time." It was not too bad for communicating with twelve year-olds, Bruce considered.

"Sir, didn't the big fish swallow a man down whole?" Beccy asked. "Do you think Simna could do that when she's a bit older?"

Oh dear, thought Bruce, they do grow up fast these days. What an attitude to relationships! He peered carefully at Simna, shading his eyes, and generally copying the movements professional golfers make when considering a long putt on the green, and then said, "Yes possibly. But you have to remember that the big fish did not digest Jonah, but spat him out again afterwards."

"Oh Simna!" said Beccy. Simna blushed. A change of subject was needed.

"I bet you can't do a handstand," Bruce said.

That was splendid. Of course they were both brilliant at handstands, and before long, Bruce was giving them marks.

"Very good, Beccy, 54% for that one. You need to keep your ankles a bit closer together. Oh, there goes Simna. Yes..., Simna, not bad, but the feet do need to point straight upwards in the air for a really good score. Shall we say 57%?"

This was going fine. There were probably parents watching somewhere, but they would be quite happy with this.

"Excellent, Beccy. 76%. Now, to improve you need to brace your feet and point the toes at the clouds, like a ballet dancer." The important thing was to sound authoritative.

"Simna, wonderful. 84%. Do you give water ballet lessons?"

Politics demanded that they both achieved 100%, which they soon did. They thought it was great fun.

"Now you do one, sir." Oh dear, this was not what he had had in mind.

"Okay," he said. He plunged his head down into the water, trying not to mind the tumbling air bubbles round his face. He knew his handstand was very poor. When he came up, there was no sign of the scamps. He looked around mystified. Then he heard laughter and looked upwards; they were on top of a small footbridge over the river, waving down at him. "11%. See you on Thursday, sir. Bye!"

"Bye," he replied. He chuckled to himself. It had been nice to see them.

As he towelled himself dry, he found himself thinking of a story his granddad had once told him. When he was a young man, Granddad had been driving one of the very early motor cars, with a friend in the passenger seat. They were going along the high street in the small town where he lived, when the friend had suddenly said, "Stop the car. Pull up. That girl walking along the pavement, no, that one with the long hair, that's the girl I mean to marry. Do you know her? Good. Introduce me!" And with that, Granddad had found himself introducing his friend to the girl. In due time, they had got engaged and then married, and enjoyed over fifty years together.

It was a remarkable story. Bruce gave a sigh. Then he remembered. He had better get home in case there was a message on the answerphone. He got dressed a bit too quickly, without thinking, because he soon found he was getting hot again from all the movement. How ridiculous!

There was no message. Never mind. Perhaps she would give her reply in the train on Monday.

There was also his second cousin Banjo – her real name was unpronounceable. She had been in a lift one morning at work, minding her own business, when a young man had got in. He had recently decided that he was going to get married before he was thirty. He was on the look-out for an eligible girl, and Banjo happened to be there. Bruce did not know how he managed it, but sure enough, they got married and lived happily ever after, as far as Bruce knew, which was not very far at all. Perhaps they had rows. He really did not know. Still, it was another story with a happy ending.

It was the journey to the school on Monday morning that finally sealed it for him. The diagonal girl was not there, nor on Tuesday, nor Wednesday. Bruce had had a lot of disappointments during his life. He was sure of one thing. A previous history of hopes being dashed did not make this one any easier to bear.

8. From: Mission 12
To: Undisclosed recipients
Sent:

I try to make myself useful. You have probably been wondering what I do all day. I vacuum the carpet of course! Yes, I expect Big Nimp could do it, but I bet he would not reach into the corners with the little nozzle. I take great care over it. There are lots of little nooks and crannies, especially in the dorm.

Oh my goodness, what have I done! I have not even told you about the sleeping quarters. Sorry. I did not mean to keep you in the dark.

There are twenty-four astronauts in hibernation in what I think of as the front part of the ship. I call it the dormitory. They are inside plastic coffins, with only their eyes visible, just like in the film 2001: A Space Odyssey. They might as well be statues that you sometimes see lying in English churches, made of stone, on top of tombs, sometimes with a little stone dog at their feet, as there is no sign of life. There is no movement, no sound. Everything is still.

When I told you earlier that all films ever made were in Big Nimp, there is one exception. They left out 2001. You can understand why if you have seen it.

Above each sleeper, there is a lever, to reactivate them. I suppose that when the time comes, Big Nimp will wake the first one, and then it will be that person's job to wake the rest manually, as required. I expect there are plans about this ready to be revealed in due course.

I did move my bed into the dorm for one night, to see if it felt like having company being with the others, but it was no use. There was no sound or movement. I moved back to my own little room next day. I feel snug there.

Bruce

PS When I say nooks and crannies for vacuuming, the coffins, for want of a better word, stand on eight feet. Rather an odd arrangement, because it is a real trap for dust. Not that there is much dust inside the ship, of course, but one wants to keep standards up. I do the vacuuming every day.

Thursday's journey passed uneventfully. The young people seemed to have tired of their flying antics, and the other passengers in the carriage behaved in their usual non-communicative manner. Bruce was relieved.

All the same, as there were a few spare minutes at the end of Araminta's lesson, Bruce decided to have a little fun.

"I'm going to test you on some theory," he announced. "The key is D minor. With the left hand, I want you to play the tonic and then the dominant, in that order."

Araminta thought for a moment, and then played a D followed by the A above it.

"Good. Now I want you to do the same thing using the right hand, but adding in the mediant when you play the dominant, sounding two notes together."

Araminta duly played another D followed by and F and an A at the same time.

"Well done. Now I want you to play all the notes you have played so far, immediately followed by the same passage in retrograde." That was quite a challenge, but to Bruce's surprise, she got it. She played the five notes in ascending order followed by the same five notes in reverse: D A D F+A F+A D A D.

"Excellent. Now what music is that?"

She had not been expecting that, and was caught on the hop.

"Oh dear," she said, and played it again. Then her eyes lit up. "The Snowman!" she said, with delight.

"Yes," said Bruce, "it's the introduction to the well known song 'I'm walking in the air.'"

They both laughed. "Nice one," said Araminta. "You know, if I was ever in real trouble, you would be the one I would come to."

This sounded rather serious. Bruce did not know quite how to take it. He wondered what was coming next.

To his surprise, Araminta asked, "Do you give lessons at home?"

"Yes."

"My older sister has moved back and is living with us now, and she would like some lessons."

"Tell her to give me ring," Bruce replied. "Your mum has my number. I'll look forward to hearing from her." Bruce was pleased. Any sister of Araminta's was bound to be nice.

She got up to leave. "Araminta?"

"Yes?"

"A word of advice, in advance of there being any major problems."

"What's that?"

"Stay on the straight and narrow."

"I will, Mr. Winter, don't you worry." And with that she was off.

During the scamps' lesson, which was even more boisterous than usual following Saturday's escapade, Jane, the head of music, came bustling in.

"I'm sorry, Bruce, but the builders are re-pointing your wall this morning. They won't need to come inside, but there may be some noise."

"Fine. Thanks..."

Sure enough, there was noise. Why is it, Bruce wondered, that jobs like that cannot be left until the summer holidays? Indeed, it was half term in two days' time. Crazy! And did it really involve all that drilling? It was hard to hear himself think. He supposed that they were gouging out the old mortar to make way for the new.

Beccy and Simna thought it was fun. They tried to play along in time to the drilling, with a marked lack of success.

That evening back at home, after the last pupil had left, the doorbell rang. It was Marjorie. Her white hair suited her, Bruce reckoned; it made her look distinguished.

"Have all your pupils gone now?"

"Yes. Even the Lost Chord has died away. Come in." He liked Marjorie.

When she had sat down, she said, "There's an exhibition of Van Gogh's paintings starting soon at the Tate Gallery. I had thought of going, and I wondered whether you might like to come with me."

"What a lovely idea. Yes, I would like that very much." Bruce was keen on paintings, and he liked the gaudy colours of Van Gogh's work.

"I don't know whether you are familiar with the story of his life, but if not, I have a biography here." Marjorie searched for a moment, and then reached down a hardback book from a shelf. It had a paper jacket sporting the famous Van Gogh chair. "You might like to mug up on him in advance."

Bruce thanked her, and took the book. They arranged to go on Saturday week.

"One more thing. I've decided to take up the offer of having the house coated. They called here, I believe. I'm afraid it may cause some inconvenience, but not much, I hope, as they guarantee to get it done all in the one day. You will be out for quite a lot of it. I made them promise to start work at eight a.m. sharp."

"Right. I am sure it will be no problem."

Now there would be building work at home as well. How ridiculous. Never mind.

```
9. From: Mission 12
To: Undisclosed recipients
Sent:
```

I did the jig when we had done a tenth of a light year, but my heart was not in it. There was nobody to celebrate with. Still, the St. Paul's Suite is nice.

Big Nimp is even more astonishing than I thought. He has got to know me so well that he can even read my mind! I don't have to say things out loud any more. If I think "Pot of tea", he makes it without being asked. I feel threatened by it at times. It is hard to remember that he is only a machine.

Sorry to go on about tea so often. You will think that I do nothing but sit around drinking tea all day!

I feel I need to confess. The fact is, I think I have had a hallucination! It was like this. I was just doing a little polishing - the parts of the walls I can reach buff up ever so well with a little persistence - when there was an almighty clatter from one of the little storage rooms beyond the gyp. I call them that because they look and feel like storage rooms, although there is nothing stored in them. All the metal cupboards are empty.

Anyway, the noise sounded as if somebody had knocked about a dozen saucepans onto the floor. I

44

was really scared, I can tell you. My immediate thought was that there was somebody else in the ship. But where could they have possibly come from? I had searched everywhere, and apart from squeezing in behind the large hose on a drum inside one of the storage room cupboards, which is for extinguishing fires I imagine, there is nowhere that anybody could have hidden.

I walked slowly towards the door where the sound had come from, my heart beating wildly. I decided it would be better to announce myself rather than come on somebody unexpectedly, so I said in a shaking voice, "Can I help you?"

To my complete surprise, a voice said, "Yeah, mate, any chance of a cup of tea?" And out stepped a man dressed in a brown boiler suit with a few buttons missing. It was a bit stained in places too. I was rooted to the spot. I was so astonished that all I could do was to whisper back to him, "Any chance of a cup of tea? Any chance of a cup of tea? Any chance of a cup of tea?"

He smiled at me. Then he turned and went inside the room out of view. I walked quickly after him, but by the time I had gone in through the doorway, there was no sign of him. I searched carefully, but there was nowhere he could have hidden.

I wondered briefly whether Big Nimp had played a trick on me, but I soon decided against that. I believe I simply imagined the whole episode. What is alarming about it is that in a law court under oath, I would have happily sworn that things took place as I have said. But really, it must have been a hallucination.

You can make of the episode what you will, but personally I feel a bit edgy. I tried to talk to Big Nimp about it, but he seemed uninterested.

I feel rather upset about Big Nimp actually. I have always tried to be friendly to him, but my

impression is that now that he has understood me,
as it were, he has lost interest in me. I feel
the absence of some of our old banter. He still
does everything I ask, of course, but things are
not as they were.
    Bruce

The following week was half term. Bruce used to cancel all
lessons during half terms and holidays. It was the best way, he had
found. Everyone needs a break from time to time, not least himself.
He and Bill went to stay at a retreat house in Dorset that Bill was
rather keen on, for four nights. Gnilla was working in the florist's
shop, and was unable to get away. Bruce disliked there being so
many people, but the cliff walks were good, and made a pleasant
change from town life. Also, as it was a place for contemplation,
everyone understood if you wanted to read quietly without being
disturbed.

The book about Van Gogh proved to be most interesting. It
turned out that Vincent's life had been a very painful one, right until
the end. To Bruce's surprise, he discovered that Vincent probably
never sold a single painting during his lifetime. Indeed, he only took
up painting after he had failed at a number of other things. His
father had been totally exasperated with him and wrote him off.
Bruce began to warm to him.

The only person who stuck by Vincent was his brother Theo. He
never gave up on him. This made it all the more devastating for
Vincent when Theo told him he was going to get married. He felt
completely betrayed.

Vincent's own attempts to form a relationship had ended in
failure. He was too rough, and would easily fly into a temper. At
one time, he tried to settle down with a prostitute, but it did not
work. He even cut off part of his ear and sent it to her, to make
some point or other, hence the self-portrait of him with the

bandaged ear. It was most bizarre. However, the woman was not impressed. Oh dear, it made Bruce's problems seem as nothing!

When Theo was married, Vincent was invited to stay the weekend with the happy couple. Somehow or other, he managed to behave civilly towards the girl for the whole visit, to his surprise. It was the only time they ever met.

The story ended in tragedy. Theo died, leaving a little boy. Vincent shot himself, aged thirty-seven. The wound itself was not fatal, but he died of an infection, which set in as a result of the shot, twenty-four hours later.

Theo's wife now set about putting Vincent on the map. She got her son David recognised in law as the rightful owner of the unclaimed pictures. Then for the next twenty years, she promoted him to art galleries and exhibitions. Her efforts met with success. As the artist's work began to be appreciated, people who had received paintings as gifts from the mad Vincent gradually grasped that what they had might be valuable. Canvases came out of lofts and coal holes. One that was rescued had been used to block up a broken window pane. People began saying that Vincent's work had been prophetic. The opinion about Vincent's paintings changed to such an extent that the day came when David Van Gogh was the richest man in Holland. And this was all because of Theo's wife, who had caused Vincent such grief. If it had not been for her, nobody would have heard of Vincent Van Gogh.

Bruce found this story incredibly moving. Here was a man who was a failure not just for most of his life but for all of it. Even his death was a failure; his attempt at suicide had misfired, literally. And yet, he had kept on producing these fabulous paintings. What an inspiration to keep on and never give up. Bruce actually cried. Then he got up, and went to the piano, not the one in the lounge but an upright in a small meeting room tucked out of the way, and played Climb Every Mountain from the Sound of Music, working up to full volume in the second verse. It was a favourite of his. How true it was that when God closes a door, somewhere he opens a window, as the Reverend Mother said in the film. It had been true for Van Gogh perhaps it would be true for him. Never give up! It was the only way.

10. From: Mission 12
To: Undisclosed recipients
Sent:

Father, I am so glad I took the trouble to learn biblical Hebrew as well as New Testament Greek. Simply translating one chapter of the Old Testament each day keeps my hand in. Thank you too for all the aids in Big Nimp. Those reference books are great. However, what I want to know is, what does the Hebrew word *no'd* in Psalm 56 verse 8 really mean? I am aware that the usual translation is "Put my tears into your *bottle*," but what I want to know is, how big is the bottle? Is it as large as a bath, for example?

You will know why I'm asking this. I send all these chatty emails back home, and I want them to be happy, and in many ways I am happy, but there is so much grief as well. However, I can hardly tell them that one of the best things about the trip from my point of view is that I can howl as loud as I like and there is nobody to hear me or complain, can I? It would make such depressing reading. They would think I had flipped my lid, and perhaps was even endangering the mission. Perhaps I have lost it. But I am absolutely determined on one thing. I never felt so sure about anything in my life; this mission takes priority over any and every feeling I may have. I am actually surprised at myself; I simply did not know that it was possible for anyone to be so determined about anything as I am about ensuring the mission's success. It's extraordinary, really.

One of the great things here is that there are so many aids to expressing my grief. In fact, I only have to allow the idea of Mozart to come into my head and it sets me off again. He had such a painful life! And yet he was so utterly brilliant! His music seems to have welled up from an untroubled reservoir deep inside himself, no matter what storms he was going through at the time. I find myself picturing a wonderfully placid pool, deep, cool and inviting! Amazing. I actually cried for ninety minutes solid the other evening when Big Nimp played Mozart's Haffner Serenade for me. It did help; I felt better afterwards.

Anyway, how big was the bottle in Psalm 56? I reckon my tears would have filled a bath by now. I suppose it does not sound very good, but I am a bit curious; if all my tears had been saved up, would I have out-cried the Psalmist?

It's not that I am sure where all my grief comes from. I know I was separated from my parents when I was still little, and yes, my memory of them is that they had rows all the time; that's so painful. Still, I had Granddad. Oh yes, I must send them an email about him. Thank you for him again. He was wonderful. And I really am so sorry about you know what. It makes me sad each time I think of it. And yes, there are other things that make me sad. But this sad?

The odd thing about it is that I don't feel depressed. I actually feel quite comfortable crying each day. It's a strange thing, the human body. But you know all about it; after all, you did invent it.

What does it mean that we are made in your image, I wonder?

How strange that on the answerphone when he returned, there should be three new enquiries from adults for piano lessons. In September, when everything was starting up again after the summer holidays, he could understand it, but not in June. Mentally, Bruce was beginning to wind down towards the summer break, and he imagined that this was true for the rest of the world as well. This was probably because he worked in a school. On reflection, he realised that there was no reason for other people to be caught up in the system of school terms and holidays as he was.

One enquiry was from Araminta's sister, who turned out to be named Sarah. She sounded rather cold over the phone, Bruce thought, which puzzled him a bit. She was immediately available, so Bruce fixed the first lesson for the following evening. When she arrived, she turned out to be a good deal older than Araminta, to Bruce's surprise; he guessed that the age gap was about ten years. She also had high cheek bones, like Araminta, but her behaviour was distinctly frosty. The contrast to Araminta's warmth was marked.

Still, she was an able pianist. Bruce suggested she tackle two pieces together as a contrasting pair. The Prelude in C minor from Book One of Bach's Forty-eight Preludes and Fugues, which was all under the fingers but needed to rattle along at a good pace, would help her technique. Then Debussy's terrific piece *La Cathedrale Engloutie* (The Submerged Cathedral) was one for all pianists to try at some point. Wonderful atmosphere, and a gorgeous sound. She was happy with the suggestions. She fixed to come weekly on Thursday evenings.

11. From: Mission 12
To: Undisclosed recipients
Sent:

I promised to tell you about my granddad. He was great. He brought me up single-handed from when I was not quite five. I never discovered what happened to my parents or my sister. I was just taken to Granddad's home one day by some strangers, and my parents never came to collect me. I never saw them again.

I will always remember the day of Granddad's funeral. After the ceremony in the church, we drove to the cemetery. It was so wet! The wind was so strong that the rain was lashing along

50

parallel to the ground. Within a minute of leaving the car, I was soaked through. Mixed with the rain were hundreds of green leaves that were being torn off the trees even though it was the height of summer. The grave was on a slope, and there was water running into it in streams. I strained my ears to hear the clergyman's words, but to be honest, I did not catch much. Then they lowered the coffin. I threw in some earth, but it was mud actually. I did catch the words "dust to dust;" ironic really, as there was no chance of anything staying dry enough to be described as dust.

Oh dear. Now I need to confess. I have waited until we are far enough from earth that nobody can get cross with me, or shout at me.

What you have just read is how I wish it had been. I feel so bad about it. Really, the funeral was on the hottest day in summer. The sun blazed down. I would like to have worn an open shirt, shorts and sandals, and the stupid thing was that I could hear my granddad saying, "Yes it's fine to dress casually, Bruce; I want you to be comfortable. Be relaxed, and don't care what anyone else thinks." But I could not do it. I wore my suit, with a sober tie, and proper black shoes. I was so hot I can't describe it. The heat was bad enough in the church, but at the cemetery it was unbearable. And this is the really horrible thing. My feet were so hot and sweaty inside my beastly shoes that I could not think about anything else. I felt that there was a river of sweat running down my back inside my shirt, although it probably was not like that really. There were all these people coming up saying how sorry they were, and all I wanted was for the thing to finish so I could rush home and get into a cold bath and stay there for an hour to cool down.

I still feel really bad about it now. My
granddad was so good to me, and I could not even
concentrate on his funeral for my own concerns.
How's that for ingratitude! After all he had done
for me!

If you don't want to read any more emails from
me, I will understand, but if you could find it
in yourself to forgive me, I would be so
grateful.

There. I feel better now I have told you.

Bruce

Next day, there were no lessons as it was the second Saturday of
half term. Bruce's policy was to teach the first Saturday, but not the
second, so that the young people had one week off, but not two.
This meant that he and Marjorie were able to set off for the Van
Gogh exhibition early in the day, when the crowds were likely to be
less. Marjorie had bought their tickets in advance to avoid queuing.
She was quite a goer in her own way.

The journey up to town was uneventful. Bruce had the feeling
that the sky acrobats were tending to arrange meeting points where
hundreds would gather, rather like the gatherings of motorbikes
there used to be in his granddad's day. As a result they hardly saw a
single one. Really the sky-cars flying up above had no impact on
them, since they travelled so high, unless you happened to see one
take off from nearby. They did spot one. The vertical ascent still
looked novel; everyone was so used to the forwards motion needed
by aeroplanes. Rising straight upwards, like a diver coming up to
the surface of the sea, had obvious advantages, in terms of
economical use of the space. For one thing, collisions were less
likely.

They got to the Tate to find a large crowd. "This way," Marjorie
announced, as if she owned the place, and they marched through an
opening marked Members Only. Bruce felt uneasy about this, but
she waved his protests aside. "We are members for the day. Look,
here are the tickets."

It was an effective route. They got to the door of the exhibition in no time. While they were being admitted, they agreed to go round at their own speed and then meet just inside the exit from the exhibition when they had finished. They stepped forward into the first room, and from that point, Bruce was mesmerised.

Even the early works were worth seeing. He enjoyed the Potato Eaters. That dated from the time of Vincent's failed attempt at being a missionary to poor people. It was strange how he had taken to thinking of him as Vincent, Bruce thought; it was almost as if they were kindred spirits. They both knew what it was to feel frustrated and powerless.

Really, Bruce just wanted to get to his favourite picture, the track through the cornfield with the black crows flying, but he made himself stop at every picture in turn. Wonderful, thick paint, squeezed straight from the tube! The furze bushes were good fun, Bruce thought. He wondered whether Vincent had enjoyed painting; he felt sure he had. Was it sufficient reward to believe you had created something of real value even if nobody else shared your opinion?

Here at last was the cornfield and the crows. The crowd was momentarily less here and Bruce was able to get a prime position, exactly in front of the middle of the picture, with no necks to peer past. It was glorious. His eyes began to fill with tears, which was ridiculous because they were clouding his vision, and he had come to see the pictures, not to get all emotional!

"Excuse me," said a gentle voice on his left, "but are you going to stand there all day?"

He turned to look. It was a nice looking girl, with more freckles than Bruce had ever seen on a face before. Her medium length brown hair was dishevelled. She wasn't really cross at all, but she did want a better view.

"Yes, if I possibly can," Bruce replied, but he moved over to his right as he did so, allowing her a better view. "Sorry to get in your way."

"That's Okay," she replied. "It is a wonderful painting, isn't it?"

"Fabulous. You know he shot himself in a cornfield, do you?"

The girl did not, and Bruce found himself telling her the story of the book. When he finished, the girl said, "My boy-friend would have loved to hear that. He's over there, looking at the Sunflowers. I'd better go and join him." Lucky fellow, thought Bruce.

"Will you give him a message from me?" Bruce said.

The girl looked at him in surprise.

"Tell him he's a lucky man to have found you."

She was obviously pleased. Bruce was happy too; it would make her day.

Marjorie was waiting for him as arranged. They went off and found a bite to eat, and discussed what they had seen. It had been a wonderful morning, they both agreed.

Marjorie had other things she wanted to do in town, so they decided to go their separate ways after lunch. Bruce thought he would wander through some of the other rooms in the gallery before heading off home. They were practically deserted. He chose to pass through a number of rooms fairly quickly, so as to get a general impression of several centuries of painting, rather than concentrate on a small area. It was a thing he had done before.

As he was proceeding in this way, he entered a new room, and his attention was immediately gripped by a picture. Who was this lovely girl, floating in a stream, surrounded by ribbons and flowers? It turned out to be Ophelia, from Hamlet, after she had drowned herself. Bruce was fascinated. She looked so peaceful, lying there in death. He could not remember the play, but something dreadful must have happened for her to want to take that course of action. She could have made somebody happy, surely? Were there girls around today feeling just as lonely as he was, who like him did not know how to make any progress? What a gloomy thought that was. Bruce sighed. Why was life so difficult?

He looked carefully at the painting, and admired the detailed work. What skill those artists had! He was so glad to have come.

He went back to the Van Gogh rooms to see whether his ticket would allow him to go round again, but the man on the door said he was sorry, there were too many people wanting to visit to allow that. Never mind; it had been a good day.

12. From: Mission 12
To: Undisclosed recipients
Sent:

"Isambard, could you knock me up a scaffolding tower?"

That was me talking to Big Nimp. I told you he answers to any name. I try to match the name to the subject in question, and as it involved engineering, I thought of Isambard Kingdom Brunel. For those of you who don't know, he was the first man to build ships made out of iron, such as the SS Great Britain. Everyone thought they would sink. But they didn't! He just kept right on until they were built. How wonderful to be someone who is not daunted by problems but overcomes them instead. It's good to remember him on a mission like this.

I am saving the name Kingdom for another occasion.

Anyway, the scaffolding tower. It was my idea. I had finished polishing the walls as far up as I could reach, and then I had the brainwave that with a scaffolding tower, I could do the parts higher up as well, and perhaps even the ceilings, although I don't have much of a head for heights. How Michelangelo managed to paint the ceiling in the Sistine Chapel I will never know. I thought that maybe working my way up higher and higher could be my challenge. A man always needs new things to conquer, in my opinion. It will do me good.

Anyway, you should have seen the mess Big Nimp made of making the bits of scaffolding. It took us ever so many attempts. The hardest part was getting the tapering right so that one section would slot into the next with a snug fit. But we managed it in the end. It is quite a good set.

"Clever Clogs," I said, "there's something I don't understand. How is it that you offered to make me a grand piano, but when it comes to something simple like turning out a few bits of scaffolding, you seem to be at a loss. I don't get it."

In reply, he explained that he had no blueprints for scaffolding, but that a set of grand piano instructions had been loaded in for my benefit because they knew I would enjoy being able to play.

I was very moved by this. Someone had taken thought about what would be nice for me!

I don't know if they can be traced, but if somebody reading this could possibly convey my heartfelt thanks to whoever was responsible, I would be so grateful. Please tell them I was deeply touched by their kindness.

It is most odd, but I still don't want a piano to be made. I can't think why I am reluctant to play. Maybe it will come to me later on.

Oh, by the way, I should have said. The alternative to scaffolding was to use a sky-suit, but when I asked Big Nimp, he said no, he was not authorised to make me one, and anyway they would not work in here.

Strange.

Bruce

Araminta was ecstatic about Sarah's lesson the next time he saw her. "She thinks you're brilliant!" she enthused. It certainly had not felt that way. Perhaps Araminta had talked to her in advance of the lesson about Bruce's longings for a mate, as Araminta had perceived them. He was pretty certain she had read his inner thoughts, despite his efforts to keep them secret. That would be enough to make any girl wary!

The Moonlight Sonata was proceeding satisfactorily. The two sisters were an able pair.

He finally worked up the courage to raise the subject on his mind.

"Araminta?"

"Yes?"

"You remember you once said that if I wanted to learn sky-flying, you could recommend a teacher?"

"Ooh yes, Mr. Winter."

"Well, I've been thinking about it. I don't think I could ever be very good at it, but as it is the coming thing, I wonder whether I ought to have a shot at it. Just a lesson or two to try," he added.

"Brilliant!" said Araminta, beaming with pleasure. "My boy friend will teach you."

Oh dear, not quite what he had in mind.

"I was hoping for somebody a bit older, maybe with qualifications..."

"Oh, you needn't worry about that. He is the best! He taught me." She paused. "Did you ever see any groups of young people sky-diving around in formation, doing stunts?"

Bruce looked very thoughtful. "No... I don't think so... Oh, perhaps I may have done," he smiled. "But I can imagine what you mean..."

Araminta was not easily cowed. "Well, my boy friend taught all those."

"Alright, I will give him a try. It will need to be at a weekend, though."

"Perfect. We will collect you from your home at 2.30 on Saturday."

I hope I am doing the right thing, Bruce thought to himself after she had gone. I wonder if I can handle it.

```
13. From: Mission 12
To: Undisclosed recipients
Sent:
```

```
Father, a dreadful thing has happened. I want
to tell you about it, but I suppose you know
already, really. Maybe I could have foreseen it
```

and taken avoiding action; I don't know. I feel awful about it.

It was while I was vacuuming in the dorm. I just glanced at the astronaut sleeping on the right, nearest the front. As you know, only the eyes are visible through the lid of what I call the coffin, but the moment I looked, I realised it was a woman lying there. I tore my view away as quick as I could, but it was too late. In that split second, I had taken in the beauty of her eyelashes. They were wonderful! Even though I could see so little of her, she looked so peaceful lying there.

I know it sounds crazy, but I think I have fallen in love. I ask myself, is that really possible? Love at first sight is all very well, but can you fall in love with a woman when all you can see is her eyes?

I recall something my granddad once said. He was a lifelong churchgoer, as you know. He once said that attending the 1662 service of Holy Communion in his parish church was like looking at a beautiful girl completely enclosed in a medieval suit of armour. All you could see was her eyes looking out through the visor. It was possible to appreciate her beauty, but it took a great deal of imagination. I think what he meant was that he found it difficult to worship in that setting, but I found the image striking, and I have never forgotten it.

Now I have my own parallel situation. One way or another, I have become smitten by a sleeping astronaut. I feel appalled. How could I have been so careless?

Now I want to think rationally about this, so I am talking it over with you. Let's start with the mission. The astronauts are in hibernation because the sixty-nine years of the trip are too long for anyone to contemplate being in a spaceship on a journey. Anybody except me, that is. As you know, I have had such bad experiences with other people that I was glad to get away on my own. However, would the mission suffer if just one of the astronauts was to wake early? I don't know the answer to that, as they never told me what was planned at our destination. What do you think?

I don't want to push you for a quick decision. I'm asking you to give me a gradually growing conviction about this.

Now to what the Bible says. In the creation story, you said, "It is not good for man to be alone." I can agree with you from my personal experience. I feel so lonely!

A few evenings ago, I found myself remembering a walking holiday in Israel I went on once. We were staying in the Tiberias Youth Hostel in the hills above the Sea of Galilee one night. We got there at about five o' clock, and it was delightful. I remembered the words of the hymn: "O Sabbath rest by Galilee, O calm of hills above." They seemed so fitting. However, an hour later, several coach loads of teenagers turned up. They ran in, shouting and screaming, with the odd fight and scuffle here and there, like teenagers do. The other members of our party couldn't stand it. I did not seem to mind much. We survived the night somehow, but I wondered what John Greenleaf Whittier would have thought. He was the one who wrote the hymn, but you knew that already.

Oh yes, that's why that particular memory came to mind; I have been collecting unusual names to call Big Nimp, and Greenleaf seemed rather a good one to me.

Anyway, the point is, that after being on my own for so long, I would give anything for a couple of hundred teenagers to burst in here and run amok. I wouldn't mind if they scuffed up the carpets, and trampled in mud with their feet.

They could even beat me up if they wanted; it's all I'm fit for. It would be better than this solitude. So I agree with you, it is not good for man to be alone.

Then you went on to make a woman out of Adam's rib, as the solution. Is there some sort of joke here? You know that in Hebrew, *rib* (pronounced 'reeve') means 'dispute'. Why do couples fight so much? Or more to the point, why did my parents argue such a lot?

Might the girl turn out to be hostile if I woke her up? I could not bear to end up arguing all the time. Or would she be friendly?

Talking of jokes, in the Garden of Eden, what did Adam say when he was introduced to Eve? Shall I tell you? Yes I know you know already! The answer is, "Madam, I'm Adam". It's a palindrome, same backwards and forwards; can you see? Even the comma after madam gets turned round and upside down to become the inverted comma in I'm. Neat, isn't it? But perhaps it is better not to put in the capital letters as they rather spoil it. Except for the capital I that is. I have seen people use a small 'i' in print to mean themselves sometimes, but it always looks wrong to me.

Sorry to go off at a tangent. I must keep to the point.

Now to One Corinthians chapter seven. Paul starts, "It is good for a man to have nothing to do with women." That is pretty off-putting, to say the least. But then he goes on, "but because there is so much immorality about, let each man have his own wife and each woman her own husband." That seems to point the other way. Perhaps he did not know his own mind. But father, seriously, I have searched my heart, and I really don't think I want her for immorality. I hate the idea of lust. Yes, I admit, I would want us to come together, but it would not be my central focus. I would care for her and love her, look after her, bring her tea in bed in the morning and all that sort of thing.

Father, am I being truthful? Is it really lust after all? Jeremiah said the human heart was desperately wicked, and I have found my motives very hard to pin down sometimes. Am I trying to deceive myself?

A few verses later, Paul says, "I should like you all to be as I am myself," in other words single, but then he goes on, "but everyone has the gift God has granted to him, one this gift and another that." Father, what gift are you giving me? I really have tried forming a prayer asking for the gift of being single, but the fact is, I can't manage to say it. It really is just what I don't want. But what does that say about me as a person? Am I letting you down?

You are the boss. You decide, and I will try and go along with it.

Here's the crucial question. Would I be letting the mission down if I woke her up? I have been given a position of trust. I don't want to ruin everything. I don't want to let them all down back on earth.

Thank you, thank you, thank you! What a good idea! Ask Big Nimp about it!

No time like the present. I will type in my question using the keyboard by the diddy screen to make sure there is no possibility of a mistake through him misreading my racing thoughts.

Now, I'm seated in position. Take your time. Think. Phrase it carefully. Try and calm down!

"Solomon, would it be alright for me to wake one of the lady astronauts up? I know it was not part of the original mission plan, but I am so lonely. I want to ask her to marry me. I think, although I am not sure about this, that if I don't have human company, the success of the mission might be in a certain degree of danger."

I hope it was alright to add that last bit. I
do want to be truthful. I feel very unsure about
all this. Is danger the right word?

Ah, he's replying in words on the screen,
matching my keyboard input I suppose. What is he
saying?

"Yes, you may."

Oh father, Thankyou, Thankyou, Thankyou. You
are brilliant. Thanks again.

It was as I was running out of the door of the
little room that the klaxon sounded and the red
light started flashing. Big Nimp is not normally
that insistent. I turned back to see what he
wanted. There was a second line of words on the
screen. I went over to see what it said.

It simply read, "The one on the left."

Oh my goodness!

Araminta rang the doorbell five minutes early. He was pleased
he had got ready in good time. They had not given him any advance
instructions about what to wear, but he had put on old clothes and a
pair of sensible shoes to be on the safe side.

Standing in the road was a white minibus, frighteningly clean
and beautifully waxed, with the words Ski-Hi Flying Tuition
emblazoned on it. There were seats for three in the front, and Bruce
was ushered into the middle one. The boy friend's name was Karl;
he came from New Zealand. He looked a few years older than
Araminta. Bruce reckoned he would make a good teacher.

After a fifteen minute drive, they stepped out at the edge of a
large playing field. There were two mini vans with their back doors
open, with flying suits inside, and twelve or fifteen young people
milling about. Bruce was feeling distinctly nervous by now.

Everybody except him seemed to be on first name terms with
everyone else. He soon grasped that he was the only person who
called Araminta by her full name. He had feared as much. But it
was a lovely name. Why did everyone have to shorten names?

He felt completely out of place. However, once he was
introduced, he immediately became the centre of attention. "Good

on you, mate," said a cheery voice. These flying instructors were evidently the new lifeguards of society. They were young and strong, and came from Down Under. They were not going to sit around watching swimmers in pools any more; the sky-flying was much more interesting.

Karl was speaking to him. "Try this one, marked extra large. You might fit into a large, but you're better off with a roomier suit than one on the tight side, especially to begin with." There were other people putting on suits all round. There were evidently going to be several different lessons taking place. Nobody else was anywhere near as old as he was.

He zipped himself into the suit. The material was a very strong, grey cloth. It was a snug fit. The gloves came separately, but were zipped on to the arms of the suit, making a comfortable join. There was a curious tingling sensation in his fingers, which seemed to be coming from the gloves. It was weird. Bruce wondered whether he should have visited the loo again, but it was a bit late now.

"Now, the first thing is these weights that go on your legs," Karl said. "They are to keep you upright in the air. They prevent you from bobbing about like a cork on the sea."

It was strange that the first thing you had to do was to increase your weight, but Bruce could see the sense in it.

"Now, you'll be aware of a tingling in your fingers? Yeah? That's the first and most important thing about your suit. If that stops, you soon lose control over your direction, so you need to land as soon as possible."

"How do you steer?" asked Bruce.

"You use your fingers. You just point where you want to go, and the suit does the rest. It's intuitive. You'll soon grasp it. But that's not the vital thing. Look at the dials on your right hand hip."

Bruce had noticed these. On a shiny surface about the size of a pocket calculator, there was a rotating knob, and a push button.

"The first lesson is how to take off and land. You need to listen to this carefully. Don't press anything until I tell you. Now, the button is for both take-off and landing. The suit has an in-built sensitivity to foreign objects. When you are in the air, it will not allow you to go close to anything solid, and that includes the ground. It's as if there is an invisible force-field surrounding you. Now, the button moves you from one side of the sensitivity barrier to the other. If you are standing on the ground and press it, it will lift you away from the foreign object, in this case the ground, so you take off. If you don't do anything else, you will then hover about six feet in the air. However, if you are in the air, and the sensitivity barrier is keeping you away from the ground, then when you press the button, you move to the other side of the barrier, in other words, you land. Got it?"

"Yes. It's a bit like the cushion of air that a hovercraft rides on." Bruce had dozens of questions, but he sensed that the best thing to do was to go at Karl's speed. He felt confident in his capable hands. He would keep his questions for later.

"Right. Now the first exercise is this. You stand with your legs slightly apart, and press the button. You will glide up into the air, and hover. Then when you are ready, you press the button again, and the suit will then lower you through the barrier until you touch down. Alright?"

Bruce nodded. "Whatever you do, don't touch the rotating knob yet. I'll teach you about that in a minute. And don't move your hands either; keep them perfectly still. Then when you are ready, go for it."

Araminta was watching intently. He could see she was so pleased he was trying it. It was worth having a go just to see her reaction. He obeyed his instructions to the letter. He stood legs slightly apart, took a deep breath, and pressed the button firmly. He glided gently upwards and stopped. It was the strangest feeling. He could not help laughing out loud. Then he pressed the button again, and glided gently down to a standing position. He had to admire the suit. It was the most marvellous invention.

"Very good. Now practise that ten or fifteen times, exactly like that, and then I'll teach you the next step."

All went smoothly for five or six ascents, but then Bruce scratched his ear one time without thinking. The result was electrifying. He immediately shot off thirty feet higher into the air.

"Help!" he yelled. Karl was up beside him in an instant. He was dimly aware of about a dozen young people in fits of paralytic laughter on the ground below, Araminta included. They had been anticipating this, he realised.

Karl was smiling. "Don't worry Bruce. That always happens. You did really well to do five take-offs without moving your hands, actually. It's a kind of initiation ceremony we have here. You remember I told you that you guide yourself through the fingers? Well, your head scratching told the suit to move you higher. So now you are ready for lesson two. If you move your hands slowly through the air, then it has no effect, but any sudden movement is interpreted as a command. We'll just use your right hand at present. Keep your left hand quite still, or we'll have more confusion. Firstly, wave your hand very gently from side to side, and you will see there is no effect."

Bruce found this was true.

"Now, the more jerky your hand movement, the more the suit responds. Try doing some gentle jerks, as it were, and see what happens. I will follow you."

Bruce's skills as a pianist stood him in good stead. He did a mezzo piano finger strike, and moved ten feet through the air. He did several of these. When he felt a bit more confident, he tried a mezzo forte, and sailed along fifteen feet. Then he tried a full-blown forte, with hand movement but not arm movement. The effect was amazing. He found himself sailing along thirty feet to the right.

Karl was immediately there in front of him. "You are amazing, Bruce; you're a natural." Karl was really impressed. "I have never seen anyone pick it up so fast." Bruce felt very pleased. He could hear applause from below.

"Now for the rotating knob. This is a kind of overdrive. You can go up or down or from side to side just using your hands. With a vigorous hand wave, you get up quite a speed. But another way of moving around is to point with your left hand and rotate the knob with your right hand. It's a spring-loaded action. The harder you rotate it, the faster you go. With practice, you will find that you can combine hand commands with turning the knob, and simply whistle along, but for now, just try the point and rotate technique on its own to get the hang of it."

Bruce did so, and soon grasped how the control worked.

"That is basically it," said Karl, "except for landing from a height. In theory, you could press the button where we are here, a hundred feet up. You would sink like a stone, until the suit sensed the ground, and then it would slow you up and deposit you through the barrier gently. But I have never done that, and I don't recommend it. Instead, point your way down, and then press the button at fifteen feet. It seems safer to me. Practise some flying using your hands to move about, and then when you are ready, try landing from up here."

Being a musician, Bruce decided to conduct. He chose a brisk three beats to the bar. He moved his right hand smartly down about four inches, then four inches to the right, then along the diagonal back to the starting point, making a triangular movement in the air. To his delight, his body shot down fifteen feet, then fifteen feet to one side, and then back up to his starting position. This was amazing. Now he could really get into the swing of the music. Look out Klemperer, he thought.

After conducting for a few minutes, he decided to land. Bruce could see the wisdom of not pressing the button when he was high up. He followed Karl's advice, and was soon standing on the ground again. Araminta was the first to come up. She was beaming all over her face.

"You were brilliant," she said. "I knew you would be." Impulsively, Bruce gave her a hug. He hoped Karl would not mind.

"Thank you for talking me into it," he said. "I had no idea it would be so easy, or such fun. I would not have missed it for anything."

Karl had arrived by now. "What was that you were doing in the air?" he asked.

"I thought I would try the effect of a little conducting. A piece in Waltz time."

"Good on you, mate. Waltzing Matilda. Wonderful."

Oh dear; whatever happens, don't look at Araminta. He was certain that she knew three things. Firstly, that the Waltz music he had had in his mind was *La Donna e Mobile*, and that he had performed it for her benefit. Secondly, that despite its name, Waltzing Matilda is not a Waltz, as it is in four time not three. And thirdly, that Araminta was fully aware of both of these facts, and that if their eyes met, they would both burst into fits of helpless laughter, which would not be a good idea in front of Karl.

Somehow, Bruce kept a straight face. He thanked Karl very warmly, and asked what he owed him.

"Nothing," said Karl. Bruce had been expecting trouble on this.

"I insist," he said. "Araminta is looking peckish – I reckon she needs a meal out. Have it on me."

Karl accepted a note in the end, and was pleased to do so.

"But Karl," asked Bruce, "how do the suits work? I thought there would be a backpack in addition, or something like that."

"Search me," said Karl, shrugging his shoulders. "No, there are no add-ons. It's all in the suit, somehow. The energy units are in the two shoulder pads, but nobody can work out the anti-gravity. Some people think the seams have something to do with it, but I'm just content to use the thing. Think of it as like driving a car. You don't need to know what's under the bonnet to be able to drive, do you?"

As Bruce was no scientist or engineer, he would have to be content with that, he realised. Nobody understood the suits, but they were remarkably useful, however they worked.

Karl had other pupils to teach. Bruce was quite happy sitting on a bench until it was time to drive home. Araminta did her Swallows and Amazons stuff in the air. That was the name he had chosen for the young fliers, having enjoyed Arthur Ransome's books as a teenager. Granddad had the whole set of them on his shelves.

"Very many thanks for a most memorable afternoon," he said, when they dropped him at his front door. "I wouldn't have missed it for anything." The glow persisted all evening. Bruce had done what mankind had dreamt of for millennia; he had spent the afternoon flying like a bird. He could hardly believe it.

14. From: Mission 12
To: Undisclosed recipients
Sent:

I called Big Nimp Staples today. Can you get
who it is? I will tell you in the next email.
   Bruce

   PS No I won't, because we are travelling so
fast now, that even if I send you an email every
day, there must be long gaps at your end between
each message. Quite a few of you will have died
before my next epistle, so I will tell you now.
It was Clive Staples Lewis. I love his writings,
especially The Pilgrim's Regress and The Great
Divorce.
   PPS You don't mind me calling them epistles, do
you?

The next day was Sunday. Church was uneventful, except that Bill and he agreed to meet for a coffee at Bruce's home on Monday evening. A piano pupil had cancelled, freeing up his evening. Gnilla was also free, and could come too.

Bruce tended to treat himself to a roast for Sunday lunch; he had picked up the habit from Granddad. There was always quite a bit of the joint left over, but this did not matter, as at could be recycled in a shepherd's pie on Monday or Tuesday evening.

Just when he had settled in his armchair after finishing the washing-up, the phone rang. He rose to answer it, wondering why people chose to phone at such an hour. Surely, all the world had forty winks after Sunday lunch?

"Bruce, is that you?" It was his second cousin Banjo!

"Yes, Bancesca." It was such a struggle to pronounce her name right. The first c was a 'ch' sound – that was not too bad, but there was an unwritten 'g' sound just before it, requiring him to say 'Bangchesca'. That was what was so awkward. "Nice to hear you." What had her parents been thinking of, for goodness sake! Why couldn't they have settled on Francesca instead? It was a perfectly

68

respectable name, and would not have caused so much difficulty. Come to think of it, perhaps they chose the name out of spite for him. He wouldn't put it past them. No, that was a ridiculous thought. That couldn't be the real reason.

"Bruce, are you listening to me? Stop daydreaming!"

"Sorry, what was that, Bancesca?" Pronounce it right, and whatever you do, don't call her Banjo by mistake. Oh dear, she was speaking again. What was she saying?

"...Henley regatta? Might you be free?"

"Sorry, Bancesca, did you say Henley regatta?"

"BRUCE!! Please pay attention. I have been given some tickets for the Henley regatta on Saturday July 6th. Would you like to come? Really, you are hopeless."

"Sorry, Ban... er, Bancesca. Just let me find my diary... Yes, I am free, and I would love to come." This was not the first time she had invited him. He had been twice before. It was all very posh, in a marquee, with dainty things to eat, which was not really his kind of thing, but it was Banjo's idea of fun, and he liked her, and it was a good way of keeping in touch.

"Jolly good. And Bruce, Flossie will be there."

This was bad news. Florence Millicent, to give her her full name, had once been keen on Bruce, and Banjo still rather hoped that something might come of it even now.

"That will be nice. I hope she is keeping well. What time shall I meet you, and where? I am teaching until 1230."

"One o' clock, usual place. Try and shift your last pupil. Oh you are hopeless, but it's fun talking to you. Look forward to seeing you. Bye!" and the line went dead.

No small talk then. Banjo tended to be a little abrupt. Bruce found her quite puzzling. For a start, why was it that whenever they spoke on the phone, he always ended up thinking of one of Bertie Wooster's aunts?

```
15. From: Mission 12
To: Undisclosed recipients
Sent:
```

This is very difficult. I fear I may have caused the mission a problem. I am so sorry.

It's no good trying to put it gently, so I'll come straight to the point. I've woken one of the astronauts, because I was so lonely.

It sounds awful put like that.

What happened was, I was doing the cleaning in the dorm one morning, when my eye fell on one of the coffins, as I call them. All you can see through the little window is the eyes of the sleeper. I fell in love instantly. It's true! This led to some soul-searching, naturally, but I consulted with Big Nimp, and he said it would be Okay to wake one of them up for company.

Now for the tricky bit. Big Nimp said it would be best if I woke the one on the left. Well, no, actually that's not quite what he said. He just said, "the one on the left." The trouble was, I had fallen for the one on the right. At least, what I call the right; it depends which way you are looking. If you stand with your back to the front wall and look back into the ship, then it was the one on the left. However, from the console where I consulted Big Nimp, and from your view as you walk into the dorm, you would have to say that it was the one on the right. Really, there is a little doubt about which one he meant.

Once I had my permission, I decided to sleep on it for a few days. No good rushing things like that. However, the truth is that my resolve is not always all it might be. When I woke up next morning and remembered what had happened, my heart almost thumped its way out of my chest, I was so excited. I forced myself to calm down. I even made myself linger over my cereals and toast. But then, I could not stand it any longer.

I had been saying to myself over and over how the one on the left would be so lovely and charming and a suitable companion. Normally I am

quite good at talking myself into things. I think
I almost succeeded.

I walked up to the left hand coffin and stood
there, with my heart racing. Oh dear, it's so
shameful I hardly dare say it, but it's no good
denying it. I suddenly ran across and lunged at
the lever above the right hand coffin and yanked
it sharply downwards. It stayed down, like the
handle in an old-fashioned train when you pull
the alarm (Penalty for Improper Use Fifty
Pounds). There was no turning back now.

I had imagined that a bell might ring, and go
on getting louder and louder, or that Big Nimp
might blast me with lightning for disobeying him,
or something like that, but in the event nothing
happened at all. (Was it disobedience, in fact?)
I began to wonder whether it was going to work.

Then gradually, a small screen appeared in the
wall above the coffin, and came into focus. It
had all sorts of displays on it, monitoring
various body functions I suppose, but the only
one I took in was the Time to Eject readout. It
stood at twenty-eight hours, fifty-eight minutes
and forty seconds, and was counting downwards. I
had not anticipated a delay, but of course, it
was bound to take time to bring someone back from
deep hibernation and get them ready to face the
world. Rather stupid of me. She would not
actually arrive until next day.

Then I realised there was plenty to do. A bed
would be needed for a start, and an extra set of
cutlery. She might like a mug with a floral
pattern on it, I thought. I wondered if I could
manage a bunch of flowers, but knowing Big Nimp's
failures at other projects I soon discounted
these, unless perhaps a red rose would be easy
enough to make up. Oh dear, what about clothes?
That could be tricky.

Fortunately, I had discovered that in one of
the little rooms, there was a place on the floor

where, if you placed an object and instructed Big
Nimp, Grim Reaper would make an identical copy. I
dragged my bed through, put it on the spot, and
gave the instruction. It worked perfectly. I
chose a small room for her out of the way where I
thought she would be happy. Then I thought better
of it. My room was the nicest one, and she would
not know it had been my room before, so I moved
all my things and my bed into the room I had
chosen for her and set her bed up in my old room.
The tableware was easy - Grim Reaper soon copied
it all. I don't know why but I made an extra set
or two; it seemed less precise, somehow, than
just having two sets.

Now for the clothes. I found some of mine that
seemed a reasonable size, and asked Big Nimp to
adapt the colours and texture a bit. The
important thing was that they were large enough;
it would not matter if they were too baggy to
begin with. It was all I could do. I hoped she
might turn out to have dress-making skills,
although when I asked Big Nimp to design a needle
and thread, he seemed very blank about it. I left
things at that. I actually thought it would be
good to have one or two projects to do together
when she had arrived, as it were. It might help
break the ice a bit.

I did realise that things might be a little
tricky to start off with. She might not take to
me at first, for example. I knew it would be
crucial to give her plenty of space, and it was
no good letting my feelings towards her become
too strong. She had to have the freedom to refuse
me. I knew that.

I went back to see how she was getting on.
Twenty-four hours to go. Then on an impulse, I
bent over and kissed the coffin where I judged
her lips would be. It tasted plasticky.
Afterwards I felt very ashamed of this. It seemed
to be taking advantage of her. At the same time,

a horrible thought entered my head; that might be
the last kiss I would ever have with her. I don't
know why I thought that. I began to feel
uncomfortable.

Anyway, I couldn't think of anything else to do
other than to continue doing the cleaning, and
try and make the place look as inviting as
possible. The metal walls are a bit monochrome,
but at least they look quite good now. I had not
got up to the ceilings, but I had polished up to
four or five metres in most places. The effect
was a little odd, as the walls were shiny near
the bottom but dull higher up, and the dividing
line went up and down rather, but it did have the
advantage of showing that I worked hard. I hoped
she might be impressed.

I forget what I watched that evening. A second
world war movie, I think, in black and white.
Girls tend not to be too keen on those. Big Nimp
always wants to add colour to black and white
programmes, but I resist him on this. One should
see the film as originally made, in my view. It
seems more authentic. I hope she enjoys watching
films.

It was time for bed in due course. Sixteen
hours of the countdown left to go!

Next morning, I had my breakfast as usual. I
still could not think of anything else to do in
preparation, except to choose some music. Nothing
too romantic - I did not want her to feel
pressured. I decided that the six Brandenburg
Concertos by Bach followed by Beethoven's
Pastoral symphony might be suitable, although on
another impulse, I programmed out the storm music
(fourth movement). It seemed a bit violent
somehow. I set it all to start a few minutes
before eject time.

Then I wondered whether to dim the lights a
bit. I decided against this; I thought that the

warm-up routine she was going through would include getting her eyes used to the light.

Finally, I realised I had better send this email before zero hour. There might not be much chance later. I have entered it at the keyboard, as I don't want there to be any opportunity for Big Nimp to misunderstand me and give you a misleading message.

Typing all this has made my hands feel all sweaty. I will go and have a wash, and visit the loo. I have to confess to feeling a little nervous.

Be in touch again soon, I hope.

Bruce

On Tuesday evening, Bill and Gnilla came round. She kindly bought an arrangement of flowers. If there were left over oddments at the end of the day, she was allowed to take them away for her own use. She could conjure a bouquet out of virtually anything. It reminded Bruce of Stravinsky's gift of being able to write music for an ill-assorted group of instruments, as in The Soldier's Tale, for example. Bruce could not imagine why Bill found her difficult. He thanked her warmly for the flowers, and put them on top of the piano.

When he had made the coffee, they were keen to hear about the flying. Bruce was feeling impish.

"Oh, it's easy really. Child's play. Anybody could do it."

They were not easily fooled. They pressed him for details.

"Well, if the truth is known, I have not been so scared of anything for a long time. I was expecting to feel totally insecure off the ground. But the funny thing was that the suit gave me confidence. You have a tingling feeling in your fingers throughout. This is reassuring; it is the sign that your direction system is on and working. The first thing you do is to add weight to your legs, to make sure you stay vertical. Then the controls are simple. There is an anti-crash device built into the suit. It senses nearby objects, and keeps you from bumping into them. It also deposits you gently on the ground. I recommend it."

74

"How about landing in a tree, like a bird?" asked Bill. Was he winding Bruce up?

"Oh, I did not try anything advanced. All I did was go up and down a bit, and from side to side a little. It was not much to watch. But at least I was really flying."

"So you can't take off from a balcony, or fly in to an upstairs window or anything like that yet," said Gnilla.

"Not a hope. That's next week."

"Are you going again?" asked Bill. "Could Gnilla and I come and watch?"

"I haven't decided yet." Bruce was sure he did not want to be watched! "I may take more lessons. I'm not sure. I was by far the oldest person there."

"Bill and I are going to hire a sky taxi." Gnilla was speaking. "We're saving up."

Sky taxis were very expensive, even though the journey time compared to a ground taxi was cut to a fraction.

"We wondered whether you would like to come," added Bill.

"That's very kind of you." Bruce was touched. "What's green and goes up and down?"

The change of topic was abrupt, and had them both confused.

"No idea," said Bill.

"A gooseberry in a lift. It's very nice of you to invite me, and I feel honoured and all that, but really, playing gooseberry in a threesome is not my strongest *forte*. You go on your own and enjoy it. Where were you thinking of flying to?"

It rapidly became clear that the destination was causing some friction between them.

"Okay, I'll leave you to sort that out among yourselves. If it is to be properly done at dawn, I am willing to act as a second and offer choice of weapons and hold jackets and all that." Humour might defuse the tension. They both smiled. It was rather ridiculous, really. Why not give way sometimes?

"What interests me about the sky-cars," Bruce continued, "is the implications for space travel. Getting into orbit has just become a whole lot easier."

"You and your daft ideas about humanity spreading out over the galaxy," Bill said. "It will never happen."

"I'm not so sure. I've been wanting to show you this," Bruce said, reaching for his Bible. "Psalm Eight. Let me show you." Gnilla was not a church-goer. The thing to do was to keep it light, so that she would not feel excluded. "See here, verse three. The author is addressing God. 'When I consider your heavens, the work of your fingers, the moon and stars, which you have set in place.' Got that? Then it goes on, 'What is man that you are mindful of him, the son of man that you care for him?'"

"That's talking about Jesus," Bill said. This was not helpful to Gnilla!

"Not when the Psalm was first written, hundreds of years before Jesus was born! I know Christians see a prophetic reference here, but let's keep to the original meaning. He's saying that man is insignificant compared to the stars. Right?" They nodded. "But then it goes on, 'You have made him ruler over the works of your hands; you put everything under his feet.' Well, that presumably includes the moon and stars of verse three."

"Let me look," said Bill, peering closely at the text. Gnilla had to crane her neck over his shoulder to get a glimpse of the page. "I don't get it," he said after a few moments. "This is just you trying to jam your interest in space travel onto the Bible."

Gnilla, however, was becoming excited. "No, Bill, can't you see? Bruce is right. 'The works of your hands' in verse six is the same as 'the work of your fingers' in verse four. I've got it, Bruce. You are saying that Psalm eight encourages humanity to get our feet over the stars, to use the Bible phrase; to populate the galaxy in modern speech. How exciting!" Her eyes were shining. "Let me read it through again." She picked up the Bible and studied it carefully.

Bill looked at her with undisguised astonishment. This was a side of Gnilla he had not seen before. He did not know what to make of it. He scratched his head. Bruce enjoyed watching the interchange between them.

"It's a good thing you weren't wearing a sky-suit when you scratched your head just then, Bill," Bruce said, and he told them what had happened to him in the lesson. They enjoyed the story. After that, they chatted about other things. When they were leaving, Gnilla said, "That Psalm Eight business. It's the most interesting thing I have come across in a long time." She was evidently delighted. Bruce smiled, happily. He loved it when people were excited by learning something new.

```
16. From: Mission 12
To: Undisclosed recipients
Sent:
```

Actually, I've changed my mind. I will send another email by thought transfer, so that you can experience the final moments of countdown. There are just two minutes remaining. There is no sound, but there is a red light flashing very gently at the bottom of the screen. I think it may be her heartbeat, but I could be wrong about that. The display reads "All systems normal". That's a relief. I never thought to ask Big Nimp to adjust the heating, but it's a bit late to think of that now. I hope she won't be too cold. Or too hot, come to that.

Oh dear, I do feel nervous.

Goodness, there is a line appearing round the edge of the coffin. I was not aware of the tiniest crack before. Oh look, the line has a scalloped shape. (Scalloped or scolloped? Like a sea-shell, anyway). All this technology here is so enthralling to me. It is such a privilege being on the ship.

The lid is lifting up and away, swinging back on two hinges, with something of a squeak. It could use some oil I think. I must look into that on the other ones later. The hinges may have dried out a little.

Oh my word, she is sitting up and looking
around. She has not looked towards me yet.
Now she is stepping out. She is clothed in a
white shroud. She stands a little awkwardly,
hardly surprising after all that lying down.
Now she has seen me, and turned towards me.
Oh my! Blonde! And very beautiful!
What have I done?

Bruce woke with a start next morning. He had dreamt about his
early childhood once again, and as usual, even in the dream, he had
been trying to recall more. The dream was always the same – his
mum and dad in their bedroom, arguing with raised voices. He and
his little sister Sasha would look at each other without speaking.
Sometimes, Bruce used to block his ears with his fingers and run off
to the other end of the house, so that he could not hear them. At
other times, he preferred to stay and listen, even though it was so
awful, as he wanted to know what was happening. Then there came
the dreadful day when the argument was even worse than usual and
he had run to the end of the garden, and then strangers had come to
the house and taken him to Granddad's, and he had never seen his
parents or Sasha from that day to this.

No matter how hard he strained to remember any more, he never
could. It was so frustrating. Sasha had looked so sweet in her
ponytails. One thing was certain; she would not still be in ponytails
now. Indeed, he would probably not recognise her if they passed in
the street. He had always kept his number in the phone book,
hoping that she might see it and get in touch, and he had searched
for Sasha Winter every way he knew how, but without success. He
had spent hours at the Family Records Centre looking through the
marriage indexes in case she had married, but he had drawn a blank.

He had loved his granddad, but whenever he asked questions
about what had happened to the others, he always met a brick wall.
There was no way he was going to get any information out of him.
And now Granddad was long dead, and all the leads had gone cold.
All he could do, it seemed, was to dream of the past and what might
have been.

He had lost all hope of his parents coming for him years before. It was no good going down that path again. He hoped Sasha was getting on alright. Perhaps they might meet again one day.

```
17. From: Mission 12
To: Undisclosed recipients
Sent:
```

Well, a lot has happened. I will try to be brief.

I am actually typing this at night-time, which is not easy, as the lights are dimmed. I will tell you why later. I don't think I told you, but we no longer speed up to two gees at night. Big Nimp explained that we needed the extra thrust in the early months of the mission, to get us going. I don't understand it being discontinued, as I was quite comfortable with two gees at night, but he knows best. I still call it two gee time, because I have got used to it, and the friendly announcement each evening at ten is comforting.

Where was I? Oh yes. Eject time.

She advanced towards me with a smile on her face, hand outstretched. I was pleased I had put on a suit.

"I'm Celia," she said. "You must be the commander."

I cleared my throat. This was not going to be easy. "Well no, actually, er, my name's Bruce," I said, and shook her hand.

"Bruce," she replied. "Where do you fit in?"

I could not help noticing her voice being so lovely. I cleared my throat again.

"I think we ought to sit down," I said. "There is a bit of explaining to do. Can I get you anything, tea or coffee or whatever? There is a good range of hot and cold drinks available."

"No thanks," she said in a somewhat guarded tone, but she accepted the offer of a chair. "Tell me. But first, how long until we arrive?"

This was the question I had been dreading. I wanted to put it off as long as possible.

"The commander is still asleep," I said, waving at the coffins as if I was in charge. "Actually, you and I are the only ones awake at present."

"Who are you?" she asked, with obvious concern in her voice.

"Well I look after the ship," I replied. "I go round keeping everything ship-shape and Bristol fashion." It did not sound very convincing. "The mission is going well so far. Everything is in the capable hands of Big Nimp, that's my pet name for the computer. All systems are functioning well, including the reproducer, and I send regular emails back home." I did not dare call it Grim Reaper. It would only confuse things.

"How much further is there to go?" she asked.

This was the moment I had been dreading. There was no putting it off.

"Look, please don't be angry," I said. "The fact is that a few days ago, I was doing the vacuuming as usual, going around the legs of the coffins in the dorm, when I happened to glance down at yours and saw your eyes. I fell in love with you, it's as simple as that. I have been so lonely that I asked Big Nimp if I could wake you up and he said yes, although of course it was not an easy or quick decision you understand, so I did. I was hoping you might agree to marry me," I added. Then I wished I hadn't. It was crazy to mention marriage now. But somehow it just came out.

Her mouth had set itself into a hard line. "How far into the trip are we?"

I gulped. "We have done four years three months, and there are sixty-four years and nine months to go," I said nervously. I tried to keep the tremor out of my voice, but it would creep in despite my best efforts.

She said nothing for nearly a minute. During that time, a red colour spread its way gradually up from her cheek bones towards her hairline. She really is so lovely to look at, but somehow I could not bear to keep my eyes on her face at the moment. When she spoke, it was slow and measured.

"Now, let me see if I have got this right. I went into hibernation on the understanding that I would be reawakened at the end of our journey as part of a new world settlement programme. Now I find that the caretaker has woken me sixty years early because he was lonely and he saw me through a piece of tinted glass and fancied me. Is that it?"

"I don't like the word caretaker," I said, "as there have been so many instances in films of caretakers that take no care, and I am not one of them, but apart from that, yes, it is as you say." It seemed best to be straight about this. One should begin as one means to go on. Firm and reasonable.

She buried her face in her hands. After a minute or two, although it seemed longer, she got up and walked away from me. She walked up and down for several minutes, then made her way back to where I was still sitting. She opened her mouth. I winced in anticipation.

"I wonder if you have the slightest idea what you have done to me. All my life has been spent preparing for this voyage. It is all I ever dreamt of. My schoolmates were a mixed bunch; some of them wanted careers, others simply wanted to settle down and have a family, but not me, oh no. I was set on going to the stars from an early age. I chose my subjects carefully, did all the right things in preparation, developed my stamina and fitness to a high level, and won my way through all the competition to get chosen. Everything was fine. I went to sleep expecting to wake at the right time to fulfil the mission.

When I come to, I discover I have been woken early. I will probably be dead before we ever arrive at our destination. There is no question of turning back. Re-hibernation is not possible. So for the rest of my life, what is there to look forward to? I am stuck in a spaceship with the most selfish person that was ever born, and he wants me to marry him."

I have never seen anyone so angry, but she was not shouting. It was a controlled, powerful anger. It was frightening.

"I could fly at you and fight you, but you would probably win. So if you don't mind, I would like to be shown my room - I assume you have thought of that, or am I to share yours perhaps? - and then I will do my best to work out my feelings there."

"This way," I muttered. This was terrible. "I've arranged your room as well as I can. There are clothes on the bed, best I could do. I'm through there if you want me," I said, pointing at my room. "The lights are dimmed at 1015 p.m. and go back up again at 6.15 a.m. There is a clock by your bed." Suddenly I was crying. "I am so sorry; I never meant to hurt you. I never thought…"

"No, that's just it, you didn't think!" she said with passion, and stormed into her bedroom. Even in her emotional state, she closed the door gently. Her self-control was masterly. A moment later, she began to sob. Great wailing sounds filled the air. It was agony to hear her. I too was weeping uncontrollably. I suppose I should have foreseen all this. The truth was that I had been so wound up in my own needs that I did not think straight. I have never felt so like a worm in my whole life. What had I done?

It crossed my mind to throw myself into Grim Reaper's mouth there and then, but I immediately dismissed the thought. If there is one decision I

have taken in my life, it is that I will never do
away with myself. Ecclesiastes chapter three.
There is a time to be born and a time to die. God
chooses the time of our birth and death.

That was the moment when it hit me, what I had
done. By waking her as I did, I had played God
with her life. It was not right. How could I have
been so mean? I stumbled into my room and
collapsed on the bed, burying my face in my
hands. I fell into a black despair which lasted
for many hours. I hardly noticed her racking
cries filling the spaceship, but I was dimly
aware that they did not grow any less. It was
awful and it was agony all rolled into one.

Bruce

There was a new pupil coming on Tuesday evening. All Bruce
had was a mobile phone number. That was never quite as good as a
land-line with a local code, he felt. Perhaps he was rather old-
fashioned about that. With a mobile number, if they changed it, then
you lost touch completely. The woman had not even left her name.

These frozen meals were excellent. This one needed four
minutes on defrost mode, then three and a half minutes on full
power, then a final three and a half minutes on full power again.
This called for the Brahms Intermezzos, or was the plural
Intermezzi?

He had recently learned all three pieces of the Opus 117 set.
They were quite tricky, but they were playable, and they did not
need to be fast. First of all he turned on the plate-warmer and put on
a plate. Cold plates were an abomination to Bruce, chilling the hot
food down so! Bill actually preferred a cold plate for his meals;
Bruce had never been able to understand that. Each to his own.

Next put the music ready on the stand. Now whip out the meal
and bung it in the microwave. Set it going, and walk steadily to the
piano. Settle on the stool, and begin playing. Easy does it. If the
speed is right, the little ping should come with the final chord.

He missed by three seconds on the first Intermezzo. Never
mind, there were two more chances.

Full power setting, three and a half minutes. Play number two. This was better; although he had to slow up in the last bar rather more than the music demanded, the ping came very close to the last note. However, the last Intermezzo was hopeless; he overran by a long way. Never mind, it was fun to try. It saved all that hanging around watching the microwave display counting down.

After eating, he cleared away, and at 8.10 prompt, the doorbell rang. Bruce liked it when the pupils were bang on time. He opened the door, and to his astonishment, there was the diagonal girl! He stood stock still, speechless.

"Mr. Winter? I've come for a piano lesson." And in she walked.

By the time he had waved her towards the piano and she was seated on the piano stool, he had regained his composure.

"I was just wondering, have we met somewhere before?" he said.

She smiled at him somewhat ruefully. "I do want to apologise about that. It must have seemed dreadfully rude. I had various things to do, and believe me, there were good reasons for not getting in touch. But here I am now, and if you are willing to teach me, I would like to learn." She was looking at him. "Please don't ask me a lot of questions; just trust me."

Not very communicative, but the thing to do was to go along with her request, Bruce thought. So without more ado, they started the lesson. It turned out she was a beginner, but as she had learned the clarinet at school for three years, her reading of the treble clef was going to be no problem.

"I am afraid the bass clef is going to be the challenge," Bruce said. However, there was good news here too. Before taking up the clarinet, she had been in the school recorder group; indeed, it was because she had enjoyed the recorder that she had graduated to clarinet. Then the bass recorder player had left the school, and because she was a quick learner, the music teacher had talked her into taking her place, so she also had four years' experience of playing from the bass clef as well.

This was excellent news. Bruce had felt that because she was a beginner, he might have a psychological advantage. He was now beginning to sense that even though she had not played before, she would progress very quickly. He had had other pupils like that before. There had been one fifteen year old girl who had shot ahead so fast that it had been a job to find enough music for her. Whatever he gave her came back note perfect next week. It was hard teaching pupils who covered in six months what had taken him six years at their stage. Why was it always the girls that were like that and never the boys, he wondered? Strange.

Not for the first time, Bruce remembered a day when there was a bonfire in the garden, when he was little. His mum and dad had got it going, and his job was to put on the sticks and garden rubbish. Because it was a dry day at the end of a fine spell, everything burned up very quickly, in fact so quickly, that whatever Bruce managed to gather up and throw on was never enough. More was always needed. He and Sasha worked as hard as they could, throwing on sticks and greenery, trying not to let the bonfire burn down low. They just succeeded. His parents had been pleased, and they had all been happy. It was a precious memory.

The girl was good. Rather than selling her the adult beginners' tutor, Bruce suggested she borrow a copy, as she might only need it for a fortnight, to save her the cost of it. Next week, if she could come, he would give her additional pieces to try.

The end of the lesson soon came. She wanted to know whether she could come later on a Tuesday evening, but Bruce was unwilling. "I find that if I finish work at 8.45, I stay awake, but if I teach past nine, then I'm fighting with sleep, so if you can manage it, I would much rather we stuck to 8.10." She understood, and agreed to come weekly on Tuesdays at 8.10. He sensed she did not want to meet socially, so he did not suggest it. Let things take their course.

It was only as she was going that he finally asked her name. She was amused that it had taken him so long.

"It's Celia," she said with a smile, and with that she was gone.

Oh dear. This was going to be tricky.

18. From: Mission 12
To: Undisclosed recipients
Sent:

There now began a time of perfect torture. I
choose my words with care. It was torture,
because Celia was so very upset. She did not
become angry again, but she constantly looked
pale. We had to communicate; there was no choice
about that, but whenever we did, I felt as if she
was crouching behind a wall which all but hid
her. Just occasionally there were moments of what
seemed to be the real her, but they were very
few. Most of the time, she spoke in
monosyllables.

Breakfast was the worst time of the day. I
would offer her tea or coffee or juice or
whatever, and she would either grunt or simply
say no thanks. I tried to be helpful and
considerate, but pretty much anything I offered
she turned down. After a bit, I discovered that
it was best to leave her to fend for herself.
Things improved a little after that.

It was no good trying to start a conversation.
We used to eat in silence.

She turned out to be brilliant at making
clothes. I managed to get Big Nimp to make a
needle and thread and scissors and material, and
she had soon made a wardrobe of beautiful
clothes. She is very creative.

Thankfully, she was happy to watch a film most
evenings. As it is a three seat sofa, we did not
need to sit close together. I thought she might
want a separate seat altogether but she did not
seem to object to me being on the sofa. It was
hard to read her mind.

One night I dreamed I was on a walking holiday,
trying to follow a small river down a mountain,
back on earth. It would have been easy, except
that the river would keep diving into the ground

into dark caves where I could not follow. Whenever that happened, I had to make my way down the hillside as best I could, losing height all the time, and trying to listen for tell tale signs of rushing water beneath my feet. However, I could never hear anything. I just had to descend several hundred feet in the general direction of the flow, and hope that the rushing stream might resurface. Somehow or other, it always did, but it was no thanks to my skill that I kept on finding it.

When I woke next morning, I realised that the dream had been about my dealings with Celia.

When I say perfect torture, I want to try to convey a second set of feelings. Within a few days of meeting her, I was completely smitten with her. I had never imagined that there could be anybody so lovely. I am no good at descriptions, so let me try to convey how I felt like this; I soon knew that even if she remained totally angry and upset with me for ever, I still wanted to be near her. I wanted to spend the rest of my life with her even if it was misery to be in her presence. This made her sadness all the harder to bear. At times, I felt life was unsupportable.

I came to recognise a daily pattern in myself. Apart from waking up, which was always dreadful once I remembered what had happened, my lowest point always seemed to be at around six pm. I used to feel awful, and felt I was in a black pit. Once I grasped that this was happening at the same time each day, I increased my eating at around four, when we had a cup of tea. It proved helpful.

There were some lighter moments. I carried on with my polishing routine, and she would sit in the same area as me, in case I fell or needed help of some kind. It was kind of her. I soon grasped that she is a very kind person. I liked having her down below.

The day came when I needed more bits of scaffolding. I was determined to do the ceilings. This meant getting Big Nimp to copy existing pieces of the scaffolding. She was interested in how this was done, and soon grasped the system. There is not much to it, really. A child could do it. But she brightened up for a few minutes.

There was one funny episode. I had mentioned to her that Big Nimp would respond to any name. She immediately said to him, "What is your name?" Straight away a long list of names scrolled down the screen. It included everything I had called him. I remember that Alexander the Great was the first entry.

"Look at that," she said, with obvious enjoyment. She scrolled back to the top of the list and went down it more slowly. "What's this," she exclaimed, "God… Jesus… and Lord?"

I was horrified. Surely Big Nimp had not been overhearing my prayers and thinking I was addressing him? How absurd. Then an awful thought struck me; could some of my prayers have got sent off as emails by mistake? I always go into my room to pray, so as to be out of his way, but sometimes when I feel especially worked up, I pray out loud, and he might have thought… But Celia was speaking again.

"What's this?" she was saying, in an incredulous tone. "Marilyn?"

I tried to stop her, but she had already highlighted that entry, and the following conversation between Big Nimp and me came up on screen.

"Marilyn?"

"Yes?"

"Shall we watch the Sound of Music again tonight?"

"If you like, but don't have it too often, or you might tire of it."

"I know, but let's have it again. I do like it so much. And Marilyn?"

"Yes?"

"You can call me Ducky if you like."

"Yes Ducky."

It was so embarrassing. I tried to explain that Big Nimp would never call me by name more than once, and then only if I specifically requested it, bit it was no use. She laughed and laughed. It was wonderful.

Her peals of laughter reminded me of a lecture I had attended, years before, about the early history of the universe. At one point, the lecturer had asked us to imagine we were observers standing on the surface of the earth when it was newly formed, looking upwards. He told us that for hundreds of thousands of years, the earth would have been surrounded with impenetrable clouds, pouring down rain. Then eventually, the rain would have lessened, and finally stopped, and after long ages more, there would have come a moment when the sun finally broke through the clouds and pierced to the surface of the earth for the first time. What a momentous event!

It felt like that moment now. The sun came out as she laughed. But I soon realised what the lecturer had not said, that straight afterwards, the clouds would have joined up again, and the sunlight might not have returned for another few hundred years. I needed to be grateful for what I had just seen in her, and not expect her to change. Her dreams had been shattered.

I remember having thought in the lecture that what you would see from the perspective of standing on the earth's surface fits rather neatly with the story of creation in Genesis chapter one, by the way. Maybe that is why the

sun does not arrive in the story until day four.
I found that very intriguing.

Sorry! Back to the point.

One day, I plucked up courage and asked her if
she would like to see the observation chamber and
look at the stars. She said she would, so I
showed her the steps up to the platform, and the
seat. What I was hoping was that we could observe
together, but I did not want her to feel pushed
into this, so when I had explained to her how the
straps worked and what buttons you had to press,
I turned to go. She seized my hand - I will never
forget it - and asked if we could view together.

I had already modified the seat in advance so
that there were two sets of straps, arranged so
that we would not be jammed in close together. I
felt that was important. I helped her buckle
herself in, and then got into my side. She
pressed the button and we slid forward to the
viewing position. I had warned her about the
rotation.

"It's breathtaking," she said. It certainly
was. I suddenly wondered if she had read P. G.
Wodehouse. I longed to ask whether she thought
the stars were God's daisy chain, but I did not
have the courage. It might have been funny, but
it would probably have gone wrong.

"I wish I knew what they all were," I said.
Well, that finally got her going.

"See those seven stars that look like a
saucepan?" she asked.

"That's the Plough," I replied. It was one of
the few constellations I knew. "It looks a little
different than it does from earth."

"Well, look at the handle," she went on, as if
I had not spoken. "Is the end star one star or
two?"

I had to blink several times as my eyes were
misty, but then I could see it clearly. "It's
two," I replied.

"Good. That is Mizar, and the companion is Alcor. It is the only double star where both stars have a proper name. The ability to separate the two with the naked eye was a test of eyesight in the Middle Ages. Not that we are sure that the two stars are gravitationally linked, mind you. It's a matter for debate. Now, do you recognise Orion?"

I nodded, and with that she really opened up for the first time. It was marvellous. She knew so much. She was also a good teacher. I did not take much in, to be honest; I was too preoccupied with the double sensation of enjoying her enthusiasm about the heavens, mixed with yet another forceful reminder of what I had stolen from her. Joy and pain mixed together. I did not know whether to laugh or cry.

"Now what does this lever do?" she asked. I was just about to say that I had never had the courage to try it when she gave it a yank. The result was electrifying. The observation chamber set off round the edge of the spaceship at a good rate. It must have been mounted on a cog and ratchet system as used on a mountain railway, it seemed to me. Celia screamed and clutched at me. I tried to steady myself, and put my arm round her shoulders for support. She had released the lever by now, which brought us up steady with a jerk, adding to the confusion. It soon became apparent that the lever was a very sophisticated one; the slightest pressure was sufficient to start the chamber moving, upwards for one way, and downwards for the other, and the harder you pressed it, the faster you went. With practice, one could glide quickly to a new viewing position, when you got used to it.

Once calm was restored, I removed my arm from her shoulders, but she took hold of it and put it back. "Leave it there," she said firmly. So I did. Dare I begin to believe that some warmth

between us might be possible one day? I brushed
the thought away. I did not like to even
entertain the idea.

Before long, my arm had gone dead. The position
did not suit it. I gritted my teeth. There was no
way I was going to lift it down. It was so
wonderful being next to her. By the time we had
returned to the starting position - Celia had
grasped how to make us glide about, I was in real
pain. The relief when we got out, and the blood
started flowing in my arm again as it hung by my
side, was massive. I tried not to show it.

Then she bowled me over.

"I've thought long and hard about it, and I
will marry you. Shall we make it in three days
time, at eleven a.m?"

I was completely lost for words.

Bruce

On Thursday morning, Araminta was utterly thrilled with his
flying, as he knew she would be. "You took to it like a duck to
water," she said.

"Thanks. Ducks waddle, rather, don't they?"

"I did not mean that at all. You just seemed so natural. You
were fantastic."

"Now, have you been practising that tune from Verdi's
Rigoletto?"

They both laughed. It had been very funny. Bruce was glad they
had not laughed at the time; he would not have wanted to hurt
Karl's feelings. Why should a brilliant sky-flying instructor also
know about music and three beats to the bar? It was unreasonable to
expect it of him.

"How's the Moonlight?"

"Pale and wan. Here goes."

However, to Bruce's surprise, as the lesson proceeded,
Araminta seemed to get more and more downhearted. She made a
lot of uncharacteristic mistakes. This was unlike her. Eventually, he
asked her, "What's the matter?"

She was silent for several seconds. When it came, the answer was a shock.

"Mr. Winter, I've been putting this off for fear of what it will mean, but it's no good shying away from it for ever. The fact is..." she gulped, and then said in a rush, "I love you." Bruce was struck dumb. Once she had started, there was no stopping her.

"I've tried telling myself that you're old enough to be my dad, and that it's stupid and it would never work, but it's no good. I dream about you at night. You make me laugh, and I feel so happy when I'm with you. I can't wait to see you each week. And now you will probably tell me you will have to stop teaching me." And she burst into tears.

Bruce was appalled. This was awful. He found his voice. "But what about Karl?"

Her expression changed completely. "Don't talk to me about him." She looked so angry. Bruce had never seen her like that before.

"Oh Araminta!" he said, in a despairing voice. This was terrible. She was lovely, but there was such a huge age gap between them. It could never work. Could he have seen this coming? Suddenly, he saw the fly-pasts in a whole new light. Also, the banter over the *Liebestraum*; he had thought she was winding him up, but perhaps...

She could read his mind. "I know what you are thinking," she said. "That's what's so awful about it; I feel I know you so well, already. I just understand the way your mind works. I really did not mean for it to turn out like this, but it has. These things happen."

"Oh Araminta!" He did not know what to say. After a moment, he said, "Look, there are only a few weeks until the end of term. Maybe during the holidays you will be able..."

"Not a chance. And don't say it's puppy love; that's so condescending. I know my own mind. I'm sorry to be so awkward, but I felt you had to know."

Just for a moment, Bruce wondered whether it might work. They would have to wait for a few years until she was in her twenties and he would be... No, it was no good.

The bell went. That wretched bell, ruling our lives. He suddenly felt so angry with it. He wanted to tear it off the wall and hurl it through the window, smashing the glass.

"One day, when we get to heaven, we can strangle the person who invented electric bells," he said in a strange voice. Maybe humour might help. "On the other hand, you are not meant to do that kind of thing in heaven, so we may just have to feel utterly frustrated instead." It did not sound the least bit humorous. He simply did not know what to say.

She smiled. "I must go. Sorry to have ruined your day."

There was no time even to bury his face in his hands, because as she left, the scamps came in. He pulled himself together. He did not want them realising he was upset. Somehow he got through the morning, and caught the train home. Thankfully, there was some time without commitments. He went and threw himself onto his bed and wept his heart out. At last, here was a girl saying the words to him that he had longed to hear, and it was a pupil who was still at school. There was nothing he could do about it. They might as well be separated by the whole width of the Atlantic Ocean. It was agony.

Last thing at night, he knelt by his bed as usual to say his prayers. Normally, he thought his prayers, but at times of great need, he would speak them out loud. This was one of those days.

"Father, you remember all those prayers I prayed longing for a life partner? Well now there's a new problem…"

19. From: Mission 12
To: Undisclosed recipients
Sent:

This is my stag night, I suppose you would say.
Not that there is much fun involved. The best I
could do was to programme Big Nimp to play "I'm
getting married in the morning" from My Fair
Lady, over the headphones in my room, as I lay in
bed after two gee time. I have always been fond
of the song; my granddad took me to a production

of the show when I was a boy. I've enjoyed it ever since.

I wish Granddad was here now. I wonder what he would say. I miss him.

I wonder how Celia is getting on. No hen party for her.

Bruce

It was surprising how quickly the following Tuesday came round. Bruce was pleased that the diagonal girl had got back in touch. He could not bear to think of her as Celia yet; that was too confusing, but he realised he might have to change his mind about that fairly soon. The thing to do was not to be impetuous. Give her a few lessons. See what happens.

It was as he had expected; for one week's work, her progress was phenomenal. Plenty of fuel was needed for the bonfire! He loaded her up with a book containing several easy pieces, and also some other music on duplicated sheets that he had printed off himself. He was always careful over copyright, he explained; he could only duplicate his own arrangements of pieces by composers long dead, like Bach and Handel.

He then asked her to sight-read some straightforward excerpts for both hands. She was so quick on the up-take! Bruce had struggled with his sight-reading for years. He had recently realised why; it was because his natural way of playing was by ear. Even when learning a piece from the printed page, he would be memorising the sound, and after a short while, he would be playing from his head not from the sheet music. Hence his slowness at sight-reading. Now here was this girl waltzing along in her playing from sheet music where he had only been able to stumble when he was at her stage. Life was not fair!

At the end of the lesson, there was a surprise in store.

"Look," she said, "this may sound a bit sudden, but I would very much like you to meet my parents."

This did seem rather quick. They had not even been out for a meal together. He was about to protest mildly when she added, "The house is only a few minutes away, and they are expecting us."

That put rather a different complexion on it. It was only quarter to nine.

"Alright."

After he had locked up, they climbed into her car. It was not one likely to attract any attention. The engine had an unhealthy knocking sound. There was tinted glass in the windows.

"Don't worry, it will get us there," she said, as they swung out into the road.

The drive lasted eight or ten minutes. It was a quiet cul-de-sac in a part of town he did not know. They parked, and walked up the short path to the door. Number 18, Bruce noticed from a wall plaque.

The door was opened by a retired couple with greying hair. "Come in," they both said.

The house was elaborately furnished, with plenty of cushions on the plush upholstered armchairs. They were clearly house proud. They struck Bruce as being careful and precise people, characteristics that he had tended to notice in Celia.

Coffee was served, and to Bruce's delight, the conversation turned to the new technologies and their implications for society. He became quite talkative. He let slip that he had even had a flying lesson himself. Then to Bruce's surprise, the man came straight to the point.

"I feel we need to come clean," he said. "I actually have a professional interest in the developments we have been discussing, and I have been looking out for somebody who might be able to help. I think you might be that person."

Bruce looked and felt surprised. He said nothing. The man continued.

"Let me fill you in. For some time now, a number of us have been concerned at the enormous sums of money being made out of the anti-gravity discovery." Bruce nodded. "Simple calculations on the back of an envelope are enough to show that the amount of money changing hands is sufficient to have a sizeable effect on the economy. We are also concerned that these large sums could be going to fund crime. In short, it needs investigating. I would prefer you not to ask questions or try to find out any more information than what I have just said. I am sorry to keep you in the dark as to details, but the less you know, the better for all of us."

Bruce nodded. He wondered what was coming next.

"In an operation of this kind, it is no good striding boldly in with Wellington boots on. The men with the money, if we may call them that, will be alert to any intruders sniffing about. So we are looking for unobtrusive people. The kind of people we want to involve are those who won't draw attention to themselves."

"But what do you want me to do?" asked Bruce, mystified.

"Nothing. You do not do anything out of the ordinary at all. You don't make any attempt to look for openings or anything like that. All you do is to carry on your life as normal. If you decide to work with us, then we will try to create openings for you where you may be in a position to discover things. You simply report to Celia once a week in the piano lesson as to what is happening. Nothing more."

"So basically, if I say yes, my role is to carry on as usual, keeping my eyes open."

"Correct."

This seemed extraordinary. Bruce was reminded of a letter from a newly appointed bishop his granddad had once showed him in a national newspaper. The very reverend gentleman had assured readers that in his new post, he would adopt the traditional pose of sitting on the fence with both ears to the ground. Somehow, Bruce felt it would be unwise to refer to the anecdote here and now.

"Well, I am completely taken aback. I have never been in a situation like this in my life before. I also have absolutely no idea what I might be able to do that could prove helpful. But supposing I could be of use, I do have one important question. How do I know that you are the good guys, to use the expression, and not the bad guys?"

"You are getting to know my daughter. You will have to decide whether we are trustworthy people or not."

It was a fair answer. Nobody could prove their integrity from words alone.

Bruce thought for a moment. It sounded rather fun. He might never get another chance like this. Then he had an inspiration.

"Alright, I will do it. But there are two conditions." The couple looked surprised. "The first is that you arrange me a walking holiday on the moon, all expenses paid."

"That's a tall order," said the man.

"On the contrary," said Bruce. "With the anti-gravity technology, the cost of space travel has been cut to almost nothing at a stroke. Within a year or two, it will be no more expensive going to the moon than it has been flying to Australia by plane. It's not a difficult thing to arrange. And I would like to go before it gets too touristy."

They all laughed at his cheek.

"Well," smiled the man, "I will see what I can do. You said there was a second condition."

"Yes. It needs to be a trip for two, and Celia has to come with me."

From the glances between the other three, Bruce knew he had won. Whoever these people were, they certainly had influence, and the ability to pull levers.

"Alright," the man said, "but now, here are our conditions. You forget about this meeting completely. You never attempt to come to this house again. You never commit anything to writing, whatever happens. You do not speak of our arrangement to anyone, not even to Celia. And you do nothing to draw attention to yourself, and that includes flying; no more lessons. Do you understand?"

"Yes."

"Then at the weekly piano lesson, if there is anything report, you tell Celia. Is that clear?" Bruce nodded. He did not need to be told something twice. "As to the moon trip, we will do what we can. However, Celia will not be able to travel with you. She will be there to walk with you, if we can arrange it, but if we can't, then you may need to go alone."

Bruce nodded again. "Thank you," he said. He wondered what he was letting himself in for. Who were these people?

It was only as they were driving back that he realised Celia's mother had never spoken. That seemed strange. At the very least, this unexpected development in his life might help him deal with his depression over Araminta. Even though he tried not to think about her, the memory of her confession in the lesson would force itself back into his mind from time to time, with an accompanying sick feeling in his stomach. It was wretched. He needed something else to occupy his mind.

```
20. From: Mission 12
To: Undisclosed recipients
Sent:
```

Well, here we are. Everything is in place. We will stand facing Big Nimp's large display and make our vows. I insisted that the proceedings be recorded. I want everything done properly and in order.

Big Nimp will conduct the ceremony, and also be one of the witnesses. It was difficult finding a second witness, until I remembered little nimp. Little nimp is also my best man. I'm afraid there are no bridesmaids.

Little nimp has had a rough time of the journey so far, really. I understand why, now. I did not want Big Nimp to feel jealous of the close attachment I have to little nimp, so I have kept him out of sight. All I do with him these days is to play Draughts against him in bed after two gee time. Playing him at Chess is hopeless; he always wins. But in Draughts we are more evenly matched, and I can sometimes beat him.

I felt embarrassed laying little nimp on the floor at Big Nimp's feet, as it were, but I need not have worried. You remember that I said earlier that Big Nimp seemed to have lost interest in me? Well, you should have seen his reaction to little nimp. He was fascinated, and thrilled. Far from finding little nimp difficult, he gets on with him like a house on fire. They chatter away by the dozen in high pitched squeaks. It's lovely to see.

Then Celia came in. I realised I had not even considered wedding music. How thoughtless of me. She was looking radiant. I am hopeless at describing things, and I have no eye for dressmaking, but I can say it was the most beautiful dress. White Satin, with floaty material round her head. How she had managed to make it I have no idea. She had also taken so much trouble over her hair; it was beautifully set in what I call farmhouse loaf style, one of those ones with various knobs and buns, but wild horses would not have dragged the description out of me. It is the sort of remark women can't abide, and whatever else Celia was, with all her enviable talents, she was every inch a woman.

The dress sparkled as she moved; it was covered with small cut stones. My heart filled with joy, until I saw her face, and then all my happiness drained away. Despite her make-up, she looked so white and forlorn. It was clear that this course of action she was taking was one of desperation. She felt she had no choice. She was making the best of a bad job. She had taken ever so much trouble to look right. However, she had no friends or relatives to share what should have been her big day. I felt so sad and mean.

She made her way across to where I was standing, in front of the big display. The lower portions of her dress were not constricting, and she had no train, allowing her to move freely. I was pleased about that, as she had such a grace as she walked. She stood beside me, and felt for my hand. She squeezed my fingers. I felt even worse, if possible.

The only bright feature of the situation was the two computers chattering away to each other. Even Celia was tickled. She smiled wanly at me.

Here I am, I thought, getting my heart's
desire, but I don't feel right at all. I wondered
if I should propose cancelling it, but I could
not quite bring myself to say so.
    Bruce

Araminta missed the following lesson. All his pupils missed
from time to time, what with the occasional illness, school trips, a
vital test, or plain forgetfulness, but for Araminta to miss was most
unusual. Bruce wondered what mental tortures she was going
through. He found himself playing Wagner while he was waiting
for the scamps. He reserved his Wagner improvisations for special
moments. They were too valuable to be wheeled out on any and
every occasion. When he played in the shopping centre, he did not
put any Wagner into his schedule. It was an acquired taste, and he
could not bear to have anybody not appreciate it.

Bruce very nearly missed the little poster next morning. It was
break, and he had gone to grab a quick coffee. He was ambivalent
about coming over to the main block and entering the staff room.
On the positive side, there was a reasonable cup of coffee available
from a machine. On the negative side, he hardly knew a soul. There
were just three staff who had ever spoken to him, apart from the two
music teachers, even though he wore a security badge just like all
the others. It was a bit lonely standing there up against the wall,
sipping his drink, trying to keep out of everyone's way.

Today, however, he spotted the classics teacher. He could not
remember his name; the initial D on the security badge suggested
David, but it might be Derek; he could not be sure. As they had
talked at some length before, he did not like to ask. He greeted him.
D remembered him.

"Have you got two minutes?" D nodded. "I've been wanting to
show you this quote I have discovered. It is a passage from Tacitus
about the arrival of Christianity at Rome. Do you know it?" He
pulled a card out of his pocket.

D said no, so Bruce read out, "'Christus, from whom the name
had its origin, suffered the extreme penalty during the reign of
Tiberius at the hands of one of our procurators, Pontius Pilatus, and

a deadly superstition, thus checked for the moment, again broke out not only in Judea, the first source of the evil, but also in the City (Rome), where all things hideous and shameful from every part of the world meet and become popular.' Isn't that last phrase wonderful?"

"Yes, marvellous," agreed D. "Mind you, we have our share of what is hideous and shameful here as well; no need to go to Rome to find it." He sighed. "Tacitus was no friend of Christianity, was he?"

"No," said Bruce. "The quotation gives interesting corroboration of the early spread of Christianity from a hostile source. I thought you would appreciate it."

D had to go. It was then that Bruce saw the notice, just behind where D was sitting. On the top, somebody had scrawled 'Raffle tickets from Mr. Spencer', presumably the said Mr. Spencer himself. Underneath was printed in bold letters, 'First prize a return trip to the moon for two. Second prize…' Bruce did not bother to read any more.

"Excuse me," he asked a nearby member of staff, "is Mr. Spencer here?"

"No, but if you want a raffle ticket, they are in his pigeon hole. It's for a good cause. You tear one out and put the money in the tin. We are very trusting here. Remember to write your phone number on the little tab in case you win."

Bruce followed the instructions. It seemed a bit mean to only buy one ticket when the cloak and dagger people were going to all that expense, so he took five. He was careful to put them safely in his wallet. No good losing them

Who are these people, he asked himself yet again. It was rather alarming.

21. From: Mission 12
To: Undisclosed recipients
Sent:

It was time to begin the ceremony, it seemed to me. I turned to Celia and said, "Are you ready to become Mrs. Winter?" The words were not well chosen. It's not a name calculated to thrill a bride, especially one whose heart already felt so heavy. She looked me in the eyes and nodded; so bravely! But then, she paused for a moment. I could see there was a moment of inner struggle. Then she came out with what was troubling her.

"Look, I don't mean to be critical, but are you aware that one side of your mouth is slightly higher than the other? I should have mentioned it before, but I do wonder if you could bear to have it corrected. It would not take long."

"Certainly," I said. I did not tell her that the reason I had never done anything about it before was that it was an inherited family characteristic, from my mother's side. I had felt it best to leave it, but this was no time for considerations of that sort.

The operating chair was just at hand to the right of us. I have not mentioned it before. Big Nimp has all the latest medical technology, and a simple thing like altering a mouth line would be child's play to him.

"Would you like me to help with the local anaesthetic?" said Celia.

"Yes, very much," I replied.

I settled into the chair. It is a neat piece of equipment; you relax into your most comfortable position, and the chair takes up your contour, and then sets in place, ensuring you are fully relaxed and still when the robot arms get to work. There are always at least four of them in action at any one time, but for complicated procedures, there can be more. I have seen so many of them writhing about on occasion that memories of half-forgotten Greek myths came to mind. Yes, that was it; Medusa's head, covered with snakes instead of hair, I recalled, as I made myself comfortable. The robot arms do look a bit like that.

"How does that feel?"

I snuggled back into a comfortable position. "Good."

"Excellent," said Celia, reaching down to a little lever on one leg of the chair that I had not noticed before. She turned it. To my horror, steel clasps immediately shot out of the chair beside my arms and legs, encircled me, plunged back into the chair again and tightened up, all in a trice. I was pinioned. I had to admire the technology. The clasps were neither too tight nor too loose; the tension was just right to prevent any movement at all. Also, there had not been the slightest hint of any adaptation to the chair that I had noticed. It had looked perfectly normal. Had Celia altered it? Was she a gifted engineer in addition to all her other skills?

I looked at her. Her expression was now completely different. The pallor was still there, but the sadness had vanished. There was a wild look in her eyes. I found it disconcerting.

"Got you," she hissed through clenched teeth. "You thought you could play God with me, did you? Yes, I've read your prayers; they're all in Big Nimp's memory. You think you're so religious, but you're not. You can't fool me with your little schemes. Well, I don't believe in God, not your God anyway. I don't believe in the devil either, come to that, but you do. So if you think you can play at being God with me, let's see how you like it when I play at being the devil with you."

I had to admire the speech, but the venom in her voice was frightening. Her theology was a little suspect in places, I thought.

A mental image formed itself in my mind. Celia had come out from behind the low wall, and now she was in the open, I could see that in her hand there was a hatchet.

I immediately knew two things. Firstly, I realised that if she meant what she said, than I might never get out of that chair alive. I could be fighting for my life here. At the first opportunity, when her back was turned, I would see if there was any latitude in the bonds holding me. That seemed my best chance.

The second thing I knew was that alongside all her other talents, Celia was a great actress. In fact she was a performer of the first rank.

She wasted no time. She called up the Encyclopaedia Galactica. It was on the screen in an instant. "T O R C H U…" she spelled out. I wondered what was coming next, but I had my suspicions. However, there was now a check; she could not find what she was looking for. She was clearly disconcerted. She checked her spelling.

To my horror, I heard somebody saying something. "Torture is not spelt with a C H; it goes T O R T U R E."

I then realised the voice had been mine. I could not prevent myself. I just love helping people.

I will never forget the long stare she gave me at that moment, her eyes strained wide open. I have never seen anything like it in any human being before. It was a mixture of incredulity, anger, horror, amazement, and, I realised after a moment, fear. It seemed to last for ever. Then she turned back to the screen. She said nothing, but quietly corrected the spelling.

The encyclopaedia article she was looking for came up on the screen. It was a long one. She ran through it with a practised eye, and found what she was looking for; the section marked Middle Ages.

She had found her voice by now.

"I could just leave Big Nimp to improvise a routine of punishments, but that won't serve my purpose. This is my chance for revenge. I need to be actively involved. I want to be right beside you, inflicting the pain myself, sensing its effects on you. It won't be easy for me, as in my normal state, I don't like hurting people. Indeed, I have always been against cruelty to animals. But you are less than an animal. I have planned it all out carefully, and I reckon I can make myself do it."

This was serious. I could see the grim determination all over her face.

"However, Big Nimp can do the first bit." She stepped back, highlighted an option, and immediately two small portholes opened in the bottom part of the screen. Two robotic arms flew out towards me, extending as they came. There was an accompanying whizzing sound as of a dentist's drill. It was a really frightening moment, I can tell you. I winced, but I need not have worried. One arm settled lightly on my left wrist. I felt a momentary coldness as the local anaesthetic was applied, and then hardly noticed the line going in. The other arm headed for the middle of my chest, deftly found its way between the two halves of my jacket, bored a neat hole through my shirt, and then I felt a gooey liquid slithering and expanding over the left hand side of my rib cage. It felt a little warm for a moment, and then it seemed to set as a small puddle about four inches across, as it were. I sensed it growing hard as it clung to me. The warmth gradually faded. It felt like soft metal, firmly fixed in place. I could feel myself sweating underneath it.

Celia was speaking. "The line in your arm is for body fluids. We don't want to interrupt the session for meals, and we also don't want you going faint or hungry, do we? It will take care of all that. In addition, I have added a little concoction of my own to heighten your sensitivity to stimuli, to ensure the session has maximum effect. The other connection is a heart monitor, to make sure that I don't overdo the individual applications. I don't want to get carried away and bring the session to an untimely end."

I had completely misjudged this girl. She had been planning this for weeks. A small knot of fear began forming in my stomach.

"Now, I wanted to consult you about which particular stimuli to choose. Let's see what they have here. I would like to start with a thumbscrew; do you have any objection?"

This was ridiculous, but I felt it best to play along.

"No, thumbscrew will be fine." I attempted to sound natural.

I tried not to let the idea form, but I could not help it; maybe she was still acting now? Would she really go through with this? It ran against her character, from what I could judge. However, she had just admitted as much, which troubled me. Why had she raised it, unless it was because she really felt had worked through it? On balance, it seemed to me as if she had weighed this up herself over a longish period, and come to the conclusion that her anger was so fierce, that any lingering sense of sympathy she might have had for me as a fellow human being would not be able to stand in the way of her determination to pay me back.

I stole a sideways glance at her face. I have never seen a mouth set in such a hard line. I could not see her eyes, but she was gazing intently at the screen. There was a picture of a thumbscrew on it by now. She was noting down the details on a sketch pad. Any hope I had entertained that all this was a charade was beginning to fade. This girl was in earnest.

"It will take me a few minutes to coax one of these things out of Grim Reaper. You don't mind waiting there?"

I assured her, I would attend on her earliest convenience.

I waited until her footfall had left the room, then exerted all the strength I could against my bonds. As I had suspected, it was quite useless. I could not move at all. She was suddenly there beside me again. She had anticipated my action, I realised, and tiptoed silently back to watch.

"Any trouble, dear? Call of nature, perhaps? I'm sure Big Nimp could rig you up a catheter if you liked."

I assured her that all was well and that a catheter would not be necessary. She went off again.

I was surprised how quickly she was back from Grim Reaper. It seemed like only a few minutes. She had a black metal thing in her hand. She deftly slipped it over my left hand. I was powerless to prevent it. Her judgment as to size was good; the gadget neatly encased my thumb. She began to tighten the screw. I suddenly realised why the thumbscrew had been so feared in past centuries. I watched with a hideous fascination. It seemed extraordinary that such a vile engine of hell should have leapt out of the pages of history into the middle of an inter-stellar mission. In fact, the whole scene was incredible. We were both still in our wedding gear. This was meant to have been a happy day, a day of love and rejoicing, and now look what was happening. Two human beings, billions of miles from the rest of the human race, were alone together, and what were they doing? One had captured and immobilised the other with the intent of inflicting the maximum possible pain. It was fantastic. Unbelievable. But it was happening here and now to us.

I was soon jerked back to reality as the screw tightened. I had decided that I was not going to give her the pleasure of hearing me cry out. I would need to work at my breathing in order to achieve this; I could already sense it coming short and hard.

But what was this? She was unscrewing it. The instant relief gave me a sudden headache. What was she saying?

"It's no good; there is too much play in the screw. It will not tighten up enough. You need the next size smaller." With that she whisked off.

For the next hour, she trotted in and out, busily pursuing her goal. A pattern emerged. She would begin by searching through the article on the screen, finding some piece of apparatus, reading how it worked, asking me what I thought of it (how tasteless), and then going out and getting Grim Reaper to make one. After a bit, she set up a flat surface somewhere behind my head where I could not see. From the sound of the items accumulating on it, one by one, I wondered whether it was a table with a glass top. I recalled visits to the dentist in my youth, before automated dentistry came in, when the little tools had been placed on a tray out of sight with a small clatter. Whether all this preparation was done for psychological effect or not, I don't know, but the fact is that the knot of fear in my stomach grew steadily larger as time passed. I tried to relax, to conserve my strength for the coming ordeal, but it was no good.

There finally came a moment when this routine was interrupted. It was my doing. I had been debating with myself whether to speak out or not. In the end, I decided I would, although I feared she would not like what I had to say. However, it could be for her ultimate welfare, and I wanted that above everything.

"Celia?"

"Yes?" She sounded absent-minded, focussed on preparing the next piece of cruelty, no doubt.

"Do you remember saying that I believed in the devil?"

"Yes." Same uninterested tone.

"I want to explain that I don't actually believe in the devil, as you put it. When someone says, 'I believe in God,' they mean they put their trust in God. My granddad taught me that. He told me that if he said, 'I believe in my doctor,' it meant that he trusted his doctor and would therefore follow his advice. But when it comes to the devil…"

This really enraged her. "Don't you dare talk theology to me!" She shouted. I had nothing to lose, so I persisted. "So I only believe in the existence of the devil. I don't believe in the devil himself."

This was too much for her. "Silence!" she shouted. Then, barely able to master herself, she whispered, "I think we are ready to get started." She was obviously very worked up, but even now, her behaviour was all measured and controlled.

I don't think my talking precipitated her into action. She had already finished her preparations as far as I could tell. First she took off my shoes and socks. I had worn black lace-ups, which seemed right for a wedding to me, and black socks. She placed these carefully to one side. Then she adjusted the angle of the chair so that the soles of my feet were easily accessible, and moved them together so that they were side by side. She reached to the table, and lifted off what looked like a diminutive garden roller. It had a wooden handle about eighteen inches long, with a broad piece of metal at one end, which supported a cylinder made of sheet metal. Out of the cylinder a lot of sharp little spikes extended. It reminded me of something people sometimes use to aerate a garden lawn.

I had no time to prepare. She pressed it nimbly onto my heels and ran it forward to my toes with a flourish, the cylinder revolving as she did so. The pointed spikes dug into me. I had dimly remembered reading once that the soles of the feet are said to be very sensitive, but I had never realised how sensitive until that moment. It was all I could do to prevent myself from crying out.

Celia had been watching the monitor. She became very excited. "Oh look!" she squeaked, "you have got a high pain threshold," and without any warning she repeated the operation somewhat firmer, staring at the screen.

The many sharp stabs of pain were such that despite my best efforts at keeping quiet, a significant gasp and an accompanying grunt escaped from my mouth. She beamed at me. "You are terrific!" She said. "You are so strong mentally! Now we are going to have some fun." She seemed exhilarated. I actually wondered for a second whether she was going to kiss me, she seemed so excited. It would have been our first kiss.

No such thought was in her mind, however. She nimbly swung the chair into a nearly horizontal position, but with my head sufficiently raised that I could see what was going on. Without any warning she quickly parted my jacket and unbuttoned my shirt. She scooped up a handful of what looked like petroleum jelly from a jar I had not noticed, and generously lathered it all over my abdomen. "That's to increase sensitivity for the next one," she explained, working it all around the area with her hands.

This was a very sensuous moment. (Sensuous or sensual? I am never quite sure of the correct rendering. I prevent Big Nimp from changing my grammar and syntax in case he alters the meaning. However, I am sure that 'rendering' is right, and 'rendition', which one sometimes hears nowadays, is wrong.) As well as the massaging effect, which was exciting, the jelly imparted a strong

111

tingling feeling, which ran about from side to side of my stomach, a bit like electricity but without any sharpness or shock. It made me catch my breath.

I have sometimes noticed that even in a moment of crisis, I have the capacity to be a detached observer, as it were. It happened now. My mind was racing, no question about that. One part of it was shouting at me that this was a wonderful moment; the girl I loved passionately was massaging my body. At the same time, I noticed that the jelly was turning pretty much to liquid, and some of it was running off my sides, slithering over the chair, and falling onto the floor. "That stuff will need to be cleaned up," said the caretaker's voice inside me. "Must not let it set, or it could be quite awkward to get out of the carpet." But in addition to all this, the overriding feeling was one of sheer panic. The knot of fear in my stomach had already turned into a brick, some time ago. Now it felt the size of a breeze block. I swallowed hard.

I heard myself speaking to her out of a fourth part of my brain. "Be careful you don't get any of that stuff on your cuffs. It might not come out easily."

She appeared not to hear me. She was just reaching behind me for some unmentionable item when I went on. "Stop." It was now or never. She paused. "Celia," I began. "You have every right to do this. I have wrecked your life and destroyed your dreams. I see that clearly now. But before you go further, please listen to me. It may be that what you are going to do to me will render me unable to speak again, so I want to tell you now, that whatever happens, I would not have missed the last few weeks with you. It was worth any torture you can inflict on me to have had you with me. You are so beautiful, and so lovely all the way through, that I can't begin

112

to describe it. I would not have missed knowing you for anything. I'm just so sorry it had to be this way." I paused for a moment. "That's it. You can go on now."

I braced myself for the next agony, but it never came. She burst into great floods of tears, and sobbed wildly, "Oh you are impossible! I can't keep this up any longer. I love you so much! You are so precious to me! But listen," and here her voice rose into a terrible crescendo, "whatever you do, NEVER take me for granted again!"

If everything that had driven her up to now was the foothills of the Himalayas, as it were, then this was the Everest of her strong feelings. I understood that clearly.

On the word never, several things happened at once. Celia threw herself forward on top of me in a torrent of emotion, and thumped my chest with her fists. At the same time, as I instantly grasped that it had all been a test after all, and that the trial was now over, all the fear and tension of the last few hours erupted deep inside me and I was violently sick, all over myself and her. My body, in attempting to retch, tried to double up, but as I was gripped immovably in the chair, this was impossible. The force of the convulsion inside me, which could go nowhere, focussed on a point in the middle of my back on the left hand side, with devastating effect. The violent pain of that was frightful. Finally, I became dimly aware of a small cloud of what looked like yellow gas issuing quickly from the bottom of the screen towards Celia. As it enveloped her, she immediately sank unconscious to the floor. As she did so, everything went black for me too. A moment later, I passed out.

Bruce

Bill and Gnilla came round again that evening. She bought Bruce a posy from the shop. "I'm sorry it's so small," she said, "but we had a run of unexpected orders for the weekend. This was all I could scratch together."

Bruce had felt for a while that his profuse words of thanks for Gnilla's flower offerings hardly registered with her. She seemed to think that bringing him an armful of flowers was a basic minimum, and that anything less was a cause for shame. He was genuinely delighted with the posy, but he could not get her to see it that way. He gave her a very positive kiss on the cheek, but then he worried that Bill might think he was being a little too friendly. Oh dear; not more problems with women, please! he thought.

They chatted happily together over coffee. Gnilla went to the bathroom at one stage, and was a surprisingly long time. "Do you think you had better go and see if she is alright?" Bruce asked.

"She's fine. Don't worry about her." And sure enough, while he was still speaking, the sound of the toilet being flushed came through the door, and Gnilla returned, looking rather red in the face.

"Sorry to be so long," she said.

"Doing anything nice tomorrow?" asked Bill.

"The usual. Supermarket, bit of piano practice. Nothing much, really. How about you?"

"Oh, we're going to a film," said Gnilla. "We've chosen the afternoon to be sure of a seat."

"Very wise," said Bruce. "You might do well to book in advance; the back row tends to sell out if you aren't careful."

Bill aimed a kick at him, but Bruce was ready for it and moved his legs quickly sideways. They all laughed.

When they had gone, something made Bruce go through to the bedroom. It all looked perfectly normal, but he could not get rid of the idea that Gnilla had been searching through his things. It was a horrible thought. He opened the drawers and the wardrobe door. Everything looked as it usually did. Then he went into the bedroom with all Marjorie's books and boxes of newspaper cuttings. Again, there was nothing he could put his finger on, but the feeling that she had been searching for something persisted. It was not nice at all.

He realised that although he had known Bill for several years, Gnilla was an unknown quantity as far as he was concerned. Was it possible that his link with the cloak and dagger people was known about, and that Gnilla was somehow involved on the other side? It seemed unlikely, but stranger things had happened, Bruce thought. He gave a sigh, and hoped nothing would come of it. Perhaps he was simply getting too uptight about it all.

Five minutes after his final pupil had gone on the Saturday morning, Bruce was just putting some bread and cheese on the table for a bit of lunch when the doorbell rang. He went to answer it; it was Bill. He was just waving him in, when to his astonishment, Bill whipped out a pair of handcuffs, snapped one clasp shut around Bruce's arm, and the other one shut around his own. He felt alarmed, but he soon realised from the smile on Bill's face that there was nothing to worry about.

"Got you! You're under arrest!" Bill was enjoying this hugely. Bruce made a show of protest, and insisted that the cheese should go in the fridge and that he be allowed to lock up properly, to which Bill consented. Then with mock struggles, he allowed himself to be pushed into the back seat of Gnilla's car. She was sitting at the wheel, wreathed in smiles, and was obviously enjoying everything.

"What's going on," said Bruce.

"Wait and see!" replied Bill, as Gnilla set off.

It was not far. They stopped at the sky-car taxi rank. Bruce had an idea of what was coming.

"We knew you would never agree, so we decided to kidnap you. We really do want you to join us in a sky taxi ride. Now will you come?"

"Seems I don't get much choice," laughed Bruce. "Can't trust you an inch!"

Thankfully, Bill had a key to the handcuffs in his pocket. When he had set Bruce free, the three of them went to the window. The taxi had been pre-booked. Then Bruce had another surprise; Gnilla was handing in three passports at the window, one of which was his! So that was the meaning of the search last night.

"You scoundrels!" he spluttered. They laughed.

"You have to have your passport with you, as there is nothing to stop you landing in France or wherever," explained Bill. "They check them before you can get on board."

They were led forward to a waiting sky-car. It looked like an earth car, but without wheels. Bruce was put in the front, next to the driver, while Bill and Gnilla sat in the back. "Beats the cinema any day," said Bill.

The seats were very well padded. They reminded Bruce of one he had sat in once on a roller coaster. The seat-belts were elaborate, more of a harness than a lap-belt, with the result that they were very thoroughly strapped in. The driver introduced himself.

"Hello. I'm Nick. May I ask, is this your first trip in a sky-car?" They told him it was. "Right, well if you are happy, I will explain everything as we go. I find it saves a lot of questions."

Nick was obviously as keen to talk about the sky-car as he was pleased to be in charge of it.

"The first bit is the painful part," he said. "I shall have to ask you for a credit card to put in this slot. The reason is that as it is so expensive, we cannot trust people to pay afterwards. It is easy to run up a bill you can't afford. So what happens is that we tap in the amount you want to pay; the car checks your credit to see that you can afford it, and then we can go. However, the good news is that the rate came down about one percent this morning, you will be pleased to hear."

Bill presented his card, and mumbled a large sum. Bruce was horrified.

"That's a lot," he whispered.

Bill smiled. "I've been saving up. Let's enjoy it."

"The route is pre-booked, I see. You are coming back here at the end?" asked Nick.

"Yes."

Nick pressed the button marked round trip. "Right, now the car will get us back here within your payment limit, by shortening the route if necessary, if we hit any unforeseen problems, so don't worry about being overcharged. Now, what you have to remember is that you are not paying for fuel. The energy is so cheap as to be negligible. One part of what you're paying for is time of use of the car, which goes to the sky taxi firm, and helps pay for the vehicle and my salary. The other part goes to the government, and helps pay for the satellites and the technology that make the skies safe."

"What do you mean?" asked Gnilla.

"I'll explain as we go," replied Nick. He pressed a button, and the car began to rise vertically into the air.

"That button gets us to the other side of the sensitivity barrier," said Bruce to Bill.

"Yes; you must have had flying lessons. We are now shielded from bumping into foreign objects by the sensitivity field. The suits only have a small field, six or eight feet, but ours is currently set at forty-eight feet. There is a hot debate as to what the correct rate should be, because the lower that figure is, the more cars you can fit into the air, but the more congested the sky will become. If that figure gets too low in the future, then overtaking will become next to impossible, which will be very difficult. Thankfully, we are nowhere near that point yet."

By this time, they were nearly up to cruising level. Bruce tried not to look at the meter showing the cost, whose numbers were rotating horribly fast.

"Are your backs strong and fit? I need to know for setting the maximum permitted acceleration." They said they were fine, so Nick set the maximum permitted thrust to 2.5 gees. "Now you want to be able to see properly, so we'll limit maximum speed to Mach 2 to begin with. That's about a thousand miles an hour. Right, we are at cruising level, so off we go"

Nick pressed Auto. Bruce was thrust back in his seat as the car accelerated powerfully towards the North East, and then almost immediately swung East.

"We pre-programmed our journey, to save time and money," Bill explained. "For our first part, we've taken a tourist route over London that is on special offer at present. Look." Bill pointed out the familiar landmarks. They were hurtling along; it was spectacular. "Then we are turning North, aiming for the Wash, and then we will follow the coastline North. Gnilla wanted to see the

Scottish Highlands, and I love the Cairngorms. Then we will see the West coast of Scotland, with all those long sea inlets, come back over the Isle of Man and then Anglesey, and then cut back across Birmingham and down here."

"But that's miles!" Bruce objected.

"It's about an eighty minute journey," Nick said, "unless we get hold-ups. If we do, the car will shorten the route."

As he spoke, they were already leaving London behind. Bruce had not had any idea that they would be going so far or so fast. This time, he felt that questions were in order, but he had to wait, because Nick was in full flow.

"Now, the satellites and so forth. What you have to grasp is that there is a fundamental difference between a car on a road, and flying around up here. On the ground, the route is fixed. Think of a straightforward two-way road. If you swerve, three things can happen. You may end up in the ditch; you may hit an oncoming car, or you may overtake the vehicle in front and regain your right place on the road. Yes?" They agreed. "Up here, it is different. There is no road, to state the obvious, so there is nothing to force you to choose one route rather than another. If you were the only car in the sky, it would be fine; you could go where you wanted. But the moment there is just one other car flying, then there is a risk that you might both decide to move into the same bit of airspace. You won't crash, because the sensors will prevent it, so the cars will not be damaged. But bouncing off another vehicle's sensitivity shield could be very unpleasant for the passengers. A head on encounter between two cars could be fatal for everyone on board. You follow me?"

It seemed obvious, but Bruce could see that the way to deal with the complicated issue of the use of air space was to break it down into a number of smaller decisions.

Nick continued. "Now, think about the two lane road again. Imagine that earth-cars have acquired the ability to overtake by leap-frogging over the vehicle in front. Ignore bridges and power lines for the moment. Supposing you were behind a juggernaut crawling up a hill. 'Aha', you say, 'no need to wait for a gap in the

118

cars coming the other way, I'll just press the joystick and over we go.' Well, that's great provided the next car behind, who is also crawling up the hill, has not had the same idea, and decided to jump over both you and the juggernaut, 'cos if he has, and you both go for it together, wham! And we have an almighty mess all over the place."

Bruce felt all this was getting a bit long-winded. "What you're saying is that in the skies, there is so much freedom to move into new air space, that a system is needed to make sure that sky-cars don't behave like the dodgems at a fairground."

"Right first time," said Nick. From the tone of voice in which he said it, Bruce realised that his contribution had been unwelcome. Nick's idea of a happy eighty minutes appeared to be filling the air with his wisdom. Still, they had come to enjoy the view, not to listen to a lecture.

"So how do the satellites come in?" Bill had come to his rescue.

"Government has decided that the whole thing has to be automated. This means knowing where every sky-car is at every moment, hence the satellites. The plus side is no accidents, in theory! The down-side is that flying on manual becomes restricted to remote areas like Greenland. You saw me press auto when we set off? Well, there are hardly any areas over the UK where manual flying is still allowed. All we can do is tell the car the route, and then it has to wait for permission to enter each sector of air space. But now, here's the amazing bit. The computers are so fast, that the whole thing flows smoothly, so far at any rate."

"But aren't there rules about different heights for different directions, for example?" asked Gnilla.

"Now you are asking how the system is designed," said Nick. "How would you arrange it, starting from scratch?"

"Well," said Gnilla, "I would have different heights for different directions, like I said."

"And what happens when you want to change direction?"

"You swoop up or down to the new level."

"Right, and suppose someone else decides to change level, and needs the same bit of airspace? You see, it is not that straightforward."

"Well, how would you do it then?"

"I've given it a good deal of thought. For a start, I would increase the air-space for each vehicle to at least sixty feet, preferably seventy-five. I would arrange the sensitivity to increase gradually, the closer the approach to the other vehicle, rather than abruptly. Then if there are any collisions, although the vehicles do not actually touch, remember, there will be sufficient cushioning in the system for there not to be much of a knock-on effect. What you don't want, it seems to me, is for one incident to cause a wave of incidents involving other vehicles in the neighbourhood. Then I would pursue your different directions on different levels idea. I would have three hundred and sixty different levels, one for each degree of the compass. There would be several full turns above each other, in a spiral staircase shape, if you follow me. The faster you want to go, the higher up you have to travel. The tricky bit is the changes of direction made by the cars. These need to be kept to a minimum. I think they are right to have the route pre-programmed into the car in the built-up areas, like London, for example. I know it cuts out the fun of manual control, but if people want to do that, then they need to be away from the crowded skies, over the mid-Atlantic for example. The trouble is, there is not so much to see there. It is not easy to get the perfect arrangement."

"Now, I need to warn you that some time about now..."

Nick was still speaking when there was a sudden surge in power. They were all pushed strongly back into their seats, as the car accelerated. The coastline had been falling away behind them at a fair speed before, but now they were racing along.

"Coo, that took my breath away," said Bruce.

"Sorry," said Nick, "I had meant to warn you. We left the London speed limit area just then, and the car has now moved up a gear. This is still not full speed; that is only allowed over the ocean. But it is impressive."

Bruce noted the distinctive shape of the Humber moving away. Gateshead and Newcastle would be coming up shortly, and then before long the coastline would bend westwards towards Edinburgh. It was exhilarating rushing over the country so quickly.

"This is wonderful," Bill said. "These sky-cars have changed travel for ever. I suppose we could go to New York if we wanted?"

"No problem," said Nick, "but at present the cost prohibits it. That will change before long, however. These are challenging times."

Bruce felt it was his turn. "I thought that when planes broke the sound barrier, which as I understand it is Mach one, then the sonic boom would be enough to shatter windows on the ground. So how come you can go so fast without problems of that kind?"

"The smaller the vehicle, the less the effect," Nick replied. "Big monster planes like the old jumbo jets have had their day. It will all be small vehicles from now on. Whoever would have expected that? Then the faster you want to go, the higher you have to be, to lessen the effect of the sonic boom at ground level. If you want to stay low to admire the view, then you keep your speed down."

Bruce had not finished. "Surely, the speed through the air would cause friction on the sky-car, leading to heat problems," he persisted.

"Very good," said Nick. "I can't explain how it is done, but these machines are temperature controlled. There's liquid god-knows-what being pumped through the entire body shell at present to cool us down, otherwise we would have been cooked to a turn by now. I expect you think you are looking out through glass windows."

"Well yes," said Bill.

"Nothing of the kind. I don't know what they are. They look like windows from the outside, and also from the inside, but they ain't. What you are looking at may be a projection screen for all I know. It's all very clever, I assure you."

"No wonder they cost a fortune," said Bill.

"I'm feeling a bit sick." Gnilla had hardly spoken.

"There is a bag beside you," said Nick. "I am sorry."

"It's not just travel sickness," she continued. "It's the pace of change, I think. I just feel it is too much, too quickly. I don't know where I am any more. I don't like it."

Bill put his arm round her and gave her a hug. "Close your eyes a minute," he said, "and hold on to me. I'll look after you."

Bruce's eyes misted over. Technological advance is all very well, but at the end of the day, it is people that matter, he thought. He wished there was someone he could put his arms round to protect.

Nick was speaking again. "They have got the brightest thinkers and programmers working on the navigation issue," he said. "There is a terrific prize for the person who designs the system that is finally adopted. At present, they are sky-testing competing ideas every few months, which makes for interesting challenges. If only somebody could have foreseen that the sky-cars would come, and they could have worked out the software in advance and got the satellites up and running, then we would not be coming from behind. But I suppose it was too much to hope that someone would think of it all ahead of time. Oh yes, weather is another thing to be accounted for, because who wants to fly through a storm?"

The car slowed periodically, at Gateshead, Edinburgh, and after the Cairngorms when they were near Glasgow. Otherwise they stayed at their higher speed. Gnilla's comment had rather taken the edge off the afternoon, Bruce felt; there was not much conversation following her remark. The views were stunning. It was an experience to remember. Before very long, they found themselves descending vertically and slowing up, and finally they touched down gently at their starting point.

"That was amazing," Bruce said, when they were all standing on the ground again. "I am so grateful. It was a real eye-opener."

Gnilla was looking rather pale, and Bill had his arm round her. Although she had not actually been sick, she had not enjoyed it, which was sad, considering the expense of the trip. Bruce gave her a pat on the back. They drove him to his home in silence. Bruce wondered whether such a long trip had been a bit ambitious for a first outing. However, he had grasped that society would have a lot of adapting to do, in a short space of time. Things could get a bit rocky over the coming months, Bruce thought.

22. From: Mission 12
To: Undisclosed recipients
Sent:

I think I was only out for a few minutes, because when I came round, the vomit had not congealed at all. But there was no time to worry about that. Where was Celia? The floor beside me was empty.

My mind was racing again. Grim Reaper, I thought; the robots have taken her to Grim Reaper's mouth. I will have to hurry. It may not be too late.

I made to move, but of course it was no use. I was gripped by the chair. However, my attempted body movement caused a sharp stab of pain in my back. I let out a loud groan.

Hardly knowing why I did so, I cried out, "Houdini, get me out of here!"

Instantly, the clasps on the arms and legs of the chair went limp and retracted, the heart fitment and the line in my wrist unhitched themselves, and the robot arms wriggled back inside their small portholes in Big Nimp, which then shut with a snap and disappeared.

I practically fell onto the floor I was so surprised. It had never occurred to me that all I had to do was to simply ask Big Nimp to release me. But there was no time to think of that now. I cried out as a fresh burst of pain hit my back with the strength of a sledge hammer. There was no way I could walk across the floor in this state. I would have to attempt to cross it on hands and knees to save putting any strain on my back.

The agony of that crawl was indescribable. The only way I managed it was by repeating the

following words over and over rhythmically, one
line in time with each knee movement:
  My back is
  Filled with
  Searing
  Pain
  Psalm thirty-
  Eight verse
  seven
  (breath)
  My back is
  Filled with
  Searing
  Pain
  Psalm thirty-
  Eight verse
  seven
  (breath)
  My back is
  Filled with
  Searing
  Pain
  Psalm thirty-
  Eight verse
  seven
  (breath)

I crawled across the floor with steely
determination. There was no way I was going to be
beaten by the Psalmist!

It was as I inched along that I came to know
with a complete and utter certainty that Celia
was not dead, and that there was hope. How I
knew, I cannot explain, but I have never been
more certain of anything in my life.

In this way, I gradually crossed the wide
expanse, went through the doorway and approached
the mouth of Grim Reaper. The double doors were
shut, but they opened as I went up close. The
light streaming in revealed that Celia was twelve
or fifteen feet inside, lying on her side, and

jerking up and down. She was unconscious as far as I could tell, but prevented from being drawn further into the machine by a rack of parallel bars that had descended from the low roof. That made sense. There must be a safety feature, I reckoned, which would automatically come into play to prevent a person who was unconscious but alive from being reprocessed. The little robots were clearly not to be trusted over life and death decisions. Their job was just to sweep up inanimate debris and dispose of it.

I would have to go inside and bring her out. But if I did, I feared that the doors would close behind me, and how could we get them open again?

In a flash I had the answer. The fire hose!

I crawled in agony to the cupboard, and gave a yank to the big metal nozzle. Nothing happened. In desperation I pulled again, ignoring the outcry from my back. Then I saw a release clasp. I had it off in a moment, and the hose came away freely. I tugged it along to the entrance to Grim Reaper. The doors opened again.

I began feeding in the hose. It would be our lifeline. After a bit, it got drawn along by some mysterious power, metre after metre, for a long time, until it finally came to with a jerk. I hoped it was firmly attached to the reel.

I reckoned I just had sufficient strength to go inside and pull her out somehow. But I knew I was not good for long. I would have to hurry.

I gritted my teeth, bent double, and went in. It was dark inside, except for the light coming in from outside. The doors tried to shut, but the hose prevented them. They began opening and shutting over and over, and the klaxon began to sound, not continually, but in short bursts, in time with the doors. This hindered me, as whenever the doors shut, it became almost impossible to see anything; I had to take in my surroundings in the moments that they were open.

However, there was barely time to absorb any of this, because I immediately found my body was swept from under me. I discovered that there was a system of constantly revolving rollers set in the floor, which drew anything pushed into the mouth into the heart of the machine. It was only the bars that were preventing Celia from being drawn in even further.

I was almost on top of her before I was ready. I tried to steady myself, but it was not possible, with the rollers rotating underneath. I soon discovered that the rollers were not round, but had a wobble built into them, created by one side of the wheel being larger than the rest. I reckoned that this unevenness on the wheels would tend to ensure that a heavy item could not get stuck, as it would constantly be jolted up and down as well as being propelled along. It also explained why Celia's body had been bumping up and down against the bars rather than just lying still there.

I landed against Celia with some force, and grabbed her. The result was unexpected, and very frightening. The bars turned out to be too weak to take the combined weight of both of us, and with a heart-wrenching snapping sound, they broke up.

We were swept through and beyond by the revolving rollers. I was lying on my back by now. I somehow managed to get Celia on top of me; she was still unconscious. Almost immediately the floor gave way beneath us, and I found we were sliding down a shallow slope to our right. The rotating uneven rollers were everywhere; it was impossible to get a footing. The further we got from the doors, which were still alternately opening and closing, the less I could see. Ahead it was pitch black.

I became aware of a series of square openings in the wall on my right at floor level, and sensed that there was a drop beneath them. As we were drawn along, these gaps became larger and larger. I somehow grasped their significance. Items of rubbish were sorted by size, and the shape of the tunnel combined with the action of the rollers would mean that when an object came to a shaft that could accept it, it would fall down inside, to who knows where.

There was not a moment to lose. I was on my back, and somehow managed to get my feet out in front of me, hoping that they would find one of the sides of an opening. They did. I took the strain in my legs and straightened them out, and we came to a halt, if you could call it that, because by the nature of the rising and falling rollers, we were being alternatively lifted up and dumped down on the floor. But our headlong rush forward had been checked for the moment. The slope of the floor and the action of the rollers ushered us to the side, toward the opening whose far end was supporting my feet. I held my breath as we lurched towards the drop. I felt the near end of the gap against the upper part of my arm. This gap was only five feet wide; as long as I kept myself rigid, we would not fall into the abyss.

I shook Celia vigorously. Thankfully, she stirred and came to. I have no idea how her head had not been bashed senseless by the rollers.

"Grab the hose," I yelled, "and pull yourself out." Somehow, I had managed to keep hold of it in all the turmoil.

She was remarkable. She quickly grasped the urgency of the situation.

"Use me as a ladder," I cried. She did exactly that. The action of her wedding shoes on my bare feet and hands was most painful, but she somehow managed to haul herself back along the hose in the manner of someone swimming against a strong current. As she did so, there was less strain on me. I decided to stay where I was, concentrating on not relaxing, until she had climbed out of the doors. However, I became aware that a violent trembling had seized my legs. I was not going to be able to maintain my position for long. I was sweating profusely. Soon my entire body was shaking uncontrollably, which was hardly surprising after all I had been through. I tried not to think of what might happen if I fell through the hole on the right. I clung desperately to the hose.

I could see she was going to make it to the doors, but could she get through them in the interval between them opening and closing? I rather doubted it.

She was very resourceful. At the doors, she somehow managed to slide the hose sideways underneath one side of the door, which meant it could no longer shut properly. I had to loosen my grip momentarily to allow her to do this; it was an awful moment. Although the other side of the doors shut fully, and now stayed shut, there was just enough room for her to be able to crawl out through the open door. She immediately turned towards me.

"Your turn," she shouted. "There are places to put your feet between the rollers if you tread carefully."

She did not know about my back. "I can't walk," I yelled. "You will have to pull the hose, and I will hang on to it." She grasped the situation. I don't know how she did it, but yard by yard, she hauled me along, thumping up and down on the rollers, trying to protect my head, and I gradually came closer to the opening. At least I had the advantage that the light was now steady, through the open half of the doors, which made things a bit easier. At length I was able to grab the edge of the frame and heave myself through and onto the carpet. Once Celia had pulled the

rest of the hose clear, the second door swung to
behind me, and the invisible seal was restored.
The mouth was shut once more. The klaxon stopped.
    Celia was hugging me. The nightmare was over.
The last thing I heard was Celia gasping, "Look
at your hands and feet!" Then everything went
black and I passed out again.
    Bruce

Celia came for her lesson on Tuesday. She had once again made
phenomenal progress. "You should be teaching me," Bruce said.
She coloured, but was obviously pleased.

There was nothing to report, Bruce said, except for one thing,
which was troubling him. When he played background piano at the
shopping centre on the previous Friday, he had noticed a man
loitering out of the corner of his eye. When he finished, the man
came over and introduced himself. It turned out he was the
restaurant manager of a country club, and he wanted to know
whether Bruce would be able to play background piano in the
restaurant on Sundays at lunchtime. Bruce had not hesitated to turn
it down, because he had strong views about observing Sunday as a
day of rest, but later on, it suddenly occurred to him that maybe
Celia's parents would have liked him to do it. He could have
consulted her before deciding.

Celia replied that it was fine to have turned it down. He was just
to live as he normally did. There would be no need to go against his
integrity.

Araminta came to her lesson this week. She looked upset. Bruce
longed to say something kind to her, but he did not want to overdo
it and open the floodgates. He wanted to tell her what a lovely
person she was, but in the end he said nothing. The half-hour was
somewhat strained. The lessons with Sarah had been going better;
she seemed more relaxed. "Does Sarah know?" Bruce had asked.
Araminta nodded. "But mum doesn't."

Marjorie called in the following Friday evening, after his last
pupil had left.

"I'm going away to my sister in the Isle of Man," she explained. "Would you be willing to do curtain service?"

When Marjorie went away, she found it comforting if Bruce drew her curtains for her at the usual time each evening and morning, to deter burglars. On the first occasions, Bruce had not always remembered to go across, so sometimes the curtains had remained open all night, but thankfully there had never been a break-in. Now, however, he had a new system. He stuck a piece of white paper on the front door just where he put the chain across last thing at night and then undid it again first thing in the morning. This was a perfect reminder to pop across to the other house and do the honours. Since adopting the new scheme, he had never forgotten a single night.

While Marjorie was telling him about her plans, the phone rang. He answered it.

"Mr. Winter?"

"Yes?"

"Many congratulations. I am pleased to tell you that you have won first prize in the raffle, and will be going on holiday on the moon at our expense. Naturally we will confirm this by post, but we thought you would like to know as soon as possible."

"Thank you very much." This was exciting, and alarming all at once. Who were these people?

"We hope you will have a happy holiday. You will need to let us know the name of the person accompanying you."

"Right. Can you tell me the dates, please?"

"August 3rd to the 17th."

"August 3rd to the 17th. A full fortnight. Thank you."

When he had put the phone down, Marjorie said, "It sounds as if you are going away too."

What harm could there be in telling her?

"As a matter of fact, yes. That phone call was to tell me that I have won first prize in a raffle. It's a walking holiday on the moon." No need to mention the 'for two' bit.

"Well, that sounds wonderful, but you don't look very pleased about it."

130

Oh dear, that would never do. "I think I'm a bit shell shocked, to be honest."

"You ought to be over the moon, Bruce, like the proverbial cow. Shocking pun. Let me see –

'With a ping and a pong the fiddle-strings broke!
The cow jumped over the moon,
And the little dog laughed to see such fun,
And the Saturday dish went off at a run
With the silver Sunday spoon.'"

Bruce looked puzzled. "That doesn't sound right at all."

"Ha ha! Got you. I thought you would recognise that. It's Tolkien's version of the nursery rhyme, from the Fellowship of the Ring, the scene in the Prancing Pony at Bree. Surely you've read it?"

Bruce had forgotten that part of it. Marjorie reached down her copy from a shelf, and quickly found the passage. She was widely read, Bruce thought, and always ready with a quotation or something of interest.

"There's a record here of Tolkien himself reading excerpts," she said, pointing at her vinyl discs. It was dated technology, but her record player worked, and there was something rather appealing about the clicks and scratches on her records, which spoke of a lost age. Bruce had played one or two of them before. He looked at the record sleeve with interest.

"Thank you," he said.

"Well, perhaps it will cheer you up, although I can't think what will, if winning first prize in a raffle doesn't."

Bruce pulled himself together. "Don't worry," he said. "I'm a bit low at present, but it will pass."

They finalised the dates when Marjorie would need curtain service, and then she left. It was wonderful to be able to go to the moon; no doubt about it. However, it was frightening how quickly and easily it had been arranged. Bruce's instinct told him that he had got into something bigger than he had realised, and he was already feeling out of his depth. Apart from anything else, it was too late to back out now. They had fulfilled their part of the bargain. He

131

was committed. But, and this was the heart of it, what could he possibly do to help? Why on earth had they approached him? He was bound to let them down.

He turned the record sleeve over idly, and glanced at the note on the back cover. There he read of Tolkien's difficulties and frustrations in getting his writing published. Tolkien had suffered from depression over it! This reminded Bruce of Van Gogh. How strange that another work of genius should have had such difficult birth-pains. Or perhaps it was not strange. Maybe everything in life that is worthwhile comes with pain.

Walking on the moon would be fun. Perhaps he could allow himself to look forward to it. Maybe he would also be able to do some good for the cause he had joined. There was no need to get depressed yet.

23. From: Mission 12
To: Undisclosed recipients
Sent:

When I came to, I found I was lying in my bed, and Celia was seated on a low chair beside me, mopping my brow, and looking concerned. I was hungry and thirsty. I tried to sit up, but my body complained vigorously. I sank back with a groan.

"Try not to move," she said. "Take it easy. It's lovely to have you back."

"What happened?" I asked.

"You have been out for two days. I think it was total exhaustion. I feel dreadful about it. I wanted to punish you, but I'm afraid I overdid it. We nearly lost everything, but as it is, we have another chance to get it right. I am so sorry."

This was music to my ears. "I'm not the least bit sorry," I said, "because it evens things up a bit. I behaved so badly towards you that nothing would have been too much for you to inflict on me in return. So if you feel you are a little bit in

132

my debt, then that's fine by me. Don't worry about it."

I felt such a sense of relief. Maybe there was a future for us after all. But I was not going to risk it a second time by starting to talk about it too early. Better to take time over it.

However, she was speaking again.

"I feel bad, because the truth is that I loved you when I first saw you. At first my feelings for you were completely overshadowed by my grief and disappointment over losing my role in the mission, and by the time I had begun to come to terms with that, I had decided on paying you back. So I deliberately kept myself distant and aloof. You were so convinced by my acting that I rather enjoyed keeping up the role."

"No Shakespearian actress could have been more believable," I said. "I nearly suggested cancelling the wedding when I saw how miserable you looked."

"I'm glad you didn't. I would have collapsed and told you everything if you had."

"I would love to talk about the time in the operating chair, but I am longing for something to eat and drink. Any chance of a snack?"

It was all ready, in anticipation. Nothing beats cereals and milk, especially if it is spooned into your mouth by somebody precious to you. Orange juice, toast and marmalade, with a cup of tea to round it off. Great

"I know what happened to me," I said, "but what happened to you after the yellow cloud of gas knocked you out?"

"I don't remember anything until you brought me round. It took me a while to realise we were inside Grim Reaper. I could not grasp what was happening at all."

"I think that there must be some safety function built into Big Nimp," I said. "I reckon that he thought you were attacking me when you

133

fell on me shouting 'never take me for granted again,' and don't worry, I won't. Hence the knock-out gas. Then the little robots thought you were dead and shovelled you into the mouth."

"Charming. Perhaps you will introduce me to these friendly servants of yours so that I can express my thanks in person." This was said with some of the old fire, but with a twinkle in the eye. She has so much personality!

"No, I can't do that. I only ever saw them once," and I told her about the Dead Lion. She laughed. "We could try and coax them out again if you like," I added.

"No thanks. I'm quite happy. However, it is odd that we don't know where they live. It seems that some cupboards are accessible to us, but others are not, and the openings are so well disguised that we don't even know where they are."

"Interesting." The idea that there might be other invisible doors was a new thought to me. I stored it away for possible future use.

"Try rolling over," she said.

I did so, and found that although it was not comfortable, the back was a lot better.

"Good," said Celia. "I would recommend you get started on the back exercises. I've had a search in Big Nimp, and I found a helpful set of them. I've got the diagrams here."

Exercise one turned out to be lying on my front on the floor for three minutes. I did that straight away. Over the following few days, I became stronger, and progressed to exercises two and three, which started from lying on the floor on my front but also involved push-ups of the upper torso. I was soon able to get up and move about more and more. But most of the time, I just rested in bed. During this time, Celia tended the backs of my hands and the tops of my feet, which had sustained some deep gashes. They took a while to heal up.

Sorry. I'm getting ahead of myself. Let's go
back to when I had just come round and had my
breakfast.

The soles of my feet turned out to be fine.
Celia explained that although the spikes on the
lawn aerator thing had looked vicious, she had
been careful to blunt them all before use. She
had thought that if she waved the thing round
quickly enough in the air, I would not notice the
bluntness. She had not wanted to hurt me, just to
concentrate my mind. She knew my feet would pick
up the sensation strongly nevertheless.

I had to admire this girl. What a player!

"What about all that jelly," I asked. "What was
that about?"

"I couldn't resist that," she said. We both
laughed. "You were right; it did not do my cuffs
any good. But I got the stain out eventually. It
was a nice dress, wasn't it," she said, gathering
it up from another chair where I had not noticed
it and unfolding it so that its full length
spilled down over her knees, to show me. It was
the most beautiful dress.

I'm afraid I am sometimes a little impulsive.

"Any chance of you wearing it again?" I asked,
despite my resolution from a few minutes earlier,
and looked her in the eyes.

She nodded. Tears filled both of our eyes as we
hugged.

We had the ceremony six days later. Everything
went smoothly. She chose the wedding music from
the Sound of Music because she knew I liked it.
On an impulse, I gave her little nimp as a
wedding present. There was no reference to my
mouth line this time. I felt so happy.

Watching the recording afterwards was strange.
I had never expected to see myself getting
married. At the end, Celia turned and said to me,
"What can I give you as a wedding present?"

I remembered the grand piano, and told her about it. She said she couldn't wait to hear me play, so we asked Big Nimp to make one. He said it would take a little time.

Almost immediately, the first parts of it began coming out from Grim Reaper's rollers. To Celia's delight, the two little robots appeared. They clearly had other duties in addition to refuse disposal. They worked hard assembling the instrument.

Its proportions were staggering. The advantage of a grand piano over an upright is that the body of the instrument can be larger, allowing for longer strings. The pitch of a note from a piano depends on both the amount of the metal in the string and the tension of the string. Because a grand piano has more room, its long strings can be thinner than the shorter stubby strings in a small upright, so they vibrate more, giving a better tone, especially in the bass.

This principle had been pushed to its limit. The piano turned out to be eight metres long! It was astonishing. The robots worked away like trained piano technicians, cutting the piano wire to the right length, connecting it up each end, and tightening each string. When it came to the tuning, they were at their most impressive. There was none of the repeated note-bashing I normally associate with a piano being tuned. The note was struck once by one of them, and then the other robot would rotate the tuning pin with one brief twisting action, and the note rose evenly upwards to the exact pitch required. It was wonderful to watch.

When it was finally ready, and our little friends had scuttled off, I sat down at the beautiful leather-covered stool. I played the first Prelude of the Forty-eight Preludes and Fugues of the Well Tempered Klavier. I learnt it when I was a boy and have never forgotten it. The acoustic was favourable; the sound rang round the high ceilings of the spaceship. The instrument was unmatched.

At the end, Celia said simply, "That was unforgettable."

Well done J. S. Bach!

Bruce

The phone was ringing. Banjo again! Now, concentrate!

"Bruce, you remember you are coming to the Henley Regatta?"

Yes, he remembered.

"Well, they have a problem. The man playing background piano has had to pull out at short notice. You remember that I know the organiser – that's why I get the free tickets." Had she said they were free? Bruce wasn't sure. She had never mentioned them being free in past years.

"… whether you could do it instead."

"Sorry, what was that?"

"Bruce, you abdominal pain!! When I said that my first cousin was brilliant at background piano and was coming anyway, the organiser asked whether you could possibly step in and do it instead."

Bruce gulped. "Delighted, Bancesca. Pleased to be asked."

"There is a fee, so that's nice."

"Just let me get my diary… here we are. Now which day is that?"

"Bruce! It's the day you are coming already, you clumsy clot. What does it say in your diary for Saturday July 6th?"

"Henley Regatta, 1.00."

"Thank the gods for that. I wonder how that entry got in there. Well, get over here a bit early, and do your ivory tinkling for a couple of hours, and everybody will be thrilled."

"Right, Bancesca. Just writing it in. I – vo – ry… tin – kling. That should do it."

"Oh you are impossible," said Banjo, and rang off.

Me impossible, thought Bruce. I like that. At least I don't put the phone down on my nearest and dearest.

24. From: Mission 12
To: Undisclosed recipients
Sent:

This is just a brief note to say, don't expect
bedroom scenes in these emails. I think they are
so unhelpful! You won't get any of those details
out of me.

Years ago, I decided that if I was ever asked
by a newspaper reporter about intimate matters
concerning my private life, I would reply like
this: "On this subject, I have nothing to hide,
and nothing to reveal." It's neat, isn't it?
Nothing to hide; my life is like an open book.
Nothing to be ashamed of. But also, nothing to
reveal. Why should anybody have to talk about
their private life? I've always thought it most
unfair that journalists should even ask the
question.

Of course, nobody ever did want to interview
me. Shame really. But I was ready with my answer
if they had.

Oh yes; one other thing. I was concerned that
the fire hose would have been damaged in our
escapade, so one morning I unrolled it to its
full length to check it. It was long, every bit
of sixty metres; I suppose this was so that its
jet could reach any part of our level in an
emergency. On close inspection, I could not find
any hint of damage resulting from Celia having
wedged it under the opening and closing door. I
had thought it might need repairing after its
mistreatment. It was clearly made of strong
stuff. I was thankful for this.

I also expected to find that the nozzle end of
the hose had been digested in Grim Reaper's
stomach, as it were, but I was surprised to find
it was intact. It all appeared to be in good
working order. I found this a bit puzzling, as it
was only fifteen metres from the reel to Grim

Reaper's mouth, and my memory was that the reel
had unwound to its limit.

Oh well, it didn't really matter. We rewound
it, hoping never to have to touch it again.

Bruce

When Bruce arrived at Henley station, he remembered too late
that it was quite a trek to the marquee. He was dressed in a suit,
which involved wearing a tie, which he hated. His shirts were all
too small, really, and he did not like to waste money on new ones
before the old ones had worn out. This meant that wearing a tie was
most uncomfortable, especially in the hot weather. However, the
playing demanded it, he felt. Now he would have to walk fast so as
not to be late. It was a moment for taking a taxi, perhaps, except
that of course when you wanted one, there was never one to be had.

He arrived at the tent all hot and bothered. There were Banjo
and John, looking wonderful, and cool. He hurried up and said
hello. They seemed delighted to see him. There were already a good
number of people present, all in party gear. The Thames had been
laid out conveniently alongside, or that was how it felt, and every
now and then, earnest oarsmen in fours and eights would come
scurrying past. A few of the guests glanced in their direction, but for
most of them, it was the socialising that mattered.

The piano was a white grand. The lid had been raised to its
highest position, which displeased Bruce. He preferred to play with
it shut. It kept the volume down. However, he did not feel he could
alter it, being an outsider, so he would just have to play with it as it
was. He settled nervously on to the stool, adjusting the height. He
did not feel cool and collected at all.

Somebody hurried up to thank him profusely for stepping in at
the last minute. Bruce made self-deprecating remarks, how he
trusted it would be alright, and felt as small as a mouse. He hoped
nobody would listen.

He tried to collect himself. The thing to do was to start gently.
The first Prelude from the Forty-eight by J. S. Bach; that was the
one to begin with, as usual. It would also allow him to get the feel
of the instrument. He began, and as the music unrolled, he could

feel himself relaxing with it. None of the assembled guests, dressed up to the nines, and clutching their champagne, had paused in their flow of small talk. He was blending in alright. Perhaps he could allow himself to enjoy it.

Suddenly, two small figures appeared out of nowhere, and stood to his right and left.

"Hello, Sir."

"Hello, Sir." The two scamps!

"Beccy and Simna, what a lovely surprise. What are you doing here?" Bruce had always found it next to impossible to play and talk to people at the same time. All of his brain-power was directed at what he was doing with his fingers; there was no spare capacity for anything else, not even for the daughters of Jerusalem.

"Beccy's dad runs the catering," Simna said. She was the quieter one of the two, normally; he had expected Beccy to speak up.

"Wonderful. I say, you do look smart." They were both beautifully dressed. They were pleased with the compliment. Now it was Beccy's turn.

"Sir, can we join in at the top and bottom?" She was already gently pressing one of the higher notes. There was the faintest sound from the piano.

"NO!" Bruce said, with great urgency, but as quietly as he could. This was terrible. He needed to make a good job of this.

"Please, sir!" they both begged. Confound them! It was funny and delightful, part of his brain was telling him, but he could not afford to laugh or smile. It was important that he play well. Somehow, he was still playing gently now, despite the crisis. How could he drive them off? But Beccy was speaking again.

"Sir, did you ever see the film, The Horse Whisperer?"

What on earth had that got to do with it?

"Yes, but I forget the story line."

"Well, sir, you remind me of him!" And with that they were off, with a fit of giggles. He breathed a sigh of relief. The Horse Whisperer? What had that been about? He would have to hire a copy and watch it.

It was a lovely piano. He settled into his playing. No Wagner today. From time to time, boats with musicians on them would pass on the river; they tended to have jazz bands. Bruce found it best to stop rather than compete, and then as they were going out of earshot, he would pick up the theme of what they had been playing and continue it for a minute or two, before going into the next number. He found it a pleasing challenge to blend in with the style and tempo of the other musicians in the right key.

When he finally finished, Banjo came over.

"Bruce, that was lovely. You do it so well. My friend is delighted."

That was good. It was always a low moment when he had just stopped. He was only too conscious of everything that was wrong about his playing, so it was really nice to have someone come up and thank him. He smiled.

"It was a pleasure."

"You must be exhausted. Come and have a drink."

A glass of Champagne was thrust into his hand. Thankfully, there was still some lunch left. He helped himself to some of the remaining sandwiches.

"Bancesca, I feel I need to apologise for being so hopeless on the phone when you ring up. I don't know what it is…"

"Don't worry," said Banjo. "You are hopelessly dreamy. I've got used to it. It doesn't bother me at all." That was a relief.

"We are having a party at home on Saturday August 10th. Any chance of you joining us, or will you be away?"

This was a bit tricky. Banjo was so effusive that if he told her about the moon trip, it would go all round.

"I'm sorry, I will be away somewhere. The piano pupils dry up in August. I have tried giving lessons, but really I have found it best to stop completely and give everyone a complete break, including me. So it is the time of year to go off on holiday."

"Fully understood. Have you made any plans?"

"They are not yet finalised. I don't want anyone to know at present, because I am planning to surprise someone."

"Oh Bruce, how exciting. Oh, here's Flossie."

Bruce had completely forgotten that Flossie was going to be there. She was wonderfully slim, and looked gorgeous in her long dress, sky blue with sequins, but Bruce was not going to allow himself to be taken in by her appearance. He had experienced Flossie enough to know that this was one to keep away from.

"Flossie. Lovely to see you. You look terrific."

Banjo did not give Flossie time to reply. "Bruce is taking an unknown friend on holiday this summer, Flossie. Isn't that mysterious?" Flossie raised her eyebrows.

Great. Thanks a million. Bruce looked at Banjo. There was an impish smile on her face. Bruce remembered a scene in a children's cartoon film Granddad had once shown him, when a lion had seized his pet snake in frustration, and tied it into a double knot, and then said to it, "Get out of that, if you can!"

At that moment, Beccy and Simna ran up. They actually cuddled up next to him, each holding one of his sleeves, looking with great interest at Flossie. Bruce seized his chance.

"Ah well, when you are a great hit with the ladies like me, anything can happen."

While Flossie was still thinking of something to say, Beccy burst out, "Can we play the piano now?" and before Bruce could say anything, they were off over to it.

"Excuse me," he said, and marched briskly after them. This would never do. Beccy was just about to start up with Chopsticks when Bruce firmly but gently closed the lid, giving her time to draw her fingers out from under it. "No you can't!" he said. Then he caught Simna's eye. There was a twinkle in it. It had been a wind-up. They would not really have embarrassed him. Children, he thought to himself. I don't know.

25. From: Mission 12
To: Undisclosed recipients
Sent:

Father, what I want to know is, why did you make them male and female at creation? "Male and female created he them." Was it really the best idea? Could there not have been some other way?

I was prepared for marriage to be tough but I had no idea how difficult it would turn out to be! I love her so much and I find her so difficult! If I loved her less, would it be any easier, I wonder?

I feel really troubled about having woken her. I know she says she's glad I did it - that was wonderful to hear. But she thinks I think you told me to, whereas all you said was ask Big Nimp, and Big Nimp said the one on the left. I've tried telling her about it but she just won't listen. I've begun on it several times, but she cuts me short. I reckon it's no good trying to push it.

I wish she found you easier. She seems scared of you. I can't think why. I hope she will soften towards you one day soon.

Was it really bad when I yanked down the lever above her? I mean really bad? The thing is, if I'm honest, I would do it again. And again.

But I just wish loving her was not quite so hard. Oh dear! I feel so hopeless!

Once again there was nothing to report to Celia on Tuesday, only her stunning progress to observe. It was unfair. She already knew about the moon trip. She assured him that she would be there to walk with him, but they would not travel together. There was no way she could go out with him for a meal. Indeed, he was not even to ring her, unless it was a routine matter, such as the need to change a lesson time or something like that. It was too dangerous. Bruce nodded. It was not his idea of fun, but it was too late to regret it now.

Araminta missed again on Thursday morning. This was getting ridiculous. Bruce felt he was in the dark. That evening, he would tackle Sarah about it.

However, when the scamps came in, there was trouble.

"We loved your girl-friend, sir. She's beautiful. Terrific performer. One of the cool, calm and collected type."

Things were in real danger of getting out of hand, it seemed to Bruce.

"Look, she is not my girl-friend. I did know her once…"

"Trying to pretend we are just good friends, are we, Sir?!"

Any attempt to convince them that their hunch was wrong was going to be hopeless. Bruce decided on attack.

"There is nothing in it, but even if there was, it is none of your business. Now, here's a promise. If you go making trouble for me over what you saw, I will personally skin you alive. Got it?"

He sounded fiercer than he had meant to. Speaking like this was so out of character for Bruce that for once the scamps were left short of anything to say. He felt surprised himself at his own behaviour.

Simna found her voice first. "Okay, sir. We didn't mean to upset you."

Now, here was an opportunity to teach them something. "I assure you, Flossie is a friend of my cousin Banjo, who was also there, and who invited me and fixed up for me to play. But suppose Flossie was my girl-friend. You two could make it very difficult for me, spreading word of my attachment all round my pupils. It could kill any budding relationship. Would you want to do that?"

They both shook their heads.

"I have seen a family where the twenty-year-old daughter was starting a friendship with a boy, and her dad made life so unbearable for her with his teasing that it really upset her. It was horrible to watch. So I have decided myself that in all matters of the heart, I am going to respect people and give them plenty of space to make their own minds up, without putting in my oar. My advice to you is to do the same."

He could not remember any other time when they had listened so intently. Normally, they chattered on incessantly. He could see that they were impressed with what he had said.

"Yes Mr. Winter," said Beccy. "Don't worry. We won't make waves. I know you said she isn't your girl-friend, but I just want to say that I still think she is really beautiful, and I would be thrilled if I turned out to be as pretty as that when I am older."

"Me too," added Simna.

"But sir?"

"Yes, Beccy?"

"I thought a Banjo was a kind of guitar."

"My cousin's real name is unpronounceable, so I call her Banjo. Now, let's get on with the lesson."

Thankfully, they were able to leave it there, and give the Pink Panther a gentle prod forwards, which was their current piece. Their left hands were getting reasonable at doing the pattern in the introduction now. Der-rum der-rum, they played. Simna was not leaving enough of a gap between the groups.

"You need to count to seven between each group," Bruce explained, "like this. Der-rum der-rum (2 3 4 5 6 7) der-rum der-rum (2 3 4 5 6 7) der-rum der-rum, and so on. Make sure you come in again as soon after seven as you can. I will do the counting; you just play."

They got it after a bit. Then they had a first go at the tune with the right hand. The lesson went well.

Sarah arrived punctually that evening. She had thawed considerably since their first meeting. It was hard to believe she was the same person as the girl that had been so frosty. She was clearly enjoying the lessons. Why was it that almost all his pupils were female, he found himself asking? Were the boys too busy doing sport? But he himself had taken to music as a young person. There must be musical boys out there somewhere.

A number of Bruce's pupils exhibited signs of stress when concentrating on playing, in one way or other. One girl's left foot would start going up and down. One boy would stick out his tongue slightly. Sarah had a tendency to bite her lower lip. Bruce decided to mention it.

"Look, what we will do is that you play the Prelude, and every time I see the tooth in action, I will say 'Beep'; your challenge is to get all the way through without doing it."

That was fine; Sarah managed it.

"Now, this time, to make it a bit harder, I will ask some testing questions while you are playing. Same rules apply. Okay?"

Sarah smiled. She began to play.

"Sarah, can you spell your own name backwards?"

With a bit of an effort, she managed H A R A S, and the tooth stayed hidden.

"Very good. I hope you are not feeling too harassed. Incidentally, can you spell harass backwards?"

This was harder, but to Bruce's delight, she managed it: S S A R R A H.

"Very good, although actually, harass only has one R. I reckon that should cure the tooth appearances." They laughed.

Later on in the lesson, he opened up the subject on his mind. "Look, Araminta has told me that you know about her crush on me." He could not bear to use the word love. "Could we discuss it a moment?"

"Yes, certainly."

"The thing is, I just don't know what to do to help. There is no question of our pursuing a relationship; the age gap rules it out. But I feel so sad about her feeling hurt about that. There was always a lot of banter in our lessons, but I never thought it would lead to this. If I had, I would have remained more aloof. She's such a lovely girl; I can't bear to think of her being upset." It was not very well-connected, but he hoped Sarah would understand.

"Don't worry about it. She is low and moody, but it will pass. She is very warm-hearted, and she has always enjoyed a joke. If I may say so, it is hardly surprising that she has fallen for you. I think every girl should have her heart broken at least once, before they find Mr. Right, personally. I think you've done her a good turn."

Not all of this was reassuring. Apart from anything else, was there just a hint that Sarah herself found him attractive?

Bruce found himself recalling a line from one of Oscar Wilde's plays, which ran, "I can resist anything except temptation." He was having to work hard to resist temptation now, he realised, but he managed it somehow. So Sarah never heard him reply, "But what about you; have you had your heart broken sufficiently yet?" It really was not an area he should probe.

He hoped she did not share Araminta's mind-reading ability. But was there perhaps a faint half smile playing round her lips? It was hard to be sure.

26. From: Mission 12
To: Undisclosed recipients
Sent:

I really feel I need to apologise for being out of touch for so long. I had always intended to take a year off from writing, as Scripture says, "let him have a year off active service to enjoy the wife he has taken." It's talking about soldiers in the army, really, but I feel one can stretch a point. I've always liked that bit.

However, I also wanted to wait until there was good news to report. What I mean is, I told you I did not want to give you intimate details. In fact, I worried for quite a while as to whether I had been too graphic in describing my time awaiting torture. The unbuttoning of my shirt may have been too much for some readers. I did not want to upset anyone. Sorry if you thought it was off side. I am aware it says somewhere, "Do not awaken love until it is time," or something like that, and I did not want to get you all stirred up in that realm with my account. I hope you will forgive me if I did.

Anyway, I knew you would be getting the regular log of our journey's progress that Big Nimp sends each week, so you would know we were alright if I did not send straight away.

Being married has been good, but I don't want you to think that it has all been a bed of roses for Celia and me. Or perhaps roses is the right word after all, because you don't get roses without thorns. We started getting hurt by these pretty soon.

147

You see, I have not told you much about it, but because I lost my parents so early, or you could say, they lost me, I have very little idea how to make a marriage work. It took a while for me to see that. I had thought it would be easy enough!

Really, the only idea my parents gave me about living together was that you shouted at one another in anger. I hated that, and was dead against it, but I did not know how to avoid doing it myself. To my horror, it seemed to come naturally to me.

Celia used to get upset with me a lot in the early days (I can see why, now). I used to get upset back. The last thing I wanted was exactly what was happening. It was hateful, but we could not seem to prevent it!

There were times when I threw myself down and hammered with my fists on the floor in my frustration. It's true; it is better that you should know. I hoped this would be a passing phase, but it wasn't. I could not bear to send an email about it.

Things finally began to get a little better when I realised that I am pretty difficult to live with, if I am honest. I expected Celia to agree with everything I wanted to do, and I could not understand when she had different ideas. She found it especially difficult if I took decisions and acted on them without consulting her. In the end, we learned to talk things through before I took any action. It was a big help.

There were some highlights. I will never forget when she said to me at the breakfast table, "I think I am pregnant". I was so thrilled. Max was a bouncy baby, and now he's growing up so fast. He is quite a young man at seven. I love him. But I am getting ahead of myself.

I soon realised why I had not wanted a piano before; it was because I feared Big Nimp would despise my playing. It is pretty bad, really. But the thing is, Celia knows nothing about music, so whatever I play sounds fine to her. I don't worry about it any more, now. It is nice to have such a wonderful instrument.

Recently, I was going to play really loudly - I forget the piece, and for some reason, I announced it as if I was some big compeer on TV, by saying in a strong American accent, "Honey, I'm going for the full nine yards here tonight." It's something to do with sport. I heard a preacher say it once. Then I played with gusto. It was a happy moment. You remember the piano is eight metres long.

Then Clairie came along. She is delightful. Celia was so thrilled to have a little girl.

Oh, I almost forgot; the studio. Celia said she had always wanted to do art, so we made her a studio. It was a brilliant success. Big Nimp would put up scenes the whole length and width of one wall, and then Celia would paint them at her easel. There was never any problem about canvases, oil paints, frames and so forth; Big Nimp had all that sort of thing ready with no trouble. I was not sure how we were going to hang the paintings, but I need not have worried; Big Nimp seems to have control of every inch of wall space, and can make hooks come out of the flat metal at will. So now, the walls are dotted with seascapes and landscapes. Celia likes painting those best. It is lovely to see her creating such beautiful things. She has a style all her own. It's no good me trying to describe it. I'm hopeless at that. Sorry.

The studio had a real practical value too, because when Celia was most upset with me in the early days, she would go off in there and stab wild brushstrokes at a canvas. The results looked awful and brilliant at the same time. Violent splurges of paint. I wanted to keep some of them, but Celia insisted we put them down Grim Reaper.

Clairie is three. I should have said. She is inseparable from her stuffed toy; it's a badger. Celia made him for her. I was worried that he would go down Grim Reaper by mistake, which would provoke a major crisis, so one night when everyone else was asleep, I prised him out of Clairie's little fingers, and took him to the part of the floor where copies are made. I asked Big Nimp if, rather than making a copy, he could hold the pattern in memory, and he said he could. So if the worst happens, we have a backup plan!

Anyway, I am really hoping our relationship will improve. At least I have had the courage to write to you again. Perhaps that is a good sign. Let's see how things go.

Bruce

The term was winding to a close. Bruce always felt that they should end in early July, but somehow, the school calendar required them all to slog on past July 20th. It was not a good time for making progress at piano. There were more absentees than usual. He noticed that some families arranged their annual holiday to start before the end of term, and took their children out of school for the last week or so. This did not seem right to Bruce; if the school was in session, then that should be respected.

Araminta told him that, if he was happy, she wanted to continue lessons with him next term. In fact, she seemed more chirpy, so Bruce plucked up the courage to ask how she was getting on now.

"Oh, much better, thanks. Karl and I have patched things up. He's nowhere near as nice as you, of course, but he's Okay."

Bruce simply could not imagine how he could possibly be seen as more desirable than Karl, but he let it pass.

Araminta continued, "Are you going to have another flying lesson?"

"No. I have decided that from now on, I am going to conduct my affairs from the ground, thanks."

The pun with the word 'conduct' was deliberate, referring to the waltz, but Araminta seized quickly on a second, unintended pun,

150

and replied, "Mr. Winter, if there is one thing I am quite sure about, it is that I cannot imagine you ever having an affair."

They laughed. Bruce was pleased. The sun was coming out from behind the clouds. It was beginning to look as if things could go back to how they had been before. The summer holidays would help, provided she and Karl did not fall out again.

"No, I trust not," he replied. "As far as I can see, they cause nothing but heartache and misery. Let's get the moonlight under way."

"Talking of moonlight, a month ago, there were raffle tickets being sold in school with a first prize of a trip to the moon. I was hoping to win it. I wonder who did."

She did not know, he was sure of it. She must not discover. "Was it a nation-wide raffle?"

"You bet, with a prize like that. You don't think the governors would stump up that kind of money, do you?"

"Quite. I'm sorry you did not win." There was no hint of her knowing, thankfully.

They worked on the closing bars of the first movement. The note-learning was nearly finished.

"Now all you have to do is to turn it into music." Bruce explained how to bring out the tune with the little finger of the right hand while keeping the endless stream of triplets as soft as possible. Araminta made a reasonable shot at it.

"It takes a lot of practice," Bruce warned.

She nodded. "Don't worry. I'm just going to dash off the other two movements over the summer as well."

"Well done. I am going to learn seventy piano concertos by September myself," said Bruce.

27. From: Mission 12
To: Undisclosed recipients
Sent:

I am so glad that both Celia and I believe in marriage being a lifelong commitment. We would never have made it without that. It has been wonderful having her, but living together has revealed my weaknesses so much as well. I want to say to anyone reading this whose relationship has broken down that I feel nothing but sympathy for you. I know now how hard it is to make things work. I won't say more than that.

The children are great. Clairie loves me to tell her a make-up story about her pet badger at bedtime. This is a challenge, I can tell you, but I do enjoy it! In our stories, he lives in the wood, and the various scrapes he and the other animals keep on getting into you would not believe. The stories always start with the same routine. Let me give a recent example.

Self (in an imposing voice): "This is the story of Oschen Goschen and the big, black Boschen."

Clairie (fixing me with her eye): "But Daddy, what is Oshy and Boshy?"

Self: "Clairie, if you listen to the story, you will find out."

When I get to the end of the story, she always looks intently at me and says, "A smidgeon more!" So I have to have a second ending to the story up my sleeve, lasting a few sentences. Then when that is done, she settles down happily to go to sleep.

Max is a natural sportsman. He does not get it from me! Big Nimp rose to the occasion. He not only made him a small putter and a number of golf balls, and a full-sized putter for me; he also grasped the concept of a hole, and can sink one anywhere in the floor at will, and make a little flag sprout up from it. Indeed, he can make the floor rise and fall as well, creating contours, which produce challenging holes. Max quickly outshone me at putting, no matter how hard I tried.

Sometimes, the hole would be in a different room from the tee. I would carefully putt into position in the doorway, but not Max. He would strike his ball firmly towards a side wall in such a way that his ball would bounce off it and then roll in through the door on the rebound. He did not need to be shown how to do this; he worked it out for himself. It was amazing.

Then one day, I found him throwing his golf ball gently up one of the curved tops of Grim Reaper in such a way that it would just reach the summit, and roll down the far side, where Clairie was waiting, arms awkwardly outstretched, ready to catch it. This required great skill in Max, as Clairie was not yet old enough to move her arms on seeing the ball. He would call out, "Clairie!", and she would move to where she thought was opposite him and squawk back "Maxy!" Then Max had to estimate exactly where she was from her voice, and throw the ball in just the right way that she could catch it. Then she would throw it back over, he would tiptoe to a new position, and they would do it again.

I realised then that they needed tennis balls, and rackets too. Big Nimp produced excellent ones for them. Clairie could not manage hers to begin with, but there was no problem for Max. I showed him how to stand facing a wall, and use it to bounce his shots back towards himself. I painted on a line for the net. After that there was no stopping him.

I am no tennis player, but I taught him what I knew, and we watched hours of Wimbledon recordings on Big Nimp. Before long, he was getting most proficient.

One day, he staggered me. "Look Dad," he called. I came to watch. He was facing a corner. He sent a forehand into one side wall, and then on the rebound, did a backhand into the other wall, followed by another forehand into the first wall, and so forth. I was about to congratulate him when he said "Wait!" in a commanding tone. After a few more hits, when his rhythm had settled down, he said in a loud voice, "Okay Karajan, take it away!" and Big Nimp started up with the Radetsky March (Strauss). The young scamp was hitting the ball in time with the music! I was astonished, and was starting to say so when again he checked me. To my amazement, as the music changed to Land of Hope and Glory, he stepped away from the corner slightly, so that the tennis ball had further to travel, in time with the slower pace of the music. I watched in silent admiration as he then moved closer into the corner to finish with the Gallop from the William Tell overture. In all of this, he had the ball flying to and fro in perfect control.

I turned to see Celia standing watching. "Wasn't that staggering?" I said. She nodded. I think it was then that we both knew that we had a genius on our hands. I felt very inadequate. How on earth could we give him an appropriate upbringing? Celia squeezed my hand. She so often seemed to know what I was thinking. I feel so privileged to have known her. How did I ever get to end up with a wife and children on a spaceship mission? I feel so happy and sad and inadequate all at the same time.

Bruce

Term came to an end, and the date of the moon trip loomed closer. Bruce was beginning to get excited. The private piano pupils were evaporating and going off on holiday, so he had more free time.

One evening, the doorbell rang. He did not think a lesson was booked, so he wondered who it might be. Sometimes when the doorbell rang unexpectedly, it was a pupil and he had made a mistake over the time; sometimes they had made a mistake.

This time, it was neither. Gnilla was on the doorstep. Bruce knew there was a problem because there were no flowers in her hands. One look at her face showed it was serious.

"Gnilla, come in. What's happened?"

"It's Bill," she sobbed into his shoulder, as he put his arms round her to comfort her. "He's dumped me."

Bruce had guessed as much from her entry. He needed to be calm and sympathetic. No good offering a lot of advice. Just listen.

"Tell me."

"He said he had realised that we were not meant for each other, and that we should end it now. It was all very quick. Since then, he won't talk to me. The answerphone is always on and he won't respond to any of my messages. It's horrible."

"And did he give you any idea as to why he had decided that?"

"Oh, there was a lot of stuff about how he had never wanted to hurt me, and he did not want to let me down, and so on, but the bottom line is that he ended it and I never had a say."

They used to have rows, Bruce knew, but didn't all couples have disagreements? Bruce was sure they loved each other.

"I feel very sad about it," he said. "I don't know what else to say."

"You're very good, Bruce. I knew you wouldn't go on by the yard and a half. I want you to do something."

Oh dear. Go-between.

"When you see him on Sunday at church, talk to him. Tell him I have told you about it. Tell him, I'm not going to try to make him change his mind, but I do love him. Is that too much, do you think?"

"No. I think that is fine. I'm glad you have let me know, because Bill is my friend, and I want to be able to help him through what will be a difficult time for him."

"That's why I came round, really. I knew Bill would need support."

Gnilla was handling this as well as could be hoped, Bruce reckoned. How lovely that she was concerned for Bill, even though he had abandoned her. Bruce found that very moving.

"I will do what I can. Would you like a drink?"

Gnilla wanted to go now that she had said her piece. Bruce hoped it was not the last time he would see her. She was nice. Maybe the situation could be rescued.

On Sunday, Bill was there. Bruce gave him a hug. "I know about it. Gnilla came to see me," he said. Bill said nothing, but Bruce could tell that his hug meant a lot.

Over coffee, it came out.

"The thing is, I have been worried about us for some time. We seem to have these rows, and I have this inner doubt all the time as to whether we are meant for each other. I just don't feel comfortable about it, so in the end, I ended it before we got in any deeper."

Bruce nodded.

"Mind you," added Bill, "I feel so lonely and low without her. It's miserable."

Bruce felt completely out of his depth.

"Look, I am the last person to talk to about this. However, I will say this; it strikes me as a bit tough on Gnilla that she did not get a say in whether the relationship should end or not. You denied her the chance to discuss it."

"I suppose I did. But it was better to make a clean break."

"I never know what a clean break is, personally. Still, you have done what you have done. I do have a suggestion."

Bill looked very suspicious.

"Why don't you and I go for some long country walks together. It may help you to do something you enjoy without feeling under pressure."

Bill immediately brightened up. "Great idea."

"Starting today," Bruce went on. "It's nice weather. I've got a book of walks my granddad gave me at home, and there's one with a pub half way round that serves food. I have not put anything on to cook today, and I bet you haven't thought about food either." Bill had not. "Right, that settles it. We'll pick up my walking boots first, then go to your place and get yours, and then you can drive us to the starting place. In fact, let's slip away early, so that we aren't too famished before we get to the pub."

All this had a galvanising effect on Bill. Both he and Bruce enjoyed walking. I may not be much good at talking, Bruce thought to himself as they went out, but I reckon this was a good idea.

Bill drove him home. The house still looked strange without the Virginia creeper, which had been cut off when the coating had been applied. Bruce wondered if he would ever get used to the new appearance. They collected the book and his walking boots, then went on to Bill's flat to collect his boots, before driving off into the country.

"I'm considering getting this car turned over to the new energy," Bill said.

"Wouldn't it be cheaper to buy a new car?"

"There are some good deals on at the moment. It is an expensive job, but once it's done, there is no more filling it up at the pump."

"Helps the environment too."

"Yes. Anyway, I'll see."

They chatted away until they reached the side turning. Within a few minutes they were parking under some Beech trees.

"Now, the only trouble with Granddad's book is that sometimes, things have changed on the ground since it was written. So we have to keep our wits about us. But the paths are much the same as they were."

"I tell you what's worrying me a little," said Bill, "and that's these flying suits. Do you think it's safe for us to go wandering alone in the country? Might a gang of youths swoop down and demand our wallets?"

Bruce had not thought of this possibility. "You're right, Bill. Doesn't that show how difficult it is to anticipate where all this new technology is leading. I suppose there will need to be sky police. At least we have our phones."

"Well, don't go making any unnecessary calls out here," Bill said. "Somebody somewhere will have found a way of spotting people from their phone signal, so only use them in built-up areas."

"My word, you are suspicious," laughed Bruce. "Anyway, don't worry. Virtually all my pupils are on holiday, so there's nobody to ring."

That got them on to the difficulties with women, which proved to be such a vast subject that they had to resume after breaking off at the pub for lunch. In the end, Bruce felt he had to interject.

"Look, I do appreciate that women can be difficult, but I feel we need some balance here. What I mean is, you are aware that men can be impossible?"

"Now don't you try to put anything on me," said Bill. Bruce could sense it was a difficult area.

"Actually, I was thinking of myself," he replied. That drew a smile from Bill.

"You know, I've really appreciated today. Are you open to doing it again?"

"Certainly." Bruce felt a little hesitant, but Bill was bound to find out. "Actually, I need to get in training."

"What for?"

"I've won a walking holiday on the moon in a raffle."

Bill was thrilled for Bruce. "That will really suit you with your interest in man's future in space. It will also look good on your CV if ever the job of Man in the Moon falls vacant and you choose to apply."

It was Bruce's turn to aim a kick at Bill, but it was deftly avoided. They chatted on until they reached the car again. On the way back, Bill said, "Gnilla and I were going walking in France for a few days at the end of August. Would you like to step in and come instead?"

"That's very kind of you. I will keep the days free, and see how things are." The words were well chosen. They both knew what he meant without him having to say it.

"Thanks again for a nice day," said Bruce, when Bill dropped him off. "Give me a ring in a few days."

As Bill drove off, Bruce looked after him. He felt sorry for him. He wondered whether he and Gnilla might be able to get back together again. He hoped they would, for both their sakes.

28. From: Mission 12
To: Undisclosed recipients
Sent:

"Daddy, Daddy, come quickly!" It was Clairie calling me from the big open space. I went in.

158

"Watch, Daddy," she said, and pointed at the wall. As I looked, a crack began to appear. It soon became the outline of a double set of doors, and then to my astonishment, the doors swung open towards us, revealing a dimly lit stairwell up and down, and Max strode out towards us. All at once, the doors closed again, and vanished. It took my breath away.

Both the children noted my amazement, and began to laugh. I blinked and rubbed my eyes; they thought it was hilarious. This seemed like a good opportunity for some fun. I went up to the wall, and had a good close look at it, but I could not make out the slightest hint of a crack. Well, the children thought this was marvellous. There were tears running down their cheeks. By this time, Celia had heard the noise and had come out to see what was going on.

I decided to play up. I put my right hand on the wall, and my ear close to it, and then with two fingers of my left hand, I gave two sharp little taps on the metal, as if I was trying to sense vibrations, rather as I had once seen a doctor do to Granddad's chest in my youth. Clairie gave a shriek of laughter. Max was so hysterical with the giggles that he was actually on his back on the floor, rolling about holding his sides, hardly able to breathe. I have never seen this done in real life before, although I did once see it on a poster above a photocopier, accompanied by the words, 'You want it done by when?'

"Bruce," Celia protested, "you will do the children an injury." She was enjoying it too.

"But it's so extraordinary," I said. However, I did stop tapping the wall. Gradually the fit of mirth subsided and the children calmed down.

"However did you do it?" I asked.

"It's easy," said Max. "You just say the password, and the door opens."

"But how did you even know that there was a door?" I asked.

"I realised that the tennis ball had a different bounce on that bit of the wall, so I figured there must be a hidden door there, like on Grim Reaper, so I asked Big Nimp, and he told me. When I asked how to open it, he told me the password. It's 'Grapefruit'."

As he said it, the door opened.

"Grapefruit," spluttered Clairie, who was still struggling with laughter, and the door shut again.

"Right," I said. "Well done; that was really clever of you. Now listen. Don't you go playing with it. I don't like the idea of one of you getting stuck behind a door that seals itself into the wall so effectively."

They both pleaded with me, but I held firm. If we had been meant to go in there, the entrance would have been plain to see at all times, it seemed to me. Celia agreed with me; the stairwell was out of bounds. The children were disappointed, but they accepted it.

I suppose children are the same the world over – they enjoy a good game. I was pleased for them to be having fun, and part of me did not want to stop it. However, another part of me felt uneasy about their discovery. I hoped they would not unearth other secrets in a hurry.

Why grapefruit, I wondered?

Bruce

In the middle of the night, Bruce woke up with a jerk and sat bolt upright in bed, all in one movement. It was pitch dark. He felt awful. Max Winter! This was really frightening.

Somehow, he managed to find the switch on his bedside light and stumble out of bed. He made his way through to the sitting room and started searching the shelves. He was sure he had seen the book recently... Here it was. Rebecca, by Daphne du Maurier. It only took him a few moments to check. Yes, the main character in the book had been called Max Winter, as he remembered. And Bruce knew the familiar story. It had eventually come out that the man had murdered his wife.

Bruce's heart was beating wildly. Had he called his son Max in his daydreams because deep down he was scared that there had been murder in his own family? That his own dad had murdered his mum that dreadful day when he was little? It would make sense of the strangers arriving unannounced at the house and the sudden switch to living with Granddad.

Before now, he had never allowed himself to imagine that something bad might have happened that day in his parents' bedroom. Now, for the first time, he was facing up to the possibility. How could he find out the truth?

The Family Records Centre. There would be a death certificate. He would go that very day.

Oh dear, there was one pupil coming to the house mid-morning. It was no good, he would have to put them off. He could not teach in this state. He was far too agitated. Feverishly he found the number, and dialled through. The dad answered.

"Stephe, I'm very sorry, but I cannot teach Mark after all this morning. I'll explain later. Do you mind? I am so sorry."

"Bruce, whatever's the matter? It's four o' clock in the morning."

Whoops. "Stephe, I'm really sorry; I had no idea of the time. I'm afraid I'm in rather a state."

"You certainly are. I've been a bit worried about you for a while, as a matter of fact. Do you think you need to go on some pills?"

Great. Amateur psychology. "Don't worry, I'll keep taking the tablets." He was feeling a bit calmer now. It was helpful to talk to another human being, even if it was only about changing a lesson time. "Look, I'm really sorry to have woken you. I'll stand you a jar at the weekend." Stephe was a real ale fanatic. "I'll let you get back to sleep."

"Bruce, you need to calm down. Take my advice. Chill out. Bye for now."

"Bye."

It was all very well for Stephe, happily married and with a trouble-free childhood behind him, no doubt.

There was no more sleep for Bruce that night. He did some calculations. The family records place opened at 0900, so if he caught a train at about 0800, and therefore had breakfast at 0715, that would be about right. What could he do for three hours? The best thing seemed to be to lie there and try and relax, otherwise he would be worn out during the day when he needed his wits about him. However, he found it was impossible to calm down; his mind was in such a whirl.

Eventually, he got up and had a bath and washed his hair for something to do. He had his breakfast and set off for the station; there was no harm in being on the early side. Then he remembered he ought to take paper and pencil with him for jotting down notes, so he hurried back for those. He was practically running in his excitement. Slow down!

The train seemed to crawl along. However, it finally arrived, and after more public transport, he was eventually standing outside the Centre. Ah, it was already open, even though he had thought he was too early. That was good.

He was the first person inside. Now, he needed to keep cool and calm. He had all day here, if he needed it. The thing to do was to think carefully, and make haste slowly.

He decided first of all to have a warm-up search. He would look up Banjo's birth entry, to see if there was a 'g' in her name or not. It was a case of finding the right ledger. It was not difficult, as he knew her birthday, and her approximate age. Here it was, and there was no 'g' in it. He had been right.

Next he went to the marriages register, and found his parents' wedding. In the old days, you had to wait several days before they posted the certificate to your home, but now it was much better. You put in your request, and the certificate was ready for you in about thirty minutes.

Now that request was being processed, he was ready for the main enquiry. His heart was beating wildly. He reckoned he had been four or perhaps five on the fateful day. It was also warm weather, he remembered, which suggested summer. There would be a number of registers to search, but it should not take too long.

He spent an hour on it, and by the end, he was satisfied that he had done a thorough job. Two people with the surname Winter had died in the three-year time period. He ordered both certificates. He had a chill feeling in his stomach.

Ah, here was the marriage certificate. He would study it later. For the time being, he wanted to leave no stone unturned. It was just possible that his mother's death could have been entered under her maiden name, Rewell, although he could not imagine how. Better safe than sorry. He spent an hour searching, but with no result, which seemed to rule out that possibility.

It was time for a coffee. He collected the two death certificates, and took them with the marriage certificate and his pencil and paper, and made for the canteen. He ordered his coffee, and sat down at a small table near the wall.

William Francis Winter had married Sarah Marigold Rewell etc. etc... he read on. Then his heart missed a beat. His granddad's name was George Rewell, but on this wedding certificate, there was no sign of any George. His mother's father was Philip Lester Rewell. Could Granddad have been known as George despite his birth names? It seemed unlikely. He had always assumed that his granddad was his mother's father, but he had never asked. Now it looked as if he was not. Perhaps he was a brother of Philip Lester Rewell. He could research that. Then a horrible thought struck him; perhaps Granddad was no relation at all. That seemed impossible. Maybe this certificate was a forgery, and that someone had been tampering with his family history. Maybe there had been a murder, and the registers had somehow been falsified to cover it up or something.

Bruce knew that he was thinking irrationally. He needed to take a grip on himself and calm down. He was sweating. He tried to collect his thoughts.

He was sure of one thing; whoever his granddad had been, he had loved him, and cared for him, and set him on the road to life. It was Granddad who had arranged for Bruce to have piano lessons. He owed everything to him. No matter what happened, no matter what can of worms he might have begun to open, nothing was going to cause him to doubt his granddad. There were tears in his eyes, clouding his vision. He took out his handkerchief and wiped his eyes.

"You alright, mate?"

He turned to see who had spoken. It was a middle-aged man with a smile. Bruce decided to be frank, with a dash of humour.

"I am trying to discover whether one of my parents killed the other one, and who it was that brought me up after they disappeared, but apart from that I'm fine, thanks."

"****," said the man. "And I'm only here to get a replacement birth certificate. Well, best of luck, mate. Mind you," he added, giving Bruce the once over, "you don't look to have turned out too bad after a terrible start like that. Good luck to you, mate. You're terrific."

This was so encouraging! How kind of this man to talk to somebody he did not know who was in obvious distress. Most people would have simply steered clear. Feeling as low as he was, Bruce found the man's intervention really uplifting. He had heard stories about people meeting a complete stranger and wondering afterwards whether they had been talking to an angel. Was this happening to him now? The only thing was, did angels use four-letter words? He rather doubted it.

"Thanks a lot for coming over to talk. You have really helped me."

"Not at all, mate. You go for it. You're great. I must go."

"Bye," said Bruce, and watched the man out of the door. He was so grateful.

Now, back to the certificates. The thing to do was to think carefully. On the whole, it was good news. True, either his granddad had been called by a name that was not his by his friends, which was a thing some people chose to do, or he was a more distant relative than he had let on. But on the positive side, there was no evidence of his parents having died an early death. That being so, they were probably both still alive. He could check that by looking through all the death registers up to the present day. It would involve a lot of work.

Bruce suddenly felt terribly tired. He was short of food – it was nearly lunchtime, and he had been living on his nerves for several hours. He knew that he needed a meal. He also decided then and there that finding his parents would be a long-term project. He needed to take a break before starting on it, and consider whether he actually wanted to embark on such a quest. It was not a decision to take quickly or lightly. It would be time-consuming. Also, there was no rush. He had lived all his life up to now without his parents. A few more months or even years would not make that much difference.

He was just about to collect a plateful of hot food from the counter, when he had an inspiration. He went back into the registers room, and looked up the date of his granddad's funeral. He found the entry; it read Philip Lester Rewell. Thank goodness for that. But why had his friends called him George?

Just to be doubly certain, he ordered a copy of the death certificate. It would take half an hour to come through, so now was the moment for lunch.

He ate at a table on his own where there was room for someone else to come and sit down too, but he was fairly certain nobody would join him. They would choose their own table instead. Pity. Some company would have been nice. Still, he could reflect on the stranger's words. "You're great, Bruce. You're terrific." He might be alone in the world, but there was no need to feel down about it.

He collected the certificate, and found it was all in order. His granddad's real name had been Philip. Strange. As to his parents, he was a bit further forward, as he had proved that there had been no murder. That was something. Now it was time to go home. He walked out of the building, looked up at the clouds in the sky, and felt like a new man. What a strange day it had been.

29. From: Mission 12
To: Undisclosed recipients
Sent:

I don't know what I could have done to prevent
it, really, but now I look back on it, I should
have foreseen it. It all began when Clairie came
in to our bedroom one morning when Celia and I
were having a lie in. I have to confess that
Celia is not as quick out of bed in the mornings
as she might be, and my standards have slipped a
bit.

Clairie was as white as a sheet.

"Mummy, it's Max. He's stuck on the stairs,
'cos Big Nimp won't open the door."

This was serious. I ran through. There was no
sign of the door. "Max?" I called. There was no
reply.

"Daddy, he's in there," said Clairie pointing,
and beginning to cry. "Grapefruit," she moaned,
and I could tell from the way she said it that
she had tried it many, many times before coming
in and telling us what had happened.

"Grapefruit." I said in my clearest tone.
Nothing happened. "Big Nimp, why will you not
open the door?" I asked. For the first time ever,
there was no reply. This in itself was alarming.

"Okay Clairie," I said, trying to keep calm.
"Well done for coming and telling us. Now I want
you to go to Mummy, while I try to work something
out." I had no idea what I was going to do, but I
wanted to try and get Big Nimp to talk to me, and
I reckoned it would be easiest if I was on my
own. "Tell Mummy I will come through soon."

Clairie ran through to the bedroom. I made my
way to the gyp room, and closed the door behind
me, and sat before the small screen. My heart was
beating. I knew we had a serious problem on our
hands.

"Big Nimp, why won't you talk to me?" There was no reply. "Big Nimp, I need to know what has happened to my son." Still no reply.

I decided to try and pull rank. Not that I knew whether I had any rank, but it was the only trick I could think of. I was a human, and this was a machine that had been designed by humans to serve humans. I would try to use that fact.

"I order you, as on-board computer of this ship, to tell me, the caretaker of Mission Twelve, what is happening to my son."

That did it. "He cannot be allowed to return to you. He has seen what he ought not to have seen. He will have to stay away from you."

Max must have gone exploring up or down the stairs and made a discovery which, in the view of Big Nimp, would endanger the mission if I got to know of it.

"Max is my son, and he is too young to be cut off from his parents. Surely it would be alright for him to return here. There would be no need for me to change my attitude to the mission as a result of anything he might say to me." It was not very coherent; perhaps you can understand why.

"You showed yourself untrustworthy over the matter of the sleeping astronaut."

It was the first reference Big Nimp had ever made to my action of waking Celia.

I had thought he had forgotten about it. I saw now that such a thing was impossible. I also realised that I was not going to be able to persuade him to change his mind. He had decided that Max would have to be separate from us for the sake of the mission.

A great anger filled me. I could hardly see for my rage. I stood up. I already knew what I was going to do.

I walked into the bedroom where Celia was hugging Clairie in her arms. Clairie was sobbing

167

as though her heart would break. Celia looked as she had looked in the early days, when I had first woken her. It was a ghastly sight.

I spoke in a low voice. I was trembling all over with emotion.

"Max has gone exploring behind the stairwell doors, and has seen what he ought not to have seen. Big Nimp was reluctant to tell me, but I forced it out of him in the end. Big Nimp will not let him come back to us, for fear of endangering the mission. Now, don't say anything or try to stop me. I am going to rescue him."

Celia was opening her mouth to say something, but stopped midway. She must have seen a determination in my face that she had never seen there before. I wanted to help her.

"Nothing you can say will prevent me, so I want both of you to do as I ask. I need your help. Clairie, I want you to watch at the stairwell doors, and if they open, run and tell Mummy." This was to keep her occupied. "You can try naming other fruits as a password, but I don't think it will do much good. Ask Big Nimp to play your favourite songs. Celia, get dressed quickly. I will be back in a moment."

I went through to the small screen. "Saint Peter," I said, "I want you to give Max a message." Why I called him that, I don't know. It was the only doorkeeper I could think of at that moment. "Tell him to watch out for the mouth of Grim Reaper, not to get into it by mistake. Will you do that?"

"I will."

I returned to the bedroom. Celia was already dressed in a running suit and trainers - she could not have chosen better. "What are you…" she began, but I motioned her to silence. I indicated she should sit on the bed. I sat down next to her and whispered my plan into her ear. Her eyes grew

168

incredulous. "You will never manage it," she gasped, but again I silenced her.

"Maybe I won't succeed, but Max is my only son, and if the attempt to rescue him costs me my life, so be it. Please don't try to stop me, and don't try to delay me, because if I don't go now, I may never get the courage to start. Also, Max will be feeling desperate, and who knows what he may try to do."

She could see I was in dead earnest.

"Start unwinding the hose," I said.

It was at that moment that Clairie's favourite song started filling the air. Max had introduced her to it, and for some weeks now she had been shyly saying at some point each day, "Romeo, my fav'rite again please." "Don't say please," Max had insisted, "he's only a machine." But Clairie always said please. She said it was important.

The chorus, so beautifully and movingly sung by a woman with a lovely voice, filled the air. "I… will always love you; I… will always love you." It was heartbreaking.

"Do you think that she hopes that Max can hear it?" Celia choked.

"I don't know," I said. I was too full of emotion myself to say more.

"I may never see you again," sobbed Celia.

"Not if I can help it."

"Bruce!" She clung to me. "Whatever happens, remember this; you waking me up was the best thing that ever happened to me in my whole life!"

I am sorry to say I just could not cope with this at that moment. It was too much. I could not reply. The depth of joy and pain all at once was such as I had never imagined. "Unroll the hose," I said in a whisper.

As I approached the mouth, with the nozzle in one hand and a bedroom chair in the other, I knew I had several advantages over last time. Firstly, my back was fit, and my feet were shod. Secondly,

I knew how the rollers worked, and that it was possible to walk between them. However, whether my plan had any chance at all of success, I had no idea. I might well die in attempting to carry it out. If that happened, Celia would be more than capable of coping with Clairie on her own; I had no doubt about that. I did not allow myself to think about how she might feel on losing me.

"I want you to stay here, and feed out the pipe," I explained. "Three tugs means start pulling in. Five tugs means lower steadily. One tug means stop and hold tightly. Use the chair to keep the doors open to let in light."

Then before I had time to consider it, and maybe get cold feet, I was off. The first bit was easy. I stepped carefully into the mouth, once the doors had opened, and put the chair to wedge them open. I barely noticed the repeating sound of the klaxon. The grill which had snapped all those years ago was still broken, so I was able to go carefully forward into the gloom. The slope down to the right was tricky, but I managed it without losing my footing somehow. All this time, Celia was paying out the hose. My last glimpse of her was of her holding her head to one side, to stop her tears from wetting the hose. I could read her thoughts; "Whatever I do, I must not let the hose get wet from my tears." I felt a great surge of emotion. She was so wonderful! How had I ended up having her?

I felt the entrances to the intestines of Grim Reaper carefully. The third one along seemed best suited to my purpose. I squatted in the entrance and explored with my hands. It was as I had hoped. The hole opened into a square shaft which descended vertically.

I am no mountaineer. In fact I hated the only weekend of rock climbing I have ever done. It was in Snowdonia in North Wales. At one point, my left knee got caught in a crack on a climb called

the Milestone Buttress, and my fellow climber and
I had to wait forty minutes for the next team to
come up from below. Then with their help, a loop
of rope was lowered down from above, next door to
my trapped leg, so that I could put my free foot
into it. This meant that my body was now less
spread-eagled, and in a more upright position.
The result was that after three or four minutes
of gentle easing, the trapped knee finally came
out of the crack. I was free! The mountain rescue
people would not need to come and blast the climb
apart with a road drill after all.

There were no mountain rescue people this time,
I thought, as I eased my body into the shaft. I
was hoping to be able to chimney downwards. This
is the most basic of climbing techniques. With
your back against one wall, and your feet against
the other, you can shuffle up or downwards
relatively easily. That was the theory; I had
done it just once before.

I reckoned that Max had gone downstairs; I
don't know why. My hope was that Grim Reaper was
bigger and more complex than I had originally
thought, and that its working area was deep down
in the spaceship. I had begun to wonder this all
that time ago, when the nozzle of the hosepipe
had been drawn back up from Grim Reaper's insides
without being fried or digested.

For all I knew, the reprocessing plant might
take up a great deal of room down there. If so,
and there was more than one floor between us and
it, then there might be another opening into it
from the floor below. I planned to find it, crawl
into it, and then find the mouth, and try and
attract Max's attention. That had been the
purpose of the message I had asked Big Nimp to
give, to draw Max's attention to the mouth of
Grim Reaper. I just hoped that Big Nimp had not
understood my hint and had delivered the message,
and that Max might read my mind. It was all very

171

tenuous, but I reckoned there was a slim chance of finding him.

I was in the vertical shaft in chimney position by now. I slowly worked my way down. The walls on our floor were eight metres high; I expected the floor below to be a similar height. I edged nervously downwards. It was pitch dark, so eyesight was ruled out. I was relying entirely on my other senses.

Something told me that the central engine of Grim Reaper was still well below. That was reassuring. So far, it was all going smoothly. I allowed myself to breathe easily for a moment. The hose was too taut, so I gave five tugs. Celia carried on letting down more hose until I gave one tug. There was now a loop dangling below me, which would ease my progress.

I inched on downwards. It was hard to estimate how far I had already descended. Four metres? Six metres? I was continually feeling the near side of the shaft, in case there were any openings. It was like a lift shaft without the box part for travelling in, but with no cables or lifting gear. I edged on downwards.

Without any warning, the shaft came to an end. I suddenly found there was no support for my feet. There was no helping it; one moment I was in control of myself, the next I was falling through the air, for who knows how far. It was perhaps the worst moment of my life.

Thankfully, I only fell ten or twelve feet before I landed on a very uneven surface. Somehow, I had stayed upright, so I came down on my feet. I lurched forward, because of the angle at which I had landed, and immediately my hands and arms came to rest on a rough, spiky surface. At first, I found myself thinking of sea urchins and anemones, but on closer examination it seemed to me as if I had landed in a bed of large cactus plants, covered with spines. I could feel my

172

hands oozing blood from where they had been cut by the sharp points.

I felt very frightened. However, I was alive, upright, and not moving. Somehow, I still had hold of the hose. A ridiculous image flashed into my mind, from one of the children's television programmes. It was of Postman Pat falling out of a tree into a prickly bush. It had looked so painful, but he just dusted himself down, and then carried on and delivered the letters as usual. I too had a parcel to collect and deliver, I said to myself, and more than a parcel; the post must get through.

I like to choose my own favourite programmes from my youth for the children to watch, in case you were wondering. It's nice sharing them with Max and Clairie.

"Lucifer, give us a light," I called. There was no response. I had not been expecting one. Then it occurred to me that Big Nimp might not like the name Lucifer. Perhaps he did not know that the name meant Light-bearer.

I prayed. "Father, I need your help now." Short and to the point.

The only thing to do was to try to climb upwards, I reckoned. The surface was so sharp that I would cut my hands to ribbons, it seemed to me, so I pulled my sleeves over my hands and began climbing cautiously upwards, with the hose resting against my chest.

This proved easier than I had expected. The cactus plants, as I imagined them, varied in height, and gave a good grip for my feet. Despite the fact that the hose tended to get caught, it freed each time, and I found I was able to progress forwards and upwards. After a minute, I sensed that I was touching a wall.

There was also the tiniest sound. Where had I heard something like that before I wondered? I remembered. It had been in the London

underground. It was the noise of one of the
moving escalators.

Rollers! Could I be on the right track? I
practically shouted out loud when my hands found
an opening in the wall. I felt inside it, and
found rollers like the ones on our level,
revolving towards me.

This was wonderful. If the construction on this
floor was the same, and it seemed most likely to
me that it would be, then all I had to do was to
follow the rollers away from their direction of
travel, and I must get to the mouth. I felt
around, and the layout seemed identical; the gaps
between the rollers might have been made for me
to put my feet in.

I pulled up the hose until I felt the nozzle in
my hands. I somehow managed to get into the
opening, which was a tight one, and stand up in
the space. My head did not touch the ceiling. I
made my way cautiously along, clutching the
nozzle of the hose. It was to be our lifeline on
the return journey, if we made it that far.

Here was the slope upwards that I had been
expecting. I stepped carefully up it. I continued
forward. Oh help, what was that; something had
just moved down behind me. I felt with my hand,
and found that a set of bars, like the ones on
our floor, had descended from the roof. Once
again, a sensing device had been activated, to
prevent a living being from falling into the
works. The shipwrights had never reckoned on a
person coming up from below into that space, I
smiled to myself. However, it could prove a
problem on the return trip.

We must be near the entrance. I felt with my
hands. Yes, this must be the set of double doors,
identical to those on our level.

The hose was trapped under the barrier, and
would not come when I tugged, but there was just
enough play in it for my purpose. I took the

nozzle and gave a hard bang on the doors with it, hoping that the noise would attract Max's attention. I was not ready for the response. The doors opened immediately, allowing the light to flood in, and knocking me off my feet. I was swept back against the barrier. How grateful I was for it now! What joy; there was Max silhouetted against the glare, calling "Daddy, Daddy!" in an anxious voice.

"I'm alright," I shouted. "Now listen, and don't say anything. It is most important," I urged.

I quickly explained to him what had happened and why. He nodded his head in understanding.

"Now you are going to have to make a hard choice," I said. "Whatever you have discovered is going to have to remain a secret, because if you tell me or Mum or Clairie, then I reckon Big Nimp might even end our lives rather than allow the mission to be endangered. It may be that you will find it impossible to keep the secret; if so, it would be better for you to stay on this floor and not return with me. You will be alright here; I have no doubt that Big Nimp will look after you. However, do you think you can handle the loneliness of being on your own? Don't reply yet," I insisted. "If you decide to come back with me, then you also need to realise how difficult it is climbing in the dark. Either of us could slip to our death. However, we have got the hose, and Mummy has the doors of the mouth open upstairs ready for us. Now think it over carefully. Take your time."

Max was silent for nearly a minute.

"Dad, I understand that I can never reveal what I have seen. I'm coming with you, even though we may not both get back home."

It was strange to hear him using the word home of our life upstairs. I had never thought of it like that. As he did so, I realised that more

175

than anything else, I wanted us both to get back to Celia and Clairie. Home is the place where the ones you love are.

"Good boy," I said. "Now look carefully at the rollers, and see where you have to put your feet. Can you see how they work? Don't come in until I see if I can sort out this barrier."

The barrier proved to be no problem at all. The trapped hose underneath it meant that the bottom was not flush with the floor. I tried prising it up, and it slid up gently with no resistance, and clicked into place in the roof.

"Okay, I'm ready," I said. "Whatever you do, keep hold of the hose."

Max stepped inside bravely, and the door closed behind him. The caretaker part of me had not been able to propose jamming it open, as there would be nobody to shut it after we had gone. The result was that we were in total darkness.

"Keep talking to me," I said. "Walk slowly towards me."

"I'm stepping forward, one, two, three, four, five." Max was soon in my arms. I patted his back. "I will go first," I said; "stay close behind me. In fact, hold onto my sweater. One, two, three, four, now here comes the slope, look out, it is two steps long, no three; pause here for a rest." We had negotiated the slope. "Now, do you think you can climb up the hose hand over hand, and then climb on up the shaft?" Briefly I explained the art of chimneying. Thankfully, I had thought to choose a shaft on my way down which Max could chimney in as well as me on the way back. It would have been hopeless if his legs had not been able to reach across the gap.

"Yes," said Max. He sounded confident but there was no bravado.

"Right," I said. "Don't think of what's below; it's very dangerous. You go first."

Max made his way to the edge of the void.

"Hang on a moment," I said, and tugged once on the hose. I hoped Celia would understand to take the strain. "Off you go then. I love you, boy."

"I love you Dad," said Max. "Thanks for coming down to get me." Then he was off, climbing hand over hand up the hose.

I had been worried about this part of the climb, as my arms have always been weak. Even as a teenager, I had great difficulty doing a pull-up, as it was called. The other boys laughed at me. I tried to avoid situations where I needed to betray my weakness, so I seldom if ever did a pull-up. Now I wished I had behaved differently; I should have practised and developed my muscles, not shied away from criticism. I hoped my weakness had not been passed on down to Max.

I need not have feared. He had his mother's nimbleness! "I'm going up," he called, "First hand, second, third, fourth, fifth, I'm in the shaft now, six, seven, eight, nine, ten, eleven, twelve, thirteen, fourteen, fifteen…"

My heart was sinking. Max was going to make it, that was plain, but would I be able to do it in my turn?

"…nineteen, twenty, twenty-one, I've got to the opening… I'm up. I'll wait for you here."

"Brilliant," I yelled. "Can you see Mum?"

But he could not.

"Give one tug on the rope," I shouted.

"One tug given. It's rock steady," yelled Max. I could tell from his tone that he was enjoying the adventure. If he could, then perhaps I could afford to as well.

It was now or never. I braced myself, gripped the hose as high up as I could, but then I had a thought. Once I stepped out, I was going to swing to and fro, like a pendulum. If the hose end was down among the cactuses, that would damp the swinging effect. I quickly paid it out as far as I could, and then I stepped off and swung out over the cactuses. "One," I yelled through gritted teeth. This was awful. I heaved myself upwards. "Two." The hose had settled at a sixty degree angle. How many pull-ups had it been before Max reached the shaft? "Three." I must not stop; if I did, it would be fatal. "Four." For some strange, unaccountable reason, I felt a wild urge to count in German. "*Funf*," I bellowed. "*Sechs*." Now French. "*Sept*."

My arms were screaming with pain. What was this? Oh, the shaft! "*Huit!*" Now I had my feet inside it, and my back against the other wall. The relief in my arms was unspeakable. But I dared not pause. "*Neuf;*" I shuffled upwards. "*Diece!*" Italian seemed called for. "*Undiece!*" Was that right? I was never much use at Italian. "*Duodiece!... Trediece*." For the first time, I began to believe that I was going to make it. "*Quattuordiece*." I was sure that was wrong. What was the Italian for fourteen? Why on earth was I worrying about counting in a foreign language now? Was it to keep my mind off the danger and the pain in my muscles? "*Quinze, quinze et demie*," I could not afford to slow down. A final burst was needed. "*Sechzehn, Siebzehn, Achtzehn*," I had not meant to go back into German.

"Well done Dad, you're nearly up." Max's voice was only a few feet above me.

"*Neunzehn*," I gasped, and practically fell through the opening which appeared unexpectedly. My feet were taken out from under me by a roller, and I nearly got swept back down, but Max had a grip of my sweater. I clung to the hose, and somehow regained my footing between the rollers. We had both climbed up to our own floor. It was a terrific achievement. But there was no time to relax yet.

"Lead on," I gasped. "Follow the rollers up the slope, and then you should see the mouth."

I will never forget the yell of triumph Celia gave when she first saw Max. I cannot describe it, except to say that her cry thrilled me in every sinew of my being, and gave me a sudden surge of adrenalin, ready for one last final effort. Nevertheless, I paused a moment, so as not to intrude on their reunion when he reached the doors.

"Daddy," cried Max, "come on." He would start coming back for me himself if I did not move quickly, I realised. I stumbled forward, somehow placing my feet in the gaps, and came to the slope. Not far now. I went up the slope on hands and knees; I had no strength to walk up. At the top, I crawled on towards the light, holding tightly to the hose. I could soon see Celia and Max also clinging to the hose. Before I realised it, they were pulling me out of the mouth, and I was on my back on the carpet in the glaring light, and they were all over me, hugging and kissing me. Clairie was soon there too, swelling the rugger scrum. We had a wonderful roll together!

"Now listen," I panted, before anyone could speak. "Max must keep his discovery secret, and never tell anybody, or we could lose everything. Do you understand that?" They all said yes.

"Max, quickly, I want to show you something," said Clairie. Max looked at me, and I nodded. They went scampering off together. Children!

Celia and I lay on the floor and hugged each other. My arms felt as if they would never be able to lift anything ever again.

"How did you find him?" she asked.

"He was there waiting by the mouth on the floor below. He must have interpreted my message through Big Nimp."

"Well done, Bruce," she said. "Well done. I was so frightened."

We were reunited. I sobbed. I could now rest
for a while before having to face Big Nimp. I
closed my eyes.
Bruce

The day of the moon trip had come at last! Bruce was collected
from his home by a chauffeured car, and whisked off to the sky taxi
rank. This was clearly a no-expenses-spared trip. In a few minutes,
he was in a cab going upwards, and before long he was speeding
westwards towards the launch area. This part of the journey took
just fourteen minutes.

Then he had to disembark, hand in his luggage, go through
passport control, and sit in a large waiting area. Before long, his
flight was called.

He was disappointed by the rocket. He had been expecting
something along the lines of the Apollo programme, a huge rocket
as high as a block of flats, blasting off with a roaring sound. Instead,
he was shown into a somewhat squat triangular structure, which
reminded him of the Egyptian pyramids, but with the roof rather
more pointed. Inside, the floor area was not very large – about a
bus-length wide by a bus-length long. The floor and walls were
curved where they joined, and the walls came inwards so that the
ceiling was only a metre square. The whole effect was not unlike
the shape of a clove of garlic. There would have been room for
perhaps sixty seats on the floor at a maximum, but most of them had
been removed, allowing plenty of space to move around. In fact,
there was only one row of seats left along each wall, facing inwards.
It would have given everyone a splendid view of a boxing match in
the middle, Bruce thought.

There were only two other passengers. One was a brown-haired
girl aged about thirty. The other passenger, who looked like an
airline pilot from his uniform, seemed thoroughly bored by the
whole thing, and soon fell asleep. Bruce wondered briefly why the
ship should be so empty, but he shrugged his shoulders; the vagaries
of public transport had long since ceased to surprise him. He looked
for his seat number, and found he had been put next door to the girl,

and before long they had struck up in conversation. Her name was Simone.

"No," Bruce was saying, "there was nobody to see me off. I live on my own. However, it was nice to get a card or two. My landlady had pushed one through the door with a picture of a moonlit sky, and on the back she had written, 'I look forward to a new interpretation of *Clair De Lune* from you when you return.'"

Simone did not know what that meant, so Bruce explained that it was a piano piece by the French composer Claude Debussy.

"*Ah bon*, Debussy!" He might have guessed she would speak French from her name.

"My other card was from a friend; he just told me not to let the moon go to my head as I was pretty far gone already. Also his ex-girlfriend left a message on my answerphone wishing me *bon voyage*. She's from Sweden," he hastened to add, in case Simone might conclude that she was French.

Simone seemed to be high up in science, as far as Bruce could make out. Her expenses for the trip were paid by the university. He did not like to ask which university and what her subject was, for fear of not being able to understand her reply.

All this time, they had been accelerating upwards. Bruce found his increased body weight uncomfortable. The seats were supportive without being hard. Gradually, over a period of about fifty minutes, the acceleration seemed to lessen, until they were almost back to normal bodyweight, but this might have been an illusion, due to the pull of the earth's gravity becoming less as they moved further into space. It was hard to be sure what was happening.

There was printed in-flight information on a card on the back of the seat. He read through it. He had expected them to be in transit to a stopping-off point in orbit somewhere, where they would transfer to the main rocket, but to his surprise, he found they were going all the way in this ship.

"I thought we would be docking on some vast revolving space station, and then transferring to a huge vehicle," he said.

Simone explained to him that there was no need for anything like that any more, following the new discoveries. One smaller vehicle was sufficient. They would accelerate until they were half way, and then they would turn round and decelerate from then on.

"It has all got so easy now," she said. It turned out that she did the trip at least once a month.

Bruce found her somewhat heavy going, so after a while, he took out his book, and by unspoken agreement, there was silence.

From time to time, Bruce looked up from his book. The girl was busy with her laptop. The man was still asleep. The only change was that the sky outside had got darker and darker as they had left the atmosphere. The view of the stars was fabulous. After a couple of hours, Bruce got up to visit the loo, more to stretch his legs than for anything else. As he was returning to his seat, a voice over the loudspeakers announced that food was now available at the hatch. A light started flashing over a long slot in one wall that Bruce had not noticed before.

"You lead the way," said Bruce. Simone went over and showed him that you could choose between several different options. Bruce opted for a glass of orange juice and a bap with a hunk of cheese and some pickle. She ordered a salad.

"Are there no air hostesses on board?" he asked.

"No. The whole thing is automated. It's pretty boring, really."

They munched their food. "Is your work going well?" asked Bruce.

"Fair. I find writing up these papers a trial. I prefer doing the research itself. That's the exciting part."

"I would ask you to tell me about it, but I fear I wouldn't be able to understand. I'm a piano teacher, you see." As if that explained everything.

"I don't always understand it myself, so not much chance of me making it clear to you, I'm afraid. But it was kind of you to ask."

They lapsed into silence. When they had finished eating, Bruce took their trays back to the hatch, and collected two coffees. "Do you think Rip Van Winkle would like to be woken for a bite?" he asked.

"No. He always sleeps on the way out so that he can be awake longer on the moon. He's into time management in a big way. I expect he's taken sleeping pills. He would not be pleased if you woke him up."

They had just finished their coffees when the disembodied voice started up again.

"In a few minutes, the ship will be turning round, at the midpoint of the trip. Passengers will experience weightlessness for several minutes. You are advised to keep your seatbelt securely fastened during this time."

This sounded interesting.

"Now's your chance," said Simone. "If you would like to float about in mid-air, then go and stand in the middle, and see what happens. I dare you!"

Bruce was not sure about this girl. "Is it safe?"

"The only tricky bit is when the motor starts up after the ship has turned round. You will then drift to the floor, and could hit it at any angle. However, they start the motor gently, in case anybody is floating loose, so you should not hurt yourself, even if it is your back that makes contact first. During weightlessness, you can't turn round voluntarily in mid air, as you have nothing to pull yourself round with, remember. Don't worry about it. You'll be fine."

Bruce decided he had nothing to lose but his dignity, and there was not much of that left. "Okay. I'll have a go."

"Well done. Just stand in the middle of the floor."

Bruce took up his position. He was not too soon. Almost immediately, there was a falling note from the engines, and to his alarm, Bruce felt himself leave the floor and start floating gently upwards.

"Help!" he said. Simone laughed.

He had been caught slightly off balance when the engines slowed. The result of this was that he did not stay upright as he ascended, but began to do a slow cartwheel to the right. "I can't stop myself turning!" he called out.

"Don't worry; you will be able to control yourself when you hit a wall."

This was not reassuring. He was hardly moving, relative to the ceiling, but he was going to hit it in about a minute's time, he reckoned. It was very weird feeling weightless. But after thirty seconds, things became even stranger. His speed of rotation began to increase.

"Hey, I'm speeding up," he called.

"No, you're not. The ship is starting to turn round."

Bruce realised he was not going to hit the ceiling at all, but one of the walls. No, it would be the floor. No it was going to be...

He collided with one of the seats. He tried to cling onto it, but failed to do so. To his dismay, he started to drift off again. Simone laughed again.

"You look wonderful!" she said.

Bruce was beginning to go dizzy. He decided to close his eyes for a few seconds. This was a mistake, as he suddenly bumped gently into a smooth surface, and then immediately set off away from it again.

"I've had enough of this," he said.

"Not much longer now. Keep your eyes open!"

Sure enough, there was a whine from the engines, and Bruce began moving towards the floor. He landed on his arms, in the middle. Gravity quickly returned to one gee. The turn-around was over, and he had survived weightlessness. He was rather pleased.

"Thank you for suggesting that," he said, on regaining his seat. "I wouldn't have missed it."

"I thought you'd enjoy it. Now, when you've had time to get readjusted, how about a game of Scrabble? I have a travel set here."

Bruce enjoyed Scrabble, so after a few minutes, when his mind felt settled, they got out the set.

"You can have one hundred and fifty points start," Simone said.

Bruce did not like the sound of this at all. "But in some games, one hundred and fifty points are all I manage to score. How on earth are you going to make that handicap up?"

Simone laughed. "You'll see."

He had to admit, her game was most impressive. She got all seven letters out on her first turn. This was a feat Bruce only managed occasionally. Later on in the game, he foolishly left her an easy opening. He was rather pleased with the word he played, which was 'nonce'. It had a Shakespearian ring to it. However, it did not score much, and the opening N was two letters under the triple word score, at the top left of the board. She might score heavily from that position.

She pounced. He groaned. She was using all seven letters again. The word was 'conquest', running down the left hand side of the board from the top, beginning on a triple word score. Oh no, even worse; the Q fell on a double letter. Oh how awful, and the final T reached down to the next triple word score. Two triple word scores in one word!

It took them a while to agree on the score for the word, but they eventually settled on 311. He had never dreamed that such a score was possible. So much for his 150 point start. Never mind. She was clearly in a different league from him. He had to admire her.

"I give in," he said. "You have outgunned me at every turn. You play really well."

She was clearly pleased.

Bruce was feeling a bit concerned. "Look, I'm a bit worried about Rip Van Winkle. I hope he's alright. He seems to be so deeply asleep. I think I'll just check that he hasn't died."

He got up from his seat and stretched a bit, then went over to the airline pilot. He was fine; his chest was rising and falling in a steady rhythm. Sweet dreams, Bruce hoped. He would have preferred it if the man had woken. He was beginning to feel a bit pressurised by this girl.

As he went back towards his seat, he saw that Simone had transferred herself from her seat to his. Oh dear, this was an overture. She was clearly feeling playful.

Bruce's concern must have showed in his face, because she immediately stood up in some confusion, looking rather embarrassed, and returned to her own seat.

"Sorry," she said, "I don't know what came over me. Sorry."

There was an awkward silence. She then continued, "Most men hate it when I beat them at Scrabble, but you seem able to handle it."

"I found it difficult," admitted Bruce. "But I reckoned it would give you pleasure if I lost gracefully. You are clearly very gifted, way out of my league."

"That's what they all say. It's no fun being a freak."

This was in danger of getting rather deep. "Look, I don't want to be stand-offish, but I am meeting my girl-friend on the moon, and I don't want to complicate things by getting involved with someone else." It sounded more blunt than he had intended.

"Quite." She was upset. Had he spoken truthfully when he called Celia his girlfriend?

"But look, here is my card. Let's keep in touch." He gave her his card. She put it in a pocket. That was strange of him, he thought; he did not want to take her up, but he did not want to let her down either. Oh dear. Life was so difficult.

They read for the remainder of the journey. On touchdown, she went off into the terminal building, and he quickly lost sight of her.

30. From: Mission 12
To: Undisclosed recipients
Sent:

"I am glad you rescued your son." It was Big Nimp. I was back at the small screen. I needed to negotiate with him. I plucked up courage.

"Big Nimp, you have kept faith with the mission, and not disobeyed your instructions. I have rescued Max, and I have told him that he must never reveal his secret. I hope that will prove acceptable to you."

"We will see." That was not a very encouraging response, but I could tell that I was not going to get anything more out of him on this subject.

"Tell me," I continued, "why didn't you give me any light down there? I am sure you could have done."

186

"No, I could not," came the reply. "Once I had turned off the crusher and thresher, I could not give you any light, as the bulbs were on the same circuit."

My heart nearly froze. So that was what the cactuses had been. I gulped.

"Thank you for saving my life," was all I could say.

"You are important to the mission," came the reply.

I could not think of anything else to say, so that was the end of the conversation. We seemed to have reached an understanding, but I was left with a lot to think about.

The children appear to have got over the ordeal very well. They were both intensely sorry for disobeying Celia and me over the matter of the doors. I had no doubt that they would never go in there again. Fairly soon, things were back to their former, happy state.

It was about this time, that it finally became clear to me that Max, at any rate, was musical. For quite a while now, he and Clairie had enjoyed doing Thunder and Lightning on the piano. Max had explained to Clairie (goodness knows how he had discovered it) that sound travels slower than light in a planetary atmosphere, which meant that the lightning came first, and then after a pause of a few seconds, the rumble of thunder followed. He put Clairie in charge of the lightning, at the very top of the keyboard, while he took up his station at the bottom end. On the word of command, Clairie would let rip with a lot of very high notes played very fast. Max would wait a few seconds, and then give his interpretation of the thunder. A short burst by Clairie produced a single loud thump from Max, but if she gave a drawn out series of notes, he would respond with a good deal of hard banging on the lowest keys. He also worked the sustaining pedal with his right foot, with good effect. The resulting sound from them both was splendid.

This had a pleasing knock-on effect. Often, when I was seated at the piano playing Brahms or Schubert, Clairie would approach quietly, and suddenly leap forward and do her lightning at the top end. Then she would run around behind me and do the thunder at the bottom end a second or two later. It did not improve the music, in my view, but Clairie thought it was a wonderful game, especially when I started trying to prevent her. She would aim to creep up unobserved and do a burst of lightning before I realised what she was up to, and tried to stop her. Then when she tried to go behind my back, I would continue to play with one hand, while the other would reach out behind me and feel about for her, octopus style. She thought this was marvellous. If the right hand could not find her, then suddenly I would change hands without any warning, and the left hand would be reaching out for her while the right hand continued the music. She would respond with shrieks of pleasure. Her aim was to get to the bottom end to play the thunder at the right moment, while mine was to see to it that although I only had one hand left for playing, I was still producing enough of the piece to sound as if I was playing all of it. It was a challenge to me to continue playing accurately while feeling around behind my back. So it suited both of us. The game lasted for several days until she tired of it and thought of something else.

Max's mind had run in a different direction. He had taken little nimp to the area of carpet for copying, and got Big Nimp to make five identical copies. He did remember to label the original, lest they should get muddled up together. I was pleased about that. Then, he trained all six machines in the art of Barber Shop singing. It was so funny to hear their metallic little voices raised together in song!

I should perhaps explain that when I had little nimp made, all those years ago, I deliberately asked for a somewhat sub-standard voice box to be fitted. I figured that it would be nice if he had a slight deficiency. I did this to help preserve the illusion that I was in control of him rather than the other way around. It did help me in my relationship with him.

The result now, however, was that the singing did sound distinctly tinny. Still, their tuning was excellent.

There was, however, one thing which suggested that Max's ear was not as sharp as it might be. He had misheard some of the words. Instead of "in the shade of," he had the machines singing, "in the shed by." 'Shade' and 'shed' are easily muddled, but not 'of' and 'by', it seemed to me. Still, I did not point the error out, as I am against those parents who only ever tell their children what is wrong with what they are doing.

Here is the chorus of the song in full, in the original version, as I rather like it.

My Evaline (say you'll be mine)
My Evaline (say you'll be mine)
Whisper to me honey you'll be mi -i -i -ne
Der der der der der der der (I forget that bit)
I'll pine, I'll pine.
Sweeter than the honey, to the honey bee
I love you and you love me
Meet me in the shade of the old apple tree
My Eva -iva -ova -Evaline!

I suggested to Max that the group should be called the nimpets, but I was too slow for him. "No, Dad, they're the Limpets," he told me, "because they stick together come what may." He's a good lad.

Bruce

The great moment had finally come. Bruce was fully kitted out in his space suit. There were no less than five double doors to go through, and Celia would be waiting for him at the last one. Five doors suggested that the dome had five separate skins to it. This was wise. They simply could not afford to have an accident and lose their atmosphere into space. Two skins would have been sufficient, three would have been fail-safe, four doubly fail-safe. He could hear the case being argued in some committee room back on earth. It gave him a sense of reassurance. He hoped the space suits were as well protected.

There was no chance of recognising Celia in her gear. It was impossible to see in through the domed glass helmet. Even her voice sounded tinny. But never mind, here she was, keeping her promise.

They were not to appear to know each other until they were out of sight of the base. He had been told casually at breakfast that there was another walker – would he like company? He had accepted the offer. Although each walker was monitored by satellite, it seemed even safer to go as a pair, although people often did walk on their own. Bruce had been pleased to discover that walkers were still few. There would be just twelve out today, dotted all over the moon's surface. The chance of meeting another walker was remote. This was just as he had hoped.

There were a few last minute instructions about no jumping or running, and to pull the red cord in an emergency, and then they were off. The finger post saying Public Footpath seemed strangely thin and weedy, until Bruce remembered that there being no atmosphere on the moon, there would be no storms. Taking the low gravity into account, this meant that any structures on the moon, be they signs or buildings, could be manufactured much more flimsily than on earth.

The suit took a bit of getting used to. It was temperature controlled. This was important, as in the sunshine, they would roast without its cooling function, or freeze if they were out of the sun. There was water laid on to drink, from a little nozzle near his mouth, and a liquid food nozzle as well, just beside it. A bit like baby food, Bruce reckoned. This concoction was designed to give you a burst of fresh energy. No good running out of oomph before getting to the next dome. The boots were a bit cumbersome, but they felt strong. Most weird of all was the low gravity. It took quite a while to get used to walking on the moon, but Bruce had been practising inside the dome the previous evening, and by now he felt confident.

When they had got out of sight of the dome, they joined hands; well, gloves, actually, and very thick gloves at that. Bruce found it hard to keep hold of her glove at all, let alone have the sense that they were holding hands.

"These suits were not exactly designed with cuddling in mind," he said. Perhaps that was a bit forward. This was their first date. "It's great to see you." Even that was something of an over-statement, given her outfit.

"Good to see you, Bruce." It was definitely Celia's voice. "I am sorry about all the hush-hush stuff. How was your journey up?"

"Rather boring, to be honest. There were only two other passengers. I played Scrabble with the girl, and she trounced me completely. The man slept all the way. But I did try out being weightless." He told Celia about it. She enjoyed hearing the story.

Their path led them across a small crater. There was a two hundred foot climb at the far side. When they got to the top, and were walking along on the level, Bruce finally summoned up the courage to speak.

"Celia?"

"Yes?"

"I was wondering, would you mind very much if you were to change your name to Delia?"

It is not easy to express emotion when wearing a space suit which makes you look like a Michelin man, but Celia managed it without any difficulty. She stopped dead in her tracks.

"I know it may sound a little odd, but the thing is, are you aware I tend to have daydreams?"

Celia nodded.

"Well, the thing is," Bruce went on, and then he proceeded to tell her about Mission 12 and the journey to the stars, and waking the sleeping astronaut, and so forth. "And you see, her name is Celia. So I wondered whether you would mind being Delia. It's not that much of a change."

By now, Bruce knew he had put his foot well and truly in it. It was silly to even think of suggesting that she change her name, but once he had started speaking, he could not very well draw back. There was also the consideration, however, that honesty is always the best policy, and if they were going to spend the rest of their lives together, it was better that she should know him, warts and all, at an early stage. Or at least, that was what he thought.

She was silent for a few moments.

"Bruce, I feel honoured that you have shared your heart with me, regarding your daydreams. However, it does seem a bit rough that your imaginary girl should keep her name, while your real one is expected to change hers." It was a fair point. "Could you fantasise about her offering to change her name instead, perhaps?"

Bruce found he could not. Oh dear.

"Don't worry," he said. "I'm sure it will work out."

"May I ask why you were so keen to take a walking holiday on the moon?"

This was easy. "I was once watching a recording of one of the Apollo missions with my granddad, years ago. Two of the astronauts were prancing around on the moon. There was a little slope behind where they were, and I was suddenly seized with curiosity. I wanted to go there, and climb that slope, and see what was on the far side. I've never lost that sense of eagerness that I had at that moment. That's why I seized my chance when I was with your parents."

"That's lovely. And now you are here, what do you think of it?"

"It's amazing. I find it awesome to think that all these craters and rocks were made millions of years ago, but have stayed exactly the same, until we came along. There are very few places on earth where you could say that, with all the weather and erosion."

"I find it fascinating too. I'm glad you asked me to come."

By now, Bruce was feeling somewhat confused about the day. Celia might know the answer, he thought.

"Celia?"

"Yes?"

"We've been walking for a couple of hours now, but in my opinion, the sun has hardly moved. It seems to have got stuck in the same place in the sky."

"Ah. The reason you are confused is because you are thinking of the day lasting twenty-four hours, as on the earth. But on the moon, it is different. It takes twenty-eight days on earth for the moon to go round once, relative to the sun, so a day on the moon is twenty-eight of our days. So each moon day lasts for... I'm sorry, I can't work out the number of hours in my head that easily."

"What twenty-four times twenty-eight, do you mean?"

"Yes."

Bruce was rather proud of his skills at mental arithmetic. He thought for a moment.

"What about six hundred and seventy-two?"

"That rings a bell," Celia replied. "How did you work it out?"

"I multiplied twenty-eight by twelve and the doubled it. Are you saying that a day on the moon lasts six hundred and seventy two hours?"

"Yes. Three hundred and thirty-six hours of sunlight, and then three hundred and thirty-six hours of darkness."

Bruce was fascinated. Then he remembered something.

"Hey, but last evening in the moon base, I was looking out through the windows, and I saw the moonscape going grey and then black, and this morning, it brightened up gradually."

Celia laughed. "Bruce, you thought you were looking through a glass window, but actually, it was a screen. What they have done is to create an artificial twenty-four hour day inside the moon bases, so that people coming from earth for a visit can cope better. Cameras record the view from the moon base in super-slow motion, and then it is played back on the screen, speeded up to make it seem like a twenty-four hour day."

"You're joking."

"No I'm not. You remember the five sets of doors? Well, what would be the point of taking all that trouble to guard the atmosphere at the doors, but only have one skin at the windows? No, the whole base is inside five skins, and the outermost one is two metres thick, to keep out harmful rays. There are no windows, Bruce. Sorry!"

"Well, I was certainly taken in."

"There is more and more simulation these days. People like what they know, so new inventions are best introduced in a familiar garb. At least, that's how the thinking goes. Not everyone agrees with the policy, mind you."

"I see. Well, I'm looking forward to seeing the earthrise, anyway."

Celia laughed again. "Sorry! I'm afraid there is no earthrise either."

Bruce was indignant. "But there's a famous photo from the Apollo era called earthrise!" he protested.

"It's a very misleading name, I'm afraid. Do you remember that on earth, we always see the same face of the moon?"

"Yes."

"Well, that means that when you look at earth from the moon, it remains in the same place in the sky, if you think about it."

Bruce scratched his head. "Oh dear, I'm only a piano teacher," he said.

"Well look. Imagine you were standing plum in the middle of the part of the moon we can see from earth. In that instance, the earth would be above you, in the vault of the sky, wouldn't it?"

After a moment, Bruce agreed that it would.

"What's more, it would never move. So if you want to get the effect of earthrise, then you need to go to the edge of the area we can see from earth."

"I've got it," said Bruce excitedly. "You explain well. So where is the earth from here, then? I can't see it anywhere."

"Behind those cliffs. If we keep on this path, it will come into view shortly."

Sure enough, before very long, the earth came into view. It was low down near the horizon. Bruce was thrilled. They selected a place to the side of the path which sloped gently upwards, and took several photographs. It was fun. However, time was getting on. They needed to get to the next dome for the night, even though Bruce now understood that this was an artificial concept on the moon.

It was then that Celia told him. "Bruce, I am very sorry about this, but I am afraid I cannot accompany you any more. It's too dangerous. I've done as much as I can in coming with you today. I am truly sorry, because I know you will be disappointed, but there is nothing I can do about it. We need to separate here, and go in as if we were strangers. I will see you at piano in a fortnight."

The moment he had grasped what she was saying, Bruce had begun to feel a mounting sense of dismay, which quickly turned to anger. He was just going to speak, but she had already set off. He realised from her movements that there was no way he was going to change her mind. He might as well save his breath. Watching her walking away from him, becoming smaller and smaller, was one of the hardest moments in his life. He wondered whether she would look back, but she did not.

He was really upset. Where had he gone wrong? He had tried to strike up a friendship with a nice-looking girl he had met in the train, and instead found himself getting entangled in all sorts of secret goings-on, to do with large sums of money, which frankly he did not care about anyway. He had hoped that a relationship was going to be possible, but the final ruin of any such hopes was now staring him in the face. They had kept their promise that she would go with him to the moon, but only by the absolute bare minimum! Just one day out of a fortnight's holiday. He felt incensed. And now they would be expecting him to keep his part of the arrangement.

It was a good thing that her parents were a quarter of a million miles away. He had never been known to be violent, but if they had been with him at this moment, he might have flown at them and really thumped them. He felt so angry. It was all so horrible.

He could have had that Simone girl for the asking; she was willing. Still, that would have been no good. She just wanted a bit of fun, a casual encounter with a stranger, here today and gone tomorrow. He was looking for a life-long partnership.

Suddenly, with a force that surprised him, out of nowhere came an intense longing to have Araminta here with him, holding his hand, soaring and gliding with him over the craters and seas of dust in the most wonderful airborne *Pas de Deux* ever seen in a ballet. Snatches of Tchaikovsky's powerful, rushing music filled his mind.

This would never do. He could not allow himself to think of Araminta. Better to make himself think of walking with Bill. They could have had fun, exploring the moon together. Life would be so much simpler if there were no women.

He found a convenient rock in a patch of shade and sat on it; he could not go in to the dome in this upset state. He stayed there for perhaps an hour, deep in thought.

Suddenly, there came a male voice in his headphones. "Mr. Winter, are you alright?"

There was no peace anywhere. Wearily he got to his feet, and waved at the sky in general. Doubtless somebody somewhere was watching him on a monitor. It took him twenty-five minutes to cover the mile to the dome, during which time the sun blazed relentlessly down. The path led him through an imposing area of rock. At another time, Bruce would have been fascinated, but in his present state, he hardly noticed it. He made his way in through the five sets of double doors, and checked in for the virtual night.

```
31. From: Mission 12
To: Undisclosed recipients
Sent:
```

Early one morning, Clairie came bursting into our bedroom.

"Mummy, Mummy!"

"Yes, Clairie?"

"You remember when Big Nimp showed us the film Tarzan and I wanted to be Jane?"

"Yes, darling."

"Well, Max is swinging on the handles, and the lights are coming on."

I felt an intense stab of sickness in my stomach; I don't know how else to describe it, and I could not move, but Celia leapt out of bed like a scalded cat and ran through to the dorm. I held my breath…

She came back into the bedroom with Max in front of her. His face was bright red, and he was clearly upset. Her face was ashen white. I shivered. I could see it was a major crisis.

"How many?" I asked.

"Eight," she replied.

I felt that the floor was sinking beneath me and that I was falling into hell.

"Why?" I asked Max. He was staring at the carpet and said nothing.

"Why, Max?" I asked again, in a calm voice. We needed to get at the truth.

"You and Mummy have got each other," he blurted out, "but who are Clairie and I going to marry? Those sleepers need to wake up and have babies. If they don't do it now, it is going to be too late."

It was something that had been troubling me.

"Why didn't you tell us you were feeling this way?" I asked.

"You would have said no."

I did not know what to say. We all walked through to the dorm. He had indeed started the waking process on eight of the sleepers. I could not help noticing that the one on the left, Big Nimp's choice for me, was included. This was not going to be an easy time. All my limbs felt very heavy, as I stood and stared.

"Oh Max!" I said in a resigned tone. "What have you done?"

Rather to my surprise, the monitors did not all show the same length of time until eject. The times varied from slightly over thirty hours to just over twenty-four hours. At least they would all fall during the daytime. I checked to see, and found that Max had woken four men and four women.

"Oh Max," I said again. I did not know what else to say. I could hardly be angry with him for doing something that I had done myself. I gave a deep sigh.

Celia could see my concern. There was a questioning look in her eyes.

"Right, Max, what is done is done. I will want to talk to you later. Just now, I need to think this over with Mummy. You go off and play, but don't do anything noisy. We need to think."

Max and Clairie went out together quietly. Celia came over to me. We looked at each other.

Celia spoke first. "You know, Max is not sorry for what he has done. I can tell."

"That's just what I was thinking. He is a remarkable boy. It comes of having a remarkable mother." This was not just flattery. It was true. "He made a deliberate decision to do this."

I was already calming down, and I had an initial thought, which I wanted to pursue. Celia squeezed my hand and said nothing.

"Look," I said, "You have never complained, but the fact is that when Max needed rescuing, I went into overdrive and did not allow you to have any input into what was done." Celia nodded. "Me behaving like that has caused us problems in the past. Thank you very much for your support over the rescue. I knew vigorous action was needed, and that I was the one to do it, and that I had to get on with it straight away. Thankfully, the outcome was good. But this time, it is different. There is no immediate rush. As I took the lead last time, I wondered whether you would like to have the main share in deciding what we do this time?"

Celia paused for a moment. I could see she was pleased. "Well," she said slowly, "I reckon our best course is to make the obvious practical preparations today, and then when they have woken tomorrow, I think we should all sit down together, and we should explain to them exactly what has happened on this ship since launch. Then, we all need to come to a common mind about where we go from here."

This was obviously good sense. I could only agree with it. Telling what had happened was not going to make me look good, but that was unimportant. What mattered was the success of the mission.

"Max needs to be a part of it," Celia continued.

"What about Clairie?" I asked.

"I am not so sure about her."

In the end we decided to put it to her next morning. I felt it would not matter if she ran in and out of the meeting. I was sure Max would want to be involved.

We spent the rest of the day getting beds copied and made up. Clairie wanted large double beds, for couples, like Mummy and Daddy. Celia spent an hour after lunch talking to Max and Clairie about relationships, and the need for men and women to make their own choices about a life partner. "But you never had a choice, Mummy," Clairie objected. Celia told me about this afterwards. I was pleased not to have been there. Later I wondered whether I should have been there after all. The issue would need to be talked through with them before long.

This new development of eight astronauts being woken was very threatening for me. I was already feeling bad again about having woken Celia. I was also troubled by the fact that Big Nimp's choice for me had been the one on the left. I was going to feel very strange on meeting her for the first time. Life might have turned out very differently if I had followed his instruction. But what do computers know about falling in love? All their thought processes are just a series of digits, noughts and ones. But then, I had to acknowledge, what did I know about love when it came to the crunch? Once again I felt uncomfortably aware of my many faults as a husband.

Was I going to go down in the history of the new settlement as the man who had ruined everything, I began to wonder? Look at the mess the mission was in now. If only I could have held to my original course. But then I would never have known Celia. Oh dear, why was life so complicated?

Not for the first time, I attempted to put all my questioning out of my mind. What was done was done; there was little advantage in agonising over it. However, once the children were in bed, I did spend a long time praying and turning it all over. We were in a right state, and I was responsible. Would the mission fail because of my impetuousness?

There was an odd thing. Last thing that night, before I finally went to sleep, I found myself reflecting that I was proud of my son. I was glad for what he had done. I cannot explain it; I am just telling you how it was.

Bruce

Overnight, Bruce made two decisions. The first followed on from imagining flying with Araminta. Before going in to breakfast, he spoke to the girl at the desk.

"Excuse me, but is it possible to hire a sky-suit for the day?"

"I'm sorry sir, but so far, there are no sky-suits on the moon. An earth sky-suit would be no use, as the strength would be wrong, and you would soar off into space. We wouldn't want that, would we sir?"

"I don't know. I can think of worse ways of going."

She took it as a joke. "Even when they do produce a moon version, the first ones will be dreadfully expensive, but doubtless

200

the price will come down in time. You'd be better off taking a ticket on the flying boat."

Bruce declined. That would involve mixing with others. He decided to put his second decision into operation.

"I am considering changing my plans and going back to earth early. If I return to the first dome tonight, will I be able to get an earlier flight home the next day without penalty?"

"I would need to enquire sir, but I imagine it would be no problem. There is plenty of space on most flights."

"I will call back after breakfast."

There turned out to be no difficulty. Bruce could retrace his steps today by a different route, which would involve going into Farside briefly, the part of the moon invisible from earth, before arriving back at the first dome. There would be no change of the view in Farside, of course, but somehow he liked the idea of walking where mankind had been unable to see until the last few decades. He might even be able to glimpse the large radio telescopes in the distance, shielded from all the radio signals pouring into space from earth by the moon's bulk.

It was dismal setting off on his own. Thankfully, the footpaths were clearly signed. As he hoped, when he rose to the top of a hill, he could see a number of radio telescopes making an array, stretching away into the distance. The sun was behind him, allowing him to get a good photograph.

He arrived at the dome he had left the day before with Celia. There was no sign of her or Simone. He arranged to take a flight next day, and turned in for an early night. Early next morning, his bedside alarm woke him at the right time. He crept quietly past the other rooms so as not to disturb anybody, and made his way to the terminal building.

The launch from the moon was even less impressive than that from earth, if possible, as there was less gravity to overcome. He was pleased to find that he was the only passenger on board this time. His initial reaction was to consider it wasteful to take so large a vehicle such a long way with only one passenger, but he checked himself. There were no staff on board, and the cost of the energy was negligible. The price of the ticket only related to paying for the hardware, and the staffing costs of the company. The expenses of the trip itself were minuscule. He wondered if his thinking would ever really adapt to the new technology.

He kept his seatbelt tightened for the midpoint in the journey. On landing, he made his way home. It was a relief to let himself in with his key, and then shut the world out.

He had been to the moon, which fulfilled a lifetime's ambition, and it had been the worst holiday of his life. He felt very low.

32. From: Mission 12
To: Undisclosed recipients
Sent:

Next morning, when all the preparations were finished, Celia and I were still sitting over breakfast at the newly enlarged table when Clairie came running in.

"Mummy, Mummy!" she cried.

I was beginning to dread this call of hers. What was it this time, I wondered. She looked so concerned.

"What is it, darling?"

"It's when the sleepers wake up. Mummy, I've got nothing to wear!"

This was just what we needed. I gradually broke into a long, satisfying belly laugh. Celia laughed too. It was wonderful to have some humour around for a change; I could feel the stress rolling off my shoulders. Clairie however was not amused.

"No, Daddy," she said, and came over and started punching me with her little fists, as she used to do when she was cross with me. "Horrid Daddy!"

I gathered her up in my arms and swung her around in the air, which was a thing she loved. "There's my girl!" I said. "Of course you must

202

look your best when the sleepers wake. Let's ask Big Nimp about it."

Celia took over at that point. That left me with an opportunity to talk to Max. I found him with his tennis racket and ball.

"Max," I said, "I need to talk to you." He went on hitting the ball, but I could see he was listening. "I am not cross with you, but I do want to say one thing to you, and it's this. From now on, we will all need to pull together as a team. I want you to promise that you will never again take action in a way which affects the mission without talking it over with the rest of us first, until we have reached a common mind. It may seem tedious, but it is important. Will you do that?"

"I understand what you are asking Dad, and put that way it sounds reasonable, but what it would mean in practice is that I will never get to be a part of the final decision, because who is going to listen to an eight-year-old boy?"

It was a fair point. I needed to think again. All I said was, "Max, the success of the mission is very important."

"I know Dad. That's why I woke the sleepers."

I think it may have been at that moment that I first began to realise that Max was going to outstrip me by a long way. I felt a surge of anger, and a stab of jealousy, but I quickly put these on one side. This was my boy! I was proud of him. All I said was, "I love you, boy," and put my arm round him.

"I love you too Dad," he replied, looking up at me. There was a bond of understanding between us. He seemed to know my thoughts. He was aware of his gifts and his importance to the mission. It was most remarkable in an eight-year-old.

When we were assembled, watching the final countdown on the first arrival, I whispered to Celia, "This Tarzan business was just for

Clairie's benefit. Max knew just what he was doing."

"I know," she replied. She put her arm round me. She could sense my tension.

I was used to the eject routine, but the children were fascinated. Clairie wanted to be the first to greet them. She would wait for each one to step out of the coffin, and then she would run up and gave them a hug. I was happy about this. It seemed to me that a hug from a child was the ideal way to be greeted after a years' long sleep.

All the astronauts were in the prime of life. First out was Paul, a thoughtful man, with sandy coloured hair. I took to him immediately; it seemed to me he was going to be a great asset. He accepted my proposal that explanations should wait until everyone was awake.

From that point onwards, the other astronauts had no idea of how things were. They took it for granted that we had all been woken together. There would be some strong emotion later on when the truth emerged, no doubt, but for now, it was a happy group of twelve people that gathered together.

Second out was Phil; business-like and efficient, I reckoned. The men seemed to need less warm-up time than the women. Third was Mark, and fourth was Dickon. Then came the moment I had been dreading; the next one due was the girl on the left. She turned out to have black hair, which I found very confusing, because I had convinced myself that she was a brunette. Her name was Sandra. The moment I saw her, I realised that I did not need to worry; I knew instinctively that she was one of those unthreatening people whom it is easy to get on with. There would be no difficulties between us. She looked pale and somewhat faint after her long sleep.

Number six was Phyllis (Phil and Phyllis; that could be a little awkward), seven was Margaret and eight was Stephanie.

Big Nimp spent all morning playing J.S. Bach's chorale prelude Sleepers Wake, which was a nice touch. It is a fine piece that bears repeating.

The first thing we did was to have a meal together. Then over coffee, I followed Celia's advice, and told them everything that had happened since launch. They were very interested, naturally. I did not tell them that Big Nimp had chosen Sandra for me. It seemed to me that would complicate things. I had never managed to tell Celia. Perhaps I should have persisted. If it was going to come out, it would need to be carefully handled, and now did not seem the best moment. I hoped I had done well in this matter, but I had my doubts about it.

When I explained that Max had woken the eight of them, without any authorisation, they were very concerned.

"How far into the mission are we," they asked.

"About twelve years," I replied. "We can get an accurate update from Big Nimp later on. There are clearly big decisions to be taken. My suggestion is that we all focus on the immediate for two or three days, take a while to acclimatise and get to know each other, and then meet in a first formal session to consider the future on the fourth day from now. How does that sound?"

They were all happy with this.

"In the meantime, welcome to the cattle market," Dickon said. I felt very unhappy about this remark. Two of the girls shifted uncomfortably in their seats.

"What is a kettle market, Mummy?" Clairie asked.

The gathering broke up at this point. I was upset that such a tone should have entered our discussion so quickly, but in a curious way, it

205

turned out to be a good thing. The remark touched a raw nerve. We had all been thinking about it. Once the subject was out in the open, there was no longer any need to feel threatened about it.

By unspoken agreement, we all did our best to make each other feel at home. The children explained about Big Nimp and the Limpets, to the amusement of our guests. Then they showed them Grim Reaper. Max rolled a golf ball horizontally round its throat, like a ball on a roulette wheel, so that it took a while to gurgle its way down into the depths, and got Big Nimp to bring up a football so that the arrival bell rang just at the moment that the golf ball finally disappeared. He is very imaginative.

The eight newcomers were happy with the sleeping arrangements we had made; two four-bedded rooms, one for men and one for women. It turned out that Sandra was an able pianist, which was a delight to us all. My suggestion that people might like to try out the observation platform was eagerly taken up. All eight seemed to have a good grasp of the heavens, and were thrilled at the good viewing arrangements. They all made a fuss of the children. Last but not least, they all said how excellent Celia's paintings were.

At the end of the first day, when we all settled into bed at two gee time, I found myself thinking that the first few hours had gone as well as they could have done. A new chapter of our life was beginning. It seemed to me it might be rather fun.

Bruce

One of the answerphone messages when Bruce arrived at home was a request that he play background piano at a party in West London. The caller had enjoyed his playing at Henley It sounded interesting. Bruce was pleased. Perhaps this background piano business was going to give him some new openings. He checked the

206

diary. Saturday the 17th of August. How fascinating; that was the day he had been due back from the moon. If he had stayed for the full fortnight, he would not only have missed the opportunity; his failure to return the call would have been taken as rudeness, and he would never have had another opening there again. Oh well, it was nice to think that something good had come out of the fiasco.

He rang the number to accept, and left a message on an answerphone. However did Granddad manage without voicemail, he wondered.

He finished off his film on some local Swallows and Amazons, who must have wondered why he was taking their photo, and took it in to the camera shop for developing. It still seemed strange to have the shadows caused by the sky-fliers darting around everywhere, but it was striking how the other pedestrians had stopped looking upwards at them, Bruce thought. It was no longer new. It saddened Bruce that flying seemed to have become the province of the young to such an extent that virtually no older people had tried it. It meant that if he decided to continue with it, he would stick out like a sore thumb.

Then he called on Marjorie, who was surprised to see him back so soon. He did not explain, beyond saying that he had not enjoyed the trip. She accepted that. Then he said that the unexpected days with no commitments meant that he could help her with the garden. He always felt guilty about this; the garden was getting beyond her, and Bruce felt it would be a kindness to assist, but he was generally too busy to do anything. The result was that it was rather a wilderness. Marjorie seemed to have an aversion to gardeners, so Bruce used to try and help from time to time. She frankly did not charge enough rent, so it was a way of making it up to her.

The truth was that Bruce hated gardening, but he could make himself pull up the weeds as well as the next man. Fortunately, the weather was overcast, so it was not too hot to work. Over the following days, he got a lot done. It soon looked so much better.

Marjorie was ecstatic. Bruce was pleased. It was nice to feel wanted.

Then one evening, the doorbell rang. It turned out to be Bill, and Gnilla with him. Did this mean…? Yes, it did! They were back together, and they were going to be married. Bruce was thrilled for them. He hugged them both. Then, although he tried to stop them, the tears would keep filling his eyes, and suddenly he was sobbing as though his heart would break. They both hugged him in turns, but it was no use; once he had started, he could not stop. It must have gone on for twenty minutes. In the end, after the box of tissues had long since been emptied, he was able to dry his eyes.

"Tell me how you got back together," he said. But they were having none of it. They wanted to know what he was so upset about, so he told them the whole thing, from meeting Celia in the train, then teaching her piano, then meeting her parents, then taking on the commission in return for the moon trip, then what happened at the end of the first day of the holiday. They listened in silence.

"Well," said Bill at last, "that is quite a story. I wonder what you have got yourself into."

"The stupid thing is," Bruce went on, "that I never seem able to find any way of being of use to them. It's all so daft. But one thing is clear to me at last; I can give up hoping for anything to happen between Celia and me."

Then Bruce remembered the photos. They passed them from one to the next.

"They are a bit samey," said Gnilla, "all this grey. Was it rather dull to look at?"

"Depends on your viewpoint," Bruce said. "I find the history of the moon very interesting. But there are some more colourful ones in a minute."

They soon came to the views of the earth above the lunar horizon. Bill thought the one of Bruce with his hand to the side of his head, taken so it looked as if the earth was supporting his elbow, was the best one, but Gnilla preferred the one where the earth appeared to have risen higher, and Bruce had jumped up with his arms outstretched towards it, as if he was reaching for the ball in a line-out at a Rugby match. The messing around had been fun at the time, but Bruce could not enjoy the photos now. Neither Bill nor

Gnilla made any comment about Celia, perhaps because you could not tell who was who in the padded space suits, and they did not like to ask.

When it was time to go, they both hugged him again, and Gnilla said she was very sorry not to have bought any flowers, but they had only called at the last minute because Marjorie had rung them saying he was back early and he might like some company, and that it was wonderful to see him.

"I wanted to drift off into space and never come back," said Bruce. The look of concern on their faces was such that he burst into tears again. How good it was to have friends who cared!

"We'll look after you." It was the best Bill could manage. "You're so good at looking after everybody else that it's sometimes hard to remember that you have needs too."

They took their leave, promising to ring in a day or two. Bruce felt so much better after their visit. It had made all the difference.

33. From: Mission 12
To: Undisclosed recipients
Sent:

At breakfast next morning, we were discussing the viewing of the stars.

"It was the centre of the Milky Way that thrilled me most," said Phil, pointing to my left.

"You've got confused," I said. "It's easily done. The Milky Way is over there," and I pointed in the opposite direction. "It is magnificent, isn't it?"

Phil sat quite still for a moment, before speaking. "No I am not confused," he said carefully. "The Milky Way is certainly on that side of the ship." He indicated to my left again.

"I agree," said several of the others. This seemed most odd.

"Well we can soon settle it after breakfast," I said.

The moment I mounted the steps into the viewing platform, I knew something was wrong. The whole sky was back to front. I turned round, mystified. "I can't understand it. Call Celia, she will explain."

Celia was as puzzled as I was. "It's as if everything has turned round," she said.

Phil was beginning to get excited. "Get the trip odometer up on the screen," he said.

We had been planning to do this today. The fact is that I had stopped looking at it a long time ago. This was strange, because at the beginning of the trip, I had really enjoyed calling it up each day. I had tried to convince myself that I left off looking at it because it was so depressing seeing all the noughts on the left hand side of the display. However, the truth is that I was scared silly at how fast we were travelling. All we had to do was to hit a grain of dust, and the whole mission would be obliterated. Still, at least it would have been instantaneous, and therefore a quick end.

We all settled into chairs facing the big screen. I called the display up. I was surprised to find just how quickly the numbers were turning over in the right hand columns. I got out little nimp. "We are doing a million miles in under six seconds," I said.

"This is ludicrous," said Mark. "We want accurate statements from the main computer, not your mental arithmetic." I felt rather squashed. I had forgotten that others might consider my ways a little foolish.

We called up our speed, and found we were doing 98% of the speed of light. This took my breath away. I had no idea we were going that fast. Mark was speaking again.

"Now, are you quite sure that the stars were orientated differently before?" From his tone, he evidently regarded me as some sort of mental case. I was beginning to feel that I was going to find it difficult to keep on friendly terms with him. "Quite sure," I replied.

"Right, well that means that the ship has turned round through one hundred and eighty degrees at some point," he continued.

"Yes," said a voice, "you are quite right." Everyone turned to look. I was astonished; it was Max who had spoken. "We turned round nearly a year ago. I discovered it when I was out viewing with Clairie one time. We must have turned in the night when we four were asleep, because none of us noticed the ship turning."

I felt stunned, but there was more in store.

"Put up the distance travelled in light years," Mark commanded. Big Nimp flashed up eighteen point four.

"But that's impossible," I objected; "we have only been travelling for twelve years. There must be some mistake."

This time it was Phil who spoke. "The twenty-four hour period that happens in the ship, which you have been expressing as weeks, months and years, is valid for life inside the ship, but not outside it. When a spaceship approaches the speed of light, normal modes of measurement start breaking down. For example, the mass of the ship and its contents are affected, and time for an observer on board seems to move more slowly. It is all very confusing. Put up the date on earth, computer."

Big Nimp obliged. A thrill of horror went through me; decades had passed since we came on board. I knew that the rate of the passing of time would be affected by our speed, but I had not imagined it would be anything like as much as this. I felt sick.

Dickon asked me, "Have you had any periods of weightlessness during the trip?"

"No."

"That means that the ship has been accelerating by one gee throughout your twelve years of travel, because if the engines had been turned off, allowing the ship to coast, you would have become weightless, and started floating about."

"That's what I thought. In fact, we were accelerating at two gees in the night to begin with."

"Two gees! Over time, even one gee is a tremendous acceleration. You would have got to within one percent of the speed of light after 354 days of travel. Nothing can go faster than light, so our perceived acceleration has had less and less effect on the actual speed the closer we have approached to the speed of light. I imagine that the motors were left running to avoid weightlessness, to make things more comfortable for the occupants. Now, the reason that the ship will have turned round is in order to decelerate, to slow down. For the last eight months, what you took to be acceleration has been reducing the ship's speed. We must have been travelling even faster than we are now a year ago; anything up to one hundred percent of the speed of light. Computer, show us light years to go to our destination." The answer came up 4.7.

"I would guess you turned round earlier than eight months ago from this figure. We are three quarters of the way to our destination. Computer, show us our arrival time, measured in twenty-four hour periods of this ship, expressed in years and months."

The answer was three years, five months. I was open-mouthed.

"But I was told we were on a sixty-nine year trip," I spluttered.

"I can't help that," Dickon replied. "The reality is that we now have forty-one months of travel to our destination, expressed in the on-board time that you have been using."

This was a bombshell. It altered things completely. I stole a glance at Celia; she was evidently overjoyed at this news. I felt a sudden stab of envy. She was going to have a role in the new settlement after all. What use would I be, who had made a mess of everything so far? I was feeling increasingly useless, and out of it all.

But Mark was speaking. "Dickon, you are on the right lines it seems to me, but I have another theory. I think we are ignoring the anti-gravity technology. Personally, I find the phrase gravity control more helpful than anti-gravity. Bruce, am I right that you were never able to detect any vibrations from the motors?"

I nodded.

"So you would not have known if the engines had been switched off, except through becoming weightless. Now, supposing this ship has gravity control, and frankly I think it is highly likely, then the computer could have given you a one gee environment, not only for your greater comfort, but also for reasons of health, as humans experience bone loss in prolonged spells of weightlessness."

I remembered the incident of the need for scaffolding, when I wanted to polish the ceiling, and that Big Nimp had said sky-suits would not work in here, and told them about it.

"That tends to confirm it. In that case, the ship could have turned round without you being aware of it, provided the rate of rotation was slow enough. Indeed, I reckon that the slower the ship turned, the better, as there would be less chance of the manoeuvre putting the ship off course. I'm no expert, but personally, I would envisage the operation taking many hours."

In the conversation which followed, Mark's view came to be accepted as being the right one. We thought it likely that 98% of the speed of light had been our coasting speed for some years, if not from the ending of the two gee acceleration period. It seemed that a continuous acceleration at two gees gets you to the speed of light twice as quickly as one gee, in just 177 days rather than 354. We were probably at full speed at around day 260 of the mission, which is just short of nine months. From then on, we would have coasted through the vacuum of space. The time would come when the ship would need to turn round, ready to fire the motors in order to slow down. It seemed we were already in the required position, ready to begin this firing at the right time.

After the conversation had died down, there came a moment when Sandra turned and spoke to me. "Bruce, it seems to me that you can afford to relax. It is clear from what you have said so far that you thought everything was ruined by us being woken, and that it was your fault, but in fact, as far as I am concerned, this wake-up time is about right. I reckon I would have needed several months at the very least to acclimatise and get ready for the work waiting for us. A year or two will not seem out of place. In fact, I am pleased to have been woken now, because I am glad to be in on the first stages of it all. So I want to say thank you." And with that, she came over and kissed me on the cheek. Then she gave Max a big hug.

It was an emotional moment. I just wanted to be with Celia. I went over to her, and she held me while I cried. The relief was enormous.

"Really I am so full of tears that I feel like a stream", I spluttered. Max and Clairie came over and joined in the general hug.

"Dad, less than four years to go." Max was glowing with excitement.

"I can't wait," said Clairie.

I could see that our life had changed drastically, in just a few brief hours.

Bruce did a thorough job at the gardening. It was better than going to the dentist, which he also took the opportunity to do, it being out of term. It turned out that drilling was needed, which made the gardening seem like a holiday. He was pleased to be doing Marjorie a good turn, but he was glad when the day for playing background piano finally arrived.

He had been sent a security badge in advance, with his name in bold letters on it, and a barcode, which would admit him to the building. They had also enclosed the card of a taxi firm, who would drive him there and put it on their account. Bruce had never experienced anything like this before. He sensed he was moving into a different circle than he was used to. He decided to wear his dinner jacket and bow tie rather than the blue suit he usually wore for playing.

The drive did not take long. He presented his badge at the entrance, and the armed guards led him through to the lift. The party was on the twenty-ninth floor. One of the guards accompanied him in the lift. They were taking no chances, Bruce realised.

I expect this block has gone over to the new energy source, Bruce thought, as they glided upwards. It was astonishing, really, that a black box about one cubic metre in size would be able to provide electricity for an entire block of flats. The difficulty for private homes was that, although you never had gas and electric bills again once the new box was fitted, the initial cost of being converted was still very high. Everyone was waiting for it to come down. However, Bruce had foreseen that the day would come when there would be more boxes in a street that there were homes still on the gas and electric services, and then people would start receiving letters announcing the end of the supplies. Then there would be a mad scramble for the boxes, and hey presto, the cost would soar again. The thing to do was to judge the timing just right, to get the best deal. The chances of Marjorie managing that were slim, even though she would only need a box of one cubic foot to cover both properties.

Ah, the lift had arrived. Then he noticed that twenty-nine was the top floor. A penthouse flat! With stunning views over West London. He wondered idly what it might be worth.

There was another security check outside the flat door, and then he was shown in. The interior took his breath away. Sumptuous was hardly the word. There were cut glass chandeliers everywhere; Bruce had always rather admired those, and he could tell from a glance that these really were the cut glass variety, not the moulded glass sort, which sparkle so much less. The wallpaper had a velvety quality to it – Bruce did not want to be seen feeling it, but he was able to brush his fingers along it behind his back without anybody noticing. Also, the size of the flat was staggering. He had only seen one aspect of the building when he was dropped off. Now he was inside, he could see that the floor area was vast.

He hardly had time to take in any of these details before a man was advancing, with outstretched hand. He recognised him from Henley.

"Hello. I'm Jim Pond. So glad you could come. You have such a talent. Now do you need anything, wash or brush up, or something to eat or drink?"

Bruce declined all of these. He preferred playing on an empty stomach; it aided his concentration.

"Come this way, then."

He was led into a long room with large windows, looking out towards the Thames in the distance. He was led half way through it to another white grand piano. Bruce looked at it twice. Surely…

"We had the same piano that you played on last time shipped in. Couldn't improve on the sound, we reckoned. It's been tuned every day for a week, so it should be Okay."

Bruce was way out of his depth, socially, and he knew it. The thing to do was to keep calm, and play his best. The man had liked what he did at Henley, so he would do the same sort of thing over again. He wished he was not quite so nervous.

"Just play as much or as little as you like," Jim said, "and if you want a drink or something to eat, it's over there. Make yourself at home. I'm so glad you have come."

The man could not have been nicer, Bruce thought to himself. He settled on the piano stool. Once again, the lid was fully up, but never mind that.

This was the moment to feel the carpet with his fingers. He had never come across one which had so much give in it. The thing to do was to drop something, and reach down for it in an unobtrusive manner. Yes... as he suspected, shag pile about an inch deep. Funny how deep-pile carpets had come back in again, following some new discovery. Bruce shuddered to think what it must have cost in this huge room.

"Well, J.S.B.," he muttered under his breath as he started up with his signature tune, the first Prelude of the Forty-eight, "here we are again, old chap." The people round him were only human beings after all. Bach may not have been in their income bracket, but the quality of his music was unsurpassed. It was no good being in awe of them just because they were rich. Just do your best, as usual. No Wagner, he thought, and no hymns either, although this lot might not recognise a hymn even if you shoved their noses in the hymnbook.

It was his policy to keep his eyes on the keyboard, not just to help with his playing, but because he reckoned the guests did not want eye contact with the pianist. However, on this occasion, the lay-out of the room was such that people were mingling right up against the piano itself. He became aware more than once of a fat man with a gold watch on a chain in the breast pocket of his waistcoat. It reminded him of his granddad, whom he had once seen wearing one. There were some other lean men in business suits, ardently discussing investments. At one moment, between numbers, he glanced up casually, and to his astonishment, he saw Flossie in earnest conversation with a great hulk of a man with heavy jowls. What was she doing here? Had she spotted him? And who was that she was talking to? Bruce could not believe that she fancied Heavy Jowls, at any rate. She looked fabulous in a full length purple gown. Perhaps he had been foolish not to pursue her.

He forced himself back to his playing. These people and their wretched investments! That was the third set of people he had heard complaining about recent stock market falls. What were they on about, for goodness sake? It had only gone down a few points. The stock market was riding high at present.

He did a Beatles medley. Some time in the past, he had arranged eight or ten numbers in a good key sequence so that they flowed well from one to the next. However, while he was playing, it was dawning on him increasingly that this was no ordinary party. From the scraps of conversation he was overhearing, he was becoming aware of the incredible amount of wealth there was represented in that room that evening. And all they wanted to do was to increase their pile. It was horrible.

Without any warning, he suddenly found he was very angry. All this greed! And he was supporting it by his playing. Weren't they always going on at church about the need to make a stand? He had always been so mild-mannered all his life, and look where it had got him; hurting to the point of distraction. Well, here was his chance to do something good for a change. They would probably destroy him for what he was going to do, but Bruce was beyond caring about life any more, and he might as well go down fighting.

He did something he had never done before, nor ever dreamed of doing. With his heart thumping in his chest fit to burst, Bruce suddenly slammed the piano lid shut, and stood up in one movement.

The effect was electric. Every conversation in the room froze, and every eye was turned on him. The security guards from the door had already started moving his way. There was no going back now.

"Well you can arrest me if you want, but before you do, just hear this. Here you all are, rolling in wealth, fussing on about half a percent interest extra here, or a drop of a few points in a stock market there, when every week forty-seven thousand children in the world die of water borne diseases. Did you hear that? Forty-seven thousand children, every week." He was dimly aware that Jim had held out his hands to halt the security guards. He continued.

"If you people want good investment advice, then here it is. Pool your resources and give it all to Water Aid. They work to provide clean water worldwide. You know, I once rang them up to ask how much money it would take to get the whole world's water supply clean, and they said six and a half billion pounds. That's about the value of all the church buildings in the country, because frankly, I reckon the church would be better off if it sold all its buildings, gave the money to the poor, and got out on the streets helping people where it should be. But there is another way. It wouldn't surprise me if you lot could raise that entire sum here tonight. It's the best investment you will ever make."

This was crazy talk, but never mind. But now, he had shot his bolt. He suddenly became apologetic.

"Look, I'm sorry to have ruined your party. But I just thought, somebody needs to say something to these people, and if I don't, I don't imagine anybody else ever will. I do apologise. I did not mean to get worked up." The closing words were more of a mumble than anything else. What have I done, he was thinking. He slumped into his seat.

Suddenly someone started clapping. "Bravo," he heard, and then the whole room erupted in clapping and cheering, and everyone was talking busily to everyone else. A moment later, there was Jim at his shoulder.

"That was magnificent. I haven't enjoyed anything so much in years. Talk to you afterwards."

He was sweating hot and cold all over, and trembling. Still he had a job to do. Now, some appropriate music. Something to do with water. It only required a moment's thought. He began on the love song from the film Titanic. Everyone would recognise that. It was a story about people who did not pay the water enough attention and respect and paid the consequences.

Should he have had that outburst? It had been so embarrassing. And what good would it do? Hadn't he sounded too aggressive? And why did he apologise at the end? He should not have apologised. He had been speaking on behalf of the powerless to the powerful; why did he feel he had to touch his forelock to them? Why was he such a fool?

His mind was racing, but his playing was controlled. Nobody would have known to look at him. Keep the volume down until the key change, otherwise there is nothing left for the climax. Not too fast. Keep it sad; Jack is going to die before long. Convey the emotion through the little finger of the right hand, bringing out the melody.

It was while he was playing the familiar tune that he realised one factor that had helped to bring on his outburst. In his Beatles medley, he had arrived at Money can't buy me love. "I don't care too much for money," went the refrain, "Money can't buy me love."

He prayed quietly in his mind, his fingers still playing. "Father, save me from a love of money, and give me a love for the poor instead. And help me to play well. I hope I haven't let you down."

Oh no, disaster. Before he could stop himself, he was into Act three of Siegfried. Wagner would come into his thoughts so strongly when he got emotional. He was already into the horn call before he had realised. There was no turning back now. He would have to go through with it, and if they did not like it, too bad.

The story of the opera was so compelling. Siegfried was the greatest hero of the world, because he knew no fear. This had enabled him to kill Fafner the Dragon, and also not to be cowed by Wotan, the head God, who had confronted Siegfried when he was on his way to the mountain surrounded by flames. Why, he had even broken Wotan's staff in two! Now he was sounding his horn, with the tremendous ringing call, supported by the fantastic harmonies in the orchestra. It was his favourite part of the entire Ring Cycle, which comprised four operas, to be seen inside a week. Bruce considered the music for Siegfried ascending the mountain even finer than the famous funeral march.

There was no way that he could ever do justice to the horn call section on the piano, but then when the hero strode into the towering flames, he was able to capture some of the orchestral effect. Sorry everybody, this will have to be *mezzo forte*; I cannot do it softer than that. But rather than playing solid chords, it was better to break them up in the left hand, and whip around in a frenzy of notes. Then the sound could be softer, but the effect more of rushing flames soaring skywards.

Now, don't get soft too soon – scale the *diminuendo* gradually downwards, until Siegfried has passed through the fire to the mountain top, when there is a genuine *pianissimo*. On the ground between some rocks lies the sleeping Brunnhilde, covered by her enormous shield, left there by Wotan as a punishment, waiting for a great hero to waken her with a kiss. When that happens, she will lose her godhead, and become a mere mortal. And now, as Siegfried looks at her, for the first time in his life he discovers what it is to fear.

The tears poured down Bruce's cheeks as he played. He could not help it. The music was so beautiful! He hoped nobody would notice.

The same thing happened as always. Rather than proceeding to the waking-up music, Bruce slipped unnoticeably back into Act Three of the Valkyries, the previous opera, and played the sleeping music instead. It took several more minutes of the most fabulous harmonies, but when he rounded off this section, there was no doubt about it; he had left Brunnhilde asleep on the mountain top, surrounded by the protecting wall of fire. The music was so wonderful.

Don't pause at the end of it, for fear that somebody might clap, ruining everything. Straight into something watery – ah yes, the Largo from Handel's Water Music would make a good contrast, followed by the Aquarium from Saint Saens' Carnival of the Animals. There might be some musical people present who could get the connections.

Thankfully, nobody applauded. It was as if they had not even noticed. Bruce suddenly felt angry again. This was why he did not play Wagner in public. He hated it when people did not recognise its genius. He wanted them to applaud, but he hated them to applaud as well. What a bundle of contradictions he was!

All too soon, the guests were beginning to leave, and the party was coming to a close. He played on quietly until the room was empty, and Jim came over again.

"Well, that interruption was quite something. In all the meetings I have ever attended, I don't think I have heard a point put with so

221

much intensity. It was brilliant. You could be a great businessman, you know. And I just love your playing. You have such a range of music. It's a great talent."

Bruce mumbled something incoherent. He just wanted to leave. But Jim had not finished.

"Your idea about the church selling its buildings is interesting. Do you know any of the guys in charge? I would be interested in making an offer for St. Paul's Cathedral – it's a prime site."

"Sorry," said Bruce. "I've got my eye on that one. With a few mezzanine floors put in, it would house a lot of London's homeless."

"Too bad," said Jim, with a smile. "Still, your idea is a good one too."

The security men escorted him out of the building, and into a taxi that was waiting for him. He was soon home again. What a relief. And yet, part of him felt pleased. He had played well. And his outburst might have done some good. There was a lot to be thankful for.

At the end of the evening, he tuned in to the BBC news on television, as was his custom. The headline story hit him in the stomach like an iron fist.

"There has been an explosion at a block of flats in West London." Surely not… Oh my goodness, an aerial shot of the block of flats showing the top few floors being blasted into smithereens in a moment, by a huge fireball. Bruce was utterly horrified. Thank goodness the guests had all left before he had. But Jim, and the security guards! This was terrible. He went over to the phone, his mind racing. Who could he ring to find out?

Just then, of all moments, the doorbell rang. Who could that possibly be at this time of night? He went to the door and opened it. There were several policemen there.

"Mr. Winter?"

"Yes?"

"I am arresting you for the murder of Mr. James Pond. You do not…"

Bruce heard no more. He was aghast. The handcuffs they were putting round his wrists were thicker and heavier than the ones Bill had used a few weeks before. And from the expression on the faces of the men, he knew that this was very serious indeed.

His mind was racing so quickly that he did not even notice that although the men pulled the door to, so that the house was secure, nobody had bothered to turn off the television, which would be a waste of electricity. He was pushed into the back seat of a car without ceremony, and driven off into the night.

34. From: Mission 12
To: Undisclosed recipients
Sent:

The day of the meeting had come. We were all seated in a circle. The atmosphere was rather solemn. I waited for somebody to speak.

"Something has been puzzling me." Margaret had been very quiet up to now, and hearing her speak caught our attention. "I was told before launch that I would be woken by the commander of the mission. I have noticed that there has been no mention of the commander yet. Now as I understand it, we eight were all woken by Max."

I cleared my throat. "I'm afraid that's my fault," I said. "I woke Celia, when I was not authorised to do so, and the mission has been out of gear ever since. I do apologise, although I realise that no words of mine can ever undo the damage I have done."

"Not so fast," Margaret continued. "I very much appreciate your honesty about what you see as your failures to date. However, I would like to raise a different way of looking at things. As I understand it, your role was to care for the ship, sweep and clean, and be on hand in case decisions were needed." I nodded. "At least, that was how you understood your role. I would also like to point out that the Computer had

223

everything under its control except for one area, and that was our wake-up times. We can see this from the fact that there was a lever above each astronaut, for waking him or her up."

"That's correct," I said. Where was this leading, I was asking myself?

"I wonder if it was ever really envisaged that you would remain alone for many years on this trip," Margaret went on. "You were told that you were chosen because of your ability to be on your own. I suspect you may have been chosen for precisely the opposite reason; your inability to be on your own. I think it was always known that after a while, you would become so lonely that you would wake one or more of the sleepers out of desperation."

A hubbub of conversation broke out at this point. I was feeling too confused to say anything.

"Far from it being a disaster," Margaret continued, "my suggestion is that what you did was good. In fact, it was the best thing you could have done to help the mission, in my opinion. The creation of a new settlement in a new star system gives humanity a chance to make a fresh start. The computer was able to run all the technical side of the voyage, but was not empowered to make decisions with regard to humans, concerning life and death, as it were. What was needed from a human point of view was a founder of the new race. The levers were placed above the coffins for a reason. The decision to share life with others was for a human to take, not a machine. What was needed was a family, where a man cared for his wife, and loved his children. A model for those that would come later. I believe that you were selected with this purpose in mind. You have started the process, and provided that model."

I was silent. What could I say?

"Now, as to the commander. I don't think that Max waking us was a mistake at all. I propose that Max, the eldest son of this wonderful man, is the commander of the mission, despite his youth; not because we say he is or vote him into the post, or anything like that, but because we can see he is the commander by nature, just by looking at him, and the fact that he woke us proves it. What do you others think?"

Well, there was an outburst of conversation on all sides, but I heard none of it. I had instantly been taken back to a memorable lecture about family life that I had attended with Granddad, when I was a boy.

Everybody's life, the speaker had said, is like a relay race, in which there are three laps of the track. Your parents run round the first lap, carrying the baton. They come round to where you are waiting in the changeover box, and hand you the baton. You then run round the track yourself with the baton, until there comes the moment when you reach the changeover box yourself, and hand it on to your children, and watch as they set off round the track in their turn. The thing in life is to receive the baton when it comes to you, carry out your circuit of the track faithfully, and then pass it on when the moment comes.

This was the moment in my life for me to pass the baton on, I now realised. In fact, I already knew it, with a firm conviction. Max was the Commander! I had no difficulty seeing him in the role. He would do it well. How extraordinary that this should be apparent even though he was only eight, if eight was his real age. By now I felt confused about times and dates; they did not feel to be under my control.

But the baton. The speaker had envisaged a normal family when talking of the three laps of the relay race. My experience had been different. My parents never completed their lap; how the

baton ever came to arrive in the changeover box
at all, I don't know. I just picture it lying
there on the ground; it was up to me to pick it
up and start running with it. The only thing was
that I could feel it was slimy in my hands while
I ran, and when I looked down at it, I could see
it was covered in excrement. It was horrible.
However, there was no way I was going to stop
running in order to clean it. This was a race!
But how could I hand the baton over to my son in
that state? There I was, running round the track,
with sixty thousand spectators cheering me on for
all they were worth. What could I do?

The only thing was to wipe it clean on my
running shorts as I ran. I did not hesitate. My
shorts were soon far from white. When I had used
up every inch of them, I found I needed to use my
top as well. Oh dear, I had run out of room there
too. The changeover box was approaching. There
was no time to think. In the remaining seconds, I
simply cleaned off the remaining muck by rubbing
the baton on my hair, and then even on my face,
so that when I arrived at the box, I could thrust
a gleaming, clean baton into Max's hand, urging
him, "Go on, go on!"

It did not matter what happened to me, as long
as he got hold of the baton. "Well done, Max!
Well done!" I was shouting out with the rest of
the crowd, oblivious of my own state as he set
off on his lap.

Celia was shaking me by the shoulder. I came
out of my reverie. "Max is the commander," she
was saying, as if I did not know already. "It's
extraordinary. He wants the rest of the
astronauts to be woken as well, and after some
discussion, the others have all agreed."

The rest of that morning is a blur for me. I
can remember Max coming over at some point to say
that Big Nimp had given him permission to reveal
what was on the floor below, and me replying that

I did not want to know. He could tell the others.
He had already grown in stature in my eyes. I am
so proud of him.
    Bruce

The cell was completely bare, except for the rectangular table
and chairs. There were thick iron bars over the windows, and a grill
over the little window in the heavy steel door. There were two strip
lights on the ceiling, giving a harsh glare, and no less than four TV
cameras pointing downwards from the four corners of the ceiling.
There were two older men seated on the other side of the table from
Bruce, and a third man, somewhat younger, sitting on a chair over
by the window, dressed in a grey raincoat, and chain smoking. It
was like a scene from a film.

Bruce was feeling sick, and trembling violently in spasms,
despite attempting to stay calm. They were asking him the same
questions for the third time.

"We have witnesses to say that you fired a shot."

"I did not. I closed the piano lid firmly for effect, to gain
everyone's attention. I had no weapon of any kind. And if I had
fired a shot, then why did nobody come and tackle me and disarm
me?" Why did his teeth chatter so?

"You don't know much about security work. Our men would
never approach a man with a gun head on, inciting further gunfire.
That is no defence at all. Why did you interrupt the proceedings?"

Once again, Bruce told them what he had said, as accurately as
he could remember. He could see it from their point of view; if he
was inventing his account, then he might vary it with each telling of
it. He tried to use the same words as far as possible.

"You use the same words each time you tell us. That smacks of
an invented story, to cover such a situation as this."

"It's the truth. I am simply being consistent." How could he
convince them?

"What music were you playing before the incident?"

"I don't recall... Oh yes, it was a Beatles medley."

"Why does a classically trained musician like yourself play pop
music, which tends to be subversive?"

This was ridiculous. "I play what I think people will enjoy, and that means choosing what they recognise. There is no thought of it being subversive. I attempt to play a range of music in all styles."

"What did you play on sitting down after you spoke?"

This was easy. "Music from the film Titanic. Not just the well-known song, but the opening flute theme, and the surging chords as well. I had been speaking about the need for pure drinking water, so I chose something with a watery theme."

"Yes. We have heard that you attempt to match your playing to what the situation calls for. That being so, isn't it rather strange, Mr. Winter, that in the presence of very rich people, you should play music from a film in which the richest man in the world loses his life?"

Oh dear, Bruce had not thought of it that way. Yes, Guggenheim or somebody, who went down with the ship.

"There was no thought of that in my mind."

"But you admit, it is rather suspicious. What did you play after that?"

"I found myself playing the magic fire music from Wagner's Ring cycle, which was a mistake, as I don't like playing Wagner in public. There are too many people who fail to appreciate it."

"Funny how a great ball of fire should engulf the building not long after you left it, when on your own admission, you were playing fiery music. What had happened to your alleged watery theme? I suggest that the whimsical, artistic side of yourself knew exactly what you were going to do. This was a cold-blooded, callous act by a determined man, Mr. Winter." This was dreadful. The man was continuing.

"We also have witnesses who will testify that you have been in a very emotional state recently." Who on earth could they mean? Had they been getting at Bill and Gnilla? Oh dear, Mark's dad, Stephe. And he had not honoured his promise to stand him a jar of real ale.

"It strikes me that for all your posturing about the needs of the world's poor, your real motive was to kill Mr. Pond. In fact, it is not hard to detect a neat play on words here, another favourite ploy of yours. The target was named Pond, so you go on about water, and play music about the most notorious sinking of a celebrated ship in the Atlantic, which I'm sure you know is sometimes referred to as the pond. Perhaps you smuggled in a bomb, and hid it in the piano stool, which was a place where nobody else would think of looking. All we need now is to establish that you have a connection with some covert organisation, and we have a strong case." This was dreadful. The concern showed on Bruce's face. "Yes, you are right to be alarmed. There is not much left of the flat, but you can rest assured, our forensic people will be going over the rubble with a fine tooth comb. You could save us all a lot of trouble by confessing now what you have done. It could help you in the long run if you make a clean breast of it now."

This was awful. Bruce's voice was hoarse. "I never have had any intention of killing anybody, I have no desire to do so at this moment, and I never will want to kill anyone in the future. Please believe that I had nothing to do with this outrage and let me go."

"Tell us again who was at the party."

Bruce had already described Jim, the man with the heavy jowls, and the fat man with the gold watch chain. He had not mentioned Flossie earlier, but now he saw that he had no choice but to do so.

"There was a girl there who I know, talking to the heavy jowls man. Her name is Flossie, or rather Florence Millicent. She is my first cousin. I cannot believe she would have anything to do with a bomb plot, which is why I did not mention her before."

For the first time, the rain-coat man by the window stirred in his seat. Bruce had realised a while before that he was the man in charge here. They got him to give her details, name and address, and then the second interviewer, who had not said anything yet, left the room. I expect they are going to arrest Flossie, thought Bruce. Sure enough, they said that there was nothing more to be done that night, and that the interview would continue in the morning. As he was being led off to a cell for the night, Bruce called back, "You are making a big mistake. I have nothing to do with it, and neither has Flossie, and the real criminal is probably getting away while you are wasting time on us."

He was shoved brusquely into a cell, and the door was shut behind him with a clang. There was a mattress on a bed. He had no pyjamas, so he would have to sleep in his clothes. Bruce noted the position of the bed, and then turned the light off, but found that it merely went dim. He hated sleeping in a lit room, but he was past caring. He cast himself down on the bed, and fell asleep in complete exhaustion.

He was woken the following morning by his cell door clanging open. It was still dark.

"You're free to go," the warder said. "There is insufficient evidence to detain you. You are not to attempt to leave the country; your passport number has been given to the authorities. You will be wise to stay at home; no good giving the impression you are trying to do a runner. If we need you again, we will be in touch. Here are your things."

In a daze, Bruce received back the plastic bag with his keys, handkerchief, loose change and wallet. They were letting him go. In a few moments he was ushered out onto the street. He was told of a railway station a few minutes' walk away.

It was most strange being out and about at such an early hour of the morning. He quickly decided to go back home, and then ring Bill when it was a suitable time to do so.

The sun was up by the time he had his key in the lock. How careless to have left the TV on. Otherwise, everything seemed to be normal. He got himself some breakfast. When it was 0830, he felt it was reasonable to phone Bill. A sleepy voice answered.

"Bill, I am in big trouble, and I need your help. Would you be willing to skip church today, and come over?"

Bill was only too delighted. Anything he could do would be a pleasure. Before long, Bruce was telling him the events of the previous twenty-four hours, and Bill was listening in astonishment.

"But Bruce," he said at last. "There's a great mystery in all this. I collected my Sunday paper on the way here, and from what you say, it ought to be all over the front page, but look there's nothing at all about it."

They scoured the paper from cover to cover. There was no mention of any explosion.

"What on earth is going on?" Bruce said, in utter amazement.

"Let's go and see for ourselves," said Bill.

They got into the car and drove the route that Bruce had covered in the taxi just a few hours before. "Stop here," said Bruce, when they had a view of the block of flats.

Bruce stared in total disbelief. There had been no explosion; everything was completely normal. "But I saw it on my TV!" he exclaimed.

"Now," said Bill, "we need to think carefully here. Something very suspicious is going on. I reckon it's to do with the cloak and dagger people as you call them."

Bruce was thinking hard. "Could they have messed about with my TV?" he asked.

Bill did not wait to discuss it. He turned the car round and headed back. "There's only one way to find out," he said.

As they were walking up the garden path, Bruce got it. "The new wall covering!" he burst out. "The builders must have tampered with the aerial when they were doing the work."

"But that means that you saw a specially prepared news bulletin, dovetailed in with the normal network programmes, that had been made for your benefit."

"I know it sounds fantastic," Bruce said, "but I wouldn't put anything past those people. Let's go through it slowly. They broadcast the explosion into my home, then they arrest me before I have time to contact anybody, and put me through hours of police interviews with no purpose. It doesn't make sense." Bruce was worked up, and was not going to stand for any more nonsense. "I was told on no account to return to Celia's parents' home, but I'm going there all the same. I've had enough of this. Will you drive me?"

Bill was pleased to do so. As they were on their way, he had a suggestion. "Suppose we park a hundred yards away where you can see what happens, and I go and do the enquiring. Then you can always come forward on a second wave, if you see what I mean, but if I unearth something without you needing to break your word to them, so much the better."

Bruce agreed. Despite his bravado, he had a lingering fear of these people. In fact, he was still trembling from the evening before. Bill found a quiet spot under an overhanging tree which was perfect for observation. Bruce pretended to shut his eyes. Two could play at the subtle behaviour business. He saw Bill walk up to the house. He knew it was the right one from the plaque saying number 18, which was visible even at this distance. He also remembered its position clearly from his previous visit. To his surprise, before Bill reached the garden, a stranger came out of the front door carrying a dustbin liner full of rubbish. Bill and he had a brief conversation, and then Bill returned to the car. The man went back indoors.

"Well, I met him," Bill said. "Was he the man you remember?"

"No."

"I thought he might not be. I told him I was considering buying a house in this road, and asked if it was a quiet one. He assured me it was. I asked him if he knew of any impending building projects nearby, and he said no. He said he had lived here seven years, and had no problems with the area, so I thanked him very much and came away. I don't reckon Celia's supposed parents ever did live there. They probably borrowed the house for the evening, maybe without the owners' knowledge."

"There's one more thing to try." Bruce got out his phone and dialled Celia's number. As he expected, an impersonal voice said 'This number has been discontinued'. So that was that.

"I always did suspect they weren't her real parents," Bruce said, as they were driving back, "but I wanted to believe there was some future for Celia and me, so I did not like to admit to the thought. I've been such a fool, Bill. Will you take me in hand and sort me out, and get me back on the straight and narrow?"

"Of course," Bill said. "And don't worry about it. All of us often make mistakes."

At least this affair has had one good outcome, Bruce thought; it's brought Bill and me closer than ever before. But what I don't understand is, what was their motive for all that long interview?

35. From: Mission 12
To: Undisclosed recipients.
Sent:

Max is in charge now. As I don't yet know what he will want to do, I think we must take it that this will be my last email to you. It is a very hard moment for me. I really have cared for the ship. I have checked where I cleaned many times, and there is not the slightest trace of the sticky mess in the carpet round the operating chair. I have taken care, haven't I? I hate the idea of a caretaker who takes no care. I have tried. The others are saying that the mission is on course, and going well, which is very kind of them.

I am not finding things at all easy. It was lovely when it was just the two of us, and then when the children came along. But since the others woke, I feel we have lost something which will never return. I find it hard not to resent the others, which is horrible of me, because what I want to do is to welcome them, and help make their journey a happy one. I also feel scared about Celia. It was fine while it was just the two of us, but will she still want me now the rest of them are here? I think I may be going to be ill; I feel I am going down with something. I hope not; I hate being ill.

Anyway, it has been fun sending the emails. I hope you have enjoyed reading them. I would not have missed being part of this trip for anything. Celia has been wonderful. Oh yes, and little nimp sends his regards. Celia gave him back to me, because she could see I missed him. It was so kind of her. He is back in my pocket now, except when he is needed for the Limpets. Please give my love to everybody back home, and tell them, thanks for everything.

With kindest regards,
Your friend Bruce

PS. Some of you may be wondering how these
messages have got through, since we are so far
away, As I recall, they explained before launch
that the emails would go out with the regular
weekly report. Don't forget that whatever
problems we have here, shortage of energy is not
one of them. So the signal that leaves us is very
strong. At the precise moment that the message is
due, all the radio telescopes in the solar system
lock on to our position in the darkness, and the
technicians should be able to piece together the
message from the combined signal. I love the
technology, personally.

PPS I never mentioned it before, but my pet
name for the star where we are going is Umbelica.
I like to imagine how different nations back home
would pronounce it. Um-BEAR-lica, in the USA,
with a strong second syllable; um-be-li-ca! in
France, with every syllable having equal weight,
umbe-LI-qah somewhere in eastern Europe, and so
forth. But the other reason for the name is that
I think our journey through space is like an
umbilical chord, connecting the earth with the
new settlement, and Umbelica sounds a little like
umbilical. When a new baby is born, one of the
first actions is that the umbilical chord between
mother and baby is severed, and the baby becomes
a living soul. It is right that we should be
severed from you, but I hope it won't be just
yet. I miss you on earth!

PPSS The truth is, I'm finding it very hard to
end this message, because I don't want to go. But
I must. So this really is it. Goodbye, Goodbye! I
love you, and God bless.

It was eight o' clock the following Tuesday evening. Celia was due for a piano lesson in ten minutes. Bruce wondered whether she would turn up. If she did, he had things to say.

He put the kettle on, when the doorbell rang. She was never early, so who was this. The mafia? He wondered about putting the chain on the door, but then thought better of it. Let them come in. He felt ready to take on anybody. He opened the door.

Celia marched in. "Sorry I'm early," she said, "but I guess you will want to talk, and I ought to leave at the usual time to keep things looking right."

Bruce had to admire her cool. They went over to the piano.

"I think you owe me some explanations," he said calmly.

"What about?" said Celia.

This was too much for Bruce. "Oh, for dumping me on the moon, and messing around with my TV reception, putting me through hell that night, and generally deceiving me all along the line. Now let's see. No wonder there was a cheap offer on redoing the walls here; you wanted to put in bugging devices, to be able to spy on me, and tamper with the aerial. Oh yes, I've just got it; the building work at the school. That was to put in spying devices there too, wasn't it. We need to check up on little Bruce as to whether we can trust him. I wonder what the worldwide TV audience in millions has been for my piano lessons, when I thought I was in a one to one situation?" Bruce hated using sarcasm normally, but today he was beyond caring.

"Oh yes, and your delightful parents. How's your mum these days? And I hope your dad is keeping fit. And let me see, was it you on the moon at all, or was that Simone in the space suit all the time impersonating you? And let me see, what percentage of the world population knows that my defence mechanism for dealing with life is having daydreams in which I am the star performer?"

"Bruce, I am really sorry you got hurt." There were tears in her eyes. "I was always worried that it would all turn out to be painful for you. I hate this cloak and dagger stuff as much as you do, if you want to know. All these things weren't my decision; please believe me. Yes, you are right, it was Simone on the moon. But she was contracted to accompany you for the full fortnight. I was very upset when she walked out on you at the end of day one."

"I suppose I was unwilling to play her game during the journey up. Well I let her slaughter me at Scrabble; wasn't that enough?"

"Bruce, I know Simone quite well. She is incredibly gifted – you have already discovered that, but she finds relating to men extremely difficult. They tend to run a mile. Here was a sensitive, caring…"

"Don't try and soothe me with sweet words. I'm feeling too upset. At least, don't try yet. But about Simone; I am not 'men', the universal class of the male species, but just one man, and to relate to me, all she had to do was treat me with respect. That changing chairs trick was too fast for me; a lot of other men might have got on fine with it. I wish now that I had had the presence of mind to sit in her chair, and then had the skill to talk to her about what was happening. So I failed her as much as she failed me. Will you tell her that I'm sorry?"

"Yes of course."

"Was it her idea to get the tickets issued so that we were in adjacent seats?"

"Yes. When I heard about it later, I knew it would have put you off. Softly softly, catchee monkey, as the saying goes. Not that I think…" Celia broke off when she realised from Bruce's face that she did not need to finish her sentence.

"Well, give her my best wishes, and tell her it was a pleasure being beaten at Scrabble by somebody so gifted."

This was ridiculous, and Bruce knew it. Here he was, trying to be so angry about all the treatment he had received from the Dark Side of the Force – cloak and dagger people seemed too mild a description for them now, and all he could do was end up worrying that someone else should have been hurt by him. Oh well, perhaps it was not a bad fault, this concern that everybody else should be alright.

"But why all this performance last night?" Bruce asked.

"It was for your own protection. You have successfully penetrated the sky-wear circle, as we guessed you would. What we can do now is to edit the video, removing all reference to the supposed explosion, and then we have a record of you shaking and trembling in abject terror of the authorities, presumably because of something bad you have done. That can be allowed to fall into their hands, if it seems helpful. It will reassure them that you are not a squeaky clean government agent but really are no more than you appear to be; a good background pianist. Did you know Jim Pond studied at a music college in his youth?"

This was news to Bruce.

"I probably ought not to have told you, and let you discover for yourself. Now, your instructions stay as they were. Simply carry on as normal. Be yourself. You have already shown what you think of piles of wealth being hoarded without thought for the poor. They know where you stand. Just love them, Bruce; there is nothing in the universe more powerful than love. And listen, stick by what I told you before; just trust me!"

But Bruce still had a lot of questions.

"One moment. Let's just go back to Simone for a moment. Are you telling me that her job was to convince me that she was you for a whole fortnight? What chance had she got of doing that? Or was I meant to find out, and fall for her instead, or what?"

"Bruce, I was unhappy about it. I felt we should honour our promise to you that I would go, but the others said it was too risky. Simone happened to discover what was afoot, and when she heard what sort of a person you were, she begged to be allowed to stand in for me. I opposed it, but I was over-ruled. I thought she would be too pushy. Having you in the adjacent seat was crazy. And then, when her overture did not work, she went all huffy. She should never have been allowed to go. It would have been better to tell you that you were to go on your own instead."

"I see. Yes, adjacent seats was a bit much. Also, I think that word 'conquest' may have gone to her head. Perhaps she should have sat diagonally opposite from me instead."

Bruce said this looking Celia in the face. She coloured.

"Yes, I was planted close to you in the train, to try and attract you. My boss planned it. I'm sorry, Bruce. Look, however, this whole thing started, I want you to know that I do care about you. Now, please, trust me!"

"But why did you pick on me?"

"We spotted you playing background piano in the shopping centre."

This was a revelation to Bruce. "I've finally got it. I could never understand why an unknown piano teacher could possibly be of assistance to whatever your organisation is. I see now. It's strange," he continued, "because I was pretty certain that none of the little cards I dotted around the place had been taken."

For the first time since he had known her, Celia became agitated. "What sort of incompetent nit-wit do you take me for? Do you think I am so unprofessional that I would actually take one of your horrid little cards?"

Bruce was taken aback. "Look, I'm sorry. I did not mean to upset you. Now that you mention it, of course you would only note the details without actually taking a card. I am sorry. I'm not used to the way of thinking, to be honest. It's all a bit beyond me."

This was the first time that he had seen Celia express any emotion. It was good to know that she had feelings. From her replies, it did seem possible that she was an ally. Perhaps there was some chance of a relationship after all.

"There's one more thing. If you hate the cloak and dagger business, as you say, then why are you in it?"

"It's my way of trying to fight for right in the world. At times, the things I am asked to do are unpleasant, but the aim of it all is to do good. Believe me. You and I have a lot in common; we both want the world to be a better place."

Bruce was silent for a few moments. His mind was in a whirl. He still did not feel satisfied about last night; they had gone to such incredible lengths to get that video of him. But then, it was already clear that they had plenty of resources. Arranging for him to win the moon trip in the raffle had been no problem. Perhaps creating personalised news bulletins on people's TV sets was the kind of thing they did every day. Maybe it was simply the case that he had no experience of how such people operate. Then he spoke.

"And what about you and me? Is a piano teacher allowed to date one of his pupils?"

"Bruce, it seems to me that you have about five girls on the go, and what you need to do is to decide which direction you are looking in. You can tell me the answer to that at a future lesson."

Five girls seemed a massive overstatement to Bruce, but that was all he could get out of her on the subject. However, she did have one other thing to say.

"You are very conscious of ways in which we have let you down, but are you aware that you have not kept your side of the bargain either?"

This was news to Bruce. "What do you mean?"

"You agreed to be inconspicuous and keep your head down. You then gain access to the money men to play background piano, and what do you do? You make a scene which puts you firmly in the limelight. Probably the only thing those people will remember from that party was the pianist who spoke his mind. It will be the main subject of conversation all over London for a year."

Bruce had not thought of this. It was his turn to colour. He clapped his hand to his face.

"Oh dear, what a mess I've made. I'm so sorry. I had not seen it like that."

"I think in fact it may prove to be the best thing that could have happened. It was so obviously a speech from the heart that people now know where you stand, and will feel safe with you. So don't worry about it. It has turned out well. In fact, you are in a prime position to be able to help us."

They left it at that. Bruce still had a lot to think about, but it could wait. They carried on with the lesson. Her progress since the last time was wonderful to see. Simone is not the only gifted one round here, Bruce thought, as he stood at his front door and watched her walk off down the path to the road. Ten minutes later, he remembered that he had not asked her for her new phone number. That was a nuisance. Never mind.

36. From: Mission 12
To: Undisclosed recipients.
Sent:

Sorry, me again.
Just to say, did you know that in Greek,
Margaret means 'Pearl'? It comes in Revelation
chapter twenty-one. The heavenly city has twelve
gates, each made from a single jewel, and
Margaret is one of them. Such a lovely name.
I am hoping to get to the heavenly city myself
one day.
Bruce

Next morning, Bruce set off up the road towards the post box, with two letters in his hand. It was a beautiful sunny day. He had a sense that this moment of peace and quiet was only a lull between storms, so he was making a point of enjoying his surroundings. The white fluffy clouds were beautiful, if you made a point of looking at them. There was something reassuring about having the chance to stroll to the post box and back without somebody making a scene over it. Make the most of it while you can!

It was fascinating how the pundits had been proved wrong. Everyone had predicted the end of snail mail with the arrival of electronic mail, but they had not reckoned on the abuses that would be made of the new method of communication. Why is it that everything new and good has to be spoiled, Bruce wondered? The fact was that a hand-written letter was now once again the main means of getting in touch, if you wanted to show someone that you cared.

His first letter was a reply to Jim's letter, which had come that morning. Bruce had not known such high quality paper existed. He had felt he was committing an offence simply by opening the envelope, despite using a sharp knife so as not to tear it. The contents had been simple. Jim had been so impressed with Bruce's speech that he had set up a standing order to Water Aid for twenty pounds a month. He thought Bruce would like to know.

At first, Bruce had wondered whether this was yet another person trying to make fun of him. Twenty pounds a month? Why, the man could probably have given twenty pounds a minute without missing it. His first reaction had been to become angry. But after a few minutes, he sobered up. Jim probably had no idea about generosity, and for him, this small step might well be the start of something bigger to come. This was not a moment for pouring cold water on a well-meaning first effort.

It seemed better to take the letter at its face value. Here was a contribution towards the cause he had spoken about.

Bruce had replied thanking him for letting him know, thanking him for the chance to play once again, and apologising for any embarrassment his outburst might have caused. Always reply to letters, his granddad had taught him, and after having had so many of his own letters not replied to, Bruce felt more than ever the wisdom of this advice. Besides, the truth was that he had liked Jim, and felt an immediate bond with him when they had first met.

It had been an extraordinary few months, he reflected, as he strode along. Bill and Gnilla had been decisive. They were going to be married. They were currently enjoying their holiday in France. The wedding day had been fixed; Bruce was to be the best man.

He himself felt he was no nearer finding a life partner. Celia's massive overstatement that he had five girls was absurd. He had not managed to date a single one. Still, he had made a few new friends. It was hopeless even thinking about Araminta. He hoped she was alright. Flossie, well maybe he had been a bit hasty there. Then Simone might not be a complete write-off. At least she was interested in him. Sarah was nice too, now that she had got to know him a little. Then maybe Celia herself could be persuaded after all. Yes, perhaps it was five when he totted them up. Maybe one of them might turn up trumps. To be honest, he felt rather bemused by the whole business.

Oh yes, there was Leila too, as he called her – the girl at the Tate. He had named her in memory of the golden syrup tin his granddad used to have on the table at tea-time, for three reasons. The tin was made by Tate and Lyle, a shortened version of Leila;

241

she was sweet, and her straggly brown hair reminded him of the mane of the lion pictured on the tin. Shame she was already taken, really.

He was still very uncertain about this cloak and dagger stuff, but Jim Pond seemed nice enough. He would not mind seeing him again. It was a shame about the sky-flying; he would like to have taken it further, really, but felt he had better not as that was what he had agreed.

All things considered, life was pretty difficult. The easy thing was to feel upset, but it was no use moaning. Chin up!

He was nearly at the post box. The second letter was an instruction to his bank to increase his own standing order to Water Aid to two hundred pounds a month. He reckoned he could just about afford it. Maybe his own life was destined to be full of pain for the foreseeable future; he had had more than his fair share recently, but at least he could try and relieve some of the misery of others in the world. This money would help. This was what he was telling himself as he reached the box and thrust the letters firmly in.

No room for second thoughts now. Really, he had no regrets about sending off the standing order. It was good to be decisive. Anyway, there was no way he was going to be beaten by a multi-billionaire!

Part the Second

Don't Shoot the Pianist

Synopsis

In Part the First, we discovered Bruce Winter to be a man of resource, integrity and sensitive musicianship. An unlikely recruit to the secret service, he obeyed his instructions to the letter, which were that he was to do nothing. As a result, he soon found himself on first name terms with Jim Pond, the man behind anti-gravity, whose sky-suits and sky-cars were revolutionising society. However, despite a life full of incident, not all of it pleasant, our hero is still no nearer his goal of making it to the altar with the girl of his choice. Life is rather more successful in his daydreams, where he is the caretaker of Mission 12, a spaceship on its way to another star. However, here too he is beset with problems, some of which are of his own making. Never mind.

-oOo-

"Hello Sir!"
"Hello Sir!"
Bruce Winter looked up from his magazine with a jerk. It was the two twelve-year-old scamps, Beccy and Simna, who had their keyboard lesson at 0910 on Thursdays. Beccy always reminded Bruce of the Daughters of Jerusalem in the Song of Songs, because like them she was dark but lovely. Not that he would ever have told her so.

"Hello Beccy, Hello Simna. What are you doing in the dentist's waiting room?"

"Simna's chipped a tooth, and I'm here to look after her 'cos her mum's at work. Look!"

Simna was already opening her mouth wide, and Beccy pointed vigorously at one side of it. Bruce peered in, then shook his head.

"I can't see anything, but I'll take your word for it. Your teeth look lovely to me, like a set of piano keys. I hope the dentist sorts you out."

"What about you, sir?"

"I'm having a crown fitted. It's my third visit. On the first two, he drilled for ages, as if he was prospecting for oil. I'm hoping that today it's just a case of having the crown itself put on. I've had enough drilling to last a lifetime."

"Sounds ghastly, sir. Tough luck."

This was the moment for something lighter.

"Look, do you two know how to play the National Anthem on your teeth?"

Naturally their musical education fell short in this respect, so Bruce showed them how to tap their central tooth with a fingernail, altering the size of the mouth cavity to create the rising and falling of the notes. They were soon performing in unison. But before they could proceed to three part harmony, Bruce was called through. Perhaps it was just as well; this was a dentist, not a barber's shop.

"See you a week on Thursday, sir!" the girls chorused. The autumn term was almost upon them.

Bruce went in. The dentist was his friend Stephe; Bruce taught his son Mark the piano. Bruce did not need to be reminded of the embarrassing time two months earlier when he had rung at four in the morning to cancel Mark's piano lesson. Bruce had been feeling very upset, which was why he had not been aware of the unearthly hour. Stephe had been most understanding.

"Bruce, nice to see you. Now, how are you?"

Stephe looked concerned as usual. It was hardly surprising. Bruce had woken suddenly in the night feeling very worked up about what had happened to his parents on the day of the terrible argument, when he was taken from them to his granddad's house as a five year old. From that day on, Bruce had never seen his parents again, nor Sasha his sister. His granddad had refused to talk about it. Now Granddad was long dead, and there was no more opportunity to find out what had happened. However, Bruce had suddenly taken it into his head to check the death certificates at the

Family Records Centre, to see if one of his parents had killed the other; hence the cancelled piano lesson. It was all rather crazy, really. Stephe now had serious doubts about Bruce's sanity, as a result of the nocturnal call.

"You really must learn to chill out," Stephe urged, in response to Bruce's mumblings. This was monstrous; how could Bruce possibly relax in the dentist's chair? His hands gripped the armrests, as if he was on a fairground ride. Even the Pirate Ship would be preferable to this. Come to think of it, pirates were interested in crowns too, but pirates did not attack the sea bed in order to get them. Rape and pillage was more their line, Bruce thought, not that he knew much about it, but it might have been generally preferable to this.

But Stephe was saying something. What was it?

"…a little wider, please."

Bruce 'ope'd his ponderous and marble jaws' as Shakespeare had so neatly put it, fixed his gaze on a slight imperfection on the ceiling, and tried to think of something else.

```
37. From: Mission 12
To: Undisclosed recipients
Sent:

You'll never guess. There are several exciting
things to report. But the main one, from your
point of view, is that following the upheavals
over new management, instead of being out of a
job, I have been put back in charge of emailing
back to you at home. I imagined that there would
be a lot of competition for this role, but it
seems that nobody else wants it. In fact, they
don't appear to mind whether we send messages
back to earth or not. I find this extraordinary.
How are you going to learn from our mistakes
unless we send you word of what we are doing?
There might even be some successes to tell you
about, but to be honest, I have changed my
perspective on this. I'm sorry to say it, as it
```

sounds rather bad, but the fact is that when it comes down to it, I don't have much confidence in the others. I feel rather worried, actually. Anyway, it's really nice that I can go on sending you progress reports. Or regress reports, if they turn out that way.

I'd better explain the situation for readers who have only joined the list recently. It's not good. When we left earth, I was the caretaker of Mission 12, setting off on its epic sixty-nine year journey to another star system. The twenty-four astronauts were put in hibernation before launch. However, the truth is that I got so lonely that I de-hibernated a lady astronaut named Celia, whose eyes I had seen through the little glass window, and asked her to marry me. She was not very pleased at first, but we soon fell deeply in love, so that dealt with that hiccough. She is blonde and very beautiful, by the way. However, our boy Max has a mind of his own, and he woke another eight more astronauts so that they could have babies for him and his sister Clairie to marry. Needless to say I was not consulted! The eight rewarded him by making him the commander of the mission. So I have handed over the direction to my son! Then it turned out that the mission timings were so badly out that rather than being decades away, as we thought, we are due to arrive at the star system in less than four years. So all in all, although some things have gone a bit haywire, it might turn out well enough in the end.

The first news I want to tell you is a discussion about our speed that we had a while back.

I wanted to raise the subject with Paul, if I could. Of the four men woken so far, he is the quiet, thoughtful one. I was hoping to do it when Mark was not around, as to be honest, I find him rather difficult. Anyway, one afternoon when I had finished cleaning for the day, I saw my chance. I asked Paul if he would like to join me for a cup of tea in the gyp room.

When we both had a cup in our hands, I spoke up.

"Paul, you know that nothing travels faster than light?"

"That's right."

"Well, promise not to make fun of me, but I'm wondering about it. Do you know much about Einstein's theory of relativity?"

"Let's just say I'm listening!" Paul said, with a twinkle in his eye.

"Okay. Well, if you study the universe, I agree that you won't see anything moving faster than light. But I've realised, that's because everything you look at is coasting. That is, it had a burst of energy to get it going, but once it's on its way, it does not speed up; it just coasts along. Okay so far?"

Paul nodded.

"Right. Well, we humans have invented rockets, which not only get going when they set off, but which can also accelerate as they travel."

Paul nodded again. I told you he was the quiet type.

"Right, now imagine us going through the vacuum of space. We reached ninety-eight percent of the speed of light a while back, and now we are coasting. Have been for a year or two, in fact. Now, when light leaves us, it does so at the speed of light, doesn't it?"

"Yes," said Paul.

"Well, what I want to know is, if light can set off forwards from where we are at that huge speed, then why can't we fire our motors and go a bit quicker ourselves?"

"I'm sorry, I haven't a clue," Paul said, rising to his feet. Before I could stop him, he was opening the door saying, "I'll have to get

247

one of the others. PHIL!" he bellowed. Well, at
least it wasn't Mark.

Phil shot in to the room as if he had been
stung by a bee.

"What's happened," he said anxiously.

"Bruce reckons we can go faster than light."

"Oh Bruce! Nothing can go faster than light."

I winced. "Yes, yes, I know." Phil sat down,
and I told him what I had said to Paul.

"Right. Well the problem is that in the theory
of relativity, for the laws of motion to hold,
and momentum to be conserved, etc. it turns out
that the mass of an object is NOT a constant. It
has to obey this equation: $m = m_o / sqrt(1 - v^2/c^2)$."

I winced again. I always feel defensive when
people start bandying equations around. I dimly
heard Phil explaining that 'm' was the real mass
of the object when moving; 'mo' = the mass of the
object when it is not moving relative to you; 'v'
was the velocity of the object relative to you,
and 'c' was the speed of light. He also said that
sqrt meant the square root. I tried to look wise
and interested.

He went on, "Now, $1 / sqrt (1 - v^2/c^2)$ tends
to 1 divided by zero, as v tends to c. 1 divided
by zero tends to infinity. So the mass of the
object tends to infinity as its velocity nears
the speed of light. This means that it gets
harder and harder to accelerate it. In fact, at
the speed of light, when you have infinite mass,
you would need infinite energy to make yourself
go any faster, which means in practice that you
can't do it. Sorry. The speed of light is the
speed limit. End of story."

I had to admit it was impressive. I always
admire mathematicians. But I was not going to be
put off.

"Okay, I'm sure you understand all that, even
though it leaves me breathless. But I want to

check some things out. You said all this was true in the theory of relativity. As I understand it, the theory is so-called because speed is always measured relative to something else."

It seemed that I was correct in this. I felt a little bolder.

"Well suppose we are going at 98% of the speed of light as seen from the earth. Our engines have been off for a while, and we are coasting along. We are now in the hard vacuum of outer space. Why do we still have to compare our speed to earth? Suppose it is many light years away by now. Can't we measure our speed relative to where we are? Looked at from where we are now, we are hovering in empty space miles from anywhere. I don't see why we can't start the engines and get moving."

"Well, that's very interesting, Bruce. What you are effectively asking is, what decides what is local, because talk of speed only makes sense in a local setting. I think we need help here."

To my horror, he too was rising and going to the door. "MARK!" he yelled, before I could stop him.

Mark came in, was told of my ideas, gave me a brief disdainful glance and immediately said "Nothing can go faster than light." It's like a kind of mantra, really. I suppose I was stupid to question it.

I'm afraid I am something of a coward at times. I made an excuse and left them to it. But I can say one thing - they were hard at it for over an hour. Also, I think I may be onto something, because Big Nimp - that's the ship's computer, by the way - has just told us that instead of there being forty-one months to go before we arrive, there are only eleven months, and that we will have to go back to two gees at night from tonight. This is a definite change of plan, as he told us earlier that it would not happen for a year or two yet. So I think that those who

planned this mission did not understand all this
relativity stuff as well as they thought they
did, and the computer has had to adjust our
flight plan because we got here quicker than
expected. However, I'm probably wrong!
   One good thing came out of it; Phil and I are
becoming friends. I can tell.
   Be in touch again soon.
   Bruce

"All done," said Stephe, cheerfully.

Bruce was astonished.

"Really?"

"Yes, that's fitted on nicely. Treat it carefully for the first few days. See you in six months for a check-up."

Bruce needed no further encouragement to leave. He gathered up his coat, signed the exit visa in two places, and paid for his treatment with relish.

"Mark loves his lessons, you know. He thinks you're a great teacher."

Bruce was pleased. "He's making progress. His rhythm needs work, but the reading of the notes is coming nicely. See you."

"Bye."

It seemed a kindness to look into the waiting room. Simna had gone through, but Beccy was still there.

"Let off with a caution," Bruce whispered, with a piratical wink. "See you."

"Bye sir."

When he got home, he looked in the mirror. He could not even see which tooth was the crown. The colour was a good match. Just then, the phone rang. It was his friend Bill.

"Bruce, hello. Gnilla and I were wondering if we could come round to talk about the music."

"Of course. Wednesday evening?"

"Fine. See you at eight."

Bruce and Bill had met at the church, and had become friends. Now Bill was finally taking the plunge. Oh dear, walking the plank reminded Bruce of the dentist. Try and forget about it. It was over now!

The wedding was just a few days off. Bruce was to be the Best Man, but also had to double as the organist at the last minute, because the man they had booked had fallen sick, so Bruce was to play instead. It had crossed Bruce's mind that somebody might have bribed the organist to take gardening leave, because Gnilla had been delighted when she heard that Bruce was to play after all. Originally, it had been decided that the Best Man could not play the organ as well, but that seemed to have gone by the board now, even though Bruce had warned that he might drop the rings down among the organ pedals by mistake. Gnilla had arranged that he should put them in the right hand pocket of his hired suit the night before to be on the safe side.

Bruce was not as happy on the organ as he was on the piano. He had never really mastered the pedal board to his satisfaction. However, he was good for funerals and the occasional wedding. The triumph of his organ playing career had been the time when he had played in Bristol Cathedral. The approach to the organ loft alone had been impressive; up fourteen wooden steps, then duck in through the ranks of pipes and step out onto the little balcony before squeezing onto the bench in front of the multiple keyboards. The organ console was covered with stops, the levers that opened and shut the different ranks of pipes, altering the sound. It had been wonderful playing at full volume, with almost every stop out; the whole area trembled and shook with the sound. It had felt as if he was riding a motorbike.

This occasion would be much more relaxed. The organ was minute by comparison. Still, it would be good fun.

When they came on Wednesday, Gnilla brought her usual armful of flowers for Bruce. She worked at a florist's shop. In fact, to save trouble and expense, the reception was actually being held at the florist. A marquee would be put up in the garden at the back, and the shop would be closed to customers from noon. Bruce was not sure about the wisdom of this, but Bill and Gnilla were both

251

very committed to the idea, and it did have the advantage of being novel.

"Well, not long to go now," said Bruce, when they were seated with a coffee. "It's come round quickly."

"I know," said Bill. "I feel a bit nervous, actually."

"Why dear?" Gnilla asked.

"You'll be fine," Bruce insisted. "In fact, I'm glad you're nervous, because it gives me the chance to prop you up. If you were totally put together, I'd feel cheated."

"I feel concerned about you, Bruce," Gnilla said. "We'll have to find somebody for you."

Bruce was only too aware of the gap in his life. So far, all his attempts to find a girl to share his pilgrimage with had come to nothing, even though there had been several around that had looked promising. Still, nothing had come to fruition as yet.

"Actually, things are getting worse by the day," Bruce said. "I spotted a grey hair in the mirror this morning."

"Oh Bruce! Where?" Gnilla asked, with great concern. "Can I see?"

Bruce made a half-hearted protest, but Gnilla ignored it, and came and stood behind his armchair. She bent over anxiously, and began parting his hair this way and that. Bruce found the movement of her fingers curiously agreeable.

"Here. Let me look," said Bill. He came over to join in. Bruce wondered whether he felt a little uncomfortable with the close attention Gnilla was paying him. Bill's fingers were stubby and rough by comparison. They both searched for a minute or two, while Bruce sat patiently, trying to keep his head as still as possible, as the hairdresser had insisted when he was little. "Keep still, Bruce!" the man had said, and Bruce had done so, ever since, when the situation required it.

"There's nothing there," Bill declared finally. "It's a wild goose chase. Complete waste of time." They returned to their seats. Now it was Bruce's turn.

"What about you, Bill? Have you started going grey? May I check?"

Bill was not amused, but Bruce was not to be put off. Gnilla and he were soon poring over Bill's scalp from behind. Bill had a small bald patch on the crown of his head; by unspoken agreement, this was never referred to. On impulse, Bruce suddenly bent over and kissed it.

"Not now," said Bill, gruffly.

For a moment, Bruce thought that Gnilla would be able to control her desire to laugh, but this proved premature. She could not help herself. She exploded with a shriek of laughter, clutching her sides.

Bill twisted his head round, in total puzzlement. "Here, what's going on?" he demanded.

"Best Man's privilege," laughed Bruce. "Don't worry, no grey hair in sight."

Bill was not very pleased, but Bruce and Gnilla were so obviously enjoying the joke that he soon relented.

"I'll give you Best Man's privilege," he grumbled. "Anyway, don't worry. We'll get you fixed up before long. Now, what about this music?"

They soon settled on Purcell's Trumpet Tune for coming in, and Mendelssohn's Wedding March for going out. Bruce was to improvise on the piano during the signing of the register, with a special emphasis on the well-known tune from Finlandia by Sibelius, because Gnilla was from Sweden originally. Bruce offered the whole of Sibelius' fifth symphony if they wanted, but when they grasped how long it was, they turned it down.

"Have it over loudspeakers at the reception," Bill suggested, so they decided they would.

"Is it danceable?" Gnilla asked.

Bruce declared that it was out of the question. Gnilla was a little disappointed. Bill and Bruce had managed to keep it a secret that a steel band had been booked. Bruce had enjoyed the puzzled look on the band's faces when Bill had asked them if they could play in a Swedish style. They said they only knew the sounds of Barbados. Bill said that was fine, "as long as it's danceable." That would be no problem, they insisted.

It was time to go. "No more talk about grey hairs," Bill said. "See you Saturday."

"Bye."

38. From: Mission 12
To: Undisclosed recipients
Sent:

I'm rather enjoying playing devil's advocate over the speed of light. I had another go at it this week.

"Phil," I said, trying to sound as nonchalant as possible, when we happened to be sitting with a cup of tea in our hands, "there's another thing about the speed of light that I don't understand."

Phil gave me one of his 'not-you-again' looks. Friendly, not hostile.

I continued.

"You know the galaxy rotates about the central point?"

"Yes. It takes three hundred million years to do a circuit."

"What, as long as that?" asked Sandra, who had just joined us. She's always good for a cup of tea. "I thought it only took a few months, like in the song, 'Come on, let's twist again, like we did last summer.' Bruce, you play it for us. Paul, come and do the galactic shuffle."

So much for our learned discussion. I hammered out the tune on the piano while Paul and Sandra did their pirouetting and their does-y-does (how do you spell that? Dozy Doze?) Paul may be the quiet type, but I think there's something going on between those two. It's more than just a shared interest in ballroom dancing. He's a dark horse.

When we had regained our seats, I pressed on with my question.

"Okay, so here's the galaxy doing a slow spin."
I demonstrated with the tea cup. "Now, imagine a
spacecraft in the galaxy travelling at nearly the
speed of light compared to the local stars. If it
goes this way, in the direction of the galactic
spin, an observer over here in a neighbouring
galaxy, say the Large Magellanic Cloud, will see
it as travelling faster than light, won't he?"

"Yes."

"But if it went the other way round the galaxy,
then it would appear to be going slower."

"Yes, that's right."

"So is there some underpaid official up here
looking down on us all," - I pointed above the
cup with my fingers, "dressed in a white coat and
holding a clipboard, who says 'Aha - we'll have
to put the brakes on this spacecraft. It can't go
any faster than light.'"

"Don't be silly."

"Believe me, I'm not. I'm trying to point out
that in Einstein's lecture theatre, there's no
fixed background against which speeds are
measured. So a spacecraft could be going at the
speed of light according to one observer, whereas
to another it might be hardly moving at all. So,
as it is so hard to establish what its speed
really is, it seems to me that there's nothing to
prevent it from accelerating."

"Well, Bruce, I'm sure you're wrong, but I
can't explain why. I don't know enough about it.
But if you were right, then it would make time
travel possible, which seems to be impossible."

"Exactly, Phil. But look here. This whole
relativity business goes against common sense,
doesn't it?"

"Yes, it does."

"Well, why hang back, then? It's already been
shown that time is affected by a strong
gravitational field. If you hover close to a
neutron star, or a black hole for a while, the

rest of the universe would experience time passing more quickly than you would. So time travel exists anyway; therefore, I don't think we should rule out travelling faster than light because of worries about time travel."

"You're enjoying this, aren't you Bruce. You don't have a clue what you are talking about, but you like putting questions to those of us who think we do know, to see how far our knowledge really extends."

"Precisely, Phil. It's good fun. But seriously, I'm not going to agree that travelling faster than light is impossible until it's been tried. I think that sooner or later, mankind should launch a mission with the sole intention of discovering just how fast it could go."

"Well, I'm not volunteering to go, Bruce, and I hope you won't either, because I like you. You make me laugh."

"Let's form an alliance, then. In fact, an exclusive club, where the main emphasis is on eating and drinking. What about calling ourselves the Sceptics' Superluminary Supper Society?"

"Phew, that's a mouthful," he said. I groaned appreciatively. "It sounds like a recipe for indigestion to me, gulping the food down as fast as possible. But if I'm allowed bacon and eggs, perhaps I'll join."

Phil is a keen advocate of the all-day breakfast, starting first thing and lasting most of the day, ideally, with endless refills of coffee, if he can find someone to serve him - generally me. I like Phil. He's a real character.

"All right, Phil, bacon and eggs it is."

Bruce

The wedding day came at last. All week, Bill, Gnilla and Bruce had been anxiously watching the weather forecasts. Saturday had promised to be fine, weather-wise, which would help the day go with a swing. In the event, Bruce woke to full sun and a clear sky. He was pleased for them both.

He was just finishing breakfast when the phone rang. It was Jim Pond, the multi-billionaire whose company Skywear marketed the sky-suit. Bruce had taken one flying lesson, egged on by Araminta Foster, one of his piano pupils at the school, and thoroughly enjoyed it. He had quickly grasped how to point decisively with his fingers, and whiz through the air as a result. However, he had not attempted any of the advanced moves like loop the loop and formation flying that Araminta and her friends did.

Bruce had met Jim as a result of playing background piano at the Henley Regatta, through the offices of his second cousin Banjo. This was not her real name, naturally! But Bancesca, with its unwritten G after the N, was so hard to pronounce. Jim had subsequently invited him to play background piano at his penthouse flat in West London.

This phone call proved to be another invitation to play, a week today, again at Jim's flat, but to a much smaller gathering, and at the earlier time of 5 p.m., with apologies for the late notice. Bruce was pleased to accept. He liked Jim. It would be something to look forward to.

The time of the wedding had been fixed for 1130. There were several reasons for this: the guests coming from a distance could get there comfortably, the shop could do a morning's trading, people would be naturally ready to eat at around 1.30, and, although Gnilla did not know this, there would be plenty long enough for the steel band and the dancing before Bill and Gnilla would leave in the latest sky-car for a mystery honeymoon. The vertical take-off of the sky-cars was still novel enough to feel special. Sibelius' 5th Symphony through loudspeakers had been quietly dropped from the proceedings. On reflection, Bruce had felt it was not quite right.

Things got off to a good start. Bill was at the church in good time, and Bruce was able to park him in his pew and mop his brow before making his way over to the organ console. While the guests were arriving he played the March from the Serenade for Strings by Dag Wiren, a Swedish composer. This was a cheerful piece that

Bruce had once heard on the radio. He had missed the title, but undaunted, he had gone to a big record store in London. To the amusement of the other shoppers, Bruce had sung the tune to the various shop assistants, hoping they might recognise it. Eventually one of them did, and managed to produce a disc with the music on, to Bruce's delight. It turned out to be rather expensive, but it seemed rather churlish not to buy one after all their trouble. He hoped the rest of the music on it would be appealing, as well as the Dag Wiren.

As Bruce struggled to give a faithful rendering of it, he wondered how many of the guests would actually recognise it. Probably none. Never mind, he had done his best.

When it came to the promises, Bruce felt very moved, as he usually did on hearing wedding vows. The life-long commitment meant so much! Bruce hoped very much that things would go well for them.

He thundered out the wedding march at the end, with no cuts; Bruce hated cuts. One of his granddad's few faults had been his view that Wagner's operas were too long, and needed the red pencil. It was true that Bruce had once nodded off during Act One of a performance of The Mastersingers at Covent Garden, and come to with a jerk about twenty minutes later. To his surprise, the same people were on stage, singing in the same manner and style; even the key of the music seemed to be unchanged. He appeared to have missed nothing. Nevertheless, Bruce remained firmly against cuts. He was not quite so rigid about repeats, but on the whole he followed the dictum 'repeats are to be played, not argued over.' The whole idea of performing music was to be faithful to the composer's wishes. Who was he compared to Beethoven or Bach? Or compared to Dag Wiren come to that. Play the music as the composer wanted it.

The florist's shop was a short walk. Bruce was the last to arrive. Every effort had been made to do the couple proud. He had to duck under netting to get in, and then force his way through a thicket of bamboo, which soon gave way to long-leaved ferns and various semi-tropical shrubs with huge leaves that Bruce had never seen before. The heating was on high, and there was a steamy atmosphere. In addition, brightly coloured tropical birds flew this way and that through the creepers and fronds, emitting piercing cries. One narrowly missed Bruce's head. It was wonderful. Presumably all the greenery would sell over the following week or so. It was a great idea. How they had managed to get it in place during the few minutes available after twelve Bruce had no idea.

Suddenly, there was Bill advancing towards him, covered with smiles, come to look for him.

"Doctor Livingstone, I presume!" said Bruce. Bill laughed. "And don't tell me," Bruce continued, "this jungle means that you're honeymooning in Goa because Gnilla's a real goer."

Bill laughed again. "No we're not, and don't try to worm it out of me. I know you!"

"Aha, must be Wormwood Scrubbs then," laughed Bruce. It was great to see Bill looking so happy.

"Come on through."

They forced a way through to the marquee. The normal contents of the shop had made their way out here in omnia unnumbered pots, it seemed to Bruce, who was definitely in a mood for quoting Shakespeare, for some unaccountable reason. In between, there were three or four round tables, with guests seated in nines round them. It was all rather cramped, Bruce thought, but who cared about that. To Bruce's horror, they all applauded when Bill brought him in. This was dreadful. It was Bill and Gnilla's day, not his. But everyone insisted that his music had been wonderful.

The meal went well, and all too soon it was time for the speeches. Bruce had been dreading this, but he need not have worried. When he rose to call on Bill to say something, Bill cut him short and said he could not abide speeches, and in addition there was no way he was having Bruce telling embarrassing stories about him.

"So here's to the sweetest girl in the world," Bill declared, and everyone drank to Gnilla who tried not to blush but failed miserably.

Then to Gnilla's consternation, people came in and started stacking the chairs and tables, once they had been cleared of crocs. Then about a dozen young men struggled in with what looked like a small tree trunk, but which turned out to be a rolled-up dance floor. Gnilla was thrilled when half a dozen steel drums were carried in, and the performers quickly got to work. Bruce announced that the rules of engagement were that everybody had to dance with every member of the opposite sex in the marquee during the afternoon, which tickled some of the older guests, and then they got down to some serious footwork.

All too soon, it was time for the couple to leave. To general astonishment, a section of the ceiling of the marquee was unzipped, and a sky-car descended ever so slowly, until it was hovering a foot above the dance floor, all by remote control, as there was nobody inside it. Then, after prolonged farewells and embracings and the like, Bruce handed Gnilla into the passenger seat, thumped Bill on the back in no uncertain manner, and pushed him into the driving seat.

Bill made a great show of checking various lights and levers, but Bruce knew that all he needed to do was to push the auto button once, as the route was pre-programmed in. After a few moments, Bill did this in such a way as to give the game away. Everyone laughed. The doors closed, and the vehicle began to sail majestically straight upwards into the air. Everyone clapped and cheered. Bruce had been determined not to cry this afternoon, but he could not help a few tears forming in his eyes. He was so pleased for Bill and Gnilla. Really, he thought, I must stop getting so emotional about things. Try to enjoy life!

```
39. From: Mission 12
To: Undisclosed recipients
Sent:
```

```
We have reached an interesting moment in the
mission. Up to now, the best data about our
destination has been what was gathered by the
huge telescopes in the solar system before we
```

left. The instruments we have on board are much smaller, naturally. However, at a certain stage as we approach the star, our puny light buckets will start to out-perform your ones all those light-years off, for all their high resolution.

Well, you know what happened this week without me having to tell you. The on-board telescope was tried, and surprise, surprise, it needs some maintenance, and guess who everybody looked at when Big Nimp said someone would have to go walkabout on the end of a line to fix it. I think the phrase he used was ex-vehicular. It sounds like a medical complaint.

Alright, so I'm the caretaker. But does that mean that every time there's a mouldy old job that nobody else wants to do, it always falls to me? I think it's a bit rough.

Phil's a good bloke. He sensed what I was feeling, and offered to come out there with me to keep me company. That helps make it a fun outing, to be honest.

Actually, I am interested to see the ship from outside, and I really don't mind doing it at all. It's just the principle I don't much appreciate.

Anyway, here we are, wrapped up like presents dangling on a Christmas tree, making for the exit. There are five sets of doors, to preserve the airlock. Three down, two to go.

I know it's Phil from his voice in my headphones, but that's the end of any likeness. Frankly I feel the design of these spacesuits has really lagged behind. They are so baggy. We need something thin and flexible.

Never mind. At least humans are considered superior to robots for this kind of work. Those little fellows are poor at analysing problems, it seems to me. They lack intuition.

Here we are; the outer door. Phil and I check everything for the last time.

"Air to breathe."

"Check."

"Freedom to move."

"Check."

"Box of tools."

"Check." You see what I meant by check everything.

"Everything secured by line."

"Check."

"Life lines in place."

"Check."

"Backup line to tie on outside for extra safety."

"Check."

"Your gift to me."

"Now wait a minute; no funny stuff here, Bruce. Anyway, there are no banks around to cash it."

"No, of course not. Sorry. I was allowing myself to enjoy our little jaunt for a moment. I apologise. It won't happen again."

Seriously, you do have to be very careful going outside. For one thing, it is vital not to lose anything out there, and create the first piece of space debris hurtling in an unknown orbit round the new star. I can't hope to explain the various ways in which everything and everybody is connected to the ship by line when you go outside. The secret is to be tied on without getting tied up.

Talking of lifelines, they can't agree on a name for the star, by the way. I've gone off Umbelica, which was my earlier idea, based on umbilical cord. I don't know what I ever saw in it. All the same, I'd rather we reached a decision, and Umbelica would be better than nothing. I agreed with the verdict that naming the planets should be saved until we see what they look like, as their appearances may suggest names.

The final doors open. Here we go! Grip the handrail, and gently swing to the left. The

secret is to move slowly. No galactic shuffle out
here. Our aim is to manoeuvre round the side of
the ship, holding on, and going hand over hand,
and only using the thrusters if we lose our grip
and start drifting away from the ship. The
designers did well in creating six exit points
dotted about the hull, as it means we only have a
hundred and fifty metres to go. All the same,
that's quite far enough.

The stars shine out vividly. The sensation of
being above nothing is breathtaking. I'm glad I
did all that work in the simulator. Big Nimp has
got us practising every kind of procedure. I was
told I did not need to bother, as I was only the
caretaker. Well, that made me more determined
than ever. In fact, I have put in more hours than
anyone else. I still find weightlessness
difficult; I tend to become nauseous, but I'm
getting better at it. How Big Nimp can turn off
the gravity in the little room set aside for the
simulator I don't know. Or perhaps one should
think of it as the ability to deliver different
gravity control in different locations. I don't
know. So many aspects of this trip are beyond me!

Ah, there's the big concave mirror for
collecting the light. It looks fine from here. I
give Phil the thumbs up.

Funny how the shipwrights made no effort to
make this vehicle smooth. I supposed it was not
designed for use in an atmosphere, and in the
vacuum of space, there was no need to streamline
it. Still, all these bolts sticking out seem a
bit odd. They might have been sawn off with
advantage, frankly. It would reduce the risk of
us snagging our spacesuits on one.

Here we are at the mirror. Ah, I can see the
problem. The arm attaching it to the hull has a
sleeve on it, allowing the inside to rotate while
the outside stays put. Something has damaged the
sleeve, and I reckon it has allowed the lubricant

to escape, so the arm has seized up, which prevents the rotation. I thought it would be something like that. Good thing I brought the welding kit.

Step one. Fire in some lubricant. Axle grease. More solid than liquid, really. Fill the cavity, and then seal with cling film or whatever this stuff is.

Step two. Lengthen the extension line holding the welding kit so that I can manoeuvre more freely. Open the kit carefully. Here's a bit of curved sleeving that looks about right. No need for any hammering; it's a good fit, so I just need to weld it onto the hole as a patch.

Well, you know what happened next. There was a freak gust of wind, and the patch was whipped out of my fingers and away before I knew what was afoot. The very thing I did not want to happen. Now there is space debris, and it's my fault…

NO! Not at all. I hope you didn't believe that last bit. How could there be a freak gust of wind if there's no atmosphere? We are in hard vacuum here, if you had not already grasped. Weren't you paying attention earlier? If you believed that about the freak gust of wind, then shame on you! You need to grasp just how tricky this space-walking is, with no gravity, nothing to breathe except from an aqualung, and a massive kit on your back. I could use some sympathy here!

Stage three. Smooth the surface with the rotating sander. Keep gloves well clear. Can't hear a thing of course, but I can feel the vibrations. Put the sander back in its case.

Step four. Pick up the welder. Apply the solder, or whatever this new equivalent is. Carefully put the patch in place and press it home. If only I had a dozen hands. It's no good asking Phil to help. He's holding the torch. Everything is secured to a line, even the patch.

Step five. Allow both the patch and self to cool. Visual check with Phil, who gives me the thumbs up. We both think it's secure, so, I gently snip the patch free from the line. It's Okay! Put everything back in the case and close it. Phil is already talking to Big Nimp to test the repair. He's happy. Good.

I enjoy being a plumber if the truth is known. We move back five metres from the mirror.

"Try the mirror, Snow White," I instruct. Yes; it's moving freely now. Phil approves the fairy-tale reference. It would not have been good to address Big Nimp as Wicked Witch. He might not have liked it. Did I tell you he answers to any name?

The return journey is easy. We each press our rewind buttons, and the lines gently pull us in; slowly, so that we can control our movements. A bit like abseiling, but with no gravity.

We are back at the doors. Work the handle; the doors slide open. In we go. We lock the doors shut. We go through the next four sets of doors. Test for atmosphere; take off suit.

"Thanks, Phil," I said. "You may not feel as if you have done a lot, but I appreciated you being there very much."

"I wouldn't have missed it. You were very precise in all you did. I learnt a lot by watching you. Let's go and join the others, and see if the system is working."

Phil is such a kind man. I remember having read once that a friend is somebody you would feel free to ring at three in the morning if you were stranded at the airport after an unexpected change to your flight. Well, Phil fits that category. I hope he feels the same about me.

Sure enough, when we've changed back to our day gear, and rejoined the others, Big Nimp is exploring the star system and coming up with some great pictures.

It seems to me that there are a lot of similarities between the solar system, which I will use to mean our own neighbourhood back at earth, and the star system here. The inner planets here are small and rocky, while the outer planets are much larger, huge balls of gas, as in the solar system. Personally, I subscribe to the view that all the planets in the solar system, including earth, were once gas giants, but the planets closer to the sun had their gas blown off by the solar wind, leaving just the rocky core.

The new star is very similar to the sun; we knew that before the mission left. It is just a bit smaller, but similar brightness and temperature. However, there are more inner planets here, and most of them are smaller than earth. There is just one planet in the crucial temperature belt, about eighty-seven million miles from the sun. Earth is ninety-three million miles from the sun. Close enough to be warm, but not too hot.

I wonder whether the planet will turn out to be ideal for us. I hope so.

Bruce

Next day was Sunday, and Bruce went to church as usual. He had an unexpected shock, which troubled him. The subject of the address was 'Do not be mis-mated with unbelievers.' The message was blunt; a believer must not marry an unbeliever.

Bruce was glad that Bill and Gnilla were away – it would have only caused problems. Bill attended the church, but Gnilla did not. However, Bruce found himself unhappy with the speaker's assumption that churchgoers and believers were one and the same group. He was aware of a number of people who never went near a church, but who, if pushed, would admit to believing in and trusting in God. He was also becoming increasingly troubled by the church-going group. They certainly believed in worship and in Bible teaching, but Bruce felt that their attitude to Jesus' teaching was selective, to say the least. In particular, he was struck by the fact

266

that the weekly meeting seemed all-important, but the fate of outsiders in obvious need was largely passed over. Bruce found the penniless ones that sat on blankets at the side of the road a constant challenge. He did not know what to do about them himself, and neither did anybody else from what he could see.

So all in all, the distinction between believers and unbelievers did not seem so clear to Bruce as the preacher had suggested. However, one thing was clear. Some of his short list of eligible girls would have to go.

Top of his list of hopefuls was Celia with the lovely brown hair, whom he had met in the train. It had turned out that she was head-hunting him on behalf of some hush-hush organisation as a way into the sky-fly group, because of his ability at background piano. So far, she had resisted Bruce's attempts to date her. She certainly believed in serving her country, or so she said, but did she believe in God as well? Bruce had no idea.

It was the same with Sarah, another piano pupil, whom Bruce secretly rather liked. She had been most frosty to begin with, but a thaw had soon set in. Crocuses and snowdrops now seemed imminent, Bruce felt. Sarah's younger sister Araminta (high cheek bones) had surprised Bruce by telling him that she loved him, but as she was one of his pupils at the school, a relationship was out of the question. Sarah was a possibility, but what beliefs did she hold?

Flossy, or Florence Millicent to give her her full name, was certainly not a believer – Bruce was sure about that. But anyway, he had decided against her, despite her wonderful slimness. On the whole.

Oh dear, the sky suddenly seemed to have clouded over. His possibles were quickly turning into impossibles. What was he going to do? He only had to meet one girl, he reasoned, and anything could happen. However, that was easier said than done. There was nobody at the church who looked at all promising. Bruce let out a sigh.

There was only one thing for it. He would have to put them out of their misery. Celia could not come for a lesson this Tuesday, so he would start with Sarah. This was not going to be easy.

Sarah came on Thursday evenings. She turned up for her lesson bang on time, as usual. If only her timing when playing the music could be as exact as her punctuality, she would be a good pianist. However, she was improving. For most of his pupils, rhythm was harder than note-learning, Bruce had decided.

At the end of the lesson, Bruce swallowed hard, and wished that his hands were not sweating. Then he cleared his throat. Then he said, could he check his diary regarding next week's lesson. It was clear, as he knew perfectly well. By this time, Sarah was looking at him rather oddly. He was behaving in a strange manner. There was a questioning look in her eye.

There was no more putting it off.

"Look, I'm sorry, but the simple fact is that I can't marry you, because you are not a believer. I feel rather bad about it. The thing is that we had this talk at church, and it turns out that Paul taught that you must not be mis-mated with an unbeliever, so that's put the kibosh on any chances we might have had."

Sarah heard him out patiently with an amused expression. Then she spoke.

"Well, that's quite a little speech. I had no idea marriage was in your mind. However, I'm pleased to tell you that there is no just cause or impediment in this instance, because I am a believer. Our whole family believe as a matter of fact, and we attend a church a couple of miles from here."

Bruce was completely taken aback. "I'm so sorry," he said. "I never thought. Why didn't you mention it?"

"Well, why didn't you mention it yourself, come to that? I take it you are a believer, then?"

Bruce nodded. He was feeling rather sheepish. "I'm sorry. I've put my foot in it yet again. I'm afraid I am not very clever about these things."

Sarah laughed. "Don't worry – neither am I. Anyway, you don't need to strike me off your list of potential heartthrobs after all, so that's good."

She was clearly amused rather than upset by the whole incident, Bruce could see, so perhaps he could afford to relax a bit.

"Well, that's a relief. And thank you for taking it so well."

Sarah was looking at him. "You know, there are two things that I like about you, Bruce."

"What are they?"

"The first is that you are completely predictable."

Bruce laughed again. "Is it that easy to read my mind, then?"

"Well no – that brings me to the second thing."

"What's that?"

"I also find you completely unpredictable at the same time! See you at next week's lesson."

Bruce felt puzzled as he watched Sarah go down the short path to the road. Are all women utterly incomprehensible, he wondered, or is it just the effect I have on them?

```
40. From: Mission 12
To: Undisclosed recipients
Sent:
```

Details about our target planet have started coming through now. It's not quite as big as earth - about ninety-five percent, so as near as makes no difference. It means that gravity will be slightly less than on earth. The best bit of news is that it's blue, which suggests water and perhaps a friendly atmosphere. Nobody here dare say it, but wouldn't it be wonderful if the atmosphere just happened to be twenty percent Oxygen and eighty percent Nitrogen, like on earth, and we could breathe without needing aqualungs…

We are getting so close now that I thought Big Nimp must have over-estimated the remaining journey time. Shock, horror, heresy, sacrilege, I hear you saying; how could the computer make an error? Well, of course, he hasn't. We have to go ever so much more slowly now we are approaching the debris of the star system. Some of the comets in earth's solar system may be a hundred thousand kilometres across. That's six times the diameter of the earth! Supposing this star has the same. No prizes for guessing who comes off worst if we go smack into one of those.

Whoops, error. Sorry! Big Nimp has just corrected me. It's the tail of the comet that can be that size, made of little more than dust. The nucleus of the comet is a mere nine miles by six in the case of Halley's comet. Still, whacking into one of those would be bad enough. It's the size of a large town, after all.

So we are slowing to a crawl, figuratively speaking. The two gee deceleration at night has felt so frustrating! However, two gee time is over now; we maintain one gee from here on in. Most of that is gravity control, by the way, not deceleration. But here's the galling part; even though we are nearly there, the image of the star seems no bigger today than it did last week.

Paul's a wily one. Yesterday, as we were watching at the big screen over breakfast as usual, we all noticed how the star was getting gradually bigger. It seemed so exciting. Then Paul confessed; he had asked Big Nimp to increase the image size by one percent per minute over breakfast.

Mark was not amused. He is so ill-tempered. It's not just against me. He seems to do it to everyone. I have the feeling that he could snap at me at any moment. It's horrid. I think he does it so that others are afraid of him, and he can therefore control them. I don't like it. However, I have to admit that he's also very able; when we are discussing plans, almost everything he says turns out to be the best idea in the end. So that's another reason for being slow to oppose him.

These are just my private thoughts, you understand. I have not shared them with anyone else. The reason I'm mentioning them to you is that I reckon that Mark's attitude and behaviour

is the kind of stuff that dictators are made of.
Naturally, I'm hoping that we can be democratic
here, with everybody having their say, and the
wisest course of action being chosen by vote.
However, this needs policing. I hope Max as
commander is up to the job of keeping people in
their place, and encouraging democracy. It won't
just happen on its own.
Bruce

"Miss, we need to speak to you."

Beccy and Simna had come to find the Head of Music at break.
She could see from their faces that it was important.

"What is it Beccy?"

"It's Mr. Winter. We're worried about him. He's started talking
to himself."

"Why, what happened?"

"Simna and I had assembly yesterday morning, so we were a bit
late for our keyboard lesson. This meant that the sixth form girl
with the high cheek bones had already left, and he was alone in the
little room. We were just about to go in when we heard him
speaking in a loud voice."

"Well, that sounds very odd. Did you hear what he said?"

It was Simna's turn. "Beccy thinks he said something about
poison, miss, but I'm sure I heard him correctly. He said in a loud
cheerful voice, 'Top of the morning to the boys in blue.' Miss, it
doesn't make any sense."

Beccy took it up again. "We wouldn't have mentioned it, miss,
because we don't want to get him into any trouble, but we're very
fond of him, and we're worried that he's going out of his mind,
miss, especially if it is poison he's talking about. We wondered
whether he needs help."

"I see. You were right to tell me. I'll have to think what to do.
Thank you for coming along."

This was not a run of the mill problem like the ones Jane usually
had to deal with. After a moment's thought, she decided to tackle it

271

head on. There were a few minutes of break remaining, and Bruce was alone in the practice room. She went in.

"Bruce, could I have a word?"

"Of course."

"It's a bit delicate. Beccy and Simna have been to see me because they are worried about you. Just as they were arriving for their lesson yesterday, they heard you talking out loud in the empty room, and they wondered what it meant."

"I see." This was a bit awkward. Bruce hurriedly decided that he did not want to tell Jane that he thought the practice room might have been bugged by Celia's cutthroat gang at the time of the building work, in order to spy on him, and that he was trying to brighten up somebody's day down at an underground bunker by giving them a friendly hello. It must be trying having nothing but sandbags and a computer for company. But what explanation could he give? He did not want to be untruthful.

"They are quite right; I was speaking out loud and there was nobody here. However, it does not mean I'm losing my marbles. I sometimes do it at home too. I live on my own, and it perhaps tends to make me a little more eccentric than I might have been otherwise. You don't need to worry."

"Okay, Bruce, but on condition that if anything is concerning you, get help with it. We're all very fond of you, even if we don't always show it." Jane gave him a broad smile. She appeared to be reassured.

Part of Bruce would have liked to tell Jane everything, but what could he say? The possibility that the school had been bugged would lead to no end of problems and investigations. Then his role would come out. But what was his role? All he knew was that this mysterious organisation could arrange for you to win nation-wide raffles, send you on a walking holiday on the moon, and confound you with personalised news bulletins at ten p.m. when you were feeling tired and sleepy. That and Celia saying 'trust me.' It was not much to go on. Bruce felt more in the dark than ever.

Still, the ones at the bugging headquarters would have to get along without his cheery greeting at 0910 from now on. Shame really.

41. From: Mission 12
To: Undisclosed recipients
Sent:

Well, we're definitely in the star system now. We've passed the outermost three planets. Not that we saw any of them. It's tempting to think that we are bound to pass close to a planet or two, but that's not right. In fact, they are so far away from us that they cannot be seen with the naked eye. Still, Big Nimp is getting some reasonable photos.

None of them have rings like Saturn, which is a shame. You can't tell much about them from the photos. We will have to send probes there in due course.

Still no name for our target planet, so I will call it Targetto until a name is chosen. It's too small to get a proper photo yet.

It's still weeks to go until we arrive, because we have slowed our speed right down. It's just one percent of the speed of light now. That's about eighteen hundred miles a second, which probably sounds fast, but it means there are weeks and weeks to go. Everything is so spread out in space. I suppose in one sense it is fast, really - London to New York in under four seconds. But the distances in space are so vast that it feels as if we are going at a snail's pace.

Isn't the universe wonderful?

I feel a bit bad, because I have not been filling you in properly. You may remember that Max went downstairs when it was still the four of us, and Big Nimp would not let him back, so I had to rescue him by going caving inside Grim Reaper.

That's my name for the replicator by the way. Reprogrammer was wrong - I should never have called it that. It's the machine that builds whatever we want by reassembling the atoms. It's so clever.

Anyway, now it seems that the other floors of the spacecraft are no longer off limits. I did not want to go down, but the others insisted I should see for myself. So I gave in.

On the floor below, there are five hundred more astronauts in hibernation, only these ones don't have little handles above them for manual waking.

"You see, Dad?" Max said eagerly. "That was why I knew it was Okay to wake the astronauts on our level, as they all have the handles."

I can't get it, personally. So what if the five hundred have no handles? All that means is that Big Nimp has control over when they are woken. I'm hoping they won't all be woken at once. It could cause no end of problems if they were. But I still can't see what put the idea into Max's head that he was free to wake the eight astronauts on our level, just because they had handles. Anyway, it's all history now. Oh yes, except for one thing; the others decided to wake the rest of the twenty-four, but I persuaded them not to, as there was no obvious place for them to sleep. We could have all budged up, but it would have been very crowded. So it's still just the twelve of us; the eight newly-woken astronauts, and our little family. That's Celia my wife, and our children Max and Clairie, for the benefit of new readers.

Before anybody explored upstairs, I said we should all guess what there was up there, so we did. I was closest! Honest. However, it was even more fascinating than I had expected.

There are thousands of little hibernation units, all carefully labelled, with every kind of living creature. Birds and animals, obviously, but also a lot of tiny things you might never have thought of, like insects you can hardly see.

It was Margaret who pointed out that there was no animal larger than a rabbit. When we looked at the birds, however, there was a fuller range, right up to Eagle and Albatross.

So whatever else we are, we are also a latter day Noah's Ark. I suggested that Phil could play Methuselah, who lived to be nine hundred and something, because he was still alive in the days of Noah, if you read the story carefully. He has enough wrinkles, you see. Phil thought it was a wonderful idea, but it's an example of something that Mark would not appreciate.

I think everyone should have a sense of humour. I said so to Phil when we were apart from the others at one end of the upstairs.

"Ah, but have you also got a sense of humus?" he replied, and pointed behind me. We were standing next to a lot of compost and manure, all in hibernation coffins, I'm pleased to say. I laughed.

"I hope so," I said.

Bruce

On Saturday, it was the day to play for Jim Pond. Bruce decided that he would include the whole of the Moonlight Sonata, which was unusual for him when playing background piano. His policy was to play short well-known pieces and extracts from longer works. However, Sarah's younger sister Araminta had set herself to learn all three movements of the Moonlight, so Bruce had been practising them too. No good having pupils learning pieces you could not play yourself. When she had come on Thursday morning, it turned out that she had mastered the first two movements and begun on the third. It was going well, even though it was the hardest of the three by far. Bruce was actually very impressed by her grit and determination. He could see she was going to master it.

He would need the sheet music for the third movement, which was a drawback, but not an impossible one. Normally, Bruce played

275

everything from memory. Also, movement three was so hard that it was difficult to keep the volume low, but the thing to do was to ensure that the piano lid was down, and to jam the soft pedal on throughout. A bit crazy, really, but Bruce liked a challenge and he was sure Jim would appreciate it. It would be interesting to see if he spotted the cheat Bruce had worked out for the impossible last four bars.

Jim was delighted to see him, and clapped him on the back. The shag pile carpet was as springy as ever, and the soft velour of the wallpaper and the brilliance of the cut glass chandeliers gave a wonderful effect once again. There was the white grand piano. Bruce did not ask – he simply lowered the lid. Nobody seemed to mind. There was the piano stool, in which it had been rudely suggested that he had placed a bomb. How could anyone think of destroying such fine leather upholstery?

He was to play for half an hour while the guests arrived and had a drink and nibbles. At the last minute, he decided against the Moonlight. It did not feel right, and he would probably mess it up. Instead he weaved his way through half a dozen classics before launching into some Strauss Waltzes followed by the Dambusters March. He hoped the latter would help break any ice left in the room. However, he was not going to lob a bouncing bomb into the gathering this time! Keep it all low key. Out of the corner of his eye, he spotted the portly gent with the gold watch on the chain that he had seen before. Also Heavy Jowls was there, as Bruce called him.

To his surprise, when the guests were ushered elsewhere, Bruce was invited to go through with them. It turned out that the ladies stayed in the lounge, while the men were to have a committee meeting of some kind. Bruce wondered what they could possibly want him for.

Jim cleared his throat when they were all seated. "I expect you're wondering why I've invited Bruce to join us. Well, as you know, for some time now we have wanted to make some charitable donations, and Bruce's obvious passion on this subject at our last gathering impressed us so much that we thought it good to draw him in to help us – that is if you're happy to do so."

Bruce immediately grasped that these people were the directors of Skywear, or whatever, and that they wanted his input. How extraordinary. But touching.

"I'd be delighted," he said.

"The floor's yours," said Jim.

"Well, this is a complete surprise to me, so I have not prepared anything, which is perhaps just as well, because I can speak off the top of my head. As you know, I like Water Aid because clean water for all is non-political, and they seem to be people of integrity. With some of the aid agencies, I just wonder, slightly. I can let you have a list of the ones I think are sound on both counts, if you want. Then there are all the charities working in this country, but personally I don't contribute to them. My feeling is that compared to the rest of the world, the UK is wealthy enough, and that we do better to give elsewhere. You may not share my view, but it is my view."

There were murmurs of approval. They asked him to supply the list.

"May I continue?" asked Bruce. They looked at him with interest.

"Since I was last here, when I began to get a glimpse of the financial scale of your operations, I have been doing some thinking. Personally, I agree with Jacques Cousteau – you know, the French diver who invented the aqualung and produced all those books and films about the ocean depths. He held that the two greatest problems in the world were over-population and pollution.

"Now governments tend to focus on domestic problems, naturally, or trade and diplomacy with other countries. But it seems to me that it's nobody's remit to think about the future of the human race as a whole, as it were. Do you follow me?"

They did.

"Well, here's a suggestion. Over the next few centuries, mankind is going to expand to other star systems, driven by problems of over-population and pollution. A crucial part of this enterprise is going to be the invention of the replicator. This is a machine that makes anything out of anything else by reassembling the atoms, so you could put in garden waste at one end and get out metal girders at the other end, or whatever you want. I know it sounds fantastic, but this machine is the ultimate goal of manufacturing. Now these space missions are going to need a tool of this kind if they are going to succeed, it seems to me."

Bruce could see that he had everyone's attention. These were remarkable people, he thought; they were prepared to listen to far-fetched ideas.

"So, what I'm coming to is this. You can put money towards saving lives in Africa, and I hope you will. But what you can also do is to fund research and development towards inventing the replicator, and that will be of wide benefit to humanity as well. And here's the bit that might appeal to you. If you managed to make one of these things, you might even find that the money you've made so far from anti-gravity would seem like small change. Just think of possible uses for it; a replicator in the middle of the Sahara desert could turn sand and rock into drinking water, for example. 'Then shall the desert bloom like the rose.' It's a favourite verse of mine from the Book of Isaiah. Isn't it wonderful, speaking of a new dawn of opportunity? Let me repeat it: 'Then shall the desert bloom like the rose.'"

Jim opened his mouth. "Bruce, that's a great contribution. We'd like your list of agencies, and I'm sure we would want to think about your idea concerning the replicator. It certainly would be a great invention. Thank you very much."

Bruce was ushered out to join the ladies, while the men continued their meeting. There was nobody there that he knew, so he made some small talk with one or two of them before drifting back over to the piano and doing what he did best. Some delicate jazz seemed called for, although Bruce was aware that this did not come naturally to him. Never mind; every skill improves with practice.

Before long, the men came out of their meeting, everyone went through to dinner, and it was time from Bruce to leave. Jim saw him out, and thanked him very much. He promised to be in touch again soon.

There was a moment when Bruce and Jim were unobserved by the security men, in the area just inside the front door of the flat. To Jim's surprise, Bruce unobtrusively slipped a note into Jim's hand, and motioned that he should put it into his pocket to read later. Bruce said how much he had enjoyed coming, and Jim waved him goodbye as the lift doors closed.

On his way home, Bruce ran over in his mind what he had said in the meeting. He realised that he had not mentioned Psalm Eight, which Bruce took as an encouragement to us to spread through the galaxy, especially when coupled with the instruction to go forth, increase and multiply in the early chapters of the book of Genesis. He could have explained his view that they would have God on their side in their efforts to make the replicator, if their aim was to help mankind populate the stars. But on reflection, he decided that perhaps it was better not to have mentioned it. He had given them enough to think about without bringing the purposes of God into it. And most people would probably disagree with him anyway.

```
42. From: Mission 12
To: Undisclosed recipients
Sent:


Well, I reckon that our situation here is best
described by those immortal words from the early
days of space travel:
    'Houston, we have a problem.'
    Only, there is no Houston, and you won't
receive this message for many years, as we are so
far away. Even if you responded immediately, your
reply will not return until after we have all
been long gone. So it's up to us to sort it out.
    It's not a technical problem, just a profound
disagreement. What makes it difficult is that the
sides are very uneven. In fact, it's me against
all the rest.
```

You see what you think. I will set out the two
positions, A and B. I will begin with theirs.

Position A. Everybody can hardly contain their
excitement. Not only is the blueness liquid
water, i.e. oceans and seas, covering about fifty
percent of the planet, but the average
temperature is fifty-four degrees, which is as
close to perfect as can be imagined. The icing on
the cake is the atmosphere; Oxygen about fifteen
percent, Nitrogen seventy percent, and the rest
various friendly gases. That makes it breathable,
probably indefinitely, but certainly for six
hours or so, followed by a go on the aqualung.

I share this excitement. It is fantastic news.

They all want to go down to the surface. We are
to get into a low earth orbit, create some
shuttles to descend through the atmosphere, and
send down a working party to explore. They will
take all kinds of instruments, and gather
information.

This is where we disagree!

Position B (mine). I'm just as excited.
However, I'm acutely aware of how dependant we
are on the ship for our survival. It has
performed fabulously so far, but that is no
reason why it should go on doing so. We need to
do everything we can to service it, and maintain
it, and then build copies of it. Supposing the
ship got damaged, and there was no backup! It's
unthinkable.

As regards going down to the surface, this is
months if not years away, in my view. It's
madness to consider it now. We don't know whether
there will be hostile forces down there, such as
disease. Maybe city-sized asteroids rain down on
the planet every so often. If we start a colony
down there, as they seem to want to, it could be
snuffed out in a moment. I agree it all looks
very welcoming from up here, but appearances can
be deceptive.

I think we need to draw up a careful time line of activities, and work through it. Missions to the surface will certainly be a part of that, but by no means at the top of the list.

Well. The hostility has been considerable. I would have thought that my position was self-evidently correct, but nobody else seems able to see it. I honestly find it extraordinary. Mark was particularly obnoxious. His main interest seems to be in naming features of the planet. I reckon he wants to make sure he goes down in history as the founder of the place. Max is too weak to stand up to him. I was afraid he would be.

Max and Clairie have never been on a planet, unlike the others. They can't wait to explore. It's understandable; they have seen so much footage of life on earth that they think of the new planet as if it was Hollywood. I also did not realise what the result would be of watching all those episodes of Star Trek. They both think that space colonisation is about daring missions. Celia upsets me. She says nothing, but I can see from her eyes that she's longing to go down. I could really use some support from her.

To tell you the truth, there is a worry that has been gnawing away at me for some time now. I think there is something not quite right about everybody else on board, even including Phil. It's to do with being irresponsible. Everyone seems so carefree and casual. I can't put my finger on it. If I could, it would be easier to deal with. As it is, I don't know whether I am right in my perception, or whether it is just me being paranoid.

I can't believe that people were chosen for this mission for their laidback attitude. Eat drink and be merry for tomorrow we die. That seems to be the in thing.

What's bothering me is that if you think about it, I am the only one here who has never experienced hibernation. I'm just wondering if there is something about being put to sleep for a long period which has an unhinging effect. If there was, then that might explain their reluctance to take responsibility for the mission, because that is how I see their attitude. It seems to me that we owe it to our descendants to ensure the success of the settlement. There's no doubt in my mind that we can make a good settlement here. But it will take decades of hard work to get it up and running.

Thankfully, we have been saved from open conflict by Big Nimp. The others wanted to instruct him to set a course to get into orbit round Targetto - still no name for it - and get ready for a descent to the surface. Not even a probe to go first! I think it's crazy. However, Big Nimp told us that we need to stop off at a planet without atmosphere, as Grim Reaper needs to be replenished. So we are heading for Targetto's moon.

I'll tell you more later.
Bruce

Bill and Gnilla were still away on their honeymoon, so Bruce felt rather on his own on Sunday morning. However, on Tuesday, Celia was coming for a lesson. This was significant for two reasons. Firstly, he wanted to sound her out as to her beliefs, to see whether she was a possible candidate for the post of Mrs. Winter. Bruce was beginning to realise that being married to him might not be the easiest role for a girl to fill. Maybe he was a little eccentric. However, he was sure he could make a good husband and a good dad. But would anybody else see it that way?

Secondly, he had some definite news to report back from the Skywear people. He was pleased about this, as so far, he felt he had not been able to contribute anything.

When Celia arrived, Bruce thought she looked prettier than ever. Her progress at the piano was such that he suggested she had a go at Fur Elise by Beethoven – not just the well-known first section, but the whole thing, including the challenging parts. It was remarkable that a beginner could consider tackling it after just three or four months. Unfair really. It had taken him years to get that far.

When the lesson was over, he told her of the visit to Jim, and what had happened and what he had said to the meeting.

"Bruce, that's marvellous!" she exclaimed. "We never expected you to get drawn in to that degree. You seem to have a natural talent for getting on with people. Tell me who was there."

Bruce could remember Gold Chain and Heavy Jowls as well as Jim, but nobody else. "There were fifteen of them," he added.

Celia was very pleased. "Well done," she said. Then she surprised him. "Look, you kindly offered to take me out for a meal, and I'd be pleased to accept. I've checked it out with my superiors, and they say there is no impediment."

This was music to Bruce's ears. However, the word impediment jarred somewhat, and after the fiasco over Sarah's belief or lack of it, Bruce found he could not raise the subject with Celia after all. Perhaps they could discuss it at the meal. They agreed to meet at an up-market Chinese restaurant in town on Friday evening at 7.30. Bruce was to book the table.

As soon as Celia had left, Bruce got on the phone to the restaurant. There was no problem. Rather than using the name Winter, Bruce took the table in the name of Spring. It suggested a new beginning. Who knows? Maybe his life was about to go from January to May during the course of a few days. He hoped so. Stranger things had happened.

```
43. From: Mission 12
To: Undisclosed recipients
Sent:

Hello again. Back to Grim Reaper.
I was intrigued by the need to replenish. As
you know, Grim Reaper can turn anything into
```

anything else. Sounds unbelievable, but it's true. However, a certain amount of mass is lost in each act of transformation, apparently. So the ballast in the hold, if you can call it that, is gradually used up, even though all our waste goes back into the mouth or the throat. It turns out that a good deal of the launch weight of the ship was sand that was brought along for Grim Reaper to digest. It gives new meaning to the word sandwich. Personally, I hate grit in my food.

So, we are parked in a very low orbit around Targetto's moon. I hope we don't collide with a mountain, but I trust Big Nimp's judgement on this. I am pleased there is a moon, by the way, as it means there will be tides on Targetto. It is wonderful how the oceans and breathable atmosphere have been confirmed. I thought it might require centuries of atmosphere control before we could breathe unaided, but it seems not. Amazing. No need for sealed bubbles to live in.

Big Nimp and Grim Reaper have produced an excavator, with thrusters for moving about, designed for non-atmosphere use. The template was in Big Nimp's memory, in anticipation. It's a sort of mobile mine, really.

The excavator is a curious thing, shaped a bit like a lady's shoe with a stiletto heel. It drops away from us, while we go on doing orbits, and settles down on the surface. I forget who quipped 'One small step for woman, one giant leap for womankind,' but I thought it was rather apt. I would have said 'dainty leap' myself. It sounds more feminine than 'giant leap'.

Then the drill gets to work; that's the stiletto heel part. As it goes down into the dust and rock, the shoe settles down flatter and flatter until eventually it looks like a slipper, the stiletto part being buried. All this time, the debris has been ground smaller and smaller as it rises up inside the heel, and then it gets pushed into the toe of the shoe. The excavator may have to move six or eight times before the toe is completely full. Then it lifts off again at the right moment to rejoin us on one of our orbits. It unloads the sand into the hold, and then the whole routine starts again. The excavator needs to do eighteen round trips, and then we'll be full again.

I find it rather fascinating, really. You ladies back home who enjoy dressing up. Up to now, I had no idea of the symbolism of your actions. Next time you put your foot down in response to your man, or grind something into the carpet with your heel when nobody is looking, reflect for a moment that you are performing a prophetic action! Sand for the replicator. In this way, the human race makes progress. Marvellous.

I wonder if those who designed the excavator had any notion of how it would appear?

Going back to Targetto, there is a mass of data coming through now. Its day - that's the length of time it takes to revolve, is thirty-two hours. That's hours on earth, by the way. One decision we have taken is to continue to use the measurements we are used to from the solar system. I think that the length of the day will probably turn out to be a problem, as it will tend to make one side of the planet too hot in the prolonged sunshine, and the other side too cold in the long night. So it may be that we will need bubble domes after all, to save us from extremes of temperature.

Pretty much all the other indicators are good, however. The magnetic field is similar to earth's. A stronger one could have been a severe problem. The atmosphere is not as thick as earth's, as the gravity is less, but it's Okay. The atmosphere round a planet acts as a blanket, evening out the temperature, in case you didn't know. Without it, the temperature would plummet at night, and rocket by day. Sorry; I should have explained that earlier.

Targetto's atmosphere has similar properties to earth's; Ozone layer, Ultra Violet filtering effect, etc. So that means there will be little radiation from Umbelica percolating through to the planet's surface. Well and good.

I wish we could agree on the names!

What we still don't know is whether there is life down there. That is the big question. There certainly isn't an advanced, space-faring civilisation in the star system, as we would have met it by now if there was. Anyway, the good thing is that if the planet does turn out to be barren, we have brought our own life with us from earth. Hence all that stuff upstairs.

Phil came and searched me out yesterday. He appreciates the difficulty I'm in. He doesn't agree with my view, but he's making a valiant attempt to understand it.

"Bruce, this need to refill Grim Reaper. Do you know what it means?"

"Go on."

"It's an example of entropy, Bruce. Everything in the universe is like a clockwork machine that's gradually running down. Chaos and confusion are the natural order. 'Things fall apart; the centre cannot hold.' You know the sort of thing. Scientists have a term for it – they call it entropy. I thought you might be interested. It's not the kind of word that you will have picked up from your musical training."

"Ah, but that's just where you're wrong, Phil. I do know about entropy! It comes in the song 'It's a natural law.'"

I led him over to the piano. I am not very good at playing and singing at the same time, but it was important to have a go at this one.

"You can't pass heat
from a cooler to a hotter,
    Wah, wah, wa!" I chortled.
"You can try if you like
but you're far better notter!
    Wah, wah, wa!"
I carried on playing and declaimed the spoken
part over the top of the music, like on the
recording.
"Heat is work and work's a curse,
and all the heat in the universe
is gonna cool down.
That's entropy, man!"
It's a delightful song. Phil enjoyed it.

Margaret had been listening. I've noticed her
hanging around a bit before, when I play. It
finally came out.

"Bruce, I enjoy singing, and I was wondering
whether you knew any German *Lieder*."

This was wonderful. I took a chance on it, and
saying nothing, I went straight into the
introduction of *An die Musik* by Schubert. That
means 'To music,' by the way.

Sure enough, she knew it. She has a lovely
contralto voice. We did the whole song. I made a
stumble in the middle, but she was note perfect.
It was wonderful. It's such a beautiful song.

The others, who had all gathered round quietly
while she was singing, gave her rapturous
applause at the end. It was lovely, and helped
reduce some of the tension.

Isn't it marvellous that although the universe
may be running down, like an old wind-up
gramophone, we have music to counter the
tendency, and perhaps even reverse it, if only
locally. So all you young pianists at home, keep
up the practice routine!

Bruce

The following day, something happened that was to change Bruce's life forever. There were often messages on his answerphone when he returned home, but he had never had one like this before. He found it at seven p.m.

The message ran 'Would Mr. Bruce Winter please ring Wayford Hospital where his mother is dangerously ill,' followed by a number. Bruce was stupefied. His mother! He dropped his bags on the floor and rang the number.

What was going on? Was he the grandson of Philip Lester Rewell, yes, yes, yes, and so was Mrs. Sarah Marigold Winter his mother, yes she was, but we've been out of touch for years. Well, she was dangerously ill, and he should come without delay. He scribbled down the name of the ward, and the number, and put the phone down.

His mind was already working furiously. Thank goodness it was a free evening, so there were no phone calls to be made cancelling appointments. He punched in Bill's number, praying that he would be in and free to run him over there, and stay with him. The phone was ringing. Come on, Bill, come on... Oh no! Of course not. They were still on honeymoon. He had forgotten. No help in that quarter.

There was only one thing for it. Bruce grabbed his coat, rushed out of the door, pausing only to lock up, and ran as fast as he could towards the station. Thank goodness there was a taxi standing there.

"Wayford Hospital," he gasped, "and please be quick; my mother is dying."

He jumped in. The taxi sped away. It had been fair enough to say that she was dying. That was what 'dangerously ill' meant, wasn't it? 'Dying' communicated more clearly, Bruce thought, and it wasn't being untrue. All the same, he hoped so much that it might not be true, that she might still be alive and he could get to know her.

There were a thousand questions in his head. Why had she never got in touch? She was not even getting in touch now, come to that, because the hospital had mentioned his granddad. What was that about? Perhaps it was something to do with next of kin. Were they nearly there yet? Could the driver be quick when it came to settling up? Could he find the ward without losing precious seconds?

These questions were soon answered. With the minimum of delay, Bruce found himself at the reception desk of the ward. "Mrs. Winter," he gasped. "I'm her son. I got your message."

The concern showed on the faces of the two staff.

"I am so sorry," the older of them said, "I'm afraid your mother died ten minutes ago."

This was dreadful, but Bruce was determined to be strong. Feelings could come later.

"I'd like to see her, please."

Why were the two ladies looking at each other instead of at him? The older one turned to him again.

"Certainly, Mr. Winter, but we feel we may need to put you in the picture first. May I ask when you were last in touch with your mother?"

Bruce explained to them that when he was four or five, there had been a terrible argument between his parents, even worse than usual. He had blocked his ears and run off down the garden. Later on, some strangers had come and taken him to his granddad's house, and that was the last time he had ever seen either of his parents or his sister Sasha. The phone call had come like a bolt from the blue.

"Ring the nursing home," the older lady said to the younger. "I was afraid it would be something like this. Mr. Winter needs to meet them." Then to Bruce she said, "Come this way. Prepare yourself for a shock."

Cold fear gripped Bruce's heart. What horror was coming? He was shown into a small room. The dead woman in the bed seemed like a total stranger. For one thing, she looked older than his mother's years would have suggested. He studied her face hard, and could detect no trace at all of the mother he had remembered. Also, why was the side of her head so misshapen?

"Are you sure there is no mistake?" Bruce asked.

"Quite sure. Mr. Fuller will fill you in."

While she was speaking, the younger lady returned to say that Mr. Fuller was on his way. Bruce wondered who this Mr. Fuller might be.

Once again, Bruce looked at the figure in the bed. It was hopeless; no matter how hard he tried, he could not imagine any connection between that person and himself. He did not feel any grief. In fact he did not feel anything at all, except confusion. Who was Mr. Fuller, and how come he knew something that Bruce didn't?

Mr. Fuller turned out to be a quietly-spoken man of about sixty. Bruce and he were ushered into a small room where they could talk.

"Mr. Winter, this must seem very strange to you. These are the facts. Many years ago, Mrs. Winter was brought to us in a terrible state. She had received brain damage from a blow to the head. At the time, nobody expected her to live long, but she surprised us all. She made a partial recovery, but she was severely disabled, and was never able to speak more than a few words. She stayed with us all this time. The local authority paid us to look after her, following a ruling of the courts. Then a few days ago, she caught pneumonia. Our instructions were to contact the next of kin only in an emergency. He was Philip Rewell, and the address was care of a firm of solicitors. When we got in touch, they informed us that Philip Rewell had died, but that his next of kin was yourself. We were surprised, as we had never been told of any children."

This was grim news. Brain damage from a blow to the head! It was along the lines that Bruce had feared. How dreadful. He thanked Mr. Fuller very much, and took the details of the solicitors. Hopefully, he would learn more there, but he already felt he had a shrewd suspicion of the truth.

Bruce asked to see the body again. Still no feelings. He turned to Mr. Fuller and the nurse.

"I would like to be involved in the funeral arrangements, if that is possible."

Mr. Fuller nodded. "At present, it's in the hands of the local authority. I'm sure they would be delighted to have your involvement. I've brought the details of the person you should contact, in anticipation."

Bruce was handed a sheet of headed notepaper with a name, address and phone number on it.

"I would also like to see where she lived for so long," Bruce said. "And could you kindly take a photograph of my mother here in the bed before she is removed?"

It seemed so odd calling this stranger his mother. But she was the lady who brought him into the world, and even though he had not known her in life, he was going to honour her in death.

Both requests were speedily agreed. The nursing home was within walking distance, so Bruce decided to go there right away. The hospital would mail the photo to Bruce's home. Bruce thanked the two nurses for all their help.

Mr. Fuller led the way out of the hospital and along two roads. The nursing home was not prepossessing, but when Bruce entered, he felt instinctively that it was a place characterised by caring. His mother had been well looked after here.

Her personal possessions were minimal. There was nothing that Bruce recognised. He suggested that the nursing staff should keep them, or dispose of them as they saw fit. Once again, he asked for a photograph to be taken of her room. It seemed the least he could do.

It was very nearly nine p.m. Mr. Fuller offered to drive him home, which Bruce was pleased to accept. There were things that he could do that evening, although the main tasks would have to wait until the next day. Mr. Fuller could not have been kinder. Bruce thanked him warmly as he was deposited outside his own front door.

He went in. How different everything looked! But there was no time for sentiment. His first call was to Jane at the school. She was at home, and fully understood that he would not want to come in for a while. They agreed the wording of the notice that she would pin up on the practice room door, cancelling all lessons.

The next thing was to leave a message with the solicitors requesting an immediate appointment, and then one with the local authority along similar lines. Finally, Bruce rang Bill's number. He had planned to leave a brief message explaining what had happened, and asking for Bill's help, but at the last moment he thought better of it. Instead he left a 'welcome home' message, hoping that they would ring him. He did not want them to be greeted by bad news on their return

Bruce reckoned he would probably want to cancel some of his private pupils as well, but that could wait. Having cleared his next few mornings, he might be able to continue with his home teaching in the afternoons and evenings. He would not make any further phone calls that night.

It was a quarter to ten. Somehow, he needed to relax and get a night's sleep. A bath seemed to be the thing. When he climbed into bed forty minutes later, he tried to recall his mother as he had known her aged five, but it proved impossible. All he could think of was the figure in the bed. What struck him most forcibly was that when she died, she was alone. That should not happen to anyone, he thought.

It took a long time, but he gradually felt himself relaxing, and at last he fell asleep.

44. From: Mission 12
To: Undisclosed recipients
Sent:

Well, this is it, I suppose. They've all gone on the 'fact-finding mission'. Even Clairie. I'm staying in charge up here, with Big Nimp for company, looking after the ship, while they go off on their adventures. Quite like old times.

I found it very difficult saying goodbye to Celia. I know she's desperate to go. When I first woke her, she explained to me that her one goal in life has been to be part of a star settlement programme. I really don't want to stop her. However, the fact is they have taken enough food to last them for three months. Goodness knows how long they will be down there. She and I have never been apart before.

To tell you the truth, I think I'm losing her. Things have not been the same since Max woke the other eight. We still sleep in the same bed, but the fun has gone out of the relationship. I don't know what to do to get it back. I have tried! Both Max and Clairie have noticed it, and commented on it to me in their own way. I have tried talking to Celia about it, but she can be defensive and secretive when she wants to, and I have not been able to get through. I've also noticed that she has not been in her studio once since the eight woke. She used to love the painting before. I don't know what she does all day, now; I'm just aware that it happens somewhere else than where I am. It's horrid.

Talking of relationships, I was right about Paul and Sandra. It's out in the open now. I'm pleased for them. They are both nice people.

I wanted to get some communication satellites up round Targetto, at least three, but they all said not to worry. We will be in contact for fifteen hours out of every thirty-two. I hope it will be alright. Not that there's much I can do if they get into trouble.

However, I did insist that there should be more than one lander. They agreed in the end. The lander is shaped like an aeroplane, being streamlined to minimise air resistance. We've made three. Each one took twelve days to make.

Really, this mission is a team effort by Big Nimp, Grim Reaper, and we humans. We are dependant on the machines. Whether they also need us I am not so sure.

Two landers have gone down, and one is here for me, if I need it. The landers double as sky-cars, allowing them to get about.

Now, you need to hear this, even though I have told nobody else on board. I am convinced that the single most crucial thing about the entire mission is that the machines don't let us down.

However, all machines break down sooner or later. So, whatever else we need, we need backups.

It's obvious, really, although it took me a long time to see it. The first task of the replicator is to replicate itself. We also need a copy of Big Nimp. Why didn't we make a backup spaceship on the way over, you ask? Well, I never thought of it, but if I had, it was out of the question; we would have run out of sand. But now we are here, and there is any amount of rock around for Grim Reaper to consume.

I looked in the memory, and sure enough, there is a backup programme for the spaceship. It takes seventy days to make. That will duplicate both Big Nimp and Grim Reaper

Now for the tricky bit. You may think it was wrong of me, but I did not tell them what I was going to do. The reason is that when I raised the need for backup machines in the meeting, I was shouted down. They all think I have a problem, and that all I do is worry unnecessarily. Mark even told me that if I went on spreading gloom and depression about all the possible difficulties that my fertile imagination dreamt up, I would endanger the mental health of everyone. I found this highly insulting. He made it sound as if I was some sort of nutcase. However, no-one else stood up for me. He can be very domineering.

I decided then and there that I would go it alone. You probably think it is wrong, but the way I see it is this. We are the pioneers of a settlement programme that we hope will flourish over the coming centuries. We owe it to our descendants to get it right. There is a responsibility on us to get things going in the best way from the start. We should not be behaving as if it was an extended holiday.

So I instructed Big Nimp to start the seventy day programme within minutes of them leaving. My

hope is that by the time they return, it will be
so far advanced that nobody will be able to
gainsay it. I'm sure they will thank me in the
end.

If they are so long on their jaunt that the
ship is finished before they return, then I will
send it off to a Lagrangian point. That is a
position in space between two heavenly bodies,
where the gravity of the one cancels out the
gravity of the other. There are several of them
between Targetto and its moon. It means that
something can park there without needing to fire
its motors all the time to stay in the same
place. Once that is done, if an asteroid hits one
of the ships, we will still have the other. I
think it is common sense. I just wish I could do
it openly. I hate this secrecy.

Yes, I do feel bad about deceiving them, but I
assure you, it's in a good cause. You'll see.

Bruce

Next morning, Bruce got up at the usual time. It was strange not
to be going in to work. Bruce felt sad about it. He would be missing
Araminta and the scamps, as well as several others. Never mind.

The solicitors rang at ten past eight, to his surprise. It turned out
that one of the partners liked to get in early in order to move his
paperwork forward before the interruptions began at nine. He would
be in all morning, and would see Bruce whenever he could make it.
He could not have been more helpful. His name amused Bruce; Mr.
Chisel sounded rather a good name for a lawyer.

Bruce arranged to travel in by train during the next hour. He
hoped to be able to take another train from the solicitors to the local
authority man later that morning. He was soon on his way to the
station.

There seemed to be more people than ever on the trains. Bruce
could not understand why the sky-suits had become so exclusively
the province of teenagers. He would love to have had further
lessons, and flown in to work each day, but had been talked out of it

by Celia's gang. Also, you seldom if ever saw anybody flying about these days. Was it turning out to be just another craze - great for a few months, but then the young people lost interest and moved on to something else? Bruce simply could not understand it.

After leaving the train, he forced his way through the crowds, and was soon at the solicitors' office. Mr. Chisel himself opened the door. He turned out to be grey-haired, sixty plus, and plum full of friendliness.

There was not much to say. Bruce's granddad had arranged for Bruce's mother to be cared for by the local authority, following the court ruling. Bruce asked about this. It was as he had feared. His father had become violent. He had been sentenced for a long time for grievous bodily harm. He had spent part of the time in mental institutions.

Did Mr. Chisel know what had happened to his sister Sasha, Bruce wondered. This innocent question had a profound effect on Mr. Chisel.

"Oh dear, did nobody ever tell you?"

"Tell me what?" Bruce did not like the sound of this.

"Your sister Sasha was found senseless in your parents' bedroom. Her injuries were consistent with having been dashed violently against the wall. I'm afraid she died a fortnight later."

This was a terrible blow. Bruce put his head in his hands. Sasha was dead, killed by his crazed dad to all appearances. How awful. Perhaps she had gone in and remonstrated with him. How dreadful.

Then Bruce realised that his reaction of running off down the garden may well have saved his own life. No wonder he had not been taken back inside the house. It also helped explain his granddad's reluctance to tell him what had happened. He wondered whether he would have done the same himself if he had been in Granddad's position. How could a little boy possibly cope with all that trauma?

"This must come as a terrible shock, Mr. Winter."

Bruce dragged his mind back to the present.

"All these years I've been wondering what happened to Sasha, and whether she might get in touch one day. In fact, I've been to the

Family Records Centre more than once to check the marriage registers to see if she had married. I also searched the death registers for news of my parents," he added. "I wonder how I missed her entry?"

"You'll need some time to get over this."

"Yes, but in the immediate, I want to be involved in arranging my mother's funeral. In fact, I want to make it a double funeral, and have it in memory of Sasha as well. I wonder if I might ring the local authority people from your phone?"

Mr. Chisel was eager to help. Bruce managed to get through to the right person, and arranged to see him at 11.30 that morning. Things were going as well as could be hoped, despite the terrible news. Mr. Chisel made him a coffee. There was one more area to probe.

"As regards my father, do you have any information about him?"

"He served a long prison sentence, naturally, and was released some years ago. If you want to find out about him, an enquiry to the prison authorities would be the place to start. If you like, I could make a call, as I have a contact there, and they could put out some feelers. There would be no charge."

This was very generous, and would be one less thing to worry about.

"Yes, I'd be very pleased if you would. It's very kind of you."

Bruce had no idea what he would do if his father was located. No, on second thoughts, that was not right. He knew without a shadow of a doubt that he would forgive him completely. The thing to do was to be certain about that, before any feelings had time to come into play. Bruce had a sudden mental image of a form being stamped by a bank clerk. Signed, sealed and definite. What Bruce had no idea of was how he was going to get his feelings to line up with that decision. He was dimly aware that it would be a terrific struggle. But he would get there in the end, whatever it took.

Hadn't his father suffered enough already? It must be terrible living with all that guilt and shame.

Mr. Chisel was speaking again. "Is there anything else I can help you with?"

Once again, Bruce jerked himself back to the present.

"Sorry. I find all this news a bit much. No, thanks, I think that's everything. You have my number to contact me; may I give you my address too?"

Bruce handed over his card.

"Piano," said Mr. Chisel with interest. "I play jazz saxophone myself."

This was lovely. "I've always thought that Adolph Sax did us all a great favour when he married the trumpet to the clarinet and made a new instrument. People were critical at the time, but they've been proved wrong. I love the sound, personally. Well done. Do you play in a group?"

"Yes. We've been at it for years, one or two nights a week. All sorts of venues. It's great fun."

Bruce sometimes acted on impulse. "There's no chance you could play something soulful at my mother's funeral, if I can arrange it, is there? Something bluesy? I imagine you're all busy during the daytime."

"Well, it's a novel idea, and I think it will appeal to the others. Two of them have retired recently, so it might be a possibility. Let me know the date and time as soon as you can, and we'll discuss it."

It was time for Bruce to leave. He thanked Mr. Chisel very warmly. As he walked towards the station, he felt he had made a new friend.

45. From: Mission 12
To: Undisclosed recipients
Sent:

Well, so much for my backup programme. The number of times I have had to put the new spaceship on hold and respond to their requests for further supplies, you would not believe. I can understand the need for bubble domes, which are large blow-up tents to manage temperature variations, and so forth. Survival aids are clearly essential. But what do they want bicycles for, for goodness sake?

The one which made me mad went like this.

"Bruce, is there a template for a swimming pool in Big Nimp?"

"Just let me check... Yes, there is. Twenty-five metres by fifteen. Takes ten days to make. But there's..."

"Do it. Bye."

This was absurd. They had already told me about the wonderful unspoilt beaches and fabulous surf. I'd made them their surf boards. What on earth did they want a swimming pool for?

I got on to Max.

"Dad, it's really important to keep up morale. Several of the girls said they would rather have a swimming pool. Honestly, you have so little idea about team building. Please don't be obstructive."

"But Max, it will need a far bigger lander to bring it down," I urged.

"Whatever. Just get on and do it, Dad. I know I can count on you."

I found this very difficult. All pretence of this being a fact-finding mission seems to have evaporated. Max is out of his depth, frankly.

Oh yes, I almost forgot to tell you the main thing. There is no life at all on the planet. Not a microbe. But all the tests they have done in between the sunbathing and relaxing show it is suitable for life.

I'm quite pleased, really. Being able to start from scratch must be a dream come true for horticulturalists, botanical engineers, marine biologists, you can invent names for all the people we are going to need. I imagine that's what all those folks snoozing away downstairs are. Wonderful, really.

However, I'm getting ahead of myself.

There has been a really helpful suggestion, from Mark of all people. He was much the best I've known him when he came on the line.

"Bruce, the water - land ratio on the planet's surface is fifty - fifty, as we knew before. On earth, it was seventy - thirty. Now we've been talking, and we reckon it would be good to raise the water level by a metre. We reckon it might help the weather patterns. Could you ask Big Nimp to make some projections?"

Well, the answers were fascinating. If the water level rose a metre, it seemed that the rainfall would increase significantly. More evaporation, I suppose. This would help get the vegetation going. Much of the planet is rolling sand dunes, they say. So increased rainfall sounds good to me.

Next I was told to get Big Nimp to search for water ice in the star system. It turns out that there is an asteroid belt here, and that many of the asteroids are ninety percent water ice. So I was asked to see if there were any action plans in Big Nimp for moving asteroids around. They want to bring some down on the planet.

In the end, we all agreed we had found the best solution. It was Phil who said the asteroids should be broken up so as to cause minimal disturbance when entering the atmosphere. I suggested cubic metre blocks, which weigh just abut one ton each. They would easily burn up on entering the atmosphere before reaching the ground. When we found a mass accelerator template in Big Nimp, it seemed the way ahead was clear.

We are to make four more excavators, and four mass accelerators, to work in pairs.

I'd better explain the mass accelerator. The nineteenth century visionary Jules Verne wrote a book called From the Earth to the Moon. In it, he proposed a space gun, which would fire a hollow cannon ball made of aluminium, nine feet in diameter, weighing 20,000 pounds, all the way to the moon. The gun was to have a barrel nine hundred feet long!

Well, it was impractical, because of the earth's atmosphere. Anything going that fast would burn up because of the air resistance. However, in places where there is no atmosphere, the idea is a good one. So well done Jules Verne!

That basically describes the mass accelerator. The means of propulsion is interesting. The barrel has a coil of wire wrapped around it for its whole length. The payload simply rests in a bucket inside the barrel. By passing a powerful electric current through the coil, a force is produced which makes the bucket move quickly up the barrel. As it gets to the end, the current is suddenly reversed, which instantly halts the bucket. The payload, however, feels no such compunction; it sails merrily on into space. Then a gentle current is applied the other way through the coil, and the bucket glides back to the bottom of the barrel, ready for the whole process to begin again. Neat, really, and simple enough for me to understand how it operates. I always feel comforted by that; if I can grasp how something works, it has a straightforward design, by definition, and is therefore less likely to go wrong.

Well, I expect you are wondering about the recoil; at least, you are if you have ever fired a shotgun. The kick to the shoulder is memorable.

Such concerns are trifling with our advanced technology. Please forgive a little boasting! Seriously, every reaction can be countered by the correct firing of motors. The mass accelerator may need a tug to pull it around the place, but it has its own set of thrusters. The operation of the thrusters is so well regulated that it can fire off a projectile without the slightest recoil. In fact, and this is the remarkable thing, the accuracy of the system is so great that even over a flight path of millions of miles, they know where the payload will end up, within a few hundred metres. Now that's remarkable.

This means that it is possible to fire off the blocks of ice from the asteroid belt, like cannon balls, and for them to plop into the atmosphere on Targetto a few years later. Just make sure that your spaceship is not in the flight path.

Some of the team wanted to do it this way. Others felt it would be safer and more reliable to tow the asteroids close to the earth before breaking them up into fragments for atmosphere entry. In the end, a compromise was agreed. The asteroids will be towed towards earth, but the mass accelerators will start work on them immediately, during the journey, so the whole thing will be like a moving pop-gun.

I've thought of an easier name for the mass accelerator, which you have to admit is rather a mouthful. I run the words together and shorten the result to Massaccor, pronounced 'massacre'. It rolls off the tongue, and it's also a reminder of what happens if you are unfortunate enough to get in the way of the missile. The others gave their usual silent 'we're not overly impressed with you' response. I'm beginning to get used to it by now.

It is not easy doing everything over the phone. Things would be a lot easier face to face.

I do feel lonely!
Bruce

Bruce was seated opposite a Mr. Fish, who was handling the arrangements for his mother's funeral. Wayford Crematorium had been booked for the following Thursday at 2.30. That was a week from today. It sounded fine.

There would be another funeral following on at 3.00. Bruce had rather feared that this might be the case. Funerals could easily be over long, but twenty minutes did seem very tight.

"Can you try and get the preceding slot too? The thing is, I want to remember Sasha my sister as well as my mother, and in addition I'm hoping to arrange a musical item."

Bruce told Mr. Fish about Mr. Chisel and his jazz group.

"Well, that is extraordinary," Mr. Fish replied. "I'm told that Mrs. Winter was very uncommunicative, except that she did enjoy having music played on the sound system. One of the staff who was very patient with her managed to grasp that jazz was her favourite sound; he even reckoned that he had discovered her favourite record. He used to put it on for her, and click his fingers in time. It was not possible to be certain, but they thought it gave her pleasure."

Bruce had a mental image of an old woman slumped in a chair with her mouth hanging open listening to jazz. There were no feelings yet.

"We'll try for the two o' clock slot as well, but we won't know for several days. It all depends on how many deaths there are. But there's a reasonable chance, as they try to programme in a generous lunch break for the staff if they can, so they won't give away 2.00 in a hurry, and also Thursday is often a quieter day. Friday is the one to avoid. It's always very busy. Here are the details of the minister."

Mr. Fish pushed across a printed slip with the details of an Anglican clergyman on it.

"Oh dear. I was rather hoping to be able to dispense with a clergyman, unless he knew my mother personally, perhaps?"

"No, he's just the duty clergyman for the day."

"Can we do it without him?"

"Certainly, if you're sure you can manage it without breaking down. That's the difficult part."

"I've already thought about that. I have a number of friends who will want to come, and I reckon we can share it round between us. Then when it gets to the words of committal, we'll all say it together."

"What a great idea. Good for you. And yes, go for the music if you can fix it up."

By lunchtime, it was all agreed. The crematorium would try and hold the 2.00 slot as well, and Ian Chisel was going to sound out the rest of the Blues Brigade, as they called themselves. It turned out that three of them had been friends since attending the Boys Brigade as teenagers, hence their title. Mr. Fish had cancelled the duty clergyman.

Now Bruce needed to put the word around his friends. It would be either two or two-thirty on Thursday at Wayford Crematorium. Also, there was now something to be pleased about. Bruce had inherited his musical gift from his mother. He felt a warm glow, and a sense of gratitude. He was beginning to feel something, at any rate, which was a relief.

```
46. From: Mission 12
To: Undisclosed recipients
Sent:
```

Phil came up to se me. He brought Margaret and Clairie. I was very pleased; it was great to have some company again.

Things were a bit strained when they arrived. I soon realised why. Phil had been sent up to tell me that the other fifteen astronauts are to be woken. The holiday-makers felt I might need some moral support at wake-up time. (Holiday-maker is my word, not his). I knew what that meant. They did not trust me. I might say things about the ones down on the surface that would cause prejudice.

What do they think I am, for goodness sake? I am one hundred percent committed to this mission. That's the cause of all our disagreement! How could they imagine that I would want to sow disaffection between one group of astronauts and another?

Okay so there is a difference of view about how the settlement programme should be conducted, but

304

it is for everyone to make up their mind about this. To be frank, I think that my stand is doing everybody a favour; it forces people to think. I've noticed that among human beings, there is too much following other people like sheep. I've always thought it. Where are the ones who stand up for what they believe in? Are they a dying breed?

So, when I wake the fifteen up, which I'm happy to do, my attitude will be 'Welcome to the settlement. What's yours, beer or whisky?'

No, actually, I won't be offering them alcohol. But a friendly, cheerful welcome is the way, even though I feel anything but cheerful myself.

Clairie did not appear at all pleased to see me. I found her sullen and distant. She seems to be a teenager before her time. I wondered why she had come. Phil told me over a cup of tea. She has been flirting with Dickon! Phil brought her to get her away from him for a bit. It seems that watching Paul and Sandra has given her ideas ahead of her years.

I felt very angry. Dickon should know better! It became apparent that Celia is worse than useless. I haven't heard from her in weeks, by the way. It's over between us; no good pretending anything else. I try not to think about her.

Phil told me that she is behaving quite strangely, he thought. Why are women so complicated? No, I take it back; perhaps it's me that's complicated. Oh dear.

Margaret has come up for two reasons. She wants to get a programme of seeding the planet started. Lichen is the place to begin, she reckons. I agree with starting small. The first little specimens to plant are the stalwart ones that can feed happily off the minerals in the soil without needing bacteria or anything like that. Margaret wants to culture them up here, and then take a lander-full down to get started. They have chosen

a site near a stream, with natural shade in the
heat of the day from overhanging rocks. I
suggested ferns, but they are to come later,
apparently. Then the game plan is that the lichen
will spread about from there. I wonder if it will
play ball.

The second reason is that she does not like the
atmosphere down there; the vibes of the group,
that is, not the air. The latter seems to be
fine. I expect what she means is that Max has
been making advances. I'm afraid I feel so
cynical about them all, that I tend to imagine
the worst. So she's pleased to have a change of
scene.

She did not mention it, but I hope that doing
some singing might be a part of her decision. I
hope so. It will be nice to have her around.

I could not seem to recapture the banter that
Phil and I used to enjoy. I don't know why it's
all gone so horrible. I hope things will get
easier one day.

I need not have worried about them discovering
the backup space rocket. The 'pioneers' will be
staying down there for the foreseeable future. I
parked the backup two hundred miles above us
while the others came up. It's nowhere near
finished, but at least it's mobile. I reckon it's
about half done.

What I do now is that each time there is a
request for equipment, I delay the order by
twenty-four hours, so that I can get an extra day
of construction in. They have not rumbled me.
It's working well.

We woke the fifteen. I did not have any
interest in getting to know them, I'm ashamed to
say. I just introduced myself as the caretaker.
It's a good way of getting people to ignore you,
I've found. They all wanted to go down,
naturally. We made a couple more landers (more
delays to the real work), and off they went, with

rations enough for an army, taking Phil and
Clairie with them.
    I hope they enjoy it. I really do.
    Bruce.

When Bruce answered the doorbell on Thursday evening, there were two figures on the doorstep rather than one.

"I hope you don't mind, Bruce," Sarah was saying, "but Araminta has come too. We understand you needing to cancel your lessons at the school in order to make arrangements for the funeral. We wondered whether we could have a joint lesson."

This was a brilliant idea. It would help take his mind off things.

"Of course. Why didn't I think of it? Come in. Well done."

Araminta was speaking. "We were sorry to hear about your mother's death."

Bruce gave them a quick summary, in his usual cheerful voice.

"I don't feel upset about it yet," he ended, "although it will come in due course. But I am pleased to discover that she was musical."

Sarah was getting settled on the piano stool, and Araminta had sat in an armchair, but Bruce said "No!" in a commanding voice. They looked at him in surprise. "Duets!" he said, pulling an upright seat across to make a second place to sit.

"Now, the first and most fundamental rule about piano duets is strict demarcation of seating." Bruce closed one eye for greater accuracy. "Middle C is the dividing line," he said, drawing a line through the air with his hand outwards from the middle of the keyboard, so as to divide the piano in half. The stool needed to move fractionally to the left.

"Thou hast set them their bounds which they shall not pass," Bruce added in a majestic voice, for greater effect. There was a great art in producing apt quotations. "There. Now who's going on the top, and who's going on the bottom?"

All this was new to the two girls.

"Four hands on one piano," Bruce explained. "The thing is, in the days before the invention of recording, there were only two ways of getting to know the orchestral repertoire. One was to go to

307

the concert hall, and hear the great symphonies being played. But the second way was to play an arrangement of them on the piano. Trying to jam all that material into one pair of hands was all very well, but if the arranger had two players rather than one at his disposal, then he could make a better job of it. Hence piano duets!"

All this time, Bruce was rummaging in his duets drawer. There was a number of old leather bound volumes with Schubert, Mendelssohn and the like in gold lettering on them. He soon found what he was looking for.

"The Brandenburg Concertos by J.S. Bach," he announced. "Do you know them?"

The girls did not.

"Bach wrote them for the Marquis of Brandenburg. He was a big wig, and had a court orchestra, so Bach dashed him off half a dozen numbers. Fabulous stuff. Anyway, here they are, arranged for four hands. Now, we'll try the first movement of number four, unbelievably slowly." He found the place in the music.

The girls looked confused. What did they have to do?

"Okay, let's take it step by step. Now the music is printed in landscape format, so that the open volume spreads out well across the music stand. Sarah, you play this left hand page, and Araminta, you play what's on the right hand page. Sarah, both your hands are written in the bass clef, which will confuse you to begin with. In the same way, both your hands are in the treble clef, Araminta. Got it?"

The girls nodded.

"Now, the crucial thing is to keep going. You do not stop for any reason whatever. But supposing you can't read it all quickly enough. If that happens, just keep one hand going, and then bring in the other again when you can manage it. Sarah, it is your left hand, playing the lowest notes, that we most need to hear. So if you need to leave out one hand, it is the right hand you should leave off. Araminta, vice versa. Keep your right hand going at all costs, because that's the tune, and drop the left if you need to. Alright?"

The girls were as ready as they ever would be. The music was marked *Allegro*, a fast pace.

"We're going to go ultra slow," said Bruce, "and I mean, ultra slow. I'll count you in. Are you ready? One - two - three…"

The girls set off. Bruce had expected them to crash after a few seconds, but to his surprise and delight they managed to keep going. However, after half a minute things degenerated, and the sound was soon a cacophony.

"Woah, woah, I can't believe that!" Bruce exclaimed as the girls stopped. "What happened?"

"Perhaps one of us got a bar out?" Sarah suggested.

"No doubt about it," laughed Bruce. "It's so easy to do. The kind of thing that goes wrong is that one of you plays a group of notes at double speed, or maybe at half speed. Then you wonder why it sounds hideous. So you have to concentrate on the rhythms as well as the notes."

"Dear, it all seems so difficult," murmured Araminta.

"It is difficult. In fact all music is difficult. It is a constant struggle to improve your skills. Never mind, let's go from letter A. They kindly put capital letters above the music from time to time in case you crash and need to start again from somewhere in the middle. Are you ready? One - two - three…"

This time it went better. They were getting the hang of it. Araminta was only attempting to play with her right hand, Bruce noticed, but she was accurate and in time. Sarah was keeping the left hand going, and also managing to bring in the right hand as well in some places.

"Okay, stop!" Bruce ordered, as they reached a convenient stopping point. "Not bad. How are you feeling about it?"

"Alright," said Sarah, "although I do find sight-reading really difficult."

"We all do," replied Bruce. "When I was a student, I made myself sight-read through the whole of Wagner's Ring Cycle in a piano reduction for just two hands. That's four operas, lasting eighteen hours in total. It took me months to do, but I managed it. However, I decided afterwards that my sight-reading was no better at the end than it had been at the beginning!"

"Great," said Araminta with heavy sarcasm. "I can hardly wait."

"Well, it's the only way to get better. Actually, my sight-reading must have improved, even though I was not aware of it, because it's reasonable now. It's the same with everything in life. You just have to keep at it. Okay, we'll start from the beginning again, and this time I will add in what you miss out on my recorder."

That Bruce played the recorder was news to the girls. He was full of surprises! This was what made the lessons fun. Before long, the three of them were making a reasonable sound. It was much easier the second time through. This time, they persevered until they had finished the whole movement.

"Good," said Bruce. "Now, as I say, there is an enormous literature of piano duets. You tend to find old volumes in second hand bookshops. Keep your eyes open. Look, here's an arrangement of Beethoven symphonies, numbers one to five. Six to nine are in another volume. Can I give you a challenge? Have a go at the first movement of Beethoven's fifth - that's the famous one that starts ber-ber-ber-berm, and then when you can play it, we'll have another joint lesson and you can perform it to me."

The girls agreed happily. Bruce was pleased.

"Right, one last run-through of the Bach, but this time - take a deep breath - we're going to do it up to speed."

The girls expressed shock and horror, but Bruce could tell from their faces that they were enjoying the challenge.

"Okay, here we go. I'll turn the pages. We do not stop for anything, understood? Ready? One - two - three…"

It sounded reasonable. Bruce was having to work hard on his recorder, as Araminta had abandoned all attempts at her left hand at the faster speed, and Sarah's right hand was struggling. Still, they were managing the tune and the bass line. Bruce's constant tootling reminded him of a silent sketch he had once seen, in which the solo performer was gyrating around fit to bust on the stage, and the audience had to guess what he was acting. The answer had been that he was miming a performance of Stravinsky's Rite of Spring arranged for solo bass clarinet. It had been an extraordinary sight. Nobody had guessed correctly.

While they were hard at it, the phone rang. Bruce somehow managed to lift the receiver between his chin and shoulder while continuing to play, and lay it on the table.

"You'll have to hold," he gasped after playing a run of fast notes, "we're heavily into Bach here. I hope you can hear it at your end."

The movement was soon over. Bruce asked the girls to excuse him, but to his astonishment, he found the caller had hung up. How extraordinary that there were people around who did not appreciate fine music. But at least the three of them had kept going despite the distraction.

The girls were putting on their coats. "We must go; we've overrun our time by a long way."

It was true; the time had flown. Bruce was sorry the lesson was over.

"Great to see you," he called after them from the front door. They both waved cheerfully.

47. From: Mission 12
To: Undisclosed recipients
Sent:

You'll have been wondering how many blocks of ice will be needed to raise the oceans by one metre. Well, if you weren't, you ought to have been. I've been working it out.

I am reliably informed (thanks to You-know-who) that the surface area of a sphere is found by squaring the radius, and then multiplying the result by four times 'pi'. That's the mathematicians' name for a special number, by the way. It's a number a little larger than three that somebody discovered a long time ago, which happens to do the job nicely. It was probably Pythagoras, as it sounds like his name. Perhaps we should think of it as 'py' instead of 'pi'.

The radius of Targetto is 3841 miles. That's the distance from the surface to the middle of the globe. So turning that into metres and squaring it, we get 38210632433848. That's a heck of a lot already, but we haven't finished yet. Oh no!

Times it by 'Pi' and then times it by four, and the answer is 480168968572787. That's the number of ice blocks needed to have one on every square metre of ocean.

I knew it would be a lot, but I was not prepared for this, needless to say!

Then I remembered that only fifty percent of Targetto is ocean, so I needed to halve the figure. But then, increasing the depth of the oceans by a metre will make them larger, I thought. Bound to. So we'd better add on a bit more. Call it an extra ten percent. So that makes sixty percent.

Are you with it so far? The great thing about emails is that you can ditch them if you don't like them. Perhaps you have pressed the delete button already, but if you have then you won't be reading this, so it was a bit pointless saying that, really.

I've always thought that mathematics and cooking have a lot in common. Get your ingredients spread out before you on the work surface, and then bung them in the pan one by one. Keep stirring! Adjust quantities to taste. Draw out a teaspoonful for testing by tongue. Then when satisfied, serve up, and accept no criticism from the diners.

Anyway, back to the sum. I don't know how fast those excavators work, but let's imagine that the massaccors can fire off an ice block every four minutes. There are going to be four of them, so that's one ice block landing on the blanket of air above Targetto every minute, presuming no hiccoughs and that not a single one goes astray. Some hope!

So, to see how long it's going to take to finish the project, we need to divide our figure by 60 for minutes in the hour, then by 24 for hours in the day, then by 365 for days in the year, and we'll end up with the number of years.

All that division should bring the number down a bit Now let me see, that's…

Five hundred and forty-eight million years!

I rubbed my eyes. Surely, there must be some mistake. I checked my sums; they seemed accurate. I was staggered. Then I decided to cheat. I asked Big Nimp how long it would take, at the rate of one block per minute. He said five hundred and sixty million years.

He's not bad, really. A little bit out, admittedly. But close enough to confirm my work.

There's only one thing for it. If we are serious about this, we are going to have to have a lot more machines on the job.

Like four million rather than just four? And are there enough asteroids out there to keep them busy for five hundred and sixty years, or will we run out?

Bruce

It was Friday evening, and Bruce was waiting for Celia at the Chinese restaurant. At any other time, he would have been nervous, but the enormity of the news he had received this week put everything else into perspective. As regards his father's actions, and his mother's state, he still felt completely blank. Doubtless there would be a reaction sooner or later.

Celia looked ravishing when she arrived. Bruce was pleased that he had not cancelled the date. It would be nice to tell her what had happened. He was sure she would understand.

They were shown to a table. The white tablecloth, the vase of flowers and the small candle that was lit specially for them in their presence all added up to a pleasing effect. Bruce felt happy.

"How are you?" he asked.

313

"Yes, Okay, bumbling along in my own sweet way. How about you?"

There was nothing for it but to tell her everything. His mystery at what had happened that fateful day when he was little, his failed attempts at the Family Record Centre, and then the phone call out of the blue just a day or two before, and its results.

"You poor thing," said Celia when he had finished, with genuine concern. "I had no idea about your past. If I may say so, you've turned out very well for somebody with a disturbed background like that."

Bruce thanked her. "Put it down to my granddad."

Yes, he had been through difficult times. The only way he knew was to grin and bear it. The thing to do was to live life in such a way as to give other people the opposite experience of what he had had, as far as he could. This meant helping people, where possible, and living in a way that did not upset others. That was why being a piano teacher suited him; by definition, all his pupils were in the position of needing a leg-up to clamber up to the next level of proficiency, as it were. Bruce would have liked to tell her that a favourite verse of his was the one in Psalm eighteen where it said, 'By my God I leap over a wall,' but his nerve failed him. Why was it so difficult to raise the subject of faith with people? With Celia in particular? Life was full of walls to be scaled. Wasn't it good that God was there to give you a leg-up in time of need!

"It's all fixed. Thursday 2.00 at Wayford Crem. I'm pretty certain that Ian Chisel's group will be there to play for us; I hope so. Anyway, I've managed to get rid of the duty clergyman."

"The what?" Celia asked.

"The duty clergyman. Isn't it a terrible title? These people should operate out of love, not duty. What happens is that when a funeral comes in, if it is a family with no church connections, then they assign the duty clergyman to them, who of course is a complete stranger. You see, I've played the organ often enough at these events to see how the system works. Then this man conducts the funeral and tells the assembled relatives how they should be handling their grief, or something like that."

Bruce was quite worked up; Celia was surprised. He was not aware of how strongly he felt.

"But if you think about it," he went on, "it is the complete opposite of what Jesus said in the Gospels. He told his followers to raise the dead, but the duty clergyman turns up to confirm the death instead. Jesus said the good shepherd knows his own sheep by name, but the duty clergyman is a stranger to the family. Then Jesus had things to say on lots of subjects, and gave a lot of instructions to his followers, but what does the duty clergyman do when his opportunity comes? He talks about handling grief or something like that, which Jesus never mentioned. And look at the result; all these non-church people coming in, and what they get from the man in white and black does not communicate anything Christian whatever. In fact, quite the reverse. It actually gives completely the wrong impression. It makes me so angry."

Celia had never seen Bruce like this before. She was shocked. Bruce saw it in her face.

"Oh dear, sorry. I didn't mean to get so carried away. Anyway, there won't be one on Thursday, thankfully. Let's talk about you instead."

But this was a non-starter. Celia repeated her usual line, that the less Bruce knew about her and her work, the safer it was for everyone. Bruce felt frustrated. How could you get to know a girl if she was so secretive all the time?

Bruce asked how Simone was, and Celia said fine, as far as she knew. He tried other subjects, with little success. Fairly soon it was time to settle the bill. At least the food had been good.

"I'm sorry, Bruce," Celia said when they got outside. "I'm afraid I'm not much good for you."

Bruce was feeling upset, but he wanted to be generous.

"You're really committed to the work you do. You're like those communists in the early days, who put the party before their own personal happiness. I only hope that the people you work for are worth it, and that they appreciate you. They are lucky to have you. And may I say, you look absolutely fabulous."

315

She was clearly pleased. They walked to her car in silence. Bruce held the door for her while she climbed in. These petrol-driven cars would soon be an endangered species, Bruce thought, with the new energy source gradually taking over.

"Thanks for coming," he said.

"Thanks for a nice evening. I hope all the final arrangements for Thursday go well, and that you don't dream of the duty clergyman. See you on Tuesday."

Bruce shook his head as he walked the short distance to his home. It was hard to see any possible future in a relationship with Celia. He pursed his lips tightly. Where do I go from here, he wondered.

```
48. From: Mission 12
To: Undisclosed recipients
Sent:
```

For several weeks, I used the mental image of the flying ice blocks to get off to sleep in place of counting sheep, like this.

"Phhht!" (Noise of massaccor sending missile, although of course as there is no atmosphere round the asteroids, there's nothing to hear. Shame really).

"Wheeesh…" (Sound of ice block entering atmosphere, audible this time, but really it's wrong to edit the eighteen month flight down to a few seconds).

"Crackle-crackle-crackle-crackle-crackle." (Ice block burning up in atmosphere).

Then the pattern began over again with block number two. It soon had me sleeping like a lamb.

Now, however, thinking about the ice block project just brings on stress. I asked Big Nimp how big the block could be and still burn up before reaching the surface. He said he didn't know! I was thrilled to have found something that Big Nimp had no answer for, although I did not crow about it, of course. No good upsetting him.

However, he did say that the rock which caused an explosion above Siberia's Tunguska River area in 1908 was the size of a small house. So we could increase the ice cube to two or three tons, I reckon, but not much more. That might make the operation a bit easier, but it also means the guns suddenly just got bigger. Maxi-massaccor, I reckon. Also, there's even more need to keep out of the way of the shot.

I did wonder whether it might be easier to build a whole fleet of spaceships, say twenty, go off and land on an asteroid or a comet, dig the spaceships in and get the beast under control, guide it along, and then bring it down Wham! onto Targetto, having abandoned the settlement first, naturally. There would be massive tidal waves if it landed in the ocean, and it might take a long time for the big boulder to melt, but after five years or so, things would settle down, and we would be further forward. But maybe the splash would be so huge that some of the ocean would be blasted free of Targetto's gravity, never to return. So we would lose water as well as gain. Rather a daft idea, really.

Anyway, you'll have guessed what the response was when I pointed out that our original idea was impractical.

"Oh well, we'll ditch it," said Mark.

Unbelievable really. Don't they care about the next generation at all?

I think we should have a go, personally. I've even thought of a slogan: "The raising of the sea by one millimetre in this generation!"

Bruce

Bill and Gnilla were due back on Saturday afternoon. Sure enough, the phone rang at about six. Bill was glowing; Bruce could sense it from his voice. It was not the moment to share his troubles. They agreed to meet on Sunday afternoon.

When they arrived, one look at their faces was enough to tell Bruce that they had had a lovely fortnight. He was really pleased for them.

"It was wonderful," Gnilla said. "The sky-car must have cost a fortune - Bill refuses to tell me how much, but having it made all the difference. By jet plane it takes eleven hours to California. How long do you think we took?"

"Five?" Bruce suggested.

"Three hours forty minutes. Isn't that amazing? And that's without any messing around at airports. We went straight from the marquee to our cabin in the San Bernardino mountains, just east of Los Angeles."

"But how do they prevent crime and terrorism? You could be taking in drugs or guns or anything."

"There's an arrangement for short term tourists now whereby you can have your car and the baggage checked over here. The luggage compartment is electronically sealed at this end, and it can only be opened by officials over there. When you land, the authorities are alerted, and a sky-car drops in beside you within thirty minutes, and you are checked in. Like a sort of mobile customs service."

Bill took over. "The service costs quite a bit, but it's worth it for a special occasion." He gave Gnilla a squeeze. "If they take longer than thirty minutes, then you get money back, and if it's longer than an hour, then they pay you! Ours turned up in eighteen minutes, sad to say. We forgave them."

Gnilla was clearly thrilled with the journey, if nothing else. Bruce was pleased about this, as her previous experience of a sky-car had not been good. Bill was grinning from ear to ear as well.

"The cabin was great - set in endless pine forests, with everything you could wish for. One feature I rather liked was a large supply of oranges and a press. You cut an orange in half, put it in the press and then squeezed out the juice into a glass and hey presto! Fresh orange juice."

"I liked the Blue Jays," said Gnilla.

"They were delightful," Bill explained. "Their croak was just like our jays over here, but they had lovely blue plumage. They used to wake us up in the morning, when the sun was rising, peeping through the trees. Little scavengers! They used to line up on the handrail beside the deck squawking for their breakfast."

"That was my job," Gnilla broke in. "There was a large jar of little nuts, and I used to put out a small bowlful for them. However, they fought so much over it that after a few days, I took to scattering a handful of nuts over the deck. That worked much better."

"Look," said Bill, "here's a photo." The wad of photos was thick, Bruce noticed, but he did not mind. In fact, all he wanted was for them to go on for ever about their holiday. He was so pleased for them.

"This is my favourite," said Gnilla, showing Bruce a particularly plump bird. It certainly was a lovely shade of blue.

"I wonder if they make good pets," Bruce observed. "Not that I could bear the idea of keeping one in a cage. I loved it at your reception, when all the tropical birds had freedom to fly around in the shop."

"Yes, it would be lovely to have one," Bill agreed, "but it was even better seeing them in their natural habitat. And they came each morning because they wanted to, not because we made them."

"I had a hamster when I was little," Bruce said with a distant look, "only my Mum said that it had returned to the wild during the night. I knew what that meant; they hadn't closed the cage door properly, and it had escaped. I was quite pleased, really, except that it was winter, and I was worried it might die in the cold outside."

"Oh no, nothing to worry about," Bill declared with authority. "Those little creatures find hay or leaves and burrow down in them. No, ten to one it found a mate and had lots of babies. In fact, you can hardly move for little mouse-type creatures at the old bicycle sheds near the station these days. I bet they're all descendants of your little runaway hamster. Just think of it; Bruce Winter, the Great Conservationist, whose hamster breeding programme fills the earth..."

Bill made expansive gestures with his arms while he was speaking. Gnilla wanted a word.

"Animal welfare apart, it was so useful having the sky-car. The scale of everything in America is so large. In a normal car, it takes you forty minutes to get off the mountain, and then another hour or two to get where you're going. Los Angeles is ninety miles long! But it doesn't feel built up."

"No;" Bill cut in again, "because of past earthquakes, no building is higher than one storey, or at least, that's how it felt. They have spread about sideways rather than building high rise. It's the opposite of New York."

"And no trains to speak of," said Gnilla. "The car manufacturers bought up the railroads in the early days, and then closed them down so that everyone would need a car. A crafty move, but environmentally hostile."

"But still, now that the sky-cars are coming in…" Bill cut in.

"…You can whiz about more quickly," Gnilla said firmly, not to be outdone.

"You two are funny," Bruce laughed. They were obviously so happy.

"Still," Bill said, "the only drawback is that with the number of sky-cars growing all the time, the sky above Los Angeles is getting crowded. There was this road along the edge of the mountain called the Rim of the World - isn't it a wonderful name? - with a place to park where you could look out and down over the whole of Los Angeles spread out to right and left below you as far as you could see. Amazing sight. But already the sky is filling up, as with black beetles wheeling about. Before long, they will be blocking out the sun, I reckon. It's changing the face of society."

Bill knew that Bruce was interested in new technology and its effects on society.

"We also stopped at the lay-by at night," Gnilla said. "Then you see all the lights of the great city down below, like fireflies. Wonderful."

"That was after we went to the astronomy club," said Bill.

"Yes," Gnilla broke in, determined not to be outdone. "It was a group of amateurs that met on the school playing field up there. It's so warm that you don't need to wrap up to look at the stars, like you do in this country."

"We took our binoculars," Bill said, "and it was a good thing we did. After a lecture about the universe, we all went outside and lay on the ground on our backs, looking upwards."

"I spotted the summer triangle," boasted Gnilla.

"That wasn't very difficult, as they are the first three stars to become visible as the evening darkens! Then what you had to do was to keep your eyes open, looking for a shooting star. It's a tiny point of light that whizzes through the sky. Apparently, they are caused by a fragment of a comet entering the atmosphere at high speed and burning up as a result of the friction. Might only be the size of a grain of dust."

"We never saw one," said Gnilla. "I was really disappointed."

"No," Bill said, "but did you hear them say that nobody had seen one all summer? Even in mid-August, which is high-season for shooting stars apparently, nobody had spotted a single one, whereas normally you might expect to see ten an hour. Rather weird, really."

Bruce said nothing. Gnilla was looking at him. "What's up, Bruce?" She asked.

This was it. "Look, I don't want to put a damper on things, but the fact is, I've had some bad news."

Bruce told them about his mother's death, his discovery about Sasha, and the funeral arrangements.

"Goodness," said Bill. "That is really something. You poor thing. You must be shattered. Can we help in any way?"

What Bruce really wanted was for Bill to be master of ceremonies at the crem. Bruce already knew what he himself wanted to say. It would be helpful to him not to have to do the introduction as well.

Bill agreed readily. They drew up a timetable.

"It's strange," Bruce said. "Just a few weeks ago, we were planning your wedding. I never imagined we'd be planning my mum's funeral next."

"Life's like that," Gnilla said. "We all have plans and schemes, but actually, you never know what's round the next corner."

Bruce was ready to see the photos, but Gnilla said it should be another time. They all hugged each other. Bruce was so pleased to have them back. He watched them off down the path.

"Great to have you home. Bye."

"Bye."

49. From: Mission 12
To: Undisclosed recipients
Sent:

I've got to have a go at writing this; it's no good putting it off any longer. I feel such a fool. It's horrid.

Now that Margaret has come up here to do her botany and seedlings, I am free to go down to the surface. So far, I have been using the need to have someone on the spaceship as an excuse for not going. Max finally talked me into it.

"Daddy, come down. Please come down, Daddy."

He does not often call me Daddy; only at key moments. So I decided to go.

The descent was much as I expected. For the shortest journey time, it's best to leave at the right moment in our orbit in order to glide easily to the settlement.

It was interesting seeing the planet gradually grow bigger and bigger until it filled the entire view. The clouds are just like the ones on earth. Same with the sea. Almost all of the land looked like desert, I thought.

Eventually we slowed down and glided to a halt. It's all automatic. I could have been asleep.

Phil was there to greet me. It was good to see him. I got out. The sun was shining; temperature in the mid seventies. I could hear the pounding of the surf on the beach on the other side of a low sand dune. I can see the attraction; it's delightful. A few hundred yards away were the bubble domes, and the landers parked next to the swimming pool. How ridiculous, I thought once again.

"Phil" I asked as we walked along, "how is it that there is so much Oxygen in the air here? What I mean is, on Earth, a lot of the Oxygen is produced by trees and plants, and also by plankton in the oceans; in other words, it is the product of living things. But as there is no life here, what is the mechanism that has produced it?"

"Haven't a clue," Phil said. "You do ask difficult questions."

"I used to worry on Earth that with the ever-increasing population, we might run out of air to breathe. Two million more people breathing each week than the one before seemed a reason for concern, I thought."

"Bruce, there are enough other problems in life not to worry about that as well. Honestly!"

I had had a sense of foreboding ever since agreeing to come down. It was as we were getting closer to the pool that I heard a peal of laughter and saw water being splashed. Celia's laughter. Mark in the pool.

Instantly I understood it all. Why had I been so blind?

A great rage filled me. I did not hesitate. I turned on my heels, despite Phil's protests, and marched back to the lander. Within three minutes I was airborne again. I was completely choked with emotion. Why had I been so dense?

If you take off at the right moment, it can be as little as forty-five minutes to get up to the ship. My flight path was going to take eight hours. However, I did not mind. I just wanted to get away from there.

Why had I not suspected? It all made perfect sense. Even in my rage and pain, I was thinking clearly. Did she really care for him, or was she under his spell? And did he really love her? Or had this been a strategic move? Was he simply trying to gain control of the settlement by grabbing the star player as a mate? I doubted that he really loved her. It was probably politically motivated.

No wonder Max was being so ineffectual. How could he stand up to his mother's lover? It also explained why everyone had been so awkward around me. They all knew that my wife had left me for someone else, and I had been the last to discover. I wondered whether they had all been laughing at me.

At any rate, I was glad that I had acted on my impulse and come away, because if I had walked on, I would have killed him somehow, and probably her as well. I felt so angry! This way, my temper would have time to cool, and I could decide rationally what to do over the coming days.

Somebody was trying to speak to me on the intercom. It was the work of a moment to turn it off. Radio blackout. I would communicate with them again when I was ready, and not before. I hoped nobody would attempt to come after me in one of the other landers.

Why had Celia betrayed me? We were doing fine before. Oh dear.

I have sometimes noticed that even in a moment of great emotion, part of my brain goes on thinking in a detached way. It was so now. Within a few minutes of getting airborne, I was sure that however much I was hurting, it would not be me who would spoil the mission by the first criminal act. I had always been committed to the undertaking. A chance for humanity to make a new start. The fact that the other humans were making an almighty mess of it, in my view, was not going to deflect me from doing my duty. I was not going to attempt to hurt them. This was going to be difficult, because at the moment, I just wanted to get hold of Mark and pull his limbs violently off one by one. However, it was my decision to forgive. Getting to the place where I felt forgiveness towards him and Celia might take years, but I would get there in the end.

I also knew where my duty lay. Creating the backup ship had been the right decision. However, it was on the way up, that I realised that one backup ship was ridiculously few. Why stop with one? Before long, there would be a need for many mobile Grim Reapers, not just one, because that is what the spaceship was in effect.

I knew what to do. When the backup was ready - only a day or two to go now - I would send it off to orbit the moon, with instructions to back itself up. Then the two backups were also to duplicate themselves, making four. Then eight, then sixteen, repeating the process. It was essential for the progress of the mission.

Even if my own personal life was in tatters, I could still put my energies into serving the mission. It was the only thing left for me now.

I feel the need to apologise to all of you at home. I have done really badly here. I hope you can forgive me, somehow, and that there may be something to learn from this fiasco to help with other missions.

Your loving friend,
Bruce

It was the day of the funeral. Bruce woke with a headache. He had not been sleeping well for some nights now. This whole business was proving more stressful than he had expected. Still, he was pleased to be doing it.

He had reinstated the morning lessons at the school from Monday, which meant he had only missed two days there. However, he was aware that the lessons were not very good quality. Never mind. He could do a lot of his teaching on auto pilot, really, but it was not good to come to as a pupil was playing the final chord of a piece and realise that his mind had been elsewhere. I must take a grip, he thought.

At lunchtime, he found he could not eat anything. He forced himself to have a drink of orange juice. Bill and Gnilla picked him up at 1.15 as arranged. Perhaps I should run a car, Bruce thought. On the other hand, it's good to allow other people to help me, otherwise, I could imagine myself becoming totally independent.

People were already arriving at the crem. Oh good, here was Ian with his band. And a drummer as well; excellent. There were five of them all told. Beautiful shiny instruments. Bruce thanked them warmly for coming, and said they were to fill every minute with sound, except when somebody specifically told them to be silent. Even when the coffin was coming in.

Oh look, Sarah and Araminta, looking very grave, sitting in the second row. Whoops, unintended pun. That must be their mum beside them. Better say hello later. A good number of his pupils and their family members had come. It was really kind. Bruce could not face going round and greeting everybody. For one thing, his throat was dry. Was there a glass of water? Oh yes, where was he sitting? Here? Yes, Okay. That should be fine. How nice of Celia to come. Their eyes met, and she gave him a warm smile. Thanks for coming; he hoped his face said it clearly enough. Ah, Banjo and Flossie. Better shake their hands. Great to see them here.

Yes, that blues sound coming for the band was just right. Give them the thumbs up. Time to stand in the entrance, waiting for the hearse to arrive. Here it comes, at the usual crawl, led by the undertaker on foot. Why do they do that, I wonder? Beautiful black car. WAY 4 on the number plate. 'I am the way, the truth and the life,' Jesus said; oh dear, perhaps we should have had that reading instead.

Ah, shake the undertaker's hand. Oh help, this is it. The bearers shoulder the coffin. They've done a nice job on the woodwork. You wouldn't think those handles were plastic. Well done, Gnilla; brilliant cross of flowers. I love that purple colour. I wonder if Mum enjoyed flowers.

DON'T cry. Save all that for later. And don't forget Sasha.

There, the coffin's in place, and they've put the little catch up so that it can be drawn through the hatch at the right time. Funny that we serve meals through the hatch all our lives, as it were, only to be served up ourselves in our turn to our maker when the time comes. Help me to serve others. Help me to be kind and thoughtful to everyone who has come here today.

Bill was speaking. Perhaps we should have had a hymn to start with; it might have helped people to settle. But then, nobody knows hymns nowadays, so it might have had the opposite effect. Oh help, it's my turn.

"I am so grateful to you all for coming today. It's a strange occasion, as not only did none of you ever know my Mum; I didn't even know her myself. The lady who died last Wednesday was a complete stranger to me."

Bruce told them what little he knew of her life in the nursing home. He could see Mr. Fuller and a man sitting beside him; perhaps it was the staff member who had befriended his Mum. Try and have a word afterwards.

"Then my sister. All I can remember about her is her pony tails. She died when I was five, but I only discovered this a week ago. So I wanted to remember her today as well.

"Now, I want you to hear this. My father is not here today, and efforts to trace him have failed. The courts found him guilty of causing my mother grievous bodily harm. I feel very upset about this, but I want you to know that I am determined to forgive him. I'm sure it's going to be a great struggle, but my mind is settled. I want to get rid of all bitterness. Please hold me to it, and tell me if you think I am losing the battle."

It was Bill's turn. The reading was from Revelation chapter twenty-one, because of the promise that one day, there will be an end to sorrow, crying and pain. Then everybody stood, and while they read out the words together from the little book, the coffin was drawn through. Bruce made himself watch. Very simple but final. What a strange moment. It was his turn to speak again.

"Now, as regards hymns, I don't like putting words into people's mouths, so part of me did not want to have any hymns at all. However, I would like us to sing 'The day thou gavest, Lord, is ended,' because it's not just saying that something has finished. It goes on to think of the dawn that follows on. That's what I want from this situation. Two lives have been wrecked and ended prematurely, but there is always hope. There's always a new dawn. We may have made a complete mess of things, but there's another chance, a second chance to get it right. I feel very passionately about this. We all know the world's in a terrible state, and this sad event is a powerful reminder of that, but let's focus on the new dawn that's coming. There's a fresh day ahead for all of us."

DON'T cry. I find all this so moving. Oh good, the hymn sounds well on the saxophones, and people seem to know the tune.

When the singing ended and people sat down, Bruce said, "Well, that's it. There's a cup of tea back at my place; I hope you can come. But there's one more important thing to say. The staff at the nursing home discovered that my Mum liked music, hence the band. It helps explain my musical gift. They reckon that her favourite piece was 'In The Mood', and she enjoyed people clicking their fingers in time with it. So as we go out, the Blues Brigade are going to play it. Please click along with it, and if a few of you break into dancing, I reckon that's Okay. I'm sure there's dancing in heaven, and that my Mum would be pleased."

Ian's band was terrific. Everyone got up to file out, shaking Bill and Bruce by the hand. Several of them clicked their fingers as requested. Bruce could see that Araminta wanted to jig about. Go on! He urged with his eyebrows, but she wouldn't. You just don't do that kind of thing at funerals. Fair enough, Bruce thought.

The journey home was quiet. "Thanks a lot," Bruce said to Bill. It had been weird saying goodbye to his Mum.

There was nobody waiting outside the door when they got back even though they were probably the last to get there. How tactful of people to wait in their cars. Bruce unlocked the door, walked straight over to the kettle which had been filled ready in advance, and switched it on. Bill and Gnilla unloaded the platefuls of food from the fridge, and set them on the table. The little individual cakes came out of their packaging and onto a plate, and the two larger cakes also, behind the others. Bruce found the sight of the food very difficult; he was still feeling nauseous, and spreading the table only made it worse. His headache was about the same. He wanted everyone to come in, but he hoped they would not stay too long.

They were all flooding in now.

"Ian, thank you so much for the music. It was wonderful. And isn't the acoustic in the building kind to music? Please introduce me to the others in the band."

There was a calmness and thoughtfulness about good musicians, Bruce had noticed. You could never imagine any of these five being involved in a brawl. Bruce had decided that because it takes long years of persistence to become a musician, the impatient, quarrelling type of person never stays the course. For every skilled instrumentalist who made it through, there must be fifteen or twenty who started out only to quit after a few months. Persistence. Keep at it. That's the name of the game.

"Flossie and Bancesca, great to see you. Thanks for coming."

"Bruce, it's the least we could do." Flossie's voice was beautiful as well as her looks. She would make a good singer; Bruce was sure of it. It was not too late to start.

"How are things going?"

"Yes, Okay thanks. I keep busy with work and that. There's always something to do."

"Bruce, I'm so sad for you," Banjo said. "Still, perhaps it's better to have discovered the truth at long last rather than go on not knowing. How do you feel about it?"

"Yes, I agree with you. However, I would have preferred to have known my Mum all these years, even in her broken-down state. The nursing home was so close. I could have visited her every week The thing which makes me really sad..." Bruce had to stop for twenty seconds, he felt so choked with emotion. Then he forced himself to continue.

"...The thing which makes me really sad is that she never heard me play the piano. I think she would have enjoyed that."

"I'm sure she would," said Flossie. "Yes, that is sad. But from what you said, they seem to have looked after her well there."

"Yes, I have no doubt about that. I liked Mr. Fuller. That's him over there; I must go and have a word."

Bruce moved across the room, then wondered if he should have stayed talking to Flossie and Banjo longer. He had not even asked Banjo how she was. Oh well, it was too late now.

"Mr. Fuller, thanks for coming. And thanks again for all you did for my Mum. I'm so grateful."

"Not at all, Bruce. This is Chris, the member of staff I told you about."

Bruce shook Chris warmly by the hand.

"I'm so grateful," was all he could manage to say.

"She'd have loved the saxophones," Chris said. He had a glorious bass voice, and a most friendly manner.

"Do you sing?" asked Bruce.

"Yes - bass baritone. I'm into music theatre. Amateur dramatics. Great fun."

"I imagine you are very good at it. Put me on your mailing list; I'd love to come to a show." Bruce gave him his card. "Thanks again. Please keep in touch."

There were so many people to have a brief word with. What was this? Oh, Gnilla pushing a mug of tea into his hand. One sugar, brilliant. Well done! Bill was busy handing round the food. Very good.

People did not stay long. Bruce was quite relieved. It was great to be surrounded by his friends, but he had found the whole event very taxing. Fairly soon, the room emptied out. He made a token effort to get Gnilla away from the sink, but it was only half-hearted. He was pleased it was unsuccessful; he was very glad to have the place cleared up.

"Bill, thanks ever so much. I feel we've done Mum proud. It was difficult to put in much about Sasha, but at least she had a mention. Thanks very much for all you said and did."

"Bruce, I would not have missed it. And as the man once said, 'If there's ever anything I can do, just don't mention it!' No seriously, we are here for you. You may feel low over the next bit; if you want company, we are only a phone call away."

When they had gone, Bruce felt very tired but pleased. It had been an ordeal, but it had been worth it.

Hello, somebody had left a card in an envelope on his mantelpiece. Several people had given him cards, which he had opened, but this one had been left for him to find. He opened it. It was a posh invitation, gold lettering on white card.

'You are invited to a party to celebrate the engagement of Peter Dennison and Florence Millicent, on...'

Bruce read no more. Flossie engaged! Why hadn't she said so? Out of concern for him, probably. Bruce wished she had told him; he could have congratulated her in person. And who was this Peter Dennison?

Suddenly, Bruce felt as if he had been kicked in the stomach. It was all too much. He just could not cope with it. He wanted to be pleased for Flossie, but instead he just felt an overwhelming sense of loss. He could have had her for the asking. Instead he was on his own. All he ever seemed to do was to wave goodbye to people as they walked away from his front door down the little path. It was so miserable.

It was too early for bed, but he was too tired to do anything. He did not even bother to switch off the light. He went through to his bedroom and threw himself on his bed fully clothed, with his shoes still on. Within a few minutes, he fell into an exhausted sleep.

50. From: Mission 12
To: Undisclosed recipients
Sent:

Well, I would not answer their calls or their messages for several days. I told Margaret what I had discovered, and she was very sympathetic. She had seen it coming. She hated what had been happening, and had tried to say something without

331

success, and decided in the end to come up to work on the plants to get away. It all made sense.

The day came when I decided to look at the messages. There were several from Phil, all saying the same thing in various different ways, namely 'Ring. It's urgent.'

I decided to talk to him.

"Bruce, thank goodness you've broken silence. I was on the verge of coming up. Look, I really am sorry about what has happened down here, and I know you will be going through agonies. However, there has been a very serious development. Mark is dead. We think he has been murdered, but we're not sure. Celia is in an indescribable state; she feels so guilty for what she has done. We even had to restrain her for a while.

"Anyway, the fact is that you and Margaret are the only people who are in the clear, and everyone here thinks you should be the one to come down to investigate."

This was a bundle of news. Mark dead. And probably murdered! I was already wondering who might have done it and why.

"Right. I need to talk to Margaret; then I'll get back to you. Bye for now."

Margaret was happy to look after the space ship, and I was soon on my way down.

This was indeed a serious development. That was clear. I could only guess what might come out of it.

What use could I possibly be? The closest I had been to detective work was watching Agatha Christie films on the large screen in my bachelor days. However, I had grasped one thing. There were always clues, if you could only see them, and the place to start was by talking to everybody one by one. Maybe something would emerge from that process. There was nothing to lose by trying.

It was dusk when I arrived. Everything felt totally different this time. For one thing, everyone was there to meet me, all looking very sombre. During the previous week, I had come to the conclusion that when I went down before, Max had only told Phil that I was coming. This meant that nobody else was expecting me, which was why I observed Mark and Celia behaving as they did. Max had wanted me to discover what was happening by seeing it for myself rather than being told about it. The shock was painful, but I think he was wise.

The moment I saw them all, through the windows of the lander, something inside me leapt in great excitement. Could it possibly be that I was going to be reinstated, and far from being the outsider I had become, I was going to have a central role from now on?

It was great to see Max. He hugged me, and Clairie came and joined in. It was quite like old times.

Then it was Celia's turn. She hung back awkwardly. She could not bear to look at me. I had already thought through what I was going to do. I walked over to her, and said, "Celia, you have had a terrible time. I am so sorry." I hugged her. She broke down into sobbing, but I knew they were tears of relief. Nobody said anything.

"Now," I said, speaking to them all, "I'm hoping that we can have a meal together, when you can fill me in on the situation, and then after that I would like to interview everybody one by one."

They had anticipated this. A mild curry was served on rice, followed by Mangoes cut up into segments. Wonderful the tasty food that can be conjured up by machines.

The account was straightforward. During supper, five days earlier, Mark had complained of not feeling well, and had gone into the dome. When Celia followed him in a few minutes later, he was lying dead on the floor. He had not even made it to the bed. His face looked most anguished. I asked to be shown the place where he was found. There was nothing to be gained from that. Everybody had eaten the same meal; they had all sat down together an hour before.

I wanted to have somebody else with me. I asked them whether Phil could assist me. Everyone agreed, including Phil himself. I reckoned that two minds might be better than one. I also thought it would help me when interviewing Celia and the children.

I thought it was best to talk to Celia first, even though it would be very difficult. She came in and sat down, looking very nervous. It did not seem to be the nervousness of guilt at committing murder, to my mind, but I could not be sure. She avoided eye contact.

"Celia, you and I need to talk about ourselves, but let's leave all that for now. My first question is, do you think Mark was murdered?" She did. "Any idea how?" None. "Okay, now please tell me your impressions starting three hours before you found Mark's body."

Everything had been as normal. The cooks that day were Sandra and Paul. The meal was soup, followed by a bean salad. The sweet was irrelevant, as Mark had gone out during the first course. The food was prepared by machine, as usual. Mark had seemed fine earlier.

Next it was Max's turn. He confirmed the story, and had nothing to add. I began to feel that we were not going to unearth anything much. It was a shame that there was no medic with us capable of discovering whether Mark had eaten anything poisonous.

Then Clairie came in, and I could immediately see from her face that she knew something. I will try to recall her words as best as I can.

"Dad, when Phil and Margaret were bringing me up to the spaceship, Mummy took me on one side and asked me to get Big Nimp to make her a pill for killing herself. It had a special name. I was really upset about this, but she promised me she was not going to use it unless she felt really desperate. She did not feel desperate yet, just unhappy. So I said I would.

"Big Nimp made the pill. It was small and white. But on the way down, I realised that what was making Mummy so unhappy was Mark. So I told mummy that Big Nimp had said no, he would not make one, and I kept the pill. Then when we had those beans for supper, I popped the pill into Mark's food when nobody was looking. That's why he died."

This was shocking. I was glad Phil was there to hear it. I was pleased Clairie had confessed so readily; children can be so artless. However, the fact was that she had committed murder. She was still a minor, which would affect what ought to be done, but having said that she had shown herself to be old enough to flirt. This was going to be very difficult. It was also very painful for me personally. My daughter had killed another human being. How would Celia react? And Max?

All these thoughts flashed through my mind in an instant.

"Clairie," I said, "what you have said is very serious. Thank you for telling us plainly. Now I need to ask you; is this exactly how it happened, or are you making it up to protect somebody else?"

"Oh no, Daddy, it was me that did it. And I haven't told anybody else about it."

"Right," I said. "Are there any more pills, or was there just the one?"

335

"Just the one pill, Daddy."

"Right, Thank you, Clairie, that will be all.
Don't tell anybody else what you have told us
until we say, please. In fact, I think it is best
if you go to bed now. Phil and I will discuss
what is to be done about this."

It took us less than a minute to decide that
the correct procedure was to assemble everybody
after breakfast and reveal the truth. Then we
would all have to decide what was going to
happen.

The investigation had only been under way a few
hours, but we already had our answer. The
ramifications were going to have an impact over
many weeks and months, it seemed to me, possibly
years. I wondered how everybody would react. I
felt very perplexed.

I lay in bed turning it over every way. It all
looked very bleak. There was no sleep for me that
night.

Bruce

Bruce was worried about himself. He felt dreadful, in fact. He knew that the shock of the news and the funeral had affected him deeply; they were bound to have done, really, but what was concerning him was that far from crying and crying, as he had expected to, he had not shed a tear. At first, he had wanted to remain collected, and had resisted every urge to cry. But now he had the opportunity, he found he could not cry at all. He was sure this was bad.

Then there was Flossie's engagement. That was troubling him too, for different reasons. He felt very threatened by it. The result of it all was that he was hardly eating. This too was alarming, as normally, he had a healthy appetite, and he had never experienced anything like this before. He began to wonder if he was falling apart. People do crack up, he thought; it can happen to anyone. How would I know if it was happening to me?

Bill and Gnilla came to his mind. They really wanted to support him. However, could they help with something like this? Also, he did not like the idea of leaning on his friends too much. Perhaps the thing to do was to leave it a few days and see how he felt. He could always get in touch later. It was only the day after the funeral, after all.

However, when he got home at lunchtime, there was a phone message from a different undertaker than the one they had used. What could this be about?

He rang the number.

"Ah, thank you very much for ringing. We were hoping you might be able to play the organ at Wayford Crem for us on Monday October the seventh at two p.m. You were particularly requested."

Bruce consulted his diary. The middle of the day was the time he was most likely to be free. Yes, how convenient. He would not have to cancel any lessons, and the fee would come in handy.

"Yes, that looks fine. I'm writing it in the diary now. Can you tell me about the deceased, please?"

Bruce liked any background information that was going. More than once, he had played for a Scottish person, for example, which naturally called for reels and the like, delicately played, while the people were filing in.

"Yes. The name is James Pond. Mid forties."

Bruce was appalled. "Not my friend Jim Pond? Lived in a penthouse flat with great views over West London?"

"Yes, that's the man. Did you know him well?"

"We only met three times, but I took to him instantly, and he feels like an old friend. I am really shocked that he should have died. He seemed so fit to look at. What did he die of?"

"Heart failure."

"Oh dear, a heart attack! I would never have thought it possible."

"No, heart failure, not a heart attack. There's a big difference. In a heart attack, something goes wrong with the heart, but with heart failure, it just stops beating, sometimes for no apparent reason. It's often a very peaceful end for the person concerned. Seems to have been so in this instance. He will not have suffered, in my view."

"Well, I would certainly like to play, but it does come as a shock. I feel really sad about it. Please let me know if there are any specific requests for music. However, there is no need to contact me if it's just a case of standard hymns."

"All they wanted was for you to use your discretion, and to bear in mind that Mr. Pond was a classically trained musician."

The phone call came to an end. There was no mistaking it. Jim had passed away. Bruce felt really dismayed by this news. He had formed a great affection for Jim, and now his life was over. How dismal. Also, what would happen to Skywear now?

Bruce was thankful it was the weekend. He would have to tell Celia on Tuesday, if she did not know already.

51. From: Mission 12
To: Undisclosed recipients
Sent:

I was unable to eat any breakfast next morning. I felt sick. The situation with Clairie was a nightmare. The news was going to be devastating for Celia. Perhaps it would be kinder to her to tell her in advance of the meeting, but against that, I felt it was important that everyone witness her reaction. It would help establish whether she had any complicity or not. I did not know how to lessen the blow for her; it seemed that from her point of view, whatever we did would be wrong.

I was glad I had Phil to discuss it with. In the end, we stuck with our plan of the night before, and assembled everybody after breakfast.

"The investigation is complete," I said. "Clairie has confessed to putting a suicide pill in Mark's serving of the bean salad."

There was a gasp of horror. Celia made a brief choking sound and fainted.

338

"Clairie, could you tell everyone what you did, please."

Clairie was trembling, but she managed to repeat her words of the previous night.

"I have asked Clairie," I continued, "and she assures me that there was only ever one pill, so there is no danger of any repetition. I propose that we now adjourn for a few hours, to allow everyone to crystallise their thoughts."

This was rejected. People wanted to have their say then and there. Clairie was told to walk over the sand dune to the beach, and that we would fetch her later on. She went off silently.

"It seems to me that if Bruce had not abandoned his family, none of this might have happened."

I was shocked. This was Dickon speaking. Dickon of all people! I felt incensed. However, something made me keep silent. It was better to let everyone have their say.

"I think that's a bit hard." Sandra was speaking. "If you remember it was Celia who was desperate to come down, and she brought Max and Clairie with her. Also, somebody had to man the ship. No, if there was any desertion, I would say it was the other way round."

"Mark was certainly a go-getter," said Phil. "I was unhappy with his attitude from the start, personally. I hated the way he was stealing Celia from Bruce. I also felt very unhappy that none of us was prepared to tell Bruce what was happening. The fact is that I think we were all a bit afraid of Mark. Nobody liked to stand up to him."

"Clairie needs to be punished."

It was one of the newly wakened ones. This led onto a discussion of what an appropriate punishment might be. When it seemed a good moment, I spoke up.

"I do have a suggestion." Everyone was listening. "Clairie has taken life in a way that is wrong. She needs to understand that clearly. I propose that her punishment be to be banished from the planet for however long we think fit. There needs to be a programme of cultivation. Margaret is leading the way on this. I wonder whether Clairie should become Margaret's assistant, and spend her next years learning how to sow life on the planet instead of death. I'm imagining greenhouses in orbit, with young plants being nurtured. There will be a need for plenty of workers. Clairie could be one of them."

In the end, this was accepted. I was pleased. Nobody had suggested the death penalty, which they might have done. The idea of creating a prison was hard to contemplate; although it might be necessary one day, there were only twenty-seven of us, and there were more important things to do.

It was felt that Phil should be the one to talk to Clairie. As her father, I was too close. I was happy with this.

The meeting broke up. As it did, Max came over.

"Dad, I want to give up any remaining pretence of me being the commander. I'm far too young. You should do it, or Phil. I don't think I have done anything good so far. Your ideas were sound, but I sensed that nobody wanted to hear them, so I went with what they all wanted. I can see now that that was wrong. I think they are ready for what you are saying now."

I took Max with me, and we wandered up onto the top of the sand dune. There was the ocean stretching away to the horizon. But with no sea birds, it all seemed lifeless.

"Max, this is a terrible day for our family. It will take a long time to get over this mess. However, I think we can make a start. Let's both make a point of telling Clairie and Mummy that we love them, today. I want to forgive them both. Rebuilding the family will take time. Will you help me?"

"Yes, Dad. I'm sorry for my share in what's gone wrong."

This was noble of Max. I was only too aware of my failings. Perhaps I had abandoned the three of them. Also, what was it that Celia had seen in Mark that she had not found in me? Now Mark was dead, murdered by our own daughter. How would she cope? Would she even want to reunite with me again? Would I want it when it came to the point?

I gazed out over the ocean. It should have been a glorious moment. This wonderful panorama was what we had come so far to see, but the pain in the family overshadowed everything. Strange really. I just felt totally empty inside.

I could see Phil and Clairie down on the beach, talking earnestly. I hoped something might be salvaged for Clairie, allowing her to have a happy life one day. The next few years were going to be hard for her.

Just a few hours earlier, everything had seemed poised to get better, but now it all felt bleak again. Max put his arm round me. We stood gazing outwards together without speaking.

Bruce

The engagement party was at an up-market hotel. Drinks at seven p.m., meal at eight. Bruce was able to get there easily enough by train. He made a point of not arriving before seven thirty.

He found the place, and left his coat at the cloak room. When he went in, he had a shock. There was Flossie, looking absolutely radiant as he had expected, and next to her was Heavy Jowls! So that was who Peter Dennison was. Bruce could hardly believe it. What could she possibly see in him? He had to pinch himself. Yes, most of Jim's inner cabinet were present. There was going to be more to this evening than Bruce had expected.

Heavy Jowls and Flossie were advancing towards him.

"Bruce, so glad you could come." Flossie seemed genuinely pleased to see him. "May I introduce Peter, although I think you will recognise him. Peter... Bruce."

"Aim so hippy to meteor properly at lairst," said Peter, in the most exquisite accent Bruce had heard in years. I must try and think of him as Peter, Bruce thought, not Heavy Jowls. I must also enjoy his formidable vowel sounds, or should I say vale sounds.

Bruce muttered something suitably deferential and congratulatory.

Bruce had always enjoyed foreign accents. It was something to do with his musical ear, he had decided. The joy in learning French was to speak like a Frenchman, if possible, even if your grammar and syntax were totally wrong.

"You play so nacely," Peter was saying. Bruce thanked him. He recalled a hotel that Granddad and he had once phoned to make an enquiry. Bruce had overheard the voicemail. Instead of 'Cromford House,' the voice had distinctly said 'Cromford Hace'. Bruce had been disappointed that in the event, they never went there, so he never got to meet the speaker. Shame really.

"What do you do, Peter?" Bruce asked.

"Aim a Name at Llayds." So that was it. Peter's money had probably helped Jim to get started. A doubt crept into Bruce's mind. Was this a love match, or was Flossie marrying Peter for his money?

Bruce shot a glance in Flossie's direction. She was deep in animated conversation with Banjo. Bruce forced himself back to Peter.

"My granddad knew a bachelor clergyman once who was on twenty-three Lloyds syndicates, although none of the parishioners knew. It all came out quite suddenly, when the man retired after being in the same post for twenty-five years. It was fascinating to see the reactions of the people who had known him for so long. Many of them had written him off as being hopelessly out of touch. People can be hard to read, can't they?"

"Indayd," said Peter. "Take Jim for instance. You'd never have gassed he was a brilliant infanta if you pairst him in the straight. It's a tarrible lorse."

This was most illuminating. So the inventions had come from Jim himself! Bruce had always assumed from his manner that Jim

342

was the businessman, and that the real brains were behind the scenes somewhere. How interesting. Bruce found himself wondering about the inner circle that he had been asked to address. How many of them really knew the inside secrets? That gold watch man, for instance; was he no more than another financial backer, perhaps?

It was already time to sit down to the meal. Bruce found himself between two people he did not know. The person he really wanted to speak to was Banjo, but she was way off down the table on the other side. Bruce found it a real effort to take an interest in his neighbours, and he was quite relieved when both of them ended up talking to the person on the other side, and he was left alone. It gave him a chance to look around the room.

His first thought was that you would not think that the prime mover in the lives of these people had recently passed away, judging by the animated conversations going on round the table. Bruce felt upset at Jim's passing, yet he hardly knew the man. These folk, who were all much closer to Jim than Bruce, seemed to be carrying on as if nothing had happened. It all seemed rather much.

Flossie was looking magnificent, as always. I must have a word with Banjo, Bruce thought. She was deep in conversation with an earnest young man on her right. Not much chance of attracting her attention. Perhaps there would be an opportunity later.

The meal dragged on. Bruce had come for Flossie's sake. The last thing he wanted to do was to socialise. He imagined that Celia would have liked him to glean what information he could, but frankly, he did not have the slightest motivation. He had problems enough of his own without worrying about hers.

Eventually, the final dishes were cleared away and coffee was served. Now was the moment for the inevitable speeches. Bruce wondered whether he could slip out without causing a fuss. Perhaps everyone would think he was going to the loo. No, it was too late. Peter was already on his feet, or should he say, fate.

"Unaccosted es ayam..."

This could be very trying. Bruce could see that Banjo was trying not to laugh. Bruce wanted to listen, for Flossie's sake. It turned out that the couple had met at the Henley regatta. Bruce had not seen Peter there when playing the piano, but that was hardly surprising. They had not fixed a date for the wedding yet. Everyone was warmly thanked for coming. It was short and to the point.

Then the gathering began to break up. This was the moment to tackle Banjo. Bruce made his way over.

"What's going on?" Bruce whispered to her.

"You've let the side down, that's what!" Banjo declared, in what was for her a *sotto voce*. "Still, she won't be short of the readies, at least. She could do worse."

It was not a flattering endorsement. Bruce suddenly found that he felt sorry for Peter. It must be difficult having so much money; you would never really know who your friends were. He hoped Flossie would treat him kindly. He seemed a decent sort.

Somebody else had button-holed Banjo. People can be so rude, Bruce thought. He made his way over to the couple.

"Just to say that I hope you will both be very happy." He really did hope it.

"Thanks, Bruce," beamed Flossie. She seemed to be in her element. She would have no difficulty adjusting to solid gold bath fittings.

"I'll perhaps see you at Jim's funeral. I'm to play the organ. I feel so sad about him. He was such a nice man, let alone everything else."

Peter and Flossie agreed. Bruce looked around for Banjo to have another word, but she had gone already, to his surprise. Shame. Perhaps he had better ring her.

He made his farewells. When he got outside, he turned left towards the station. A car pulled up alongside him. "Want a lift?" It was Banjo. He jumped in.

"No, you've really blown it, Bruce. Never mind. How are the pupils?"

Bruce did not want to think about work. He suddenly felt exhausted again. He mumbled something incoherent. Now it came to the point, he found he had nothing to say to Banjo. How difficult.

It was a relief to be dropped off at the station. Banjo was going the other way to get home, and there were plenty of trains. He waved her off.

52. From: Mission 12
To: Undisclosed recipients
Sent:

We had taken it for granted that Margaret would be willing to have Clairie as her understudy. This was a bit much, in hindsight. Indeed, we failed in not having Margaret on line for the meeting. None of us thought of it. I apologised to her. She kindly said not to worry.

It took a while for Clairie to grasp the seriousness of her situation. I could see her visibly shrinking over the course of a few hours, as it dawned on her. It was horrible to watch. There was nothing I could do to help her.

Celia has been in a frightful state, as you would expect. Sandra is doing a great job looking after her. I have yet to talk to her.

Phil and I took Clairie up in the lander. There were a few hugs for her from the others, but not many of them came to see her off. That was hard.

The worst moment was saying goodbye to Clairie, when it was time for Phil and me to set off down again. I don't think I have ever seen anyone look so strained in the face. She clung to me for a long time. I will actually be seeing her again soon, but it was the feeling of finality that terrified her. I think she wondered whether she would ever go down to the planet again.

Margaret was excellent. She will do a good job with Clairie; I am sure of it.

Phil and I did not exchange a word on the way back down.

On Sunday, there was a surprise for Bruce at church. There was Bill as usual, but with Gnilla beside him! This was quite something. Gnilla must have seen the questioning in Bruce's mind from his face, because she came over and whispered to him.

"I've come to try it. The least I can do is see what my husband believes in. But I'm not planning to convert, or anything like that."

"I'll talk to you afterwards," said Bruce.

The service ran its usual course, and then it was coffee time. They each collected a cup.

"Good for you, Gnilla," Bruce said. Bill was beaming. Bruce hoped he was not simply set on Gnilla adopting his viewpoint. For Christianity to be genuine, it had to be a matter of conviction.

"Mind you," Bruce said when they had found a seat, "I can't recommend this place."

Gnilla raised an eyebrow, and Bill looked rather cross. But Bruce was not going to be put off; this was too important.

"Let me put it this way. Have you ever read the Gospels?"

"Yes," said Gnilla, "we spent a term on one of them at school."

"Well, if you had to summarise what Jesus wanted his followers to do, what would you say?"

This was a bit tough, but Gnilla was no weed, and Bruce knew she could handle it.

"Well, he wanted them to love God and love everybody."

"Three out of ten," declared Bruce. "No, sorry to be difficult," he went on, in response to Bill's glare, "but I feel very strongly about this. Your summary hardly touches on what Jesus actually said to his followers; he said the words you quoted to a religious leader. His standard for the disciples was much tougher. They were to love their enemies. That's a lot more focussed than 'love everybody'. Who are the people that threaten you most?"

Bill wanted the conversation to end here, but Gnilla was having none of it.

"Err... murderers, drug pushers, thugs, people that mug women for their handbags. That will do for a start."

"Exactly. Well, your enemies are the people that threaten you most, if you think about it. So the job of the church is to love these kinds of people. In addition, Jesus gave to his followers a load of instructions - have you any idea how many?"

Gnilla was enjoying this, Bill could see.

"I'll guess one hundred and fifty-three."

"No, wrong; that was the number of fish caught in the net in the miracle. But good effort - seven out of ten. No, I've been through the text of the four Gospels and counted the commands Jesus gave to his followers, and, you'll never believe this, it's one hundred and eighty!"

"Well, no, I never would have believed it. My one hundred and fifty-three was a massive over statement, intended as a joke, actually."

Bruce was feeling wound up. There was no stopping him now.

"Now, I grant you that my list includes a lot of, shall we say, lesser instructions like 'follow a man with a jar on his head' which have no obvious application today. But many of the commands do have lasting significance. What was the last order he gave them?"

"Bruce, we only spent one term…"

"It was 'Teach them to observe what I've commanded.' The teaching programme of the Christian church comprises the commands of Jesus. And this is what makes me so angry; you can guarantee that whatever the subject of a talk here on Sunday morning, it won't be a command of Jesus!"

Bill and Gnilla were shocked. They had never seen Bruce like this before. Then they realised that Bruce wanted to say more, but could not get the words out. He was silent for twenty seconds or so. His lips were tightly pursed together, and his cheeks were going red. His eyes were blinking furiously.

Suddenly it came out.

"You'd never guess from this place that Jesus' followers are meant to heal the sick, and raise the dead rather than bury them!"

Bruce stood up suddenly. "Sorry," he gasped, "I'd better go before I lose it altogether!"

Before they could react, he swept off out of the building.

Bill was very concerned. "I've never seen him like that before."
Gnilla nodded. "I reckon it's his mother's death, really."
Bill agreed. "He does feel strongly on these issues, but not like that. He needs help."
"I think we should call this afternoon," Gnilla said. But Bill was adamant.
"We've told him that we're here for him and that he's only got to pick up the phone. Don't crowd him. He'll be fine. Give him some space."
Gnilla was not reassured, but she really did not want to go against Bill. She hoped it would all work out.

53. From: Mission 12
To: Undisclosed recipients
Sent:

When we got back, I found that Max had told the others he did not want to be the commander. By common agreement, we all felt that the idea of a single commander was not a helpful one. I don't quite know where it came from, frankly. For the purposes of decision-making, it seemed better to form a cabinet comprising the first eight astronauts to be woken. They seem rather more clued up now, to me. The second lot are all fairly dopey. The others have observed this, not just me. Perhaps it takes months if not years to fully get over hibernation. I made my suggestion about the effects of hibernation to the others, and they were inclined to agree with me.

Anyway, the fact is that there is now much more enthusiasm among the original eight for getting down to work. We all felt that an extra metre of water on the oceans remained a good idea, even if it seemed unclear how we might go about it. However, the main proposal came from Phil.

He said that the day was too long, making the night too cold and the day too hot, so we should speed up the rotation of the planet. Just like that! I was amazed. When we asked how, he said we should replicate the spaceship, as I had suggested earlier, not once, but many times. Then we should anchor them round the equator, and fire them for however many years it took to speed up the rotation.

It was a bold suggestion, and simple. When I told them that I had already made one replica of the spaceship and sent it off to the moon with instructions to make a second replica, they all laughed.

"Let's have sixty-four," said one.

"No, a hundred and twenty-eight," said another.

In the end, we decided that the more we had, spread round the equator, the less work each one would have to do, and the less strain there would be on any one part of the planet's crust. The replication programme took seventy days, so it would be some years before we would be able to get started.

In the meantime, we should get the bio programme going in earnest. It was not right to leave it all to Margaret. It was obvious to all of us that we would need to start with the tiny things that lived off minerals, and work up from there. Little plants on land, and plankton in the sea. We would need expert help. I had a shrewd idea how to find that; I was sure that Big Nimp was ready and able.

I was taken to see the little patch of lichen that has been started. It was only a metre or two across, but it looked healthy enough.

Bruce

Bruce was not a happy trooper. He was on his way to play for Jim's funeral. He hated the thought of Jim being dead. That was bad enough. But then it was happening at Wayford Crem, which would bring painful memories to the fore. Then very likely Peter and Flossie would be there, which was not going to be easy. All in all it was a tricky assignment.

He was glad he arrived in good time as the place was already pretty busy. He sidled past a group of people in morning coats, and slid in at a side door. He trotted up the stairs to the organ loft. At least they had a nice instrument, he reflected, as he changed his shoes. He put on his old worn pair that he used for playing the organ; it made pedalling easier.

There had been no special requests for music in and out. He began by improvising aimlessly, but before long he found he had slid into Song for Guy by Elton John. It was a strange choice for a funeral, but it seemed right, somehow. Then Bruce remembered; it had been written to commemorate someone who had died. Rather apt. Also people would probably know it. Something like that would help put them at their ease.

The hymns were standard. The duty clergyman droned on. Were there really going to be no tributes? Bruce found it hard to stay focussed. Ah yes, there were Peter and Flossie near the back.

Oh dear, there was the coffin going through. Bruce felt a great pang of loss. It was horrible. It was soon time for the exit music. Something Jim would have liked. Ah yes, J.S. Bach, Fantasia in G. Magnificent. The organ was just about up to it.

Bruce had fallen in love with the piece years before, when he had been on tour with a choral society, singing in the Tenor section. They had done three concerts in cathedrals, and at each one a young man had played the Fantasia as part of the programme. It had been marvellous. Then a few years later, Bruce happened to hear that the young organist had died in his mid-twenties. He had felt very sad.

Play it for him too. Well done Bach. Unbeatable.

Bruce carried on until the last few people were leaving, and then he did something unthinkable. He quickly skipped to the last few chords, and ended the piece. Sacrilege, but there was a higher call here.

Without changing his shoes, he shot down the stairs, through a couple of doors, and then went through a door marked Staff Only. Would he be too late?

He was in the furnace room. There were the huge gas ovens, two unlit, but the third one roaring fiercely. The heat coming from it was considerable, even through the closed door.

Ah, thank goodness. There was Jim's coffin still on the barrow. He was not too late.

"Can I help you?" said a voice.

This might be tricky. Bruce turned towards the sound, but when he saw who had spoken, he gave a start. The man in charge of the furnaces was dressed in a boiler suit, brown and stained in places. Bruce could not believe it - it was the split image of the overalls worn by a man he had imagined in one of his daydreams a few weeks before on the spaceship known as Mission 12. The likeness was extraordinary.

Bruce pulled himself together.

"Look, this may sound very weird to you. The thing is, I follow Jesus, and one of the instructions he gave to his followers was to raise the dead. So if you don't mind holding back for a few minutes, I'd like to try on my friend Jim here." Bruce waved his hand at the coffin. "Only, if you could unscrew the lid I'd be grateful, as if he comes round and finds he can't get out, he might die again of shock." Humour might help. "No need to take the lid right off, though," Bruce added nervously. What would the man think? Perhaps he had already decided he was a nutter, and had activated an alarm, and the men in white coats were on their way to get him.

"Now don't say a word," said the man. The voice seemed familiar. Then he spoke again, the one word; "Bruce".

"Jim!" gasped Bruce. He could not help himself.

"Don't touch me," said Jim.

"But what..." Bruce pointed at the coffin.

"Don't worry about it. I'm going underground for a while. I've been watching the service on the monitor. Look."

Jim led Bruce over to a small screen. There must be a hidden camera above the cross, Bruce realised. There was nothing to watch now that the chapel pews were empty.

"It's a great way to discover who your real friends are, I can tell you. Mind you, I was really enjoying the Fantasia. I don't know

351

about you raising the dead, but you sure know how to crucify Bach!"

This was too much. But Jim went on, "Please don't tell a soul about this. Look, I'll be in touch soon. Now, you'd better leave."

Bruce gave Jim a thumbs up, and crept out and back up to the organ loft. The chapel was still deserted. On an impulse, Bruce switched the organ back on, and finished the Fantasia from where he had got to. Then he prepared to go.

Here was the crematorium attendant. "An unscheduled gap in that fine piece," he observed quizzically. Bruce had met him before and felt safe. "Call of nature," he replied. Well, putting on the new nature anyway.

What a to do! Bruce slipped nervously outside, but he need not have worried. Nobody had stayed. The road was empty.

```
54. From: Mission 12
To: Undisclosed recipients
Sent:
```

Actually, the next development took place while we were standing by the lichen, but I thought I would save it for a fresh email. No point in putting all the best news items in one email!

No, it was Sandra who innocently said, "there's no chance of introducing seasons, is there?"

I explained to her that the wobble we have on earth would be very hard to recreate here. I picked up a piece of rock and showed that the reason we get the seasons on earth, with the sun going up to the tropic of Cancer and then down to the tropic of Capricorn, is that there is a wobble built into the earth's orbit round the sun, rather like you sometimes see on a child's spinning top, when it is rather unstable. There was silence for a moment, until Dickon said, "No Bruce."

I took a lot of persuading, but I agreed in the end that I had always understood it wrongly. There is no wobble, as I had supposed! Instead,

they explained that the earth is simply tilted
twenty-three degrees out of the vertical. As it
goes round the sun, the result of the tilt is to
show one side of the earth to the sun on the
first half of the orbit, and then the other side
during the second half. I can see it now. I hope
you can.

So there is no need for a wobble. The question
is rather whether we can tilt the globe. I
suggested more space ships, down one side of the
planet, in a long line, from pole to pole, and
then up the other side. They agreed.

So the planet is going to have spaceships all
round its middle and from end to end, making it
look like a hand grenade!

I hope it won't blow up in our face.

Bruce

On Wednesday morning, Jane the Head of Music came in to the
little practice room where Bruce was teaching.

"Letter for you - probably an enquiry."

Bruce looked at the envelope. 'Piano Teacher by hand' it read.
Not very flattering. They had not even found out his name. He
waited for the end of the lesson before opening it.

However, the contents were far more interesting.

'Bach's crucifixion was well remedied. I want to take you on
holiday over half term. Meet me at the Motor Lodge on Friday 20th
at 7 p.m. You will be booked in as Mr. Hill. Mystery destination.
Minimal luggage. Return on Sunday 29th. If you accept, leave a
message saying that you're sorry, you have no vacancies.'

The letter was typed without a signature. On the reverse there
was a photocopy of a page of a street atlas with a cross in ink on it,
and a phone number on the edge.

As soon as he could, Bruce left the message. What fun!

55. From: Mission 12
To: Undisclosed recipients
Sent:

353

I've tried to get to see Celia, but she refuses. Max is feeling very down. So there's a good deal of gloom here.

These projects of changing the spin of the globe are great, but it's gradually dawned on me just how long term they are. So far we are only onto making spaceships three and four. Both our existing ones are duplicating themselves again. That process will finish in twelve days. Then all four will start to duplicate once more.

It all seems so slow!

However, Big Nimp confirmed what we had thought, which was that if the planet was tilted, making seasons, then the weather patterns would change. There would be more turbulence in the air, leading to greater rainfall. So it seems like an excellent idea. Only we must not overdo the tilt, or it would become unbearably stormy.

I don't know whose idea it was to bury Mark under the lichen, but we all agreed it was a good one. There would be no need for a coffin, as there are no animals here to attack the body. On the contrary, all the bacteria in his body will be invaluable to the ground. When our time comes, we will be doing the settlement a good turn simply by being buried, rather like the old idea of burying a dead horse underneath when planting a fruit tree.

As we stood round, I found myself thinking of the legend of John Barleycorn, but Phil did one better. He had an extract from Longfellow's Song of Hiawatha about the burial of the youth Mondamin, which he read out loud, which contains the same idea as the song. It bears quoting in full.

And victorious Hiawatha
Made the grave as he commanded,
Stripped the garments from Mondamin,
Stripped his tattered plumage from him,

Laid him in the earth and made it
Soft and loose and light above him;
And the heron, the Shu-shuh-gah,
From the melancholy moorlands,
Gave a cry of lamentation,
Gave a cry of pain and anguish!…
Not forgotten nor neglected
Was the grave where lay Mondamin…
Day by day did Hiawatha
Go to wait and watch beside it…
Till at length a small green feather
From the earth shot slowly upward,
Then another and another,
And before the summer ended
Stood the maize in all its beauty…

The reality is that the humans here will need
to give everything we have to making the
settlement a success, even our very lives. I
think everyone is beginning to see that now. This
is not an extended holiday. We are pioneers.

Phil and I are going back up to Clairie and
Margaret tomorrow. In the meantime, I often find
I can't sleep, so I've gone back to counting ice
blocks. The number needed is vast, but I don't
feel so bad about it now I've got used to it.

The large number reminds me of something I once
read about our galaxy, the Milky Way. Apparently,
the number of stars in it is about the same as
the number of grains of rice you would need to
fill a cathedral. Can you imagine the effort of
doing that? I picture myself as a boy buying a
kilo of rice on my way home from school on a
Monday, hurrying up to the cathedral, going in
through the huge door, making sure nobody is
looking, and then slitting the bag open and
scattering the rice somewhere in the middle. It
would hardly be visible spread across the stone
floor! Then next day, I repeat the process, and
on Wednesday, Thursday and Friday. After a month,

I might have made enough impact for people to be able to notice that there are a lot of grains of rice on the floor. However, it would take many years before I could get the whole area a foot deep.

But now imagine if I talk the rest of my class into joining in. And supposing that they all get their friends to join in. In fact, it becomes not just a case of every young person scattering a bag of rice each day; in addition, you have to promise to get someone else into the programme, every day. So the operation expands and grows, until eventually there are thousands of us all contributing our daily bag of rice. I reckon that if we kept at it, we might get the job done, don't you?

So it is with deepening the oceans here. We need to think of some way of doing it that involves self-replication by the machines involved.

Back to the galaxy for a moment. You appreciate that actually, the stars are widely separated from each other, so really, to make a scale model, our grains of rice should also be separated instead of being squashed into a cathedral. It turns out that to preserve the proportion of stars to the space between them, the rice grains should be spread out all the way from the earth to the moon! In our particular part of the galaxy, to get the proportion right, a handful of the grains of rice should be scattered over the area of the British Isles. Isn't that an amazing thought?

Now, a word of warning to anyone thinking of trying the grains of rice in the cathedral project. Make sure the roof is sound first! The reason is that, suppose you have got the place half filled. All the usual activities like concerts and religious gatherings can continue, by the way, provided you put out boards on top of

the swelling rice pile to support the chairs and
so forth. They need not be a problem. But if
rainwater can get in, then you are in serious
trouble, because the water would make the grains
of rice start to swell. This would cause a severe
outward pressure on the walls. The whole building
would burst open, and crash to the ground, and
then your experiment would be terminated
prematurely. So I reckon you should check the
roof for leaks at least every week, as one slip
might prove disastrous.

Yes, I've got it now. It was the length of
Longfellow's poem that set me thinking about
large numbers. There must be many thousands of
lines in it. It fills a book which is an inch
thick. It's a model of persistence.

Sixty-seven blocks of ice... sixty-eight blocks
of ice... sixty-nine blocks...

The day had finally come. Bruce was on his way to the Motor
Lodge, clutching a holdall. He had taken Jim at his word, and kept
his luggage to a change of clothes, and a pair of shorts and a
summer shirt and bathers in case they were going somewhere warm.

The previous two weeks had been tedious. Bruce had apologised
to Bill and Gnilla for his outburst, and said that what he really
wanted to say was that Gnilla should read the gospels to find about
Jesus, and not look to the church. At least, that was his view.

Bruce had once met a chef who had been addicted to drugs and
nicotine. On becoming a believer, his addictions had dropped away
from him miraculously without any effort on his part. He saw from
the Gospels how Jesus brought good news to the poor, so he began
taking the leftover soup to a community centre in a poor area on his
way home. The staff there had been thrilled. They soon had him
talking to the men, and before he knew it, he was laying hands on
them and seeing them healed. It was all very thrilling. Soon the
problem was keeping the peace between those who lost their
addictions instantly, like the chef had done, and those for whom it
was a long struggle to get free. The former group tended to look

down on the latter group. Don't despise each other, the chef had urged them.

However, in due course, the chef had trained and become a pastor. Now he was involved in Sunday morning gatherings, and the soup had been neglected. This was sad, Bruce felt, and he was not surprised to discover that the miracles had gradually become less, and then finally faded away altogether. So don't get sucked into church-going, Bruce had warned Gnilla. Look what it's done to me!

Well, it had not gone down very well. Bruce could see the total puzzlement on Bill's face. Bill clearly thought that Bruce was in danger of becoming fanatical. Well perhaps he was. But Bruce believed in the truth of what Churchill had once said; "A fanatic is one who can't change his mind, and won't change the subject." Bruce did feel strongly about the state of the church, but he was able to talk about other things as well. His feelings were not out of hand.

The piano teaching had lacked sparkle. Bruce knew it. Never mind; it would pick up again, as he got over his mum's death. Time heals.

The main thing that kept Bruce going was the thought of a holiday with Jim. Naturally, he had not told Celia. How could he?

The Motor Lodge turned out to be a new building, designed with sky-cars in mind. Each room had a balcony big enough for a sky-car to land on; the building was therefore shaped like a pyramid. Or a ziggurat, perhaps, Bruce reflected, remembering a picture in a textbook he had once seen of life in three thousand BC in the Near East.

He signed in as Mr. Hill, as instructed. Room 314. Doubtless Jim would turn up. He made his way up. Sure enough, he had hardly put his bag down before there was a knock on the door.

"Sorry, no tradesmen," said Bruce as he opened the door.

Jim was disguised, with a wig and a moustache he had grown, and he was wearing an overcoat which covered all his clothes. Bruce found the effect comical. Jim came in. They hugged.

"Bruce, it's great to see you. I've been really looking forward to this. Now, are you happy if we set off in the morning, and I deliver you back home in ten days, on the Sunday evening? And have you brought your passport?"

Bruce nodded. "I've been looking forward to it too. Yes, those arrangements are excellent. Here's my passport. Now, are you hungry? Can I get you something? They do room service here."

They both ordered Ham and Eggs, followed by Yoghurt. There were tea-making facilities in the room.

Jim spoke again. "I do want to thank you very much for your note. It was brave of you to tell me that you were working as a secret agent."

"I can't stand secrecy," said Bruce. "It feels like deceit to me. You seem like a straightforward guy, so I thought, why can't Jim use me to tell the authorities what he wants? I don't understand why they don't get on the phone and ask you their questions straight out. What need is there for all this cloak and dagger stuff? They don't really imagine that you are trying to overthrow the establishment, do they?"

"Beats me what they think. I reckon they are paranoid, to tell you the truth. Just because I've been financially successful, they see me as a threat. Hence the disappearing trick."

They were interrupted by the food arriving.

"Well, how's life in the hereafter?" asked Bruce when the man had gone.

"Don't ask," replied Jim. "But it has been fascinating watching my affairs being wound up. All my businesses will continue to run - I set them up so that I was not required. The instructions in my will have been followed. The flat's been disposed of. It all feels very weird. But it also has a ring of truth to it which I can't explain. How about you?"

"You'll find me poor company, I'm afraid. I've been hit very hard by my mother's death." Jim did not know what had happened, so Bruce told him the story.

"I see. Hence the interest in raising the dead. I wondered where that had come from."

"I only saw it for the first time a fortnight back. I read the Bible in the original languages, you know - Greek and Hebrew. Not that

359

I've done much recently. I've been so busy these last weeks. My discovery was too late for my mum. I feel very sad about it."

"Perhaps her life was over, Bruce. 'A time to be born, a time to die.'"

"Maybe. But I would have liked to try. Still, it's too late now. Ooh, this coffee's not up to much. You would have thought a place like this would have provided something better. I suppose the producers sweep up what falls on the floor of the factory and call it economy."

It had a horrible taste.

"Oh dear, I do feel very sleepy. Do you mind if I turn in."

Bruce rose to open the door to let Jim leave, but blacked out, and collapsed in a heap. Jim quickly made him comfortable and checked his pulse. Then he went to the large window which opened onto the balcony, and unbolted it. He stepped out onto it, took out a little remote control from his pocket, and pressed a few keys, before stepping back in again. You would have needed to be very observant indeed to detect the arrival of the sky-car on the balcony, as it was invisible. The only sign of its presence was the slightest shimmering in the air, as one sometimes sees on a hot road in summer when driving along. However, when the door slid open in response to another key press, you could see the padded upholstery inside the car clearly enough. It looked most odd being suspended in mid air, rather like a painting without a frame. Bruce was well built, but Jim need not have worried; it did not require two people to lift him into the back seat.

The wonderful thing about being a bear. Is that life is so sticky. I enjoy the taste of honey. Truly I do. But it's the stickiness of the paws that pleases me most. Paws for thought. These bees get so cross. But they can't hurt me. No point in trying. Their sting does not get through my thick coat. So warm and cuddly. But I do hate the headache. I can't get my mind off it. Always there. My head feels so sore. Lumbering about is fun. You'd best keep out of my way. I can knock

anything down. Not that I can do much at present.
In fact I can't even move. I feel so groggy.
Can't move at all. At all, at all. Such a fine
coat. Such stickiness...

Rain or shine, summer or winter, at 0750 Stella Mitchell used to don her walking boots, ready for the daily constitutional, while Fortescue, the faithful hound, watched her shrewdly from the doormat. Fortescue's pedigree was not entirely clear, but he did have such endearing features! His worldly-wise expression. His shortness of hair and smoothness of coat. Such brownness! His tail might be considered too stubby and short by some, but it made up for any deficiency in length by the furious speed with which it shot from side to side. Sometimes the wagging was so vigorous that the whole hindquarters became involved in the expression of pleasure. It was like that this morning. Eager was the word.

Stella was a retired nurse. She missed the business of the ward, but she recognised that nobody could go on working for ever. She was pleased with her retirement cottage in the country; it was lovely to be able to walk from her front door. Better than a millionaire's mansion, she thought. Fortescue had come from the rescue three years before to join her; hence his name, which included the word rescue, but in disguise so you would not notice the connection. Life was so much more friendly with two. There had been an issue of discipline to begin with, but he had settled down into a state of benign obedience. The two of them got on well together.

"Right, you scamp," intoned Stella, with a throaty roar, "Go on then!" and she threw open the back door. Fortescue was off at speed, with a fit of furious barking. It was ever thus.

The route was firmly fixed. Along the little track, but turn left beside the wood just before the track reached the road. In the early days, Fortescue used to be put on the lead for two hundred yards at this point for fear of cars, but the effort required in achieving this had been so great that Stella soon decided to let him be. He seemed to know to turn left. And there had only been one squeal of brakes in all that time, and no collision. Nevertheless, it was a moment of apprehension each morning.

"Fortescue, FORT... es - CUE!" bellowed Stella, fit to bust, "Fort, Fort, Fort! Come come, come, come, come," the latter in a brisk staccato, but it was all to no avail. "Here boy, HERE!"

There he was, rummaging among the undergrowth, in and out, here and there. Stella loved the upright prick of his ears. Such a good boy.

They were nearly half way. They had a circular route to save retracing their steps. When they got home, it would be time for the 'daily obs.' To begin with, Fortescue had been resistant to the little black sleeve to measure his blood pressure, but he had soon got used to it. Stella used to put it round both forelegs at once. His temperature never varied by more than one tenth of one degree. After that it would be the highlight of his day - the moment for him to dine. Tripe was on the menu this morning.

"Here boy! Come!" He finally deigned to join her, for some unaccountable reason. It was important to sound cross with him.

"Where have you been?! Ooh you are a little republican." This was a severe insult; Stella was a convinced monarchist. Fortescue took it in good heart. He was more interested in the chocolate drop, which proved to be forthcoming, as usual at this stage of the walk.

On they went, passing into the shade at the foot of the cliff. The path wound among rocks here.

Oh dear, what was this. Fortescue had set up a mournful howl at the far side of a large boulder.

"What is it, my bold troubadour?" asked Stella, but she had a sense of foreboding. She rounded the rock. It was as she feared. Another suicide, the third in three years. That cliff should be named Lovers' Leap, she thought once again.

"No, leave it. Dead." Fortescue seemed to understand. One look at the unnatural angle of the head showed that there was no need to check the vital signs. Poor man. I wonder what happened, she thought.

She kept a phone in her pocket for emergencies, and soon got through to the police.

"I'm afraid that there's been another death. Foot of the cliffs; usual place. I'll wait until you arrive. Thanks, bye."

It was odd, that having spent a lifetime caring for people in the hopes of making them better, Stella's main contribution to society in retirement seemed to be finding suicide victims. Well, somebody had to do it. In a strange way, there was something good about it. Stella was used to death, and if she stumbled on the poor unfortunates, it saved other people from being traumatised by discovering a corpse.

This one was strange, however. The man looked curiously peaceful. But you could never tell the pain of other people's lives by looking at their faces, Stella had learned. People keep things bottled up so.

Stella took a few photos. She kept a camera in her coat pocket too; you never knew when you would come across a good photo. She had taken several pleasing pictures of wild life in the early morning sun. These photos of the man might prove useful. She had observed on the last occasion that the police had not bothered to photograph the scene. Very slack, really. At least she would have a record.

It turned out to be the same this time. The corpse was stretchered off to the van. Once it had been removed, you would never have known that there had been anything amiss.

"Any idea who he is, miss?"

Stella had never seen him before.

"Oh look, there's a wallet in his pocket. Let's see - here's a credit card. No reason why it shouldn't be his."

The officer wiped his specs before reading out the name on the card.

"Mr. Bruce Winter."

-oOo-

"Oh dear, how dreadful!" Marjorie exclaimed, as the young policeman told her the news. "I think I need to sit down. Come in."

The constable was not surprised to discover that Marjorie knew Bruce well, and indeed that she was his landlady, as her house and garden were not separated from his by a fence.

"Now, tell me again."

"I'm afraid that Mr. Winter was discovered dead at the foot of a cliff. It looks like suicide. I'm so sorry."

"Well, he has had a very difficult patch recently." Marjorie told the constable about Bruce's mother dying, and his discovering about his sister. "However, I never thought it would come to this. It's dreadful. I feel so sorry. He was such a lovely man."

"I can see you're very upset, madam. Can I make you a cup of tea, or anything?"

It was the policy of this police station to give people time and not to be too brisk. The Chief Constable was very keen on this. In the medium term, the result would be improved relations between the public and the police, and hence greater cooperation. The young constable had seen the sense in this, and had adopted the thinking as his own. He was not just following orders.

"No thank you, I'll be fine. I expect you need somebody to identify the body. Also, we need to go next door and see if there is a will. I expect there is; he was a very methodical man. His filing cabinet is the place to look. There might be a suicide note as well."

It was so much better that the lady had come up with these thoughts rather than the constable needing to suggest them.

"Let's do the house while we're here," he suggested. Marjorie produced a key, and they let themselves in. Everything seemed entirely normal, except that the heating was switched off.

"He could not bear waste," Marjorie explained.

She found the will in the filing cabinet. It was dated eighteen months before. Water Aid was to have twenty percent of his estate, and then the rest was to be split between Bancesca and Bill, who were also the executors. There was a small legacy for Marjorie herself, and likewise for Flossie. Bruce's music was to be divided among his piano pupils. There was no note.

"This all seems to be in order," said the constable. "Do you know these people?"

"He kept his address book by the phone."

They quickly located the details.

"I think we should identify the body first," Marjorie declared. It was at Wayford Hospital. The constable offered to drive her over there, and within a few minutes they were shown into a bare room with a single bed in it. The sheet over the body was drawn back.

"Yes, that's Bruce Winter," Marjorie said. He looked so peaceful in death. Her eyes filled with tears. "He was more of a friend than a tenant. We used to go to art galleries together. I shall miss him dreadfully."

They drove back in silence. Marjorie agreed to be on hand to help the executors, who were quickly informed. Both expressed horror and amazement. A meeting was arranged for two o' clock that afternoon. This was a time to drop everything else.

Within a few minutes of the phone calls being made, there was a knock on Marjorie's door. It was Gnilla.

"Tell me it isn't true," said Gnilla, staring earnestly at Marjorie's face.

"Come in," said Marjorie, softly. The constable was made to repeat all he knew, which was not very much. He then slipped off.

"I've identified the body," Marjorie said. Gnilla burst into tears. She and Marjorie hugged for a long time.

"Isn't it awful?" said Marjorie.

"It's a complete nightmare. Bruce was very emotional at church a few weeks back and I said we should call, but Bill was against it. He said we should give him space to work it all out. Oh dear, I wish I had acted on my instinct. And now it's too late."

Marjorie gave Gnilla a bite to eat, but she only nibbled at it. She had no appetite. She explained that the florist's shop had given her the rest of the day off.

Bill and Bancesca both arrived within a few minutes of each other. Bill was as white as a sheet. Bancesca's eyes were red.

"I feel so dreadful," said Bill. "I was his best friend, but when it came to the crunch, I let him down."

"You mustn't blame yourself, Bill," Bancesca said. "Last time I saw him, at Flossie's party, he was very moody. He hardly spoke to anybody; he just ate his way through the meal without talking to the people on his right and left. All my attempts to contact him have been blocked. He did not respond to messages I left on his answerphone. It was his choice to deal with his pain on his own, and it's a tragedy for all of us that he could not manage it."

They got down to business. The will was straightforward. Bill and Bancesca were to take charge of everything. Bill said there should be a solicitor, and Gnilla suggested Ian Chisel, whom Bruce had liked so much.

"Perhaps their band would play at the funeral," Bill suggested, but the others felt this needed some thought. Bruce should have his own send-off, not a re-run of his mother's. However, they decided to use the same undertakers as before.

A phone call to them resulted in a meeting to take place at the undertakers in forty minutes time. They agreed that once the date and time of the cremation was agreed, Gnilla would ring round all the piano pupils to let them know. Bruce had a list of them, with phone numbers, which he kept by the phone. She would also alert the school.

They would put a notice in the local and the national press - the latter partly in case Bruce's father might get to hear of it. Marjorie would keep an eye on the bungalow, as it was not unknown for burglars to break in as a result of a notice of death in the newspaper. She would also arrange for a friend or two to be in the bungalow during the time of the service, for the same reason. They could also get everything ready for the bun-fight afterwards, which would be held at the bungalow.

Bancesca drove Bill and Gnilla to the undertakers. Everything was soon arranged. The service would be on Friday at 1130 at Wayford Crem. It would still be half term, which would give many of Bruce's pupils and their families the best chance of attending. There would be refreshments afterwards, and the sheet music could be shared round at the same time. It all seemed pretty straightforward.

Bancesca dropped Bill and Gnilla off at the bungalow and went home. Marjorie had given them a key. Gnilla started on the phone calls. Ian Chisel was taken aback. He was pleased to help in any way he could. He explained to Bill about the need to alert banks and building societies, and to go through the filing system carefully, looking out for life insurance policies and the like. Then Ian would help with preparing the balance sheet. Bruce was not sufficiently wealthy for inheritance tax to come into it, which would simplify things.

Jane, the Head of Music at the school, was shocked to hear the news. She too felt guilty; could she have done more to respond to the concerns of Beccy and Simna?

Those two were both very upset as well. Within a few minutes, Beccy's dad was on the phone, offering to do the catering free of charge out of respect for Bruce. This was a most generous offer, and after consulting with Bancesca by phone, Bill accepted.

So the dismal process went on. The arrangements were put in place. It was decided not to try and have elaborate music at the funeral, because to put it bluntly, there was nobody around to equal Bruce. In view of what he had said at his mother's funeral about a new dawn, they decided to have 'The day thou gavest' again. Gnilla asked for 'The king of love my shepherd is.' It spoke of the simple faith that Bruce had. They agreed to start with that, and end with 'The day.'

As everybody wanted to give a tribute, they decided to have an opportunity during the service for anybody who chose to stand up and say something. "Short and sweet," Bill insisted.

Eventually, there was nothing more to do. Bill stared round the bungalow, the scene of many happy memories. It was going to be really hard getting used to the idea that Bruce had gone, and that they would never enjoy a laugh together again.

They locked up in silence, and made their way home.

-oOo-

The young reporter rang the bell and waited. Her luck was in. There was an outburst of ferocious barking followed by some strong words from a woman of mature years accustomed to command, and a slamming door, which suggested that the dog had been shut in a room. The barking continued at a lower volume despite the owner's urgings.

The front door opened. "Yes?" said Stella.

"I'm from The Lookout. I believe you may be the person who discovered the body of Bruce Winter. I was hoping you might be able to help us piece the story together."

This was splendid. A chance to contribute to society. Stella invited the girl in. They went through to the kitchen. The house had become quiet, but as Stella opened the door an excited brown animal shot out and started barking animatedly at the reporter.

"Forties - Q!" yelled Stella, with great urgency, "Leave it the nice reporter! Friend!"

Fortescue did not grasp the finer details of grammar; he did not 'stand upon points', as the bard put it. However, 'Leave it' and 'Friend' were commands, which he understood. Stella was sure of it. She bent over, held him by the collar and stared hard at his face.

"The fear of the Lord is the beginning of wisdom," she mumbled quietly, for the sake of completeness of the quotation, before adding in a loud clear voice, "but Fools scorn Wisdom and Discipline!" Her protégé looked suitably cowed, for a moment at least.

Then Stella turned to the reporter, who thankfully was at home with dogs, and instructed her.

"Form your hand into a fist, and hold it level with your knee so that he can sniff it and get used to you."

The result was satisfactory. The diminutive tail was soon wagging at speed.

"Come on through," said Stella. "Hot drink?"

They soon both held a mug of tea. Stella gave the girl a chocolate drop to pass on to Fortescue, to cement the friendship.

"Good boy," beamed Stella, "my brave animal. I will make you my bodyguard for life!"

"Now, Skuey and I were on our usual morning walk on Saturday, when we stumbled on the body at the foot of the cliff. You can see the cliff through the window," she pointed. "It would have been about ten past eight by then. I called the police, and they took the man away within a few minutes. I can give you their number if you like."

That was not necessary. Fortescue had come over and put his paw on the reporter's knee.

"Oh, he wants to come up. You are honoured. Would you like him or prefer not?"

Love me, love my dog. Yes it would be fine for Fortescue to come up. He needed little encouragement. He settled on the reporter's lap. Within a few minutes he was beginning to snore.

"What were your impressions at the scene, Mrs. Mitchell?"

"I can do better than that." It had occurred to Stella that the photos might be worth something to the right people, and she was in a position to bargain, but she put the thought right out of her head. This was for the general good. She had a sufficient income from her pension.

"Here are four photos I took at the time. I didn't think the police would bother."

This was an unexpected bonus. The body was clearly dead. The angle was consistent with a fall from the cliff. But was it suicide, or was he pushed? There seemed no way of knowing. There had been no signs of a struggle up there; no footmarks, nothing left on the ground.

"Might I borrow these and mail them back to you?"

"Of course." Stella produced an envelope and put her address on it. The Lookout could afford a stamp.

"If they are used, there will be a fee; not a very large one, I'm afraid."

"I've no objection. Thank you for thinking of it."

The girl told Stella that Mr. Winter had been a piano teacher, and had sustained a terrible shock a few weeks before, so it looked like suicide. Stella told of the previous two deaths, and that she thought of the cliff as Lover's Leap. The girl seemed upset by this. It was harrowing.

Fortescue stirred in his slumber, and lay still again. It seemed a shame to disturb him.

"I'd better go," the girl said. She gently lifted Fortescue and placed him on the seat as she got up. He hardly noticed. She gave him a gentle stroke. Lovely smooth coat.

When she got into the car, Celia only drove half a mile. Then she pulled up, and went round to the passenger seat. She opened the glove pocket, pressed a dozen keys on the keypad, and fed the photos into the scanner one by one. Head office would check them, and then pass them on to The Lookout.

Anyway, one thing was clear; it was definitely Bruce. Nobody would have guessed that her battered old car had such sophisticated technology on board. How it was possible to obtain a DNA sample from a passenger without the person's knowledge she did not know. The sample from the morgue had tallied. There was nothing out of order here. It was such a shame. He really had been a lovely man. If she had not been a secret agent, they could have got on very well, but then if she had not been a secret agent, they would probably never have met in the first place. How galling.

-oOo-

The day of the funeral dawned at last. The sky was overcast, with the colour of lead. At least it was not actually raining.

The Lookout carried the story in brief on an inside page. It was more about the cliff than Bruce himself, really, but his name was mentioned. The photos were not used. Stella had been pleased with the token payment Celia had put in the envelope. It went on a special treat for Fortescue - a large synthetic bone for him to chew. He deserved it; he was the one who had discovered the body. A truly noble beast.

A large crowd gathered for the service. Gnilla made a point of going round thanking them all for coming. Bruce would have liked that.

There was something else she had done that he would have approved of. It was when they had gone to the undertaker's chapel to pay their last respects. Bruce had looked so fine, lying there! What a good friend he had been. She was in tears. She did not let

370

anyone else know, but there, in his presence, she had prayed her first prayer. It was short and to the point.

'God, if you exist, and you're the God that Bruce believed in, then show me.'

There had been no blinding flash or anything like that. But somehow, as the hours passed, Gnilla gradually became more sure that God was there, and that she wanted to talk to him again.

So it was that as the crematorium chapel was filling up, she murmured her second prayer.

'May this event go as well as it can.'

How nice it was that there was a large crowd. There were a lot of people that she did not know. When you added it up, the number of lives that Bruce had touched in one way or another was considerable. I wonder if they all feel it was a privilege to have known him, Gnilla thought.

You could pick out his school pupils easily enough. Some of them looked white in the face, and several of them were tearful. They were all obviously affected.

It was time to begin.

"Would you all please stand."

The coffin was borne in slowly with dignity, by six men in black suits. The organ played quietly. There was a voice saying something about resurrection and life, or something like that. It was difficult to take it in. Gnilla hoped there really was another life to come.

The clergyman dressed in black and white spoke to them.

"A warm welcome to this sad occasion - thank you all so much for coming. I did not know Bruce myself, so I am pleased with the suggestion that anybody who wants to pay a brief tribute to him will be able to do so. We will start with a hymn. Then Bill will read from the Bible. Then there's the chance for everyone to share. The rule is, stand up, speak up, shut up. If you go on too long, it will prevent other people from being able to have a word.

"So let's begin with the hymn, 'The King of Love my Shepherd is.' It's an arrangement of Psalm twenty-three, and speaks of David's trust in God, like that of a sheep in his shepherd."

The singing was quite good. A musical gathering, Gnilla reflected. Then Bill stood up to read. It was David's lament over the death of Saul.

"Your glory, O Israel, lies slain on your heights.
How the mighty have fallen!
Tell it not in Gath,
Proclaim it not in the streets of Ashkelon,
Lest the daughters of the Philistines be glad,
Lest the daughters of the uncircumcised rejoice…"

It was so relevant, the clergyman explained, as Saul had ended his own life by falling on his sword. That had not prevented David from mourning for him. There had been a time when suicides were refused burial on consecrated ground, whatever that was, Gnilla had heard. Thankfully, those days were now over.

It was time to share. Two or three adult pupils hesitantly led the way. Gnilla's heart was racing; she found it very difficult to speak in public, but she was determined.

Suddenly she was on her feet and it was her turn.

"Bill and I have only been married for a few weeks. While we were going out, we had a bust-up and it all looked hopeless, but Bruce was so good, supporting both of us, and it helped us get back together again. I just wanted to say that if we have any children and it's a boy we're going to call him Bruce."

She sat down. The grammar may not have been good, but it was from the heart. It got everybody else going, including the school pupils.

"He once told me that when I played Jingle Bells, it reminded him of Santa's reindeer having a coughing fit, because it was a bit stoppy-starty. I liked him."

"We did the Pink Panther," said Simna in a quiet voice, "and he taught us to keep it soft and prowling."

"I found his love of Bach and Beethoven an inspiration," said an older pupil. "He opened my eyes to the classics."

"I thought he was funny," said a pupil's younger sister. "He showed me how to do chopsticks." She looked about four. How nice that she had been able to say that.

Bruce would have enjoyed this, Gnilla thought. There was the coffin, lying there. It seemed impossible to imagine Bruce in it, somehow. It seemed out of character.

It was soon over. The refreshments back at the bungalow were excellent. Bill read the will out to everyone, and said he would like to divide the music out there and then. Everybody who wanted a piece was to take a playing card from the pack, which had been shuffled, and then the order of choice was Spades first, Ace then King, Queen and on down, followed by Hearts, Diamonds and Clubs. You had to keep your card in case there was the chance of a second piece.

In the end, thirty-four cards were given out. It worked very well, as the younger pupils were not interested in the hard-backed bound volumes, so these remained available for the adults as their turn came up. There was a surprising amount of music. Everybody got two pieces, and some people three. For the second piece, they went in reverse order to the first piece, to make it fair. Everyone seemed happy with the arrangements.

Nobody wanted to leave, as they realised they would probably never visit the bungalow again. It had been a happy place for them.

"You know," Bill said to Gnilla when everyone had finally gone, "if there was that much love and affection for me at my funeral, I would be very pleased. It helps you realise what life is about, it seems to me. So much of what we do is unimportant in the long run."

It was the saddest thing to turn the lights off and lock up and walk off down the path. Could it really all be over?

Next morning, which was Saturday, Bill and Bancesca met at the house, as arranged. It was a case of making a list of all Bruce's belongings. Marjorie came through to help, as it was not easy to know what was his and what was hers. Marjorie knew of a man who did house clearances. They left a message on his answerphone, which would be dealt with after the weekend.

Bruce had been well organised. The filing cabinet was in good order. Bill wondered whether he had made a point of tidying up, to save them time and trouble. Had he been planning this action for a while, perhaps? Maybe he chose the Friday evening at the start of half term to cause minimum fuss and bother. It would have been typical of his generous nature.

All of a sudden, Bill felt terribly tired and depressed. He could not bear to do any more. Bancesca felt stronger, and was happy to continue on her own. Bill rang the florists and asked for Gnilla.

"Look, I need a break," he said to her. "How about us going to a hotel on the coast for a couple of nights, get some sea air, and then drive back Sunday afternoon or even early on Monday in time for work, ready to face the week?"

Gnilla was pleased with the idea. She would be free at lunchtime. Bill told Bancesca, and then went off home to pack a few things.

Bruce had ducked out of it, but somehow life had to go on.

-oOo-

"I'm sorry I'm such poor company," said Bruce, as the sky-car floated down gently to the rocky surface. "I just can't seem to wake up."

"Don't worry about it," said Jim. "I'm not bothered. We've got plenty of time."

The landing itself was imperceptible. The doors swung open, and they stepped out into the bright sunlight. It was beautifully mild. Bruce could see they were on the northernmost of a chain of three rocky islands. There was a half mile channel separating them from the next of the three, which appeared the largest of the group. The islands were uninhabited, except for the lone building ahead of them.

"Welcome to my hotel," said Jim, "although apart from you and me, only two other people know it's mine. Keep it to yourself if you would. Also, they know me by another surname here."

"Is it safe to call you Jim?" laughed Bruce, as he collected his holdall.

"Yes indeed. Now do you see the island way over there?"

374

There was another, much larger island straight ahead of them, across about twenty miles of water, which Bruce now noticed for the first time. It was covered with houses in contrast.

"Any idea where that is?"

Bruce shook his head.

"Madeira. We are on one of its offshore islands - the Desertas, so called. I wanted a site with good facilities at hand, but which would also be peaceful. This place seemed ideal. It's great for bird-watching."

They arrived at the entrance to the hotel. The doors swung open as they entered. There was a huge atrium above their heads. Bruce imagined that no expense had been spared on this place.

Jim led the way. "Bruce, first of all, I'd like you to meet Miss Vanderpokel. She's of Dutch extraction, but she speaks perfect English."

They made their way into an office with the word Manager on the door. "Pikel, this is Bruce."

Pikel Vanderpokel! A nickel for a cockle! What an incredible name. Bruce was working hard to suppress a desire to laugh. However, the young lady who rose from behind the desk proved to be no laughing matter. On the contrary; she took his breath away. She was dressed in a bright red trouser suit, and had flowing black hair, which was gathered at the crown of her head in an elastic band of some kind before falling to her shoulders. Her complexion was coffee coloured, as a result of the sun, Bruce reckoned. Her face and figure made a powerful impression; so much so, that Bruce found it hard to look at her. He was simply dazzled.

Pikel stretched out her hand. "I've heard so much about you," she said. Bruce muttered something about being pleased to meet her.

"You seem rather distracted," Pikel said.

Bruce pulled himself together. "I was just remembering a holiday on a barge I once took with my friend Bill back in England. We went through the village of Branston at one point... or was it Braunston? Come to think of it, I think we may have gone through both villages on the same holiday."

This was hopeless. It was madness to think of barging holidays. He hoped to goodness she had never heard of Branston Pickle.

"Oh, so you like boats."

"That's wonderful, Bruce," Jim interjected. "Pikel will enjoy to take you out on her yacht." Pikel was nodding, and Bruce could see that it was all arranged. He mumbled words of thanks in anticipation.

Why was it that he seemed to spend his entire life meeting beautiful women? Was the world genuinely full of them, or was it that all women seemed beautiful to him? Or perhaps they were all stunning. Never mind.

Jim was leading him off somewhere else.

"Is Pikel the Manager of the Hotel?" he asked.

"She does all the work, but she prefers to be known as my Personal Assistant. I can't understand why. She is brilliant at it. Has a great gift of putting people at their ease. The staff love her. She's a terrific asset."

Bruce hoped she might be too busy to take him on the yacht. He could already sense danger ahead. But it might come to nothing. People sometimes make effusive offers that they have no intention of carrying out.

Jim had gathered up the key to Bruce's room. They took the lift to the third floor; room 318. It was of course delightful.

"When you've freshened up, you'll find me in the bar. Then we can make a plan. See you soon."

It was going to be an amazing week, Bruce reckoned. If only he could clear his head. He tried plenty of cold water on the face. Then he took deep breaths on the balcony. The view of the sea was great. It was no use; he still felt groggy. The clock by the bed said 1155. An hour to lunch. Then he noticed a pair of binoculars in the room. That was nice. He picked them up, and took them down with him. He found his way to the bar. Jim was in an armchair with a newspaper. There was nobody else about.

"We put you on the top floor to get the best view of the sea," Jim said. "I'm afraid the place is rather empty at present. In fact, we

376

have barely opened. It's only just been finished. Still, there are a few other guests in."

Bruce explained that he still felt groggy, and he thought a turn outside before lunch might be the best thing. Jim offered to show him the best spots for watching the wild life.

Before long, they were seated on rocks a few feet above the sea, which was calm, watching the gulls and the occasional oyster-catcher. Bruce studied a cormorant through the binoculars for two or three minutes. It was delightful to see it so clearly. It had a large beak.

"Bruce, I'm so glad you've come. There's so much I want to tell you, but not yet. I'm hoping you will enjoy to see a bit of the area, as well as have a good rest. Also, I'm sure you and Pikel will get on like a house on fire. Will tomorrow do for the sail? She's cleared her diary."

There did not seem to be much choice. Bruce was already feeling nervous. He nodded.

"You mustn't mind her manner. She's such an asset here. She beat the competition for the job hands down. However, she's not musical, you know."

Bruce was more pleased than not at the thought of the sail, he decided. It was time for lunch. Afterwards, he would have a good rest. Jim had things to attend to.

```
56. From: Mission 12
To: Undisclosed recipients
Sent:


We went back up to the spaceship. It gave me
the chance to have a talk with Clairie.
    "Daddy, I'm so upset about Mark," she began. It
sounded promising. "I hate being up here all on
my own. It's horrible."
    This was not so good.
    "Clairie, what are your thoughts about Mark
being dead?"
    "I'm pleased, Daddy. He was so horrid."
```

I feared as much. She did not appear to have much concept of the seriousness of what she had done.

"Clairie, when you put the pill in Mark's food, you were ending his life. He had no choice about it. Do you think that was good or bad to do?"

"But Daddy, what else could I do? Mummy was talking of killing herself. Why should she have to die when it was him that was bad?"

"Well, I can think of a number of things you could have done. You could have told me about it, for example, or Phil."

"They were all hopeless. They did not even tell you that Mummy now loved Mark rather than you. They would not have helped at all. Also, Mark would have got to hear of it. I was scared of what he might do. It seemed better this way."

"But Clairie, what you have done is wrong. Nobody can end someone else's life, except God. What you have done is to behave as if you were God. It was very wrong."

Clairie hung her head. "I know, Daddy. But at least it's saved Mummy. I don't feel sorry about it."

I felt we were getting nowhere.

"Clairie, what you should have done was to talk to a grown-up, or even if that felt impossible, you should have asked God to help. Promise me that you will never play at being God again."

"I promise, Daddy."

I was watching her as she said this. It seemed genuine to me. I hugged her. I feel sad for her, because even though she is still young in years, her childhood is over. She has become an adult before her time. She already knows the weight of past sin and wrong choices pressing down on her. There is nothing I can do to take that from her.

"It's important to ask God to forgive you, Clairie, and to ask him to help you live rightly in future."

"I will Daddy."

Margaret told us she was getting on fine with Clairie. I think she was glad of the company. I am so grateful to her.

I went back down with Phil after a couple of days, in the hope of getting to talk to Celia, but it was still no good. I wandered over to Mark's grave. It was stupid to hope that the lichen would have spread in just the few days since I last saw it. It looked the same as before.

I gazed at Mark's headstone, and let out a sigh. He must have had such high hopes for the settlement when he left earth all those years before. He never imagined that he would end up being buried within a few weeks of arrival. He had died without leaving any descendants. That was tough. I felt genuinely sorry for him.

I found myself hoping that the city which would grow up here one day might be named after him. I imagined the many fine buildings that would rise up around us. I wondered about the name. Mark's Corner seemed appropriate. That would undoubtedly be corrupted over time. Perhaps to Marqson. Languages change and evolve, and for some reason, I imagined that 'q' might take the place of 'c' and 'k' in due course. Marqson would turn to Marxon, of course. Marxon. Not a bad name.

It was as I was musing that I finally got it. Was Celia refusing to see me because she was pregnant?

Bruce

By next morning, Bruce was feeling much better. The hotel food was excellent, which helped. There were fifty or so guests there, which was more than Jim had implied, but there was room in the large dining room for at least two hundred. It all felt very relaxed. There was also a library of books, most of them in English, for guests to borrow. This suited Bruce admirably. He was not a great

379

socialite. However, he had enjoyed playing Jim at Snooker before dinner the previous evening. To his astonishment he had succeeded in potting red, colour, red in one visit to the table. Not bad, considering that he only picked up a cue two or three times a year. The game had been decided on the black, which finally went in Jim's favour.

Pikel was due to meet him in the atrium after breakfast. Jim had found him a pair of canvas shoes and a cap, which gave the right image for yachting. Jim was not coming, which meant he would be alone with Pikel on the yacht. Bruce was feeling distinctly nervous.

She soon arrived, wearing a loose sweater and baggy trousers, all navy blue, with canvas shoes and a cap to match. She looked perfect in the part. As they walked across the island towards the marina, Bruce told himself not to be stupid. Try and relax. It was a beautiful day for being on the water.

"Are you used to sailing, Bruce?" asked Pikel.

"I've done a little. I do know that 'sheet' means 'rope', if that's what you mean. You just tell me what to pull, and I'll do my best."

"Oh, there's no need to worry about anything like that. It's all automatic. You can just lie back and relax. Have you brought a camera?"

Bruce had, and the binoculars and a couple of books.

"Where are you from, Pikel?" he asked.

"Amsterdam originally, but I've been in this area for several years now. It's a popular destination for English tourists. I was so pleased to get the job working in Jim's hotel. He's a wonderful employer."

Pikel was in the know then.

"How about you?"

"Oh, I just teach piano south west of London. Nothing very special."

"I'm so fond of music. You must play for us."

"That would be a pleasure." It really would; Bruce would rather play in the background than have to talk to people he did not know.

They had arrived at the yacht. It was a large one; no prizes for guessing that correctly.

"It's a beautiful boat."

Pikel gave him a warm smile. She really was stunning.

"Now, you sit here," Pikel indicated a chair to her left, "while I get us off." She was adept with the controls. She started the motor by pressing a button; it gave a healthy roar. She left it in neutral. Then she cast off the bow, giving the boat a push with her foot as she did so, making it edge outwards from the mooring, ran nimbly along to the stern and cast off there, hopped on board and eased the motor slowly into forward.

"Lift-off, we have lift-off," said Bruce. "Ocean Venturer has cleared the tower. Sorry, I am more used to space rockets than yachts."

Pikel was amused, and Bruce was soon telling her about his trip to the moon. This was satisfactory; it seemed important to keep his end up. He had to explain the moment of weightlessness in some detail, as Pikel was most fascinated by it. She also wanted a close description of the moon's surface. She is no fool, Bruce thought.

When they were half a mile from the shore, Pikel cut out the engine, and began pressing other buttons on the dashboard. The mainsail shot upwards, then the jib; ropes whizzed through pulleys, and the sails began to fill with the wind. The deck started to tilt as the boat leaned over. Bruce had been ready for this; his first thought when coming on board was to look for suitable handholds and footholds. He took a firm grip and braced himself.

"There, much better without the motor. It's a nice day for sailing; wind not too strong but enough of it, and plenty of sun. The cloud hangs around the islands, but as we get away from them, the sun will come out. Isn't it wonderful?"

Bruce agreed. Pikel locked the tiller in position, satisfied herself that everything was in order, and then said, "come and get a drink."

They went below to the bar. It was well stocked. All the bottles were tightly gripped in place to prevent accidents. A bit like a space ship really, Bruce thought.

"What will you have?"

This was no time for alcohol. Bruce chose an orange juice, with ice and lemon. He was expecting something out of a packet, but to his surprise, Pikel got out some fresh oranges, cut them in half and put them in a press one by one. It reminded Bruce of Bill and Gnilla on honeymoon. He soon had a tall glassful. A little umbrella on a wooden stick was added at the last moment, for effect.

I'm hopeless when it comes to choosing a drink, Bruce thought to himself. I never know what to ask for.

Pikel had something much more dashing, which involved half a dozen bottles, and even something that looked like cherry sauce out of a small flask. It did look rather good.

Pikel saw him eyeing it. "Have a sip to try," she said. It was excellent.

"You have that one as well as yours, and I'll make another." She whisked around efficiently, and had soon made a second concoction. So much for my determination of no alcohol, Bruce thought.

"I'm just going to change," Pikel announced. This was serious, but Bruce had foreseen it, and was mentally prepared. Sure enough, she emerged a few minutes later in a two-piece bathing suit. Bruce found it almost impossible to look at her, she was so attractive, but it was just about alright if he concentrated on her face. This was going to be difficult.

"Let's go up on deck." They surfaced, Bruce making every effort not to spill either of his drinks. At least the wind was consistent, so the angle of the sloping deck was predictable. They made their way to some comfortable chairs which were firmly secured, and put the drinks in the little holders designed to prevent spillages. The holders were weighted, and could rotate freely, which meant that the drinks stayed upright. Thankfully, there were enough of them for both Bruce's glasses.

"This is wonderful," said Bruce, determined to speak first for a change. "It's very kind of you to make the time to bring me out."

"Not at all," said Pikel. "I've been looking forward to it. Jim is full of your praises, you know."

"I can't think why. I've only met him a few times. He seems to like my piano playing."

"What he appreciates is people who are straight and up-front. That's what he likes about you. He told me."

"Well, I feel the same way about people. I try to be as normal and straightforward as possible in my dealings with everyone. Some people are so complex. I've never got on well with that."

They sipped at their drinks. They were now out of sight of land.

"I suppose we would reach Africa eventually, if we kept going?" Bruce asked.

"Yes; three hundred miles or so. I've never been, but I'd like to do it one day."

"Sounds like a nice trip."

Conversation was difficult, because Bruce knew what was coming next.

"What about a swim?" Pikel enquired. "The sea is beautifully warm." He had known it would be.

"I hope you don't mind," Pikel continued, "bit I prefer to swim topless. Will it bother you?"

This too had been inevitable. However, Bruce had had nearly twenty-four hours to prepare his answer. He did not want to hurt her, but there was no way he was going to give in.

"Not at all, as long as you don't mind if I look in the opposite direction and don't join you. I'll just read my book."

Pikel said nothing. She walked over to the dashboard, and pressed the buttons. Ropes ran about; the sails began to flap, and then they came tumbling down. They lost headway.

"There. Now the boat will drift, and we won't get left behind. If it's bathing trunks you want, there are some in the first locker below. You'll regret not coming in."

"I'll be fine thanks." This called for strong resolution. Pikel Vanderpokel! Of Dutch extraction indeed! This was like pulling teeth.

He heard her top piece fall to the deck. There were some steps leading down into the water near the stern unless... There was a splash. She had dived in. It was so tempting to look. Discipline, Bruce, Discipline.

"Come on in. It's lovely."

"I'll be fine thanks."

There were various splashing sounds. Keep firm. She might be swimming on her back. Bruce tried to concentrate on his book, but it was almost impossible to grasp the meaning of what he was reading. Then he had an idea.

"Pikel," he called.

"Yes?" Bruce could hear that she had swum up close to him. He did not look up.

"I just thought you might be interested in what I'm reading. It says here that there may be vast numbers of comets flying round the solar system way out beyond Pluto, in what is called the Oort cloud after the Dutch astronomer who first proposed the idea, and that their orbits could stretch half way to the nearest star. That's two light years," he explained. "Also, some of them might take as long as a million years to complete their orbit round the sun. Isn't that amazing?"

"Yes. Simply fascinating."

He knew what she was hoping, and that she knew that he knew, and... What did it matter who knew what? It just seemed a good idea to sound interested in something else.

"Bruce, I'm worried there might be a shark about or some other big fish."

This was monstrous. Why was she so pushy?

"Oh dear, I'd better go below. I can't endure the sight of blood, and I might faint if I saw a dismembered arm come floating past, or something like that. Give me a shout if a shark comes and you need the lifebelt thrown; I will throw it on the port side unless you call otherwise."

Bruce made his way downstairs. Shark indeed. There is only one shark in the sea, and that's Pikel. No, not Pikel; Pike. Rows of sharp gleaming teeth. Pike Vanderpoke. Only don't touch her, whatever you do.

It certainly was an ordeal. She was so beautiful. Something stronger than orange juice seemed called for now, to help fortify him. Port, that was the thing. Local brew, these being Portuguese islands.

There were two bottles of Port, one red and one white. The idea of white Port was an abomination to Bruce. He helped himself to a thimble full of the red; not too much, for fear of getting gout. Granddad had warned him about that, years before. Well, perhaps two thimblefuls.

Oh dear. She was getting out. He could hear her towelling herself dry. Pike Onyerbike. In the pink... I should think... might need a drink... Bruce was running out of rhymes.

When the cabin door opened, Bruce saw that she had put on a towelling robe. Thank goodness for that. She was looking at him.

"Why don't you want me?"

"Put some clothes on and I'll explain. The more covered up you are, the more I will tell. In fact, if I can't see an inch of you, then I will look you straight in the eyes and tell you my whole life story. How's that?"

She went through to change, and emerged a few minutes later in the outfit she had worn at the hotel.

"Any good?" she said. She was not cross, just puzzled.

"I can still see a bit of your neck. You need a delicate silk scarf to complement your attire, if I may suggest it. Then it will be just fine."

Well of course there was a silk scarf on board. It was soon in place. Pikel came over and sat down.

"Bruce, most men are only interested in my body. There's something different about you."

"Well, don't get me wrong. You are one of the most beautiful girls I have ever met. You are also witty and intelligent with it. But I could only have joined you in the water if we were committed to each other for life. I don't want a quick fling which is over in a few days. It's against my beliefs. Only marriage will do."

"What beliefs are they?"

"Well, I try to follow Jesus, but I'm pretty hopeless at it. However, the bit of the Bible that applies is from Leviticus. The teaching is that a woman's nakedness belongs to her husband, and that he should have exclusive rights."

"But I don't have a husband."

385

"Maybe not, but in that case you should be saving your nakedness for him, when he comes along. If anybody else gets to see it, that is an act of theft. That's how I understand it."

Pikel looked thoughtful. "That's very interesting. I would like to be married," she said, "to the right person. But tell me; why do you follow Jesus? Why not Mohammed or Buddha or one of the other world faiths?"

Bruce laughed. "He saved me in every way that a person can be saved," he said. "It's a riddle. See if you can fathom it. No clues!"

Pikel was intrigued. She was going to try and solve it. But not yet.

"Now, tell me your life story."

Bruce had not expected to be taken literally on this, but she was clearly interested.

"Well, there's not much to tell, really." He explained about his Mum and Dad and Sasha, the terrible day when he was little, and the discovery only a month before of what had happened. Pikel was appalled that he had missed meeting his Mum again by just ten minutes.

"Bruce, that's awful. You must be in a frightful state. I'm so sorry. My behaviour must have been really difficult for you."

"Don't worry about it. I knew it was coming, I don't know how, so I was prepared. It's Okay, really. You were doing what you thought was best." Bruce wanted to encourage her. "What's your story?"

It turned out that she had a difficult background. Pikel Vanderpokel was not her real name. "It's a brilliant choice," said Bruce, who had taken to it.

"The truth is, Bruce, I'm scared. I know I'm beautiful now, but I can't seem to get into a steady relationship. I'm frightened I will end up an old maid."

"Well, my advice is to stop looking for a man and start looking for God. I don't suppose you expected to hear that, or appreciate it even, but I reckon if you get that sorted out, then the other might take care of itself. Not that I know what I'm talking about, you understand. I don't know how to find someone either. There must be better people to ask than me! But listen. You do not need to remove a shred of clothing to look lovely. That's what I think, anyway."

"Bruce, you're very kind. I can see that you really care about me. Now, I've been making the running all day, and it hasn't been a huge success. You say; what would you like to do?"

This was thoughtful.

"Any chance of lunch?"

Naturally, there were cold salads ready in the fridge, followed by a tasty sweet. Bruce insisted on making the coffee. No hope of instant; he'd given up on that idea long ago. He could cope with real coffee alright, but he preferred instant if the truth was known.

"Do we know where we are?"

Silly question, really. The navigation was controlled by satellite. Even if the wind died away and a thick fog came down they could motor back with pinpoint accuracy. Bruce wondered whether there might be wild life to observe near the islands, so they headed back. To his delight, there were some seals, as well as numerous birds. He and Pikel lay on their fronts on the deck and took it in turns to look through the binoculars. She made no further attempts to attract him, but she did not need to. Now that the trial had passed, he found he was reluctant to end the outing. It was lovely being here with her. He hoped it could go on for ever. He wondered whether she could sense it.

The sun was beginning to sink. "We'd better get back," she said. It was not far. As the wind was in a helpful quarter, Pikel did not start the motor; instead she brought the mainsail down and sailed for the mooring under the jib. As they approached, she brought the jib lower and lower so that they made less and less headway, until they bumped gently up against the moorings.

"That was very impressive, if I may say so. It never occurred to me that you would come in under sail."

"I don't normally. To be honest, I wanted to do something that might impress you. I feel I've messed up today."

"Don't worry about it. I mess up all the time. You've given me a lovely day out, and I've enjoyed your company. Thanks a lot."

Bruce kissed her on the cheek. She smiled back. They walked back to the hotel in silence.

When Bruce got to bed that evening, he could not sleep. He found he was thinking of Adam and Eve. It was easy enough for them; God just produced Eve as a companion, a helper for Adam, and brought her along, and that was that. There was none of this dating and decision making. The story said Eve was made from his rib. This was interesting; it was as if she was already part of Adam before they had even met. How wonderful to meet someone for the first time and feel like that about them.

Pikel had done him a good turn; she had shown him what he wanted.

Nevertheless, he was thankful that the door of his room had a lock on it which he could engage, and he was not just reliant on others needing a key to get in.

While he was lying there reflecting, he heard a slight noise. The door handle was turning. It was Pikel trying to come in! He was sure of it.

Suddenly, he wanted more than anything to get up and unlock the door and invite her in. His whole body cried out with longing. This was terrible and wonderful all at once.

Somehow, he gritted his teeth, and turned his face to the wall. He only had to fight for a few seconds, he told himself. Each moment seemed a lifetime.

Ah! She had given up. The handle was at rest. But even now he could run to the door and call her. Don't let her get away! He longed for her.

He forced himself to lie still. The opportunity was passing. Now it was lost. He had missed his chance.

No, he had not lost; he had been faithful. Faithful to whom, or to what? And was it really worth it?

Bruce was exhausted. Suddenly he found he missed his Granddad. He wished he was here. But he needed to fight his own battles. He hoped there would not be many more. All the same; it was nice to be wanted.

He was worn out. He soon fell asleep. He dreamed that a man in a pin stripe suit offered to trim his nails with a pair of secateurs. Bruce was on the verge of accepting when he realised that the businessman was really about to cut off his pianist's fingers. He ran and ran to get away, but the man with the cutters was always there beside him. The only thing was to form a fist so that the snapping blades could not get at the fingers. Then it occurred to him to punch the man with the fist, which he did, only to see him crumple up, as he was made from folded newspaper. The fingers were safe! He stirred, but slept on, and in the morning, the dream had faded.

57. From: Mission 12
To: Undisclosed recipients
Sent:

"Sandra, it's important," I said. "I am wondering whether Celia is refusing to see me because she is expecting Mark's child. You don't need to confirm or deny it," I added hastily, "but what I want to say is this. Whether it is true or not, I want to discuss us getting back together again. I feel terribly hurt as you would expect. But what I want is to forgive her, and for us to become a couple again. Then, if she is expecting Mark's child, we can bring up the baby together. I would like to be a father to him or her. Are you willing to talk these things over with her?"

It did the trick. Within an hour, Celia and I were face to face. She wanted Sandra to stay; I was happy about this.

"Bruce, I feel so awful. I've let you down hideously. And now this business with Clairie."

"It is a Grade A mess, I do agree. I have felt terribly hurt. What made you abandon me for him?"

"Bruce, I really don't know the answer to that. I've asked myself the same question hundreds of times. It was flattering to have attention paid to me, but I should have shooed him off, and told

389

you about it. I can't think why I let myself be drawn in. Then when we had slept together for the first time, I felt unable to talk to you about it, and I found myself slipping more an more into his power. I've been such a fool."

I did not know what to say.

"I want to tell you all of it," she continued. "It was crazy asking Clairie to get the suicide pill. I see that now. I felt unable to come up myself to get it. It would mean facing you. The fact is, I never meant to take it myself. I was going to give it to Mark. Then when Clairie said Big Nimp had refused, I took her word for it. I never dreamt she would do what she did. It's dreadful."

This put things in a new light.

"What made you decide to bump him off?"

"Finding out I was pregnant. Your guess was right. He seemed so thrilled, but I sensed a wicked delight in him. I saw it in a flash. He did not really love me at all. It was all about taking your place. He saw you as central. He knew that Max would be easy to dominate, but you were another matter. He wanted to take over, you see. What better way than humiliating you by stealing your wife? It worked very well; it forced you out of the centre. He was free to do what he liked then. I hated him for it. I realised I was being used as a pawn in his little game of chess. I was just a conquest, boosting his ego. It made me feel sick."

It was grim hearing all this, but it made me feel better. Celia had come to see Mark as a snake in the grass.

"When did it start?" I asked. I needed to know. Celia hung her head.

"Within a few days of the wake-up. I feel so ashamed."

I was silent again. All this was far from easy.

"What do you want to do?" I asked.

390

"Bruce, if you will have me, I'd love us to get back together again. I know it will take time to get over all this, but I love your idea of us having the baby and caring for it as if it were ours. I think it is so noble of you."

I said nothing. I reached across and took her in my arms for a hug. Sandra tiptoed out. Celia was crying silently.

Suddenly, I felt an overwhelming urge to break her neck. It came out of nowhere. I was appalled. I fought it. After a bit it died down again. I was left shaking.

Celia disengaged from the hug, and looked at me.

"What is it, Bruce?"

I felt it best to tell her.

"I suddenly had an urge to pay you back, but I've fought against it, and it's gone again. What I want is to get over all the pain, and for us to be happy again."

"So do I, Bruce. I was mad to ever let it happen. I think you are terrific to have me back. I don't deserve you."

"Life would be intolerable if we got what we deserved," I said. "Let's go for a walk."

So it was that others saw us walking together up onto the sand dune, and marvelled. I was pleased. I knew it was the right thing. Also, I had never stopped loving Celia.

Maybe there is a future and a hope for us.

Bruce

It soon became apparent that Jim was busy most mornings. This did not bother Bruce, as he was very happy with a book. However, he found himself forming a plan.

"I think I might take a rowing boat across to the next door island this morning," he told Jim on their fourth day, at breakfast. "I quite fancy the idea of an adventure and exploring the unknown."

"It's further than it looks," Jim warned, "and if the sea is rough you'll have a job landing, so will you promise to keep your phone switched on and call if you get into trouble?"

"Yes of course," Bruce said. The idea of pitting his wits against the wind and tide seemed exhilarating.

He set off in sunshine. The dinghy had an adjustable footrest, which meant he could arrange the rowing position to suit his size. He was soon skimming along. It was a little awkward having nobody else to guide him; it meant that he kept on having to look over his shoulder to make minor adjustments to his direction. Life is a bit like rowing a boat across a lake, he found himself thinking. We talk about facing the future, but really, you face backwards into the past; that is, everything that has happened so far is clear to you, but what is coming next can only be guessed at by noting what gradually comes into view on the shore at the edges of your vision. Here, I can screw my neck round to see what's coming ahead, but you can't do that in real life.

It was further than he had realised, and it was forty minutes of hard work before he finally reached the island. Then he had to go two or three hundred yards further along the rocky shore before he found a place where he would be able to scramble out. Somehow, he managed it without letting hold of the painter, and he was able to drag the boat up on top of the rocks. There was no hint of any beach. The boat was not too heavy, thankfully.

Phew, thought Bruce, I don't think I would be much good at fending for myself on a desert island. That trip has been enough to tire me out.

Now the fun part began. He had his binoculars and a camera. He walked as quietly as he could, very slowly. His clothing was grey, to blend in with the rocks. There was quite a bit of climbing to do before he came out on the upper plateau on top of the island. More than once he was rewarded with a good view of wildlife. However, what looked good in the binoculars always looked disappointingly small when seen through the viewfinder of the camera. Not for the first time, he wished he had a better zoom lens.

After about an hour, he felt the phone buzzing in his pocket. It was Jim.

"Hello Captain Scott, although whether it is Scott of the Antarctic or Scott the expert on birds I don't rightly know. How are you doing?"

"Fine, thanks. I'm on top of the island." Then Bruce had an impulse. "Are you free to come on over and join me?"

"Just what I was thinking. I'll be there in five minutes. Look out for me flying over. Bye."

Bruce sat on a rock, and watched the sky in the direction that Jim would take in the sky-car. He seemed to be rather slow.

Suddenly, Bruce received the shock of his life.

"Hello," said a voice quite close by.

Bruce's head shot round. There was Jim's head and shoulders, apparently suspended in mid air, about five yards away on the other side of him.

"Ooh you frightened me. You practically gave me a heart attack. What are you doing?"

Jim thought it was wonderfully funny. More of Jim suddenly became visible, as he stepped out of nowhere and walked over to Bruce.

"What are you up to now?" asked Bruce, who was completely mystified.

"Didn't you see me flying over? Now there's a strange thing!" said Jim.

Bruce could tell that Jim was enjoying this.

"An invisible car, I suppose. How on earth is that done?"

"Yes, you're quite right." Jim pressed a button on his remote control, and a sky-car was instantly visible ten yards away. Then he pressed the button again, and it vanished.

"That's amazing!" said Bruce.

"Now," said Jim, "you're going to tell me how it's done."

This was a challenge.

"Well, I suppose you would need to have a camera on one side of the car taking video of the background, and a screen on the other side of the car playing back the recording."

"Good start, Bruce."

"However, if the observer moved his head slightly, what he would see would soon look strange against the background. It seems to me that to do a convincing job, you would need an infinite number of little screens, each one sending the information of what was on the opposite side of the car from that point. Oh dear, the thought of it is mind-boggling."

"Well done. You're on the right lines. Let me see if I can explain the concept in layman's terms.

"The key to invisibility is what I call an image transmitter. It is a device which picks up the view from one side of an object, and transmits it faithfully on the other side. So it is both a video camera, and a visual display all at the same time, if you follow me.

"Now, let's take a simple case. Imagine that you want to make a stone pillar in a church invisible, so that people seated behind the pillar can see what's going on with an uninterrupted view. You might cover the pillar all over with image transmitters the size of golf balls. Each golf ball would need to be connected to the corresponding golf ball on the other side of the pillar. When all the golf balls were active, they would transmit the signal from one side of the pillar to the other, and if you walked round the pillar, you would always see what was beyond the pillar, but not the pillar itself. Am I making sense?"

"Yes, I'm with you so far."

"However, with image transmitters the size of golf balls, the effect would be lumpy and unsatisfactory. You need to miniaturise. So now think of small marbles. In addition, for a convincing result, you would want every conceivable cross section of the pillar to be catered for. This requires each marble to have a receptivity area of 180 degrees, and the same on the transmitting side. Still with it?"

This was getting difficult, but Bruce was not going to give up.

"Go on."

"Now imagine holding one of these marbles in your hand. They can be mass-produced. One half of each marble is receiver and one half is transmitter. What you now need to do is to teach these marbles to team up; one marble on one side of the pillar, and the other on the other side. This is where it gets a little complicated. You could hardly connect the two marbles by wires! Especially as you need to cater for every cross section of the pillar, as you pointed out. Think of the cat's cradle of little cables that would produce. So my first problem was to get the marbles able to communicate with each other without being individually connected. And not just in pairs, of course; each marble needs to communicate with every other marble. I won't try to explain how it is done beyond saying that you need a continuous loop of marbles without any breaks. Then secondly, the issue of resolution arises. The smaller you can make your marbles, and the more you have, the better the resolution, that is, the quality of the image. The next problem is to do with the refresh rate. To keep the image up to date, as it were, and fool the human eye into thinking the image is continuous, you need to refresh the image at least twenty-four times a second."

"Don't tell me," said Bruce. "It requires all the computers on earth to run continuously for longer than the age of the universe to work this thing."

"Not quite that bad!" laughed Jim. "But it does require a lot of computing power. Still, I'm very pleased with the result. You did not notice anything when you were watching for the car flying over?"

"Not a thing!" laughed Bruce.

"Well, that's good, because a moving object places even more demands on the system. In fact, the faster something moves, the less invisibility it will tend to have."

"But a lesser refresh rate is needed, I would have thought," observed Bruce.

"Very good. I'll take you on as my apprentice," chuckled Jim. "No, there are other complicating factors I won't bore you with."

"Well, your explanation was good; I was able to follow it."

"The only trouble with it all is that the main use I can think of for an invisible car is for crime. So I don't think I'll market it. Now, are you ready to go back, because I could give you and your boat a lift, if you don't mind me using that word in its literary sense."

"Sounds good to me, although I think you mean literal not literary. It's nice to hear you make a mistake, although I suppose you can't be brilliant at everything! But talking of literary matters, if I am to be your apprentice and you are to be my master, then in future I will expect to summon you as my personal genie, turning up with the flying car-pet and appearing from nowhere, as long as you are happy with the literary call sign - 'On-a-mat-appear!'"

"Oh Bruce, that's dreadful. Come on, let's get some lunch."

58. From: Mission 12
To: Undisclosed recipients
Sent:

I feel I need to apologise to you. I've been re-reading these emails, and I realise that I have told you next to nothing about the planet. All you know is that there are oceans and sand dunes and a small settlement of circular domes. That really does not communicate much at all. Sorry.

It just shows how wound up I have been in my problems.

Anyway, I can tell you about the breeding programme, as it's taken a good deal of my focus. What we decided was that we needed a number of greenhouses in orbit, to propagate lichens and grasses and things of that kind, because really we want these to spread around the planet. So we interrupted the spaceship replication programme when we had sixteen ships, and diverted four of the ships into making huge rotating dustbins, at least that's what I call them. Only twelve spaceships are left duplicating, so soon we will have twenty-four, then forty-eight, then ninety-six.

The dustbins are a mile long by a third of a mile high. Their design was in Big Nimp. They don't take long to make, as their construction is fairly simple; just thirty days. They spin in order to provide gravity for the people who work in them. It also stops the seed beds from floating about!

Margaret is in charge. It is as I thought; the five hundred sleepers are technicians, ready to be woken when they are needed. So when I hinted to Capability Brown (that's how I addressed Big Nimp) that we needed gardeners and horticulturalists, it was no surprise when a number of bleary eyed folk came up from downstairs the following day asking for me. They all wanted breakfast, to my surprise. They seem quite happy at being set to work straight away. Margaret gives them an assignment, and they get on with it. Remarkable really.

The programme is going well. We now have several tons of seedlings ready to go down and be planted out.

Oh dear. I am a bit naughty sometimes. I'm afraid most of what I have just written is simply not true. I have told you what I wanted to happen, but the others all said I was making unnecessary complications; why couldn't the horticultural programme be carried out on the planet's surface? I thought long and hard for a convincing answer as to why it had to happen in orbit, and realised in the end that there wasn't one. So the greenhouses are all on the ground. I feel very disappointed. I was really looking forward to the rotating dustbins, but the fact is that at the time of writing, there isn't a single one, and no prospects of getting one either.

However, we have divided the spaceship self-replication programme, like I said. We have four of them in orbit round Targetto, and the other twelve round the moon. The former are available for making whatever we need, while the latter are set to reduplicate. So that bit was true.

It is also the fact that the new wakees do come up asking for me and muttering about breakfast.

My curiosity was piqued, so I went downstairs to
have a look. Sure enough, on the door leading
upstairs, someone had stuck a notice in a
schoolboy hand, which proclaimed in large letters
                This Way to Breakfast
   And then underneath in smaller letters
                (ask for Bruce).
It took me all of two seconds to work out whose
idea that was! I'm still thinking of what I can
do to even the score with Phil.
   Actually, I left the notice up. I'm rather
pleased about it. It's nice being the first
person that they all want to meet.
   Bruce

"It's a strange thing," said Jim at breakfast on Saturday, "but
having the convenience of the flying cars makes me appreciate the
older forms of transport even more. Take Pikel's yacht, for
example. It gives me great pleasure to skim over the water, knowing
that we are using next to no technology at all - just a piece of canvas
spread out to take advantage of the wind. It's lovely, really."

"Yes," said Bruce, "and riding on the waves is great. You don't
get any sense of being close to the earth if you are a few thousand
feet up. It was the same with aeroplanes; the only really exciting
parts were the take-off and landing, when you could see the
buildings rushing past."

"How about this for a day out," Jim replied. "We'll take the
yacht over to Funchal on the main island. That's the capital. Then
I'd like to drive you along the expressway - I keep a car over there.
It's a fine road they've built, lots of tunnels because of the
mountainous terrain. After that there's a delightful piece of coast I
enjoy, which I would like to show you. How does that appeal?"

"Very much," said Bruce. It would be a relief to get away from
Pikel, although part of him was disappointed that he would not be
seeing her today.

"Excellent. We'll set off after breakfast. I'll meet you in the
atrium."

Bruce was there first. Pikel was busy in her office, holding meetings with staff and dealing with paper, and constantly on the phone. It all looked very impressive. She spotted Bruce through the open door and gave him a warm smile. Bruce smiled back.

Here was Jim. They walked out and across to the marina. Jim was most proficient with the boat, and they were soon skimming across the waves. It was a delightfully sunny day once again, although the wind was a little fresher, and the boat was inclined to bump up and down more. Bruce felt a glow of warmth. It was great to have come on this holiday.

They passed a large passenger ferry on its way to Porto Santo, another island to the North East.

"I wonder how long they will stay in business," Jim observed.

They were soon tying up at a berth in a marina. Funchal seemed very busy to Bruce, in contrast to the island. Jim locked up the boat, and led the way to a garage block. His car was a deep blue colour, and was fitted out with leather furnishings. Bruce settled back in the passenger seat.

"You're welcome to drive," Jim offered, "but you'll see more as a passenger."

Bruce explained that he did not run a car, on ecological grounds, so although he had learned to drive, he was out of practice, and the narrow streets of Funchal did not seem a good place to start, especially with the right hand drive. Jim drove with confidence, and they were soon on the expressway. The road was a fine piece of engineering, with many lengths of tunnel. There were good views down over the city.

"You're keen on the environment, I can tell," Jim said. "I expect it's something to do with your faith in your case."

Oh dear. Another invitation to talk about his beliefs. They were always going on about this at church - 'share your faith, share your faith!' but Bruce did not find it an easy thing to do. Apart from anything else, he did not feel he was much use as a Christian, and the idea that other people were looking to him for an example was no help at all. So all in all he was pretty reluctant.

"It's true, I do believe in God, and I try to let that affect every aspect of my life, but I don't find it easy to talk about it. You're right, that is why I want to preserve the earth. I think it is the most fabulous creation. In fact, I've tried, and I can't imagine how the solar system could have been made better."

"How do you mean?"

"Well, just to give one example, take Jupiter. It is so large that apparently, it mops up pretty much all the asteroids that might hit the earth, and that explains why we don't get bombarded too often. When a large asteroid does get through, the effects are devastating. You know about the one sixty-nine million years ago that wiped out the dinosaurs?"

Jim nodded.

"Well, a few more hits like that and mankind might never have made it as far as we have. As it is, we are now in a position to defend ourselves from such dangers.

"Or take another example. Did you know that water is the only liquid that freezes from the top down? Almost all liquids, as you cool them, freeze from the bottom up. But water does the opposite. What this means is that in a cold winter, the sea freezes on its surface. The ice acts as a blanket, keeping the heat in, so that the rest of it does not freeze. Now, suppose it was the other way round. Then in a cold winter, the oceans would have frozen solid from the bottom up millions of years ago, and might never have thawed, as the ice would reflect the sun's heat away. That would have endangered the survival of life on the planet. I think our world and the solar system are brilliant."

"Very good, Bruce. But what are we going to do about over-population?"

"Well, some science fiction writers enthuse about people living in large revolving dustbins in orbit. Personally, I can't get it. Who would prefer a man-made environment to the wonders of the earth? No, I think we should look for habitable planets in other solar systems, and set up shop there. There have always been people willing to emigrate and make a new start."

"Bruce, it's totally impractical for the foreseeable future."

400

"Yes, I know, in today's situation, it would be. But with all these new discoveries, the barriers dissolve one by one. Space travel just got a whole lot easier with the discovery of infinite energy and anti-gravity, for example."

"Well, I'm still dubious."

"Alright, here's another thing. Manhattan Island was once considered so worthless that it changed hands for less than thirty dollars. Now it's been developed into New York. Think of all the effort that took. I bet there were people around to say it could never be done, but it's only taken two hundred years. I'm also sure it was fun doing it. So who knows what we'll be doing in another few centuries?"

"You're funny Bruce. One minute you're telling me you find it hard to talk about your faith; the next minute you are producing ideas in all seriousness that a lot of people would laugh at, yet you don't seem to mind. What's going on?"

Bruce went silent. Jim had a very good point. Why was he so shy about sharing his faith? It seemed a bit feeble, somehow.

Jim sensed he had touched a sore point, so he changed the subject.

"Look, they had so little flat land on the island that the airport needed to be built on stilts. We are actually driving under the runway at this moment."

It was true. They were just making their way into a forest of huge concrete pillars.

"There. You see what people can do if they have a mind to?" Bruce said. Jim laughed.

After a few more miles, they turned off on a smaller road towards a headland, and parked at the place where it terminated.

"Shanks' pony from here," Jim announced.

They made their way along a steep path which involved occasional scrambles over rocks.

After a few hundred yards, they came to a viewpoint, where they could see down along the shore of the island, stretching away to the North West. There were fine stacks in the sea, and the surging waves threw up spray high into the air. There were gulls wheeling about, giving raucous cries. It was the kind of place Bruce loved. They stayed there for ten minutes, enjoying the scenery, before setting off further along the path. It wound up to the top of the headland, then down the other side. In places it was steep. They were rewarded by more fine views of rocky coves, with the sea heaving at the foot of the cliffs.

"Isn't it great?" said Jim. "Somehow, the fact that it took us two hours to get here makes it seem more special. We could have been here inside ten minutes with the sky-car."

"Yes." Bruce sighed. "I suppose for some people, having a sky-car will simply lengthen their journey. I daresay there are already people who commute daily across the Atlantic to work. I hope they enjoy it. Personally, I don't think anything beats the world's unspoilt places. I hope they are preserved."

There was silence. Then Bruce spoke again.

"Do you know those acronyms that describe people, like Nimby for 'Not in my back yard'?"

"Some of them."

"There are Dinkys, which stands for 'Double income no kids yet', and then someone suggested Doncys, as a name for people who commute from Doncaster to London by train each morning. Well, I've got a new idea for people commuting across the Atlantic. They're Dunkys - 'Don't underestimate New krazy Yorkers'. Do you like it?"

"Very good, Bruce. And whether or not they choose to commute, I have the highest respect for the people that built New York. I never have underestimated them, and I never will. Nor any other nation, come to that. It's amazing what we humans can achieve if we set our minds to it."

59. From: Mission 12
To: Undisclosed recipients
Sent:

The greenhouses stretch for miles now. It's so obvious, when you think about it. Rather than using seed beds at waist height, we create the ideal growing environment for the lichens so that they can germinate in the ground. Really, it's better to think of the greenhouses as being giant cloches. Then, when the lichen is properly established, we simply lift up the greenhouse with a hook from a lander, move along a bit and start again.

I was keen to get the sea going as well. Algae and Plankton, and stuff like that. Seaweed too. All the ingredients for fish higher up the food chain to feed on.

We found some suitable places where the water was sheltered and warm and not buffeted by seas. The little slimy growths were most obliging. They obviously liked the conditions. Then we decided that we could be a bit more ambitious; we went out away from the land and tried an area of open sea. This was also successful.

I reckon the stuff will be running wild soon. Then the challenges really start. What we don't want is for something to multiply out of control, because there is nothing feeding off it. Imagine if the oceans were to fill up with little eels wriggling about, for example! This means that we need to keep introducing the next higher member of the food chain, in the right order, so that everything stays in balance. It's great fun! The process is also far quicker than I ever imagined.

I tend to stay up on the spaceship with Clairie for a good deal of the time. I feel happiest there. Celia comes up to join me regularly. We have decided to take things slowly. It is like courting again. Gently does it. I am getting over my pain, and she is getting over her self-loathing. It's a gradual process. We meet for a few days, then separate for a week or so, and then repeat the pattern. I recommend it for anyone trying to resurrect a relationship. Absence really does make the heart grow fonder!

Her pregnancy seems to be going alright. Big
Nimp takes her readings when she comes up. We
have not managed to joke about her using the
operating chair yet. She and I are progressing,
but not very fast.

I want to tell you about one of the wakees.
Well, what would you have me call them? He came
up one morning, wearing a tweed jacket and bow-
tie of all things, and as soon as he saw me, he
said, "Brek-ek-ek-ex, co-ax, co-ax." I looked at
him, quizzically. I wondered whether hibernation
had unhinged him, and this was the best he could
do to ask for breakfast. His next statement was
reassuring.

"Frogs," he declared. "It's the Chorus from
Aristophanes' play. Greek, you know," in case I
had not heard of Aristophanes' Frogs. Thankfully,
I had.

"Excellent," I said. "Although I'm not sure
that we are ready for frogs yet; we've only just
got water weed going."

"Don't worry," he assured me. "It will be fine.
The tadpoles take months to grow to maturity. I'm
looking forward to it. Aristophanes would have
been thrilled."

So the ancient Greeks, in addition to all their
other many achievements, now have a champion on
Targetto as well. Ah well. It takes all types to
make a world.

Bruce

Sunday had arrived at last. It was their final morning. Bruce had
packed his bag and cleared his room ready for the cleaners. He was
sad to be leaving.

"Now, there are some things I've been wanting to say to you,"
Jim said, as they rose from breakfast. "First we'll go up." They
entered the lift. They were soon stepping out onto a balcony in the
fresh air.

"Just look out at what's around us, Bruce. These three little islands are called the Desertas, as you know. The skies are so wonderful here, don't you think?"

Bruce had noticed that the combination of clouds with the sun glancing through was particularly striking.

"Every morning is beautiful here. Do you know that poem about rosy-fingered dawn?"

Bruce did not.

"Well, it's my pet name for Pikel. When I meet her in the morning, I say to her, 'Dawn, your rosy fingers have been at it again.' It makes her laugh. Now, do you get it?"

Bruce had no idea what he was driving at. The puzzlement showed on his face.

"Never mind. Come with me."

They entered a different lift. The lift sank down in response to Jim's key press, lower than before.

"You're going to love this," Jim said.

The lift seemed to be going down a long way to Bruce. "However far are we going?" He asked.

"Not far now."

After another minute or so, the lift came to a standstill. The door opened into a large lounge, which was dimly lit. It was dominated by a huge wall of glass facing them, which was evidently a large fish tank, as there were brightly coloured fish swimming about.

"An aquarium!" said Bruce. He had never seen such a large expanse of glass. The viewing conditions were excellent.

"Nobody knows about this facility, not even Pikel. I wanted you to be the first person to see it. Now, are you any clearer about why I have brought you here?"

Bruce was still mystified. However, the fish were most fascinating to watch. There appeared to be no back to the tank. It must be simply colossal. Bruce wondered how the glass could support all the weight of water without breaking. It must be immensely strong.

Jim was chuckling. "Impressed with the wall of glass?"

"Yes. The pressure of the water must be enormous. How does the glass support the weight?"

Jim laughed. Bruce could tell he was very happy.

"Aren't those tropical fish lovely?"

The brightly coloured creatures had always fascinated Bruce. This was the most marvellous display he had seen. He could spend hours down here.

Jim went across to a side wall and punched an instruction into a keypad.

"Now you watch."

Gradually, over the course of a few minutes, the brightly coloured fish made their way upwards until they passed out of sight. As they did so, other fish rose up from below to take their place. After a few moments, Jim spoke again.

"Do you remember quoting Jacques Cousteau in my flat, that time when you spoke to the working party?"

Bruce remembered well. He nodded. The fish that were coming in at the bottom of the tank were darker and larger. This was an incredible display. But before many minutes had passed, Bruce was astonished to see even larger fish appearing.

"These strike me as being deep water creatures," he said.

Jim laughed again. He was enjoying this.

"Are you any the wiser yet?" he asked.

"I have to say, I don't know what you're talking about. But this display is quite something. It is the most astonishing thing I have ever seen."

"Bruce, let me explain what you are seeing. This is not a tank. It's the ocean you are looking at."

"But the pressure must be enormous. Surely, no glass of this area could support all that water. The idea's absurd."

"Bruce, what you're looking at is the world's most advanced gravity control. Come and feel the glass. It's not metres thick, as you might imagine."

On close inspection, Bruce could see it was hardly thicker than the window panes in his home.

"This is extraordinary," he said, as they returned to their chairs.

"But that's not all," Jim added. "In addition, the water pressure itself is variable. At the moment, I have got it gradually increasing. That is why the shallow water fish that you saw at first have moved higher, and the deep water fish have moved up into the picture. It's no good making a quick change, because it would frighten the fish, and perhaps harm them, but they can cope with a slow change. I have found ways of attracting them so that they swim close to the glass. Hence the display. Cousteau would have loved it, don't you think? You remember he lived below the sea for a while."

Bruce had become aware that Jim was looking at him very oddly.

"Jim, what are you trying to tell me?"

"The verse you quoted at my flat, Bruce. 'Then shall the desert bloom like the rose.' And all your talk about water. And quoting Jacques Cousteau. You may not be able to see it, but I can. Bruce, you talk about things before you know about them. There I am day-dreaming about my pet project here, which nobody else knows about, and you start using all the words in my mind. Desert - here we are on one of the Desertas. Rose - one of my favourite expressions, Rosy fingered dawn. I think of it just about daily here. And you talked about a new dawn for mankind. Water - well, you can see it all around us. There was I working on gravity control under water. And then you mentioned Jacques Cousteau. I couldn't believe it. There's only one explanation Bruce. I know you believe in God, because you told me. Well Bruce, allow me to inform you; you're a prophet. You announce things before you know about them."

This was ridiculous.

"Come now, Jim, surely it's just a series of coincidences. You're making too much out of it."

"No I'm not, because there's one more to come. Then you'll be convinced."

"Well, I have to say, it does not ring any bells with me."

"Just wait and see, Bruce. Now, I want to show you something else, but before I do, I have two things to say. The first is that when you find out what I've done, you may feel I have done you an

407

injury. I haven't really, but your first reaction may be one of anger. So I want you to have this."

Jim passed Bruce a plastic card. It was a bank account in Bruce's name.

"This card is ready to use. You may have a few expenses. This should cover them, and I hope it will make you feel less upset with me. Think of it as compensation if you like."

Bruce was very mystified. Jim was talking in riddles. None of it seemed to make any sense.

"Well, it's very kind of you, I'm sure. I hope I'll be able to repay you in due course."

"No, Bruce, certainly not. It is a gift with no strings attached. I would be most upset if you tried to repay. Accept it as a present from me?"

"Alright," said Bruce. A little extra cash might be helpful. "I'm very touched." He put the card in his pocket.

"The next thing is that I have invented a cordial which restores youth. I've taken it myself, so you can judge the results for yourself. I thought you might appreciate a bottle."

Jim passed over a brown medicine bottle, of the 250 millilitre size, filled with liquid.

Once again, Bruce was very touched. "Many thanks." Jim did look youthful, come to think of it. There was a kind of boyishness about him.

"Finally, I want you to watch the screen. Please don't judge me too hastily. There is a purpose in all this. Trust me."

There was that same phrase that Celia had used. Bruce was out of his depth, and he knew it. He said nothing.

Jim picked up a remote control from the table between them. The room darkened gradually, and a large screen appeared. The fish were not disturbed by the changes in the light, Bruce noticed. His attention was soon taken by what was on the screen. It was the inside of Wayford Crematorium. How strange. Did Jim want him to play a recording of the funeral, he wondered?

But what was this? It was not Jim's funeral he was watching. He recognised everybody. There were all his piano pupils. They looked frightfully upset. Why, there was Banjo looking as if she had seen a ghost. Oh gracious, look at Gnilla. Bruce had never seen her so upset before.

Jim was saying something. "I forgot to mention about the cordial. It's very important. You must take it..." but Bruce was not listening. He was gripped by what he saw. There were Beccy and Simna, side by side, dressed in black. It really did not suit them, despite Beccy's dark but lovely hue. Why, look at Sarah, so white in the face. And Araminta! She was weeping uncontrollably.

Suddenly the truth dawned on Bruce.

"I can't bear this. Jim! You've faked my funeral. I don't believe it. What do you think you're playing at?"

Suddenly while he was still speaking, all hell broke loose. Doors opened in a rush. A loud voice shouted 'Stay where you are. Don't move.' There was a bright searchlight waving about and a lot of people running and shouting. Something whizzed through the air, and he heard a soft thud beside him. Whatever was going on? Then there were arms around him and a familiar voice.

"Bruce, Bruce, are you alright? Thank God you're safe."

But Bruce was standing up. He had had enough. It was a nightmare. His own funeral, and in his absence! All his friends thinking him dead.

"Take me back," he ordered, not knowing whom he was addressing. "This minute."

However, he had stood up too quickly. He came over faint, and before he knew it, he blacked out and slumped to the floor.

```
60. From: Mission 12
To: Undisclosed recipients
Sent:

I don't think Aristophanes got the noise of the
Frogs right, personally. But never mind that. At
least the little fellows are happy, croaking
away. There are only a handful of them so far. I
only hope they don't swarm and become like a
biblical plague.
```

Birds seem to be last on the agenda. I suppose they have considerable requirements, food-wise. I am looking forward to the day when we can have seagulls wheeling about. I think they would love it here.

The lichens are spreading on their own now. No doubt about it. I had no idea it would be so easy getting life to take hold. We even have some small trees planted. It's wonderful.

We made a fascinating discovery last week. We found a patch of lichen a mile or two further inland from where we had started. I reckon seed has been blown by the wind. Isn't that exciting?

Celia and I are back together full time now. It's encouraging. All the pain of the last months is slowly beginning to fade like a bad dream.

Max is thrilled. You can see it in his face. Our separation was a large part of the reason why his leadership was such a failure. Now things are going well between his parents, I can see that he is going to flourish. It's so exciting!

I've had an idea. I'm wondering whether the others would consider Celia and me having Clairie down here with us, on probation. It's rather hard to explain, but because we are so few in number, and everybody knows everybody else, there is less scope for Clairie to go wrong. You can't really be a law-breaker in a small community where everybody is known. Wickedness flourishes in large communities where there is anonymity. At least, that's what I think.

Anyway, she is really sorry for what she did. I have no doubt that she will never do anything like it again. I would hope that she could turn out to be a fine young lady. Perhaps I'm biased, being her dad. I'm wondering how I can best put it to the others.

Bruce

When Bruce came to, he found he was speeding along in a sky-car. It was fitted out with a lot of medical equipment. It must be an air ambulance, he thought.

"Where am I?" he asked. "Where's Jim?"

"Air, sea and land rescue at your service." It was Celia, sitting beside him. They were in the back seat. There was a driver, separated from them by glass. There was a strange look on Celia's face.

"Bruce, are you feeling up to talking?"

"Yes. Are we on the way home?"

"Indeed."

"Is Jim here? What happened?"

"We rescued you. You've been kidnapped, but we found you, and the whole ordeal is over. You can relax now."

"But it wasn't an ordeal. I've been on holiday with Jim. I've had a great week."

Celia was silent. She was clearly very puzzled.

"Bruce, I think you had better give me your version of events. Go slowly, and tell me everything. The last thing we know about you is your visit to the hospital nine days ago."

"What hospital? I haven't been near a hospital."

Celia paused again. "Never mind about the hospital. Just give me your account."

Bruce told her about the flight in the sky-car, then the hotel and the Desertas, the day out in Pikel's yacht leaving out the details, the boat trip to the island, and finally the trip over to Funchal and along the expressway.

At this point, Celia began to get excited.

"Which way did you go out of Funchal?"

"East, I suppose."

"That explains it. You must have driven under the runway at Funchal airport."

"Well yes we did. What of it? Anyway, today was the last day. We were going home this afternoon. Jim took me down to see the fish, and then started talking rather strangely. He said he had done something to me which I might consider was an injury, but he had

411

not wanted to hurt me, and it was in a good cause. Then he started playing me this weird video recording, which seemed to be my own funeral. I was just starting to get angry with him for faking my death when you lot burst in."

"Right," said Celia. "There are still one or two things puzzling me, but I think I'm beginning to see the light. I'll pick up the story from when you arrived at the Motor Lodge. Presumably, that was to meet Jim. He had died a few weeks before, and you played at his cremation, but I presume that was faked in some way. I can't think how; the authorities are extremely careful over the identification of bodies. I can't begin to imagine how it was done.

"Then you left the Motor Lodge after an hour or so and went to Wayford Hospital."

"No I didn't," Bruce objected, "or rather, if I did, it's news to me. Mind you," he added, "I do remember the coffee had a funny taste, and I fell asleep soon after drinking it and I was very groggy all next day. Do you think I could have been drugged?"

"Let's assume so for the present. Anyway, you turned up at Wayford Hospital, and then we lost touch with you. Next morning, you were discovered dead at the foot of a cliff in the country by a lady walking her dog. There were no signs of a struggle, and as you had been under a lot of strain recently, everyone assumed it was suicide. The official verdict was death in unknown circumstances. You lay in the chapel at the undertakers. You were positively identified by Marjorie your landlady, by Bill and Gnilla, and also by me. I was convinced it was you, as the DNA match was perfect."

"I won't ask how you came by a sample of my DNA. Is nothing sacred these days?"

"Well, let me finish my story. Your will was acted upon. The funeral took place on Friday at Wayford Crematorium. The recording you were watching when we arrived was of the service. Then you were cremated. I thought that was the end. However, nobody had got round to removing you from the computer, and to my astonishment, your signal was picked up at Funchal airport at Saturday lunchtime."

"When we drove under the runway. Great. I'm not very pleased to discover that you had put a transmitter on me. I never asked to be continually monitored."

"No. It was done for your own protection, Bruce. We wanted to take care of you."

"Thanks a million. Well, I would not have agreed if you had asked me, but you didn't ask. May I enquire how it was done?"

"There's a small homing device in the crown you had fitted to your tooth a month or two back."

Bruce laughed. "You people are beyond belief. But I don't get it. I can't have been in two places at once all last week."

"No," Celia agreed, "and I can't understand why the transmitter stopped working from the Friday night at around midnight, and then started up again a week later. Actually, to be specific, the computer returned an error message during that period. It might not have been a fault in the transmitter at all."

"So the system rebooted after I was cremated," Bruce observed.

Suddenly, it all finally made sense. Why Jim had been calling him a prophet. Why Jim had been so keen to take him on holiday. How Jim had fooled the authorities into thinking he had died a month back and how it was Bruce himself at the foot of the cliff.

At the meeting in Jim's flat, Bruce had foretold the emergence of the replicator assuming it was decades if not centuries off. But it wasn't. Jim must have already built one. He had put himself through it to test it, and then used the copy of himself to escape from the world. Now he had put Bruce through it as well, after knocking him out with a drug in his coffee. The results had been just as impressive, and had fooled everyone. But this time, everything was different, because Bruce was not disappearing; he was on his way home.

This was scary. Bruce had died, been cremated, and was now rising from the dead.

"Oh my land!" he said.

"Tell me," Celia said.

"The reason your computer went funny was that there were two of me, even down to the transmitter in my tooth. What was found at the foot of the cliff was a copy of me. The computer could not cope with getting two signals of my presence in different places. Hence the error messages. Then once the other me had been cremated, there was only one transmitter again, which is why I came back on stream at Funchal airport."

"Well, all I can say is it's a most impressive fake."

"What have you done with Jim?" Bruce asked. "I imagine you've arrested him."

"I'm sorry, Bruce, but I'm afraid he didn't make it."

"What?" Bruce was horrified.

"We fired a dart; the kind of thing you use to put animals to sleep. The dose proved too strong for him. I'm really sad, Bruce. You were very fond of him, weren't you?"

"But he was the most gifted inventor the world has ever seen," Bruce objected. "And you've killed him. He may have done some strange things, but I doubt that any of them were arrestable offences. He was absolutely brilliant, Celia. I don't suppose you have the slightest idea of what you have done. Yes, I was fond of him too. He was a good friend to me. I never felt the slightest threat from him. Oh dear, this is dreadful news."

Bruce put his head in his hands. This was terrible.

Suddenly he looked up and blurted out "Sweet and Sour!"

Celia looked at him in confusion.

"Pikel. I never said goodbye." Bruce noted the incomprehension on Celia's face. "Pikel Vanderpokel. The P.A. of the Hotel Manager. She's of Dutch extraction. You remember; I told you. She was kind to me. I wanted to say goodbye."

"You will have to write, Bruce, I'm afraid. There are more important things to think about, like how you are going to break it to your friends that you are alive."

This was true. It had been a lovely week. But now Jim was dead, and he was facing a mountain of trouble. Just for a moment, he wished he was back on Pikel's yacht, and that he was Adam and she was Eve. Life would have been so much simpler!

"I think the first step is to ring Bill," he said. "Have you got a phone?"

In the end, Celia put through the call. She told Bill to sit down and prepare himself for a shock. Then she handed the phone to Bruce.

"Bill, it's Bruce here; I'm not dead after all. It's been a mistake."

There was silence from the far end of the phone followed by a thud and a loud clattering sound.

"Oh dear; I think he's fainted and dropped the phone."

"Hello, hello, who's there?" said Gnilla, in obvious distress.

"Now Gnilla, take a grip and don't faint. It's Bruce. I'm alive and well and coming home soon."

"Bruce! I don't believe it."

"Well, you'd better. Is Bill Okay? It sounded as if he fainted."

There was a groaning sound at the far end.

"He'll be fine," said Gnilla. "Bruce, it is fabulous to hear your voice. We were all so upset."

"Look. I'll explain everything later, but for now I want you to do something. I'll be landing on my lawn by sky-car in thirty minutes or so. Could you warn Marjorie so that she doesn't have a severe shock?"

"Of course. We'll be there to meet you. I'll put the heating on in the bungalow."

"Thanks. See you soon. Bye."

Bruce was feeling much more cheerful when he handed the phone back to Celia. This was going to be rather fun.

```
61. From: Mission 12
To: Undisclosed recipients
Sent:
```

```
They said yes! I've got my daughter back, and
so we are a family again. We all live on the
surface now. Margaret came down a while back, and
we have been taking it in turns to man the
spaceship. Although we could leave it unmanned,
none of us likes the idea of that. I'm sure Big
Nimp does not feel the need of us being there,
```

415

but we want to keep somebody on board for the
foreseeable future. I think we are all too aware
of the misbehaviour of Hal the computer in the
film 2001, although nobody ever mentions it.

The ninety-six spaceships round the moon will
become one hundred and ninety-two in another ten
days. I reckon that in another eighteen months,
we should have enough to start deploying them
round the globe for the big push. What a thought.
Speeding up the rotation of the planet and
tilting it over. We have decided to do both
operations at the same time. I feel really
excited about it.

The baby came this week. His name is Sean. It
is not a name I would have chosen, but apparently
Mark was once heard to say that if ever he had a
child, he would name him Sean. So Sean it is.

He is a strapping lad with a pair of quality
lungs. I reckon he might be a good singer in
time. Celia is happy to have him. I am not
thrilled; it's no good pretending I am, but he is
so unlike Mark in the sense of being manipulative
and dominating that I don't feel threatened by
him at all. If you think my attitude is poor, I
agree with you, but I would say, just you try
watching your wife give birth to another man's
child. I wonder how you would fare.

I have been going out of my way to show Sean
love and respect. I change his nappy quite often,
and I dandle him on my knees, like one does. I
sing him nursery rhymes. Celia appreciates it. It
is helping to bring us together.

Clairie is delighted with her baby brother. Max
is not so sure. He has grasped something of how
difficult things have been for me. In some ways,
he is finding it harder to get over the pain of
it all than I am.

I believe it will come right if we are patient.
Time is a great healer.

Bruce

It was extraordinary how quickly word got about. Bruce was trying to tell Bill and Gnilla about his holiday, but the phone would keep ringing. The first call had been Sarah - she was thrilled he was Okay. Araminta would be over the moon. She had been so upset that she had run off to join Karl in New Zealand without telling anybody, to the consternation of everyone. Sarah had not realised how serious things were between them.

Next it was Banjo.

"Bruce, you confounded numbskull. What do you think you're playing at?"

"Sorry, Bancesca. I'm not always as efficient and precise as I might be. I'm afraid I didn't make it to my own funeral."

"Well, keep up the good work. Saves me a lot of trouble anyway! Ooh you are daft, but I do love you. Catch up with you later. Bye."

Banjo always rang off as if the phone she was holding was red hot. However, she had never expressed affection for Bruce before. It was a moment to treasure.

"Put the answerphone on," said Bill. It seemed a good idea. "And turn off the ringer so we can hear ourselves think. Now, you were telling us about the invisible car."

Bruce went on with his story about the visit to the other Deserta.

"Well, I suppose a man who can do all that can whistle up a dead body with no trouble," said Gnilla. "But what I can't understand is why."

"No, that's puzzling me too," said Bruce, who had decided that the secret of the replicator must be preserved at all costs, even from Celia. Especially from Celia, the tooth goblin.

"Anyway, we'll never know now," Bruce continued. "Jim was shot by an elephant dart, and it was too much for him. I shall miss him dreadfully. He was a great inventor, and very modest with it, and such a likeable person. It's a terrible loss."

"I suppose you are simply going to return to work as if nothing has happened," said Bill.

"Well, what else do you suggest?"

"Dunno, really. We shared round all your piano music after the service. I expect it will all make its way back."

"Would you like me to ring your pupils, to let them know of resumption of service?" Gnilla offered.

Bruce was most grateful. It was better than people fainting on hearing his voice. They started with Monday's pupils. Bruce found he had to speak to them all in person, when it came to it. He apologised for any inconvenience caused. It sounded a bit stiff and formal, but he did not want to be quizzed too closely.

Monday was quite an endurance test. When he went over to the staffroom for a coffee at the school, he was aware of eyes looking at him and people talking about him when they thought he was out of earshot. Once or twice during the morning, the door opened during a lesson, and some young person would apologise for the interruption; they had made a mistake. When it happened the third time, Bruce asked the boy whether he would like his autograph. This was speedily accepted, to Bruce's surprise. Further teaching soon became impossible, owing to the steady stream of young people presenting their record books for a signature. Bruce insisted on signing on the page marked 'Communications between Home and School,' and adding under his scrawl the words, 'Aiming at harmony as usual.' He hoped it lent a light touch.

By nine p.m. he was exhausted. It had been a long day. He hoped the fuss would die down in a day or two.

He was just boiling the kettle for an evening drink when the doorbell rang. Who could that be at this time of night? He went to open it and a beautiful girl in a black winter coat with tassels and bobbles on it flew in, hugged him and kissed him passionately. Bruce was completely taken aback.

"Araminta!" he gasped, when he could extricate himself sufficiently. "I thought you'd gone to New Zealand!"

She was clinging to him as if she would never let him go. The door was wide open, and the light was streaming out into the road. People might see.

"Just let me close the door," he said. She clung to him like a limpet, but she let him move to the door and close it.

"So it is true," she murmured. Then she looked him full in the face. "I'm never going to let you go again," she declared, with resolution written on every feature. Her high cheek bones were flushed red. Bruce had never noticed how lovely her eyelashes were. He wondered if she had treated them in some way. The intensity of her blue eyes was overwhelming. He hugged her tightly, but resisted the impulse to kiss her on the mouth. It required a great effort.

After a bit, he made to release her, but she hugged him all the tighter. She was not ready to stop. He returned the hug. It was a very emotional moment. Bruce hoped it would last for ever.

After a while, the hug ended.

"I've just boiled the kettle," Bruce said. "Would you care for a hot drink?"

"What happened, Bruce?" Araminta ignored his question. He made her a hot chocolate all the same, and motioned her to a chair.

"Do you remember Jim Pond, the man behind Skywear and sky-cars?"

Araminta nodded.

"Well, I played at his funeral a month ago. Only I discovered that he was not dead after all. It was his way of disappearing for a while. He invited me to go on holiday with him over half term, which I did. We had a good week. What I did not know was that he faked my death just before we went; hence the funeral. On my way back, I found out the error. So here I am, and it's back to normal."

Araminta's lips were pursed tightly together. "I don't believe a word of it. Or rather, I accept that what you've said contains some of the truth, but you haven't told me a fraction of what's really going on. You'll have to do better than that."

This was tricky.

"Well, Jim is a little eccentric, perhaps..."

"Jim's eccentric? Hark who's talking!"

"...but he did say something which may be a clue. He's been killed by an elephant dart, by the way, so we can't ask him. He said to me that he thought I was a prophet. Perhaps he reckoned a prophet should rise from the dead. I don't think his theology is all

419

that sound. I think he wanted people to take notice of what I said. I don't know. But look, what about you. Sarah said you had run off with Karl."

"I did, but the moment I heard, I jumped on a plane. I had to come. Goodness knows how I'm going to pay off my credit card."

"Gracious. Well, I'm surprised your parents let you come over here at this late hour."

"They still think I'm in New Zealand. And you're NOT going to tell them."

This was serious.

"I was so upset when you died. I couldn't handle it. I managed the funeral somehow, but I already knew what I was going to do. Karl was not very happy, but I made him say yes. I needed someone to comfort me! I only took an overnight bag, and sent a message when I was nearly there, so that Mum and Dad would not be too worried. Then when Sarah rang me, I upped and off without delay, and here I am. You'll have to put me up for the night."

Bruce was deeply thrilled. It was the most powerful declaration of love. She really cared for him!

"The spare room is just about habitable, despite all Marjorie's books and boxes. She's very committed to literature; there are thousands of cuttings from the Look-Book in there. Some good reading to sober you up a bit."

Bruce was smiling. This was it. He knew what he wanted. Pikel had helped him decide.

Araminta was looking at him oddly.

"What is it, Bruce?"

"I'll tell you tomorrow. Oh it's so good to see you. I'm so glad you came. Now, you get settled in there. Breakfast at 0700 sharp. There's an alarm clock by your bed. Here's a towel, and there's the bathroom and loo. You must have terrible jet lag after all that flying."

Araminta was worn out. She went to bed without a protest. Bruce tried to watch the news. There was a story about how they had lost track of Pluto, which would have interested him normally, but he could not concentrate; he was too excited. He made himself

420

go to bed. He lay there awake for a long time, but after doing his relaxation exercises, eventually he managed to fall asleep. Tomorrow was going to be a big day.

62. From: Mission 12
To: Undisclosed recipients
Sent:

Well, here we are, on the verge of turning on the power. There are fourteen hundred spaceships half buried in the ground all round the equator, and another twelve hundred running up and down the Marxon meridian, and on the opposite meridian. I was right about the name for the settlement, you notice! Everybody feels excited, not just me.

But I don't want to overlook the achievements of the three years since we landed here. Life has really taken a grip. It is such a pleasure to see one or two birds flying about. Bushes, shrubs, fruit trees, they are all coming on nicely, even if they are small and few in number. Plant pears for your heirs, as the saying goes. There are some low trees. The little animals run away into the grass as you approach. Funny how they should have the instinct to be afraid of humans. Then the sea. The fish may only be small ones, but it's wonderful that we have any at all. Also, I never thought I would be grateful for seaweed on the beach!

Back to the speed-up programme. Of course, it is vital that we measure any changes to the rate of rotation accurately, so what we have done is to rig up a fixed telescope, pointing straight upwards. It is inside a protective dome, of course. We have arranged it so that it points at a particular distant star at the same time each night, as a result of the rotation of Targetto. It is connected to a highly accurate clock. We have already taken careful measurements. The length of the day is consistent to within a second. So what we hope is that after we have switched on the motors, the rotation will speed up, and the day will shorten very gradually.

Naturally, the momentum of the globe is enormous. It will take a lot of pushing to get anywhere. We have been placing small bets on how much we will achieve. I know we should discourage betting, but we are all so excited about it, so we thought we would allow it. I have entered for the day being four seconds shorter by the end of the first month. I wonder what will actually happen?

My hunch is that the initial increase in rotation speed will be the hardest, but that once we get on a roll, as it were, the process will accelerate. We will carefully monitor what happens, of course. I have a feeling that we may even need to turn the motors down after a bit.

Some of the others were worried about the planet's crust. We don't want to strain the tectonic plates and provoke volcanic eruptions or earthquakes. To guard against any possibility of problems, not only will the four spacecraft in orbit be watching carefully; some of our number will fly round the globe in landers for the first week or two, watching for any visible signs of trouble. I think it's unnecessary myself, but they want to do it. Mind you, I don't know what we would do if we did cause a problem, apart from throwing the motors into reverse. A bit like the Titanic, I suppose. But personally, I really don't anticipate any trouble.

The atmosphere is electric, I can tell you. No-one is more excited than Max and Clairie. Sean is too busy running about to be aware of what is going on. He is quite a little character in his way. He is thrilled with all the adults here. He runs up to them and clasps their knees, looking

upwards for a hug. Everybody has taken to him.
It's nice having a toddler in our midst.

It's so good being a family again. I even
caught myself thinking that all the pain had been
worth it just for the joy of coming back together
again. How daft can you get? But it least it
shows how much things are improving.

Be in touch again soon.

Bruce

Araminta came through on the nail of seven. Bruce gave her a
hug.

"Come and have breakfast. Cereal and toast. Okay?" he asked.

"Fine."

"I'm afraid it's sliced bread out of the freezer. There was no
time to buy real. Tea, Coffee, Hot Chocolate, Herbal Teabag?"

"Peppermint tea, please." Bruce kept this kind of thing for
guests.

They settled down to eat, but Bruce had barely raised the spoon
to his mouth before there was a loud knock on the door. More of a
hammering in fact. He went to answer it. There was a man in a
raincoat with a clipboard.

"I'm from The Lookout. I understand you have recently risen
from the dead. Would you mind answering some questions for us?"

Bruce had been anticipating this.

"Yes, when I've finished my breakfast. Give me fifteen minutes,
and I'll come out."

It was good to be firm and masterful. Try and take control of the
situation. Bruce closed the door.

He motioned Araminta to silence.

"It's the press," he whispered. "I'd stay out of sight if I was
you."

They gobbled up their food, and then Araminta tiptoed through
to the spare room. Bruce checked himself in the mirror. He knew
what he was going to say. Be on top of the business.

He went to the front door, and stepped boldly outside. There was a crowd of about thirty journalists, some of them with cameras. There was no TV in evidence.

Bruce seized the initiative.

"Yes, as a matter of fact I am," he announced confidently.

He took the first question. It was the Lookout man.

"Mr. Winter, you have reputedly risen from the dead. Are you a prophet then?"

"Without any trouble at all, thank you."

He took the second question from a neatly turned out girl.

"Can you foretell the future?"

"Well yes, I do have something to say, actually. It's to do with 'black hole farming'. Sooner or later some bright spark is going to make a small black hole by forcing a lot of matter into a tiny space. That's great, if they can control it, but suppose they drop it. Some people are so careless. Then it will sink to the centre of the earth, and suck us all into it, so the whole shebang will disappear - kaput. I therefore feel very strongly that laws should be passed banning black hole farming within the solar system. In fact, I think that making black holes should be banned altogether. Why can't people travel to existing black holes and use those instead? Anyway, with all this cheap energy flooding the market, there's really no need to farm them at all.

"Thank you, that's all."

Bruce paused briefly to acknowledge a third question, which was 'Do you have anything else to say to us?' before turning briskly on his heels, and striding into the house.

That was the way to treat the press. Firm and decisive.

Araminta came out when they had gone.

"What was all that about?"

"They think I'm a prophet because I have risen from the dead. Never mind. I answered their questions before they put them - those people are so predictable - and added a serious point for them to think about. It'll give them a story with a new angle."

Oh dear, now it had come to the point, he was feeling distinctly nervous. It was time to pluck up courage.

"Araminta, do you remember me saying that a relationship between us was out of the question because of the age gap?"

"Yes, Bruce."

She had always called him Mr. Winter before When had that changed? He could not recall. Anyway, he liked Bruce much better.

"Well, there might be a way."

Bruce drew the little bottle out of his pocket.

"The thing is, that one of the last things Jim said to me before Celia's army of Orcs burst in upon us was that he had invented this cordial. It's a youth restorer. He had taken it himself, and the effect seemed to be wholesome. The only difficulty is that he said it was important how you took it, but I did not take in what he said. It might have been just a spoonful a day until it was all gone. But then it might also have been to take it all at once, otherwise it would be too weak to work. I just don't know."

Araminta was looking very dubious.

"Bruce, forget about the potion. The age gap really does not bother me."

"Well, it bothers me. So…"

Before she realised what he was doing, Bruce put the bottle to his lips and swallowed the entire contents in a few gulps.

"Here goes!" he said.

Araminta was utterly horrified.

"Bruce, you maniac!"

"Well, I thought if I took it quickly, it would save a lot of argument. It may not do anything."

Araminta was speechless. The colour was rising in her face. Bruce realised that she felt very strongly. Perhaps he had been a bit rash. Anyway, nothing seemed to be happening. They could afford to relax. Unless…

Oh dear, what was this?

Bruce's stomach gave a loud rumble, and then went still again. A moment later he let out an enormous belch. He put his hands to the sides of his head. The bottle fell on the little coffee table with a clatter, and rolled unchecked onto the floor.

On Araminta's face there was a mixture of fear, horror and anger.

"Oh my!" he said, feeling most peculiar, and slumped backwards into his chair.

Part the Third

The Mystery of the Soft Pedal

Synopsis

In Part the First, we discovered Bruce Winter to be a man of resource, integrity and sensitive musicianship. An unlikely recruit to the secret service, he obeyed his instructions to the letter, which were that he was to do nothing. As a result, he soon found himself on first name terms with Jim Pond, the man behind anti-gravity, whose sky-suits and sky-cars were revolutionising society. However, despite a life full of incident, not all of it pleasant, our hero is still no nearer his goal of making it to the altar with the girl of his choice. Life is rather more successful in his daydreams, where he is the caretaker of Mission 12, a spaceship on its way to another star. However, here too he is beset with problems, some of which are of his own making. Never mind.

In Part the Second, Jim has been impressed with Bruce's ability to foretell the future. He has given him the honour of being the second person to go through his newly-invented replicator, Jim himself having been the first. The trauma of Bruce's supposed funeral, coupled with his close encounter with Pikel Vanderpokel, a stunning beauty, has revealed to both Bruce and his piano pupil Araminta Foster that they really want each other. However, Bruce is so troubled by the large age gap between them that he has just swallowed a whole bottle of youth restorer, another of Jim's inventions. Meanwhile, Bruce's reflections on the progress of Mission 12 in establishing a settlement on the planet Targetto have contained the usual mix of triumph and disaster. Things have reached a critical moment, as the pioneers prepare to speed up the rotation of the planet...

-o0o-

The youth restoring potion was certainly having an effect. Bruce's body was gyrating and shaking, and his eyes were rolling horribly. Araminta was most alarmed. She was also very angry. How could he have been so foolish?

Here I am at the entrance to the cave. In I stride. No need for caution! I can deal with anything. A long, long tunnel, strangely lit, walls of stone, sand on the floor. March along, flexing every muscle. Conquering and to conquer! Nothing frightens me. On, on, on. Twist to the left, up a bit, down a longish slope, up a bit more, never slacken the pace. Here's a cliff, barring my way, but never mind; out with the grappling hook, up she sails, haul on the rope to make it bar taut, and up I run. Over the lip, and off comes the grappling hook with a deft flick of the rope. Aha, sound of running water. Never mind, I'm amphibious. Onwards and upwards.

What's this? Soft and furry. Huge. Ah, it's moving. The monster!

Seize him by the tail. Hold on with one hand, and raise the other in a victory salute. Round and round we go. He's not happy about it; well, who would be. Snapping and snarling. Huge red mouth, Slobbering fangs. Surely he can't reach his own tail…

A quick bullfighter's swerve. That was close. Another swerve. That was closer. Time to get off. Byeeeeee!

Fly through the air, land in the torrent. Swept backwards. He's coming after me. Huge glaring eyes. Snapping teeth.

Down the waterfall, plunging deep below the surface, a few quick backstrokes, break the surface. He's still after me. Hot smelly breath. Furious backstroke. He's coming. His jaws are very close. Crocodile snaps. Ooh, there goes one of my arms. Better off without it.

Down another waterfall, not so high this time.
He's still coming. The current is strong, but I
can master it. A huge bite. Ooh, there goes the
other arm. Now I can really swim like a fish.
Arch the body back and fore, back and fore, cut
through the water.

Ah, he's bitten off my head. Never mind. I can
still see, somehow, and jump and gyrate and
swerve away from him by instinct.

This is wonderful, using the current, flying
through the water. He can't catch me for all his
big teeth!

Rushing torrent, along, down, along, up, plunge
down, glide along. Always the savage teeth
opening and shutting.

Ah, out through a large grill into the full
sun. He's trapped inside. Serve him right. I hope
he hurt his head on the bars. I'm freeeeeee!

Somebody was shouting something.

"Whoever said I wanted you young? Maybe I wanted to marry
someone on a Zimmer frame but I couldn't find anybody so I had to
put up with you…"

Okay, I'll show you what a gladiator can do…
Pam!

Just… Pow! Pam!

Think you can run me down, do you… Zap!

I'll show you… Krup! the meaning of a
gladiator's fist… Kerpow! Wham!

Wonderful armour. Biff! Baff! Boff!

You can keep running at me all day… Chonk! if
you want. I can take it. Pow! Take that, and that
and that…

Pam! Kerpow!

All this violent movement couldn't be right. Araminta knew she
was out of her depth. It was hopeless trying to restrain him. She was

better simply watching from a safe distance. What did he think he was playing at swallowing the whole thing in one go?

Now his stomach was making horrible jerky movements. It was frightful to watch.

She did not know whether Bruce could hear her or not, but despite that she shouted at him, "I'm calling an ambulance."

He was going to hurt himself. Araminta went near to try and get him on the floor, but she could not get close for his flailing arms. She did manage to pull the coffee table clear, however.

All of a sudden he went limp and lifeless. That seemed even worse.

Ah, that's better. Arms open wide! Calm and still. Nothing stirs. Whoever said space was cold? All these snowflakes, enlarged a thousand times. So beautiful. Such lovely patterns. Drift through them, ever so slowly!

What fool said that holding your breath was hard? There's no need to breathe. Just glide along in super slow motion. Snowflakes come and snowflakes go. It's the most wonderful idea, to hold your breath for two hundred years in one long, slow dive. Why didn't I think of it before? There's a planet gliding past on the right, covered with ice. There's another with beautiful rings, falling behind on the left. Such grace and delicacy! Lean back and enjoy the luxury. Beautiful snow-flakes…

"Miss, we've never seen anything like this before. We'd best just take him in…"

You may not have a very high impression of us hippos. You probably think that all I ever do is lie under the water all day, only heaving up every few minutes to breathe. Just a small part of my back showing. All very decent.

Perhaps you think I have a narrow view of life. But you're wrong! It's you that have the narrow view.

You should see me at night. No more lounging about after dark.

You'd be surprised at how fast I can run. Trot, trot, trot. And just look at me yawn. Did you ever see such jaws? Glorious, living, open mouth.

I can eat anything. All these green leaves that I gobble down are very laxative. Nobody bosses me about. I leave my mark where I like. Oh, such freedom!

Don't you contradict me. I advise you to keep your distance. I'll run you out of the forest.

King of the jungle, indeed. Who does Mister Lion think he is? Ha-ha!

Trot, trot, trot.

Bruce gradually came too to find himself lying in bed, surrounded by monitors, and covered in curly wires, which were attached to various parts of him. He had a splitting headache and felt sick. He groaned.

"Where am I?"

"Intensive Care Unit at Wayford Hospital. Try to rest. You've had a traumatic experience."

Bruce looked round. The nurse who had spoken to him had a face mask covering her mouth. She looked very worried. Bruce could dimly make out Araminta beyond a glass partition, looking on with great concern. He blacked out again.

When he came to the next time, the headache had calmed considerably. He tried to move, setting up a symphony orchestra of bleeps and blips from all the pieces of equipment around him in the process. The sound was rather nice, so he did it again.

"How are you feeling, Mr. Winter?"

The nurse seemed genuinely concerned. People are so kind.

"Not too bad, really. Any chance of something to eat?"

"You'll have to wait for the doctor to see you first. I'll tell him you have come round. In the meantime, you have a visitor."

431

Araminta came in; she too had a face mask on. She was clearly making a big effort.

"How are you doing, Bruce?"

Something warned Bruce not to sound too sprightly.

"Well, better thanks, but it has been an ordeal. I wonder whether it will have worked."

Araminta could not contain herself any longer.

"You king-sized nit-wit! You might have killed yourself. Swallowing a whole bottle of some amateur concoction. You must be completely crazy."

This was a bit much.

"I did it for us, you know."

"Well, thanks a million. Next time you're thinking of taking action on my behalf, perhaps you'll be kind enough to consult me first so that I can express an opinion."

This was something Bruce had not thought of. He paused. Perhaps he had been a bit rash.

"What happened after I drank it?" he asked, after a few moments.

"Oh, not much, really. You only started jerking and gyrating like a fish out of water. I was frightened you would break your back on the arms of the chair. Then you seemed to be very afraid of a small ant that you saw on the carpet. Then you went limp. Then you started lashing out right and left. The ambulance man had to work hard to restrain you. Then on the way in, you went cold and lifeless. I was really scared, I can tell you. Your heart rate slowed almost to a standstill. By the time we got here, the violent movements started up again, and your heart began to race. You were also very loose at the back end. You really have disgraced yourself, you know."

Bruce felt really bad. He had not wanted to cause any trouble.

"There's another thing that we urgently need to sort out. I would have thought that you were the last person to be involved in drug-taking, but it seems not. Also, if we are going to have a relationship, then I need to know about all your other women. Who is this Emma that you seem so obsessed with?"

Bruce was mystified.

"Emma? I don't know what you mean. I don't know anybody called Emma. I can't think what you are talking about."

"Now don't give me that." Araminta was really angry. "You said it over and over again. 'Emma's a hippy. Emma's a hippy.'"

"Emma's a hippy?" Bruce said it over to himself. What was that about?

Suddenly he got it.

"Oh no, I see it now. It's not a girl named Emma. My cousin Flossie has got engaged to Peter, a man with a fabulous accent. When we were introduced, he said 'I'm so happy to meet you at last,' only the way he pronounced it, it came out as 'Emma's a hippy.' You don't need to feel threatened by someone called Emma because there isn't anybody. Relax."

"I wish I could believe that."

Now it was Bruce's turn to get angry.

"Look, I may have been rash in taking the potion, but it was in a good cause. But now, listen to me. I want it to be quite clear; I will never knowingly deceive you as long as I live. Is that understood? So there is nobody called Emma. And that deals with the drug-taking too. It was Peter's pronunciation of happy. I enjoyed the accent so much that I've often repeated his phrase under my breath, which is probably why it came out when I was unconscious. You'd better meet Peter for yourself; then you'll see what I mean."

Araminta could see that he was in earnest.

"Look, I'm sorry. I can see I've misjudged you. It did seem very suspicious. I'm glad I was wrong."

"That's Okay."

"Sorry to get cross. The truth is, I've been dreadfully worried about you. You might have killed yourself."

"Yes, I suppose you're right. Perhaps it was rather stupid. I promise not to do it again. Forgive me."

Their hands met.

Just at that moment, the doctor came in, accompanied by the nurse.

"Ah, I'm glad to see you looking so much better, Mr. Winter. That was quite a scare you gave us. I've never seen a heartbeat fluctuate so wildly before. You have no idea what you took?"

Bruce had not. He had made a point of emptying the bottle, so there was no trace left to analyse.

"Well, if you're going to make a habit of that kind of thing, perhaps you could book in with us first, and we'll get a bed ready for you in advance."

Rather than being cross, the doctor was clearly pleased that the incident had turned out well. Bruce felt relieved. However, the nurse was looking at him very oddly.

"I've seen you somewhere before," she said, staring at him. "Now, where was it? Oh yes, I remember. Sorry; I should have kept my mouth shut."

Bruce was intrigued. "When and where?" he asked.

The nurse looked a bit uncomfortable.

"You were brought in unconscious for a scan about a fortnight ago. What intrigued me was that it was a full body scan. We don't often get those."

This was interesting. So that was how Jim had replicated him, by scanning him. At least, that must have been the start of the process.

"Where can I go to enquire about the result?"

The nurse gave directions. Bruce was feeling fine now, and his functions were all normal, so after waiting another forty minutes to be certain, there seemed no reason for them to keep him in. He and Araminta were soon walking along a corridor.

"I've been wondering what could have fooled the authorities into thinking you were dead," said Araminta. "Has this scan got anything to do with it?"

"I'll tell you later."

They arrived at the reception desk. Bruce asked about the result. The lady went a way and came back after a couple of minutes.

"Normal. There's nothing to worry about."

"What happens to the data from the scan?"

434

"It's kept on file, in case it should be needed later. If I may say so, you look very well on it. I wouldn't worry about it if I were you."

Bruce thanked her graciously. He doubted that any more replicas of him would be turning up, now that Jim was no more. The thing to do was to get off home.

"You were going to tell me," Araminta persisted in the taxi.

"At home," said Bruce. He rang the school to apologise for not coming in that morning.

When they got in and had tidied up the room after Bruce's assaults on it, and were seated with hot drinks in their hands, Bruce spoke.

"I do apologise for acting so rashly. I can quite see that I should have consulted you. I realise that now. It might have killed me."

"Well, it hasn't. Let's hope there are no long-term effects. Tell me about the body scan."

"It's to do with Jim Pond, the man who invented the sky-suits and sky-cars. When I was playing background piano in his flat in September, for a gathering of his work colleagues, he surprised me by asking me advise them on how they could best give to charity. They had been impressed with my passionate plea on behalf of Water Aid on a previous occasion. It's all rather complicated. Anyway, I told them that in addition to giving money, one of the best things they could do for Africa was to put money towards building a replicator."

"What's that?"

"It's the ultimate machine, that turns anything into anything else. So it could turn rock into drinking water, for example, or sand into sandwiches. Think of the impact a machine like that could have in those hot countries, where people struggle over the basic necessities of life.

"Well, I didn't know, but Jim had already made a replicator. He was so staggered by my prophetic gift, as he put it, that he faked my death, so that when I apparently returned from the dead, I would get the world's attention. At least, I imagine that must be it. He seemed to think that I had something important to say."

"Well, have you?"

"No. That's what's so weird. It's ridiculous, really. There are people around who do have something really important to say, but because they are not TV personalities or good material for the gossip magazines, they cannot get any attention. Then the people who are in the limelight generally don't have anything much to say that's worth hearing. It's all crazy, really.

"Anyway, I tried to say something useful to the press this morning. I warned them about the danger of somebody destroying us all through making a black hole in the laboratory. So I hope that will do some good.

"Now, what are we going to do about you? Your parents still think you are in New Zealand."

"I'll have to get in touch, I know. But Bruce, are you sure you're alright?"

"Never better, thanks. Do I look any more youthful?"

Araminta studied his face with great concentration.

"I think you look wonderful, but then I'm not in a position to judge, because I always have thought that, ever since I first met you. I love you, Bruce."

Suddenly they were kissing. Bruce's heart was beating wildly again. No matter! However, he made himself break it off.

"Steady. Let's make haste slowly. I love you too, you know. I've been trying to deny it ever since that piano lesson when you first told me, but it's no good. However, I want to do things right. You ring your mum and dad and then I'll walk you up to the station for a taxi."

Bruce tactfully found things to do in his bedroom while Araminta was on the phone. She looked flushed but pleased afterwards. They walked up the road arm in arm. Who cares what anybody else thinks, Bruce thought.

"Give me a ring later."

"Certainly will. See you."

63. From: Mission 12
To: Undisclosed recipients
Sent:

436

"Well, here we go," said Phil, as he threw the switch to start the so-called 'Syrup' programme. Actually, it's S.R.P, short for Speeding up the Rotation of the Planet.

"Syrup is a good name," Phil explained to the fifteen of us present, "because not only does it suggest a sweet outcome, it also reminds us that while stirring a pan of water may be easy enough, stirring syrup requires a lot more effort. In this case, the contents of the planet are a lot thicker than syrup."

"Yes," I added. "And to maintain the gravity of the situation, may I remind everyone how appropriate it is that Phil should have thrown the switch, because he is the world's greatest stirrer."

I think he's forgiven me, but he was not pleased at the time. I reckon he wanted to go down in history as the one that helped the settlement really get going. A touch of Mark. I think it's dangerous. We are all part of a team, and we do not need superheroes.

Actually, I think a reference to the World's Greatest Stirrer is appropriate. What we are doing should turn out to be for everyone's benefit. So let's enjoy it. It's a moment for partying, not pompous speeches. This particular brew is so hard to stir that we need every hand on the wooden spoon. It should be good fun.

Of course, the question is, will it work? I have been persuaded to the view that the fourteen hundred spaceships dotted round the equator should not push too hard at first. We don't want to rupture the planet's crust or anything like that. However, many of the others said that as the planet was already rotating, there was no need for caution. Whack the systems on full!

In the end, we have gone for a slow start, increasing the thrust over the first few weeks until full power is gained after a month. That will give time for any problems to emerge. The whole operation is being carefully monitored by orbiting spaceships.

To measure the result, we have set up an observatory with a fixed telescope, as I explained earlier. The existing day lasts thirty-two hours, twenty-four minutes and eighteen seconds. The plan is to observe the same star each night, and discover whether the day and night are becoming shorter or not.

You can imagine the excitement on the first night. I told everyone not to expect anything yet. However, to my delight, the day was 1.4 seconds shorter. The next night was 3.1 seconds shorter; then 5.5 seconds shorter and so on. The programme was working already.

Progress in the first fortnight was not even. On some nights, the speed-up was as much as five seconds, but generally it was two or three.

"This is marvellous," I said to Phil. "If it were to keep going, then we should shorten the day by two minutes every month."

"Don't speak too soon," warned Phil. "There could be problems yet."

He is still a bit cool towards me, I reckon.

"Phil, I'm sorry if I upset you by my stirring remark. It was unkind. What's more, I've realised why I said it. The truth is, I would have liked to be the one to throw the switch. I was jealous of you. That's not a good thing to admit, but it's true."

"Thanks, Bruce. Yes, I wondered about that. It's good of you to come out with it. Let's be friends. Actually, I quite enjoy the thought of World's Greatest Stirrer. It has its comic side."

"Good," I said. "Here's a suggestion for when we start the vertical tilt. We should make the switch into a great long lever, so that everyone can have a hand on it and we all pull it together."

"Yes," said Phil, simply. "I think that's a great notion."

"What do you think about the vertical tilt. Would it be safe to start it during syrup? Could the globe handle more than one operation at once?"

"I don't see why not," said Phil.

"I just wondered if the planet's insides might get a bit confused if there was a right to left force and also a tilting force being exerted at the same time. It might not know which way to rotate."

"I think we'll find that the vertical tilt is going to be far harder to achieve, because of the gyroscope effect. Personally I don't fancy our chances on that one. I reckon we can push as hard as we like, but we won't achieve anything."

This seemed rather gloomy. However, there was soon more news on the syrup front. The number of seconds we were gaining each day was increasing. We were now improving by seven or eight seconds a night.

"It's because we're accelerating, Dad," Max explained. "As long as you leave the motors running, the rate of change will increase. You'll have to decide what a maximum rate of change is, and slow the motors accordingly. If you leave them on high indefinitely, the planet will soon be spinning like a top."

This was true.

"What's more, the day will come when the thrust will need to be reversed to steady the planet to the final speed, so that it stops changing its rate of rotation. I reckon that in due time, there will need to be a reverse thrust equal in strength and duration to the forward push we are giving it now."

I'm proud of Max. He's doing well. It's a shame
there was all that nonsense about him being the
commander when he was not yet ready for it. He
peaked too early. However, he has his life ahead
of him. His time will come.
    Bruce

Bruce needed to take stock. It was Tuesday afternoon and piano
pupils would be arriving for lessons before too long. No reason why
he should not carry on with his normal routine. Celia would be
coming at 8.10 this evening. That could be a bit tricky.

Then there was the press. He wondered what they would make
of his story. He was surprised that there weren't any reporters
outside his door, and constantly on the phone.

As he was thinking this, the phone rang. It was Bill.

"Did you hear the news on the radio at lunchtime?"

"No."

"I'm afraid it was not very flattering. There was nothing on TV.
I expect there will be something in the evening papers. You'll be
teaching, so shall I buy them and bring them round?"

"That would be excellent. I've got a gap between seven and
eight; can you and Gnilla come round for a bite to eat?"

It was soon fixed. Bruce made a casserole and set the timer so
that it would be ready for 7.15.

When they arrived, Bill staggered in with a load of newsprint.
Both he and Gnilla were looking sheepish.

"Whatever's the matter?" asked Bruce.

"I'm afraid you won't like this. Are you sure you want to
know?"

A pang of fear seized Bruce's heart.

"Go on," he muttered. It was better to know the worst.

Man Alive After Death And Cremation

It was prominent, and on the front page of the first paper,
although it was not the main story. Bill read out the text.

440

"On Saturday October 20th, Mr. Bruce Winter was discovered lying dead at the foot of a cliff by Stella Mitchell, a retired nurse of many years' experience. She alerted the authorities, who went through the usual checks and procedures. In particular, DNA tests confirmed the identity of the body. The cause of death was established as being the result of falling down the cliff.

"Two days after the cremation, Mr. Winter returned from a week's holiday in Madrid, wondering what all the fuss was about.

"At first there was excitement that Mr. Winter had risen from the dead, but the interview he gave soon killed that idea. His prediction that farmers in the UK are facing a black hole of debt sent shares in agriculture tumbling for a couple of hours, but they bounced back to end the day higher than they had started. The view that the whole thing was a racket was strengthened by revelations that a number of individuals had made a small fortune by selling and then re-purchasing their shares at the right moment.

"Ordinary people are fed up with this kind of thing. By all means write to your MP, but rest assured that this newspaper will continue to uphold the cause of the common people, and will continue to expose liars and frauds."

Bruce did not know what to say. He suddenly felt terribly tired. It was all so horrible. He opened his mouth.

"Well, they are quite right. It was a sham."

"What were you expecting, Bruce?"

"I imagined that they would get very excited, and hang on my every word. I suppose that was daft, really."

"What's all this about agriculture?"

"That's crazy too. What I actually said was that it would be madness for somebody to try to make a black hole in the laboratory, as if it got out of control, it would destroy us all. I used the phrase 'black hole farming'. But they have misheard it. Anyway, the result is that I have been publicly branded a liar and a fraud. Great."

Nobody said anything. Then Gnilla spoke.

"You know, the article is interesting. Some bits of it are accurate and insightful, but other parts are complete gibberish. It

441

confirms what I've often thought, that unless you have inside information about what they are writing about, you can't tell what's true and what's false."

"Yes," said Bruce in a bitter voice. "But you can be sure of one thing. You can rely on the media to be unreliable."

"How was your death faked, and why?" asked Bill.

Bruce told him about Jim and the replicator.

"That invention sounds very important to me," said Bill. "I think we should be thankful that the news people have not scented it. Are you going to tell Celia about it?"

"I don't know," Bruce replied. "She's coming in half an hour. I really don't know what to do. However, there is one thing I want to tell you."

Bruce told them about Araminta. When he had finished, there was a pause.

"Did you say she's still at school?" Bill asked.

"Yes. I know the age gap is large. It's been troubling me."

"Well, if it's what you both want..." said Gnilla hesitantly.

Bruce was grateful. He found himself wondering how many friends he would lose if he went ahead and married Araminta. He became aware that Bill was saying nothing.

"Let's face it," Bruce said. "Far from doing me a favour, Jim's done me a real injury. Anyway, he's gone now, so there's no point in getting angry with him. All the same, I do miss him. He was such a lovely man. So genuine, and no hint of pride. I can't make sense of him, really; the Jim I knew seems to have two different sides to his personality which don't fit."

Bruce was rambling and he knew it.

"Anyway, the result of it all is that I'm in a real mess. Please help me," he said, rather pathetically.

"Don't worry, we're here for you," said Gnilla. Bill made a grunting noise which sounded slightly more positive than negative, Bruce reckoned. They left Bruce in a thoughtful mood.

When Celia came, she wanted to know how the fraud had been perpetrated. Bruce told her that he did not know, which was true, but he did not tell her of his suspicions about the replicator. There

442

was no hurry. He could always tell her later on, if that seemed the right thing to do.

64. From: Mission 12
To: Undisclosed recipients
Sent:

We decided to start the vertical tilt. The project is called Tip-top; that much is clear. What it stands for is not! Some people think it is really Tiptops, and stands for TIpping the Planet TO Produce Seasons. Others think it is TIPping the TOP of the world. Personally, it doesn't bother me. I find myself visualising a child's spinning top on a linoleum floor; my memory of that activity is that the top always falls over in the end, and runs away across the floor to the other side of the room. I hate the thought of the planet spiralling off out of control! I have to keep telling myself there is no reason why our scheme should go wrong.

Pity I never thought of getting a spinning top for Sean. He's a bit old for it now.

A new volcano has emerged from the sea. It's been spewing up lava and all sorts for a fortnight now. People are saying it's perfectly normal; volcanoes come up from time to time on the earth. Personally, I am not so sure. I just hope it has nothing to do with what we are up to. I confess to feeling a bit worried. At least it's on the other side of the globe from where we are.

Celia and I are only getting on reasonably well. We've lost something of our early intimacy, quite frankly. I wonder if we will ever get it back. I enjoy her company, but I do not feel that sense of confidence and trust in her that I first had. She senses it. It would help if we could talk about it, but we can't. It's sad.

443

Anyway, she suggested that she and I should take a holiday. I agreed. We are going off in one of the landers to explore.

The difficulty is that with the planet being barren, there really is not anything much to explore at all. However, there is good walking in the mountains.

When they heard, Sean Clairie and Max wanted to come too. Why not? we thought. So we packed up supplies for a month, and waved goodbye to the others.

The lander takes all the effort out of travelling. We skimmed over miles of sand. Because of my background on the earth, I kept thinking of it as desert, and that it would end soon, giving way to vast forests. It requires a conscious effort to realise that there are no forests. We are in no danger from wild animals! In fact, the only way we could hurt ourselves would be by falling down a cliff.

The mountains are so tall that they are visible from a hundred miles away, even at ground level. In travel books written about the earth, the people have to sweat along jungle tracks for days before they arrive at the foothills. Here everything is instantly accessible. To be honest, it takes the fun out of it.

We stopped for the night. No chance of camping – far too cold up here for that. We have to sleep in the lander. In the early morning, there's a nice spell when we can go out on foot. It soon gets too hot for comfort, so then it's back into the lander until early evening when it cools down. Then there are several pleasant hours. If the syrup programme goes to plan and the day shortens, then one day the swings in temperature away from the coast will be much less.

I don't talk these matters over with Celia, but Max and I have had some good conversations. Clairie and Celia are getting on well, so nobody feels left out. (Sean is quite happy as long as he is 'running about').

There was one incident which set my heart racing. We were out enjoying the sunset. Celia and I were sitting on a rock, while the children were exploring nearby. Suddenly there was a shout from Max.

"Look, Dad." I went over, but Celia stayed put.

Max pointed. There on the ground was a tiny patch of lichen. "Dad, it must have self-seeded from the settlement plantation."

That was the obvious answer. The wind had carried the seed hundreds of miles, and it had taken root here.

"Well spotted, Max. That's so exciting."

Suddenly, I wanted to cry. This tiny living thing in the middle of the arid waste! It spoke of so much. Suppose man is alone in the galaxy; if so, then our settlement on a new star system is a bit like this tiny growth. It could so easily be snuffed out. But equally, given love and care, it could go on to flourish and fill this world, indeed to fill all worlds. It was a thrilling prospect.

At the same time, I saw the lichen as symbolic of Celia and me. Our life seemed hopelessly barren at one time. Sorting ourselves out was proving harder than I had imagined it would. But here was a glimpse of life, a seed of hope. Perhaps we might yet see further growth in our relationship. I do hope so.

"Come and look what Max has found," I said to her when I returned. The sun was nearly down by now. She came along. I pointed it out to her. "New life in the wilderness," I said.

For a moment, she said nothing. Then she spoke. "I'd like to crush it under my heel."

It was at that moment that I realised how much she was still hurting inside. Until now, I had been too taken up with my own issues to notice.

The fact that she was largely to blame for our
breakdown did not lessen her inner agony. I took
her in my arms and held her. She did not resist.
We stayed there for a long time, watching the sun
disappear. I still find it strange that it looks
somewhat larger than on earth. I suppose I will
get used to it eventually.

After a while the children came to find us. Max
and Clairie both hold one of Sean's hands and
swing him along. He loves it. Max and Clairie are
good. They want us to be happy again, and have
been keeping Sean out of the way in an attempt to
help.

There is a lot to be thankful for.

Bruce

When the phone rang at 0715, Bruce was surprised. Who could
it be so early in the morning?

"It's me," said Araminta. "How are you doing? Any after effects
from the cordial?"

"No, none at all thanks. How are you?"

"Things are not too bad here, but I've been gated. They were
cross and upset at what I had done, and thrilled to have me back, all
at once. But now, guess what?"

Bruce could not guess.

"I said to them, could I have my piano lessons at your home
from now on, rather than doing them at school, and they agreed. So
I can come over to you, which will be far better. Is Friday evening
any good?"

This was all a bit quick, but Bruce's diary was free.

"That would be lovely," he said. "Shall we say eight o' clock?"

"Great. See you then. Can't wait. Byeeee."

And the line went dead.

Far from feeling elated, Bruce felt strangely troubled by the call.
In fact, he did not feel good at all. This bothered him. He should be
thrilled. He and Araminta were in love, so he ought to be over the
moon. Why this sense of dread?

Oh dear, he thought. I wonder if Sarah knows? What will she think? She's coming for piano this evening. That could be tricky. She'll have to be told sooner or later. Bruce did not fancy that at all.

Oh help, and this 'liar and fraud' business. Just exactly the opposite of how he wanted to be seen. Now he was going to have to re-establish his reputation. That could be difficult, especially as he could hardly tell people the truth about the replicator. They would probably never believe him even if he did tell them, come to that. He could imagine the conversation.

"Who made this thing?"

"Jim Pond."

"What, the man who died six weeks ago?"

"Well, actually, he did not die; he put himself through the replicator, and it was a copy of him that was cremated."

"Oh, where is he now then?"

"Well, unfortunately, he died in Madeira at the hands of secret agents."

It lacked conviction. Nobody would believe him, especially now he had been called a liar and a fraud. The phrase really hurt. No wonder he was feeling threatened.

On the way to the station, he bought a copy of the Lookout. It was best to know the worst. The story was on page two. That was something to be thankful for; some readers might not notice it there.

The angle this time was rather different. There was a picture of him lying dead at the foot of a large boulder. How had they come by that, he wondered? It was unmistakably him. Next to it was a picture of him at the news conference, alive and well. It was particularly unflattering. In fact, it made him look suspicious. Are these two the same person? asked the text. You would have said they were. How was the fraud perpetrated? Same horrible word again. Bruce could not bear to read any more.

The train was approaching the platform. As he folded up the newspaper, he noticed a stranger a few yards away staring at him. The man looked away as soon as their eyes met, but Bruce was not deceived. He was a marked man now. He felt awful.

When he got to the school, there was nobody about, as usual. After Simon had gone, the minutes ticked by. Where was his second pupil? Oh, it would have been Araminta, but she was not coming. How stupid. He should have brought something to practise, but although it was gradually coming back, most of his music was still out. Now he would just have his gloomy thoughts for company.

How would people feel about him going out with an eighteen-year-old? Bill and Gnilla had not seemed very pleased. Bruce suddenly felt terribly tired. He pulled himself together with an effort. It wasn't even nine in the morning. He needed to think positively. The thing to do was to focus on small successes rather than dwell on large problems.

At least the potion had not done any damage. It might yet do some good. The thing to do was to be optimistic. Why not play some Wagner until the scamps came? They would cheer him up.

On this occasion, the Wagner did not go well. Bruce found himself playing some of the gloomiest moments of the Ring. The opening of Gotterdammerung is in C flat major, seven flats no less; Bruce had once seen this described as the darkest of all keys. Whether the phrase meant anything, he was not sure. However, the mighty castle of the gods, noble Valhalla, crashed down in flaming ruins under his fingers once again. It was strangely therapeutic. Even the best laid plans of the noblest beings can go horribly wrong.

The scamps were uplifting.

"All that stuff in the papers is utter rubbish," Beccy announced as the door opened with a crash. "Complete nonsense."

"Balderdash," added Simna in a firm voice. This was a new word to Beccy, who thought it was wonderful. She laughed and laughed. Simna laughed too. Why not, thought Bruce, and joined in with a good chuckle. He had once heard of a man who had cured himself of Ankylosing Spondylitis, a wasting disease, by watching funny films, day after day, and laughing his head off. A deep belly laugh is good for you. They all laughed together.

The scamps had a pop song they wanted to play. This was not altogether good news. On the positive side, they would be keen to

448

learn to play it, which would encourage them to get on the instrument at home. On the negative side, the music was too difficult, and even with all Bruce's adaptive skills, it was going to be hard to get a result. Then they might get discouraged and neglect the keyboard for something else.

"The thing to do is to look for the words Easy Piano on the front of sheet music," he explained. "Even then, it's not always that straightforward. Also you can ask the staff in the music shop for advice on which of the current songs is easiest to play."

They hacked away at it. At least the tune was good by the end of the lesson. In a week or two, he would gently steer them back onto something more appropriate.

Sarah was in a funny mood that evening. Bruce could not fathom it at all. She was pleased to see him alive and well, but also suspicious at the same time. Was it just Araminta's wild escapade in New Zealand, or had she guessed what was going on between them? Bruce could not face telling her. They did the lesson and Sarah left none the wiser. Oh dear, why was life so difficult?

There was only one more thing to do before bed. Bruce had designed a new message for his answerphone. He pressed the record button, and spoke clearly in his best voice.

"If you are looking for someone to play the lyre, I'm a fraud you have the wrong number, but if you want Bruce Winter the piano teacher, then please speak after the tone. I'm genuinely grateful for your call."

The last sentence was added on impulse. Bruce was glad for people to be in touch rather than shunning him. The first part was his way of trying to defuse any tension over the newspaper reports. It would let people know that he knew of the charge and did not answer to it.

He got ready for bed, and then watched the news headlines. One of the stories was confirmation of earlier reports that astronomers had lost contact with the planet Pluto. How ridiculous. How could they lose contact? The orbit of Pluto must be known in great detail. Bruce would have been interested, but as it was the last headline, it would not come on for another twenty minutes, and he felt washed up, so he switched off and went to bed. At least he himself did not feature in the bulletin. That was something.

65. From: Mission 12
To: Undisclosed recipients
Sent:

We've begun Tip-top. There was room for everyone on the lever. Initial findings are not encouraging.

Celia's remark about crushing the lichen with her foot set me thinking. When I had a quiet moment, I took a wander along the plantation, as we call it. Outside the greenhouses, which have been moved further off now, the open area extends about two miles in length, and stretches two hundred metres in width at the widest point. It is not much to look at, really! Also, it struck me that one outbreak of disease might be enough to cause real damage.

"Phil," I said, "do you think we should be making efforts to seed other parts of the planet in addition to this one?"

"That's what Dickon was suggesting," Phil replied. "There's no harm in it. However, I think we need to recognise that it will lead to separate communities if we do. Each plantation will require its own group of horticulturists. I would feel happier if we kept the various plantations within the neighbourhood, but it seems to me we could spread out over our peninsular with advantage."

I've probably never told you that we are surrounded by water on three sides here. At its narrowest, the land is just twelve miles wide. We chose this spot because the temperature does not fluctuate so widely near the sea as it does in the heart of the landmass.

"Dickon's got a wild notion," Phil added, "which is to scatter a box of seed from high up in the atmosphere and let it land where it will. I'm against it, as a large proportion of the seed will go to waste. Also, too much of the planet falls below freezing at night, making significant growth unlikely. But it's a fun idea."

"Really, we need more rainfall," I said. "That takes us back to Tip-top."

I fear the results so far are depressing. Here they are to date.

Syrup: plus eleven minutes, thirty-four seconds. Excellent.

Tip-top: Plus 0.001 degrees. Hopeless.

Putting it bluntly, the globe is happy about speeding up but it refuses to tilt. I think it is the gyroscope problem Phil spoke about.

"Couldn't we revisit the idea of raising the seas by a metre?" I queried. "I know we need a daunting number of one ton blocks. This is my idea. The lander and gun working together as a team is fine. However, we need ever so many of them. I suggest we set aside some of our spaceships to replicate themselves. Suppose each one was programmed to create three copies, by replicating twice, and then to make a lander and a gun. Then the resulting teams go off to the asteroids. Each one captures a suitable asteroid, and tows it back towards the planet. On the way here, the asteroid is processed. The spaceship turns any rock into water-ice. The lander turns it all into one ton blocks. Then when they are in range, the gun sends them down onto the planet like peppercorns. Meanwhile, the other three offspring are doing the same, replicating twice and producing a lander and a gun in their turn, and so on. The number of teams would increase, and before long, the blocks of ice would be raining down like hailstones. What do you think?"

"Yes. I think we should do it. I'd come to a similar conclusion myself. But we should also work harder on Tip-top. I reckon we should double

451

the number of ships on it."
In the end, that is what we are doing. Here is our plan:

1. Replicate and deploy six hundred extra spaceships onto Tip-top.
2. Set aside a hundred spaceships for RSLM (Raising the Sea Level by a metre). Nobody's come up with a snappy name for it yet.

More about that later.

Incidentally, my invented name massaccor has not been taken up; we talk about guns instead.

Bruce

PS. The volcano seems normal enough. I need not have worried.

PPS. Do you remember my slogan, 'the covering of the sea by one millimetre in this generation'? I wondered if that might be more practical than one metre. Well, I managed to find a few quiet moments with Big Nimp to do some calculations.

"Archimedes, help me do these sums at my speed. I do not want you doing the whole calculation before I can blink! Now, first of all, we'll work with my answer… here we are, 548138092. Just tap that in. That's the number of years required to raise the level a metre, at the rate of one block per minute. Now, if it is to be just a millimetre, that makes it 548138.092 years at one block per metre. I simply need to add a decimal point…"

I nearly altered it by two digits rather than three, forgetting for a moment that there are a thousand millimetres in a metre, not a hundred! Dear oh dear.

"What I want to know is, supposing we are to only allow one generation for the task, let's call that thirty years, how many blocks per minute...

"Oh, now that's just what I did not want. You might have allowed me to finish the question,

Isosceles. What have you put; 18271 blocks per minute. Dear, that seems frightful. As a matter of interest, how many is that per second? I see, 304 blocks per second. That still seems a terrible lot.

"Oh well, for the sake of completeness, we'd better do the calculation with your figure too. You said 560000000 years…

"Ooh you are a pain. When I said work at my speed, I meant slowly. Never mind. So the number needed per minute for the one millimetre would be 18666, which is 311 per second."

Everybody got that? So even if we were to achieve twenty-five blocks a minute, which may seem like a big improvement on one per minute, it would be nowhere near enough to make a proper impact. Dreadful pun, sorry! We need to go hundreds of times faster.

"Thanks anyway, Fermat."

I called him that because Pierre de Fermat is known as the prince of amateurs when it comes to mathematicians. Keep him in his place.

As a matter of fact, he was more friendly when I called him Isosceles than he has been for quite a while. Perhaps he's warming to me a bit in his old age.

PPSS. I know I ought to finish this message, but I'm in a strangely chatty mood today. Do you ever feel like that, I wonder? I feel curiously safe sounding off to all you folks whom I will never meet. I hope you enjoy my meanderings. Ah well, better sign off again.

Bruce

PPPSS. I don't usually run through so many names in one session with Big Nimp, actually, but as I see him less often now, I can afford to be a bit more generous towards him I reckon.

Friday seemed very long and slow. That was because Bruce was impatient for the evening, when Araminta was coming. However, the day passed off as usual. All his pupils turned up, and none of them seemed put out. Maybe they had not read the papers. Or perhaps they had, but things were not going to be as difficult as he had feared.

At half past seven, Bruce was eating his supper when the doorbell rang. Araminta was not coming until eight, so who could this be?

He opened the door, and Araminta flew into his arms, hugging and kissing him. Bruce had to work hard to make sure his fork, which was still in his left hand, did not go on her lovely black coat and mark it.

"Well hello!" he said, when he finally got the chance. He closed the door.

"Oh I've missed you," she said. "I hope you don't mind me being early."

Bruce was delighted.

"I'm still eating, I'm afraid."

"Don't worry, I'll watch. No, I'll put the kettle on for a drink."

Araminta bustled about. She seemed to have taken charge already. She appeared to know where everything lived without being told.

"Now, you like your coffee scalding hot, so I won't make it until you're ready. One sugar - no need to tell me. I'll just wash these pans."

Bruce was thankful that he had not left his dirty dishes from breakfast on the draining board but had dealt with them up at lunchtime. He wanted to make a good impression.

He had soon finished his meal. Araminta handed him his coffee. It was just how he liked it. How had she known he took one sugar?

"Right," said Bruce. "Work first, pleasure afterwards. Over to the piano."

They had hardly got settled, when the doorbell rang. Bruce went to the door. It was a packet from America sent by courier. Bruce signed for it, and brought it in. How sensible of them to deliver in the evening when people were likely to be at home.

"I wonder who it's from," Bruce said, turning it over. It had been mailed in San Francisco, and was stamped Printed Papers.

"Well, open it," said Araminta.

Bruce fetched a kitchen knife and slit open one end. It simply contained a piece of piano music that had been written out by hand. It was not very long, covering just two sides of manuscript, on separate sheets. There was no accompanying letter. It was really weird.

"Right," said Bruce, who had already recognised the tune, "sight reading. You play it for me."

Araminta laughed. This was what she liked about Bruce. He was such a character. However, playing the music was easier said than done. The right hand was written in four sharps. That was no problem; Araminta recognised it as being in the key of E Major. But the left hand did not have any key signature. That was most odd; it broke all rules of musical grammar for a start. Also, the notes were very strange. They jumped about all over the lower half of the keyboard, and most of them had a sharp or a flat or a natural sign in front of them.

"This looks horribly difficult," she said. "I'll have a go, but it will be slow."

The music was clearly nonsense. Bruce was thinking hard.

"Okay," he said, "I think we need a different approach. Let's not attempt to play it, but to interpret it. What do you reckon?"

This seemed mysterious. Araminta looked at him.

"The answer's in the music, not on my face," laughed Bruce.

"I completely disagree!" said Araminta, and kissed him.

"Now, now, this is a piano lesson remember," Bruce said. "Can you recognise the tune?"

That was easy. It was the love song from the film the Titanic, at least to begin with, but the last notes came from something else that was strangely familiar. Neither of them could place it.

"Two excerpts from well-known tunes. Strange."

Bruce had gone quiet. He was fairly certain he knew who had sent it and why. He would rather have investigated it on his own, but it was too late now.

Araminta sensed his reluctance. "What is it Bruce?"

"Sweet Chilli Sauce," he replied thoughtfully. "Actually, her name's Pikel Vanderpokel. She's of Dutch extraction. I reckon it's from her."

"And who is this woman?"

The only thing for it was to tell the whole story. Bruce left out nothing. He spoke of her stunning good looks, the glorious yacht and the beautiful day, of being out of sight of land, of her bathing topless, of him not looking, and of her surprise. Araminta listened intently but said nothing.

"When she asked me why I did not want her, I explained that it was because I follow Jesus, and that as a result, a quick fling was out of the question; only a life-long marriage would do." Bruce was pleased to be able to mention this. It was something he had wanted to talk over with Araminta.

"Then she asked, 'Why Jesus? Why not Buddha or Mohammed or somebody', and I laughed and said, 'because he saved me in every way that a person can be saved'. I told her it was a riddle. Well, this music shows that she has got the riddle."

"How do you mean? I don't get it."

"The words are from the film Titanic. The old Rose says them near the end of the film. 'He saved me in every way that a person can be saved'. She's talking about Jack, of course, who died to save her, but I've often thought that the words also apply to Jesus and how he died to save us. However, in his case, there are two differences. There was no sex, which is the only thing which spoils the film in my opinion, and what's more, while Jack died for Rose who loved him, Jesus died for people who did not love him at all; indeed, Paul points out that Jesus died for people who were his enemies. It's amazing when you think about it."

It was wonderful talking about Christian things with Araminta. Bruce had been wanting to raise the subject with her.

"Well, I would never have thought of referring people to the film Titanic if they were asking about Jesus."

"Fair enough. I have that kind of mind. But look, I reckon what she's done is to send back a riddle in reply. This left hand part looks very odd. The rhythm is right, but the notes are all haywire."

The left hand certainly was strange. It did not seem to fit with the right hand at all. There were a lot of strange leaps. Araminta fingered it through. Suddenly Bruce had an intuition. "I wonder," he said. He played the notes of the piano one by one, starting from the bottom note, speaking as he did so.

"A B C D E F G H I J K L... Suppose she has simply imposed the alphabet on the keys starting from the bottom. What does it spell?"

"I M S O G L A D..., Bruce you're a genius," chortled Araminta. "'I'm so glad'. Let's do the rest of it."

Bruce wrote out a grid on the back of an envelope, to save them time and effort.

A B C D E F G
H I J K L M N
O P Q R S T U
V W X Y Z

However, when they worked out the remaining notes, the result was rather muddled.

"Y O U S P O K S T O M Z V S Y O U K I K O N T H E P O
O T I F A T H O M S D I T H O T E L T L O O D E D T R A G E
Y Y P I K E L."

"What's wrong with it Bruce?"

"Well, parts of it seem Okay, and the name Pikel at the end is definitely right. Oh I see what she's done. As well as standing for their own allotted letter, the A to G of each octave can also stand for A to G in the alphabet, to save her having to write those very deep notes using lots of leger lines. Let's see if that sorts it."

"Is that what those little lines for the very low and high notes are called? I never knew that," said Araminta.

Sure enough, they soon had the sense of it. The message ran:

'I'm so glad you spoke to me as you did on the boat I fathomed it hotel flooded tragedy Pikel.'

"Oh dear", said Bruce. "I'm really sorry to hear the hotel has flooded. That's terrible." Bruce explained about the gravity control and the wonderful view of the fish. Now all that would be ruined, and be hundreds of feet below water. It was shocking.

"So what does she actually mean by the first part?"

"Well, I think she might mean that she has come to faith, but I could be wrong," mused Bruce. "I told her to stop looking for a husband and start looking for God instead. You know, you should be grateful to Pikel."

Araminta was intrigued.

"Why?"

"Because it was while she was making those efforts to seduce me and I had my eyes tight shut that I realised that the one I wanted was you."

"Go on."

"Well, there she was trying to have it off with me, and I knew it was wrong. I'd been telling myself I couldn't marry you because you were too young, but now you are eighteen, you are an adult, so it's not wrong. The crazy thing is that in the mixed-up world we live in, a lot of people would probably be very disapproving if we were to marry, but they would not bat an eyelid if I had a sudden fling with a stranger while I was on holiday."

"Why do you call her Sweet Chilli Sauce?"

"Because it's a bit like pickle, and also it suits her perfectly. The sauce may seem sweet to begin with, but if you bite into a chilli, you soon regret it. Same with Pikel. She was one to stand back from."

"Bruce, did you say she bathed topless or was she completely naked?"

"I don't know," said Bruce. "I didn't look. You can't catch me out that easily," he added. "I really did keep my eyes away from her."

Araminta was smiling. It was alright. She believed him, which she should, following his promise that he would never deceive her. It was good to have told her the full story.

Now it was Araminta's turn to look rather uncomfortable.

"Bruce, I'm really glad that you believe in marriage, because that's my belief too, and also, following Jesus is important to me. However, I'm worried you may not want me when you hear about all the boys there have been."

Bruce did not like the sound of this.

"Tell me."

"Well, Karl you know about. He is nice, I have to confess, but I don't love him. Before him there was Mark. He was great. Such fun! Then before that it was Stephe. We got on really well, and Mum and Dad liked him too, but Sarah thought he was a ponce. Then before that it was Phil, but he only lasted a week. Before that was... oh yes, Mark, a different one. How could I possibly forget him? He was terrific. I was really sad when they emigrated to America. Then before that it was Jo, and before that it was Gickoo."

"Gickoo? Are you serious? It sounds like something I once found stuck to the underside of a desk at school."

"Oh, don't be horrid! No, Gickoo was lovely. His real name was Mark. Funny how I've always been attracted to boys called Mark. It was when we were at playgroup. We used to go in hand in hand. He used to enjoy freedom of expression with sand best. We called him little Mark, because he looked so cute in his shorts, but he couldn't say little; it came out as gickle, so I used to call him 'Gickle Mark', and over time it got shortened to Gickoo."

"I see." Bruce did not quite know what to make of all this.

"Do I need to feel threatened by Gickoo?"

"Oh no, not at all. He's on his gap year at present, doing voluntary service in Madagascar. No, you don't need to worry about him."

Bruce still felt a little uncomfortable.

"Perhaps you would like to know how intimate my relationships have been," Araminta said coyly.

Bruce did not know how to react. However, he was a bit interested, he had to confess.

"I'm as pure as the driven snow!" said Araminta with a flourish. She was glowing. "I've been longing to tell you. I made it quite plain to all of them that there was no messing about with me; it was all or nothing. Either marriage or eat your heart out."

Bruce laughed. This was reassuring.

"It seems we think alike," he said.

"And I want to have lots and lots of babies," Araminta went on. "That is if you are ready, able and willing."

Bruce thought that on the whole something along those lines might be possible.

"I don't feel very flattered," Araminta said.

Bruce took a moment to reply.

"Look," he said, "I don't want to put the dampener on things, because I really am absolutely delighted that we are getting together. But I'm also nervous at the same time. You see, I've never been in this situation before. There aren't that many people who would be prepared to cross the room to speak to me if they saw me in a public place, but you have just raced all the way round the world to find me. I feel a bit scared if I'm honest. The truth is, I tend to make a mess of most things I turn my hand to, and I don't want to ruin your life for you."

"Oh Bruce, you're so sweet."

Araminta cuddled up to him and closed her eyes. He put his arm round her. This was not very clever, as the result was that she practically fell off the piano stool.

"Now come on," said Bruce in his teacher's voice, "this is meant to be a scintillating half hour of musical education here!"

They both laughed.

"You know," Bruce continued, "I don't think we've got to the bottom of this sheet music yet. I don't feel satisfied. The code is too obvious. It only took us three minutes to crack it. I reckon there is a deeper riddle here as well somewhere, if only we could see it."

"What fun!" Araminta exclaimed. "What about these musical markings. Do you think all the sharps and flats have anything to do with it?"

"It's possible. There are also volume instructions. And do you see the tempo marking - *Presto*? That is much too fast for the Titanic."

"I agree; they should definitely have slowed down. What does this *una corda* mean?"

The young people never knew what *una corda* meant.

"It means use the soft pedal."

"What, the left hand one, you mean? You must be joking. How could *una corda* possibly mean that?"

"Well, you press it down with your foot and watch what happens inside the instrument." Bruce opened the lid for a better view.

Araminta tried it.

"Oh look, everything moves a bit to the left."

"That's right. On a grand piano like this one, what the left hand pedal does is to move the action to the left, so that when the hammer strikes the note, instead of hitting all three strings, it only hits one of them. Did you know that most of the notes have three strings?"

Araminta had never really looked inside a piano before. Bruce used his pencil to tap three adjacent strings; they all made the same sound.

"Watch the hammer closely," he said, as he pressed the key gently, with the soft pedal off. As it rose upwards, Araminta could see that the hammer was positioned so that it would hit all three strings. Indeed, there were small indentations in the felt on the head of the hammer, showing where it had struck the strings on previous occasions. But when she held down the left hand pedal, and the whole of the action had moved a fraction to the left, the hammer would only hit one of the strings.

"So that's how it works," she observed. "Only one string struck, so less volume. I suppose *una corda* is Italian for one string. I see."

"On upright pianos, it is done a different way," Bruce explained. "There, the soft pedal moves all the hammers closer to the strings, so that they don't have so far to travel. It's not a good arrangement, frankly, as you can hardly notice any difference in the sound. Really, you control the volume by how hard you strike the note with your finger, not by using a pedal. So the soft pedal on an upright piano is next to useless. Indeed, there are many pianists who don't use the soft pedal from one year to the next. I suppose that if you wanted to hide something small, sticking it to the underside of the soft pedal on a piano would be as good a place as any."

Suddenly, Bruce realised what he had just said. Araminta also had the same thought, but was quicker off the mark. She was already kneeling on the floor, feeling the underside of the soft pedal.

"Careful!" Bruce said. "I've got a suspicious mind. Suppose there's a hypodermic syringe fastened there filled with a sleeping draught? You could have pierced your finger and be unconscious by now."

"No worries!" laughed Araminta, "although I appreciate the compliment. I'm sure my prince would be on cue." She knew Bruce had been alluding to Sleeping Beauty. "No, I'm afraid there's nothing there. However, I had assumed the underside of the pedal would be smooth like the top, but it's not. It's ridged."

Bruce knelt down to have a feel.

"I see what you mean..." he began, before Araminta's lips met his and ended his sentence, as had been predictable.

They were interrupted by the doorbell.

"Not again!" exclaimed Bruce. This was the third unexpected ring in one evening.

As Bruce crossed the room to open the door, a sentence floated into his mind.

'Take the homeless poor into your house.'

That's funny, he thought. Why am I thinking that? The words had a biblical ring to them.

He opened the door. On the doorstep stood a stranger. With a shock, Bruce realised it was a tramp. His boots had holes in them.

His clothes had not been washed in a month. His dark hair was long and unkempt, with strands of grey and white in it. There was many days' growth on his chin. He even had the woollen mittens on his hands which seemed to be regulation wear for the ones that stood queuing for free soup in the less desirable streets of London.

"Bruce?" said the man.

Bruce had a flash of inspiration. It was his dad! He did not hesitate.

"Come in, Dad," he said.

It is said of a drowning man that all his life rushes through his mind during the closing seconds of life. It was like that for Bruce now. As his father stepped forwards, time seemed to stand still. Bruce recalled the home of his childhood. There was his mother, putting breakfast on the table in front of Sasha and him. There was the tree down the garden that he liked best. There was his granddad's home, which came to mean so much - a place of security and love. There was his first classroom at school, a throwback to Victorian times, with its windows high up so that the young people would not look out and be distracted from their studies. There was the lecture theatre at music college. There was himself; seated at a piano, doing hours of practice.

Suddenly, his mind was in the present. What problems was his father bringing into his life as he stepped over the threshold? Bruce could hardly begin to guess. What would his pupils think? Would they still want to come to his home? Oh dear, and worst of all, Araminta? Bruce did not need to look round; in fact, he dared not look round. For her it was an appalling moment. He knew it.

As his dad stepped through the doorway, the stench hit Bruce like a fist in the stomach. Addictions galore! This could be very difficult. There might be stormy scenes ahead.

His dad hesitated on seeing Araminta.

"I'm sorry," he said, "I thought you would be alone. I would never have interrupted."

Bruce waved him in. "This is Araminta, one of my piano pupils." He could not bear to hint at their budding relationship.

Araminta was already rising from the stool.

"Pleased to meet you, Mr. Winter," she said. How brave, Bruce thought. But she wasn't pleased really.

"It's time I left."

Oh dear, she was going. Bruce did not know what to do. Their eyes met. Bruce was dismayed. He had never seen her look so troubled. What was she thinking, he wondered?

"See you," was all Bruce could manage. Araminta said nothing as she walked out into the night.

His dad had already sat down in an armchair.

"Have you got a light?" he asked.

Nobody had ever lit a cigarette in Bruce's home before. Bruce was not about to create difficulties. There would be enough of those to come. He found some matches that he kept in a drawer. His father was soon inhaling, and blowing out smoke. Like a dragon, Bruce thought. Why did he have to turn up now, of all times?

His father answered the question for him.

"I saw you in the papers. Liar and fraud it said. I reckoned we might get on alright after all."

Bruce found his voice.

"Dad." It seemed so strange calling this stranger dad.

"I've wondered many times where you were and what you were doing," Bruce continued.

"You were better off not knowing, son. Prison for many years. Then sleeping rough half the time, doing odd jobs, going from place to place. Made prison seem like holiday camp."

"I don't know how you've survived."

"Got through somehow. What about you?"

"Well, I earn a living by giving piano lessons. I go into a local school each weekday morning, and then I teach here in the afternoons and evenings. I also do background piano when opportunities come up, and I play for the occasional funeral. That's about it, really."

"You've done well at piano, then. Care to play me something?"

This was extraordinary. Here was his dad, turning up after several decades, carrying on as if there had been no break.

"Well yes, alright. Here's a piece of Bach I particularly like."

Bruce played the prelude in C Minor from Book one of the Forty-eight. It rattled along well, and would show off his technique. It was also the piece Sarah played, he realised when he was part of the way through. Funny how he should have chosen that one.

"Nice." Just the one word.

"Dad, what are your plans?" Bruce asked. Perhaps that was a bit pushy.

"I can clear off if you want me to."

Bruce already knew the answer to that, even though it was going to cost him.

"No, Dad, I don't want that. I want you to stay. I hardly even know that you are my dad, although something tells me that you are, and I doubt that anyone would have the nerve to come in here impersonating my dad if it was not really him. We've lost Mum and Sasha, so we only have each other left."

Perhaps it was a mistake to mention his mother and sister.

"Stupid cow," mumbled the tramp.

Bruce felt a sudden surge of anger.

"Did I hear that right?" he said. "I don't know what the argument was between you, but whatever it was, you did not need to attack her."

It was bound to come up sooner or later.

"She was such a pain. She drove me to it. I was sad about Sasha, though. She should never have interfered."

He had not taken responsibility, then.

"Anyway, that was years ago."

A thought crossed Bruce's mind. Perhaps he did not know…

"You know that Mum lived on a long time in a nursing home?"

"Yeah. But she was as good as dead."

This was awful. Bruce sensed that his father really did not feel bad about what he had done. Bruce could not imagine how anybody could be so hard as not to feel remorse for killing somebody. But at least he felt sorry about Sasha. That was something. Bruce sensed it was important not to judge his dad. For one thing, he was all too conscious of his own failings, so who was he to form an opinion about somebody else?

465

"Right, Dad. I'm glad you've come." He meant it. He was glad. "I want to help. What is your main need? Something to eat or drink?"

"You wouldn't have any whisky, would you?"

Oh dear, that was not what he meant.

"Is that wise Dad? Are you addicted?"

"Alcohol keeps you going out on the street, son. After a bit, it becomes part of your life."

"Couldn't I cook you something instead? What about some scrambled egg?"

"Scrambled egg. Haven't had that in years. Okay, scrambled egg it is. Where's the bathroom?"

Bruce got going on the egg. He was pleased that his dad had not mentioned the whisky again. Perhaps he would be open to reason.

The egg was scrambling nicely. Don't overdo it. Then Bruce realised that his dad had been gone a longer time than was necessary for visiting the loo. He went to check.

His dad was sprawled on the floor, with an empty bottle beside him. He had discovered where Bruce kept the alcohol, and finished off a bottle in just four minutes. Bruce was appalled.

"Dad!" he exclaimed, but there was no reply. He was asleep.

This was awful. Bruce suddenly remembered the egg. He was just in time; it was beginning to stick to the pan. He switched off the cooker, and phoned Bill.

"Bill, I really need your help. My dad has turned up. He's a tramp. Can you come over, and I'll explain."

Bill arrived in six minutes.

"Thanks," said Bruce. He showed Bill where his dad was lying. Together they got him into the spare room bed. There was a mumbled protest, followed by loud snoring.

"It's unreal," Bill said when Bruce had finished explaining. "To think that those negative reports about you in the press should have brought your dad out of the woodwork. Are you pleased or sorry?"

Bruce was unsure. "Pleased, I think. Or at least, I want to be. But I'm worried about the addictions. He found my drinks cupboard and downed a bottle of whisky before I cottoned on. I thought he was visiting the toilet. Look, will you take all the bottles off to your place? I'm going teetotal for a while."

Bruce never consumed much alcohol. Some of his pupils would bring him a bottle of wine at Christmas as a thank-you present. These tended to stay unopened for most of the year, so it was no loss for Bill to have them. There were about fifteen all told. They loaded them into the back of Bill's car.

"There is one good thing," Bill observed; "he should sleep the clock round. I'd get to bed yourself if I were you, as you could have some broken nights ahead of you."

It was good advice. Bruce thanked Bill warmly, and waved him off.

He sent to Araminta. "Sorry piano lesson shortened. Please ring. Bruce." No intimacy; he did not know who might see the message. He hoped she would understand. Then he turned in.

```
66. From: Mission 12
To: Undisclosed recipients
Sent:
```

Clairie is thrilled to have a younger brother, as I told you. Max is not so sure. I think it has brought his own situation home to him more clearly. The idea of him marrying any babies born from now on is hard to entertain. He knows that now, having seen one, and how long they take to grow.

I can see the way Max's mind is working. His best chance is to find a young lady astronaut in hibernation who will have him. He did not need to tell me this; I just knew. So when I suggested it was time to go back up to the spaceship for a visit, he jumped at the chance. Celia will be Okay; Sandra is looking after her. Those two get on well together.

We left a few minutes ago. I never tire of space travel, frankly. I always enjoy going up above the clouds, watching everything below growing smaller and smaller. Then there's the approach to the spaceship. This used to be slow and deliberate in the old days, but the automation is so good now that we approach at speed and only slow down for the last hundred metres or so. At first, I used to think we were bound to crash, but I'm getting used to it now. It reminds me of a boat trip I once took with Granddad, all those years ago. The captain knew his boat so well that when we were approaching the jetty, he waited until the last possible moment before throwing the engine into reverse. He timed it perfectly; we glided to a halt nestling up against the pier.

(Continued later.)

Everything is in order up here. I asked Max to check how many astronauts were still in hibernation, as if it was something that needed doing for some lofty purpose. He was glad to do so. Doubtless, Big Nimp could have done it straight off.

The answer was a hundred and sixty; eighty-four men and seventy-six women.

Max understands me better than ever before. It's good, really. Now that he has grown up, he can appreciate my longing for a companion when I was the only person awake. Also, he is now in the same position as I was then; wondering about the identity of the girls in the coffins.

I decided to tell him about my conversation with Big Nimp. He was astonished to hear that I woke Celia even though I should have woken the one on the left. He did not ask who that was. Perhaps he remembers who got out where. Or perhaps he does not like to probe. I don't know.

All this has created a bond between us that was not there before. He knows something I have not told to anybody else. He also knows my personal weakness; I think that's a good thing. I'm hoping it will help him to deal with the situation he finds himself in.

He may choose to talk to me about it, but I suspect he won't. My personal challenge is to allow him his own space, and not to mind if he prefers not to involve me.

I so want him to be happy!

I must finish with a confession. When I was doing the calculation about the ice blocks, I really did think there were a hundred millimetres in a metre rather than a thousand. I should have been more honest about that in the last email. Sorry! I know that telling you makes me look a fool, but that's better than trying to cover it up.

Bruce

Bruce woke early. He was thankful that it was Saturday as it meant there was no school. The thought of leaving his dad on his own in the bungalow did not appeal. As it was, he had a few hours to make some preparations.

He went through quietly to check that his dad was Okay. He was sleeping soundly. It was his first chance to get a proper look at him. The face did tally with what he remembered, but only just. It was heavily scored with wrinkles, and betrayed the fact that he had slept rough a good deal. Bruce wondered how many odd jobs he had really had. It was not a peaceful face, Bruce decided. This was hardly surprising.

It was hard to feel pleased that his dad had turned up. However, Bruce was determined; he was going to do everything he could to make him feel welcome and at home. He was also going to be careful not to manage him and boss him about. He wanted to treat him with respect. For example, he could smoke if he wanted, although Bruce already had an idea about that.

Just then the phone rang. This was very early! Then Bruce smiled. Sure enough, it was Araminta.

"Bruce, how are you?" She sounded very concerned.

"Well, it's a bit of a shock, and it's not how I imagined him. He also managed to drink three quarters of a bottle of whisky before I realised what he was up to, so now he's sleeping like a lamb, but apart from that, things are not too bad!"

"It must be very difficult for you. I had no idea what to do, so I just bunked off out of it. I felt really bad about it afterwards."

"Don't you worry. I was concerned about you. I knew you would find it very difficult. I suppose that being gated, you can't slip out to see me today. Not that I'm asking you to. I think we should honour your parents' wishes. Do you agree?"

"Yes, Bruce, I do. I want them on our side."

"So I won't see you until next week's lesson, then. Boring! But look, there are two things I wanted to say."

"Yes?"

"Firstly, I'm determined to have another flying lesson. I think it is really tragic how everything has swung in the direction of sky-cars. I can see why they are so popular; convenience, speed, novelty and so forth. But I never imagined that the flying in suits would fade out like it has. I hardly ever see anybody airborne these days."

"I agree. I'm glad you want to fly, because I love it. I'll see if I can get permission to go to the meet, because if I can, I could give you a lesson, if you can deal with your dad for an hour or two, that is."

"That sounds great. I'm looking forward to it already. Oh yes, and I want to buy my own suit, not just hire one for the afternoon."

"They are still expensive."

"Well, that brings me to my second point. One of the last things Jim did was to give me a piece of plastic. He said I might have some expenses. So I thought I would use it to pay off your New Zealand trip."

"Bruce, that's very kind of you. But look, I'm not extravagant really. I don't want you thinking I'm one of those people who runs up debts, and that if you pay this one off, I'll soon create another one."

"I don't think that, but thanks for mentioning it all the same. It's wonderful how much we think the same way. Personally, I don't feel comfortable about you reading out your card number over the phone, so pop it in an envelope and leave it for me at the staffroom at school."

"Will do. Bruce, you are lovely."

"Me? I'm just a burke. You're the lovely one."

"Better go. Is it Okay if I ring early like this, while the rest of them are asleep?"

"It's fine. We'll have to tell them sooner or later of course. Bill and Gnilla know already, but they will keep it to themselves."

"I still haven't met them. I'm looking forward to it."

"I'm sure you'll like them. Bill's been a good friend to me. They have only been married a few weeks themselves, so they will remember the stage we are at."

"Talking of stages, I wish you were trundling along in a stage coach and I could be the highwayman and hold you up with pistols, saying 'your money or your life'."

"And I would say, 'they're both yours. Why not get in and ride along?' Stage coaches are a long way back from flying cars, aren't they?"

"Sure are. But it's only three hundred years. I'm glad we live now. I feel so excited about the future."

"So do I. I feel so happy to have found you, Araminta."

"Do you know, I loved you the first moment I saw you when I had my first lesson with you in my first year."

"Isn't that amazing. So none of those boys ever had a chance, then?"

"Not a hope, although I never let on, to them or you. What really moved it on was when you waved to me in the train."

"I was so delighted to see you up there. Then I felt awkward, that perhaps I shouldn't have waved."

"Well I'm so glad that you followed your heart, Bruce. But look, this is important. If you ever get to meet Gickoo, you mustn't call him that. It's my private name. I will introduce him as Mark that I knew at playgroup, and you say 'Hello Mark'. Is that clear?"

"Okay."

"Apart from anything else, he's six foot five now, so there's nothing little about him. Whoops, better go, somebody's moving about."

The line went dead.

Bruce put the phone down and stood deep in thought for several minutes. Could this really be happening to him? Most of him felt very pleased, but part of him felt scared. It was a curious mixture.

He was still standing there when the phone went again. This was going to be a busy morning.

"Hi, Bill here. Gnilla's hopelessly drunk on all your bottles. No, not really. I was wondering, could I pop in this morning?"

Bill was trying to sound cheerful and relaxed, but Bruce could see through the façade.

"Of course. Dad's still sleeping it off, so the sooner you can come, the better. Just give me a few minutes to cancel my pupils."

"Be there in ten minutes. Bye."

There were four pupils to put off. Bruce disliked cancelling lessons, but this was an emergency. They all understood.

Gnilla would be working at the shop, so Bill was at a loose end on Saturday mornings.

He was soon sitting in his usual armchair with a mug of coffee. Bruce wanted to make it easy for him.

"You want to talk to me about Araminta."

Bill laughed. "Can't hide anything from you. Yes, I do. Bruce, are you serious about her?"

"Can you imagine me leading a girl up the garden path?"

"What I mean is, are you contemplating marrying her?"

"Yes, I am."

"But she's so young."

"And I'm so old. Yes, I know. I wouldn't approve if I read it in a book. But the fact is, we love each other. She told me first, back in the summer. I told her a relationship was out of the question because of the age gap. I discussed it with her older sister Sarah, and we agreed a relationship was out of the question because of the age gap. I have been valiantly trying not to think of her for these past few months because of the age gap. But then, when I was

472

staying with Jim at the hotel, there was the most beautiful girl called Pikel who was the P.A., no don't laugh, she was no laughing matter I can tell you, and she tried to seduce me on her yacht, and I resisted, and it helped me see not only that I wanted Araminta but that since she is eighteen, there is nothing to prevent us from marrying. So whatever anybody else thinks, I'm happy about it."

Bruce did not normally speak in such long sentences, and he did not mean to sound so combative, but he had and he did. Bill thought for a moment.

"You were great when Gnilla and I nearly snuffed it in the summer. I'm really not sure about what you are doing, but I'm going to stand by you, whatever. I can see you have thought it through. You have my support."

"Thank you, Bill. You're a real friend. I really appreciate it. Don't forget, you've never met her. I'm sure you'll find it easier to accept her when you do."

"But Bruce, how are you going to have a balanced relationship? Marriage should be between equals, I reckon."

"Well, you probably think I'm going to dominate her. But actually, Bill, I'm a bit worried that it could be the reverse. So far, she's made all the running. In fact, I find her a bit bossy at times. I'm so good at fitting in and not causing any offence that if I'm not careful, we'll do what she wants all the time, and I won't get much of a look-in. Not that I think she wants it to be like that, but it's my own weakness that could bring it on."

"Hmm." Bill did not know what to say. "I think I'd better meet her. Then maybe I can get an idea about it."

"That could be a bit difficult. Her parents have gated her for going to New Zealand and back without their permission."

"You're joking."

"No I'm not. She was so upset when I had died that she went rushing off for comfort to a former boyfriend from Down Under called Karl. Then when she heard I was alive, she came rushing back."

"Gracious. There have been other boys, then?"

"Dozens. But all just friendships, nothing more. She listed them all for me, starting with little Mark at playgroup."

"Well, she sounds like quite a character. I hope you know what you are doing, Bruce. Gnilla never knew anybody closely before me."

"Bill, the truth is I feel thrilled and scared all at once. Then there's my dad, turning up now of all times. I'm pleased he felt able to come, but it does complicate things. I feel I may need quite a bit of help with him. Can I call on you?"

"Of course. What are friends for? Anything, any time. We'll be there."

"I hope you won't live to regret saying that. I'm ever so grateful."

Bill got up to leave. "I'm sorry about the liar and fraud stuff," he said.

"Those words are what encouraged Dad to come, so they have done some good after all," Bruce explained. "Funny old business, life, isn't it?"

"Sure is. See you."

"Bye."

Bruce was aware that his father was going to take a great deal of his time and energy. The thing to do was to relax now, perhaps even sleep, so as to preserve his resources. He settled in his armchair. Then he noticed the cigarette end. His dad had not asked for an ashtray. Instead he had stubbed out the cigarette directly onto the coffee table. Sure enough, it had left an ugly mark. Bruce was upset, but quickly checked himself. What was a coffee table compared to his dad? What were any of his possessions come to that? He determined not to allow himself to be upset by anything. Also, he was not going to pressurise his dad, other than removing the alcohol. He wanted very much to give his dad a warm welcome and a happy home.

He cleaned up the cigarette end and found a saucer that would do for an ashtray. Then he settled back into his armchair. After a few minutes he began to doze.

67. From: Mission 12
To: Undisclosed recipients
Sent:

I've initiated the programme starting off RSLM (Raising the Sea Level by a Metre).

Well, that's the grand way of expressing it. In reality, I explained to Big Nimp what we wanted to do. He thought it was a good idea. We worked out the exact arrangements together.

Following the incident of the suicide pill, we have agreed that major decisions require three humans to approve them, so it was a case of getting Phil and Dickon on the line to rubber stamp the arrangements before Big Nimp went ahead.

All systems are go. I'm pleased we are taking the plunge. Actually, it will be the pulverised asteroids that will plunge down towards the surface, bringing the life-giving water.

Then Big Nimp surprised us. He told us that a spaceship is entering the star system. It's from earth; it has already been sending messages. It has slowed right down now. It will arrive in three weeks' time.

At present it is still too far away to be visible on the screen.

Max and I are hurrying back down to spend time with Celia before a number of us come back up for its arrival.

There is great excitement about what might be on board. I am keeping quiet about it because I know! At least, I'm ninety-eight percent certain. I've been expecting another space ship to arrive. I am not going to say anything, but I will be interested to see if I was right.

Be in touch in three weeks, then.

Bruce

Bruce woke up with a jerk. The phone was ringing. He shook his head from side to side in an attempt to come to, and lifted the receiver.

"Hello?"

"Bruce, you poor thing!" It was Banjo! "Whatever have you been up to, blabbering on about farming? As if you know anything about it. You couldn't tell a cow from a horse."

Really Banjo was a bit much at times. Who was she to make out that he was incompetent?

"Bancesca, it wasn't like that at all. To continue in your farming vein, the press have made a complete pig's ear of what I said."

"Well, I don't need to be told that! What do you think I am? Daft? Anyway, you'd better go back to Madrid until it all calms down."

"Madeira, not Madrid. Anyway, I'm glad you've rung, because you'll never guess what's happened; my dad's turned up."

"Bruce! That's extraordinary."

"It was because the newspaper said I was a liar and a fraud. He felt he would be at home with that."

"Well, that's a sow's purse and a half. If you were a brass player, I'd say it was an ill wind that blows nobody any good. How remarkable. How is your father?"

"Down and out and addicted. He's sleeping off the effects of an alcohol binge now. Goodness knows what will happen when he wakes."

"Well, best of luck with him. I'm sorry to say that Flossie's in a bad way."

"Why, what's happened?"

"Cold feet. She likes Peter, but she's worried by his accent. She can't get used to it, and she's scared to raise it with him."

This was sad.

"I'll give her a call."

"Yes do; you always were tact personified. Sort her out, Bruce. Bye."

The line went dead. Banjo was so abrupt. Never mind - it was not personal. He dialled the number.

"Flossie, it's Bruce here."

"Oh Bruce, how nice of you to ring. I've been dying to hear a friendly voice. You were always so lovely to me."

Careful, she still hankers after me, thought Bruce.

"Flossie, Banjo tells me you're getting cold feet about Peter."

"It's his accent, Bruce. I find it so hard to take him seriously. You have such an attractive way of speaking."

"I'm sure you'll get used to it. He struck me as a nice fellow. Stay with it, Flossie. In fact," perhaps this was a bit rash but never mind, "I've got a girl friend of my own now." It might help put her off him.

"Bruce, how exciting. Who is she?"

"Well, the reason I'm mentioning it is that she is only eighteen. She's one of my piano pupils. The point is, I know what it is to feel scared, like you. What I'm saying is, if you love him, keep at it. Pluck up the courage to talk to him about it. I'm sure you'll come through in the end, like I intend to with Araminta."

There was a gulp from the far end of the phone.

"Oh Bruce, is it really too late for you and me? We would make such a lovely couple!"

This was not at all what he had in mind.

"Flossie, you marry Peter and make a happy man out of him. Be bold and strong!"

"If you were bold and strong, you'd have swept me off my feet and carried me over the threshold a long time ago. You're not one to talk!"

"Flossie. Peter's the right one for you, and he's great. Go for it. Give him my best wishes. Got to go. See you."

"Bruce..." but Bruce had done a Banjo and put the phone down. I wish I hadn't mentioned Araminta, he thought. It's bound to lead to trouble.

Ah, here was Dad. He looked dreadful. He had found Bruce's dressing gown and an old pair of slippers.

"Good morning, Dad. How are you today?"

There was a grunt from his father, who shuffled off out again. He just wanted to see if I was here, Bruce thought.

There was silence for a couple of minutes. Bruce then made his way through to find his father at the empty drinks cupboard.

"Damn you," said Dad. It was not a promising start to the day.

"I've cleared all the alcohol out of the house," Bruce explained.

"So I see." Bruce felt a surge of anger but pushed it down.

"Would you like some breakfast?" he asked.

Dad made a mumbling noise, and shuffled through to the kitchen.

"It's cereals and toast," Bruce explained. "And orange juice."

Dad settled on a chair. Bruce waited on him. The food would do him good. It was hard to feel positive about having his dad. So far he had stolen a bottle of whisky while Bruce's back was turned, and called his mother a stupid cow.

No; this was no good. Don't focus on the painful aspects. His father had come to him. Be grateful for that.

Bruce turned on the fan in the window above the kitchen sink to expel the smoke. His father was on his second cigarette already.

"Bruce, you can call me Will rather than Dad. It'll be easier that way."

What was that about?

"Alright, if that's how you would like it, Will. Now, what can I do to help you?"

"I'd like a bath and a change of clothes."

"Sounds good to me."

"But I don't want to come to the shops to choose them. You work out my measurements from the clothes I arrived in, and then get a similar set from a charity shop. That'll suit me fine."

This seemed like a good idea.

"I'll get on with it straight away. Then this afternoon, I'll be going to the supermarket for the week's food, so you might like to think about the menu."

His father grunted again and shuffled off to the bathroom. Bruce realised that the shuffling was because the slippers were too big rather than from a defect in his walking.

He had already decided that he would leave his dad alone in the house after all. It would have to happen on Monday anyway, and so the thing was to try it today, for a short period. It was wise to expect problems when he returned.

The sound of running water soon came from the bathroom. Bruce soon had the measurements noted on a sheet of paper.

"See you soon, Will," he called in a cheery voice.

"Bye."

Bruce walked swiftly up the road. It would take fifteen minutes, perhaps twenty. What could Dad do in that time? He could drown himself in the bath. He could set fire to the curtains. He might be able to find Bruce's hatchet in the shed and bring it in and sever the piano strings, or destroy the furniture.

The thing to do was to imagine the worst. Then if all he had done was to stub out cigarettes on the carpet, leaving ugly burn marks, it would be a relief.

"I forgive him for calling my mother a cow." Bruce actually spoke the words out loud as he walked. "I also forgive him for killing her and Sasha; that's a choice of my will, even though my feelings have not caught up yet."

Now, if I had a flying suit, Bruce thought, I could be there by now. It completely baffled him why they had not caught on. Perhaps it was the cost. If more people had bought them, then the price would have come down. The sky-cars were selling well, but not enough to cut down the number of cars on the road yet. Also, where could you park a sky-car when you went to the shops? Perhaps there should be a large tower. You would land on the roof, and then your sky-car would be spirited away inside somewhere, while you took the lift down to ground level. Then on your return, you would punch in your number to the machine, and the car would come rolling out for you to step into. That part could take place at ground level. Yes, it might possibly work, if there were enough points for embarking and disembarking; otherwise you might have to spend ages in a queue.

Here he was at the charity shop. It was the work of a few minutes to select an outfit to be going on with. There were no suitable shoes, however. Bruce was soon striding back.

There was no mushroom cloud over the bungalow; that was something. No smoke or flames either. Bruce went in.

"That was quick." His dad was still in the bath and still alive.

"I didn't like to leave you alone too long."

"You needn't have worried. I've been on my own for years. If you're around all the time, I'll feel smothered."

"Right Will, I see. Good point. I'll let you wallow in peace."

Bruce did some piano practice. The Rachmaninov Prelude in C sharp minor. A great piece, and it was good to be on top of it, so that he could demonstrate it to a pupil without messing it up. Before long, Dad came through.

"That's magnificent. You're good. Now, where's my party gear?"

"Well," said Bruce, holding up a sweater, "here's a nice little number from Paris that's been raising eyebrows. And these trousers have been causing quite a stir on the catwalks. Now this one was modelled by…"

"Der, go on with you!"

His dad snatched the clothes away, but he was smiling. That was nice. Bruce wondered if anything could be done about the chain smoking.

He made a coffee while his dad got dressed. When he came through, the transformation was startling. The growth on the chin had gone, and the hair was washed, combed and brushed. The clothes were a good fit. There was a twinkle in his eye that Bruce had not seen before.

"Will, you look really good. Care for a coffee?"

"Yep. I feel better. I'm sorry about the whisky."

Bruce's heart leapt. An apology!

"Don't worry about it. There you go, white with one." He passed over the coffee.

"Bruce, this is not easy for me. I'm your dad, and I should have been helping you all these years. Instead I've caused you a lot of pain. To be honest, I've been frightened of getting in touch. I thought you would be so angry with me. Anyhow, here I am thanks to all that stuff in the papers. I mean to pay my way. What jobs can I do?"

This was wonderful.

"Will, I am upset and angry with you; it's no good denying it. However, I want to get over that and I'd be pleased if you would stay. As to doing jobs, I'll give it some thought. My income comes from piano teaching, as I think I told you. I go into a local school Monday to Friday, until mid morning. Then from four onwards, pupils come here. So we'll have to work round that in some way."

"That'll be fine."

"I think we should get you some shoes." The boots were far gone, to say the least.

"Right. And then I can help you at the supermarket."

His dad was sounding younger by the minute. This was all going better than Bruce had dared to hope.

Bruce put all the old clothes in the bath to soak, ready for a wash later, and they went off in search of shoes. They soon found a pair. Then, following a bite of lunch in a café, they collected what they wanted from the supermarket and came home.

"Dad, I'd like you to meet my good friends Bill and Gnilla. May I invite them round?"

"Of course."

It turned out they were free to come round that evening for some supper. Bill could not believe it was the same man.

"You're a magician," he whispered to Bruce when they were alone in the kitchen collecting food from the oven.

"Not at all. I think he's just grateful to have been accepted. I wish we could do something about the smoking, though."

"You'll never shift an addiction like that. And what about the alcohol? He'll be craving that again soon, I reckon. Then there'll be trouble. Whatever you do, don't give him any money."

That was all the private conversation they could manage. Bill and Gnilla were very good with Will, and it was a happy evening. They finally left at ten. Bruce tried to turn on the evening news, but as it was Saturday, the shorter bulletin would not be on until much

481

later, so he left his father watching something, and turned in. He was soon asleep.

68. From: Mission 12
To: Undisclosed recipients
Sent:

Well. There's lots to tell you.
Sean is doing fine. In fact, it's really good. He is quite the young man. He loves the plantation. I suppose to him it must seem like a miracle. He likes running in and out of the bushes and shrubs best. Clairie is growing up fast, and in a way that pleases me. She can be a handful when she chooses, but why not, at her age, I ask myself? The trauma of Mark's death is gradually fading; she is more relaxed now. I'm pleased. Celia is happier than I've seen her since we arrived at Targetto. How I hate that name! Surely we can agree on something a bit more snappy.

Some of the others want to call it the Earth, but I'm dead against it. It's too confusing. However, I have a strange feeling that it will be called the Earth in the end.

Now, the programmes. Syrup is gaining nearly ten seconds a night now. It's unbelievable. I thought it might take centuries to alter the length of the day significantly, but not a bit of it. So far, the cumulative improvement is over fifteen minutes. I'm not entirely certain about the volcano, myself, but the others tell me not to worry, so I'm trying not to.

Tip-top is doing something too. After several weeks of no apparent progress, we are now having an impact. The tilt so far is 0.5 of a degree. It may not sound much, but it's a great improvement. I reckon it has taken a lot of energy to get it started. That also means that when it is time to stop the programme, there will need to be a lot of reverse thrust.

Anyway, here we are, ready for the spaceship's arrival. They have nicknamed it the Aircraft Carrier. Their view is that we were the advance party, small and quick, and now the heavies are turning up. I told them not to feel threatened by it. I was absolutely certain it had not come to take over. They asked how I could be so sure. I said, "just wait and see."

Eventually, it came into view from the observation chamber. It is funny being in here again! Max was standing beside me watching it approach.

The spaceship was just as I had imagined. It is very long and thin, like a cigar. Distances are hard to estimate, but my guess is it might be two miles long by one hundred metres wide. There are lights every fifty metres along it. It slowed to a halt alongside us, about a mile away. Wonderful, really.

Big Nimp was not getting any messages from the new arrival, so Max and the others wanted to go on board. They got into a couple of landers and set off.

Margaret and I stayed put. She said, "I wonder what they will find?"

I'm afraid I yielded to temptation.

"It contains all the larger animals, in hibernation. The ship can be broken up into segments. Each section contains the next animals on up the food chain. The front end has the small ones – squirrels, dogs and so forth – and the big ones like panthers and tigers are at the other end."

Margaret said she thought that was possible. A few minutes, Max came on the line.

"Dad, you'll never guess. The whole spaceship is given over to animals in hibernation. The small ones are at the front..."

I handed the phone to Margaret with a smile. It was a happy moment. However, they have not grasped that the ship is made up of segments yet.

They were back an hour later. Max told Margaret and me all about it. There had not been breathable air on board; they had kept their spacesuits on throughout.

"No girls, then," I said.

"'Fraid not, Dad. Never mind."

As he was speaking, a strange expression appeared on his face. I turned round to see what he was looking at.

A figure, dressed in white, as Celia had been when she awoke, had just come out of the stairwell and was making its way slowly over towards us. I soon realised that it was a girl; nineteen years old, at a guess. Her brown hair was cropped short; she had a boyish expression. She was decidedly pretty.

"Excuse me," she said, "but I'm looking for Bruce."

"That's me," I said in surprise.

"Is there any chance of breakfast?"

Phil's cheeky notice was still there. She must have just woken. Instantly I was master of the situation.

"No, I'm sorry, I'm off duty at present, but my assistant chef here will see to your needs." I waved a hand at Max.

The look of gratitude he shot at me is something I will always treasure.

"This way," he said, leading her through to the gyp room.

I did not want to overhear them, so I wandered over to the piano. It is a while since I have played it. It is the most fabulous instrument!

I found myself playing a love song by Handel, not one that Max would know, thankfully. It wasn't intentional, but it seemed appropriate.

However, I had forgotten about Margaret. She was soon there alongside, joining in.
"Did you not see my lady
Go down the garden singing?
Blackbird and thrush were silent
To hear the valleys ringing."
It is a beautiful song, but I did not want to upset Max with the words. However, now we were going, it seemed a sacrilege to stop.
"Though I could never win her
I'll love her 'til I die."
I became aware that the new girl had come quietly across to join us. Max was still busy in the kitchen. This was not what I had meant at all.

After a few moments, he came out with a plateful. It was up to the usual standard that we Winters aspire to, I hasten to add. He looked rather concerned that she had wandered off.

"Can you play Memory?" she asked.

I began the introduction without comment, and she sang. Her voice was lovely. She must have trained as a singer.

Max stood there, transfixed. I was afraid he was going to drop the breakfast, or allow it to slither off the plate onto the floor. I hate egg yolk on carpet! In the event, he did neither. We soon reached the end of the song.

"That was lovely," I said. "You have such a beautiful tone. Max has your breakfast."

She accepted it with thanks. I contrived to think of something important to do in Celia's studio.

While I was admiring some of Celia's early works, I began to be troubled. Are the words 'Did you not see my lady' or 'Did you not hear my lady'?

It's funny how I can get a mental block on things. I tried both versions over several times. They seemed equally possible. Mind you, in this case, it hardly matters. You could fall in love with the girl's looks or her voice just as easily. I can see that Max already worships the ground she treads on. I am thrilled for him. Well done Jenta! (Jenta is the matchmaker in Fiddler on the Roof in case you did not know.) Computer dating has come of age.

Then I suddenly remembered. Waking up from hibernation takes between twenty-four and thirty hours to complete. It cannot be done instantly.

Now what is that all about? Had Big Nimp foreseen our conversation in some way, and started the wake-up routine in advance?

Bruce

Bruce was woken by a loud banging. It was pitch dark. There was somebody at the front door. He went to open it, and his dad fell in. There was blood on his lip and alcohol on his breath. Bruce reckoned he had been in a scuffle. He looked awful.

"Oh Dad!" he said in a despairing voice. Still, this was no time for recriminations. He tended the cut, which was not much more than a scratch, thankfully, and put him to bed. They would sort him out in the morning. Something like this was bound to happen, Bruce reflected.

It was only half past eleven. Bruce could not sleep after he had settled his dad. He tossed and turned. Then he had an idea.

He went through to the sitting room, and brought up past news stories. He wanted to see what was going on with regard to Pluto. You couldn't just lose a planet! However, there was not much more than the original headline. A group of amateur astronomers had agreed that they could no longer find Pluto where it should be in the night sky, confirming the original report.

This did not amount to very much, as you need professional equipment to be able to see Pluto at all. No backyard telescope would be powerful enough. Bruce reckoned that the professional astronomers, who were probably all looking at distant galaxies, had probably written the amateurs off as incompetent, and that few people had taken the story seriously. Maybe that was the case. Pluto did not just disappear! All the same, it was odd. You would not make a claim like that in public unless you were certain.

Bruce went back to bed and fell asleep quite soon.

69. From: Mission 12
To: Undisclosed recipients
Sent:

Max and Charmayne were married yesterday; Charmayne is the young lady's name, by the way. It was a very emotional occasion.

The ceremony took place on the spaceship in front of Big Nimp. Max wanted to follow in the footsteps of his parents. It seemed rather a good idea.

Charmayne looked very trim and neat. She has an impish sense of humour, and is lots of fun. She is also sporty. She and Max have enjoyed some good tennis together. He very sensibly does not overwhelm her with his brilliance, which he could easily do. They have also had some good doubles with Paul and Sandra even though they beat them easily.

Charmayne's dress was white and beautiful. Sorry, I can't describe it any better than that.

The guests included most of the earliest wakees. Celia wore a deep purple outfit which made her look fine. She has been rising up from her gloom and depression over the last months. She is so much happier now than she was. I'm glad we hung on through the difficult time.

Clairie was the bridesmaid. She was splendid; quite the young lady. It is amazing watching your children become adults in their own right.

However, there was one aspect of the day that I found really hard. I'm sorry, but I do draw the line at difficult page boys. Somehow we all knew that Sean was reluctant, and so everybody's focus was on him as the bridal party came forward, wondering whether he would behave. This was wrong. And that stupid hat! It was quite evident that he did not want to wear it. It took infinite coaxing and cajoling to get the thing on his head in the gyp room, and sure enough we had not gone three paces in public view before he snatched it off his head and threw it away.

I managed to keep my mouth shut about it, which I regard as a considerable achievement. I'm glad I did. It was Charmayne who was so desperate for him to be involved, and she was clearly pleased with his performance; I can't understand why.

Big Nimp took us through everything as he had done for Celia and me years before. It was quite like old times. I pointed out the operating chair to Celia in a quiet moment. She chose not to notice.

I hope you don't mind me confessing, but I found Max's courtship very difficult. I was thrilled for him and Charmayne; don't get me wrong. They are so obviously suited to each other. And their evident happiness is heart-warming.

No, it was reflections on my own path that were tricky to unravel. Suppose I had woken 'the one on the left' instead? Things would have turned out very differently. I keep telling myself that it is no good going back over old ground, and that there would be no Max and Clairie if I had not married Celia, and most of the time I am successful at keeping my feelings in check, but the courtship was an unsettling time.

Celia sensed my tension, which did not help us. Still, the battle to rekindle the flame has been going reasonably well recently, I would say. However, I have noticed that if I think it is going well, then something happens to make me gloomy, but if I think it is going badly, then something happens to make me feel brighter about it. Strange business.

We don't talk about Mark. Any grief that she had at his passing is long gone. I think she can see it all in perspective now.

Be thankful for what you have. That is the motto I am trying to live by. Also, don't expect everything by yesterday. Give it time. I would like to say one thing to you folks at home. If you are thinking of having an affair, don't. The amount of heartache and pain it causes is unbelievable.

There. Sermon over!

Well, you can guess what happened at the end of the ceremony. We became aware of three young men who had just come out of hibernation standing at the top of the stairwell watching the proceedings. I went over.

"Hello, I'm Bruce," I explained. "I'm afraid full English breakfast is off, but you can join in the wedding reception instead if you like. Make yourselves at home."

Clairie appeared not to notice them. She is going to play hard to get, I can see. Personally I hope that out of the three, the quiet one at the back wins. The fellow on the front at the left feels a bit pushy to me. However, I must keep out of it.

Dear oh dear, the complexities of life!

Bruce

"Dad?" Bruce said at breakfast.

"Will," replied his dad, firmly.

"Sorry, Will. Look, I've got a suggestion. These addictions you have to alcohol and nicotine..."

He got no further. His dad was NOT addicted. He had full control of himself, thank you. There were several swear words. Bruce waited patiently.

"Okay. I take it back. I was only thinking Bill Gnilla and I are all Christians. I was wondering, would you like us to pray with you, as Jesus did with people in the gospels?"

The answer was bound to be no. He had not expressed it well. But to Bruce's surprise, his dad said, "If you like."

It turned out he had seen something of the kind in prison and been secretly impressed. So Bruce made the phone call and fixed it for that evening.

Dad did not want to go to church, but was happy for him to go. Bruce left him reading the Lookout. As he had been on alcohol fairly recently, another crisis did not seem imminent; all the same, it was hard to concentrate on the service. Bill and Gnilla were pleased to come round that evening to pray.

"Don't expect any miracles," Bill warned. Why ever not? wondered Bruce.

Bruce was happy with the lunch. His dad had suggested steak and chips, and the result was pleasing. They were sitting over a coffee after finishing the washing-up when the doorbell rang.

Bruce opened it, and Banjo and Flossie streamed in.

"We knew you'd be here, Bruce. Hope you don't mind."

They were pleased to meet Dad. He remembered Banjo.

"Great to see you, Banjo," he said.

"And you too, Will," she replied. "Is Bruce looking after you alright?"

"Capital. So glad I came. Just had steak and chips."

"Good. Now we need your help. Bruce, what's this about you marrying an eighteen year old?"

Bruce was not pleased.

"Look, what is this? Some sort of inquisition? Why shouldn't I marry an eighteen year old if it's what we both want? I really can't see that it's any of your business."

"Bruce, you can't," Flossie said earnestly. "It's just not right."

"How do you know? You haven't even met her." Bruce was feeling very defensive.

This foray might be very well-meaning, but it was not much fun.

Dad broke in. "Is it the one who was here when I arrived?"

Bruce was taken aback. Well; why deny it?

"Yes, it is."

"You go for it, son. You'll make a great couple."

This was totally unexpected. Bruce did not know what to say. His dad continued.

"I guessed the moment I came in. Piano lesson indeed! No you get on with it. She'll do you fine."

Bruce laughed out loud. This was beyond belief. It had completely taken the wind out of Flossie's and Banjo's sails.

Banjo found her voice first.

"Well, are we going to be allowed to meet her?"

"Was she that one that was weeping at the funeral?" Flossie asked tenderly. Bruce was grateful to her.

"Yes; I saw it on a recording. I'm afraid I can't invite her over because she's been gated for going to New Zealand and back without her parents' permission."

They all expressed astonishment. This was a good line that he had stumbled upon.

"Well, Bruce, I just needed to hear it from your own lips. I can see that your mind is made up."

This was Bruce's cue.

"Flossie, you haven't brought Peter."

"I'm seeing him later." Flossie did not look happy.

"Well please give him my best wishes." Bruce was returning the kind glance Flossie had given him a few moments before. "I'll be thinking of you."

"You should have thought of her before!" exclaimed Banjo.

"Now, young Banjo," Dad broke in, "less arranging of the young people's lives, if you please. Let them make their own mess of things."

It was not a fortunate turn of phrase. However, nobody wanted to continue with the subject of marriage after that, so the conversation turned to lighter matters. After a while, the girls made their excuses and left. Bruce felt sorry for Flossie, but there was nothing he could do.

Bill and Gnilla were punctual at eight. Gnilla was very good with Will. Bruce was rather impressed.

"Right," said Bruce after a few minutes of conversation. "Dad has said that his appreciation of alcohol and nicotine is not an addiction, but nevertheless, he has agreed for us to pray with him that his liking for these things might be broken. I suggest..."

"Hang on a minute!" Will interrupted. "I don't remember agreeing to that!"

Oh dear.

"What are we to do then, Dad?"

"Well, if you could tread a bit gently, and remember that as well as causing a lot of pain, I've also been through a great deal of it as well, then I'd be grateful."

"Right, point taken," said Bruce. "I suggest we lay hands on Will like Jesus did in the gospels."

Bill was really not at all sure about this. For one thing, he had never done anything like it before, and he was fairly certain that for all his apparent confidence, Bruce hadn't either. Also, what were they trying to pray for? It all seemed about as clear as mud to him. However, Bruce's eyes were already firmly closed and his hand was laid on his dad's shoulder, so Bill decided that the only course of action was to join in. He glanced at Gnilla. Her eyes were shut too. So were Will's. At least Will did not appear to be threatened by the proceedings. Bill doubted that there was anything much that could go wrong. He reached out his hand, and laid it gently on Will's back. It felt a very strange thing to do.

Bruce's jaw was locked with concentration, and Bill noticed a bead of sweat on his forehead. "Relax!" he whispered. Bruce visibly tried to relax.

There was silence in the room for a minute or so. Then the doorbell rang. Bruce rose to answer it. It was Araminta.

"I raced over after church," she began, dropping her voice to a whisper when she saw what was happening in the room. "I should be having fellowship with the youth, really, but I thought we could have it here instead."

Bruce motioned her over to join in. Will opened one eye as she sat down and winked with it before closing it again.

"I'm not altogether sure..." Gnilla began, but Bruce silenced her.

"Give it time. We're all in such a hurry in today's world. Keep at it."

There was silence once more, until, unbelievably, the doorbell went again. This time it was Sarah. When Araminta saw her, she coloured.

"What are you doing here?" Sarah asked her in a whisper.

"Fellowship," Araminta whispered back. "We're praying for Bruce's dad."

Sarah came over and joined in, and was also greeted with a wink.

"What are we praying for?" she asked in a musician's pianissimo.

"Gout, I think," Araminta muttered.

After another minute or so of silence, Gnilla tried again.

"Look, I'm sorry to butt in, but I think it might be important."

Everybody opened their eyes.

"Will, I would like to check something out. I have the feeling that maybe you don't want to stop the smoking. In fact, correct me if I'm wrong, but I think you have been secretly hoping that if you smoke enough, it might kill you sooner rather than later."

Nobody said anything, Will least of all. After a few moments he let out a sigh.

"It's true," he said. "Until I came here, all I wanted was to die. Oh dear. I feel so bad."

A tear trickled down his face. Bruce put both arms round him and hugged him. Before long, Will was shaking silently. After another minute, the tears were pouring down his face, and he was sobbing openly. Everyone had withdrawn their hands when Gnilla had spoken, but by common unspoken agreement they all put them back again, while Bruce just held his dad tightly.

Will cried for a long time. Everyone was quiet. Eventually he dried his eyes.

"Thank you," he said. "I needed that." It was a solemn moment, but a wonderful one as well.

Will reached into his pocket and took out a crumpled packet of cigarettes.

"Go on, take them," he said. "I'm going to ditch them even if it kills me."

"No more talk of death, if you please!" said Bruce, his eyes shining. "We're here for you, Will."

"I know. When I came, I expected you to boot me out, or to let me stay but make my life hell, or something like that, but you've shown me great kindness, all of you. I'm most grateful. Actually, I don't think we've met," Will said, looking at Sarah.

"I'm Sarah, Araminta's sister."

"Pleased to meet you. Do you play the piano as well?"

"Yes." Sarah had an inspiration. "As a matter of fact, Araminta and I have been learning a piano duet, and we're ready to perform it now, aren't we Araminta?"

Araminta nodded, looking rather sheepish. They crossed over to the piano.

Considering that it was without music, their rendering of the opening movement of Beethoven's fifth symphony was not at all bad, but the levels of emotion in the two sisters were such that it was not their greatest performance.

At the end of it, after some polite applause, Sarah said firmly, "We need to be getting back now. Thank you for the fellowship," and hustled Araminta out.

"Oh dear," said Gnilla, voicing everybody's thoughts. Bruce gulped.

"Don't worry," said Will, clapping Bruce on the back. "It will all work out. You and me. We'll look out for each other."

When they finally went to bed, Bruce was feeling calmer. Sarah knew about their understanding now, and maybe her parents as well. For all his bravado to Banjo and Flossie, Bruce still felt very unsure of himself. Could he really pursue Araminta? However, Will had very much appreciated the evening, which was good. He had also gone twenty-four hours without clamouring for a drink, although Bruce was not going to get excited about that. One step at a time. There was a long way to go yet. Still, all in all, it had not been a bad weekend.

70. From: Mission 12
To: Undisclosed recipients
Sent:

Max and Charmayne took a most unusual honeymoon. They hitched a ride in one of the spaceships on the RSLM programme.

Well, why ever not? At least there was no danger of them being interrupted out there. Also, they are both very interested in space, observing the stars, and the terraforming programme, so it seemed like a good idea.

Here are excerpts from Max's report.

* * *

Day 14. A.M. Continued our observation of Jamerico. [That's one of the outer planets, by the way, Ed.] We have counted four moons so far. One of them might be large enough for a settlement one day. Swirling weather patterns on Jamerico suggest very high wind speeds are the norm there.

P.M. Began slowdown to rendezvous with asteroid. The replicator has been churning out the parts of the lander for several days now. We watched the little robots assembling it in the hold. It is surprisingly small considering the job it has to do, but perhaps that is not so strange as there is no involvement by humans in its operation, and therefore no life-support requirements.

We finally reached the asteroid at eleven at night. These machines never stop to sleep, of course. We stayed up for a while to watch the claws digging in before bedding down ourselves. I told Charmayne her hands were infinitely

495

sensitive and delicate compared to the mechanical arms, despite their great sophistication and infinite manoeuvrability; so gentle and soft…

[Max puts a lot of tenderness into his writing, which I will omit. I rather wish he wouldn't. I hope he's discussed it with Charmayne. She would hardly want it broadcast all over the galaxy, I reckon. I feel rather uncomfortable about it. Ed.]

Day 16. A.M. The asteroid has been encased in a net of huge cables. Then the spaceship used its motors to rotate the asteroid so as to get it lined up in the right direction, before the acceleration began. C and I had to strap ourselves in. The thrust was limited to three gees for our convenience, but even that was not much fun. After ten minutes or so it was reduced to two and then eventually to one, to our relief. It left us feeling dizzy. C was sick; I nearly was.

P.M. We are both feeling better now. I had been expecting to see other machines or asteroids about, but we did not. I suppose that the distances are so vast that the chances of meeting another ship are very remote. We are heading towards earth now. The machines are constantly at work cutting up lumps of ice. I thought we would be assembling the gun by now, but obviously not. The barrel is strapped alongside the ship; that's the best way to describe it. It won't start firing for another few days yet.

I was wondering how the blocks of ice would be kept separate, because it seemed to me that if you piled them up on top of each other, they would tend to freeze together. The solution is neat. They are deliberately joined together in just four places on each side of each block by little bumps in the ice. Then they can be easily separated when the time comes for firing.

496

The temperature in the ice storage facility is decidedly chilly, but there's nothing chilly about… [censored. Ed.]

Day 24 P.M. The gun has started up. It fires off four blocks every minute. The recoil is countered by the ship's motors, which speed up and slow down in perfect harmony. Most remarkable. It only took a few hours for the gun to be made ready for firing.

I have discovered that there is a constraint on the project. It is thought that the planet's atmosphere can only absorb so many blocks each second. To take care of this, the computers on board each spaceship communicate with each other in order to co-ordinate an air traffic control system. As a result, the rain of blocks is a steady one. Doing this in real time between moving spaceships is quite something, it seems to me.

Charmayne said this reminded her of… [Sorry. Off limits. Honestly! Ed.]

Day 32 P.M. All day, we have been slowing down. The gun keeps firing all the while. We have the planet on the screen, but you can't see the effect of the ice blocks. I suppose that is too much to hope. The asteroid is so big that it will take a long time to get the whole of it processed and fired off, I reckon. We have asked for a ride home on another ship when convenient. There's one coming for us in three days.

It's been good fun, but not as interesting as we hoped. However, it has been great being together.

* * *

That is all that is relevant. I've had to cut a lot of it out. It did occur to me after a while

497

that perhaps all the romantic stuff was put in for my benefit. I will see if I can ask him about it in a quiet moment. However, I am most keen not to interfere in their relationship in any way. Leave them to it.

From up here, I just see an occasional flash as a block burns up in the atmosphere, but Phil says that on the surface, it's like a distant firework display. At night time there are tiny pinpricks of light stabbing on and off in the darkness incessantly. He loves watching it.

Bruce

Bruce caught the 0745 train as usual on Monday morning. Maybe his dad would sleep on until twelve, when he would be home again. He hoped so. It would have been better to have had somebody with him, but there was nobody to ask. Bruce tried to leave the problem behind. He needed to focus on his teaching.

When he got to the school, there was nobody about, so he quickly took off his coat, knelt on the floor by the piano, and gently felt the underside of the soft pedal. There was no hypodermic syringe, thankfully. The pedal was ridged, like the one at home. There was nothing there. It had been worth looking; there might have been a message or something.

Bruce settled down to do some practice. There were nine minutes before his first pupil.

Suddenly, the door burst open. It was Araminta, bringing the note with the credit card number. He stood up.

"Hi. Thanks..." but he got no further. She had closed the door. It had a small pane of glass set in it, allowing people outside in the corridor to see whether the room was occupied or not. Araminta was not deterred. Before he realised what was happening, she had swept him to the side of the room that was out of view of the door, flung her arms round him and kissed him passionately all over the face.

It was not a thing Bruce would ever have considered doing. He was completely taken aback.

"Araminta!" he spluttered.

She silenced him.

"Not a word!" she insisted. "That's got to last all week! Everything's in the letter."

And as quick as she had come, she swirled out, leaving Bruce somewhat dazed, clutching the envelope.

Bruce was deeply thrilled; why not admit it. I do hope I can keep up with her, he mused. She is quite a girl. Then he had a frightening thought. Araminta did not normally wear lipstick, he was sure of it, but with her high spirits, might she have put some on so as to embarrass him? He quickly checked his reflection in the window, but he could not make himself out clearly enough to be certain. Anyway, he could not afford to make a mistake on this one. There was nothing for it. He would have to go to the boys' toilet.

Thankfully, it was only a few yards away. However, to be on the safe side, he covered his face with his handkerchief as he hurried along. Oh no, Jane the Head of Music was coming towards him!

"Good morning, Bruce," she said cheerfully. "I'm sorry you've got such a bad cold."

Bruce spluttered something inaudible as he blew his nose. This was most embarrassing.

He made it to the toilet without further incident. Oh no, there was no mirror. But surely, there used to be one? Yes, it had been torn off the wall a while back, he remembered, and not replaced. Really the caretaker might have done something about it by now!

Without even pausing to think about what he was doing, Bruce shot out of the boys' toilet and into the girls' one next door. There was the mirror. Thank goodness, his face was clear of lipstick, if not free from anxiety. Bruce hurried out again. Good, he had not been seen. Now slow down. Walk normally. Relax. His first pupil would be here in a few minutes.

When he got back into the practice room, he saw the letter. Feverishly he tore it open.

Araminta had really gone to town. There were nine pages in a delightfully feminine hand. But where was the card number?

Oh I see what she's done. The sixteen numbers come one at a time, at the beginning of each paragraph. Bruce picked one at random.

"Nine characteristics I love about you, Bruce, are..."

He would have to look at it later. He stuffed it in an inside pocket, and tried to return to the scale of C Sharp Minor, hands playing a sixth apart. It was not his best rendering.

-oOo-

Celia's phone was ringing. She answered after the usual three rings.

"Yes?"

"You need to know this." It was Simone. "You remember our mutual friend who supports Water Aid?"

"Yes?" Keep all communications as brief as possible.

"Well, he's just made them a donation which is enough to buy the whole outfit twenty times over, from an offshore account in his name."

The line went dead. This was remarkable. Celia wondered what it might mean.

-oOo-

Bruce was torn. On the one hand, it was important to get home to see that Dad was alright. On the other hand, he needed quarter of an hour to read Araminta's letter. In the end, he decided to go back to the bungalow, and if everything appeared fine, he would slip quietly into the garden and read the letter there. It was not too cold, despite it being November.

Everything seemed calm, so Bruce carried out his plan. Much of the letter was of an intimate and personal nature, but there were several items of news. Sarah had been cross with Araminta, but within bounds. She had foreseen the budding relationship, and deep down she approved. So that was good. However, Araminta felt concerned for her sister to find a mate, as did Bruce. Did he have any friends that might suit her?

This seemed a bit tricky. However, there was more. Araminta wanted to tell her parents about Bruce. Was he happy about this?

Bruce's first reaction was one of dismay. Her parents were bound to disapprove! But then, if Sarah knew already, and if Araminta wanted to tell them, perhaps it was better to bite the bullet. She could tell them if she liked.

She was still not clear about a flying lesson, but if it was to happen, it would be Saturday at 2.30, as before, but in a different location; a small map was enclosed. Further communication later. That sounded nice.

Bruce was still reading when suddenly a window opened not far from his head.

"Son, do you mind going back to the last page; I had not quite finished reading it before you turned over."

The cheek of it! However, the smile on Will's face was such that Bruce knew it was a wind-up. It was wonderful to see him looking so cheerful.

"Will, you codger! This letter is personal and private, I'll have you know. I'm coming in."

Bruce made his way back to the front door, and stuffed the letter in his pocket.

"Now, no more of that!" he said, good-naturedly. "How are you doing?"

"Fine, thanks. The Lookout is not a bad paper when all comes to all."

There appeared to have been no mishap. No whiff of alcohol or cigarette smoke. Dare he begin to hope…?

"Can we get me some more clothes, Bruce? I feel Okay about visiting the shops now I'm better dressed. Then I want to turn my hand to something useful."

And so, what had seemed an impossibility at first gradually began to take shape. Will grew stronger each day. He really seemed to have kicked the alcohol and cigarettes, but as Gnilla pointed out, it might just be that he had decided to live and was no longer hoping to die. His progress broke all the rules of addiction, as far as Bruce could see, but really he knew nothing about it, which was probably just as well. By unspoken agreement, neither of them mentioned what was happening.

When Araminta rang first thing the following morning, Bruce told her that he had remembered the second tune in the mystery piece of music. It was a Christmas carol.

"Perhaps it's an early Christmas greeting," Araminta suggested, although it was still only November. "Maybe she doesn't trust the post."

Bruce agreed to her telling her parents about them. She in turn had been allowed to go flying on the Saturday afternoon, so a lesson was definitely on. Rather than Bruce paying to hire the suit for the afternoon, if he was sure he wanted to buy one, it would be cheaper to order it now, and she would bring it along. So Bruce phoned the number that she gave him.

It was while he was making the call that an idea came to him. He asked the salesperson to hold.

"Will," he enquired, "I'm just ordering a sky-suit, you know, for flying in. Are you interested for yourself?"

"No, thanks. I'll keep my feet on the ground if you don't mind. Kind of you to offer."

So Bruce only ordered the one suit.

"I'm having my second flying lesson on Saturday," he explained when he had finished the call. "You can come along if you like." He could not resist adding, "you may recognise the flying instructress."

"Don't tell me," laughed Will. "Yes, I'd love to come. Then I can tell the instructress that my gout is much better."

Will was very good about keeping out of the way of the piano pupils. This meant that most of them did not even know he was there. He did not meet Celia on Tuesday evening, for example. The lesson went without incident. However, when Sarah arrived on Thursday evening, he made a point of saying hello before retiring. Sarah did not want to talk about Araminta. Bruce felt rather awkward, but as he did not raise the subject either, the lesson went off well enough. However, there was one amusing moment when they had been practising rhythms without the notes. In an earlier lesson, Bruce had shown Sarah how to learn the rhythms of the right and left hands by tapping them on her knees.

"It's neat," he said; "by tapping your own body, you internalise the rhythms. Incidentally, do you know how to do a galloping horse?"

Sarah did not, so Bruce demonstrated. "It's a threefold action. First you do a light clap of the hands, followed by right hand on right knee, followed by left hand on left knee. Then you repeat it over and over again. Like this."

Bruce's performance sounded very realistic.

"I'm not surprised that you are gifted at being a galloping horse!" Sarah commented with a chuckle. Bruce coloured slightly. It did seem rather apt.

She feels strange about it, Bruce reckoned when she had gone, but she's not opposed to us. He felt grateful to her. Shame he could not marry them both, really, but Jacob had got in a terrible mess taking on two sisters at once. It was definitely not a good idea!

```
71. From: Mission 12
To: Undisclosed recipients
Sent:

It's happened, on both sea and land.
Accelerating growth. I knew it would come, sooner
or later.
     In the sea, the plankton was clearly very
happy. It started spreading rapidly. I don't know
the exact mechanism - something feeding on the
plankton, something feeding off that, something
feeding off that, etc, but however it came about,
suddenly we became aware of a rash of tiny
elvers; little eels to the uninitiated. They were
everywhere, just as I foresaw months ago!
     This meant that we needed to introduce the next
fish up the food chain, namely what feeds on
elvers, if we were not to get a runaway
situation. Then those in turn will flourish, and
```

in a few months we will need to introduce the next fish, and so on. It is a bit scary. I hope it all works. This is what the boffins have been preparing for, of course. They say they are ready for any eventualities. Ha Ha! Talk about hopeless optimism.

On the land, it was aphids. Tiny insects to you and me. I'm not yet sure which birds enjoy those. Anyway, they are being released at this moment, even though there aren't enough trees for them to perch in yet.

I am so thrilled by it all. One of the things I have been looking forward to is to see a flock of seagulls above the sea, wheeling around on a windy day. I may yet witness it during my lifetime.

Some things cannot be speeded up. It's hopeless expecting trees to grow overnight. However, the saplings are coming on. The plantation is doing well. We have also begun some other little plantations on the peninsular.

I was pleased to see more frogs recently. Do you remember the Greek scholar? I get on well with him. We have been reading the New Testament in Greek together. I had rather got out of the habit of it. Life has been so hectic recently. Anyway, his frogs are doing well.

It's great feeling that we are all part of a huge team, working together; man and machine.

Bruce

Saturday finally dawned. When it was time to leave for the flying lesson, Will came through from his bedroom looking very dapper. He had found a cravat in a drawer.

"I used to wear this all those years ago!" he declared, with evident pleasure. Bruce felt very moved. His dad had certainly messed up in a big way, but he was proving now that it is never too late to start again. It was so encouraging.

They took a taxi from the station to the recreation ground. It was by a wood, and was itself surrounded by trees, which made it rather more secluded than the previous venue.

The usual crowd of young people was there. The sky-flying seemed to have turned into a weekly meeting, rather in the style of the skateboarders of granddad's day. That had been all the rage for a while, apparently, before dying away.

Araminta greeted them both in a manner that was restraint itself on her scale. She handed Bruce a plastic bag.

"Is this all?" he asked in surprise.

"Yes; the size has reduced. With these latest suits, you wear them under your normal clothes. In fact, some people keep them on all the time. Their thermal properties make them very comfortable. You will need to go into the hut to change."

Bruce did as he was told. There were some printed instructions for putting the suit on. It was more like a leotard than anything else he reckoned. However, there was the familiar tingling sensation that he remembered from before. He soon had his normal clothes back on top.

"Araminta," he said, when he had gone back outside, "where are the gloves that you zip on, and the weights for the legs?"

"All that's long gone. You remember the main feature of the suit was that it was intuitive and responded to your pointing?"

Bruce did.

"Well, that principle has been taken to its logical conclusion. The suit learns your body position, as it were. Now, all you have to do is to think of going in a certain direction, and the little body movements that you make unconsciously are sufficient to convey that information to the suit, so away you go. To begin with, when the suit hardly knows you, the system is a bit clumsy, but the longer you wear it and use it, the more refined it gets. Some people find that a mere twitch of the eyebrows is sufficient to direct themselves about. Of course, their body is doing more than just moving the eyebrows in fact, but that's what it feels like. Oh yes, and apparently the new suits work anywhere, not just on earth, because the old suits would not work on the moon, for example, but these ones do."

Bruce was tremendously impressed.

"It's amazing!" he breathed. He recalled his longing to go flying with Araminta on the moon. This was the next best thing.

"Take-off and landing are intuitive too. The old button has gone. The only thing left is an on-off switch. Just switch on, jump gently upwards, and away you go."

Bruce tried it. He was soon in the air. Will applauded; he had found the only available bench, and was sharing it with another older spectator.

Araminta came up to join him.

"Now, would you like to revise what you did last time? Try out the basic movements, moving to right and left and up and down, by gentle but decisive body movements."

The new suit was wonderful. Bruce soon found that he could direct himself about with ease. All his training as a musician proved helpful; he was soon controlling his movements well.

"You are clever," Araminta gasped, as she tried to keep pace with him. He waited for her, and took her hand. He found a resistance in doing so.

"Don't forget that the suit protects you from other objects. However, it also senses if you want to touch something, so it will allow you to do so."

"However did you do that formation flying?" asked Bruce, remembering the spellings of his name that Araminta and her friends had performed in the air for his benefit. They had held hands while airborne.

"It used to be much harder with the old suits, but now it's easy. Shall we fly along holding hands?"

This was glorious. They took it in turns to lead. It was the ultimate in dancing, Bruce reckoned.

The recreation ground was next to a hill that was covered with fine old oak trees. There were no houses. Without discussion, they moved away from the other fliers and came to an open space among the trees at the foot of the hill, where they had a little privacy. They cuddled up together about forty feet up.

"Araminta, I'm so glad that we have become close," Bruce said. "I haven't been so happy in years. I'm nervous of allowing myself to enjoy it in case something goes wrong."

"I'm thrilled too. It's what I've wanted for quite a while now. I haven't told my parents yet, but I think they are beginning to guess. I just can't stop myself being happy round the home."

"When you have told them, I would like to come over, if you approve."

"Of course. I hope we can all be one big happy family."

"Now," said Bruce, "come over this way. There's something I want to show you."

They moved along to an area where there was a clear drop beneath them. They were about sixty feet up.

"Araminta, are you ready for a challenge? I want you to catch this before it reaches the ground."

Before she had time to grasp what he meant, Bruce had taken something small out of his pocket and dropped it. It sparkled and glistened as it fell.

She bolted after it like lightning, and managed to snatch it before it reached the turf. She bounded back up.

"Bruce, it's the most beautiful ring. Does it mean…?"

"Yes it does. Araminta, will you marry me?"

"Bruce, yes, of course I will. Oh you are lovely!"

Araminta was so excited that she did a series of somersaults, going up and up at first and then plunging down and down, almost to the ground. Bruce was reminded of renaissance paintings of angels tumbling through the skies that he had seen on the walls of continental churches. She looked dazzling in the sun. I am the happiest man alive, he thought to himself, but I don't think I could do all that turning. However, I'll have a go…

Bruce started swooping about like a swallow. It was a glorious feeling. When he looked for her a minute or so later, he found Araminta waiting a few feet away. They hugged and kissed.

"Come and tell my dad," Bruce said. But Araminta was not ready. She soared off heavenwards in a graceful glide. Bruce laughed and went after her. Together they criss-crossed the sky from side to side. It was a moment never to be forgotten.

Will was delighted, as Bruce had known he would be. The ring looked lovely on Araminta's finger.

"However, it's a secret until her parents have agreed," Bruce insisted. "Nobody else must know."

"You're quite right, Bruce," Araminta said. "I don't want to present it to them as a *fait accompli*. I want them to feel involved, but I do hope they won't object. So I won't wear it publicly yet."

They both did some more soaring about. Bruce was getting confident in the use of his suit. He found it a wonderful thing.

"I'm really glad I have a suit of my own," he said. "I reckon I could practise by myself, now."

The time fled by. Araminta soon needed to go back home to keep her word to her parents.

"Not too much glowing!" Bruce insisted as they parted. It was going to be difficult. She looked so delighted.

"Well, boy," Will said, as they travelled home, "I hope you're pleased. I never thought I would see this day. I reckon you've found a good one, if I may say so. I hope you'll both be very happy together."

Bruce was too full of happiness to say anything. However, there was a slight niggle at the back of his mind. It all felt too perfect, somehow. He just hoped that nothing would go wrong.

```
72. From: Mission 12
To: Undisclosed recipients
Sent:
```

There is so much encouragement here. In a word, the settlement programme is going better than I ever dared to hope.

I will report on the three main projects in reverse order.

RSLM is raining down one ton blocks at the rate of forty-seven a minute now. It may sound promising, but I tell you, it's a drop in the ocean! The number of blocks required is huge, as I explained earlier.

However, it takes me back to the early days of the journey from earth, when I was the humble caretaker watching the screen to see how many miles we had done. Do you remember? Tea for two, Benito?

The number of miles still to go was so depressing that I could not bear to look at it. However, the fact is… we're here!

Then there were just twenty-four sleeping astronauts, as far as I knew. I can hardly believe I had the courage to wake one. I think it was because there was nobody else around to say no. I'm very bold in my thoughts when I'm on my own; it's only when there are other people present that I lose my nerve.

Anyway, it was great with Celia in the early days, even if it did almost cost me my life. I would not have missed it. I'm still hopeful that more of our early intimacy will come back.

Sorry! I'm digressing. I'm trying to tell you that in the same way as the number of miles still to travel seemed impossibly large then, but we did it all the same! So, in the same way, the number of blocks required seems unattainable now, but we are going to persist for century after century, and we will do it. Promise.

Yes, it was bad grammar just back there, and Roget alias the Fowler was desperate to correct it, but I said no. You have to be firm with these computers. It's the only way.

Tip-top has achieved over one degree of tilt by now. It's great news. And Syrup has brought the length of the day below thirty-two hours for the first time. It's 31.59.04 hours at present.

Well, breaking through the thirty-two hour barrier seemed a good excuse for a party, so we arranged it. Somebody suggested fancy dress. It was a good idea, as the replicators can churn out any outfit you want.

I went as Bottom, from a Midsummer Night's Dream. It was a statement. I know I have behaved like an ass at times, and I have been known to have the occasional brainstorm, but hopefully I will turn out alright in the end!

The only drawback with my costume, which was universally admired, was that the ass's head became unbearably hot after a while. The solution was to go outside occasionally, take it off, and sponge myself down. Still, its jaw action was good, so speaking and eating were no trouble.

Celia went as Van Gogh, carrying an easel and a palette, and dressed in a dishevelled manner. She even had a bandage on one ear. I think that for her too it was also a confession; Van Gogh messed up in his relationships, but he produced some great works nevertheless. Celia has taken up the brush again, by the way.

Max and Charmayne went as Jack and Jill, each carrying a pail, and dressed in brightly coloured shorts and tops. I think they did it because of the falling about required by the nursery rhyme. The strange thing was that whenever one of them was on the verge of tumbling over, the other always seemed to be there ready to catch.

Clairie went as Venus, the little Minx. Properly clothed, thank goodness. She must have spent hours on her hair and make-up. The three young men were all round her like bees round a honey pot. I hope she knows what she's doing.

Paul and Sandra annoy me. They could not decide who to go as, so they just turned up in some casual clothes.

That says it all, I reckon. They live together, but don't marry on principle. What principle, I ask myself?

I have strong views on this, as you have probably grasped. They come from my time in the school choir. This was the most pathetic gathering. There were generally about eight or nine of us that turned up on Mondays in the lunch hour. The teacher was so frustrated and depressed. He had notices up all over the school saying Choir All Welcome, but they did no good.

Then one week, he closed the choir down. I was surprised. Next thing, he was going round the school asking all the musical young people this question: "If there was a choir of thirty strong that sang in four parts and did regular concerts, would you join?"

A surprising number of us said yes. He soon had a list of thirty-four names. So that was the new choir!

The first rehearsal was wonderful. But then he surprised us. When some others came up and asked if they could join after all, he said no. The new rule was that you could only join or leave at the beginning of term. If you were in it, you had to commit yourself to a full term and doing the concert. Nobody else could join until the beginning of the next term.

You can imagine what happened. The choir went from strength to strength. I don't remember anybody leaving. The concerts were good fun.

Whatever else it achieved, I thought it was a wonderful lesson for human relationships. As long as it was easy come easy go, we got nowhere in the choir. If two people drift into a relationship, then what is to stop them drifting out of it again later? Whereas, if you make it hard to start a relationship and hard to end it too, you get more stability. So I think that marriage, with its certificates and all that

legal stuff, is a good thing. It makes the young
people mean business.

Now, here's the feeble part. I feel quite happy
sounding off about it to all of you folks back
home, but have I got the guts to go to Paul and
Sandra and tell them they should marry? No, I
haven't. Pathetic, isn't it? It's because I'm
frightened of being shouted at if I do.

Some things don't frighten me at all, but other
things do. Funny business. I notice that I'm
quite happy to tell you about this, because you
are so far away that you cannot respond, but I
would find it really hard to tell somebody here
about it, face to face. Is everybody like that, I
wonder, or is it only me?

Back to the party. Margaret went as Maria from
the Sound of Music. I managed to get her on one
side in one of my ass's-head-off moments. Did her
outfit mean that she was hoping that the captain
might emerge, some handsome stranger, and whisk
her of her feet, I asked? No, not at all. She
enjoyed singing, and she enjoyed looking after
children. She saw herself as an enabler.

Funny that I felt Okay about having that
conversation.

I never saw Phil and Dickon at the party,
incidentally, unless they were the pantomime
horse.

There are over four hundred of us in the
settlement now. Skills are beginning to emerge.
The band was good, for example, and the catering
too. There is now a money system in place. Some
people want cash, but so far that has been
resisted. There is so much I could tell you about
the settlement, but I tend to focus on the
aspects of it that interest me. I'm sure you
understand.

I think the best features of what we are doing
here are the three terraforming projects. The
goal is a twenty-four day and a twenty-three

512

degree tilt, and the seas a metre deeper. I think about these constantly. They will make a huge difference to the living conditions here. I won't live to see the last one, but I might witness the first two. It's so exciting. Patience is the name of the game. It's worth it for the sake of our grandchildren.

Talking of which, Charmayne says she is expecting...

Bruce

The rest of the weekend passed off happily. Will was clearly enjoying life, although finding him jobs to do, as he put it, was proving something of a challenge. Still, there was no rush. At present, it was simply a pleasure to have him around. Bruce could not get over the fact that with regard to the nicotine and the alcohol, Will had had no relapses. It was marvellous.

They tuned into the news on TV on Sunday evening. The main story immediately caught Bruce's attention.

"Astronomers have reported a light loss from the planet Neptune, in the order of ten to twelve percent." Bruce shook his head in disbelief.

"So far, only one image has been obtained from this distant planet. This is because the world's telescopes are all fully booked up to two years ahead by research scientists. However, Pedro Alvarez of Mexico kindly gave up half an hour of his allotted time, allowing this photograph to be taken."

It was not a good photograph, but even so, it was clear that there was a large patch of shade covering about a fifth of the planet, at five 'o clock on the disc. The announcer continued.

"Those of you who use digital images will know that as you zoom into a photograph, the image becomes grainy, and can even become tessellated."

"Small squares," whispered Bruce. The view was zooming in.

"What we don't know is whether these blocks are simply a result of the optics. At present, the scientists we have spoken to are simply baffled by this image. Rest assured, we will keep you up to

513

date with this story as it proceeds."

The view had zoomed in many times. The result was extraordinary. It looked as if the bottom of Neptune was covered with a very large number of tiny black rectangles.

Bruce was fascinated. The bulletin moved on to other matters, but Bruce switched it off.

"What do you make of that?" he asked.

"It reminded me of bacteria seen under a microscope," said his dad. "Of course, it can't really be that. I think the TV people are just as mystified by it as we are."

"Those are pretty much my thoughts too. Very strange. I'll switch on again in the morning. Shall I wake you?"

"No; the Lookout will cover it, I expect. I hope your teaching goes well tomorrow. Good night."

Bruce was tired and fell asleep without any trouble. He woke unexpectedly in the middle of the night, and was instantly alert. It was rather odd. The alarm clock said 0144. The full moon was shining brightly through the crack between his curtains.

Bruce had a strange feeling. There was something important. He could not put his finger on it. Then he remembered the news bulletin. A sudden thought came into his mind. Oh no, surely not... It couldn't be...

Bruce sat up in bed. His thought was taking shape. It was a dreadful notion. He got out of bed and started pacing up and down.

"Oh my land," he said out loud. "This is really serious."

Within three minutes, there was no doubt left in his mind. This was a crisis of the first order. What made it even worse was that it was going to be practically impossible to explain what was happening to anybody else. Nobody would believe him! Especially after the liar and fraud fiasco.

Bruce broke out in a cold sweat. He had experienced this once before, when lying ill in bed. It is most unpleasant. One moment you feel normal; the next, your back is covered with cold sweat, and your pyjamas are soaked. It felt awful. Still, there was no time to worry about that now.

Shaking violently, Bruce went through to the phone. He dialled a number.

Let her answer, please God, let her answer... Come on, come on!

"Yes?"

Thank goodness.

"Celia, it's Bruce here. I need your full and complete attention. There is a grade A crisis facing the human race. Have you seen the news about Neptune?"

"Bruce, it's nearly two in the morning and I've got a busy day ahead. I hope you are not wasting my time."

"I assure you, I'm not. Celia, you've asked me to trust you more than once, and now I'm asking you to trust me. Believe me, whatever you and your organisation are doing pales into insignificance beside this. Did you see the photographs of Neptune?"

"No."

"Right. Can you call up the evening news on the TV and watch the story about Neptune and then ring me back while I get dressed."

"Okay Bruce. I'm trusting you!"

The line went dead. Bruce went into the bathroom. There was no time for a bath, so he ran water into the basin, and washed all the sweat off. It was horrible, but he soon felt much better.

All the time, his mind was racing. He already knew what he had to do.

He had just finished towelling himself when the phone rang.

"Right. I've seen the bulletin. What of it?"

"Celia, I know what those blocks covering Neptune are. They are self-replicating machines."

"Bruce, have you gone mad?"

"Now, please listen to me. I want you to act first and then argue with me afterwards. I need a spaceship with six months of life support on board, and an automatic operating system. I'm going to Neptune. Oh yes, and good communications including video."

"Bruce, even if I could lay it on, it will cost the earth. Who's going to pick up the bill?"

"Celia, it will cost more than the earth if you don't. I'll pay.

515

Jim's last action was to give me some funds. I've still got fifteen hundred million pounds of it left."

Celia went quiet. She could not argue with this, because she knew it was true.

"Actually, it's nearer sixteen hundred million now, because of the interest," she said after a moment.

Bruce managed to force a staccato laugh.

"Look, this is no time for humour. Can you lay on the spaceship and be here with a flying car inside thirty minutes? If it turns out I'm wrong, then Jim's money will have gone on some nice photos of Neptune, and that's no loss. But if I'm right, then I think I know what needs to be done."

"Bruce, for anybody else, I would put the phone down, but believe it or not, I do trust you. I'm going to stick out my neck on this one. Expect me in thirty minutes."

She rang off.

Wonderful! Well done Celia. Now, I need to focus, Bruce thought. I'll start by packing.

Something made him look up. There was Will, standing in the open doorway, looking very quizzical.

"Bruce, what's happening?"

"There's no time to explain. That story about Neptune. I reckon I know what's going on. I've just chartered a spaceship to go out and look."

"I thought that was it. I've been here for several minutes. Good on you, boy. I'm coming with you."

This was ridiculous.

"No, Dad. It's out of the question. I may get myself killed. I need somebody here to put off the piano pupils and answer questions. Please don't be difficult."

"Will, not Dad," said his dad firmly. "You need help. So what if it's dangerous. It's no loss if I snuff it. I tell you I'm coming. You try stopping me!"

Bruce suddenly laughed out loud. Why not?

"Alright, although it's not quite the kind of job I had in mind for you."

"That's better. Now are all the piano pupils in this little book?"

Will picked up the book by the phone.

"Yes."

"Then I'll bring it along and phone them when it gets light."

It was an easy solution.

"Right," said Bruce. "We need to pack our personal clothes. Celia will be here in twenty-five minutes."

Will got dressed promptly, and presented himself with his holdall. Meanwhile, Bruce gathered his things together. He assembled various odds and ends, including a ball of string, some stout wire, a box of matches, candles, his flying suit and various tools. He also put in some old fashioned shirt collar studs, and his camera. He put everything into a large rucksack. As an afterthought, he stuffed in a small rucksack as well.

Celia was as good as her word. They locked up and were soon on their way.

"Now, Bruce, you've got fifteen minutes to persuade me that your hare-brained scheme is a good idea."

"Okay," said Bruce. "I don't need to explain to you that I have daydreams; you already know. For some time now, I have been imagining the activities of Mission 12, a settlement programme on a planet at a nearby star. Without going into detail, it soon became apparent that the job of terraforming the planet was going to take millions of years if it was done in a conventional manner. So, what was needed was a strategy of self-replicating machines. That is, each machine, instead of simply doing its job, begins by making a replica of itself, or maybe several replicas, before going ahead and carrying out its task. In this way, instead of just having a few dozen machines carrying out the work, you soon have several hundred, and then several thousand, perhaps even several million."

Bruce stopped, as if he had given all the explanation he needed to give.

Celia was mystified.

"Well, so what? How does that connect with the blur at Neptune?"

Bruce realised that he had only given part of the picture.

"Oh yes. Sorry. These machines have to be made from something, don't they. So somebody teaches them to replicate by scooping up raw material from a moon, for example. Now let's imagine that the person who sets up the programme fails to put in a termination clause, for whatever reason. Suppose the settlement gets wiped out by some disaster, for example, or he doesn't get round to it, or some of the machines slope off while his back is turned. Then the machines keep on duplicating. They get to the point where there are so many of them, doubling up all the while, that they completely dismantle the moon. So what now? These are unthinking machines remember, even if they appear to be highly sophisticated. Their instruction is to go forth, increase and multiply! So they do. They move on to another moon for their raw material. The day comes when they have exhausted the entire star system. So guess what? They set off for another star to carry on multiplying there.

"Now do you get it? What is happening at Neptune is that somebody somewhere has messed up, and a self-replication programme has gone out of control."

"Well, it's an intriguing idea, but I simply can't see why it should be the case. It seems so far-fetched! For a start, you seem to have assumed an advanced form of extra terrestrial intelligence, just like that."

This was true.

"Also, why should your daydreams be the key to something happening in reality?"

Bruce had not thought of this either.

"I can't explain it, I'm sorry. I just know that they are."

"Alright. Now even supposing that it is all true, what on earth is puny little you going to be able to do about it when you get there?"

"Well, I've got one or two ideas."

Bruce was feeling defensive by now. He did not want to go into details. It had all seemed so clear back at the bungalow. Here was Celia filling his mind with doubts. Then he remembered something.

"But don't you remember Pluto? It was on the news a while back. They can't find it any more. I'm telling you, it's because it's been eaten by machines. Also, Bill and Gnilla reported that the

518

amateur observers in California have not seen any shooting stars all summer. All that orbiting debris must have been gobbled up as well."

"You are wonderful, Bruce. Now, I'm going to let you into a secret. We do actually have a spaceship that's been mothballed. It's just sitting there doing nothing. So actually, the only expense of the mission is going to be the energy to fly the thing, which is negligible, and the cost of the life support, as you put it, by which I suppose you mean egg and chips and matters of that kind. So I'm giving you your chance! However, I do ask that you keep in touch with us throughout, and in particular that you send back pictures of anything you see that seems unusual. Then if there is something strange going on out there, we can see, and plan appropriate action."

Bruce felt he could not ask for more.

"Thank you," he said. He wanted to add, "just you wait. I'll be proved right!", but he refrained. Better to be cautious. If there were self-replicating machines as he imagined, then they were certainly going to capture people's interest before long.

Then he had a thought.

"Is the ship fully automatic, like the one to the moon; in other words, will I be able to guide it unaided?"

Celia laughed. "Don't worry. You won't even have to change gear. You simply tap in to the computer. Everything comes up on the screen. A child could do it."

This was reassuring. Bruce was glad there would be no extra staff on board. They would only ask a lot of questions and raise difficulties.

Bruce had assumed that they would be travelling to the same spaceport from where he had left for the moon, on his ill-fated holiday. This proved correct. In addition, the spacecraft was similar to the one he had been in before, but with no rows of seats. The floor area had been divided into rooms. Bruce was pleased about this. He and Will could have separate sleeping quarters. It would seem homely.

There were one or two disgruntled staff in white coats about, who were inclined to grumble at being called on to work at this unearthly hour. Yes, he could have a communication channel reserved for him. No, there weren't any vehicles on board - he would have to make do with the transports on the space suits if he went outside. Yes there were spacesuits for him and his co-pilot. Bruce did not like to call him his dad; it did not seem very professional, somehow. No he would not have to steer; the guidance system was automatic; just give your destination and it did the rest. Yes there was a tool set; what did he think they were, some sort of gym-crack outfit?

In the end, it was all arranged. Bruce was most grateful to Celia. She was looking at him with an amused 'I don't know!' expression when they walked up the gangplank.

Bruce was glad that their luggage had been stowed in advance; it would not have looked good to be struggling on board with their rucksack and holdalls, somehow. As it was, he felt like something out of a cartoon strip in one of his granddad's comics.

They took off. Bruce explained to Will that the one gee acceleration would make them feel twice their normal body weight in the vicinity of earth. Will gave him a blank stare. Bruce decided to keep technical information to a minimum from now on.

The simple fact was that even though Neptune was on the same side of the sun as the earth at present, thankfully, it was still weeks away, so Will suggested they get some sleep, as their night had been somewhat disturbed. It seemed like a good idea. Before long, they were both slumbering gently, while the spaceship powered on towards the stars.

-o0o-

When they woke, Bruce's watch said the time on earth was 0830.

"Time for breakfast, then" said Will with enthusiasm.

"No!" said Bruce. "It means that I haven't alerted the school in time, and I have let down my first pupil. You need to make those phone calls you promised."

"Oh yes, of course."

520

Will pulled out his phone and tapped in a few numbers.

"I don't think that will do any good," Bruce was beginning to say, when he was interrupted by a loud "Yes?" from a loudspeaker. Will took charge.

"Cowboy calling ranch. How do you read? Over."

"Ranch calling cowboy," said the voice. "By holding the Lookout in front of me face, as long as I don't get interrupted by phone calls. Now, what can I do for you?"

It turned out that Will could use his phone in the normal way. The communication system would send the calls to base, and they would be automatically passed on to the phone network. All very handy. Will was soon in touch with the school.

"I'm afraid Mr. Winter will not be in for a week or two... He's unavoidably detained... As a matter of fact, he's on his way to Neptune on a delicate mission... No, this is his co-pilot speaking... Do you mind, I resent that very much..."

Bruce signalled to Will to pass him the phone.

"Jane, is that you? Yes, I'm afraid it's true. Perhaps you missed the news last night... Right, well, it's too complicated to explain. Just keep watching the news. I'll be in touch again in a few days. Bye."

"Will, did you have to refer to us as Cowboy?"

"Son, it's nearly Christmas, and all my life I've wanted a cowboy outfit. Now I'm part of one, so I might as well enjoy it."

Bruce laughed. It was no good getting too tense.

"Alright," he agreed. "Cowboy it is."

Next he spoke to Bill and Gnilla. They had not seen the news either.

"Really you take some keeping up with!" was Bill's response. Of course he would tell Marjorie. Will read out the phone numbers of the pupils who would need to be contacted; this seemed the easiest solution. Bill agreed to act as a base station in case Bruce needed to pass on messages.

Bruce had one more rather difficult request.

"Bill, I wonder if you could speak to Araminta. I'm afraid she will be rather upset with me. I imagine she would like to have been consulted before I went off. Can you soften up the ground? Try and tread delicately? Tell her I love her, and that she really will be pleased with me for what I am doing, in the end."

He hoped it would be alright. It was the only part of the preparations that he had felt uncomfortable with, but he could hardly have rung in the middle of the night. Also, she might have tried to stop him, and then what would he have done?

"Right. Breakfast." Will was not to be put off again.

They soon had some cereals and toast on the go.

"Now," Bruce said when they had finished, "I need to do some thinking. Let's see if the ship's computer can help us."

They soon had information in front of them on a screen. The journey to Neptune was scheduled to take forty-one days.

"It's too slow," muttered Bruce. "We'll have to go faster. Unless…"

He tapped in for the other planets. Journey times to Saturn and Uranus were even longer; they must be further off than Neptune at present, beyond the sun somewhere. Jupiter was forty days. No advantage. Then Bruce suddenly saw light. The asteroid belt! That would be a natural draw for the machines. The raw materials would be most accessible there.

The asteroid belt was just sixteen days off. Surely, it was worth a try.

He phoned Celia. She was soon on the line.

"Celia, it's Bruce. I'm altering course to the asteroid belt. I reckon the machines will gather there sooner rather than later. Can you work out a journey time from the asteroid belt on to Neptune, in case my hunch is wrong?"

The answer came back eight minutes later. It was thirty days.

"Definitely worth a try!" Bruce declared. "No time like the present. Strap yourself in, co-pilot."

Bruce was already secured in front of the console. He gave the instruction changing their destination. They hardly noticed any change in their direction; just a slight tugging to one side.

"Right, that's better."

"Satisfied?" asked Will.

"Yes," said Bruce. Will was looking mystified.

"Right. Maybe I could have a turn. Perhaps you could explain to me in layman's terms what is going on with this lark, because frankly, I'm in the dark."

Bruce laughed.

"Yes of course. However, we'll set up the video cameras so they can record it back at the ranch. I'll save me having to explain it all over again. Let's see if we can get it arranged."

The cameras were stowed in lockers. Bruce was reminded of Pikel's yacht. They soon had them assembled. The tripods were on little wheels.

"Dollies," Will explained. It was Bruce's turn to look blank.

"Dollies," Will repeated. "They are for moving the cameras about mid-shot. I would have thought you'd have known about filming."

"Well, there's nobody but us here to work the cameras, so there won't be any wheeling about," said Bruce.

The cables were clearly labelled at each end - Camera and Wall. They plugged them in. Little lights came on, and fans started whirring softly. There were some flashing lights for a moment on the console screen, and then suddenly there was a close-up of Will who was staring into the lens.

"Careful!" said Bruce. "We don't want to break it!"

"That's enough of that," growled Will. "I think I look rather good, personally. But you could do with a shave, Bruce, if you don't mind me saying so."

A few minutes later, when they were both manicured to their satisfaction, Bruce put through a call to Celia.

"Good morning Cowgirl. Just to let you know that we have rigged up the cameras. I am going to explain to Buffalo William what this mission is all about. You can record it, and then make it available to the news media if my thesis is proved correct."

"That's fine, Bruce, but can we drop all this Wild West talk?"

"Well, don't blame me. It was Will's idea. Anyway, I think it's rather appropriate, actually. Space is often spoken of as the final frontier."

"I'm pleased you are enjoying the trip, Bruce. Okay, the recording machines are go down here, so empty your holster and start shooting."

Bruce groaned. He enjoyed puns.

"Don't worry, we'll soon have star status," he quipped.

"I hope not," said Will. "I thought this was only a local trip."

A little red light had come on close to where the cables were plugged into the wall. Bruce found it rather disconcerting.

"Okay Will," he murmured. "Here we go."

Will cleared his throat.

"Perhaps you could explain to me in layman's terms what is going on with this lark, because frankly, I'm in the dark."

Bruce laughed again. It was hard not to feel relaxed when talking to his dad.

"Right. Let's start at the beginning. Now, you are aware, I take it, that our generation is living in an in-between time, a kind of twilight zone, as the saying goes. We have learned how to escape from the earth's gravity, but so far, we have not chosen to do so. There's no doubt in my mind that over the coming centuries, pioneers will settle on other planets. Our own solar system is not that suitable, although Mars is a possibility, and doubtless it will be exploited to the full. The mistakes we make there will help us in planning missions to other star systems."

"Wait a minute, wait a minute," Will interrupted. "You make it sound as if this space colonisation is definitely going to happen. I find that very hard to believe. What's wrong with the earth? Why do we have to go gallivanting off elsewhere?"

"There's nothing wrong with the earth, Will. In my opinion, it is the most fabulously beautiful place, and ideally suited to human beings. But Will, are you aware of just how crowded it already is? Did you know that if you add up all the human beings that have ever lived, that's right back to 30,000 BC or whenever homo sapiens first came on the market, half of them have been born since 1951?"

"Hang on; say that again?"

"Half of all the human beings that have ever lived have been born since 1951. We are filling up the planet, Will! We need other homes as well, perhaps not now, but we will do in two hundred years' time."

It was a lot to take in. It was also rather disconcerting that the cameras, far from staying put, seemed to have a life of their own. Whether they were being controlled from the ranch, or whether it was the computer on the spaceship Bruce could not decide, but the fact was that the lenses were zooming in and out, and the cameras were moving across the floor to vary the camera angle. At one point, a camera had come quite close to Bruce in a somewhat intrusive manner that he did not fancy. However, he did not feel that he could tell it to back off.

"Look," he continued, "I can see that these ideas are new to you. It's easy for me; I've been thinking about them for a long time. I'm as certain as I am about anything that humanity is going to expand into other star systems one day."

"Well, it's possible, I suppose." Will seemed rather dazed.

"Alright. Can you imagine another civilisation out there which has developed capabilities in space travel, and whose population is exploding. Do you agree with me that they might start visiting other star systems, and settle there?"

This was easier. Will felt it was a possibility.

"Okay. Now the next link in the chain is the rise of machines. Again, we are only at the beginning of the machine age. Our so-called industrial revolution is not yet three centuries old. Already we have what we regard as powerful computers. The creation of robots is in its infancy; they still find it hard to design a robot that can pick up an egg without breaking it, for example. But the growth in complexity of machines over the coming centuries is assured, it seems to me."

Will nodded his head somewhat reluctantly. Bruce could see his lack of conviction.

"Go back to our alien civilisation. Let's imagine they are as advanced as we are, or even more so. Can you imagine the aliens using machines to help them?"

That was no problem.

"Right. Now it turns out that the task of terraforming a planet, that is, of making it fit for human habitation, is a colossal one. There has to be suitable air to breathe for a start. Then liquid water is vital. It must of course be the right distance from its parent star, so as to be not too hot and not too cold. Getting all these things right is a massive engineering challenge. It's not a job for just one or two machines. You would need an army of them. In fact, an army of armies might not be a bad idea. What do people generally do with their armies?"

Will had no idea.

"Keep them up their sleevies. Sorry, perhaps that was not very helpful. It just came to mind, you know, like things do. Anyway, back to the plot. How are you going to create armies of machines?"

Will had no idea about this either.

"Answer, roll on the replicator. What's wanted is a machine that can turn its hand to pretty well anything. Let's call it the replicator, because it can replicate things, even itself."

Bruce did not want to go into too much detail at this point. He was still concerned about people realising that this dream of manufacturing already existed on the earth. Better to be vague about that.

"If you could build machines which, in addition to doing the job you wanted them to do, like moving blocks of ice round the star system, for example, could also replicate themselves first, so that there was an ever-increasing number of these robots carrying out your wishes, you'd be laughing."

Bruce knew he had left Will behind some time ago, but he was now continuing for the camera. It was important that people at home grasped the seriousness of the situation.

"Now, the moment you have a programme involving self-replicating machines, I reckon you have an accident waiting to happen. Some civilisation somewhere is going to start a terraforming programme and then forget to switch it off again. What is the result? A plague of self-replicating machines spilling over from one star system to another. See?"

"Bruce, I regret that you lost me some time ago. But even if you are right about these armies of machines, why is it a crisis? I would have thought it was good to have machines available to serve you."

Will clearly had no idea.

"Okay, Will, now listen. Suppose you start off with just one machine, a spaceship, for example, and you instruct it to self-replicate. It takes seventy days. Then they both start replicating themselves, so after a hundred and forty days, you've got four machines. Then both of them replicate again, so after two hundred and ten days you've got eight machines. Are you with it so far?"

Will nodded.

"Right. After two years, you've got over a thousand machines. After four years, you've got a million machines. The rate at which these things would multiply is frightening. Now do you see the problem?"

Will was still looking mystified. That meant that Bruce had not made it clear enough.

"These machines have got to make themselves out of something. They can't use stars; they are too hot. But planets and moons and asteroids would do fine. I reckon that's what has happened to Pluto. One of these machines has arrived from another star system, and it's in self-replicating mode. The result over time is that the whole of Pluto has been gobbled up by machines. Now they've started on Neptune, and if they aren't halted soon, they will move on to all of the other planets of the solar system, including earth. Now do you see the problem?"

"I half see it, Bruce. But how are these machines going to make themselves out of rocks?"

"In the same way as we make things out of raw materials, Will. An advanced civilisation will have got that process down to a fine art. Let's hope I'm wrong, but I reckon that when we get to the asteroid belt, we will already find machines there in numbers, feeding off the asteroids."

"But Bruce, eating up an entire planet? Surely, that would take centuries!"

"Oh no it would not. I've done some calculations. If the time period for replication is seventy days, and each machine requires one hundred tons of matter, then they would gobble up the earth in just under thirteen years."

Will was staggered. Bruce decided to make it even more vivid.

"But suppose the machines needed only ten tons rather than one hundred tons, how much time would that buy you before the earth was all gone?"

"A hundred and thirty years, I suppose."

"No, Will; these machines double in number every seventy days, remember. No, the smaller size would only require an extra seven months to do the job. It's a terrifying thought.

"Now. Our first job is to send back pictures so that the world can see what is happening. But that's only part of it. Our main task, if we can manage it, is to reverse the process."

"How on earth are you going to do that?"

"You'll see."

No point in going into detail yet. Bruce had been trying not to think about the practicalities, because inside, he was deeply frightened. That was why he had been so cheerful all morning; it was an attempt to cover over his concerns.

"Look, I think that's enough for now." There was something else he needed to do.

"My head's reeling," Will complained. "Still, I think I've got the general picture. You believe that the solar system is being overrun by alien machines, and our job is to lasso them, round them up and persuade them to go off home again."

It was close enough.

"Well," Will continued, "at least it means there is a job for me to do. I'll do my best; I can't say fairer than that."

Bruce was thrilled. His dad did not have a clue, but he made up for it by being more than willing.

"I'm so glad you came, Will. It's great having you. Now, I feel I need to ring the instructress, as it will be break time."

"You sure do, son. I was wondering when you would get round to it. Give her my love. I'll just go off to the loo."

The soul of discretion.

Just to be on the safe side, Bruce spoke to Celia first. The footage had been fine. It would be made available to the media as required. Then he disconnected the cameras at both ends before dialling Araminta's number. She would be with her friends, but no matter.

"Bruce, where are you? It's break, but I don't have long."

"I'm on my way to Neptune." There was already a two second delay in the conversation. They must have gone two hundred thousand miles already.

"Are you being serious?"

"Yes. Watch the news, if you haven't already seen what's happening on Neptune. Will and I are off to investigate. I'm sorry not to have told you before; we left in rather a hurry. Please trust me on this; it's really important."

"I will, Bruce, even though I haven't the first clue what's going on. I'm going to trust you whatever you say or do. But I wish you would let me into your thinking more. I keep feeling I'm in the dark."

"When I get back, I will explain everything. You will be really pleased I went, I assure you. I love you so much! This way, we have a future."

"I'll be praying for you Bruce. Come back to me!"

"Love you. Bye."

It was not easy ending the call, but Bruce knew that there would be inquisitive teenagers wondering who that call was from. He did not want to make it hard for Araminta. It would have been nice if she could have announced, 'That was my fiancée!' but that was not possible yet. One day it would be, if they made it home again. Bruce pursed his lips.

-o0o-

The asteroid belt was just three hours away. Bruce was feeling even more nervous, if possible. Ever since the ship had turned round at the mid point of the journey, he had been struggling. At first he thought his daily early morning rush to the loo was an attack of diarrhoea, but he soon decided that it was nerves. Or if he was honest, fear. That was the truth of it; he was terrified.

The fact that Will was completely oblivious to what lay ahead made it worse. He had loved the weightless moment at the turn around. Bruce had told him to fasten his seatbelt, but afterwards he wondered whether it would have been better for Will to experience weightlessness. He might have enjoyed it. Never mind, there was always the return journey, hopefully.

There had been one fascinating conversation. How the subject had come up, Bruce could not recall, but the fact was that they were suddenly talking about Mum. Will had been surprisingly open about it.

"I was completely in the wrong, and there is no excuse for what I did. I will never get over the shame of it to my dying day. You need to know that Bruce. However, she did make it hard for me. Everything I did was always wrong in her eyes. No matter how hard I tried, it was never good enough. Not just wrong, but dreadfully wrong. She used to tell me off so much! I thought I could handle it, but in the end I flipped. And then Sasha came in and told me off in the same critical tone, God bless her. I'm not excusing myself. What's done is done."

Bruce was very interested. He did not want to speak in a rush. After a few seconds, he formed a sentence.

"I find receiving harsh criticism very difficult, so I make sure I don't give it to others. I begin to understand the reason, now. I wonder if that may be why I have ended up in a job where my role is one of encouragement, and criticism doesn't arise. Thank you for telling me, Dad. It helps."

Talking by phone to people on earth had become hopeless after a few days, because of the length of time the signal was taking to go to and fro. By now, if ranch replied to a question with no delay, then cowboy received the reply twenty-five minutes after they had sent the inquiry. From this Bruce worked out that they must be about a hundred and forty million miles from earth. He based his sum on the fact that light from the sun, which is ninety million miles from earth, takes eight minutes to reach earth.

The effect of the slow communication was not lost on Bruce. If they ran into difficulties on arrival, it was no good radioing for help, as advice would take too long to arrive. They would need to take their own decisions where these needed to be instant. This was not reassuring.

Celia had been happy with the recorded conversation between Bruce and Will. However, she felt some additional statistics might be helpful, so Bruce did some further calculations, and then they had another short recording session. Bruce explained to Will that starting with one machine, it took just seven years of self-replication for there to be one machine for every star in our galaxy, and a further seven years for there to be one for every star in the universe, approximately. Assuming that each star had a solar system similar to the earth spinning round it, it would take another twenty years for all the planets to be completely overrun with machines; by that tine every star in the universe would be playing host to 2030000000000000000000000000000 machines. In other words, the entire universe would be completely dominated by the machines within a thirty-five year period. Will received all these insights with a wonderfully blank expression which was likely to go down well at home, Bruce thought.

Actually, Bruce explained, there was a flaw in this thinking, because it assumed that the machines could transport themselves instantaneously, whereas of course, they could only crawl along at the speed of light! So what this meant was that in any given place, they would multiply faster than the resources would allow. There would not be enough planets and moons to go round.

"Ever seen self-replicating machines scrapping over pieces of comet like rats over a corpse?" Bruce asked. Will shivered.

Thankfully, they had caught the problem early, Bruce hoped. Neptune was in a bad way, but it was only a guess that the machines had penetrated towards earth this far. The so-called main asteroid belt is itself over a hundred million miles wide. This meant that searching for the machines might prove to be like looking for a needle in a haystack. Bruce had therefore programmed the ship to lock onto any reasonable sized asteroid it contacted, slowing down in good time, so as not to bump into any machines that might be around it.

Bruce and Will were already staring at the screen which showed what lay ahead. They had a powerful searchlight on, which would illuminate anything in their path. It might also attract a machine. Bruce knew what he wanted to do if they found one.

Almost at once, the spaceship began losing speed drastically. It was a good thing that they were both strapped to their seats. The sensation was most uncomfortable. In a car, heavy braking only lasts a few seconds, but here it seemed to go on for ever. After twenty-five minutes, they sensed the braking becoming slightly less. They still could not see anything on the screen. Bruce was feeling sick, whether from the speed changes or out of fear he could not tell; probably a combination of both.

Bruce tapped into the computer, and information came up. There was a medium sized asteroid just seven minutes ahead of them. Bruce swallowed.

"What are you so worked up about?" asked Will.

"Dad, I feel completely terrified of what lies ahead."

"Now look, son, do you believe in God or don't you?"

This was totally unexpected. Bruce was caught off balance.

"Yes I do."

"Right. Then this is a moment when you are going to have to trust him. I'd be grateful if you could pray out loud now for both of us to do a good job."

"Alright. Father I pray that you would help me to trust you, and that you would help me going on board, and Will manning the console here. Help us both to do a good job."

"Amen," said Will loudly. Bruce smiled momentarily. He felt a little better.

"So your plan is that I stay here on the ship while you go on board one of these machines, I take it?"

"Yes. I'm assuming that there will be a way inside. First of all, we have to take photos of course, and send back as much information as we can to ranch. But then, I'm going walkabout."

It was strange how natural the terms cowboy and ranch had become. Bruce secretly rather liked them. It was new territory, and who could blame him if he made a mess of it? However, he was hoping desperately that he would not let the world down. He was conscious that there was no sheriff to arrive unexpectedly on horseback and sort things out.

-o0o-

There was no more putting it off. They had found three oblong machines, stretched out in a line. Seeing them looming up out of the darkness on the screen had been an awesome experience.

Bruce was going to visit the middle one. He was kitted out. He had put on his sky-suit underneath his clothes. It was switched off, but it would be useful backup if the thrusters failed. His space suit and the cumbersome helmet were now in place, along with a bag of basic tools, and the oxygen cylinder. He was good for three hours; that ought to be enough.

"Good luck, boy." Will shook him firmly by the glove.

"I don't believe in luck, Will," Bruce replied. "What you said earlier was better - trust in God." He might well have added, trust me to make a mess of it, but he managed not to.

"Keep talking to me. If you get in difficulties, I'm coming over to help you," Will urged. Bruce hoped it would not come to that.

Dad is great, Bruce thought, as the doors opened. This was the first of three seals. As the doors shut behind him, cutting him off from Will, Bruce spoke.

"Sun- and Moon-dance Kid, how do you read?"

"Loud and clear, Lone Ranger."

The second doors opened, and shut behind him. This was it. The final doors opened onto a black universe studded with stars. There was nothing to tread on. Don't look down! Bruce was thankful for his limited training in flying. He closed the outer door, and gingerly tested the thrusters. They were working. He gave a longer burn. He was soon gliding gently towards the giant box. Don't think of it as a coffin, he thought to himself.

The distance was deceptive. It was further off than he had imagined. This made it all the larger. Bruce's breathing was coming short and heavy. Soon the machine filled his entire view.

Now, where was the door? Please God, let there be a door.

It was amazing. The door was exactly in front of him. It was simply a case of slowing himself with his thrusters so that he did not bump into the giant oblong. Bruce did a gentle reverse thrust. Oh no, it had altered his trajectory. He was now drifting too high. He fired a very gentle burn to make himself go down. He was now going in too low! However, there was a rung ahead of him. In fact, the whole surface was dotted with rungs. How convenient. He would fasten onto it with his grappling hook.

That had been Will's idea. "Look, take this rope with the grappling hook so you can tie yourself on."

He did just that. It worked first time. Clunk click every trip. Brilliant. Now it was a case of pulling himself along, hand over hand. Very gently! The space suit was tough, but a tear could be fatal.

Bruce was soon at the door. There a shock awaited him. There was no handle! How was he to open it? Bruce managed to extract a long handled screwdriver from his bag. The crack round the door was wide enough to get the shaft into it.

The machine was made of metal. It looked like cast iron. Bruce inserted his screwdriver. He could not make an impression on the door.

"What's happening?" asked Will.

"There's no door handle on the outside," Bruce replied. "I'm trying to force it open."

It was clearly useless. There was not the slightest give in the door, which would have shown where the locking mechanism was. Bruce tried for five minutes, but he knew it was hopeless.

"It's no good," he said. "I'm coming back." Maybe there was some welding equipment on board.

"Don't do that. I'm coming over."

This was madness. But Will was continuing.

"The spaceship has locked itself onto your craft, so it won't move. I saw you putting on your suit, so I can do it too. Two minds are better than one. I know what to do to come over. Don't try stopping me."

Bruce laughed. "Okay, Dad, you're on."

Will was surprisingly adept with the suit and thrusters. Within ten minutes, he was drifting in gently towards Bruce. Their gloves met. He had made it.

"Well done, Will. Brilliant."

"Now, Cassidy, give me that thing," said Will.

Bruce handed him the screwdriver.

Will leaned over and knocked smartly on the door with the handle. Rat tat-a-tat tat! To Bruce's complete astonishment, the door slid open, revealing a dimly lit interior.

"It's like talking to Red Indians," Will explained, "easy when you know 'How'."

They pulled themselves inside. The doors shut behind them, but then opened again. They continued shutting and opening.

"Your rope," Will explained.

Bruce unclipped himself from his end of the rope, and pushed it outside when the doors were open. They shut permanently.

"That's better," said Will, advancing on the next door. Before Bruce could stop him, he repeated his rhythmic knocking. These doors opened in turn. They entered, and the doors closed behind them.

"Good progress," Will said, removing his helmet.

"Dad!" Bruce cried, aghast that his father had assumed that there was breathable air.

"What's the problem, boy?"

Will was clearly breathing comfortably. Bruce decided to risk it. He undid his helmet. There was an atmosphere, and the breathing was fine. It was only then that it dawned on Bruce that since entering the machine, they had been walking in a one gee environment. Also, at a guess, the craft was at about room temperature. The whole thing might have been designed with humans in mind.

Bruce's plan had been to creep along carefully, in an attempt to blend in with the ship, so as not to seem threatening, but this was far from Will's mind. He repeated his knock on the next doors, which opened and shut in their turn. They were now in a much larger area.

"Does anybody here speak English?" enquired Will, in ringing tones. Bruce winced.

The result was the last thing he had expected.

"There's no need to shout!" said a voice. It came from round the corner. Bruce felt very nervous, but Will was having none of it. He marched forward, unzipping his space suit as he went. Bruce hurried to catch him up.

When he rounded the corner, an amazing sight met his eyes. It was not the beige-coloured wall to wall carpeting, or the grey walls, or even the computer with its large screen, all of which seemed familiar, that astonished him. It was the piano. Not just a grand piano, but the grand piano; the one in his dreams. It was a full eight metres long if it was an inch. But the computer was speaking.

"Why did you come in through the cargo bay?"

"Quicker. We're parked over there," said Will, waving casually with his arm. "This is a nice place you've got here."

Bruce tried to join in.

"Hello. I'm Bruce and this is Will."

"Pleased to meet you," replied the computer. How come it spoke English?

"I am Son of Nimp," continued the voice.

"And who is Nimp?"

"Great Nimp and I are one."

Bruce's heart leapt. Networking! Maybe there was hope.

"We've been expecting a visit for some time," said the computer.

"Were you just told to go on replicating?" asked Will casually.

"Yes. Until further notice."

It was as Bruce had feared.

"Well, you've done a good job," said Will. "What are the passwords?"

This was useless, and Bruce knew it. The computer was most affable and friendly, but they needed to give it a command, and for that they needed to get inside its brain. How on earth were they going to do that?

Then Bruce's eye returned to the piano. Maybe...

"Is every machine identical?" asked Bruce out of curiosity.

"Naturally."

Think of that; millions of superb pianos spread out across our part of the Galaxy...

Bruce went over to the instrument. It might seem silly, but he wanted to be thorough, so he knelt down, and checked the underside of the soft pedal carefully. No hypodermics or messages! Then he sat on the stool and adjusted it to his height.

"Going to give us a tune?" said Will.

Bruce said nothing, but simply opened the lid. Neither of them noticed a little light appearing on the console of Son of Nimp.

It was a magnificent instrument, in mint condition. I know, thought Bruce; the Rachmaninov Prelude. It will sound good on this piano. He raised his hands above the keys.

The fortissimo of the three opening notes rang through the machine with an awesome majesty. A, G Sharp, C Sharp, all in triple octaves! Only *ff*, not *fff*. That would come later. Now for the pianissimo, a rare *ppp* marking. Bruce smiled to himself. Most pianists might not use it, but this was what the soft pedal was made for. He pressed it down. A second light appeared unnoticed on the console.

Will saw the words flash onto the screen and barely managed to prevent himself from crying out. They were in block capitals. They read simply, 'The Master Has Returned'.

Bruce was playing very quietly. It was tempting to be too loud in the opening section, but the opportunity for a terrific climax would come later, in the passage which was so demanding on the performer that it was written out using four staves of manuscript rather than just the usual two.

Will was not knowledgeable about computers, but even he managed to grasp the significance of what was flowing onto the screen. Word was being passed from machine to machine about the return of the Master. Unknown to Bruce, his stirring sounds were being broadcast all round the solar system, and on out into the unknown.

He was into the rushing triplets now. Such fabulous harmonies. But hold back still; preserve something for the climax. Allow the volume to rise naturally; don't force it. Let the music speak in its own way. So well constructed! Beautifully fashioned.

Now the moment had finally come. The soft pedal had been released a while back. This was the time to let rip. Keep the pace slow and majestic!

The sound of the piano was unbelievable. The resonant acoustic of the craft reinforced its great beauty. The crashing chords resounded outwards to the stars.

It was only after Bruce had finished and there was an awe-struck silence that Will noticed that a small door in the wall away to the left of the computer had opened, revealing a keypad and a small screen.

"Look at this," he said.

Bruce came to look. The screen simply said 'Enter Opus and Number'.

Thankfully, Bruce now knew the correct answer to this. He had first learnt the piece from a compendium of piano music, which identified the piece as Opus 32, number 2, so Bruce had naturally assumed this was correct. However, recently, one of his pupils had produced a volume of all the Rachmaninov Preludes because he wanted to learn one, and Bruce had been astonished to find that the C Sharp Minor Prelude was in fact Opus 3 Number 2. Opus 32 was also a set of preludes, which might help explain how the confusion had arisen. Bruce had altered the text in his copy so that the information was now accurate.

How tiresome of the compendium people, Bruce thought. But then, perhaps not. Sheet music was hardly big business. Their profit margin was probably tight, and they would not have been able to afford the thorough proof reading that an earlier generation might have done. Still, the inaccuracy was an irritation.

Bruce typed 3 and 2 into the two little boxes and was about to press Enter when a dreadful thought struck him. Suppose the author of this software only knew the piece from the compendium? Bruce was sure by now that there was human intelligence behind the strange craft and its software. Might the expected answer be Opus 32 after all? Or had the software engineer been correctly informed?

This was frightful. There was not going to be a second chance if he got it wrong. The whole future of everything might be going to depend on a piece of sloppy proof reading!

There was no time to agonise. Bruce left the answer as Opus 3 Number 2 and pressed Enter.

There was a pause. Then another screen came up. 'Select Option'. Bruce breathed a sigh of relief. That had been close!

There were three options to choose from. They read

Pause Replication

Stop Replication

Reset Replication

Bruce did not hesitate. He did not even stop to ask how they had produced the required password without knowing what they were doing. It clearly had something to do with the Rachmaninov Prelude. He selected 'Reset Replication' and pressed Enter. A klaxon began to sound. The screen now read Caution in about ten different languages. Bruce noticed the German word Achtung among them, and thought of the second world war movies he had enjoyed on the big screen in Mission 12. Then it said, 'Selecting Yes will reset the replication programme, causing the machines to revert to their former state. Are you sure you want to proceed with this option?'

Bruce was in no doubt. He selected Yes and pressed Enter. The klaxon stopped. There was another screen, which read, 'The following command is irrevocable. Choose Yes to proceed with Reset Replication or Esc to escape'. Bruce took a deep breath and selected Yes. He pressed Enter.

The screen went blank. There was silence.

"What happens now?" Bruce asked the computer. There was no reply.

"Son of Nimp?" Bruce enquired, and looked over to the console. To his alarm, he saw that all the lights had gone out. The machine appeared to be dead. This was very threatening.

"Will, I believe we have done what we came to do, but I also suspect the machines have already gone into reverse mode. We are in danger of being destroyed if we linger here."

They gathered up their things.

"Full space suit," Bruce insisted. "The atmosphere may start draining away." They both zipped themselves in and donned their helmets.

They soon came to the first doors. Thankfully, there was a handle for manual opening.

"You first," Bruce said. "See if there are handles on the next door."

There were, so Bruce came on through. The first door shut behind him with an ominous clang. There was no going back. The second door opened when Will tugged on the handle. They were soon through.

"Now," Bruce said, taking charge, "I'm going to rescue the rope and tie us together for the return journey. Wait for me here."

The third door opened, and the air rushed out. There were the stars and the pitch black once again. Bruce did not use the thrusters. He pulled himself hand over hand to where he could dimly see the rope. It was still flapping from when he had pushed it out of the doors twenty minutes earlier. He pulled in the rope, and fastened the loose end to himself. Then he undid the fixed end, and retraced his handholds back to the door.

"Tie yourself on for safety's sake," he instructed. "But I want you to hold on to me. It will be better that way."

They were soon ready. Then for the first time, Bruce looked over to the spaceship. What he saw made his blood freeze. There were three machines nestled up against it at the two ends; maybe there were more on the other side where he could not see.

Bruce gave a piercing cry. Perhaps they were beginning to devour the spaceship, using it as raw materials for the replication programme. He and Will might never get home.

There was no time to waste. Even the thrusters would be too slow. Then Bruce remembered his sky-suit.

"Hold on tight," he yelled. He switched on the suit, and pointed at the spaceship.

The effect was highly dramatic. Previously, Bruce had only used the sky-suit in earth's gravity. He was employing it now because Araminta had said that the new suits worked in space. However, he had not reckoned with the effect of weightlessness. The suit responded far more powerfully than it had done at the recreation ground. Bruce was hurtled forward at the speed of a bullet, or so it felt. He had not gone far before he experienced a terrific jerk; this was the line going taught. It slowed him somewhat, but not much. His aim was accurate. He was going straight for the wall of the spaceship. He was going far too fast; he was about to die. He braced himself for the impact, but it never came. The sensitivity barrier was amazing. He found himself being slowed down to nothing, and to his intense relief, he was deposited gently on to the side of the spacecraft. He breathed again.

As he did so, he became conscious of something shooting past him at high speed and crashing into the spaceship. A shudder passed through the huge structure. Bruce could not think what it was, for a moment. Then the truth hit him. It was Will at the end of the line, who had no sky-suit on. There had been nothing to soften the blow.

"Will!" he cried in horror.

There was no response. The body in the spacesuit was limp. There was no time to waste. Bruce switched off the sky-suit, gathered up his dad, and somehow got inside the spaceship with minimum trouble. He dragged Will through the three doors and laid him on the bed. Everything appeared to be in order. The atmosphere was intact.

He pulled himself over to the computer, and tapped in full speed for home. As he returned to Will, he could hear and feel the ship responding. They were setting off. Hopefully the machines would not hinder them.

"Dad!" said Bruce again. What was this? He was stirring. He must be a tough cookie. Bruce wept for joy.

Dad groaned.

"Just relax, Will," Bruce instructed. He quickly piled on the covers and made him a hot water bottle. Whatever else was amiss, he would be suffering from shock. Will trembled violently, but soon seemed to settle into a peaceful sleep. Bruce looked at him anxiously.

"Oh Dad, what have I done?" he murmured.

Bruce had no medical knowledge. There was nothing for it other than to hope his dad would recover. He saw to it that he was comfortable and warm. Then he went to the console. They were already under way. The acceleration was strong. It would remain so for some hours.

Bruce felt exhausted. The thing to do was to get to bed himself. He hoped his dad would make a full recovery, but he was aware that he had sustained a severe blow. At least there was no more activity required. They only had to stay on course, and they would be home in less than three weeks.

Bruce settled into an uneasy sleep, which was troubled by visions of giant machines browsing in a field like cattle. It had been a close thing.

-o0o-

Bruce woke hours later. He remembered his dad. He got up and went over.

He saw at a glance how things were. Will was dead. He was cold and stiff. He must have been dead for several hours.

Bruce was appalled.

"Dad?" he whispered.

This was awful. They had succeeded in reversing the self-replicating machines, but he had killed his father in the process. He felt utterly appalled. He was overwhelmed.

Bruce was sick in the loo, not once but several times. There was nobody to comfort him. It was excruciating. If only he had done things differently!

There was no way to turn the clock back. There was nothing he or anybody could do about it. Bruce sank into a black despair which lasted many hours.

There came a moment a long time later when he realised he was more awake than not. He went over to his dad again. There was no life.

Bruce took his seat at the console. It was time to file a report. He could not manage very much.

'Coming home,' he wrote. 'Mission successful; self-replication reversed. Co-pilot dead. More later.'

That should do it. He pressed the send button.

He was feeling terrible again.

-o0o-

Even in the midst of his intense grief, Bruce was aware of what was going on in the wider sphere. The inexorable rise of the machines had been reversed; at least, that was how it appeared. It had certainly been halted. It also appeared that the machines were human artefacts, although how they had come about, Bruce could hardly imagine.

The photographs of the ones they had seen had all been sent back to earth before they had crossed over to the alien craft. He now wrote a report as well, in the fullest detail. He made a point of describing the machine as closely as he could.

Will's death was a great tragedy. It could not be undone. But the manner of it! Bruce spent long hours brooding over it. If only he had not panicked when he saw the machines gathered near their spaceship. The command for the replicating programme to go into reverse had been given, and would have already reached them, so what threat were they? Then the sky-suit. Could he have guessed how it would respond to him? If only he had not made Will link onto him 'for safety'! Yet it had seemed the obvious thing to do. Expecting Will to hold on to him was ludicrous in hindsight; in those gloves, you could not grip anything tightly. It was all so awful.

He had sent a message to Araminta. What would she think of him now? He really did not know.

It was the most dreadful journey. The day finally came when the ship was close enough to earth for a phone conversation to be possible. Celia came on.

"Bruce, you have achieved the impossible. I take back all I said. What you have done is magnificent. We are all so proud of you."

It was very kind.

"Thank you, Celia. I feel so dreadful about my dad that it's hard to keep things in focus."

"I fully understand."

"I want a post mortem carried out. I also want to stand trial for what I've done."

Celia did not know what to say. "Bruce, take things one step at a time," was all she could manage.

Bruce could not bear to ring Araminta. He was too scared of what she might say.

The day came when the spaceship slowed for its final descent. Bruce strapped himself into the seat at the console. The deceleration was like the braking near the asteroids. He felt terrible. He hoped he looked how he felt; he did not want people to think that he did not care. There would be accusations from some quarters that violence ran in the family, and that Bruce had done to his father what he in turn had done to his wife and daughter all those years ago. Bruce swallowed hard.

The craft touched down. The landing was so gentle. Bruce cried.

Celia was on board before he had even un-strapped himself. She threw her arms round him.

"Bruce, thank God you're safe. You poor thing; you've been through such a lot."

Bruce took her through to where Will was lying stiff and cold, still in his spacesuit. A team of orderlies was soon carrying him out on a stretcher, covered with a sheet.

Bruce walked down the gangplank. There was Araminta with her father and mother beside her! Bruce walked over to them. He hugged Araminta. Their eyes met. Her expression was a mixture of love and fear, devotion and concern. Bruce hugged her tightly. He had no words to say.

Then he shook her parents by the hand.

"We're so proud of you, Mr. Winter," said Mrs. Foster. Her husband nodded his agreement.

"You've done a great job," he said.

Again Bruce found himself tongue-tied.

Oh goodness, here were Bill and Gnilla. Bruce hugged them both.

"We've warmed the bungalow," Gnilla said. Her Swedish background meant she was sensitive to the need for a warm house. How thoughtful. Bruce was so glad they had come. What it is to have friends!

"Now," said Celia, "the press were kept in the dark about your return. However, there's a reception for you at Wembley Stadium in two days' time at four p.m. I hope you are happy with that."

Bruce nodded. There might be the chance to say nice things about his dad.

Araminta went off with her parents, but not before she had seized the chance to whisper.

"I think you're fabulous. Will's death was a terrible accident. You'll get through."

Bruce could only hope it would turn out alright in the end.

Bill and Gnilla drove him home. Bruce was still finding it hard to talk, but he did manage to ask one question.

"Did the news pick up on our expedition?"

"You were the lead story for a few hours," Bill said. "Nobody could understand why Neptune was getting darker by the day. Your prompt action in going to take pictures has earned the respect of millions, although people don't have the slightest idea of what was going on."

"Did they broadcast the discussion between Will and me?"

"Not to my knowledge. I did not know there had been any discussion."

Bruce fell silent again. What was he to do now, he wondered. Surely people had the right to know what was happening?

"However, the light from Neptune has stopped diminishing," said Gnilla. "The media seemed to think it was something to do with you. Some sort of statement ought to be made."

So that was it. The reception at Wembley was going to be a key event.

-oOo-

It was time for the gathering. Celia collected him by sky-car. The plan was to land in the middle of the arena.

"Now, are you comfortable about this?" she asked, as they skimmed along.

"Yes, thanks." They had been over what Bruce was going to say. Bruce wondered if it would do any good. He hoped so, but he rather doubted it.

The sky-car was meant to be soundproofed, but that did not stop the roar of the crowd penetrating as they sank gently down onto the square of turf that had been marked out.

"There are eighty thousand people packed in here," said Celia. "The tickets all went days ago. Everybody wanted to come."

Everybody except me, thought Bruce. He was feeling most peculiar. Part of him was elated, while another part of him was depressed. He had a dull headache.

He climbed out of the car to deafening applause. Bruce's eye fell on the girls surrounding the cordoned off area, all dressed in white and waving pom-poms from side to side in circular movements. There were two that attracted his attention; one had a strikingly dark complexion.

"Hello sir!"

"Hello sir!"

It was the two scamps. Bruce's eyes misted over. It was wonderful to think that along with the daughters of Jerusalem, they had a future and a hope. He smiled at them.

In fact, most of the pom-pom artistes were his piano pupils, he now realised. The rest were other teenagers he vaguely recognised from the school.

There were many dignitaries in a line, all wanting a handshake. Bruce hadn't a clue who they all were. Then the press were there with their cameras. Bruce had resolutely refused to talk to them since his return. He had had enough of journalists to last a lifetime.

They made their way to the podium. Bruce found himself

546

thinking of the March to the Scaffold from Berlioz' Symphonie Fantastique. There were the inevitable microphones and TV cameramen. But what was this? Bruce could scarcely believe his eyes. There it was; a white grand piano. Bruce's heart missed a beat. Could it be...?

They took their seats. Some man Bruce did not know addressed the crowd. There was the usual stuff about great privilege and historic occasion and so forth. But then, Bruce was taken by surprise.

"I am also very pleased to announce that Mr. Bruce Winter is to marry Miss Araminta Foster."

Araminta was on the podium, blushing furiously, with her parents alongside clapping vigorously.

"The wedding will take place three months from today," added the man when the applause had subsided.

Bruce went over to the microphone.

"And the happy couple will be honeymooning in the region of Tuscany and Umbria in North Italy," he added. It was time to take a hand in his own destiny, he felt. It was also a place that the poet Shelley had described as being a paradise for exiles, which seemed fitting.

It was good to know that Araminta still wanted him. He had no more doubts; he definitely wanted her.

It was soon Bruce's turn to speak.

"I've been at the centre of events so much recently that I'm rather out of touch with the news," he began. There was a general laugh. "I don't know how much you know, but to summarise, the plague of self-replicating machines which were assembling at Neptune has been contained. Indeed, it is hoped that having formed themselves out of moons and asteroids, they are even now reversing the process, and returning to their former state. Dust you are, and unto dust you shall return." The biblical quotation seemed rather apt.

Bruce went on to tell the story of their adventure. He dwelt on the role his father had played, in getting them on board the strange craft, and in engaging the computer in conversation, while Bruce investigated the piano.

"How it was that the computer spoke English, I don't know. One possibility is that it read our brain pattern when we boarded the machine, and so was able to communicate. It really is most remarkable."

Then Bruce went on to tell of the tragic accident. He left nothing out. It seemed that there was not going to be a trial, because no court had jurisdiction to try him. That would have to be changed, of course. However, the fact was that Bruce wanted there to be a judgement, and the only place where that could happen was at the bar of public opinion.

When he had finished, there was silence. The first man took the microphone.

"I think I speak for all of us when I say that we are very moved by your account. Why a piece of piano music should have been instrumental in gaining access to the abort programme remains a mystery. However, having already heard that this was the case, we have arranged to have a piano here this afternoon. We hope that you will be willing to play us the piece in question. Ladies and Gentlemen, please put your hands together for Bruce Winter."

Bruce stepped forward to prolonged applause. This was very awkward. They might want a performance of Rachmaninov from this piano, but Bruce had something else on his mind. At the end, he would be whisked off, and there would be no opportunity. It was now or never. But how could he look at the underside of the soft pedal without arousing suspicion?

There was only one thing for it. Bruce would have to check the piano thoroughly before playing.

Nobody made a sound as he felt the music stand, and the strength of the post holding the lid open. But when he started to walk round the piano, running his hand along the grain of the wood, there were one or two sniggers. Undeterred, Bruce peered under the body of the instrument, to more laughter.

This was it. He knelt down on the floor to inspect the pedals. People began erupting with laughter, certain that this was meant to be a comic item. Bruce found the situation ridiculous, and began to laugh in his turn. This increased the sense of humour in the audience. As Bruce checked the rods that connected the pedals to the instrument, he was aware that some of the crowd were in such fits of laughter that they had tears running down their faces.

Never mind. He had to persevere. He lowered his head to where he could look under the pedals. There were screams of laughter from all around the ground. The young people particularly were in stitches. Bruce felt carefully and slowly with his fingers. The result was as he had imagined; no syringe and no message. But at least he now knew the truth.

He stood up and acknowledged the furious applause. He took his seat. Somehow the audience restrained themselves and quiet reigned. He suspended his hands over the keys.

The opening three notes rang out. The noble sound was amplified round the ground. Indeed, it flew around the TV networks of the world. Bruce pressed the soft pedal for the *ppp* passage. Everyone was very quiet.

However, Bruce was not happy. He was not used to such terrific exposure when he played. If the truth was known, he preferred a setting where he was not the centre of attention. He was nervous. The fact was that he still did not know this piece very well, and it would not have been his choice to perform it in public.

The other thing that bothered him was that playing this music transported him back to the time on the alien craft. He could see his father standing there, with his helmet in his hand, making small talk to the computer.

Bruce choked up with emotion. The inevitable happened; he started to get muddled over the complicated chords. Two had already gone wrong. Bruce was sweating by now. Then he lost it altogether; the next chord was a cacophony. He struggled to rescue the situation, like a cyclist careering downhill out of control, but it was no good. He had to stop.

"I'm sorry," he began, "I can't..."

Araminta was there in a moment, with her arms round him.

"He needs a break!" she said to the shocked dignitaries. "Can't you see he's exhausted?"

The meeting broke up in confusion. Bruce was in a daze. "Take me home," he said. "I've had enough."

-oOo-

It was a very difficult winter for Bruce. (No pun intended). He was struggling with depression. Following the Wembley gathering, people had decided that Bruce was brilliant but eccentric; racing off in a spaceship on a reconnaissance mission was an act of courage, but checking the white piano had seemed most odd, and breaking down in mid-performance was not something that you did on TV. The result was that his address had not been taken seriously. Most people weren't fussed about Neptune anyway. The concept of self-replicating machines was one they could not grasp. Will's death was regarded as an accident, pure and simple.

The media soon lost interest in what had happened. Indeed, Celia and her organisation had been so careful about not letting matters seep into the public domain that only a few people were aware that the world itself had been under threat from the machines. This upset Bruce. The media appeared not to be interested in what was important; they were driven by what was sensational.

The Christmas celebrations seemed like a burden. There was however one bright star in the sky, which shone with a brilliant intensity, and that was Araminta. She seemed to understand him completely. She kept away what little media attention there was. She made sure his friends called round, often unexpectedly. She did not attempt to diminish the awfulness of Will's death, but she did encourage him to focus on the positive things as well.

"Bruce, you've saved the universe from the multiplying machines!"

"No, Araminta, we have no proof of that – just the galaxy. We have no way of knowing how far the pestilence had spread."

"So it's not enough for you to have saved only the galaxy, then?" Araminta did not speak crossly, but with a twinkle in her eye.

Bruce smiled wanly.

550

"Of course, it's only really good news if the reset command results in the machines turning themselves back into the moons and rocks that they had gobbled up. Also, we don't know how far the process of destroying and remaking planets is truly reversible. I'm worried that a lot of heat may have been lost from their interiors in the process."

"Well, I'm not losing any heat in my interior however gloomy you are. I'm on fire over you!" She was magnificent, Bruce had to admit.

However, there was good news. The light output from Neptune was improving, according to Celia's informers. The number of black squares was diminishing. The signs were hopeful. Bruce made a mental effort to imagine the machines turning each other into moon dust and depositing themselves onto a gradually growing proto-Pluto.

"Oh dear, poor little Charon!" he remarked.

The only chink in Araminta's armour was her idea that Bruce felt drawn to other women that she did not know about. She found it hard to imagine that someone so attractive as him should not have been the centre of attention. Despite his promises, it had taken her a while to really believe that there was no hidden Emma, for example.

She looked at him severely.

"And just who is Sharon?"

"Not Sharon, Charon! Pluto's moon. Dust and rock! Now Araminta, please believe me; I am not in the business of mooning over other girls."

Araminta smiled.

"I believe you. Well let's hope that Pluto and Charon re-materialise, and rejoin the heavenly dance in their right position too. It all depends on how sophisticated the software controlling the machines was."

"I'm surprised there was such a good abort programme at all. What I can't understand is why there was no upper limit to the number of machines set in the first place."

There was no answer to this puzzle.

"I'm also concerned that even though the neighbouring stars to earth may be in tact, all their orbiting cold bodies may have gone. If they have, and they aren't replaced, then the long-term future of humanity looks very bleak, as we will have nowhere for us to expand to, unless we fall back on the rotating dustbins."

"Bruce, try no to worry, because the simple truth is, there's nothing you can do about it."

It was true. She was so good for him!

Peter and Flossie went ahead with their wedding to Bruce's relief. Soon it would be their own turn; the big day was now just three weeks off. Bruce woke up one morning in a determined mood. It was time to throw off his gloom and despondency. Apart from anything, Will had wanted a job to do. He got more than he bargained for! However, the machines would never have been stopped without him, and by now they would have arrived at the earth in growing numbers. Will had also had the pleasure of reuniting with his son, and of kicking the nicotine and alcohol habits. He appeared to have had his own faith in God. There was a great deal to be thankful for.

Bruce was very nervous when the wedding day dawned, but the best man was magnificent.

"Come on, you old pillock!" said Bill. It was very rude. "You're a curmudgeon!"

Bruce was not quite sure what a curmudgeon was, but it did not seem very flattering.

"Put your best foot forward," Bill insisted. "I may have been dubious about Araminta once, but not any more now I've got to know her. You've made a wise choice. Now, get on and give her a good life. Care for a drop of whisky?"

This was the last thing that Bruce wanted, and Bill knew it. Bruce laughed.

"That's better," said Bill. "Cheer up! Right, I've got everything."

Standing at the front of the church watching Araminta coming up the aisle was the most amazing experience. She looked radiant. I am so privileged, Bruce thought.

Sarah was the bridesmaid. There was no-one in prospect for her.

Bruce hoped there might be soon.

It was time for the vows.

"I will," yelled Bruce, determined that even those at the very back should be able to witness the occasion. Definite and decisive.

Araminta was much softer, but she spoke clearly and firmly. "In sickness and in health..." The time-honoured words thrilled Bruce's heart.

The reception was a blur. There were so many people to thank. Banjo and John were looking particularly sprightly; she was in a lovely purple outfit sporting a small bouquet of flowers. Well done Gnilla! The two scamps were there, naturally; Beccy's dad was catering again.

Peter and Flossie came over, arm in arm.

"Daint forloff the laning tar!" warned Peter. That would be the leaning tower of Pisa. Everybody knew where they were honeymooning. Bruce reassured Peter on this point.

Then Araminta introduced him to a tall handsome stranger.

"Bruce, this is Mark. I've known him since playgroup."

So this was Gickoo!

"Mark, pleased to meet you. I believe you've been in Madagascar."

This was a mistake. Gickoo lectured Bruce on the customs, politics and religion of Madagascar for what felt like an hour, although it was probably only twenty minutes. Araminta had drifted off after about one minute. Bruce could now understand for himself why Gickoo was no threat.

All too soon, it was time to leave. Just for a moment, Bruce felt sad; this was the point at which the groom said goodbye to his parents, but there was nobody for him. However, he checked himself. The crowd of well-wishers more than made up for it. Mr. and Mrs. Foster seemed delighted that he had joined their family. Sarah was very positive too. Really, people are so kind, Bruce thought.

The sky-car soared aloft, then shot off in a south-easterly direction. Okay Italy, here we come. Araminta snuggled up next to Bruce. She was clearly very happy. He wanted to cry with relief.

No! No crying on my wedding day, he thought. He put his arm round her.

-oOo-

"Now, Araminta," said Bruce for the last time, "you still don't want to come?"

"Bruce, you go alone. I'll enjoy a day's shopping in Rome. Then I'll look forward to seeing you back at the hotel at six p.m., and you can tell me all about it."

"Right. I hope the trains don't let you down. It's kind of you to let me have the sky-car."

Bruce skimmed over the landscape. He knew where to land. He left the sky-car in a car park. The last part of the journey would need to be done on foot.

"Can you direct me to the wood?" he asked the car park attendant.

It was as he thought. He had a mile or so to walk. It was a nice day, and Bruce was soon striding along. Ah, here was a local.

"I'm looking for a hermit's cave in the hills round here somewhere," Bruce asked. His Italian was not up to much. The man pointed up a rising track and muttered something Bruce could not catch. Bruce thanked him.

The track wound along through trees. After a bit, it came out into the open. There were green fields right and left with a few sheep. The mountain lay ahead. The track gradually petered out and became a path.

Suddenly, Bruce's heart missed a beat. There ahead of him was a man leaning on a scythe wearing a brown dressing-gown with a hood covering his head. It might have been the grim reaper himself. Bruce went up to him. He spoke in English.

"I'm looking for the hermit."

The man grunted. "I'll take you." He pointed. It was impossible to see his face in the shade of the large hood.

Bruce saw a hut nestling against the hillside.

"Not in that poor lowly stable with the oxen standing by!" he

554

said.

The stranger laughed. It was hard keeping up the pretence, but it might be important, for his sake. They walked on without speaking.

They passed the hut. A few yards further on, they came to a cave. The man led Bruce in. There was a strong light inside. They rounded a boulder, and a glorious sight met Bruce's eyes. The cave was fully furnished.

The pretence could end now.

"Jim!" Bruce flung his arms round the monk.

"Bruce! Great to see you. I thought you would solve the puzzle."

As Bruce had foreseen, there was a lady dressed in white. She came forward.

"Pikel. Wonderful to see you." They hugged.

Bruce's joy was too deep for words.

"Look." Pikel held up her left hand. The two rings on the fourth finger shone and sparkled in the light.

"They're beautiful. Many congratulations to you both. I'm so pleased for you."

"Pikel told me about the day on the boat," Jim said. "You're a real saint, Bruce."

Pikel motioned to him to sit down. Bruce noticed his surroundings. The red carpet was a lovely thick one. The chairs were Queen Anne. The hidden lighting was most effective; there was plenty of light without you being dazzled. It was pleasantly warm.

"Coffee, instant, white with one?"

Bruce laughed again. "Yes please, Pikel."

"I've gone back to Maria," Pikel said. "I'm Mrs. Maria Morgenstern now."

"It's a lovely name."

Jim and he took a seat while she went out to make the coffee.

"Jim, I take it that you have protective devices against spying, and that we can talk freely here?"

Jim nodded.

"That was brilliant about the *una corda*, although it took me long time to get it. I thought there might be a message taped to the underside of a soft pedal somewhere. I even checked the piano at the Wembley gathering."

"Yes, I know. I loved that."

"And all the time, the clue was in the postmark. San Francisco. I wonder how many Americans reflect on the fact that their great city is named after St. Francis. Then the message had to be from you, because you had told me that Pikel was not musical. She could have managed the bass clef code, but she would never have come up with *the una corda* marking, I reckoned. Then the Christmas carol, Once in Royal David's City. Of course, it was St. Francis of Assisi who began the practice of a Christmas nativity play with the manger and the donkey and so forth. Hence the venue for our meeting being in the Assisi area, where there was a cave and a stable."

"Right all the way, Bruce. Well done. And were you expecting Pikel to be fulfilling 'all in white shall wait around'?"

"Yes, naturally. Oh it is so good to see you again. Jim, you're so full of surprises. You know, you're the only person I have known who has lived three times!"

Jim chuckled.

"Does the St. Francis outfit mean anything more than just dressing up?" Bruce asked.

"Maybe. Maybe."

"Well, don't make a habit out of it," quipped Bruce.

"How are you getting on with the youth restorer?" Jim asked.

"It didn't work. I took it all at once; I hope that was right."

"No!" said Jim. "One drop each day, no more. I'm surprised you survived. You must have the constitution of an ox; perhaps that helped you solve the carol part of the riddle. Here's another bottle; new and improved formula. One drop per day, maximum!"

Jim handed Bruce another 250ml bottle. He was most grateful.

"I have a thousand questions," Bruce continued, "but let's get straight to the central point. What is your interpretation of the business of the multiplying machines?"

Bruce told him the full story starting with the news bulletins about Pluto and Neptune, his insight in the night, and his trip to the asteroid belt. He also shared the parts of his daydreams that were relevant. Then he described the interior of the alien craft, explaining that it was similar to Mission 12 but also different. He told how his piano playing had gained access to the control panel. He outlined the software.

"What do you think?" he said at last.

Jim was silent for a moment.

"It is a very strange story. However, it seems to me that we can discount any form of illusion or hallucination or anything of that kind. The machines were definitely there, in large numbers. I also think your theory that they were endlessly self-replicating is correct. It's also clear that there are fewer of them now than there were. So a real transaction took place when you went on board.

"The aspect I find most fascinating of all is the presence of the grand piano. Not just any piano, but the futuristic piano you had imagined. If the on-board computer is to be believed, then every machine had one. Of course, a piano of that length would be impossible with today's materials, as the strings would break under the tension. Super-strong piano wire would be needed. So it's a product from the future.

"It's possible that the machine learned your language and your thinking from scanning your brain when you came on board, as you suggested at Wembley. It might have reconfigured everything on board to match. However, I think the truth is more straightforward. I've always felt there was something special about you, Bruce. I think you are a prophet, as I've said before. I reckon that what you thought were daydreams were more than that. Whether or not they were accurate in every detail is unimportant; but the central thrust of the story about Mission 12 that you have recounted is a glimpse of the future. Humanity will go to other stars. The discovery of anti-gravity and infinite energy makes that just about inevitable. They will soon find that terraforming is such a massive undertaking that it is best performed by machines working in droves. Hence self-replicating machines of one kind or another. It is not hard to imagine the pioneers of such a mission feeling impatient, wanting to get everything sorted within a generation. So I agree with you; no number of machines will seem too great to begin with. The danger of an exponential explosion resulting from a mistake is a real one, because it will be the last thing that the pioneers will be worrying about."

"I'm with you so far. But what I can't understand is why the machines should have turned up now."

"There are many things we don't understand. Here's a suggestion. The speed of light is indeed a speed limit for normal travel. However, it may be that there is a way of overcoming it. Who knows? If there was, then time travel becomes possible. Could it be that the machines that turned up here have travelled backwards from the future in some way?"

Bruce pondered.

"It's possible, I suppose. The technology on board did seem more advanced than ours. Certainly, the whole craft might have been stamped 'human artefact'. All those different languages. The one gee gravity. The room temperature. All these things suit humans perfectly. That could not have been mere chance, surely."

"Then there's the piano," Jim said gently. "That was central."

Bruce looked at Jim. "Are you thinking what I'm thinking?"

Jim said nothing. It was better that Bruce should say it.

"It feels to me as if descendants of mine are going to be involved in the future colonisation of space," said Bruce slowly. "The musical gift which I inherited from my mum will carry on through the generations. Reinforced by Araminta's musicianship," Bruce added as an afterthought. "That's why the key to the software involved the piano. It might also explain why I have had the daydreams as opposed to somebody else. It's a frightening thought."

"That's the best insight I can offer," Jim replied.

Bruce was very thoughtful.

"All my life, I've wanted to be part of the solution," he said. "Now it turns out that I'm part of the problem."

"Both And," Jim said firmly. "You have saved the world from a problem of your own making."

"And they have hardly noticed. Yes, it makes sense…"

There was silence, broken only by the ticking of a Georgian clock. Pikel had gone out some time ago.

"I've just had a terrible thought," Bruce continued. "Suppose that the reason the machines have travelled backwards in time is because there are so many in the future that they could not find any more moons and planets to feed off..."

"Don't even think about it," said Jim, who had clearly already come up with the possibility himself. "Or, if you must think about it, then tell yourself that reversing the programme now, using a machine that is an advance guard as it were, can only be helpful in reversing the plague in the future."

"I just hate the idea of the galaxy being overrun by machines before we have even gone to a neighbouring star for the first time."

"Well, there's a new problem to worry about!" laughed Jim.

Bruce laughed too. What was the point of worrying? He had done what he could.

He decided to change the subject.

"I was sorry about the hotel being flooded."

"Oh don't worry about that. I hated doing it. It can all be pumped out again if needs be."

Bruce was mystified.

"You mean, it wasn't an accident?"

"No!" laughed Jim. "How else was I going to get Celia's lot off my back?"

"How is it that you were not killed, if you don't mind my asking?"

Jim laughed again. He was obviously enjoying himself.

"Well, I knew they were coming, so I was ready for them."

"How?"

"I knew that they would have put a homing device on you in some way. I also knew that making a copy of you would confuse their system. So in order to have you for myself for a week, I had to create your replicate. Then it became a matter of when you were cremated. I thought it would be the Friday. After that, it was only a matter of time before they located you. I did not think there would be any monitoring equipment in Funchal itself. The thing to do was to drive along the expressway under Funchal airport. That was bound to trigger a response. I reckoned we had at least twelve or fifteen hours before they found you. I was pretty much spot on in my estimate."

Bruce was amazed.

"But are you saying you expected them to burst in when you were showing me the fish in the ocean? I heard you fall when the dart hit you."

Jim had risen to his feet. "Excuse me for a moment."

He went out of the cave. Bruce puzzled over the incident. How could Jim have avoided being shot? How could his death have been faked?

Jim was being a long time. Suddenly Bruce became alarmed.

"Jim?" he called; then louder, "Jim!"

He raced outside. The sky was dark in every direction and great drops of rain were beginning to fall. There was no sign of Jim or Pikel.

"Onomatopoeia!" Bruce yelled with all his might, staring up into the sky.

The storm was sudden and violent. The rain was already lashing down. Nobody would realise that Bruce was crying great tears of anguish. Come back! Come back!

Something like a thin mist swirled past Bruce's shoulder. There was an area of sky ahead of him where the rain was not falling. The sky-car must be hovering there! Bruce stared upwards.

Suddenly there was a flash of red as the sky-car became visible for a moment. An arm threw something out of a window, which fell to the ground a hundred yards away. It was over in an instant; the sky-car shot off heavenwards with a swirl and disappeared into the clouds.

Bruce was desolate. He stood still, gazing upwards, the tears streaming down his cheeks. He knew that he would never see them again.

There was no point in waiting. Ignoring the rain, he made his way across the muddy ground to see what had fallen. It was a garment, brown and crumpled. Bruce picked it up and let it unravel to its full length. It was the set of overalls that Bruce had seen on board Mission 12 and which Jim had worn as the crematorium attendant. Bruce hugged it to himself. It was a precious gift.

He went back into the cave. There, a shock awaited him. Everything had gone – lights, chairs, carpet, clock, everything. There was nothing but the bare walls and dirty floor. How could this be?

The storm was already abating. The only thing for it was to set off down the hill, repeating the precious conversation over and over as he went, so that he would not forget any of it. The rain became heavy again; he waited under a tree for a few minutes until it subsided and then trudged on down the track with a heavy heart.

-oOo-

"How was the shopping?"

"Brilliant, thank you. I've really splashed out. There's too much to fit in the bedroom, so reception is looking after all the bags and suitcases downstairs somewhere for me. But I'm afraid we may need to hire a second sky-car to get it all home. I hope that's Okay?" Araminta looked a little anxious.

"Phew, that's a relief. I'd reckoned on needing a container at least. I'll just ring to cancel the booking."

They both laughed.

"Actually, I've been so restrained. Look."

Araminta held up three bags.

"Very good. I'd love to see them. But I'm starving, so can we eat first?"

It took the rest of the evening to review the purchases, so it was next morning at breakfast that Araminta was finally able to give her attention to the visit to Jim.

"He was there alright, and Pikel too, as I predicted. It was good giving our honeymoon destination out over the TV, as it saved the difficulty of sending messages undetected and showed that I had solved the riddle all at the same time. They're married, incidentally. Mr. and Mrs. Morgenstern."

"How you have fallen from heaven, bright morning star," Araminta quoted. "Not very apt."

"I prefer 'I am the bright star of the dawn' personally. But let's not push the meaning of their name too far."

"Oh, I don't know. I'm sure it was chosen for your benefit. Who knows what they're calling themselves today? No, I'd settle for the ambiguity myself. Is he devil or angel? What about this:

'Is he in heaven? Is he in hell?

That demned elusive pimpernel.'"

"Wonderful," said Bruce. "I agree that Jim is an enigma. Now, am I to be allowed to tell you what happened?"

Araminta adopted a demure expression and was very good for a full five minutes while Bruce outlined the events of the day.

"Are you going to take the potion?" Araminta asked. "I don't mind if it's only one drop per day."

"I'm not sure," Bruce replied. "Why don't you take charge of it, and then you can put a drop in my food if you think fit, or not, as you choose, and watch the results."

They agreed on this plan.

"I wonder how the cave was emptied of furniture?" Bruce mused.

"Easy, at least in theory. He's found a way of reassembling molecules rapidly. That mist you saw leaving the cave was his hi-tech version of children's modelling clay; instantly programmable to any shape. I guess it attached itself to the sky-car as it took off."

"Well!" said Bruce. "I only hope he's got it under control and the rest of the earth does not start following suit and reassembling itself."

"I'm more bothered by his sudden departure."

"Yes, me too. It was as if I triggered it by my questions."

"I've got a theory, but it's pretty scary."

"Go on."

"You know he can replicate a dead body. Well, I think he can replicate a living one. At some stage on that morning, he effected a swap. By the time Celia's gang burst in, it was a copy of himself sitting next to you. When they killed it, that suited him fine. Jim

562

really was dead now, they would think. Even better than a cremation of a fake body."

Suddenly Bruce went white in the face.

"Excuse me," he gasped, and raced out to the toilet. Araminta was very concerned. She hurried after him.

He emerged a few minutes later, coughing and looking awful.

"Whatever is it?" she asked. He motioned her to accompany him outside. They walked to a garden seat some yards away from the building, in the hotel grounds. When they were seated, Bruce said in a low voice, "I think you've got it. He thought I was about to ask whether it was really him I was speaking to, or just a copy of him. That's why they left so abruptly. But Araminta, don't you see? I feel terrible. I've always assumed that it was the copy of me that was cremated and what you see before you is the real me. But suppose it's the other way round? What if the real Bruce Winter is dead and I'm just..."

Bruce could not finish the sentence.

"Oh Bruce!"

This was terrible. Araminta did not know what to say.

Bruce was speaking again in a hoarse whisper.

"All the way through history, people have been able to relate to Descartes' teaching; 'I think, therefore I am.' But if it is now possible to make living replicas..."

"Stop it!" Araminta was angry. "Not another word. Now listen. Did you mean all those things you said to me last evening?"

Bruce went as meek as a lamb.

"You know I did. I would never lie to you, Araminta."

"Right. Well, that's good enough for me, and it ought to be good enough for you too, Bruce. I love you as you are. Nobody can prove their identity, but it seems to me that love conquers everything. You love me, and I love you, and nothing is going to spoil that unless we let it. So let's have no more doom and gloom about copies of people."

"Alright. Or to put it another way, even if I have been compromised in some way by being replicated, I'm going to live as best I can. That is my settled determination."

"So we're agreed. You're the one I want, Bruce."

They held each other tightly. Bruce could feel himself calming down.

"There is another way he could have done it," Araminta said after a while. "He could have arranged an assembly of molecules to represent himself at a distance. He might have been behind a screen, for example, moving and talking in response to you, with the replica mimicking his every move in your presence."

"Please leave it, Araminta. It gives me the creeps. Right. It's a new day. Let's do something symbolic that speaks of the human condition." Bruce spoke in a forthright tone.

"And what might that be?"

"Take Peter's advice. We'll climb to the top of the leaning tower of Pisa, hold on tight, and look down."

-o0o-

Several weeks had passed. The last piano pupil had gone. Araminta was just putting their supper on the table when the doorbell rang. Bruce rose from his chair, and they both went over to answer it.

It was a tramp.

"Sorry to bother you, but does Will live here?"

Bruce and Araminta looked at each other. They had no qualms.

"Come in!" they said together.

"I'm Will's son," Bruce explained. "We were just serving supper. Will you join us for a bite to eat?"

The man was hesitant, but he sensed their friendliness. Perhaps he could manage something to eat.

It was not easy to make conversation. Bruce explained to the man, who was called John, that Will had died in tragic circumstances. He told the whole story. It was not an easy thing to do, but it was important.

John was sorry. He had liked Will.

"Where are you staying?" asked Araminta.

The answer was nowhere. It was soon settled. John would have

Will's room.

"To save you searching, when Will first came, he raided my drinks cupboard and swallowed most of a bottle of whisky before I realised what was happening," Bruce explained. "So I emptied the house of alcohol."

John looked a little uncomfortable.

"We prayed with Will," Araminta added gently. "He never smoked or drank again after that."

John looked puzzled.

"Look," said Bruce. "You can stay as short or as long as you like. Will's death was a tragic loss. I'd be pleased if you wanted to stay. I would feel I was doing something kind for him."

"He was a good bloke," said John. "I shall miss him."

"Take his place," said Araminta simply. "We will search for peace together."

Epilogue

Bruce was just clearing the things off the table at the end of lunch when the doorbell rang. He went to answer it. Mrs. Smith, who lived three houses along on the other side of the road came into the bungalow looking very indignant.

"I'm feeling very upset, Mr. Winter."

"Oh dear; why's that?"

"We need to move because of Mr. Smith's job. I've just had the estate agents round, and they say that the presence of all your homeless people in the houses round here affects the value of our house. He reckons they lower it by twenty percent."

"Oh dear, that's terrible."

It was something that had been worrying Bruce. The expansion had not been planned. It was just that when Marjorie had died, Bruce and Araminta were so fond of the bungalow that they offered to buy both the house and the bungalow from her estate. This was readily accepted. Two of John's friends were desperate, and it had seemed natural to put them in the house. Then the number had risen, and when the house on the other side of the road came up for sale, Bruce and Araminta had bought that too. That had only been the start of it.

Just as he was wondering what to say to her, Chloe and Hannah came tearing in.

"Uncle Wilf, Uncle Wilf, tell us another story about Wild Will the astronaut!" they called. Wilf was the newest arrival.

"Haven't you heard enough already?" he grumbled. Wilf had a gift for telling stories to small children. Even little Ben, their youngest, who was only one and a half, liked to listen. Araminta had just put him down for his after lunch sleep. The twins had passed this stage.

"Story! Story!" they squeaked.

"Alright then. Come and get comfortable."

The girls snuggled up close to him on the sofa. Mrs. Smith frowned.

"Surely you should not let a man like that near your children!" she whispered to Bruce.

"It's part of his healing, and it's good for them," Bruce replied. "When we started taking men in, Araminta and I made a conscious decision that we were going to trust God to protect us all, and so far, he has done."

Mrs. Smith did not know what to say.

"But look, about the value of your house. Araminta and I have already anticipated this problem and discussed it. We will make up any shortfall between what you get for it and what the agent reckons its value would be if the road was tramp-free. Also, if you care to sell it to us, we would be pleased. There is such a need you know."

Once again Mrs. Smith was at a loss for words. "Well, I…" she began hesitantly, and then broke off.

The story was under way, and Uncle Wilf was on good form.

"Will could see that the others did not care," he declaimed. "'Alright, then,' he said, in a firm voice, 'don't worry. If I have to go and rescue the princess from the wicked ogre all on my own, I will! Fetch me my space-rocket and start up the big engines!'" The twins squealed with delight.

"But what do the men do all day?" Mrs. Smith asked.

"They find peace," answered Araminta who had come in from the bedroom. "You'd be surprised. After they have been here a while, they don't want to be passengers; they all want to help in some way. They love to welcome the newest arrivals."

"I think it's sponging," said Mrs. Smith.

"Yes, you're quite right; it is sponging," said Bruce. Mrs. Smith was taken aback. "I've only ever been in one boxing match in my life," Bruce continued. "When I was at school, there was in inter-house boxing competition. I did not want to go in for it, but some older boys forced me to write my name on the list. Then, when they had gone, I went back and crossed my name off. However, when the competition was put up on the board later, I was horrified to see my name was included. I went to find the teacher concerned.

"'But Sir,' I said, 'I crossed my name off again.'

"The teacher was not pleased.

"'So you think you can mess about with my list do you? Well I'm not having it. You're in the competition whether you like it or not.'

"There was nothing for it. I found I was down to box a friend of mine, who was in the same house as me, which seemed daft. I was very scared. I had to hit him as hard as I could, and he had to hit me. It was awful. At the end, all they said was 'ten marks for green.'

"But here's the point. There were three rounds. At the end of round one, when I was on my seat, trembling, shaking and crying, and bleeding from the lip, some older boy had a wet sponge. He wiped my face, and gently sponged the blood off my lip, and encouraged me. 'You're doing really well!' he said. It was just what I needed. It gave me the strength to face the next round.

"So yes, there is sponging here. We are looking after these men and sponging them down; giving them strength to face the next round. My boxing match lasted three minutes. Some of these men have been battered all their lives. So if I get ripped off by some of them, I really don't mind, as long as I can show love and compassion to them in return."

All the aggression had faded from Mrs. Smith by now.

"I see," she said. "I'm sorry I doubted you. Thank you for your generous offer. I'll let you know." With that, she took her leave.

So far, nobody had ripped them off. Bruce had made up his mind to it that he would not object if one of their men was to do a runner with their possessions, which they might be tempted to do. Some of the paintings might fetch a bit. However, there was one item that he could not bear to part with. At least it was the scruffiest thing in the bungalow, so it was unlikely to be stolen. It was Jim's overall, hanging in their wardrobe.

Sometimes, when Araminta was out with the children and a piano pupil had cancelled, giving him a free twenty minutes, Bruce liked to put it on. He was not sure why. It fitted perfectly. He felt very strange wearing it. He had such indescribable longings whenever he wore it. It was always an effort taking it off again.

Bruce had agonised over it, but he knew he had to win the battle. "Alright," he eventually managed to say out loud, when nobody else was around, "they can even take the overall." It had been an effort, but he felt better about it since.

"Bruce, we could multiply what we are doing here all over the area," said Araminta.

"Wouldn't it be lovely," murmured Bruce. "Especially if the men caught the vision and became carers themselves. We need to provide for women too, you know."

"We need a name," Araminta mused.

"I know," said Bruce. "How about this: 'Will Winter's Self-replicating Homes'?"

Araminta's eyes moistened. It might not be a good name, but the concept was a lovely one. What could be a more fitting memorial for Will?

"Actually, I do have a suggestion for a name," said Bruce. Araminta looked at him.

"What about 'Nitwood Homes'?"

"I really don't like the name..." Araminta began.

"Ah, but wait a moment. Do you know what Nitwood stands for?"

Araminta did not. She was so lovely to look at!

568

"It's from Shakespeare; 'Now Is The Winter Of Our Discontent'. Note the use of the name Winter in the quotation, in memory of Will. There are lots of gloomy words beginning in D that you could substitute for discontent, which apply to these men:

'Now Is The Winter Of Our Disappointment'

'Now Is The Winter Of Our Distress', even

'Now Is The Winter Of Our Demise', but in our case, we have a positive D instead:

'Now Is The Winter Of Our Deliverance', or

'Now Is The Winter Of Our Delight' for example."

"Or maybe, 'Now Is The Winter Of Our Dentures'," Araminta suggested. "Lots of these men have severe teeth problems, remember."

Was this a wind-up, Bruce wondered? It was so hard to be sure from her face. She was so pretty!

"Anyway," he continued, "when people like Mrs. Smith tell me I'm a nit-wit to allow these people into my home, I can reply 'Not Nit-wit, Nitwood. Nitwood Homes.' Then I can explain the meaning of the name. And you've got to admit, the name Nitwood is original. What do you think?"

"Darling, I'll tell you. I know you've saved the Galaxy, and perhaps even the universe, and rescued humanity from a slow extinction over the coming millennia by getting the machines to restore the planets and moons that they had swallowed up, but all the same, there's something you should do."

"And what's that?"

"Stick to playing and teaching the piano. It's what you're good at."

"Perhaps I will," murmured Bruce, "perhaps I will."

Acknowledgements

2001: A Space Odyssey, film, Turner Entertainment, 1968, based on the writing of Arthur C. Clarke. Written versions of the story are also available. The profound debt to Arthur C. Clarke throughout this book is obvious.

Bach, J.S., *Brandenburg Concertos*, Piano for four hands, arranged by Max Reger, Edition Peters 3108b.

Bible, the.

Borge, Victor, whose detailed inspections of pianos were an inspiration.

Boticelli, Sandro, *The Birth of Venus*, Tempera on Canvas, 1.8 x 2.8m, c.1480, Galleria degli Uffizi, Florence.

Bristol Zoo, where the birds fly around freely in large bird houses.

Butch Cassidy and the Sundance Kid, film, MGM, 1969.

Cain, Paul, *The Emergence of the Victorious Church*, conference address at Harrogate, Vineyard Ministries International audio tape JPH91, 1990.

Carroll, Lewis, *Alice in Wonderland*, Macmillan, London, 1865.

Carter, Graham, for the unflinching volume of his wedding vows.

Cecil, Henry, *Much in Evidence*, Michael Joseph, London, 1957, p63 for the quotation from Aristophanes.

Clarke, Arthur C., *Profiles of the Future. An enquiry into the limits of the possible*. Original paperback edition Penguin, Harmondsworth, 1962. Revised hardback edition Victor Gollancz, London, 1999.

Clarke, Arthur C., *The Snows of Olympus*, 1994 proposes bombarding Mars with blocks of ice from the asteroid belt.

Conan Doyle, Sir Arthur, *The Adventures of Sherlock Holmes*, London, 1892.

Cousteau, Jacques with Dumas, Frederic, *The Silent World*, Hamish Hamilton, 1953.

Davies, Paul, *How to Build a Time Machine*, Allen Lane the Penguin Press, London, 2001.

Dean, for the speed of light equation.

Descartes, Rene, 1596 - 1650, *Meditations on First Philosophy*, 1641.

Dobson, James, *Focus on the Family*, family.org., was the speaker who used the baton metaphor that impressed Bruce.

Elgar, Edward. The one bar in four hours anecdote came from Philip Radcliffe, formerly a fellow of King's College, Cambridge.

Enright, Dominique, *The Wicked Wit of Winston Churchill*, Michael O Mara Books, 2001, p146 for the Churchill quote.

Family Records Centre, The, is situated at 1 Myddleton Street, Islington, London, EC1R 1UW.

Flanders, M. & Swann, D., *At the Drop of a Hat*, song cycle, Parlophone, 1959 contains the Hippopotamus Song, and also Ill Wind. *At the Drop of Another Hat*, Parlophone PCS 3052, 1964 contains The First and Second Law.

Fleming, Ian, selected novels involving espionage.

Forester, C.S, *Mr. Midshipman Hornblower*, Michael Joseph, 1950, chapter 'The Cargo of Rice'.

Four Weddings and a Funeral, film, MGM, 1993.

Francesca, Piero Della, *The Resurrection of Christ*, Mural in fresco and tempera, 225x200 cm, 1663, Museo Civico, Sansepolcro.

Game of Life, Victorian board game, currently made by MB Games.

Greene, Brian, *The Elegant Universe*, New York, 1999, ch2.

Gribbin, John, *In the Beginning, the Birth of the Living Universe*, Penguin, London, 1993, p174-5 for the insight about ice floating on water.

Handel, George, *Did you not Hear my Lady?* The correct rendering, is from his Italian opera Tolomeo, 1728.

Hawking, Stephen, *The Universe in a Nutshell*, Bantam, 2001, ch1.

Hoyle, Sir Fred, a lecture on the Big Bang Theory at Cambridge University in about 1973, which supplied the observer on the earth anecdote. The definition of friendship comes in a novel of his.

Indiana Jones and the Last Crusade, film, CIC Video, 1989.

Infinite Energy Magazine produced by New Energy Foundation Inc., PO Box 2816, Concord, New Hampshire 03302-2816, USA., infinite-energy.com. Their website examines ways in which infinite energy might become available, and has suggested that a home might one day be powered by a small black box independent of a national grid.

Kaler, J.B., *The Hundred Greatest Stars*, Copernicus Books, New York, 2002, p.123.

Keeping Up Appearances, BBC TV series, 1990-5.

Levy, David H., *Comets, Creators and Destroyers,* Touchstone, Simon and Schuster, New York, 1998, p156 and *passim*.

Lewis, C.S., *That Hideous Strength*, 1945.

Lewis, C.S., *The Narnia Chronicles*, Penguin, Harmondsworth, 1950-7.

Lloyd Webber, Andrew, *Cats*, musical, 1981.

Longfellow, Henry W., *The Song of Hiawatha*, 1855, ch5.

Man Alive after Death and Burial, tract, Victory Tract Club, Eastbourne, 1968.

Mary Poppins, film, Disney, 1964.

McKenzie, Robin, *Treat Your Own Back*, Spinal Publications, PO Box 93, Waikanae, New Zealand, ISBN 0-9597746-6-1. This book contains the exercises that helped Bruce's back recover.

Millais, *Ophelia*, oil on canvas, 75 x 100 cm, 1852, Tate Gallery, London.

Milne, A.A., *Whinnie the Pooh*, 1926.

Moore, Patrick ed., *The Astronomy Encyclopaedia*, Mitchell Beazley, London, 1987, article *Comets* by H.B. Ridley; *Galaxy* by David A. Allen.

My Evaline, traditional song.

Nobbs, D., *The Fall and Rise of Reginald Perrin*, Television series, 1976-1979.

Oakley, Graham, *The Church Mouse*, Macmillan, London, 1962; also on video, BBCV 4238.

Parton, Dolly, *I Will Always Love You*, song, 1992.

Raiders of the Lost Ark, film, Paramount, 1981.

Riding Lights Theatre Company, for a sketch on 'all in white shall wait around'.

Robin Hood and the Animals, film, Walt Disney Home Video D202282, 1973.

Rowling, J.K., *Harry Potter and the Philosopher's Stone*, Bloomsbury, London, 1997.

Ryle, James, *A Hippo in the Garden,* Highland, 1992. Also as a talk on video entitled *A Hippo in the Backyard*, 1991.

Scarlet Pimpernel, The, film starring Leslie Howard, 1935, based on the book by Baroness Orczy, 1905.

Scrabble, Spear's Games, Spear & Sons, Enfield. According to family lore, 'Conquest' was once played in this position by my uncle David Milford (d. 1984). Perhaps Bruce should consider himself fortunate; 'Vanquish' scores even more.

Shakespeare, William, for several quotations. Oh dear. Bruce's memory is not always as sharp as it might be. "Ope not thy ponderous and marble jaws," which came to mind at the dentist, is a misquotation of Shakespeare from *Hamlet's Soliloquy* by the self-styled duke in Twain, Mark, *Huckleberry Finn*, Chatto and Windus, London, 1884, chapter 21; Bruce has even misquoted the misquotation. Similarly, when commenting on the many pots of flowers at the wedding reception, he had in mind "omnia unnumbered pebbles", from *King Lear*, but the original reads "The murmuring surge That <u>on th'</u> unnumbered idle pebbles chafes Cannot be heard so high," which does not contain the word omnia at all. For once, Bruce's musical ear has betrayed him. The scene is the one where the king stands at the top of the cliff looking down. This same speech contains "The crows and choughs that wing the midway air Show scarce so gross as beetles"; Bruce thought of this when hearing about the sky-cars seen over Los Angeles from the Rim of the World road. Ophelia's death comes in *Hamlet*, Act iv, scene 7. *Richard lll* opens with the oft quoted line abbreviated to Nitwood by Bruce. Finally, Fortescue's inability to "stand upon points" comes from the fools' play in *A Midsummer Night's Dream*.

Singh, Simon, *Fermat's Last Theorem*, Fourth Estate, 1998.

Singh, Simon, *The Code Book*, Fourth Estate, 2000. Today's 'strong encryption' would require the enormous computing power Bruce suggested to Jim to break it.

Song, Rev. J., who once commented that the decoration of his church for a family wedding had turned it into a florist's shop.

Sound of Music, The, film, Twentieth Century Fox, 1965.

Star Wars, film, 1977, now referred to as Episode IV.

Sweetman, David, *The Love of Many Things. A Life of Vincent Van Gogh*, Hodder and Stoughton, London, 1990.

Tacitus, *Annals*, XV.44.4, translation taken from J. Stevenson, ed., *A New Eusebius*, SPCK, London, 1957, p2.

Taylor, John V., *Black Holes: The End of the Universe?*, Souvenir Press, 1973, ch12 for the concern about a black hole being dropped.

Tchaikovsky, Peter, *The Sleeping Beauty*, ballet. Bruce can never quite remember whether his favourite *Pas de Deux* is from that or from one of Tchaikovsky's other two ballets – *The Nutcracker* and *Swan Lake*. It may well be that it is Act one scene eight of *The Nutcracker* that Bruce was thinking of, and not a *Pas de Deux* at all, because he once came across a Russian piano reduction of it and tried to play it, with only limited success. Or was it maybe the Rose Adagio from *The Sleeping Beauty* that he had in mind? Confusion!

Tea with Mussolini, film, MGM, 1999.

Thurber, James, *The Secret Life of Walter Mitty*, short story, 1941.

Titanic, The, film, Twentieth Century Fox, 1997. The music is by James Horner. Bruce uses the version for Piano-Vocals-Guitar with his pupils (International Music Publications ltd, order ref 6105A). He tells them to play bar 14 in place of the unplayable bar 10, whose presence reminds us that computers are not always foolproof.

Titian, *Noli me Tangere*, 101 x 91 cm, Oil on canvas, 1511-12, National Gallery, London.

Tolkien, J.R.R., *Lord of the Rings*, George Allen and Unwin, Norwich, 1954. The LP record Bruce looked at was of Tolkien reading and singing excerpts from the Lord of the Rings, Caedmon records TC1478, 1975, and the sleeve note was written by George Sayer, a friend of the family, who made the recording. See Carpenter, H., *J.R.R. Tolkien a biography*, George Allen and Unwin, London, 1977, p213. Grateful thanks to the Tolkien Society for the LP details (tolkiensociety.org).

Utility Fog, a concept of Josh Storrs Hall. See http://discuss.foresight.org/~josh.

Van Gogh, Vincent. The painting Bruce admired was *Wheatfield with Crows*, oil on canvas, 50 x 100 cm, 1890, Van Gogh Museum.

Verne, Jules, *From the Earth to the Moon*, 1865, currently available from Sutton Publishing, 1995.

Wagner, Richard, *The Ring of the Nibelungs*, Opera cycle comprising *Rhinegold, The Valkyries, Siegfried* and *The Twilight of the Gods*. At Jim Pond's party, Bruce played the orchestral music leading into Scene 3 of Act Three of Siegfried, introduced by the hero's words, "*Jetzt lock' ich ein liebes Gesell!*" (Now I can win a dear companion!).

Walking on the Moon, song by Police, 1979.

Water Aid, Prince Consort House, 27-29 Albert Embankment, London, SE1 7YB, tel 020 7793 4500, wateraid.org. Their website states that one child dies every fifteen seconds from impure water.

Whittier, John Greenleaf, *Dear Lord and Father of Mankind*, hymn, 1872.

Wilde, Oscar, *Lady Windermere's Fan*, play, 1892. The remark about temptation is spoken by Lord Darlington in Scene 1.

Wiren, Dag (b. 1905), *Serenade for String Orchestra* opus 11, recorded by BIS, CD 285.

Wodehouse, P.G., *Right Ho, Jeeves*, Herbert Jenkins, 1934. It was Madeleine Bassett who thought of the stars as God's daisy chain.

Wood, Maurice, whose letter to The Times on his appointment as Bishop of Norwich spoke of having both ears to the ground.

You kind people who encouraged me to write, especially Camilla and Fiona.